DATE DUE

SORCERERS UNDER FIRE

Siuntio had the right of it: this time, the stolen life energy of those Kaunian captives was hurled straight at the blockhouse, a deadly dart of sorcerous force. The lamps flickered in a strange, rhythmic pattern. Then the walls started to shake in the same rhythm, and then the floor beneath Pekka's feet. The air felt hot and thick in the lungs. It tasted of blood.

The paper on which her cantrip was written burst into flames. One of the secondary sorcerors screamed. Her hair had burst into flames, too. A comrade swaddled her head with a blanket, but the flames did not want to go out.

"No!" Siuntio shouted, a battle cry that might have burst from the throat of a man half his age. "By the powers above, no! You shall not have us! You shall not!" He began what had to be a counterspell. Pekka had never imagined such a thing—one determined mage, all alone, trying to withstand the massed might of many, a might magnified by murder.

Ilmarinen's voice joined Siuntio's a moment later. They were the finest sorcerors of their generation. For an instant, just for an instant, Pekka, marshaling in her mind what she could do to aid their magecraft, thought they might have fought the Algarvians to a standstill. But then the lamps went out altogether, plunging the blockhouse into darkness. With a shriek of bursting timbers, the roof fell in. Something hit Pekka in the side of the head. The dark went black, shot with scarlet.

RULERS OF THE
DARKNESS

HARRY TURTLEDOVE

A TOM DOHERTY ASSOCIATES BOOK
NEW YORK

This is a work of fiction. All the characters and events portrayed in this book are either products of the author's imagination or are used fictitiously.

RULERS OF THE DARKNESS

Edited by Patrick Nielsen Haydon

A Tor Book
Published by Tom Doherty Associates, LLC
175 Fifth Avenue
New York, NY 10010

www.tor.com

Tor® is a registered trademark of Tom Doherty Associates, LLC.

ISBN: 978-0-7653-3382-7

Library of Congress Catalog Card Number: 2001058465

First edition: April 2002
First mass market edition: May 2003

P1

Dramatis Personae

(* shows viewpoint character)

ALGARVE

Almonio	Constable in Gromheort
Ambaldo	Colonel of dragonfliers in southern Unkerlant
Baiardo	Mage attached to Plegmund's Brigade
Balastro	Marquis; minister to Zuwayza
Bembo*	Constable in Gromheort
Carietto	Brigadier in Trapani
Domiziano	Captain of dragonfliers in southern Unkerlant
Ercole	Senior lieutenant with Plegmund's Brigade
Fronesia	Woman at court in Trapani
Frontino	Warder in Tricarico
Gastable	Mage in Gromheort
Gismonda	Sabrino's wife in Trapani
Gradasso	Lurcanio's adjutant in Priekule
Lurcanio	Colonel on occupation duty in Priekule
Mainardo	Mezentio's brother; King of Jelgava
Malindo	Scholar in Trapani
Mezentio	King of Algarve
Oraste	Constable in Gromheort
Orosio	Captain of dragonfliers in southern Unkerlant
Pesaro	Constabulary sergeant in Gromheort
Raniero	Mezentio's cousin; King of Grelz
Sabrino*	Colonel of dragonfliers in southern Unkerlant
Saffa	Sketch artist in Tricarico
Solino	General in Durrwangen
Spinello*	Major on leave in Trapani for wound
Turpino	Captain in Wriezen
Zerbino	Captain in Plegmund's Brigade

FORTHWEG

Baldred	Slogan writer in Eoforwic
Brivibas	Kaunian in Gromheort; Vanai's grandfather
Brorda	Count of Gromheort
Ceorl	Soldier in Plegmund's Brigade near Hohenroda
Daukantis	Kaunian in Gromheort; Doldasai's father
Doldasai	Kaunian courtesan in Gromheort
Ealstan*	Bookkeeper in Eoforwic; Vanai's husband
Ethelhelm	Half Kaunian band leader in Eoforwic
Feliksai	Kaunian in Gromheort; Doldasai's mother
Gippias	Kaunian robber in Gromheort
Hengist	Sidroc's father; Hestan's brother; in Gromheort
Hestan	Bookkeeper in Gromheort; Ealstan's father
Leofsig	Ealstan's deceased brother
Nemunas	Kaunian refugee leader in Zuwayza
Penda	King of Forthweg
Pernavai	Kaunian in Valmiera; Vatsyunas' wife
Pybba	Pottery magnate in Eoforwic
Sidroc*	Soldier in Plegmund's Brigade near Hohenroda
Vanai*	Kaunian in Eoforwic; Ealstan's wife
Vatsyunas	Kaunian in Valmiera; Pernavai's husband
Vitols	Kaunian refugee leader in Zuwayza
Werferth	Sergeant in Plegmund's Brigade near Hohenroda
Yadwigai	Kaunian girl with Algarvian army in Unkerlant

GYONGYOS

Arpad	Ekrekek (King) of Gyongyos
Borsos	Major; mage in western Unkerlant
Frigyes	Captain in western Unkerlant
Hevesi	Soldier in western Unkerlant
Horthy	Gyongyosian minister to Zuwayza
Istvan*	Sergeant in western Unkerlant
Kun	Corporal in western Unkerlant; minor mage
Lajos	Soldier in western Unkerlant

| Szonyi | Soldier in western Unkerlant |
| Tivadar | Captain in western Unkerlant |

JELGAVA

Ausra	Talsu's sister in Skrunda
Donalitu	King of Jelgava; now in exile
Gailisa	Talsu's wife, living in Skrunda
Kugu	Silversmith in Skrunda
Laitsina	Talsu's mother in Skrunda
Stikliu	Friend of Talsu's in Skrunda
Talsu*	Prisoner from Skrunda
Traku	Talsu's father; tailor in Skrunda
Zverinu	Banker in Skrunda

Kuusamo

Alkio	Theoretical sorcerer; married to Raahe
Elimaki	Pekka's sister
Ilmarinen	Master mage in the Naantali district
Juhainen	One of the Seven Princes of Kuusamo
Leino	Mage; Pekka's husband
Linna	Serving woman in the Naantali district
Olavin	Banker; Elimaki's husband
Parainen	One of the Seven Princes of Kuusamo
Pekka*	Mage in the Naantali district; Leino's wife
Piilis	Theoretical sorcerer
Raahe	Theoretical sorcerer; married to Alkio
Renavall	One of the Seven Princes of Kuusamo
Siuntio	Master mage in the Naantali district
Uto	Pekka and Leino's son
Vihti	Sorcerer in Naantali district

LAGOAS

| Brinco | Grandmaster Pinhiero's secretary in Setubal |
| Fernao* | Mage on duty in Kuusamo |

Janira   Cornelu's lady friend in Setubal
Pinhiero   Grandmaster of Lagoan Guild of Mages
Vitor   King of Lagoas

ORTAH

Ahinadab   King of Ortah
Hadadezer   Ortaho minister to Zuwayza

SIBIU

Balio   Fisherman running eatery in Setubal; Janira's
father
Brindza   Cornelu's daughter in Tirgoviste town
Burebistu   King of Sibiu
Cornelu*   Commander; leviathan-rider in Setubal
Costache   Cornelu's wife in Tirgoviste town

UNKERLANT

Addanz   Archmage of Unkerlant
Ascovind   Collaborator in Duchy of Grelz
Gandiluz   Soldier contacting irregulars in Grelz
Garivald*   Irregular fighter west of Herborn
Gundioc   Captain in southern Unkerlant
Gurmun   General of behemoths at Durrwangen bulge
Kiun   Soldier in Leudast's company
Kyot   Swemmel's deceased twin brother
Leudast*   Sergeant in Sulingen
Merovec   Major; Marshal Rathar's adjutant
Munderic   Irregular leader west of Herborn
Obilot   Irregular fighter west of Herborn
Rathar*   Marshal of Unkerlant traveling to Cottbus
Razalic   Irregular in forest west of Herborn
Recared   Lieutenant in Sulingen
Sadoc   Irregular fighter west of Herborn; would-be
mage

Swemmel	King of Unkerlant
Tantris	Soldier contacting irregulars in Grelz
Vatran	General in southern Unkerlant
Werbel	Soldier in Sulingen
Ysolt	Cook in Durrwangen

VALMIERA

Amatu	Noble returned from Valmiera
Bauska	Krasta's maidservant in Priekule
Gainibu	King of Valmiera
Gedominu	Skarnu and Merkela's son
Krasta*	Marchioness in Priekule; Skarnu's sister
Lauzdonu	Noble returned from Valmiera
Merkela	Underground fighter; Skarnu's wife
Palasta	Mage in Erzvilkas
Raunu	Sergeant and irregular near Pavilosta
Skarnu*	Marquis; fighter in Ventspils; Krasta's brother
Terbatu	Marquis in Priekule
Valnu	Viscount in Priekule
Zarasai	Underground fighter; a nom de guerre

YANINA

| Iskakis | Yaninan minister to Zuwayza |

ZUWAYZA

Hajjaj*	Foreign minister of Zuwayza
Ikhshid	General in Bishah
Kolthoum	Hajjaj's senior wife
Qutuz	Hajjaj's secretary in Bishah
Shazli	King of Zuwayza
Tewfik	Hajjaj's majordomo
Qutuz	Hajjaj's secretary in Bishah

GREAT NOR

E Q U

NIWAYZA

GYONGYOS

DERLA

FORTHWEG

ORTAH

BALATON
ISLANDS

DUCHY
OF
GRELZ

BOTHNIAN
OCEAN

NARROW SEA

LAND OF THE ICE P
BARRIER MOUNTAINS

One

Leudast looked across the snow-covered ruins of Sulingen. The silence seemed unnatural. After two spells of fighting in the city, he associated it with the horrible din of battle: bursting eggs, the hiss of beams as they turned snow to sudden steam, fire crackling beyond hope of control, masonry falling in on itself, wounded behemoths bawling, wounded horses and unicorns screaming, wounded men shrieking.

None of that now. Everything was silent, eerily so. Young Lieutenant Recared nudged Leudast and pointed. "Look, Sergeant," Recared said, his unlined face glowing with excitement, almost with awe. "Here come the captives."

"Aye," Leudast said softly. He couldn't have been more than two or three years older than Recared himself. It only seemed like ten or twelve. Awe was in his voice, too, as he said it again: "Aye."

He hadn't known quite so many Algarvians were left alive in Sulingen when their army at last gave up its hopeless fight. Here came some of them now: a long column of misery. By Unkerlanter standards, their tall enemies from the east were slim even when well fed. Now, after so much desperate fighting cut off from any hope of resupply, most of them were redheaded skeletons, nothing more.

They were filthy, too, with scraggly red beards covering their hollow cheeks. They wore a fantastic mix of cloaks, Algarvian tunics and kilts, long Unkerlanter tunics, and any rags and scraps of cloth they could get their hands on. Some had stuffed crumpled news sheets and other papers under their tunics to try to fight the frigid winter here in the southwest of Unkerlant. Here and there, Leudast saw Algarvians in pathetic overshoes of woven straw. Snug in his own felt boots, he almost pitied the foe. Almost. King Mezentio's men had come too close to killing him too many times for him to find feeling sorry for them easy.

Lieutenant Recared drew himself up very straight. "Seeing them makes me proud I'm an Unkerlanter," he said.

Maybe the ability to say things like that was part of what separated officers from ordinary soldiers. All Leudast could do was mumble, "Seeing them makes me glad I'm alive." He didn't think Recared heard him, which might have been just as well.

Most of the Algarvians trudged along with their heads down: they were beaten, and they knew it. A few, though, still somehow kept the jauntiness that marked their kind. One of them caught Leudast's eye, grinned, and spoke in pretty fair Unkerlanter: "Hey, Bignose—our turn today, tomorrow yours."

Leudast's mittened hand flew up to the organ the redhead had impugned. It was of a good size and strongly curved, but so were most Unkerlanters' noses. He waved derisively at the Algarvian, waved and said, "Big up above, big down below."

"Aye, all you Unkerlanters are big pricks," the captive came back with a chuckle.

Some soldiers would have blazed a man who said something like that. Leudast contented himself with the last word: "You think it's funny now. You won't be laughing so hard when they set you to work in the mines." That struck home. The Algarvian's grin slipped. He tramped on and was lost among his fellows.

At last, the long tide of misery ended. Recared shook himself, as if waking from a dream. He turned back to Leudast and said, "Now we've got to get ready to whip the rest of King Mezentio's men out of our kingdom."

"Sure enough, sir," Leudast agreed. He hadn't thought about what came after beating the Algarvians in Sulingen. He supposed thinking about such things before you had to was another part of what separated officers from the men they led.

"What state is your company in, Lieutenant?" Recared asked.

"About what you'd expect, sir—I've got maybe a section's worth of men," Leudast answered. Plenty of companies had sergeants in charge of them these days, and plenty of regiments, like Recared's, were commanded by lieutenants.

With a nod, Recared said, "Have them ready to move out tomorrow morning. I don't know for a fact that we will move tomorrow, but that's what it looks like."

"Aye, sir." Leudast's sigh built a young fogbank of vapor in front of his face. He knew he shouldn't have expected anything different, but he would have liked a little longer to rest after one fight before plunging into the next.

They didn't go north the next morning. They did go north the next afternoon, tramping up roads made passable by behemoths wearing snowshoes. Here and there, the snow lay too deep even for behemoths to trample out a usable path. Then the weary troopers had to shovel their way through the drifts. The duty was as physically wearing as combat, the only advantage being that the Algarvians weren't trying to blaze them or drop eggs on their heads.

One of Leudast's troopers said, "I wish we were riding a ley-line caravan up to the new front. Then we'd get there rested. The way things are, we're already halfway down the road to being dead." He flung a spadeful of snow over this shoulder, then stooped to get another one.

A few minutes later, the company emerged from the trench it had dug through a great drift. Leudast was awash in sweat, his lungs on fire, regardless of the frigid air he breathed. When he could see more than snow piled up in front of him, he started to laugh. There a few hundred yards to one side of the road lay a wrecked caravan, its lead car a burnt-out, blasted ruin—the Algarvians had planted an egg along the ley line, and its burst of sorcerous energy had done everything the redheads could have wanted. "Still want to go the easy way, Werbel?"

"No, thanks, Sergeant," the trooper answered at once. "Maybe this isn't so bad after all."

Leudast nodded. He wasn't laughing any more. The steersmen on that ley-line caravan were surely dead. So were dozens of Unkerlanter troopers: bodies lay stacked like cordwood by the ruined caravan. And more dozens, maybe hundreds, of men were hurt. The Algarvians had gained less by winning some skirmishes.

When the regiment encamped for the night in the ruins of an abandoned peasant village, Lieutenant Recared said, "There are some stretches of ley line that are safe. Our mages keep clearing more every day, too."

"I suppose they find out if the ley lines are clear by sending caravans on them," Leudast said sourly. "This one wasn't."

"No, but it will be now, after the mages cancel out the effect of the energy burst," Recared answered.

"And then they'll find another cursed egg a mile farther north," Leudast said. "Find it the hard way, odds are."

"You haven't got the right attitude, Sergeant," Recared said reprovingly.

Leudast thought he had just the right attitude. He was opposed to getting killed or maimed. He was especially opposed to getting killed or maimed because some mage hadn't done his job well enough. Having the enemy kill you was part of war; he understood that. Having your own side kill you . . . He'd come to understand that was part of war, too, however much he hated it.

In good weather, on good roads, they would have been about ten days' march from where the fighting was now. They took quite a bit longer than that to get there. The roads, even the best of them, were far from good. Though the winter solstice was well past, the days remained short and bleak and bitterly cold, with a new blizzard rolling in out of the west every other or every third day.

And, though no redheads opposed them on the ground, the Algarvians hadn't gone away and given up after losing Sulingen. They kept being difficult whenever and wherever they could. Unkerlant was vast, and dragons even thinner in the air than soldiers and behemoths were on the ground. That meant King Mezentio's dragonfliers could fare south to visit death and destruction on the Unkerlanters moving up to assail their countrymen.

When eggs fell, Leudast dived into the closest hole he could find. When Algarvian dragons swooped low to flame, he simply leaped into the snow on his belly and hoped his white smock would keep enemy dragonfliers from noticing him. It worked; after each attack ended, he got up and started slogging north again.

Not everyone was so lucky. He'd long since got used to seeing corpses, sometimes pieces of corpses, scattered in the snow and staining it red. But once the Algarvian dragons had been lucky enough to take out a column of more than a dozen Unkerlanter behemoths and the crews who served their egg-tossers and heavy sticks. The air that day was calm and still; the stench of burnt flesh still lingered as he tramped past. Dragonfire had roasted the behemoths inside the heavy chainmail they wore to protect them from weapons mere footsoldiers could carry. Even the beasts' snowshoe-encased hooves and the iron-shod, curving horns on their noses were covered with soot from the flames the dragons had loosed.

"Last winter, I hear, the Algarvians were eating the flesh of slain behemoths," Recared said.

He hadn't been in the fight the winter before. Leudast had. He nodded. "Aye, they did, sir." After a pause, he added, "So did we."

"Oh." Beneath his swarthy skin, beneath the dark whiskers he'd had scant chance to scrape, Recared looked a little green. "What . . . was it like?"

"Strong. Gamy," Leudast answered. Another pause. "A lot better than nothing."

"Ah. Aye." Recared nodded wisely. "Do you suppose we'll . . . ?"

"Not these beasts," Leudast said. "Not unless you want to stop and do some butchering now. If we keep going, we'll be miles away before we stop for the night."

"That's true." Lieutenant Recared considered. In thoughtful tones, he remarked, "Field kitchens haven't been all they might be, have they?" Leudast started to erupt at that, then noticed the small smile on Recared's face. King Swemmel expected his soldiers to feed themselves whenever they could. Field kitchens were almost as rare as far western mountain apes roaming these plains.

The regiment ate behemoth that night, and for several days thereafter. It was as nasty as Leudast recalled. It was a lot better than the horrible stuff the Algarvians had been pouring down their throats in the last days at Sulingen, though. And, as he'd said, it was ever so much better than nothing.

A couple of nights later, thunder rumbled in the north as the Unkerlanter soldiers made camp. But it couldn't have been thunder; the sky, for once, was clear, with swarms of stars twinkling on jet black. When the weather was very cold, they seemed to twinkle more than on a mild summer night. Leudast noted that only in passing. He knew too well what that distant rumbling that went on and on meant. Scowling, he said, "We're close enough to the fun to hear eggs bursting again. I didn't miss 'em when we couldn't, believe you me I didn't."

"Fun?" Werbel hadn't been in the company long, but even he knew better than that. "More chances to get killed, is what it is."

"That's what they pay us for," Leudast answered. "When they bother to pay us, I mean." He'd lost track of how far in arrears his own pay was. Months—he was sure of that much. And he should have been owed a lieutenant's pay, or a captain's, not a sergeant's, considering the job he'd been doing for more than a year. Of course, Recared should have been paid like a colonel, too.

Werbel listened to the eggs in the distance. With a sigh, he said, "I wonder if they'll get caught up before the war ends."

Leudast's laugh was loud, raucous, and bitter. "Powers above, what makes you think it'll ever end?"

Sidroc was glad Forthwegians had the custom of wearing full beards. For one thing, the thick black hair on his chin and cheeks and upper lip went a little way toward keeping them warm in the savage cold of southern Unkerlant. Coming out of Gromheort in the sunny north, he'd never imagined weather like this. Had anybody told him even a quarter of the truth about it before he knew it for himself, he would have called that fellow a liar to his face. No more.

For another, the beards the men of Plegmund's Brigade—Forthwegians fighting in the service of their Algarvian occupiers—wore helped distinguish them from their Unkerlanter cousins. Unkerlanters and Forthwegians were both stocky, olive-skinned, hook-nosed, both given to wearing long tunics rather than kilts or trousers. But if Sidroc saw a clean-shaven face, he blazed at it without hesitation.

At the moment, he saw very little. His regiment—about a company's worth of men, after all the hard fighting they'd been through—was trying to hold the Unkerlanters out of a village called Hohenroda. It lay somewhere not far from the important town of Durrwangen, but whether north, south, east, or west Sidroc couldn't have said to save his life. He'd done too much marching and countermarching to have any exact notion of where he was.

Eggs crashed down on the village and in front of it. The log walls of the cabin where he was sheltering shook. He turned to Sergeant Werferth. "Those Unkerlanter buggers have every egg-tosser in the world lined up south of here, seems like."

"Wouldn't surprise me," Werferth answered. If anything ever did faze him, he didn't let on. He'd served in the Forthwegian army till the Algarvians destroyed it. Sidroc had been only fifteen when the Derlavaian War began three and a half years before. Werferth spat on the rammed-earth floor. "So what?"

That was too much calm for Sidroc to handle. "They're liable to kill us, that's what!" he burst out. Every once in a while, his voice still broke like a boy's. He hated that, but couldn't help it.

"They won't kill all of us, and the ones who're left'll make 'em pay a good price for this place," Werferth said. He'd signed up for Plegmund's Brigade as soon as the recruiting broadsheets started going up on walls and fences. As far as Sidroc could tell, Werferth didn't care for whom he fought. He might have served the Unkerlanters as readily as the Algarvians. He just liked to fight.

More eggs burst. A fragment of the metal casings that held their sorcerous energy in check till suddenly and violently released slammed into the wall. Timbers creaked. Straw from the thatched roof fell down into Sidroc's hair. He peered out through a tiny slit of a window. "I wish we could see better," he grumbled.

"They don't build houses with south-facing doors in these parts," Werferth said. "A lot of 'em haven't got any south-facing windows at all, not even these little pissy ones. They know where the bad weather comes from."

Sidroc had noticed there weren't any south-facing doors, but he hadn't thought about why. Questions like that didn't interest him. He wasn't stupid, but he didn't use his brains unless he had to. Hitting somebody or blazing somebody struck him as easier.

Werferth went to the other little window. He barked out several sharp curses. "Here they come," he said, and rested his stick on the window frame, the business end pointing out toward the Unkerlanters.

Mouth dry, Sidroc did the same. He'd seen Unkerlanter charges before—not too many, or he wouldn't have remained among those present. Now he had to try to fight off another one.

It was, he had to admit, an awe-inspiring sight. King Swemmel's soldiers formed up in the frozen fields south of Hohenroda, out beyond the range of the defenders' sticks: row on row of them, all in fur hats and white smocks. Sidroc could hear them howling like demons even though they were a long way off. "Do they really feed 'em spirits before they send 'em out to attack?" he asked Werferth.

"Oh, aye," the sergeant answered. "Makes 'em mean, I shouldn't wonder. Though I wouldn't mind a nip myself right now."

Then in the distance, whistles shrilled. The ice that ran up Sidroc's back had nothing to do with the ghastly weather. He knew what was coming next. And it came. The Unkerlanters linked arms, row on row of them. The officers' whistles squealed once more. The Unkerlanters charged.

"Urra!" they bellowed, a deep, rhythmic shout, as snow flew up from their felt boots. "Urra! Urra! Swemmel! Urra! Urra!" If they couldn't overrun Hohenroda—if they couldn't overrun the whole cursed world—they didn't know it.

No doubt because they were drunk, they started blazing long before they got close enough to be in any serious danger of hitting something. Puffs of steam in the snow in front of them showed that some of the men from Plegmund's Brigade had started blazing, too. "Fools!" Werferth growled. "Bloody stupid fornicating fools! We can't afford to waste charges like that. We haven't got any Kaunians around to kill to give us the sorcerous energy we need to get more."

They didn't even have any Unkerlanters to kill for the same purpose. The local peasants had long since fled Hohenroda. The men of Plegmund's Brigade were on their own here.

Or so Sidroc thought, till eggs started bursting among the onrushing Unkerlanters. He whooped with glee—and with surprise. Plegmund's Brigade was made up of footsoldiers; it had to rely on the Algarvians for support. "I didn't know there were egg-tossers back of town," Sidroc said to Werferth.

"Neither did I," Werferth said. "If you think our lords and masters tell us everything they're up to, you're daft. And if you think those eggs'll get rid of all those Unkerlanters, you're even dafter, by the powers above."

Sidroc knew that too well. As the eggs burst in their midst, some of Swemmel's men flew through the air, to lie broken and bleeding in the snow. Others, as far as he could tell, simply ceased to be. But the Unkerlanters who still lived, who could still move forward, came on. They kept shouting with no change in rhythm he could hear.

Then they were close enough to make targets even Werferth couldn't criticize. Sidroc thrust his right forefinger out through a hole in his mitten; his stick required the touch of real flesh to blaze. He stuck his finger into the opening at the rear of the stick and blazed at an Unkerlanter a few hundred yards away. The man went down, but Sidroc had no way to be sure his beam had hit him. He blazed again, and then cursed, for he must have missed his new target.

The Unkerlanters were blazing, too, as they had been for some little while. A beam smote the peasant hut only a foot or so above Sidroc's head. The sharp, tangy stink of charred pine made his nostrils twitch. In drier weather, a beam like that might have fired the hut. Not so much risk of that now, nor of the fire's spreading if it did take hold.

"Mow 'em down!" Werferth said cheerfully. Down the Unkerlanters went, too, in great swaths, almost as if they were being scythed at harvest time. Sidroc had long since seen Swemmel's soldiers cared little about losses. If they got a victory, they didn't count the cost.

"They're going to break in!" he said, an exclamation of dismay. They might pay a regiment's worth of men to shift the company's worth of Forthwegians in Hohenroda, but that wouldn't make the detachment from Plegmund's Brigade any less wrecked. It wouldn't make Sidroc any less dead.

"We have three lines of retreat prepared," Werferth said. "We'll use all of them." He sounded calm, unconcerned, ready for anything that might happen, and ready to make the Unkerlanters pay the highest possible price for this miserable little place. In the abstract, Sidroc admired that. When fear rose up inside him like a black, choking cloud, he knew he couldn't hope to match it.

And then, instead of swarming in among the huts of Hohenroda and rooting out the defenders with beams and with knives and with sticks swung clubwise and with knees in the crotch and thumbs gouging out eyes, the Unkerlanters had to stop short of the village. More eggs fell among Swemmel's men, these from the northeast. Heavy sticks seared down half a dozen men at a time. Algarvian behemoths, fighting as they had in the old days before sticks and eggs were so much of a much, got in among the Unkerlanters and trampled them and gored them with iron-encased horns.

And the Unkerlanters broke. They hadn't expected to run into behemoths around Hohenroda. When they fought according to their plans, they were the stubbornest soldiers in the world. When taken by surprise, they sometimes panicked.

Sidroc was heartily glad this proved one of those times.

"Run, you buggers, run!" he shouted, and blazed a fleeing Unkerlanter in the back. Relief made him sound giddy. He didn't care. He felt giddy.

"They've got snowshoes," Werferth said. "The Algarvian behemoths, I mean. They didn't last winter, you know. The Algarvians hadn't figured they'd have to fight in the snow. It cost 'em."

Werferth didn't just like fighting, he liked going into detail about fighting. Sidroc didn't think that way. He'd joined Plegmund's Brigade mostly because he hadn't been able to get along with anybody back in Gromheort. A lot of the men in the Brigade were similar misfits. Some of them were out-and-out robbers and bandits. He'd led a sheltered life till the war. Things were different now.

Some of the behemoth crews waved to the defenders of Hohenroda, urging them out in pursuit of King Swemmel's men. Sidroc had no intention of pursuing anybody unless his own officers gave the order. He muttered under his breath when shouts rang out from inside the village: "Forward! South!"

Those shouts were in Algarvian. Algarvian officers commanded Plegmund's Brigade, and all orders came in their tongue. In a way, that made sense: the Brigade had to fight alongside Algarvian units and work smoothly with them. In another way, though, it was a reminder of who were the puppets and who the puppeteers.

"Let's go," Werferth said. He would never be anything more than a sergeant. Of course, had Forthweg's independent army survived, he would never have been anything more than a sergeant, either, for he had not a drop of noble blood.

Sidroc winced and cursed as the icy wind tore at him when he left the shelter of the peasant's hut. But he and his comrades were grinning at one another as they formed up and advanced toward the behemoths and toward the tumbled Unkerlanter corpses in the snow.

The Algarvian behemoth crews weren't grinning. "Who are these whoresons?" one of them shouted to a recognizably Algarvian lieutenant among the Forthwegians. "They look like a pack of Unkerlanters."

"We're from Plegmund's Brigade," the lieutenant answered. Sidroc followed Algarvian fairly well. He'd learned some in school, mostly beaten in with a switch, and more since joining the Brigade, which had ways of training harsher yet.

"Plegmund's Brigade!" the redhead on the behemoth burst out. "Plegmund's bloody Brigade? Powers above, we thought we were rescuing real Algarvians."

"Love you too, prickface." That was a trooper named Ceorl, like Sidroc in the squad Werferth led. He always had been and always would be more a ruffian than a soldier. Here, though, Sidroc completely agreed with him.

Major Spinello eyed the approaching Algarvian physician with all the warmth of a crippled elk eyeing a wolf. The physician either didn't notice or was used to such glances from recuperating soldiers. "Good morning," he said cheerfully. "How are we today?"

"I haven't the faintest idea about you, good my sir," Spinello replied—like a lot of Algarvians, he was given to extravagant flights of verbiage. "As for myself, I've never been better in all my born days. When do you propose to turn me loose so I can get back into the fight against the cursed Unkerlanters?"

He'd been saying the same thing for weeks. At first, the healing mages had ignored him. Then he'd been turned over to mere physicians . . . who'd also ignored him. This one said, "Well, we shall see what we shall see." He pressed a hearing tube against the right side of Spinello's chest. "If you'd be so kind as to cough for me . . . ?"

After taking a deep breath, Spinello coughed. He also had the Algarvian fondness for overacting; with the energy he put into his coughs, he might have been at death's door from consumption. "There, you quack," he said when he let the racking spasm end. "Does that satisfy you?"

Perhaps fortunately for him, the physician was harder to offend than most of his countrymen. Instead of getting angry—or instead of continuing the conversation through seconds, as some might have done—the fellow just asked, "Did that hurt?"

"No. Not a bit." Spinello lied without hesitation. He'd taken a sniper's beam in the chest—powers above, a sniper's beam right through the chest—down in Sulingen. He had the feeling he'd hurt for years to come, if not for the rest of his life. That being so, he could—he had to—deal with the pain.

"I was listening to you," the physician said. "So that you know, I don't believe you, not a word of it."

"So that you know, sirrah, I don't care what you believe." Spinello hopped down from the infirmary bed on which he'd been sitting and glared at the physician. He had to look up his nose, not down it, for the doctor overtopped him by several inches: he was a bantam rooster of a man, but strong for his size and very quick. He also had a powerful will; under his gaze, the physician gave back a pace before checking himself. Voice soft and menacing, Spinello demanded, "Will you write me out the certificate that warrants me fit to return to duty?"

To his surprise, the physician said, "Aye." He reached into the folder he'd set on the bed and pulled out a printed form. "In fact, I have filled it out, all but the signature." He plucked a pen and a sealed bottle of ink from the breast pocket of his tunic, inked the pen, and scrawled something that might have been his name or might equally have been an obscenity in demotic Gyongyosian. Then he handed Spinello the completed form. "This will permit you to return to duty, Major. It doesn't warrant you as fit, because you aren't fit. But the kingdom needs you, and you're unlikely to fall over dead at the first harsh breeze. Powers above keep you safe." He bowed.

And Spinello bowed in return, more deeply than the physician had. That was an extraordinary courtesy; as a count, he surely outranked the other man, who was bound to be only a commoner. But the physician had given him what he wanted most in all the world. He bowed again. "I am in your debt, sir."

With a sigh, the physician said, "Why a man should be so

eager to rush headlong into danger has always been beyond me."

"You said it yourself: Algarve needs me," Spinello replied. "Now tell me at once: is it true the last of our brave lads have had to yield themselves in Sulingen?"

"It's true," the physician said grimly. "The crystallomancers can't reach anyone there, and the Unkerlanters are shouting themselves hoarse at the victory. Not a word about the price we made them pay."

Spinello cursed. The Algarvians had fought their way into Sulingen the summer before—fought their way into it and never fought their way out again. South beyond the Wolter River lay the Mamming Hills, full of the cinnabar that made dragonfire burn so hot and fierce. Take Sulingen, storm over the Wolter, seize the mines in the hills—it had all seemed so straightforward.

It would have been, too, had the Unkerlanters not fought like demons for every street, for every manufactory, for every floor of every block of flats. And now, even though Swemmel's men had, as the physician said, surely paid a great price, an Algarvian army was gone, gone as if it had never been.

"I hope they send me west again in a tearing hurry," Spinello said, and the physician rolled his eyes. Spinello pointed to the closet at the far end of the room. "I'm sick of these cursed hospital whites. Is my uniform in there?"

"If you mean the one in which you came here, Major, no," the physician replied. "That one, as I hope you will understand, is somewhat the worse for wear. But a major's uniform does await you, aye. One moment." He went over to the closet, set a hand on the latch, and murmured softly. "There. Now it will open to your touch. We couldn't very well have had you escaping before you were even close to healed."

"I suppose not," Spinello admitted. They'd known him, all right. He walked over to the closet and tried the latch. It did open. It hadn't before; he'd tried a good many times. With a squeak of dry hinges, the door opened, too. There on hooks hung a tunic and kilt of severe military cut. The tunic, he saw to his pride, had on it a wound ribbon. He was entitled to that ribbon, and he would wear it. He got out of the baggy infirmary clothes and put on the uniform. It was baggy, too, baggy enough to make him angry. "Couldn't they have found a tailor who wasn't drunk?" he snapped.

"It is cut to your measure, Major," the physician answered. "Your former measure, I should say. You've lost a good deal of flesh since you were wounded."

"*This* much?" Spinello didn't want to believe it. But he couldn't very well call the physician a liar, either.

Also hanging in the closet was a broad-brimmed hat with a bright feather from some bird from tropical Siaulia sticking up from the leather hatband. Spinello clapped it on. His head hadn't shrunk, anyhow. That was a relief.

The physician said, "I have a mirror in my belt pouch, if you'd like to see yourself. We don't keep many in infirmaries. They might dismay patients like you, and they might do worse than dismay others, the ones unlucky enough to receive head wounds."

"Ah." Contemplating that was enough to make Spinello decide he hadn't come out so bad after all. In unwontedly quiet tones, he said, "Aye, sir, if you'd be so kind."

"Of course, Major." The physician took it out and held it up.

Spinello whistled softly. He *had* lost flesh; his cheekbones were promontories just under the skin, and the line of his jaw sharper than it had been since he left his teens—an era more than a dozen years behind him now. But his green eyes still gleamed, and the attendants who'd trimmed his coppery mustache and little chin beard and side whiskers had done a respectable job. He tilted the hat to a jauntier angle and said, "How ever will the girls keep their legs closed when they see me walking down the street?"

With a snort, the doctor put the mirror away. "You're well enough, all right," he said. "Go back to the west and terrorize the Unkerlanter women."

"Oh, my dear fellow!" Spinello rolled his eyes. "A homelier lot you'd never want to see. Built like bricks, almost all of them. I had better luck when I was on occupation duty in

Forthweg. This little blond Kaunian, couldn't have been above seventeen"—his hands shaped an hourglass in the air—"and she'd do anything I wanted, and I do mean anything."

"*How* many times have you told me about her since you've been in my care?" the physician asked. "Her name was Vanai, and she lived in Oyngestun, and—"

"And every word of it true, too," Spinello said indignantly. He took a cloak from the closet and threw it on, then dealt with shoes and stockings. He was panting by the time he finished dressing; he'd spent too long flat on his back. But he refused to admit how worn he was, even to himself. "Now, then—what formalities must I go through to escape your lair here?"

He presented the certificate of discharge to the floor nurse. After she signed it, he presented it to the nursing station downstairs. After someone there signed it, Spinello presented it to the soldier at the doorway. The man had won the soft post with a right tunic sleeve pinned up short. He pointed along the street and said, "The reassignment depot is three blocks that way, sir. Can you walk it?"

"Why? Is this a test?" Spinello asked. Rather to his surprise, the one-armed soldier nodded. He realized it made a certain amount of sense: you might browbeat a doctor into giving you a certificate, but no one who couldn't walk three blocks had any business going off to the front. The soldier signed the certificate quite legibly. Spinello asked him, "Were you lefthanded . . . before?"

"No, sir," the fellow answered. "I got this in Forthweg, early on. I've had two and a half years to learn how to do things over again."

With a nod, Spinello left the infirmary for the first time since being brought there and headed in the direction the disabled soldier had given him. Before the war, Trapani had been a gay, lively city, as befit the capital of a great kingdom. The gray gloom on the streets now had only a little to do with the overcast sky and the nasty, cold mist in the air: it was a thing of the spirit, not of the weather.

People hurried along about their business without the strut

and swagger that were as much a part of Algarvian life as wine. Women mostly looked mousy, which wasn't easy for Spinello's redheaded compatriots. The only men in the streets who weren't in uniform were old enough to be veterans of the Six Years' War a generation before or else creaking ancients even older than that.

And everyone, men and women alike, looked grim. The news sheets the vendors sold were bordered in black. Sulingen had fallen, all right. It had been plain for a long time that the town would fall to the Unkerlanters, but no one here seemed to have wanted to believe it no matter how plain it was. That made the blow even harder now that it struck home.

Big signs outside the entrance named the reassignment depot. Spinello bounded up the marble steps, threw the doors wide, and shouted, "I'm fit for duty again! The war is won!"

Some of the soldiers in there laughed. Some of them snorted. Some just rolled their eyes. "No matter who you are, sir, and no matter how great you are, you still have to queue up," a sergeant said. Spinello did, though he hated lines.

When he presented the multiply signed certificate of discharge to another sergeant, that worthy shuffled through files. At last, he said, "I have a regiment for you, Major, if you care to take it."

That was a formality. Spinello drew himself up to stiff attention. "Aye!" he exclaimed. The catch in his breath was partly from his healing, partly excitement.

The sergeant handed him his orders, as well as a list of ley-line caravans that would take him to the men who held the line somewhere in northern Unkerlant. They were waiting for him with bated breath. They just didn't know it yet. "If you hurry, sir, there's a caravan leaving from the main depot for Eoforwic in half an hour," the sergeant said helpfully. "That'll get you halfway there."

Spinello dashed out of the reassignment depot and screamed for a cab. He made the ley-line caravan he needed. As he glided southwest out of Trapani, he wondered why he was in such a hurry to go off and perhaps get himself killed. He had no answer, any more than the physician had. But he was.

* * *

Marshal Rathar wished with all his heart that he could have stayed down in southern Unkerlant and finished smashing the Algarvian invaders there. They were like serpents—you could step on them three days after you thought they were dead, and they'd rear up and bite you in the leg. Rathar sighed. He supposed General Vatran could handle things till he got back. King Swemmel had ordered him to Cottbus, and when King Swemmel ordered, every Unkerlanter obeyed.

As it was, Rathar wouldn't reach Cottbus as fast as Swemmel hoped and expected. Now that the Algarvians had been crushed in Sulingen and driven back from it, more direct ley-line routes between the south and the capital were in Unkerlanter hands once more. The trouble was, too many of them weren't yet usable. Retreating Algarvian mages had done their best to sabotage them. Retreating Algarvian engineers, relentless pragmatists, had buried eggs along the ley lines that traveled them after the Algarvian mages' efforts were overcome.

And so, Rathar had to travel almost as far out of a straight line to get from the vicinity of Sulingen to Cottbus as he had when coming south from Cottbus to Sulingen when things looked blackest the summer before. The steersman for the caravan kept sending flunkies back to Rathar with apologies for every zigzag. The marshal's displeasure carried weight. After Swemmel—but a long, long way after Swemmel (Rathar was convinced only he knew how far)—he was the most powerful man in Unkerlant.

But the marshal wasn't particularly displeased, not when he didn't want to go to Cottbus in the first place. He said, "I do prefer not getting killed on the journey, you know." The steward who'd brought him news of the latest delay had been pale under his swarthy skin. Now he breathed easier.

When the steward left the caravan car, a breath of chill got in, remind-ing the marshal it was winter—and a savage Un-kerlanter winter at that—outside. Inside, with all the windows sealed, with a red-hot coal stove at each end of the car, it might as well have been summer in desert Zuwayza, or possibly summer in a bake oven. Rathar sighed. Unkerlanter caravan cars were always like that in winter. He rubbed his eyes. The hot, stuffy air never failed to give him a headache.

He yawned, lowered the lamps, and went to sleep. He was still sleeping when the ley-line caravan silently glided into Cottbus. An apologetic steward shook him awake. Yawning again, the marshal pulled off the thin linen tunic he'd been wearing and put on the thick wool one he'd used in the caves and ruined houses that had been his headquarters buildings down in the south. For good measure, he added a heavy wool cloak and a fur cap with earflaps.

Sweat rivered off him. "Powers above, get me out of here before I cook in my own juices," he said hoarsely.

"Aye, lord Marshal," the steward said, and led him to the door at the end of the car. He had to go past a stove to get there, and did come perilously close to steaming. Then the steward opened the door, and the frigid air outside hit him like a blow in the face. Cottbus was well north of Sulingen, and so enjoyed a milder climate, but milder didn't mean mild.

Rathar sneezed three times in quick succession as he walked down the wooden steps from the ley-line car—which floated a yard off the ground—to the floor of the depot. He pulled a handkerchief from his belt pouch and blew his large, proudly curved nose.

"Your health, lord Marshal," his adjutant said, coming to attention and saluting as Rathar's feet hit the flagstones. "It's good to see you again."

"Thank you, Major Merovec," Rathar answered. "It's good to be back in the capital." *What a liar, what a courtier, I'm getting to be,* he thought.

Merovec gestured to the squad of soldiers behind him. "Your honor guard, sir, and your bodyguard, to make sure no Algarvian assassin or Grelzer turncoat does you harm on the way to the royal palace."

"How generous of his Majesty to provide them for me," Rathar said. The soldiers looked blank-faced and tough: typical Unkerlanter farm boys. They were, no doubt, equally typical in their willingness to follow orders no matter what those orders were. If Swemmel had ordered them to arrest him, for instance, they would do it, regardless of the big stars on the collar tabs of his tunic. Swemmel stayed strong not least by allowing himself no strong subjects, and Rathar knew he'd won a good deal of fame for his operations in and around Sulingen.

If Swemmel wanted to seize him, he could. Rathar knew that. And so he strode up to Merovec and the unsmiling soldiers behind him. "I have a carriage waiting for you, lord Marshal," his adjutant said, "and others for the guards here. If you will come with me . . ."

The carriage was only a carriage, not a prison wagon. The troopers got into four other carriages. They took station around the one that carried Rathar. No, an assassin wouldn't have an easy blaze at him. The marshal didn't particularly worry about assassins. King Swemmel, now, King Swemmel saw them behind every curtain and under every chair.

Cottbus by night was dark and gloomy. Algarvian dragons still flew over to drop eggs on the Unkerlanter capital. The darkness helped thwart them, even if they didn't come nearly so often or in such numbers as they had the winter before. Algarvian behemoths and footsoldiers had almost broken into Cottbus then. They'd been pushed back a good way since, which meant a longer, harder journey for King Mezentio's dragonfliers.

"Well, what sort of juicy court gossip have you got for me?" Rathar asked his adjutant.

Major Merovec stared; even in the darkness, his eyes glittered as they widened. "N-Not much, lord Marshal," he stammered; Rathar was normally indifferent to the petty—and sometimes not so petty—scandal that set tongues wagging at every court on the continent of Derlavai . . . and every court off it, too.

Horses' hoofbeats muffled by snow on stone, the carriages entered the great empty square around the royal palace. Surrounding the square were statues of the kings of Unkerlant. Swemmel's loomed, twice as tall as any of the others. Rathar wondered how long the outsized image would endure in the reign of Swemmel's successor. That was not a thought he could ever speak aloud.

Inside the palace, lamps seared eyes used to darkness. The king had trouble sleeping, which meant his servitors hardly slept at all. "His Majesty will see you in the audience chamber," a messenger told Rathar.

The marshal hung the ceremonial sword of his rank on brackets in an anteroom to that chamber. Unsmiling guards patted him with intimacy few women would have dared use. Only after enduring that could he go on. And then he had to prostrate himself before the king and, face against the carpet, recite his praises until given permission to rise.

At last, King Swemmel gave it. As Rathar climbed to his feet—a knee clicked; he wasn't so young as he had been—the king said, "We wish to continue the rout of the cursed Algarvians from our land. Punish them! We command you!" His dark eyes flashed in his long, pale face.

"Your Majesty, I aim to do just that," Rathar replied. "Now that their army in Sulingen is no more, I can shift soldiers to my columns farther north. With luck, we'll bag most of the redheads still in the southwestern part of the kingdom, trap 'em as neatly as we did the ones who'd reached the Wolter."

He knew he was exaggerating—or rather, that he would have to be very lucky indeed to bring off everything he had in mind. The Algarvians would have a lot to say about what he did and what he ended up unable to do. Getting his sovereign to understand that was one of the hardest jobs he had. So far, he'd managed. Had he failed, Unkerlant would have a new marshal these days. Rathar didn't particularly fear for himself. He did doubt the kingdom had a better officer to lead her armies.

Swemmel said, "At last, we have them on the run. By the powers above, we shall punish them as they deserve. When King Mezentio is in our hands, we'll boil him alive, as we served Kyot." Kyot, his identical twin, had fought him for the throne and lost. Had he won, he would have boiled Swemmel—and, probably, Rathar with him, though he might have contented himself with taking the soldier's head.

As far as Rathar was concerned, his king was putting the unicorn's tail in front of its horn. The marshal said, "This war is still a long way from won, your Majesty."

But Swemmel had the bit between his teeth and trampled on: "And before we do, we'll give Mezentio's cousin Raniero, the misnamed King of Grelz, an end to make Mezentio glad he's just being boiled. Aye, we will." Gloating anticipation filled his voice.

Rathar did his best to draw the king back from dreams of revenge to what was real. "We have to beat the redheads first, you know. As I said, I want to keep biting chunks out of their forces in Unkerlant. We bit out a big chunk when we took Sulingen back, but they can still hurt us if we get careless. I aim to pin them against one river barrier after another, make them fight at a disadvantage or else have to make a whole series of difficult retreats. . . ."

Swemmel wasn't listening. "Aye, when Raniero falls into our hands, we'll flay him and draw him and unman him and—oh, whatever else strikes our fancy."

"We almost ought to thank Mezentio for him," Rathar said. "One of our own nobles on the Grelzer throne in Herborn would have brought more traitors to the Algarvian side than Raniero has a hope of luring."

"Traitors everywhere," Swemmel muttered. "Everywhere." His eyes darted this way and that. "We'll kill them all, see if we don't." During the Twinkings War and even after it, there had been a good many real plots against him. There had also been a good many that existed only in his fevered imagination. Real plotters and imagined ones were equally dead now, with no one to say who was which. "Traitors."

To Rathar's relief, Swemmel wasn't looking at him. Almost desperately, the marshal said, "As I was telling you, your Majesty, our plans—"

Swemmel spoke in peremptory tones: "Set all the columns moving now. The sooner we strike the Algarvians, the sooner they shall be driven from our soil." Did he mean the soil of Unkerlant or his own, personal soil? Rathar often had trouble telling.

"Do you not agree, your Majesty, that your armies have had more success when you waited till everything was ready before striking?" Rathar asked. He'd had trouble getting Swemmel to see that throughout the war. He didn't want more trouble now.

Swemmel, of course, cared nothing for what his marshal wanted. Swemmel cared only for what he wanted. And now, glaring down at Rathar from his high seat, he snapped, "We have given you an order. You may carry it out, or someone else may carry it out. We care nothing about that. We care only that we should be obeyed. Do you understand us?"

Sometimes, a threat to resign would bring Swemmel to his senses when he tried to order something uncommonly hare-brained. Rathar didn't judge this would have been one of those times. The king wouldn't have summoned him from the south for anything but a show of unquestioned allegiance. And Swemmel would remove him and likely remove his head if he balked. Rathar looked down at the carpet and sighed. "Aye, your Majesty," he said, casting about in his mind for ways to say he obeyed while in fact doing what really needed doing.

"And think not to evade our will with plausible excuses," King Swemmel barked. He might not have been a very wise man, but no denying he was clever. Rathar sighed again.

Back before the Derlavaian War broke out, Skarnu had been a marquis. He still was a marquis, when you got down to it, but he hadn't lived like one for years. And, if the Algarvian occupiers of his native Valmiera ever got their hands on him, he wouldn't live anymore at all. This was what he got for carrying on the fight against the redheads after King Gainibu surrendered.

Had he made his peace with the conquerors, he could have been living soft in the familial mansion on the edge of Priekule, the capital. Instead, he found himself holed up in a dingy cold-water flat in Ventspils, an eastern provincial town of no great distinction—indeed, of no small distinction he could think of.

His sister still lived in that mansion. He growled, down deep in his throat. Krasta, curse her, had an Algarvian lover—Skarnu had seen them listed as a couple in a news sheet. *Colonel Lurcanio and the Marchioness Krasta*. Lurcanio, curse him, had come too close to catching Skarnu not long before. He'd had to flee the farm where he'd been living, the widow he'd come to love, and the child—his child—she was carrying. He hoped Lurcanio's men had only been after him, and that Merkela was safe.

Hope was all he could do. He didn't dare write to the farm outside the southern village of Pavilosta. If the Algarvians intercepted the letter, their mages might be able to use the law of contagion to trace it back to him. "Powers below eat them," he muttered. He wanted to pour out his soul to Merkela, but the enemy silenced him as effectively as if they'd clapped a gag over his mouth.

He went to the grimy window and looked down at the street three stories down. Wan winter sunshine filtered between the blocks of flats that sat almost side by side. Not even sunshine, though, could make the cobbles in the streets, the worn slates of the sidewalks, and the sooty, slushy snow in the gutters and in the corners by stairways anything but unlovely. The wind shook bare-branched trees; their shifting shadows put Skarnu in mind of groping, grabbing skeleton hands.

Blond Valmierans in tunics and trousers trudged this way and that. From what Skarnu had seen, nobody in Ventspils did much more than trudge. He wondered if he could blame that gloom on the Algarvian occupation, or if life in a provincial town would have been bloody dull even before the invaders came. Had he lived his whole life in Ventspils, he suspected he would have been gloomy most of the time himself.

Up the street came a couple of Algarvian soldiers or constables. He didn't recognize them by their red hair; like a lot of his countrymen, they wore hats to fight the cold. He didn't even recognize them by their pleated kilts, though he soon noticed those. No, what set them apart was the way they moved. They didn't trudge. They strutted, heads up, shoulders back, chests out. They moved as if they had vital business to take care of and wanted everybody around them to know it.

"Algarvians," Skarnu said with fine contempt. If they weren't the most self-important people on the face of the earth, he didn't know who was. He laughed, but not for long. Their pretensions would have been funnier if they hadn't dominated all the east of Derlavai.

And then they came up the stairs to his block of flats. When he saw that, he didn't hesitate for a moment. He grabbed a cloth cap, stuffed it down as low on his head as it would go, and left his flat, closing the door behind him as quietly as he could. His wool tunic would keep him warm for a while outside.

He hurried to the stairs and started down them. As he'd thought he would, he passed the Algarvians coming up. He didn't look at them; they didn't look at him. He'd gambled that they wouldn't. Their orders were probably something like, *Arrest the man you find in flat 36.* But there wouldn't be any man in flat 36 to arrest when they got there. If Skarnu hadn't seen them coming . . .

Vapor puffed from his mouth and nose as he opened the front door and went out onto the street. He was already hurrying up the sidewalk in the direction from which the redheads had come—a clever touch, he thought—when he realized he didn't know for a fact that they'd been after him. He laughed, though it wasn't funny. How likely that this block of flats held two men the Algarvians wanted badly enough to send their own after him instead of entrusting the job to Valmieran constables? Not very.

A youth waved a news sheet in his face. "Algarvians smash Unkerlanter drive south of Durrwangen!" he cried. The news sheets, of course, printed only what King Mezentio's ministers wanted Valmiera to hear. They'd stopped talking about Sulingen, for instance, as soon as the battle there was lost. They made the victories they reported these days sound like splendid triumphs instead of the desperate defensive struggles they had to be.

Skarnu strode past the vendor without a word, without even shaking his head. He turned a corner and then another and another and another, picking right or left at random each time. If the Algarvians came bursting out of the block of flats hot on his trail, they wouldn't have an easy time following him. He chuckled. He didn't know himself where he was going, so why should the redheads?

That didn't stay funny long, though. He had to pause and get his bearings—not easy in Ventspils, since he didn't know the town well. In Priekule, he could have looked for the Kaunian Column of Victory. That would have told him where in the city he was . . . till the Algarvians knocked it down. The victory it celebrated was one the Kaunian Empire had won over the barbarous Algarvic tribes—a victory that still rankled the tribesmen's barbarous descendants more than a millennium and a half later.

Though he took longer than he should have, he finally did figure out where he was. Then he needed to figure out where to go. That had only one answer, really: the tavern called the Lion and the Mouse. But the answer wasn't so good, either. Were the Algarvians after him in particular, or were they trying to smash all the resistance in Ventspils? If the former, they might know nothing of the tavern. If the latter, they were liable to be waiting in force around or inside it.

He muttered under his breath. A woman passing by gave him a curious look. He stared back so stonily, she hurried on her way as if she'd never looked at him at all. Maybe she thought him a madman or a derelict. As long as she didn't think him one of the handful who kept the fight against Algarve alive, he cared nothing for her opinion.

I've got to go, he realized. The Lion and the Mouse was the only place where he could hope to meet other irregulars. They could find him somewhere else to stay or spirit him out of Ventspils altogether. Without them . . . Skarnu didn't want to think about that. One man alone was one man helpless.

He approached the tavern with all the caution he'd learned as a captain in the Valmieran army—before the Algarvians used dragons and behemoths to smash that army into isolated chunks and then beat it. He couldn't see anything that looked particularly dangerous around the place. He wished Raunu, his veteran sergeant, were still with him. Having been in the army as long as Skarnu was alive, Raunu knew far more about soldiering than Skarnu had learned in something under a year. But Skarnu was a marquis and Raunu the son of a sausage seller, so Skarnu had led the company of which they'd both been part.

After twice walking past the doorway to the Lion and the Mouse, Skarnu, the mouse, decided he had to put his head in the lion's mouth. Scowling, he walked into the tavern. The burly fellow behind the bar was a man he'd seen before—which meant nothing if the man was in bed with the Algarvians.

But there, at a table in the far corner of the room, Skarnu spied a painter who was one of the leaders of the underground in Ventspils. Unless he proved a traitor, too, the Algarvians didn't know about this place. Skarnu bought a mug of ale—nothing wrong with Ventspils' ale—and sat down across the table from him.

"Well, hello, Pavilosta," the painter said. "Didn't expect to see you here today." That sounded polite, but harsh suspicion lay under it.

Skarnu's answering grimace was harsh, too. He didn't care to have even the name of the village he'd come from mentioned out loud. After a pull at the ale, he said, "A couple of redheads came into my block of flats an hour ago. If I hadn't spied 'em outside, they would've nabbed me."

"Well, we can't expect the Algarvians to love us, not after we yanked those Sibian dragonfliers right out from under their noses," the local underground leader said. "They'd want to poke back if they saw the chance to do it."

"I understand that." Like the painter, Skarnu kept his voice low. "But are they after underground folk in Ventspils, or me in particular?"

"Why would they be after you in particular?" the other

man asked. Then he paused and thumped his forehead with the heel of his hand. "I keep forgetting you're not just Pavilosta. You're the chap with a sister in the wrong bed."

"That's one way to put it, aye," Skarnu said. It was, in fact, a gentler way to put it than he would have used. It also avoided mentioning his noble blood—common women could and did sleep with the redheaded occupiers, too.

After a pull on his own mug of ale, the painter said, "She knew where you were down in Pavilosta—she did, or else the Algarvian she's laying did. But how would she know you've come to Ventspils? How would the redheads know, either?"

"Obvious answer is, they're squeezing somebody between Pavilosta and here," Skarnu said. "I had a narrow escape getting out of there; they might have stumbled onto somebody who helped me." He named no names. What the other fellow didn't know, King Mezentio's men and their Valmieran stooges couldn't squeeze out of him. Skarnu wouldn't have been so careful about security even during his duty in the regular Valmieran army.

"If they've got hold of a link in the chain between here and there, that could be . . . unpleasant," the painter said. "Every time we take in a new man, we have to wonder if he's the fellow who's going to sell the lot of us to the Algarvians—and one fine day, one of them will do it."

Someone Skarnu had seen once or twice before strolled into the Lion and the Mouse. Instead of ordering ale or spirits, he spoke in casual tones: "Redheads and their dogs are heading toward this place. Some people might not want to hang around and wait for them." He didn't even look toward the corner where Skarnu and the painter sat.

Skarnu's first impulse was to leap and run. Then he realized how stupid that was: it would make him stand out, which was the last thing he wanted. And even if it didn't, where would he go? Ventspils wasn't his town; aside from the men of the underground, he had no friends and hardly any acquaintances here.

After a last quick swig, the painter set down his empty mug. "Maybe *we'd* better not hang around and wait for them," he said, with which conclusion Skarnu could hardly disagree.

Skarnu didn't bother finishing his ale. He left the mug on the table and followed the other man out. "Where do we go now?" he asked.

"There are places," the painter said, an answer that wasn't an answer. After a moment, Skarnu realized the underground leader had security concerns of his own. Sure enough, the man went on, "I don't *think* we'll have to blindfold you."

"I'm so glad to hear it." Skarnu had intended the words to be sarcastic. They didn't come out that way. The Unkerlanters might have the Algarvians on the run in the distant west, but here in Valmiera the redheads could still make their handful of foes dance to their tune.

Fernao was studying his Kuusaman. That was, he understood, a curious thing for a Lagoan mage to do. Though Lagoas and Kuusamo shared the large island off the southeastern coast of Derlavai, his countrymen were in the habit of looking in the direction of the mainland and not toward their eastern neighbors, whom they usually regarded as little more than amusing rustics.

That was true even though a lot of Lagoans had some Kuusaman blood. Fernao's height and his red hair proved him of mainly Algarvic stock, but his narrow, slanted eyes showed it wasn't pure. Lagoans also did their best not to notice that Kuusamo outweighed their kingdom about three to one.

Outside, a storm that had blown up from the south did its best to turn this stretch of Kuusamo into the land of the Ice People. The wind howled. Snow drifted around the hostel the soldiers of the Seven Princes had run up here in the middle of nowhere. The district of Naantali lay so far south, the sun rose above the horizon for only a little while each day.

Down on the austral continent, of course, it wouldn't have risen at all for a while on either side of the winter solstice. Having seen the land of the Ice People in midwinter, Fernao knew that all too well. Here, he had a coal-burning stove, not the brazier he'd fed lumps of dried camel dung.

"I shall shovel snow," he murmured: a particularly apt paradigm. "You will shovel snow. He, she, it will shovel snow. We shall shovel snow. You-plural will shovel snow. They—"

Someone knocked on the door. "One moment!" Fernao called, not in Kuusaman but in classical Kaunian, the language he really did share with his Kuusaman colleagues. Just getting to the door took rather more than a moment. He had to lever himself up from his stool with the help of a cane, grab the crutch that leaned by the chair, and use both of them to cross the room and reach the doorway.

And all of that, he thought as he opened the door, was progress. He'd almost died when an Algarvian egg burst too close to him down in the land of the Ice People. His leg had been shattered. Only in the past few days had the Kuusaman healers released what was left of it from its immobilizing plaster prison.

Pekka stood in the hall outside. "Hello," she said, also in classical Kaunian, the widespread language of scholarship. "I hope I did not interrupt any important calculations. I hate it when people do that to me."

"No." Fernao smiled down at her. Like most of her countrymen—the exceptions being those who had some Lagoan blood—she was short and slim and dark, with a wide face, high cheekbones, and eyes slanted like his own. He switched to her language to show what he had been doing: "We shall shovel snow. You-plural will shovel snow. They will shovel snow."

She laughed. Against her golden skin, her teeth seemed even whiter than they were. A moment later, she sobered and nodded. "Your accent is quite good," she said, first in Kaunian, then in her own tongue.

"Thanks," Fernao said in Kuusaman. Then he returned to the classical tongue: "I have always had a knack for learning languages, but yours is different from any other I have tried to pick up." Awkwardly, he stepped aside. "Please come in. Sit down. Make yourself at home."

"I wish I were at home," Pekka said. "I wish my husband were at home, too. I miss my family." Her husband, Fernao knew, was no less a sorcerer than she, but one of a more practical bent. As Pekka walked past, she asked, "Were you using the stool or the bed? I do not want to disturb you."

"The stool," Fernao answered. Pekka had already sat down on the bed by the time he closed the door, hobbled back across the chamber, and carefully lowered himself onto the stool. He propped the crutch where he could easily reach it before saying, "And what can I do for you this morning?"

He knew what he wouldn't have minded doing, not for her but with her. He'd always reckoned Kuusaman women too small and skinny to be very interesting, but was changing his mind about Pekka. That was probably because, working alongside her, he'd come to think of her as colleague and friend, to admire her wits as well as her body. Whatever the reason, his interest was real.

He kept quiet about it. By the way she spoke about Leino, her husband, and Uto, her son, she wasn't interested in him or in anyone but them. Making advances would have been worse than rude—it would have been futile. Though a good theoretical sorcerer, Fernao was a practical man in other ways. Stretching out his legs in front of him, he waited to hear what Pekka had to say.

She hesitated, something she seldom did. At last, she answered, "Have you done any more work on Ilmarinen's contention?"

"Which contention do you mean?" he said, as innocently as he could. "He has so many of them."

That got him another smile from Pekka. Like the first, it didn't last long. "You know which one," she said. "No matter how many strange ideas Ilmarinen comes up with, only one really matters to us now."

And that was also true. Fernao sighed. He didn't like admitting, even to himself, how true it was. Here, though, he had no choice. Pointing out the window—the double-glazed window that helped hold winter at bay—in the direction of the latest release of sorcerous energy the Kuusaman experimental team had touched off, he said, "That was fresh grass, summer grass, he pulled up from the middle of the crater."

"I know," Pekka said softly. "Fresh grass in the middle of—this." She pointed out the window, too, at the snow swirling past in the grip of the whistling wind. More softly still, she added, "It can mean just one thing."

Fernao sighed again. "The calculations suggested it all along. So did the other experimental results. No wonder Ilmarinen got angry at us when we didn't want to face what that meant."

Pekka's laugh was more rueful than anything else. "If Ilmarinen had not got angry over that, he would have got angry over something else," she said. "Getting angry, and getting other people angry, is what he enjoys more than anything else these days. But . . ." She stopped; she didn't want to say what followed logically from Ilmarinen's grass, either. In the end, she did: "We really do seem to be drawing our energy in these experiments by twisting time itself."

There. It was out. Fernao didn't want to hear it, any more than he'd wanted to say it. But now that Pekka had said it, he could only nod. "Aye. That is what the numbers say, sure enough." For once, he was glad to be speaking classical Kaunian. It let him sound more detached, more objective— and a lot less frightened—than he really was.

"I think the numbers also say we can only draw energy from it when we send one set of animals racing forward and the other racing back," Pekka said. "We cannot do any more meddling than that . . . can we?" She sounded frightened, too, as if she were pleading for reassurance.

Fernao gave her what reassurance he could: "I read the calculations the same way. So does Siuntio. And so does Ilmarinen, for all his bluff and bluster."

"I know," Pekka said. "I have had long talks with both of them—talks much more worried than this one." Maybe she found Kaunian distancing, too. But she added, "What if the Algarvians are also calculating—calculating and coming up with different answers?"

For effect, Fernao tried a few words of Kuusaman: "Then we're all in trouble." Pekka let out a startled laugh, then nodded. Fernao wished he could have gone on in her language, but had to drop back into classical Kaunian: "But most of their mages are busy with their murderous magic, and the rest really should get the same results we have."

"Powers above, I hope so!" Pekka exclaimed. "The energy release is dreadful enough as is, but the world could not stand having its past revised and edited."

Before Fernao could answer, someone else knocked on the door. Pekka sprang up and opened it before Fernao could start what was for him the long, slow, involved process of rising. "Oh, hello, my dear," Master Siuntio said in Kuusaman before courteously switching to classical Kaunian so Fernao could follow: "I came to ask if our distinguished Lagoan colleague would care to join me for dinner. Now I ask you the same question as well."

"I would be delighted, sir," Fernao said, and did struggle to his feet.

"And I," Pekka agreed. "Things may look brighter once we have some food and drink inside us."

A buffet waited in the dining room. Fernao piled Kuusaman smoked salmon—as good as any in the world—on a chewy roll, and added slices of onion and of hard-cooked egg and pickled cucumber. Along with a mug of ale, that made a dinner to keep him going till suppertime. "Would you like me to carry those for you?" Pekka asked.

"If you would be so kind—the plate, anyhow," Fernao answered. "I can manage the mug. Now I have two hands, but I would need three." Till not too long before, he'd had an arm in a cast as well as a leg. Then he'd needed four hands and possessed only one.

Pekka had built a sandwich almost as formidable as his own. She did some substantial damage to it before asking Siuntio, "Master, do you think you will find any loopholes in the spells we are crafting?"

Siuntio gently shook his head. He looked more like a kindly grandfather than the leading theoretical sorcerer of his generation. "No," he said. "We have been over this ground before, you know. I see extravagant energy releases, aye, far more extravagant than we could get from any other source.

But I see no way to achieve anything but that. We cannot sneak back through the holes we tear in time—and a good thing we can't, too."

"I agree," Fernao said, gulping down a large mouthful of salmon to make sure his words came clear. "On both counts, I agree."

"I don't believe even Ilmarinen will disagree on this," Siuntio said.

"Disagree on what?" Ilmarinen asked, striding into the dining hall as if naming him could conjure him up. With a wispy white chin beard, wild hair, and gleaming eyes, he might have been Siuntio's raffish brother. But he, too, was a formidable mage. "Disagree on what?" he repeated.

"On the possibility of manipulating time along with extracting energy from it," Siuntio told him.

"Well, that doesn't look like it's in the math," Ilmarinen said. "On the other hand, you never can tell." He poured himself a mug of ale and then, for good measure, another. "Now this is a proper dinner," he declared as he sat down by Fernao.

"Do you truly think the question remains unanswered?" Fernao asked him.

"You never can tell," Ilmarinen said again, probably as much to annoy Fernao as because he really believed it. "We haven't been looking all that long, and neither have the redheads—excuse me, the Algarvians." Fernao had red hair, too. Ilmarinen went on: "A good thing the Algarvians are too taken up with killing people to power their magic to look anywhere else. Aye, a very good thing." He emptied the mugs in quick succession, then went back and filled them again.

Two

A guard clattered his bludgeon against the iron bars of Talsu's cell. "Come on, you cursed traitor, get up!" the guard shouted at him. "You think this is a hostel, eh? Do you?"

"No, sir. I don't think that, sir," Talsu replied as he sprang off his cot and stood at attention beside it. He had to give a soft answer, or else the guard and maybe three or four of his comrades would swarm into the cell and use their bludgeons on him instead of on the bars. He'd got one beating for talking back. He didn't want another one.

"You'd cursed well better not," the guard snarled before stamping down the hall to waken the prisoner in the next cell after not enough sleep.

Talsu was glad when he couldn't see the ugly lout any more. The prison guard was as much a Jelgavan as he was: a blond man who wore trousers. But he served Mainardo, the younger brother King Mezentio of Algarve had installed on the Jelgavan throne, as readily as he'd ever served King Donalitu. Donalitu had fled when Jelgava fell. His dogs had stayed behind, and wagged their tails for their new masters.

Another Jelgavan came by a few minutes later. He shoved a bowl into Talsu's cell. The barley mush in the bowl smelled sour, almost nasty. Talsu spooned it up just the same. If he didn't eat what the gaolers fed him, he would have do make do on the cockroaches that swarmed across the floor of his cell or, if he was extraordinarily lucky, on the rats that got whatever the roaches missed—and got their share of roaches, too.

The cell didn't even boast a chamber pot. He pissed in a corner, hoping he was drowning some roaches as he did it. Then he went back and sat down on his cot. He had to be plainly visible when the guard collected his bowl and spoon. If he wasn't, the guard would assume he'd used the tin spoon to dig a hole through the stone floor and escape. Then he would suffer, and so would everyone else in this wing of the prison.

As always, the guard came by with a list and a pen. He scooped up the bowl and the spoon, checked them off on the list, and glared through the bars at Talsu. "Don't look so bloody innocent," he growled. "You're not. If you were, you wouldn't be here. You hear me?"

"Aye, sir. I hear you, sir," Talsu answered. If he didn't sit there looking innocent, the guards would decide he was insolent. That rated a beating, too. As best he could tell, he couldn't win.

Of course you can't win, fool, he thought. *If you could, you wouldn't be stuck here.* He felt like kicking himself. But how could he have guessed that the silversmith who taught classical Kaunian to would-be patriots in Skrunda was in fact an Algarvian cat's-paw? As soon as Talsu wanted to do more than learn the old language, as soon as he wanted to strike a blow against the redheads who occupied his kingdom, he'd gone to Kugu. Who was more likely to know how to put one foe of the Algarvians in touch with others? The logic was perfect—or it would have been, if Mezentio's men hadn't stayed a jump ahead.

Algarvians had caught him. They'd said he was in their hands. But they must have decided he wasn't that important, because they'd given him to their Jelgavan henchmen for disposal. Thanks to the fears of Jelgava's kings, her dungeons had been notorious even before the redheads overran the kingdom; Talsu doubted they'd improved since.

After breakfast, the Jelgavan guards retreated to the ends of the corridors. Cautiously, captives began calling back and forth from one cell to another. They were cautious for a couple of good reasons. Talk was against the rules; the gaolers could punish them for it no matter how innocuous their words were. And if their words weren't so innocuous but did get overheard . . . Talsu didn't like to think about what would happen then. For the most part, he kept quiet.

His corridor's exercise period came at midmorning. One by one, the guards unlocked the cells. "Come along," their sergeant said. "Don't dawdle. Don't give us any trouble." No one seemed inclined to give them trouble: they carried sticks now, not truncheons.

Along with his fellow unfortunates, Talsu shuffled down the corridor and out into the exercise yard. There, under the watchful eyes of the guards, he walked back and forth, back and forth, for an hour. The stone walls were so high, he got not a glimpse of the outside world. He had no idea in what part of Jelgava the prison was. But he could look up and see the sky. After spending the rest of the day locked away from light and air, he found that precious beyond belief.

"All right, scum—back you go," the guard sergeant said when the exercise period was over. Now Talsu stared down at the stone paving blocks so the guards couldn't see his glare. The Algarvians hadn't built this prison, or the others much like it scattered over the face of Jelgava—Jelgavan kings had done that, to keep their own subjects in line. But the redheads were perfectly willing to use the prisons—and the guards, as long as they kept their jobs, didn't care whom they were guarding, or for whom, or why.

Talsu sat back down on his cot and waited for the bowl of mush that would be dinner. It might even have a couple of bits of salt pork floating in it. *Something to look forward to,* he thought. The worst part of that was noticing how seriously he meant it.

But a guard strode up to the cell before dinnertime. "Talsu son of Traku?" he demanded.

"Aye, sir," Talsu said.

The guard made a check on his list. He unlocked the door and pointed a stick at Talsu's chest. "You will come with me," he said. "Interrogation."

"What about my dinner?" Talsu yelped. He really had been looking forward to it. They wouldn't save it for him. He knew that all too well. Instead of answering, the guard jerked his stick, as if to say Talsu wouldn't need to worry about dinner ever again if he didn't get moving right now. Having no choice, he got moving.

Even his interrogator was a Jelgavan, a man who wore the uniform of a constabulary captain. He did not invite Talsu to sit down. Indeed, but for his stool and those on which two armed guards perched, the room had nowhere to sit. One of the guards rose and positioned a lamp so it shone straight into Talsu's face. It was bright enough to make him blink and try to look away.

"So," the constabulary officer said. "You are another one who betrayed his lawful sovereign. What have you got to say for yourself?"

"Nothing, sir," Talsu answered. "Nothing I could say would get me out of the trouble I'm in, anyhow."

"No. There you are wrong," the interrogator said. "Give us the names of those who plotted with you and things will start looking better for you in short order. You may rest assured of that: I know whereof I speak."

"I don't know any names," Talsu said, as he had the first time they'd bothered questioning him. "How could I know any names? Nobody did any plotting with me. I was all by myself—and your man got me." He didn't try to hide the self-reproach in his voice.

"You assert, then, that your father knew nothing of your treason."

It wasn't treason, not in Talsu's eyes. How could turning on the Algarvians be treason for a Jelgavan? It couldn't. He didn't think the constable felt that way, though, so all he said was, "No, sir. You ask around in Skrunda. He's made more clothes for the Algarvians in town than anybody else there."

The interrogator didn't pursue it, from which Talsu concluded he'd already asked around, and had got the same answers Talsu had given. Now he tried a new tack: "You also assert your wife knew nothing of this."

"Of course I do," Talsu exclaimed in alarm he didn't try to

hide. "I never said anything about it to Gailisa. By the powers above, it's the truth."

"And yet, she has plenty of reasons for disliking Algarvians—is that not so?" the interrogator went on. "Is it not so that she saw an Algarvian soldier stab you before you were married?"

"Aye, that is so." Talsu admitted what he could hardly deny. "But I never told her about anything. If I had told her about anything, she probably would have wanted to come with me. I didn't want that to happen."

"I see," the Jelgavan in Algarvian service said in tones suggesting Talsu hadn't helped himself or Gailisa with that answer. "You are not making this easy. You could, as I have said, if only you would name names."

"I haven't got any names to give you," Talsu said. "The only name I know is Kugu the silversmith's, and he's been on your side all along. I can't very well get him into trouble, can I?" *I would if I could,* he thought.

"Perhaps we can refresh your memory," his interrogator said. He rang a bell. A couple of more guards strode into the chamber. Without a word, they started working Talsu over. He tried to fight back, but had no luck. One against two was bad odds to begin with, and the fellows with the sticks would have intervened had he got anywhere. He didn't. The bruisers had learned their trade in a nastier school than he'd known even in the army, and learned it well. They had no trouble battering him into submission.

When the battering was done, he could hardly see out of one eye. He tasted blood, though no teeth seemed broken. One of his feet throbbed: a guard had stamped down hard on it. His ribs ached. So did his belly.

Calmly, the interrogator said, "Now, then—who else knew that you were plotting treason against King Mainardo?"

"No one," Talsu gasped. "Do you want me to make up names? What good would that do you?"

"If you want to name some of your friends and neighbors, go ahead," the interrogator said. "We will haul them in and question them most thoroughly. Here is paper. Here is a pen. Go ahead and write."

"But they wouldn't have done anything," Talsu said. "I'd just be making it up. You'd know I was just making it up."

"Suppose you let us worry about that," the interrogator said. "Once you make the accusations, things will go much easier for you. We might even think about letting you go."

"I don't understand," Talsu said, and that was true: he had trouble understanding anything but his own pain. The Jelgavan constabulary captain didn't answer. He just steepled his fingertips and waited. So did the guards with sticks. So did the bully boys who'd beaten Talsu.

It would be so easy, Talsu thought. *I could give them what they want, and then they wouldn't hurt me anymore.* He started to ask the interrogator to hand him the pen and paper. What happened to the people he might name didn't seem very important. It would, after all, be happening to someone else.

But what *would* happen to him? Nothing? That didn't seem likely. All at once, he saw the answer with horrid clarity. If he gave the Algarvians—or rather, their watchdog here—a few names, they would want more. After he gave them a first batch, how could he refuse to give them a second, and then a third? How could he refuse them anything after that? He couldn't. Had Kugu the silversmith started by making up a few names, too? Talsu gathered himself. "There wasn't anybody else," he said.

They beat him again before frog-marching him back to his cell. He'd expected they would. He'd hoped his armor of virtue would make the beating hurt less. It didn't. And he didn't get the bowl of mush he'd missed when they took him away. Even so, he slept well that night.

The blizzard screamed around the hostel in the barren wilderness of southeastern Kuusamo. It left Pekka feeling trapped, almost as if she were in prison. She and her fellow mages had come here so they could experiment without anyone else but a few reindeer noticing. That made good sense; some of the things they were doing would have wrecked good-sized chunks of Yliharma or Kajaani even if they went perfectly. And if some of those experiments escaped control . . . Pekka's shiver had nothing to do with the ghastly weather.

But, while the blizzards raged, Pekka and her colleagues couldn't experiment at all. If the rats and rabbits they were using froze to death the instant they went out of doors in spite of the best efforts of the secondary sorcerers, they were useless. That limited the amount of work the mages could do.

When Pekka said as much over supper one evening, Ilmarinen nodded soberly. "We should use Kaunians instead," he declared. "No one cares whether they live or die, after all: the Algarvians have proved as much."

Pekka winced. So did Siuntio and Fernao. That Ilmarinen spoke in classical Kaunian to include Fernao in the conversation only made his irony more savage. After a moment, Siuntio murmured, "If we succeed here, we'll keep the Algarvians from slaughtering more Kaunians."

"Will we? I doubt it." But Ilmarinen checked himself. "Well, maybe a few, and will we also keep Swemmel of Unkerlant from slaughtering his own folk to hold back the Algarvians? Maybe a few, again. What we will do, if we're lucky, is win the war this way. It's not the same thing, and we'd be fools to pretend it is."

"Right now, winning the war will do," Fernao said. "If we do not do that, nothing else matters."

Siuntio nodded in mournful agreement. He said, "Even if we do win the war, though, the world will never again be what it was. Too many dreadful things have happened."

"It will be worse if we lose," Pekka said. "Remember Yliharma." A sorcerous Algarvian attack had destroyed much of the capital of Kuusamo, had slain two of the Seven Princes, and had come too close to killing her and Siuntio and Ilmarinen.

"Everyone remembers wars." Siuntio still sounded sad. "Remembering what happened in the last one gives an excuse for fighting the next one."

Not even Ilmarinen felt like trying to top that gloomy bit of wisdom. The mages got up from the table and went off to their own chambers as if trying to escape it. But Pekka soon discovered, as she had before, that being alone in her room was anything but an escape.

Sometimes the mages would stay in the dining hall after supper, arguing about what they had done or what they wanted to do or simply chatting. Not tonight. They drifted apart and went upstairs to their chambers as if sick of one another's company. There were times when Pekka *was* sick of her comrades' company, most often of Ilmarinen's, then of Fernao's, and occasionally even of Siuntio's. Tonight wasn't one of those angry times. She just didn't want to talk to anyone.

Instead, she worked on two letters side by side. One was for her husband, the other for her son. Leino would be able to read his own, of course. Her sister Elimaki, who was taking care of Uto, would surely read aloud most of the one written to him, even though he was learning his letters.

The letter to Uto went well. Pekka had no trouble writing the things any mother should say to her son. Those were easy, and flowed from her pen as easily as they flowed from her heart. She loved him, she missed him, she hoped he was being a good little boy (with Uto, often a forlorn hope). The words, the thoughts, were simple and straightforward and true.

Writing to Leino was harder. She loved him and missed him, too, missed him with an ache that sometimes made her empty bed seem the loneliest place in the world. Those things were easy enough to say, even though she knew other eyes than his would also see them: functionaries serving the Seven Princes studied all outgoing correspondence to make sure no secrets were revealed.

But she wanted to tell her husband more. She couldn't even name the mages with whom she was working, for fear that knowledge would fall into the Algarvians' hands and give them clues they shouldn't have. She had to talk about personalities in indirect terms, a surprisingly difficult exercise. She had to talk about the work in which they were engaged in even more indirect terms. She hadn't been able to tell Leino all that much about it even when they'd been together. He hadn't asked, either. He'd known when silence was important, and respected the need for it.

We've had simply appalling weather lately, she wrote. *If it were better, we could do more.* That seemed safe enough. Most of Kuusamo had appalling weather through most of the winter. Hearing about it wouldn't tell an Algarvian spy where she was. And bad weather could interfere with any number of things, not all of them things in which a spy would be interested.

I hope to be able to see you before long. She'd been told she might be able to leave for a little while in the not too in-definite future. But even if she did manage to get away, could Leino escape his training as a proper military mage at the same time? She thought he should have stayed in a sorcerous laboratory, improving the weapons Kuusaman soldiers would take into battle. But the Seven Princes thought other-wise, and their will counted for more than hers.

Sighing, she stared down at the page. She wanted to tear it up and throw the pieces in the wastebasket. She had to be able to do better than the words she'd put down, the words that seemed so flat, so useless, even so stupid. What would Leino think when he saw them? That he'd married a halfwit?

He'll understand, she thought. *I'm sure he's learning plenty of things he can't tell me, too.* Most of her believed that. Just enough had doubts, though, to leave all of her upset and worried.

She jumped when someone knocked on the door. Spring-ing away from her letters was something of a relief. Even ar-guing abstruse theoretical calculations with Ilmarinen seemed more appealing than trying to say things she couldn't say without having them cut out of her letter before Leino ever saw it.

But when she opened the door, she found Fernao standing there, not Ilmarinen. The Lagoan mage leaned on his stick and had his crutch stuck under his other arm. "I hope I am not disturbing you," he said in careful classical Kaunian.

"Not even a little bit," Pekka said in Kuusaman. She started to repeat that in the scholarly tongue, but Fernao's nod showed he'd followed her. "Come in," she went on, in Kaunian now. "Sit down. What can I do for you?"

"I thank you," he said, and made his slow way into her chamber. She took a couple of steps back, not only to get out of his way but to keep him from looming over her quite so much: Lagoans were almost uncouthly tall.

Maybe Fernao sensed what she felt, for he sank onto one of the stools in the room. *Or maybe he's just glad to get off his feet,* Pekka thought. Had she been injured as Fernao was, she knew she would have been. She turned the chair on which she'd been sitting to write away from the desk. "Shall I make you some tea?" she asked. She couldn't be much of a hostess here, but she could do that.

Fernao shook his head. "No, thank you," he said. "If you do not mind, I can talk with you without thinking I am once more a student bearding a professor in his den."

Pekka laughed. "I often have that feeling myself around Siuntio and Ilmarinen. I think even the Grandmaster of your kingdom's Guild of Mages would have it around them."

"Grandmaster Pinhiero is not the most potent mage ever to come out of our universities," Fernao said, "but he would speak his mind to anyone, even to King Swemmel of Unkerlant."

Lagoans had always had a reputation for speaking their minds, regardless of whether doing so was a good idea. Pekka asked, "Would that make Grandmaster Pinhiero a hero or a fool?"

"Without a doubt," Fernao answered. Pekka chewed on that for a little while before deciding it was another joke and laughing again. Fernao continued, "Every time I see how far you Kuusamans have come, it amazes me."

"Why is that?" Pekka knew her tone was tart, but couldn't help it. "Because you Lagoans do not think Kuusamo worth noticing at all most of the time?"

"That probably has something to do with it," he said, which caught her by surprise. "We did notice you when it came to declare war against Algarve—I will say that. We would have done it sooner had we not feared you might take Mezentio's side and assail us from behind."

"Ah." Pekka found herself nodding. "Aye, I knew people who wanted to do exactly that." She remembered a party at Elimaki's house. Some of the friends of Elimaki's husband, Olavin the banker, had been eager to take on Lagoas. Olavin was serving the Seven Princes these days. Pekka suspected most of those friends were doing the same thing.

"Did you?" Fernao said, and Pekka nodded again. He shrugged. "Well, I can hardly say I am surprised. It would have been . . . unfortunate had that happened, though." Even as Pekka wondered how he meant the word, he explained: "Unfortunate for Lagoas, unfortunate for the whole world."

"Aye, you are likely to be right." Pekka glanced over her shoulder at the letters to Leino and Uto, then back to Fernao. "May I ask you something?"

As if he were a great noble, he inclined his head to her. "Of course."

"How do you stand it here, cut off not just from your family but from your kingdom as well?"

Fernao said, "For one thing, I have not got much in the way of family: no wife, no children, and I am not what you would call close to either of my sisters. They never have understood what being a mage means. And, for another, the work we are doing here matters. It matters so much, or may matter so much, I would sooner be here than anywhere else."

That was a more thoughtful answer than Pekka had expected. She wondered how long Fernao had been waiting for someone to ask a question like hers. Quite a while, she guessed, which might also be a measure of his loneliness. "Why have you not got a wife?" she asked, and then, realizing she might have gone too far, she quickly added, "You need not answer that."

But the Lagoan didn't take offense. Instead, he started to laugh. "Not because I would rather have a pretty boy, if that is what you mean," he said. "I like women fine, thank you very much. But I have never found one I liked enough and respected enough to want to marry her." After a moment, he held up his hand. "I take it back. I have found a couple like that, but they were already other men's wives."

"Oh," Pekka said, and then, half a beat slower than she might have, "Aye, I can see how that would be hard." Was he looking at her? She didn't look over at him, not for a little while. She didn't want to know.

"You have things you were doing, I see." Awkwardly, Fernao levered himself to his feet. "I shall not keep you. May you have a pleasant evening." He made his slow way to the door.

"And you," Pekka said. She had no trouble looking at his back. But, when he had gone, she found she couldn't continue the letter to Leino. She put it aside, hoping she'd have more luck with it in the morning.

Ealstan enjoyed walking through the streets of Eoforwic much more these days than he had a few weeks before. True, the Algarvians still occupied what had been the capital of Forthweg. True, King Penda still remained in exile in Lagoas. True, a Kaunian whose sorcerous disguise as a Forthwegian was penetrated still had dreadful things happen to him. And yet . . .

SULINGEN was scrawled in chalk or charcoal or whitewash or paint on one or two walls or fences in almost every block. Up till now, a lot of Forthwegians had been sullenly resigned to Algarvian occupation. King Mezentio's men looked like winning the war; most people—most people who weren't Kaunians, anyhow—had got on with their lives as best they could in spite of that ugly weight hanging over them. Now, even though the Algarvians still held every inch of their kingdom, some of them didn't.

A couple of Algarvian constables strode past Ealstan. Their height and red hair separated them from the Forthwegians their kingdom had overcome. So did the pleated kilts they wore. And so did their swagger. No matter what had happened to their countrymen down in Sulingen, they showed no dismay.

But a Forthwegian behind Ealstan shouted, "Get out of here, you whoresons! Go home!"

Both Algarvians jerked as if stuck with pins. The shout had been in Forthwegian, but they'd understood. They whirled, one grabbing for his club, the other for his stick. For a dreadful moment, Ealstan thought they thought he'd yelled. Then, to his vast relief, he saw they were looking past him, not at him. One of them pointed toward a Forthwegian whose black beard was streaked with gray. They both strode purposefully by Ealstan and toward the older man. He stared this way and that, as if wondering whether flight or holding still was more dangerous.

Before he had to find an answer, someone from farther up the street—someone behind the constables now, someone they couldn't see—cried out, "Aye, bugger off!"

Again, the Algarvians spun. Again, they hurried past Ealstan. Again, they seized no one, for more insults rained down on them whenever they turned their backs. Algarvians often had tempers that burst like eggs. These redheads proved no exception. One of them shook his fist and shouted in pretty fluent Forthwegian: "You fornicating bigmouths, you yell much more, we treat you all like stinking Kaunians!" To leave no doubt about what he meant, his partner stuck his chin in the air and drew a forefinger across his throat.

"Shame!" Ealstan yelled. That might have got him into trouble, but other Forthwegians were also yelling, and yelling worse things. As Ealstan knew too well, most of them cared little about what happened to the Kaunian minority in Forthweg, but they all cared about what happened to them.

The constable who'd shouted the threat was the one who'd taken the stick off his belt. Cursing now in his own language, he blazed between a couple of Forthwegians standing not far from him. His beam missed them both, but bit into the wooden wall of the wineshop behind them. The wall began to smolder. The Forthwegians fled.

So did everyone else on the street. Ealstan wasted no time ducking around the first corner he came to. He kept on running after that, too, the hem of his long wool tunic flapping just below his knees. "Those bastards have gone daft!" another man making himself scarce said.

"What's daft about it?" Ealstan returned bitterly. "They probably get a bonus for anybody they blaze."

When the other fellow didn't argue with him, he decided he'd made his point. Having made it, he went right on trotting. He didn't know whether a new round of rioting was about to flare up in Eoforwic, and didn't care to stay around to find out. That was the trouble with people feeling feisty: no matter how much trouble they stirred up, they still couldn't get rid of the Algarvians.

"One of these days, though," Ealstan murmured. "Aye, one of these days . . ." He heard the longing in his own voice. Mezentio's men had been sitting on Forthweg for three and a half years now. He smiled when he passed another scribbled SULINGEN. Surely they couldn't hold down his kingdom forever.

His own block of flats lay in a poor part of town, one already scarred again and again by rioting. He wouldn't have minded seeing another round of that if it meant throwing Mezentio's men out of Eoforwic. Since he didn't think it would, he was glad things seemed quiet.

The stairwell smelled of stale cabbage and staler piss. He sighed as he trudged up toward his flat. He'd been used to better in Gromheort before he had to flee the eastern town and come to the capital. As a matter of fact, he could afford better here. But staying in a district where no one cared about you or what you were and no one expected you to be anybody much had advantages, too.

He walked down the hall and knocked on the door to his flat—once, twice, once. A scraping noise came from inside as Vanai lifted the bar that held the door closed. His wife worked the latch and let him in. He gave her a hug and kissed her. The magecraft that hid her Kaunianity and made her look Forthwegian made her look astonishingly like a particular Forthwegian: his older sister, Conberge. He'd needed a while before that stopped bothering him.

"We could stop using the coded knock, you know," he said. "Now that you don't look Kaunian anymore, there's not much point to it."

"I still like to know it's you at the door," she answered.

That made Ealstan smile. "All right," he said, and sniffed. "What smells good?"

"Nothing very exciting," Vanai told him. "Just barley porridge with a little cheese and some of those dried mushrooms I got from the grocer the other day."

"Must be the mushrooms," Ealstan said, which made Vanai smile and nod in turn: both Forthwegians and the Kaunian minority in Forthweg were mad for mushrooms. Ealstan reached out and stroked her hair. "You must be glad to be able to go to the grocer's yourself."

"You have no idea," Vanai said. Ealstan couldn't argue with her. Until she no longer looked like what she was, she'd had to stay holed up inside the flat. Had an Algarvian spotted her on the street, or had a Forthwegian betrayed her to the redheads, she would have been taken off to the Kaunian district—and then, all too likely, shipped west so her life energy could help power the sorceries the Algarvians used in their war against Unkerlant.

Ealstan went into the kitchen, pulled the stopper from a jar of wine, and filled two cups. He carried one of them back to Vanai and raised the other in salute. "To freedom!" he said.

"Or something close to it, anyhow," Vanai answered, but she did drink to the toast.

"Aye, something close to it," Ealstan agreed. "Maybe something getting closer, too." He told her how the Forthwegians had given the Algarvian constables a hard time.

"Good!" she said. "I wish I'd been there." After a moment, the fierce smile slipped from her face. "Of course, if I'd been there looking the way I really do, they'd have been just as happy to throw rocks at me and yell, 'Dirty Kaunian!' "

Her eyes held Ealstan's, as if challenging him to deny it. He looked away. He had to look away. The most he could do was mumble, "We're not all like that."

Vanai's gaze softened. "Of course not. If you were like that, I'd be dead now. But too many Forthwegians are." She shrugged. "Nothing to be done about it, or nothing I can see. Come on. Supper should be ready."

After supper, Ealstan read a book while Vanai cleaned the dishes and silverware. He'd brought a lot of books home while she was trapped in the flat—reading was almost the only thing she'd been able to do while he went out and cast accounts and got them enough money to keep going. He read them, too. Some—the classics he'd had to study in his academy in Gromheort—proved much more interesting when he read them because he wanted to than when they were forced down his throat.

When Vanai came out of the kitchen, she sat down on the sofa beside him. She had a book waiting on the rickety table in front of the sofa. They read side by side for a while in companionable silence. Presently, Ealstan slipped his arm over Vanai's shoulder. If she'd gone on reading, he would have left it there for a while and then withdrawn it; one thing he'd learned was that she didn't care to have affection forced on her.

But she smiled, set down her book—a Forthwegian history of the glory days of the Kaunian Empire—and snuggled against him. Before long, they went back to the bedchamber together. Making love was the other thing they'd been able to do freely when Vanai was trapped in the flat—and, because Ealstan was only eighteen even now, they'd been able to do it pretty often.

Afterwards, they lay side by side, lazy and happy and soon to be ready to sleep. Ealstan reached out and ran his fingers through Vanai's hair. Some people, he'd heard, eventually grew bored with making love. Maybe that was true. He pitied those people if so.

When he woke the next morning, rain was drumming against the bedchamber windows. Winter was the rainy season in Forthweg, as in most northerly lands. Yawning, Ealstan opened one eye. Rain, sure enough. He opened the other eye and glanced over at Vanai.

He frowned. Her features had . . . changed. Her hair remained dark. It would: she regularly dyed it. But it looked straight now, not wavy. Her face was longer, her nose straight, not proudly hooked. Her skin had matched the swarthy tone of his. Now it was fairer, so the blood underneath showed through pink.

Before long, the rain woke her, too. As soon as her eyes opened, Ealstan said, "Your spell's worn off." Those eyes should have seemed dark brown, but they were their true grayish blue again.

Vanai nodded. "I'll fix it after breakfast. I don't think anyone will come bursting in to catch me looking like a Kaunian till then."

"All right," Ealstan said. "Don't forget."

She laughed at him. "I'm not likely to, you know."

And she didn't. After they'd washed down barley bread and olive oil with more red wine, Vanai took a length of yellow yarn and a length of dark brown, twisted them together, and began to chant in classical Kaunian. The spell was of her own devising, an adaptation of a Forthwegian charm in a little book called *You Too Can Be a Mage* that hadn't worked as it should have. Thanks to the training she'd had from her scholarly grandfather, the one she'd made did.

As soon as she spoke the last word of the charm, her face—indeed, her whole body—returned to its Forthwegian appearance. Kaunians in Eoforwic and throughout Forthweg used that same spell now. A lot of them had escaped from the districts in which the redheads had sealed them so they'd be handy when Algarve needed the life energy they could give. Mezentio's men weren't happy about that.

Ealstan was. He kissed Vanai and said, "If these were imperial times, you'd come down in history as a great heroine."

She answered in Kaunian, something she seldom did since taking on a Forthwegian seeming: "If these were imperial times, I wouldn't need such sorcery." Her voice was bleak.

Ealstan wished he could disagree with her. Since he couldn't, he did the next best thing: he kissed her again. "Whether you are remembered or not, you are still a heroine," he said, and had a demon of a time understanding why she suddenly started to weep.

* * *

Bembo cursed under his breath as he prowled through the streets of Gromheort. Oraste, his partner, didn't bother keeping his voice down. Gromheort lay in eastern Forthweg, not far from the border with Algarve, and a good many locals understood Algarvian. The constable kept cursing anyway.

"Miserable Kaunians," he growled. "Powers below eat them, every stinking one. They *ought* to have their throats cut, the filthy buggers, what with all the extra work they've piled on our backs."

"Aye, curse them," Bembo agreed. He was tubbier than he should have been, no braver than he had to be, and heartily disapproved of anything resembling work, especially work he'd have to do.

Oraste, for his part, disapproved of almost everything. "They're liable to cost us the war, the lousy, stinking whoresons. How are we supposed to scoop 'em up and send 'em west when they start looking like everybody else in this fornicating kingdom? The way things are going over in Unkerlant, we need all the help we can get."

"Aye," Bembo repeated, but on a less certain note. The idea of rounding up Kaunians and sending them toward the battlefront to be killed made his stomach turn unhappy flipflops. He did it—what choice did he have but to obey the sergeants and officers set over him?—but he had trouble believing it was the right thing to do.

Oraste had no doubts. Oraste, as far as Bembo could see, never had any doubts about anything. He waved now, not the usual extravagant Algarvian gesture but a functional one, one that took in the street ahead and the people on it. "Any of these bastards—*any* of 'em, by the powers above!—could be a Kaunian wrapped in magic cloaking. And what can we do about it? What can we do about it, I ask you?"

"Nothing much," Bembo answered mournfully. "If we start using Forthwegians the way we use the Kaunians here, this whole kingdom'll go up in smoke. We haven't got the men to hold it down, not if we want to go on fighting the Unkerlanters, too."

"It's war," Oraste said. "You do what you have to do. If we

need Forthwegians, we'll take 'em. We can sell it to the ones we don't take: if the Kaunians weren't wolves in sheep's clothing, we can say, we wouldn't have to do this. The Forthwegians'll buy it, or enough of 'em will. They hate the blonds as much as we do."

"I suppose so." Bembo didn't particularly hate anybody—save, perhaps, people who made him work more than he cared to. Those people included Sergeant Pesaro, his boss, as well as the miscreants he all too often failed to run to earth.

"Look at 'em!" Oraste waved again, this time with a sort of animal frustration. "Any one of them could be a Kaunian. Any one, I tell you. You think I like the notion of those lousy blonds laughing at me? Not on your life, pal." He folded his beefy hands into fists. When he didn't like something, his notion of what to do next was pound it to pieces.

And, whenever he got into that kind of mood, he'd sometimes lash out at his partner, too; he wasn't always fussy about whom or what he hurt, so long as he was hurting someone or something. To try to placate him, Bembo pointed to a man whose beard was going gray. "There. That fellow's a genuine Forthwegian, no doubt about it."

"How d'you know?" Brooding suspicion filled Oraste's voice.

"Don't you remember? He's the one who had a son disappear off to powers above know where, and his nephew murdered his other son. He couldn't get anybody to do anything about it, because the nephew was in Plegmund's Brigade."

"Oh. Him. Aye." The fire in Oraste's hazel eyes faded a little. "Well, I can't say you're wrong—*this* time."

Bembo swept off his plumed hat and bowed as deeply as his belly would permit. "Your servant," he said.

"My arse," Oraste said. He pointed to the man with whom the assuredly genuine Forthwegian was speaking. "How about him? You going to tell me you know for sure he's no Kaunian, too?"

"How can I do that?" Bembo asked reasonably as he and Oraste came up to the two men. The other fellow certainly looked like a Forthwegian: a white-haired, white-bearded, rather dissolute-seeming old Forthwegian. "But what else is he likely to be? He's a blowhard, I'll tell you that."

Sure enough, the old man was doing most of the talking, his companion mostly listening and then trying to get a word or two in edgewise. As Bembo and Oraste came up to them, the geezer waved his forefinger in the other man's face and spoke in impassioned Forthwegian. Bembo couldn't understand more than one word in four, but he knew an irate, hectoring tone when he heard one. The fellow the old man was talking to looked as if he wished he were elsewhere.

Oraste rolled his eyes. "Blowhard, nothing. He's a stinking windbag, is what he is."

"Aye, that's the truth." Instead of walking past the windbag, Bembo slowed and cocked his head to one side, frowning and listening hard.

"Are you daft?" Oraste said. "Come on."

"Shut up." Bembo was usually a little afraid of his partner, and wouldn't have dared speak to him like that most of the time. But a moment later he gave a decisive nod. "It is. By the powers above, it is!"

"Is what?" Oraste asked.

Bembo started to point, then thought better of it. "That old Forthwegian—he's *not* a Forthwegian, or I'll eat my club. Remember that noisy, smartmouthed old Kaunian whoreson we first ran into in Oyngestun? We've bumped into him a few times here in Gromheort, too."

After another couple of paces, Oraste nodded. "Aye, I do. He's the one with the good-looking granddaughter—or he said she was his granddaughter, anyway."

"That's the one. And that's him," Bembo said. "I recognize his voice. Whatever magecraft he's using, it doesn't change that."

Oraste took one more step, then spun on his heel. "Let's snag the son of a whore."

Had Bembo seen two constables bearing down on him, he would have made himself scarce. Maybe the sorcerously disguised Kaunian didn't see him and Oraste; the fellow was still doing his best to talk the other man's ear off. He looked absurdly astonished when the Algarvians laid hold of him. "What is the meaning of this?" he demanded—in good Algarvian.

That made Bembo beam. That smartmouthed Kaunian spoke Algarvian—he was supposed to be some sort of scholar. Bembo said, "You're under arrest on suspicion of being a Kaunian."

"Do I look like a Kaunian?" the old man said.

"Not now," Bembo answered. "We'll take you back, throw you in a cell, and wait and see if the magic wears off. If you still look ugly this same way tomorrow, we'll turn you loose. How much you want to bet we don't have to?"

To his surprise, the other Forthwegian, the genuine Forthwegian, tapped his belt pouch. Coins rang in there. "Gentlemen," he said, also in fluent Algarvian, "I'll make it worth your while if you forget you ever saw this fellow."

"No." Oraste spoke before Bembo could. Bembo, like a lot of Algarvians, didn't mind making some money on the side; his constable's salary didn't go very far. But he nodded now. He didn't want money. No, that wasn't quite true—he wanted money, but he wanted this old Kaunian's head more.

And so he, too, said, "No. We're going to take this fellow in and deal with him."

"You are making a serious mistake," the old man said. "I tell you, I am as much a Forthwegian as Hestan here."

Hestan there didn't say another word. He didn't call the old man who looked like a Forthwegian a liar, but he didn't claim he was telling the truth, either. Oraste started hauling the fellow off toward Gromheort's gaol, which was more crowded now than it had been when Forthweg ruled the city.

"What have we got here?" an Algarvian gaoler asked when the constables frog-marched their prisoner into the building. "You catch him filching somebody's false teeth?" He laughed at his own wit.

Bembo said, "Suspicion of Kaunianity. Lock him up and see if he still looks the same tomorrow. The magic isn't even good for a day at a time, from everything I've heard."

"Aha—one of those." The gaoler brightened. "How'd you catch him? Can't tell much by his hair, I'd say—white's still white."

"I recognized his voice," Bembo said proudly. "I'd run into him before, when he looked like what he really is. He made himself enough of a nuisance that he stuck in my mind."

"I am a Forthwegian," the old man said. "I am not a Kaunian."

"Shut up," the gaoler told him. "We'll find out what you are." He turned to a couple of his assistants, who looked to have been shooting dice before Bembo and Oraste came in with their captive. "Strip him—don't leave him anything he can use to make more magic and make more work for us. Then throw him in a cell. Like the constable says, we'll find out what he is."

"Aye," one of his assistants said. They did as they were told. The old man squawked protests and tried to fight back, but he might have been a three-year-old for all the good it did him. The assistant gaolers led him away. Even though he was naked, he kept on squawking.

"Now . . ." The gaoler reached into a desk drawer and pulled out some forms. "The paperwork. If he really is a Kaunian, you'll get the credit. If he's not, you'll get the blame."

"Blame? For what?" Bembo clapped a hand to his forehead in melodramatic disbelief. "For bothering a miserable Forthwegian? Where's the blame in that?"

"There's no blame for bothering a Forthwegian," the gaoler agreed. "But if that old bugger turns out not to be a Kaunian, you get the blame for bothering *me*." He favored the constables with a singularly unpleasant smile, the sort of smile that made them scurry out of the gaol in a hurry.

Once they'd got outside, Oraste gave Bembo the same kind of smile. "You'd better not be wrong," he said. Bembo wanted to scurry away from his partner, too, but he couldn't. He had to smile himself, and nod, and go on with his shift.

As soon as they came on duty the next day, they hurried to

the gaol. The gaoler didn't start cursing the moment he set eyes on them, which Bembo took for a good sign. "Well, you boys got it straight," the gaoler said. "He was a Kaunian."

Oraste thumped Bembo on the shoulder, hard enough to stagger him. Bembo heard something Oraste missed. *"Was?"* he asked.

"Aye." The gaoler looked sour. "Sometime during the night, somebody gave him drawers and a tunic so he wouldn't freeze. He twisted 'em up and hanged himself with 'em. That killed the spell along with him. Like I say, he was a Kaunian, all right."

"Filthy bastard," Oraste said. "We could have got some use out of his life energy."

"That's right," Bembo said. "Killing yourself like that ought to be punishable by death." He laughed. After a moment, Oraste and the gaoler did, too.

"I've sent the forms off to the constabulary barracks," the gaoler said. "You deserve the credit, like I told you yesterday. That turned out to be a nice bit of work." Bembo beamed and preened and strutted. He hadn't much minded hearing that the longwinded old Kaunian was dead. Now that he knew he'd get the credit for capturing him, he didn't mind at all.

Back in the days when he was a peasant like any other peasant in the Unkerlanter Duchy of Grelz, Garivald had looked forward to winter. With snowdrifts covering the fields, he'd spent most of his time indoors and a lot of that time drunk. Aside from taking care of the livestock that always shared the hut with his family and him, what else was there to do but drink?

But he had no home now, only a miserable little shelter, not even worth dignifying with the name of hut, in the middle of the forest west of Herborn, the capital of Grelz. Munderic's band of irregulars still held the woods, still held away the Algarvians who'd overrun Grelz and the Grelzer puppets who served them, but irregulars had a harder time of it in winter than they did in summer.

Garivald came out of his shelter to look up through the

pines and the bare-branched birches to the sullen gray sky overhead. It had snowed the day before. He thought it was done for a while, but you never could tell. He took a couple of steps. At each one, his felt boots left a clear track in the snow.

"Footprints," he growled, vapor puffing from his mouth at the word. "I wish there were a magic to make footprints go away."

"Don't say things like that," Obilot exclaimed. She was one of a handful of women in Munderic's band. The women who ran off to fight the redheads and their local cat's-paws commonly had reasons much more urgent than those of their male counterparts. Obilot went on, "Sadoc's liable to get wind of it and try to cast a spell to be rid of them."

"That might not be so bad," Garivald said. "Odds are, whatever magecraft he tried wouldn't do anything."

"Aye, but it might go wrong so badly, it'd bring the Algarvians down on our heads," Obilot said.

Neither of them spoke of the benefits that would follow if Sadoc's spell succeeded. Neither of them thought Sadoc's spell, if he made one, would succeed. He was the closest thing to a mage Munderic's band boasted. As far as Garivald was concerned, he wasn't close enough. He had no training whatever. He was just a peasant who'd fiddled around with a few charms.

"If only he knew when to try and when not to," Garivald said mournfully. "He might be good enough for little things, but he won't stay with those. He won't even take a blaze at them. If it isn't huge, he doesn't want to bother with it."

"Who doesn't want to bother with what?" Munderic asked. The leader of the irregulars was a big, hard-faced, burly man. He looked the part he played. His temper suited him to it, too. Scowling, he went on, "Who doesn't, curse it? We all have to do whatever we can."

Obilot and Garivald looked at each other. Garivald owed Munderic his life. If the irregulars hadn't plucked him from Algarvian hands, Mezentio's men would have boiled him alive for making songs that mocked them. Even so, he didn't want to give Munderic this particular idea, and neither, evidently, did Obilot.

Munderic saw as much, too. His bushy eyebrows formed a dark bar over his eyes as he scowled. "Who doesn't want to bother with what?" he repeated, an angry rumble in his voice. "You'd better tell me what you were talking about, or you'll be sorry."

"It wasn't anything, really." Garivald didn't want to antagonize Munderic, either. They'd already had a couple of run-ins. To his relief, Obilot nodded agreement.

But they didn't satisfy their leader. "Come on, out with it!" he barked. "If we're going to make the invaders and the traitors howl, we've got to do everything we can." His glare was so fierce, Garivald reluctantly told him what he and Obilot had been talking about. To his dismay, Munderic beamed. "Aye, that'd be just what we need. Footprints in the snow make it hard for us to raid without giving ourselves away. I'll talk to Sadoc."

"There's no guarantee he'll be able to do anything like that, you know," Obilot said. This time, Garivald was the one who nodded.

"I'll talk to him," Munderic said again. "We'll see what he can do. If we've got a mage here, we bloody well ought to get some use out of him, don't you think?" He stamped away without waiting for an answer.

"If we had a mage, we could get some use out of him," Garivald said after the irregulars' leader was out of earshot. "But we've got Sadoc instead."

"I know," Obilot said. They exchanged wry smiles. Garivald knew a certain amount of relief. He'd quarreled with Obilot not so long before, too.

I never wanted to quarrel with anybody, he thought. *I just wanted to live out my life back in Zossen with my wife and my son and my daughter.* But Zossen lay a long, long way to the west—fifty miles, maybe even sixty. He didn't know if he'd ever see his family again. Obilot was no great beauty, but she wasn't homely, either. He didn't want her angry at him.

He'd been away from Annore for most of a year now. Had Obilot decided to slip under the blankets with him, he wouldn't have thrown her out. But she hadn't. She didn't slip under the blankets with anyone, and she'd knifed a man who tried too persistently to slip under the blankets with her. The other women in the band of irregulars acted much the same way. Garivald looked toward her, but glanced away before their eyes met. *What'll you do next?* he thought sourly. *Start coming up with love songs?*

Obilot said, "Maybe nothing'll come of it." She didn't sound as if she believed that.

"Aye. Maybe." Garivald didn't sound as if he believed it, either.

A couple of days later, Munderic gathered the irregulars together in the clearing at the heart of their forest fastness. "We've got to go out and sabotage a ley line," he said. "There's heavy fighting around Durrwangen, south and west of here. If the regular army can take it back, they strike the Algarvians a heavy blow. And the redheads know it, curse 'em. They want to keep Durrwangen, same as they wanted to keep Sulingen. But they've got real supply lines into this place. The more we can do to keep men and behemoths and eggs from getting there, the better we serve Unkerlant. Have you got that?"

"Aye," the irregulars chorused, Garivald among them.

"We've found a stretch of ley line the Grelzer traitors don't guard well," Munderic went on. "We'll plant our eggs there. And we've got a new way of making sure the bastards who call Mezentio's precious cousin Raniero King of Grelz can't follow us. Sadoc will hide our tracks in the snow." He waved to the man who would be a mage.

"That's right," Sadoc said. He was a bruiser himself, maybe as much a bruiser as Munderic. "I'm sure it'll work." He stared from one of his comrades to another, challenging them to disagree with him.

Nobody said anything. Garivald wanted to, but Sadoc already knew what he thought of his magecraft. *Maybe he won't make a hash of it this time,* Garivald thought, his mind almost echoing Obilot's words. Unfortunately, it also echoed his own mournful coda. *Aye. Maybe.*

When night came, the irregulars left the forest and crossed the farm country around it. Garivald hoped Munderic was right when he said he knew about a length of ley line that wasn't well guarded. Some of the men supposed to be serving King Raniero really stayed loyal to King Swemmel of Unkerlant, and aided them when and as they could. But others hated Swemmel worse than the Algarvians; those Grelzers, as he'd found to his dismay, made fierce, determined foes.

Clouds scudded across the sky. Every so often, he got a glimpse of the moon, riding high in the northeast. Stars appeared, twinkled for a moment, and then vanished again. Obilot came up alongside Garivald. "Sadoc had better be able to hide our trail," she said in a low voice. "If he can't, the traitors will follow us home."

Garivald nodded. The earflaps on his fur cap bobbed up and down. "I've been thinking the same thing. I wish I hadn't."

Sometimes, the snow was deep, drifted. The irregulars had to bull through the drifts or else find a way around them. Garivald kept muttering under his breath. Even if Sadoc could sorcerously erase footprints, could he get rid of these signs of passage, too? Had Munderic thought about that? Had Munderic thought about anything but hitting the Algarvians a good lick? Garivald doubted it.

If a Grelzer company on patrol caught them out here in the open, they'd get slaughtered. He hung on to his stick—which had once belonged to a redhead who now had no further use for it—and hoped that wouldn't happen.

After what seemed like forever but the moon insisted was well before midnight, the irregulars came to the lines of shrubbery that marked the path of the invisible ley line. The shrubs kept men and animals from blundering into the path of an oncoming caravan. Garivald's heart thudded as the irregulars pushed through them. This time, no Grelzer guards shouted a challenge. Munderic had known whereof he spoke there, anyhow.

Some of the irregulars carried picks and spades as well as their sticks. They started digging a hole in which to conceal the egg they'd brought to destroy the caravan. The ground was frozen hard; they had a demon of a time excavating. Garivald could have told them they would. They probably knew it for themselves, too, but had to do the best they could. They planted the egg and heaped snow over it. With luck, the Algarvians in the lead caravan car wouldn't see it till too late.

"Let's go," Munderic said when the job was done well enough—and when he didn't feel like waiting anymore.

"Back the way we came, as near as we can," Sadoc added. "I'll get rid of all the footprints at once."

"He'd better," Garivald murmured to Obilot as they started off toward the forest. "We're in trouble if he doesn't, unless a blizzard blows up and sweeps our tracks away."

"I don't think one's coming," she said. "This isn't a hard winter, the way last year's was. Just—cold." Garivald nodded. It felt the same way to him. That didn't mean he couldn't freeze to death out here, only that freezing would take longer.

He was weary by the time the irregulars got back to the edge of the woods. Twilight hadn't touched the edge of the sky, but couldn't be far away. He hadn't heard the egg burst. Neither had Munderic, who was unhappy about it. "Something's gone wrong," the leader of the band kept saying. "Powers below eat me if something hasn't gone wrong."

"Maybe the caravan got stuck in a snowdrift," someone suggested.

"No, I'm sure something's buggered up somewhere," Munderic said fretfully. Garivald feared he was right. Munderic rounded on Sadoc. "Even if it didn't work, we don't want the foe to know we've been out. Get rid of those tracks, like you said."

"Aye." Sadoc nodded. He stooped in the snow and began to chant. The tune was one children used in a hide-and-seek game. Did that mean Sadoc was a fool, or that he truly could hide the footprints? Garivald waited and hoped. Sadoc chanted and made passes. With a last dramatic one, he cried out in a loud, commanding voice.

He'd gathered power to him. Garivald could feel it in the air, as if lightning were building. All at once, it was released—and every footprint, all the way back to the ley line (or at least as far as the eye could reach) began to glow with a soft, shimmering iridescence.

Munderic stared, then howled like a wolf. "You idiot!" he roared. "You dunderhead, you turd-witted son of a poxed sow, you—" He leaped at Sadoc. The only thing that kept him from murdering the inept mage was realizing—after he'd been pulled off—that glowing tracks in the snow weren't too much more visible than ordinary ones. The irregulars fled for their shelters in the clearing. Their new tracks didn't glow, for which Garivald thanked the powers above. He didn't think Sadoc would be working more magic any time soon. He thanked the powers above for that, too.

Krasta's foot came down on an icy patch on the sidewalk of the Avenue of Equestrians. She sat down on the pavement suddenly and very hard. An elderly Valmieran man started toward her to help her up, but she was cursing so foully, he beat a hasty, embarrassed retreat.

Her curses didn't bother a couple of Algarvian soldiers on leave in Priekule. The kilted redheads hurried over to her and hauled her to her feet. "You being all right, lady?" one of them asked in Valmieran with a trilling Algarvian accent.

"I am very well. And I thank you." Krasta was very conscious—even smugly conscious—of her own good looks. She was also very conscious that the redheads, given an inch, would cheerfully take a mile. If she were old and homely, they might well have walked right past her. Giving them her most haughty stare, she went on, "I am the Marchioness Krasta, and the companion to Colonel Lurcanio."

Her own rank probably meant very little to the soldiers in kilts. The Algarvian colonel's rank meant they couldn't take any liberties. They weren't too drunk to realize it, either.

"You being careful, milady," one of them said. They both bowed, sweeping off their broad-brimmed hats in unison. And then they went away, perhaps in search of a woman who had no way, polite or otherwise, to tell them no. They probably wouldn't have to search too far.

Rubbing her tailbone, Krasta walked on in the opposite direction. The Avenue of Equestrians had always been Priekule's main shopping thoroughfare, with shops of all sorts catering to the most fastidious—and expensive—tastes. It still was, but now only a shadow of its former self. The Algarvian occupiers had methodically plundered Valmiera for more than two and half years. It showed.

They'd been methodically doing other things for more than two and a half years, too. Another Algarvian soldier came by, his arm around the waist of a blond Valmieran girl. He, of course, wore a kilt. But so did she, one that didn't come close to reaching her knees. A lot of Valmieran women—and a fair number of Valmieran men—had adopted their conquerors' fashions.

Krasta sniffed. She kept right on wearing trousers. She'd occasionally worn kilts before the war—as much to shock as for any other reason—but never since. Despite the Algarvians who used the west wing of her mansion as their own, despite an Algarvian lover, in some ways she felt her Kaunian blood more acutely these days than ever before. That was odd, especially since she'd long been convinced Algarve would win the Derlavaian War.

From behind her, someone called, "Congratulations on still having any money to spend, milady!"

She turned. Up the street toward her came Viscount Valnu. He was strikingly handsome, and would have been even more so had he not looked quite so much like a genial skull. He was one of the first men Krasta knew who'd started wearing kilts. She looked him up and down, then shook her head. "You've got knobby knees," she said in the tones of one passing sentence.

Nothing fazed Valnu. His grin grew more impudent yet. "I've got a baby's arm holding an apple, too, sweetheart."

"In your dreams," Krasta said with a snort; she knew the truth there. She waited for Valnu to come up to her. "And what are *you* doing here, if you haven't got any money?" Nobody came to the Avenue of Equestrians without money; the street offered poor folk nothing.

Valnu patted her on the backside. She couldn't decide whether to slap him or start laughing. In the end, she didn't do anything. The viscount made outrageousness part of his stock in trade. Blue eyes flashing, he answered, "Oh, I manage to scrape a couple of coppers together every now and then. I have my ways, so I do."

He might have meant he was a gigolo. He might have meant he was something with a harsher name; everyone who knew him knew his versatility. But he might just have meant he'd had a good run at dice, or that some rents from properties out in the provinces had come in. You never could tell with Valnu.

Needling him a little, Krasta asked, "And what's new with the Algarvians?"

"How should I know, darling?" he said. "You see more of them than I do. That house of yours is swarming with beefy redheads in kilts. Do you like their legs better than mine? Or will Lurcanio fling you in a dungeon if you even look at anyone but him?" He bared his teeth in happy, even friendly, malice.

Since she couldn't tell *what* Colonel Lurcanio might do, she was usually circumspect when she looked at anyone but him. "I don't invite them to grand, gruesome orgies at my mansion," she said.

"You don't need to. They're screwing all the maidservants anyhow," Valnu answered. Krasta's chief serving woman had had a baby by Lurcanio's former adjutant, so she couldn't very well deny that. At least Valnu hadn't come right out and said that Lurcanio was screwing her. From him, that was unusual delicacy.

Krasta had trouble holding her thoughts on any one thing. Her wave encompassed the Avenue of Equestrians and the whole city. "I'm so sick of dreariness!" she burst out.

"Things could be better," Valnu agreed. He waited till a

couple of more plump, staring Algarvian soldiers enjoying leave in the captured capital of Valmiera went by and got safely out of earshot before adding, "Things could be worse, too. Those fellows are probably in from Unkerlant, for instance. It's a lot worse there."

Unkerlant, to Krasta, might as well have been a mile beyond the moon. "I'm talking about places where civilized people go," she said with a sneer.

"Kaunians go to Unkerlant, the same as Algarvians do," Valnu said in a low voice, almost a whisper. "The difference is, some Algarvians come out again."

The ice that ran through Krasta had nothing to do with the patch that had made her slip. "I saw that news sheet—broadsheet—whatever you want to call it." She shuddered. "I believe it. I believe everything it says."

One of the reasons she believed the horrors the sheet described was that it was written in her brother's hand. She hadn't told Valnu about that, nor Lurcanio, either. A lifetime of cattiness had taught her the importance of keeping some things secret. Lurcanio was after Skarnu as things were.

And you still let him sleep with you? she wondered, as she did every so often. But Algarve was stronger than Valmiera, and Lurcanio had proved himself stronger than she was—a shock that still lingered. What choice had she had? None she'd seen then, none she saw now.

As if to rub salt in the wound, Valnu said, "The redheads keep on falling back in southern Unkerlant. I don't think Durrwangen will hold."

"Where did you hear that?" Krasta asked. "It's not in any of the news sheets."

"Of course it's not." Valnu bared his teeth, mocking her naïveté. "The Algarvians aren't fools. They don't want anybody here finding out things aren't going quite so well. But *they* know—and they talk among themselves. And sometimes they talk where other people can listen. Me, for instance." He struck a pose so absurd, Krasta couldn't help laughing.

But that laugh congealed on her face as a couple of constables came up the Avenue of Equestrians toward Valnu and her. They weren't Algarvians; they were the same Valmierans who'd patrolled the city before the kingdom fell. They wore almost the same dark green uniforms they had then. Their cap badges, though, were crossed axes, and crossed axes were also stamped on the brass buttons that held their tunics closed. Something seemed stamped on their features, too: a hard contempt for their own kind. They glared at her as they tramped past.

She glared, too, but only at their backs. Turning to Valnu, she complained, "They have no respect for rank." However angry her words, she didn't speak very loud: she didn't want those grim-looking men to hear.

"You're wrong, my sweet," Valnu said, and Krasta gave him a sour look as well. He blithely ignored it, as he blithely ignored so many things. Wagging a finger in her face, he went on, "They do indeed respect rank. As far as they're concerned, the Algarvians have it, and everyone else is scum. The Algarvians agree with them, of course."

"Of course," Krasta said dully. That wasn't too far removed from her own thoughts of a moment before. The Algarvians had strength, and if strength didn't give rank, what did? *Blood,* she thought, but the redheads had the strength to ignore that if they chose. "They *will* win the war, in spite of everything," she murmured. Now her glance toward Valnu was almost beseeching; she wanted him to tell her she was wrong.

He didn't. He said, "They may. They may very well. They've already taken more knocks than they ever expected, but they're still strong, too. And their mages don't care what they do—we know about that. If they win, there's liable not to be a Kaunian left alive in Forthweg by the time they're through."

Before the war, Krasta hadn't thought much about the Kaunians in Forthweg. When she did think of them, it was as backwoods bumpkins in a distant, backward kingdom. They were blood of her blood, aye, but distant cousins she would just as soon have forgotten. Poor relations. But the Algarvians seemed bound and determined to teach the lesson that even poor relations were relations after all.

Something crossed Krasta's mind. She didn't like thinking about these things—truth to tell, she didn't like thinking at all—but she couldn't help it. And she blurted forth the horrid notion as if to exorcise it: "What if they run out?"

Valnu patted her on the head. "My occasionally dear, you must not say these things, lest you risk losing your proud reputation as a featherbrain." She let out an indignant squawk. He ignored her and leaned forward so that his mouth was right by her ear. He teased her earlobe with his tongue for a moment, then whispered three words: "Night and fog."

"What?" The teasing tongue distracted her. She was easily distracted. "What's that got to do with anything?" She'd seen NIGHT AND FOG painted on the windows or doors of shops that suddenly closed for no reason anyone could find, but found no connection between the phrase and her own frightened question.

Viscount Valnu patted her again and gave her a sweet smile, as if she were a child. "I take it back," he said, fond indulgence in his voice. "You really are a featherbrain."

"I ought to slap your face," she snapped. She didn't know why she didn't. Had anyone else spoken to her so (except Colonel Lurcanio, who hit back), she would have. But Valnu made a habit of saying and doing preposterous things, to her and to everyone he knew. His panache had kept him out of trouble so far, and kept him out of trouble now.

He said, "Here, let's do something that's more fun instead," took her in his arms, and gave her a thoroughly competent kiss. Then, bowing as extravagantly as an Algarvian, he turned and sauntered up the Avenue of Equestrians as if he had not a care in the world. Knees aside, he looked better in a kilt than most redheads.

Krasta hadn't bought anything—a shockingly unusual trip to the Avenue of Equestrians. Even so, she went back to her carriage, which waited in a side street. Her driver, surprised at her coming back so soon, hastily hid a flask. "Take me home," she told him. But would she find any shelter there, either?

Three

Winter was the rainy season in Bishah. The capital of Zuwayza rarely got much in the way of rain, but what it got, it got in winter. Sometimes, at this season, it also got cool enough at night to make Hajjaj think wearing clothes might not be the worst idea in the world.

The Zuwayzi foreign minister's senior wife patted his hand when he presumed to say that out loud. "If you want to put on a robe, put on a robe," Kolthoum told him. "No one here will mind if you do." Her tone suggested than anyone living in Hajjaj's home who did mind any eccentricity he happened to show would answer to her, and would not enjoy doing it.

But he shook his head. "My thanks, but no," he said. "No for two reasons. First, the servants *would* be scandalized, no matter what they said. I'm an old man now. I've been through too many scandals to invite another one."

"You're not so old as all that," Kolthoum said.

Hajjaj was far too courteous to laugh at his senior wife, but he knew better. His hair, having gone from black to gray, was now going from gray to white. (So was Kolthoum's; they'd been yoked together for almost fifty years. Hajjaj didn't notice it in her, for he saw her through the eyesight of a shared lifetime, where today and the lost time before the Six Years' War could blur into each other at a blink.) His dark brown skin had grown wrinkled and leathery. When it did rain here, his bones would ache.

He went on, "The second reason is even more compelling: so far as I know, we haven't got any clothes here. I have this style and that—short tunics and long ones and kilts and trousers and who knows what useless fripperies—in a closet next to my office down in the city, but I don't need to bother with such foreign nonsense in my own home."

"If you're feeling chilly, it isn't nonsense," Kolthoum said. "I'm sure we could have a maidservant fix you something out of a blanket or curtains or whatever would suit you."

"I'm fine," Hajjaj insisted. His senior wife looked eloquently unconvinced, but stopped arguing. One of the reasons they'd got on so well for so long was that they'd learned not to push each other too far.

Tewfik, the majordomo, walked into the chamber where they were sitting. Next to him, Hajjaj truly wasn't so old as all that: Tewfik had served his father before him. Bowing, the clan retainer said, "Sorry to disturb you, lad"—he was the only man Hajjaj knew who could call him that—"but a messenger from the palace just brought you this." He handed Hajjaj a roll of paper sealed with King Shazli's seal.

"I thank you, Tewfik," Hajjaj replied, and the majordomo bowed again. Hajjaj wasn't upset that he hadn't heard the messenger arrive; sheltering behind thick sandstone walls, his home, like any clanfather's, was a compound well on its way to being a little village. He put on his spectacles, broke the royal seal, unrolled the paper, and read.

"Can you speak of it?" Kolthoum asked.

"Oh, aye," he said. "His Majesty summons me to his audience chamber tomorrow morning, that's all."

"But you'd see him tomorrow anyhow," his senior wife observed. "Why does he need to summon you?"

"I don't know," Hajjaj admitted. "By tomorrow morning, though, I should find out, don't you think?"

Kolthoum sighed. "I suppose so." She reached out and patted her husband on the thigh, a gesture having more to do with sympathy than with desire. It had been a long time since they'd made love. Hajjaj couldn't remember just how long, in fact, but their companionship hardly needed physical intimacy anymore. One of these days, he would have to wed a new junior wife if he sought such amusements. Lalla, recently divorced, had been more expensive and more temperamental than she was worth. One of these days. As he neared seventy, lovemaking seemed less urgent than it had a couple of decades earlier.

He fortified himself with strong tea the next morning before his driver took the carriage down from the foothills and into Bishah proper. It hadn't rained lately, which meant the road wasn't muddy. It also wasn't dusty, a more common annoyance.

Men shouted back and forth on the roof of the royal palace. They weren't guards; the Zuwayzin liked King Shazli well. They were roofers: when the rains came, even the royal roof leaked. Unlike his citizens, Shazli didn't have to wait his turn to get things set right.

As he'd said he would, the king awaited his foreign minister in the audience chamber, a less formal setting than the throneroom. Shazli was about half Hajjaj's age. Hajjaj thought well of him: for a man so young, he was no fool. Only a gold circlet showed the king's rank—the Zuwayzi custom of nudity made display harder.

Bowing, Hajjaj said, "How may I serve your Majesty?"

"Before we talk business, we can take refreshment," Shazli answered, by which Hajjaj knew the business wasn't a desperate emergency—the king, unlike his subjects, could put aside the rules of hospitality if he chose. Shazli clapped his hands. A serving woman brought in tea and date wine and honey cakes enlivened with chopped pistachios.

While they nibbled and sipped, Shazli and Hajjaj were limited to polite small talk. Presently, the wine drunk and the cakes diminished, the maidservant came back and carried off the silver tray on which she'd fetched them. Hajjaj watched her swaying backside with appreciation but without urgency. That wasn't just his years; he'd seen so much bare flesh, it didn't inflame him as it did most Derlavaian folk.

"You will be wondering why I summoned you." Rituals completed, Shazli could with propriety get down to business.

"So I will, your Majesty," Hajjaj agreed. "As always, though, I expect you will enlighten me."

"Always the optimist," King Shazli said. Hajjaj raised an eyebrow. He'd been his kingdom's foreign minister since

Zuwayza regained her freedom from an Unkerlant embroiled in the Twinkings War after the earlier ravages of the Six Years' War. Few men who'd spent their whole careers as diplomatists retained much in the way of optimism by the time they got old. Shazli's wry chuckle said he did know that. He reached under a pillow next to the one against which he reclined and pulled out a sheet of paper. Passing it to Hajjaj, he said, "This was brought to our line under flag of truce and, once its import was recognized, flown straight here by dragon."

Like any Zuwayzi, Hajjaj carried a large leather wallet to make up for his dearth of pockets. As he had for Shazli's summons, he took out his spectacles so he could read the document. When he was through, he peered over the lenses at his sovereign. "Unkerlant has never been a kingdom renowned for subtlety," he remarked. "The Unkerlanters would always sooner order than persuade, and they would sooner threaten than order . . . as we see here."

"As we see here," the king agreed. "All-out war against us—'war to the knife' was the phrase they used, wasn't it?— unless we leave off fighting them and go over to their side against Algarve. They graciously allow us three days' time before our reply is due."

Hajjaj read the document again. Shazli had accurately summarized it. Inclining his head, the foreign minister inquired, "And what would you have of me in aid of this, your Majesty?"

"Can Swemmel do as he threatens?" Shazli demanded. "If he can, can we hope to withstand him if he hurls everything he has against us?"

"I hope you are also asking General Ikhshid these same questions," Hajjaj said. "I am not a soldier, nor do I pretend to be."

"I am consulting Ikhshid, aye." King Shazli nodded. "And I have some notion of what you are and what you are not, your Excellency. I'd better, after all these years. I want your view not as a man of war but as a man of the world."

Reclining against cushions didn't make even a seated bow

easy, but Hajjaj managed. "You do me too much credit," he murmured, thinking nothing of the sort. After a few seconds, he shook his head. "I don't believe King Swemmel can do it," he said. "Aye, the Unkerlanters crushed Algarve at Sulingen, but they're still locked with Mezentio's men from the Narrow Sea in the south to the Garelian Ocean here in the tropic north. If they pull enough men from their lines to be sure of crushing us, the Algarvians are bound to find a way to make them pay. Algarve can hurt them worse than we'd ever dream of doing."

"Ikhshid said the same thing when I asked him last night, which does somewhat relieve my mind," Shazli said. "Still . . . My next question is, is Swemmel so mad for revenge against us that he'd do anything to harm us, not caring what might happen to his own kingdom?"

Hajjaj clicked his tongue between his teeth and sucked in a long, thoughtful breath. No, his sovereign was no fool. Far from it. Though a rational man himself, Shazli knew Swemmel of Unkerlant wasn't, or wasn't always. Swemmel did some unbelievably foolish things, but he also did some unexpectedly clever ones, not least because nobody else could think along with him.

After a second longish pause, Hajjaj said, "I don't believe Swemmel will forget the war against Algarve just to punish us. I would not swear by the powers above, but I don't believe so. The Algarvians, over the past year and a half, have made themselves very hard for any Unkerlanter to forget."

"This is also General Ikhshid's view," King Shazli said. "I am glad the two of you speak with a single voice here, very glad indeed. If you disagreed, I would have more hesitation about rejecting the Unkerlanter demands out of hand."

"Oh, your Majesty, you mustn't do that!" Hajjaj exclaimed.

"How not?" Shazli asked. "Will you tell me I misunderstood you, and that you want Zuwayza to bow down to Unkerlant after all? If you will tell me that, I shall have certain things to tell you: of that you may rest assured."

"By no means," Hajjaj said. "All I ask is that you not send Swemmel a paper as hot as the ultimatum he has given you.

In fact, you might be wisest not to send him any reply at all. Aye, I believe that's best. Do nothing to inflame him, and our kingdom will stay safe."

By the nature of things, Zuwayza would never be a great power in Derlavai. The kingdom had not enough people, not enough land—and much of the land it did have was sun-blasted desert, in which thornbushes and lizards and camels might flourish but nothing else did. Hajjaj's ancestors had been nomads who roamed that desert waste and fought other Zuwayzi clans for the sport of it. Though generations removed from a camel-hair tent, he'd learned the old songs, the brave songs, as a boy. Counseling prudence came hard. But he reminded himself he was no barbarian but a civilized man. He did what needed doing.

And King Shazli nodded. "Aye, what you say makes good sense. Very well, then. If you will be so kind as to let me have that, . . ." Hajjaj passed the paper back to the king. Shazli tore it to pieces, saying, "Now we rely on the Algarvians to keep Unkerlant too busy to worry about the likes of us."

"I think we may safely do that," Hajjaj replied. "After all, the Algarvians have the strongest incentive to fight hard: if they lose, they're likely to get boiled alive."

Colonel Sabrino shook his head like a wild beast, trying to get the snow off his goggles. How was he supposed to see down to the ground if he couldn't see past the end of his nose? The Algarvian officer was tempted to take off the goggles and just use his eyes, as he did in good weather. But even then, his dragon could fly fast enough to make tears stream from his eyes and ruin his vision. The goggles would have to stay.

The dragon, sensing him distracted, let out a sharp screech and tried to fly where it wanted to go, not where he wanted it to. He whacked it with his long, iron-shod goad. It screeched again, this time in fury, and twisted its long, snaky neck so that it could glare back at him. Its yellow eyes blazed with hatred. He whacked it again. "You do what I tell you, you stupid, stinking thing!" he shouted.

Dragons were trained from hatchlinghood never to flame their riders off them. As far as humans were concerned, that was the most important lesson the great beasts ever learned. But dragonfliers knew how truly brainless their charges were. Every once in a while, a dragon forgot its lessons. . . .

This one didn't. After another hideous screech, it resigned itself to doing as Sabrino commanded. He peered down through scattered, quick-scudding clouds at the fight around Durrwangen.

What he saw made him curse even more harshly than he had at his dragon. The Unkerlanters had almost completed their ring around the city. If they did, he saw nothing that would keep them from serving the Algarvian garrison inside as they'd served the Algarvian army that reached—but did not come out of—Sulingen.

Could Algarve withstand two great disasters in the southwest? Sabrino didn't know, and didn't want to have to find out. He spoke into his crystal to the squadron leaders he commanded: "All right, lads, let's give Swemmel's men the presents they've been waiting for."

"Aye, my lord Count." That was Captain Domiziano, who still seemed younger and more cheerful than he had any business being in the fourth year of a war that looked no closer to an end than it had the day it started: further from an end, perhaps.

"Aye." Captain Orosio didn't waste words. He never had. The other two squadron commanders also acknowledged the order.

Sabrino's laugh was bitter. He should have led sixty-four dragonfliers; each of his squadron commanders should have had charge of sixteen, including himself. When the fight against Unkerlant began, the wing had been at full strength. Now Sabrino commanded twenty-five men, and there were plenty of other colonels of dragonfliers who would have envied him for having so many.

Back in headquarters far from the fighting, generals wrote orders a full wing would have had trouble meeting. They always got irate when the battered bands of dragonfliers they had in the field failed to carry out those orders in full. Sabrino got irate, too—at them, not that it did him any good.

All he could do was all he could do. Having spoken through the crystal, he used hand signals, too. Then he whacked his dragon with the goad again. It dove on a large concentration of Unkerlanters below. The dragonfliers in the wing followed him without hesitation. They always had, since the first clashes with the Forthwegians. *Good men, one and all,* he thought.

A few of the Unkerlanters blazed up at the diving dragons. A few tried to run, though running in snowshoes wouldn't get them very far very fast. Most just kept on with what they were doing. Unkerlanters were a stolid lot, and seemed all the more so to the excitable Algarvians.

Sabrino's dragon carried two eggs slung beneath its belly. He released them and let them fall on the foe. The other dragonfliers in his wing were doing the same. Bursts of suddenly released sorcerous energy flung snow and Unkerlanters and behemoths in all directions. Whooping, Sabrino ordered his dragon high into the air once more. "That's the way to do it, boys," he said. "We can still hit 'em a good lick every now and again, curse me if we can't."

He knew a moment's pity for the Unkerlanter footsoldiers. He'd been a footsoldier, toward the end of the dreadful slaughters of the Six Years' War a generation before. Having somehow come through alive, he'd vowed he would never fight on the ground again. Dragonfliers knew terror, too, but they rarely knew squalor.

Captain Domiziano's smiling face appeared in Sabrino's crystal. "Shall we go down and flame some of those whoresons, too?" the squadron leader asked.

Reluctantly, Sabrino shook his head. "Let's go back to the dragon farm and load up on eggs again instead," he answered. "It's not like flying down to Sulingen was—we can get back here again pretty fast. And that'll save on cinnabar."

Along with brimstone, the quicksilver in cinnabar helped dragons flame farther and fiercer. Brimstone was easy to come by. Quicksilver . . . Sabrino sighed. Algarve didn't

have enough. Algarve had never had enough. Her own sorcery had turned and bit her, helping Lagoas and Kuusamo
drive her from the land of the Ice People, from which she'd
imported the vital mineral. There were quicksilver mines
aplenty in the Mamming Hills south and west of Sulingen—
but the Algarvians had never got to them. And so . . .

And so, as reluctantly, Domiziano nodded. "Aye, sir.
Makes sense, I suppose. We'll save the dragonfire we've got
for fighting with Unkerlanter beasts in the air."

"My thought exactly," Sabrino agreed. "We don't always
get to do what we want to do. Sometimes we do what we
have to do."

Surely King Mezentio had been doing what he wanted to
do when he launched the Algarvian armies against Unkerlant. Until then, Algarve had gone from one triumph to another: over Forthweg, over Sibiu, over Valmiera, over
Jelgava. Sabrino sighed again. The first summer's campaigns
against the Unkerlanters had been triumphant, too. But Cottbus hadn't quite fallen. A year later, Sulingen hadn't quite
fallen, and neither had the quicksilver mines in the Mamming
Hills. And now Mezentio's men did what they had to do in
Unkerlant, not what they wanted to do.

No sooner had that gloomy thought crossed Sabrino's
mind than dour Captain Orosio's face replaced Domiziano's
in the crystal. "Look down, sir," Orosio said. "Curse me if
our soldiers aren't pulling out of Durrwangen."

"What?" Sabrino exclaimed. "They can't do that. They've
got orders to hold that town against everything the Unkerlanters can do."

"You know that, sir," Orosio answered. "I know that. But if
they know that, they don't know they know it, if you know
what I mean."

And he was right. Durrwangen was an important town,
and the Algarvians had put a sizable army into it to make
sure it didn't fall back into Unkerlanter hands. And now that
army, men and behemoths, horse and unicorn cavalry, was
streaming out of Durrwangen through the one hole in the
Unkerlanter ring around it, tramping north and east along

whatever roads the soldiers and animals could find or make in the snow.

"Have they gone mad?" Sabrino wondered. "Their commander's head will go on the block for something like this."

"I was thinking the same thing, sir." But Orosio hesitated and then added, "At least they won't be thrown away, like the men down in Sulingen were."

"What? I didn't hear that." But Sabrino was arch; he'd heard perfectly well. And he could hardly deny that his squadron commander had a point. So far as he knew, not a man had come out of Sulingen. The Algarvians down here would live to fight another day—but they were supposed to have been fighting in Durrwangen.

"What do we do, sir?" Orosio asked.

Sabrino hesitated. That needed thought. At last, he answered, "We do what we would have done even if they'd stayed in the city. We go back, get more eggs, and then come and give them whatever help we can. I don't see what else we can do. If you've got a better answer, let me hear it, by the powers above."

But Orosio only shook his head. "No, sir."

"All right, then," Sabrino said. "We'll do that."

News of the Algarvians' retreat from Durrwangen had already reached the dragon farm by the time Sabrino's wing got back to it. Some of the dragon handlers said the commander in Durrwangen hadn't bothered asking for permission before pulling out. Others claimed he had asked for permission, been refused, and pulled out anyway. They were all sure of one thing. "His head will roll," said the fellow who tossed meat covered with powdered brimstone and cinnabar to Sabrino's dragon. He sounded quite cheerful about the prospect.

And Sabrino could only nod. "His head bloody well deserves to roll," he said. "You can't go around disobeying orders."

"Oh, aye," the dragon handler agreed. But then, after a pause, he went on, "Still and all, though, that's a lot of boys who can do a lot of fighting somewhere else."

"Everybody thinks he's a general," Sabrino said with a snort. The dragon handler tossed his mount another big gobbet of meat. The beast snatched it out of the air and gulped it down. Its yellow eyes followed the handler as he took yet another piece of meat from the cart. The dragon was far fonder of the man who fed it than of the man who flew it.

Despite his snort, Sabrino remained thoughtful. He and Orosio had said about the same thing as the dragon handler had. Did that mean they were on to something, or were they all daft the same way?

In the end, it probably wouldn't matter. Regardless of whether his move proved foolish or brilliant, the general in charge of the Algarvian forces breaking out from Durrwangen *would* be in trouble with his superiors. Being right was rarely an excuse for disobeying orders.

As soon as his beasts were fed and had fresh eggs slung beneath them, Sabrino ordered them into the air once more. He hoped they wouldn't meet Unkerlanter dragons. They'd been flying too much lately. They were tired and far from at their best. He wished they could have had more time to recover between flights. But there were too many miles of fighting and not enough dragons to cover them. The ones Algarve had needed to do all they could.

As if drawn by a lodestone, Sabrino led his dragonfliers back toward the Algarvian soldiers breaking out of Durrwangen. They were doing better than he'd thought they would be. Their retreat, plainly, had caught the Unkerlanters by surprise. Swemmel's men were swarming into the city they'd lost the summer before. Most of them seemed willing to let the soldiers who'd defended it go.

Sabrino and his dragonfliers punished the Unkerlanters who did attack the retreating Algarvians. Corpses, some in long, rock-gray tunics, others in the white smocks that made them harder to see against the snow, sprawled in unlovely death. Sabrino snorted at that, this time mocking what passed for poetry in his mind. He'd seen too much fighting in two different wars, and the next lovely death he found would be the first.

Down below, the Algarvian army kept falling back. It retreated in excellent order, without the slightest sign of disarray from the men. But if they were in such good spirits, why had their leader ordered them out of Durrwangen in the first place? Couldn't they have held the important town a good deal longer? Sabrino had plenty of questions, but no good answers to go with them.

On the defensive. Sergeant Istvan didn't like the phrase. Gyongyosians were by training and (they said) by birth a warrior race. Warriors, by the nature of their calling, boldly stormed forward and overwhelmed the foe. They didn't sit and wait inside fieldworks for the foe to storm forward and try to overwhelm them.

So said most of the men in Istvan's squad, at any rate. They'd come into the army to force their way through the passes of the Ilszung Mounts and through the endless, trackless forests of western Unkerlant. They'd done a good job of it, too. Unkerlant was distracted by her bigger fight with Algarve thousands of miles to the east, and never had put enough men into the defense against Gyongyos—never till recently, anyhow. Now . . .

"We just have to wait and see if we can build up reinforcements faster than those stinking whoresons, that's all," Istvan said. "If you haven't got the men, you can't do the things you could if you did."

"Aye, he's right," Corporal Kun agreed. Kun always looked more like what he had been—a mage's apprentice—than a proper soldier. He was thin—downright scrawny for a Gyongyosian—and his spectacles gave him a studious seeming. He went on, "Istvan and I had to put up with this same kind of nonsense of Obuda, out in the Bothnian Ocean, when the Kuusamans had enough men to get the jump on us."

"And me," Szonyi said. "Don't forget about me."

"And you," Istvan agreed. They'd all been on Obuda together. Istvan went on, "We've seen the kinds of things you have to do when you haven't got enough men to do everything you want. You sit and you wait for the other bugger to make a mistake and then you try and kick him in the balls when he does."

Kun and Szonyi nodded. The two of them—weedy corporal and burly common soldier with tawny hair and curly beard that made him look like a lion—understood how to play the game. So did Istvan. The rest of the men in the squad . . . he wasn't so sure of them. They listened. They nodded in all the right places. Did they really know what he was talking about? He doubted it.

"We are a warrior race. We shall prevail, no matter what the accursed Unkerlanters do." That was Lajos, one of the new men. He was as burly as Szonyi, a little burlier than Istvan. In the small bits of action he'd seen since coming up to the front, he'd fought as bravely as anyone could want. He was nineteen, and sure he knew everything. Who was there to tell him he might be wrong? Would he believe anyone? Not likely.

Istvan took off his gloves and looked at his hands. His nails were raggedly trimmed, with black dirt ground under them and into the folds of skin at his knuckles. He turned his hands over. Thick calluses, also dark with ground-in dirt, creased his palms. Scars seamed his hands, too. His eyes went, as they always did, to one in particular, a puckered line between the second and third fingers of his left hand.

Kun had a scar as near identical to that one as made no difference. So did Szonyi. So did several other squadmates, the men who'd served under Istvan for a while. Captain Tivadar had cut them all. The company commander would have been within his rights to kill them all. They'd eaten goat stew. They hadn't known it was goat; they'd killed the Unkerlanters who'd been cooking it. But knowledge didn't matter. They'd sinned. Istvan still didn't know if his expiation was enough, or if the curse on those who ate of forbidden flesh still lingered.

Someone approached the timber-reinforced redoubt in which Istvan and his squad waited. "Who comes?" he called softly.

"The fairy frog in the fable, to gulp you all down."

With a chuckle, Istvan said, "Come ahead, Captain."

Tivadar did, slipping from tree to tree so he didn't show himself to any Unkerlanter snipers who might be lurking nearby. Nodding to Istvan, he slid down into the redoubt. "Anything that looks like trouble?" he asked.

"No, sir," Istvan answered at once. "Everything's been real quiet the past couple of days."

"That's good." Tivadar checked. He wasn't much older than Istvan—he couldn't have been thirty—but he thought of everything, or as close to everything as he could. "I hope that's good, anyhow. Maybe Swemmel's boys are brewing up something nasty out of sight." He turned to Kun. "Anything that *feels* like trouble, Corporal?"

Kun shook his head. "Nothing I can sense, Captain. I don't know how much that's worth, though. I was only an apprentice, after all, not a mage myself." In the squad, he put on airs about the small spells he did know. Putting on airs with the company commander didn't pay.

"All right," Tivadar said. "The last time they struck us with sorcery, even our best mages didn't know what they'd do till they did it, curse them."

He was all business. Having purified Istvan, Kun, Szonyi, and the rest, he acted as if they *were* ritually pure, and never mentioned that dreadful night. Neither did any of them, not where anybody not of their number might hear. The shame was too great for that. Istvan thought it always would be.

Kun usually mocked whenever he saw the chance. He was a city man, and his ways often seemed strange and slick and rather repellent to Istvan, who like most Gyongyosians came from a mountain valley where the people were at feud with some neighboring valley when they weren't at feud among themselves. But Kun didn't mock now. In tones unwontedly serious, he said, "That was an abomination. The stars will not shine on men who murder their own to power their magecraft."

"Aye, you're right," Lajos boomed. "The Unkerlanters fight filthy. It's worse than eating goat's flesh, if you ask me."

He waited for everyone to nod and agree with him. In most

squads, everybody would have. Here, the agreement was slow and halfhearted. It was badly acted by men who wanted to seem normal Gyongyosians but had trouble doing so. Lajos didn't realize that. Istvan hoped the motions of the stars would grant that he never did. The young trooper grunted and shifted uncomfortably, knowing things had gone wrong and not understanding why.

Szonyi said, "Captain, when can we take the fight to Swemmel's men again? We drove 'em through the mountains and we drove 'em through the woods. We can still do it, any time we get the orders."

Tivadar answered, "If the men set over me tell me to go forward, go forward I shall, unless I should die serving Gyongyos, in which case the stars will cherish my spirit forevermore. But if the men set over me tell me to wait in place, wait in place I shall. And if the men set over you, Trooper, if they tell *you* to wait in place, wait in place you will. And they do. I do."

"Aye, sir." Szonyi dipped his head in reluctant acquiescence. He was a man of his kingdom—and, like Istvan, a man of the countryside. Given his way, he would go straight at a foe, without subtlety but without hesitation, and keep going till one or the other of them couldn't stand up anymore.

"Remember, boys, you have to stay alert all the time," Tivadar warned. "The Unkerlanters are better in the forest than we are. We couldn't have come so far against 'em if we didn't have 'em outnumbered. They don't always need magic to have a go at us—sometimes sneakiness serves 'em just as well."

He climbed out of the redoubt and headed off along the line to the next Gyongyosian strongpoint. Istvan wished his countrymen had enough men to cover all the line through the forest they held. They didn't, especially in winter, where staying out alone might so easily lead to freezing to death.

"The captain is a pretty good officer," Lajos said.

"Aye, he is," Istvan agreed, and all the other veterans in the squad chimed in, too. Lajos let out a small sigh of relief. Not everyone thought he was an idiot all the time, anyhow.

Kun said, "If we can keep what we hold now when the war is over, we'll have won the greatest victory against Unkerlant in almost three hundred years."

"Is that a fact?" Istvan said, and Kun nodded in a way that proclaimed it was not only a fact, it was a fact anyone this side of feeblemindedness should have known. Istvan sent his corporal a look a little less than warm. Kun returned it: not quite so openly this time, for Istvan outranked him, but unmistakably nonetheless.

Szonyi sniffed, for all the world like a hound taking a scent. "More snow coming," he said. "Won't be long, either. You can taste the wind."

Istvan had plenty of practice gauging the weather himself. He opened and closed his mouth a couple of times, as if he were taking bites out of the air. The chill of the wind—a wind that had suddenly picked up—the feel of the moisture it carried . . . He nodded. "Aye, we're for it. Coming out of the west, from behind us."

"Blowing right into the Unkerlanters' faces," Szonyi said. "Seems a shame not to hit 'em when we've got that kind of edge. We could be like mountain apes, gone before they even knew we were there."

"Aye, I see the resemblance, all right." Kun planted the barb with a self-satisfied smirk. Szonyi glowered at him. Istvan kept the two of them from quarreling any worse than they usually did.

Whether right about striking or not, Szonyi was right about the storm. It blew in that night, snow swirling around the trees and through their branches till Lajos, on sentry-go, complained, "How am I supposed to see anything? King Swemmel and his whole court could be out there drinking tea, by the stars, and I wouldn't know it unless they invited me to have some."

"If Swemmel was out there, he'd be drinking spirits." Istvan spoke with great conviction. "And the son of a whore wouldn't invite anybody to share." But he could see no farther than Lajos. If the Unkerlanters were gathering in the forest not far away, he might not know it till too late. He might not, but Kun would. He shook the onetime mage's apprentice out of his bedroll.

"What do you want?" Kun asked irritably, yawning in his face.

"You've got that little magic that tells when somebody's moving toward you," Istvan answered. "Don't you think this would be a good time to use it?"

Kun eyed the snowstorm and nodded, though he warned, "The spell won't say whether the men it spies are friends or foes."

"Just work it," Istvan said impatiently. "If they're coming toward us from out of the east, they're no friends of ours."

"Well, you're bound to be right about that," Kun admitted, and worked the tiny spell. A moment later, he turned back to Istvan. "Nothing, Sergeant. Remember, the snow gives the Unkerlanters as much trouble as it gives us."

"All right." Istvan used a brisk nod to hide his relief. He knew he shouldn't have been so relieved; it wasn't proper for a man from a warrior race. But even a man of a warrior race might have been excused for being unwilling to wait and receive a blow from the enemy.

Kun said, "We'll get through another day. That will do." He sounded none too fierce himself, but Istvan didn't reprove him.

Now that Vanai dared go out onto the streets of Eoforwic once more, she wished she could find some books written in classical Kaunian. But they'd long since vanished from all the booksellers' shops, those dealing in new and secondhand volumes alike: the Algarvians forbade them. The redheads had aimed to destroy Kaunianity even before they'd started destroying Kaunians.

Vanai suspected she might have been able to get her hands on some had she known which booksellers to trust. But she didn't, and she didn't care to ask questions that might draw notice to herself. She made do with Forthwegian books.

My magecraft makes me look like a Forthwegian, she thought. *Even Ealstan sees me this way almost all the time. I speak Forthwegian almost all the time. People call me Thelberge, as if I really were a Forthwegian. Am I still Vanai?*

Whenever she looked in a mirror, her old familiar features looked back at her. Her sorcery didn't change the way she saw herself. In the mirror, she still had fair skin, a long face with a straight nose, and gray-blue eyes. But even in the mirror, her hair was black. Like any Kaunian with a grain of sense, she'd dyed it to make it harder for the Algarvians to penetrate her disguise.

Am I still Vanai, if the world knows me as Thelberge? If the world knows me as Thelberge for long enough, will the Vanai inside me start to die? If Algarve wins the Derlavaian War, will I have to go on being Thelberge for the rest of my life?

She didn't want to think about things like that, but how could she help it? If the Algarvians won the war, would Eoforwic stay shabby and battered, its people—even real Forthwegians—scrawny, for the rest of her life? She didn't want to think about that, either, but it looked like being true.

A lot of the graffiti that said SULINGEN had been painted over, but Vanai knew what rectangles of fresh whitewash meant. She smiled fiercely every time she saw one. The Algarvians had pasted recruiting broadsheets for Plegmund's Brigade everywhere they could, as if to mask the importance of the defeat they'd suffered from the Forthwegians and maybe from themselves.

Up on the hill at the heart of the city stood the royal palace. Vanai hadn't thought about King Penda very often back in the days before the war. She hadn't thought much of him, either, but that was a different story. Like most Kaunians in Forthweg, she hadn't been enamored of the rule of a man not of her blood, and a man who strongly preferred those who were of his own blood.

These days, a large Algarvian flag, red, green, and white, flew about the palace. An Algarvian governor ruled Forthweg in Penda's stead. Things surely had been less than ideal before the war. Now they were a great deal worse than that.

Vanai shook her head. Who could have imagined such a thing?

Eoforwic had several market squares. It needed them, to keep so many people fed. The one closest to her block of flats was perhaps the smallest and meanest in the city, which meant it was larger than the one in Gromheort and dwarfed the tiny square back in Oyngestun.

Vanai bought barley and beans and turnips: food for hard times, food that would keep people going when nothing better was to be had. Even the beans and barley were in short supply, and more expensive than they should have been. If Ealstan hadn't brought home good money from casting accounts, the two of them might have gone hungry. By the pinched and anxious looks on the faces of a lot of people in the square, hunger was already loose in Eoforwic.

She stayed watchful and wary as she carried her purchases back toward her flat. She'd heard stories of people knocked on the head for the sake of a sack of grain. She didn't intend to be one of them.

A blocky Forthwegian man stood in the middle of the sidewalk, staring east and pointing up into the sky. Vanai had to stop; there was no polite way around him. But she didn't turn and look. For all she knew, he'd come up with a new way to distract people and then steal from them. If that did him an injustice, then it did. *Better safe than sorry* ran through her mind.

Then the Forthwegian shouted something that made her change her mind: "Dragons! Unkerlanter dragons!"

She was just starting to whirl when the first eggs fell on Eoforwic. "Get down!" screamed somebody who must have gone through such horror before. Vanai hadn't—the Algarvians hadn't reckoned Oyngestun important enough to waste eggs on it—but she wasted no time in throwing herself flat on the slates of the sidewalk . . . and on top of the precious food she'd bought. Even with dragons overhead, she couldn't afford to lose that.

More eggs burst, seemingly at random, some far away, others only a couple of blocks off. Along with the roars from the bursts came the almost musical tinkling of shattered glass hitting walls and pavements and shattering further and the screams of men and women either wounded or terrified.

Now Vanai did look up. The dragons were hard to see. It was a cloudy day, and their bellies were painted a gray that made them look like nothing so much as moving bits of cloud themselves. The eggs their dragonfliers released were easier to spy. They were darker, and fell straight and swift.

One seemed to fall straight toward Vanai. It got bigger and bigger—and burst only half a block away, close enough to pick her up and slam her back down to the ground with shocking and painful force. Her ears were stunned, deafened, she hoped not forever. A tiny sliver of glass tore a cut in the back of her left hand. But a full-throated scream drowned out her yelp.

The man who'd warned of the Unkerlanter dragons lay writhing on the sidewalk. His hands clutched at his belly, from which blood poured: a flood, a torrent, a deluge of blood. Vanai stared in helpless, dreadful fascination. How much blood did a living man hold? More to the point, how much could he lose before he stopped being a living man?

His shrieks faded. His hands relaxed. The blood poured off the edge of the sidewalk into the gutter. Vanai gulped, fighting sickness.

Almost as soon as it began, the Unkerlanter attack ended. The dragons had flown a long way. They couldn't carry very many eggs, or very heavy ones. As soon as they'd dropped what cargo of death they could bring, their dragonfliers guided them back toward the west once more.

Vanai picked up her groceries and hurried past the stocky man's corpse toward her block of flats. A couple of other bodies lay beyond that one. She tried not to look at them, either. A wounded woman cried out, but someone was already tending to her. Vanai went on without feeling the bite of conscience.

Eoforwic boiled like an anthill stirred by a stick. People who'd been inside their homes and shops when the eggs started falling came rushing out to see if loved ones and friends were all right or simply to see what had happened.

People who'd been on the street rushed toward their homes and shops to make sure those were still standing. Here and there, physicians and mages and firefighting crews had to push their way through the chaos to do their duty.

All things considered, the Algarvian constables on the streets did a pretty good job of opening the way so help could get where it was going. They weren't subtle or gentle about it: they screamed abuse in their language and in broken Forthwegian and Kaunian, and they used their bludgeons to wallop anyone who proved even a split second slow in grasping what they meant. But Vanai didn't think Forthwegian constables would have acted differently. They did what needed doing on the spur of the moment; whys and wherefores could wait.

Vanai let out a great sigh of relief when she found her block of flats undamaged but for a couple of broken windows and no fires burning anywhere close by. She carried the barley and turnips and beans up to her flat, set down the sacks in the kitchen, and poured herself a large cup of wine.

She'd got halfway down it, a warm glow beginning to spread through her, when she started worrying about Ealstan. What if he didn't come back? What if he couldn't come back? What if he were injured? What if he were . . . ? She wouldn't even think the word. She gulped down the rest of the wine instead.

Hour followed hour. Ealstan didn't come. *There's no reason for him to come,* Vanai told herself, over and over again. *He's doing what he has to do, that's all.* That made perfect sense. Eoforwic was a big city. The Unkerlanter raid had killed or wounded a relative handful of people. The odds that Ealstan was one of them were vanishingly small. Aye, it all made perfect logical sense. It didn't stop her heart from racing or her breath from whistling in her throat with anxiety.

And it didn't stop her from leaping in the air when she heard the coded knock at the door, or from crying out, "Where *were* you?" when Ealstan came inside.

"Casting accounts. Where else would I be?" he answered. Vanai's expression must have been eloquent, for he added,

"None of the eggs fell anywhere near me. See? I'm right as rain."

Maybe he was telling the truth. Maybe he just didn't want her to worry. She didn't say anything about the cut on her hand, for fear he would worry. What she did say was, "Powers above be praised that you're safe." She squeezed the breath out of him.

"Oh, aye, I'm fine. All things considered, it wasn't much of a raid. I wonder if any of those dragons will get home again." Ealstan sounded dispassionate, but his arms tightened around her.

She squeezed him again. "Why did the Unkerlanters bother, if they didn't do Eoforwic any harm?"

"Oh, I didn't say that," Ealstan answered. "Haven't you heard?"

"Heard what?" Now Vanai wanted to shake him. "I was bringing groceries home when it happened, and I came straight here afterwards. How could I have heard anything?"

"All right. All right. I'll talk," Ealstan said, as if she were a constable pounding the truth out of him. "Most of their eggs fell around the ley-line caravan depot, and a couple of them smashed it up pretty well. The Algarvians will have some trouble moving soldiers through there for a while."

"Soldiers or . . . anybody else," Vanai said slowly. She couldn't bring herself to come out and mention by name the Kaunians the Algarvians sent west to be sacrificed so their life energy could power the redheads' sorceries.

"Aye, or anybody else." Ealstan understood what she meant. He set a hand on her shoulder. "With that sorcery you worked out, you've done more to make that hard for Mezentio's men than all the Unkerlanter dragons put together."

"Have I?" Vanai considered that. It was a pretty big thought. "Maybe I have," she said at last. "But even if I have, it's still not enough. The Algarvians shouldn't have been able to do what they did in the first place."

Ealstan nodded. "I know that. Anybody with any brains knows it. They never would have been able to, either, if so many Forthwegians didn't hate Kaunians." He gave Vanai a quick kiss. "You need to remember that not all Forthwegians do."

She smiled. "I already knew that. I'm always glad to hear it again, though—and to see proof." This time, she kissed him. One thing led to another. They ended up eating supper later than they'd intended to. They were both young enough to take that kind of thing for granted, even to laugh about it. Vanai never stopped to wonder how rare and fortunate it was.

Commander Cornelu guided his leviathan out of the harbor at Setubal and into the Strait of Valmiera. The leviathan was a fine, frisky beast. Cornelu patted its smooth, slick skin. "You may be as good as Eforiel," he said. "Aye, you just may."

The leviathan wriggled its long, slim body beneath him. It was far more sinuous, far more graceful, than its blocky cousins, the whales. It didn't understand what he'd said—he didn't think it would have understood even if he'd spoken Lagoan rather than his native Sibian—but it liked to hear him speak.

He patted it again. "Do you know what kind of compliments I'm paying you?" he asked. Since the leviathan couldn't answer, he did: "No, of course you don't. But if you did, you'd be flattered, believe me."

He'd ridden Eforiel from Sibiu to Lagoas after the Algarvians overran his island. Going into exile in Lagoas was vastly preferable to yielding to the invaders. Without false modesty, he knew Sibian-trained leviathans were the best in the world. Eforiel could do things no Lagoan leviathan-rider could hope to get his mount to match.

But Eforiel was dead, slain off his home island of Tirgoviste. After making his way back to Lagoas again, he'd had this new beast for a while, and he'd worked hard to train it up to Sibian standards. It was getting there. It might even have already arrived.

The leviathan darted to the left. Its jaws opened for a moment, then closed on a mackerel. A gulp and the fish was gone. Those great tooth jaws wouldn't have made more than two bites of a man—maybe only one. Like dragonfliers, leviathan-riders had, and needed to have, great respect for the beasts they took to war. Unlike dragonfliers, they got respect and affection in return. Cornelu wouldn't have wanted anything to do with dragons.

"Nasty, stupid, bad-tempered beasts," he told the leviathan. "Nothing like you. No, nothing like you."

With a flick of its tail, the leviathan dove below the surface. Magecraft, grease, and a rubber suit protected Cornelu from the chill of the sea. More magecraft let him breathe underwater. Without that spell, leviathan-riding would have been impossible. His mount could stay submerged far longer than he could.

Veterinary mages kept promising a spell to let leviathans breathe underwater, too. That would have changed warfare on the sea. Despite endless promises, though, the spell had yet to make an appearance. Cornelu didn't expect it during this war or, indeed, during his lifetime.

One stretch of ocean looked very much like another. Cornelu thanked the powers above that the day was clear: he had no trouble guiding his leviathan north, toward the coast of Valmiera. Along with him, the beasts carried two eggs hung under its belly. The Algarvians thought they could ship more or less safely in the waters off Valmiera. His job was to show them they were wrong.

Every so often, he glanced up at the sky. Ever since Mezentio's men seized Valmiera, their dragons and the Lagoans' had clashed above the strait that separated the island from the mainland. Now one side seized the upper hand, now the other. He'd had too many Algarvian dragonfliers attack him to want to let another one see him before he spied the enemy dragon.

Each time he looked today, the sky was empty. The Lagoans said a lot of Algarvian dragons had flown out of Valmiera lately, headed west. Maybe they were right, though Cornelu had trouble trusting them a great deal further than he trusted Mezentio's men. If they were, the war in Unkerlant was making the Algarvians forget about everything else.

Toward evening, the Derlavaian mainland rose up out of the sea ahead of Cornelu. He tapped his leviathan in a particular way. As it had been trained to do, it lifted its head out of the sea, standing on its tail with powerful beats of its flukes. Cornelu rose with the leviathan's head, and could see much farther than he could while closer to the surface.

Seeing farther, however, didn't mean seeing more here. No Algarvian freighters or warships glided along the ley lines. No Valmieran fishing boats used the ley lines, either, nor did any sailboats scud along without the power bigger vessels drew from the earth's grid of sorcerous energy.

Cornelu cursed under his breath. He'd sunk an Algarvian ley-line cruiser, along with other, smaller craft. He wanted more. With the Algarvians holding down his kingdom with a hand of iron, he hungered for more. The Sibian exiles fighting out of Lagoas were among the fiercest, most determined foes the Algarvians had.

But what a man wanted and what he got were not always, or even very often, one and the same. Cornelu had learned that painful lesson all too well. For this foray, he carried not one but two crystals. Making sure he'd chosen the one attuned to the Lagoan Admiralty, he murmured the activating charm he'd learned by rote and spoke into it: "Off the coast of Valmiera. No vessels visible. Proceeding with second plan." He'd also learned the phrases by rote. Lagoan was related to Sibian, but not too closely: its grammar was simplified, and it had borrowed far more words from Kuusaman and classical Kaunian than had his native tongue.

In the crystal, he saw the image of a Lagoan naval officer. Lagoan uniforms were darker, more somber, than the sea-green he'd worn while serving Sibiu. The Lagoan said, "Good luck with second plan. Good hunting with first." He'd evidently been briefed that Sibiu spoke his language imperfectly. After a small flare of light, the crystal returned to blankness.

The leviathan twisted in the water to catch a squid. Cornelu didn't let the motion disturb him as he replaced the first crystal in its oiled-leather case and drew out the second one from its.

Again, he murmured an activation charm. He spoke this one with much more confidence. It was in Algarvian, and Algarvian and Sibian were as closely related to each other as a couple of brothers, closer even than Valmieran and Jelgavan. He didn't know how the Lagoans had come by an Algarvian crystal: taken it from a captured dragonflier, perhaps, or brought it back from the land of the Ice People, from which Mezentio's men had been expelled.

However they'd got it, he had it now. He didn't speak into it, as he had into the one attuned to the Admiralty. All he did was listen, to see what emanations it would pick up from other Algarvian crystals aboard nearby ships or on the mainland.

For a while, he heard nothing. He cursed again, this time not under his breath. He hated the idea of going back to Setubal without having accomplished anything. He'd done it before, but he still hated it. It seemed a waste of an important part of his life.

And then, faint in the distance, he caught one Algarvian talking to another: "—cursed son of a whore slipped through our fingers again. Do you suppose his sister really is tipping him?"

"Not a chance—you think she's not watched?" the second Algarvian replied. "No, somebody slipped up, that's all, and won't admit it."

"Maybe. Maybe." But the first Algarvian didn't sound convinced. Along with the crystals, Cornelu had along a slate and a grease pencil. He scribbled notes on the conversation. He had no idea what it meant. Someone back in Setubal might.

After sunset, sea and sky and land went dark. As the Lagoans doused lamps to keep Algarvian dragons from finding targets, so Mezentio's men made sure Valmiera offered nothing to beasts flying up from the south. Cornelu found himself yawning. He didn't want to sleep; he'd have to orient himself again when he woke, for his leviathan would surely go wandering after food.

A fish leaped out of the sea and splashed back into the water. The tiny creatures on which fish fed glowed in alarm for a moment, then faded. Cornelu yawned again. He wondered why people and other animals slept. What earthly good did it do? Nothing he could see.

His captured Algarvian crystal started picking up emanations again. A couple of Mezentio's soldiers—Cornelu gradually realized they were brothers or close cousins—were comparing notes about their Valmieran girlfriends. They went into richly obscene detail. After listening for a while, Cornelu wasn't sleepy anymore. He didn't take notes on this conversation; he doubted the Lagoan officers who eventually got his slate would be amused.

"Oh, aye, she aims her toes right at the ceiling, she does," one of the Algarvians said. The other one laughed. Cornelu started to laugh, too, but choked on his own mirth. Back in Tirgoviste town, some Algarvian whorchounds like these two had seduced his wife. He wondered if Costache would present him with a bastard to go with his own daughter if he ever got back there again. Then he wondered how he would ever get back to Tirgoviste—or why he would want to.

Along with frustrated lust, frustrated fury made sure he wouldn't fall asleep right away. At last, to his relief, the two Algarvians shut up. He lay atop his leviathan's back, rocking gently on the waves. The leviathan might have been dozing, or so he thought till it chased town and caught a good-sized tunny. He liked tunny's flesh himself, but baked in a pie with cheese, not raw and wriggling.

Maybe the chase changed the emanations that reached his crystal. In any case, a new Algarvian voice spoke out of it: "Everything ready with this new shipment? All the ley lines south cleared?"

"Aye," another Algarvian answered. "We've been leaning on the cursed bandits who make life such a joy. Nothing will go wrong this time."

"It had better not," the first voice said. "We haven't got any Kaunians to spare. We haven't got anything to spare, not here we don't. Everything gets sucked west, over to Unkerlant. If we don't bring this off now, powers above only know when we'll get another chance, if we ever do."

Cornelu wrote furiously. He wondered if the Lagoans back in Setubal would be able to read his scrawl. It didn't matter too much, as long as he was there along with the notes. Mezentio's men were planning murder, somewhere along the southern coast of Valmiera—murder doubtless aimed across the Strait of Valmiera at a Lagoan or Kuusaman coastal city.

Then a new voice interrupted the Algarvians: "Shut up, you cursed fools. The emanations from your crystals are leaking and someone—aye, someone—is listening to them."

If that wasn't a mage, Cornelu had never heard one. And the fellow would be doing everything he could to learn who and, even more important, where the eavesdropper was. Quickly, Cornelu murmured the charm that took the crystal down to dormancy again. That would make the Algarvian mage's work harder for him. Cornelu was tempted to throw the crystal into the sea, too, but refrained.

He did rouse the leviathan and send it swimming south again, as fast as it would go. The sooner he got away from the Valmieran coast, the tougher the time Mezentio's minions would have finding him and running him down. He glanced up at the sky again. He would have trouble spotting dragons, but dragonfliers wouldn't enjoy looking for his leviathan, either.

After a while, he activated the crystal that linked him to Lagoas. The same officer as before appeared in it. Cornelu spoke rapidly, outlining what he'd learned—who could guess when the Algarvians might start slaying?

The Lagoan heard him out, then said, "Well, Commander, I daresay you've earned your day's pay." A Sibian officer would have kissed him on both cheeks, even if he was only an image in a crystal. Somehow, though, he didn't mind this understated praise, not tonight.

Skarnu had got out of the habit of sleeping in barns. But, having escaped the latest Algarvian attempt to grab him in Ventspils, he'd gone out into the country again. A farmer risked his own neck by putting up a fugitive from what the redheads called justice.

"I'll help with the chores if you like," he told the man (whose name he deliberately did not learn) the next morning.

"Will you?" The farmer gave him an appraising look. "You know what you're doing? You talk like a city man."

"Try me," Skarnu answered. "I feel guilty sitting here eating your food and not helping you get more."

"Well, all right." The farmer chuckled. "We'll see if you still talk the same way at the end of the day."

By the end of that day, Skarnu had tended to a flock of chickens, mucked out a cow barn, weeded a vegetable plot and an herb garden, chopped firewood, and mended a fence. He felt worn to a nub. Farmwork always wore him to the nub. "How did I do?" he asked the man who was putting him up.

"I've seen worse," the fellow allowed. He glanced at Skarnu out of the corner of his eye. "You've done this before a time or two, I do believe."

"Who, me?" Skarnu said, as innocently as he could. "I'm just a city man. You said so yourself."

"I said you talked like one," the farmer answered, "and you cursed well do. But I'll shit a brick if you haven't spent some time behind a plow." He waved a hand. "Don't tell me about it. I don't want to hear. The less I know, the better, on account of the stinking Algarvians can't rip it out of me if it's not there to begin with."

Skarnu nodded. He'd learned that lesson as a captain in the Valmieran army. All the stubborn men—and women—who kept up the fight against Algarve in occupied Valmiera had learned it somewhere. The ones who couldn't learn it were mostly dead now, and too many of their friends with them.

Supper was black bread and hard cheese and sour cabbage and ale. In Priekule before the war, Skarnu would have turned up his nose at such simple fare. Now, with the relish of hunger, he ate enormously. And, with the relish of exhaustion, he had no trouble falling asleep in the barn.

Lanternlight in his face woke him in the middle of the night. He started to spring to his feet, grabbing for the knife at his belt. "Easy," the farmer said from behind the lantern. "It's not the stinking redheads. It's a friend."

Without letting go of the knife, Skarnu peered at the man with the farmer. Slowly, he nodded. He'd seen that face before, in a tavern where irregulars gathered. "You're Zarasai," he said, naming not the man but the southern town from which he'd come.

"Aye." "Zarasai" nodded. "And you're Pavilosta." That was the village nearest the farm where Skarnu had dwelt with the widow Merkela.

"What's so important, it won't wait till sunup?" Skarnu asked. "Are the Algarvians a jump and a half behind you, hot on my trail again?"

"No, or they'd better not be," "Zarasai" answered. "It's more important than that."

More important than my neck? Skarnu thought. *What's more important to me than my neck?* "You'd better tell me," he said.

And "Zarasai" did: "The Algarvians, powers below eat them, are shipping a caravanload—maybe more than one caravanload; I don't know for sure—of Kaunians from Forthweg to the shore of the Strait of Valmiera. You know what that means."

"Slaughter." Skarnu's stomach did a slow lurch. "Slaughter. Life energy. Magic aimed at . . . Lagoas? Kuusamo?"

"We don't know," answered the other leader of Valmieran resistance. "Against one of them or the other, that's sure."

"What can we do to stop it?" Skarnu asked.

"I don't know that, either," "Zarasai" replied. "That's why I came for you—you're the one who managed to get an egg under a ley-line caravan full of Kaunians from Forthweg one of the other times the stinking Algarvians tried this. Maybe you can help us do it again. Powers above, I hope so."

"I'll do whatever I can," Skarnu told him. When he'd buried that egg on the ley line not far from Pavilosta, he hadn't even known the Algarvians would be shipping a caravanload of captives to sacrifice. But the egg had burst regardless of whether he'd known that particular caravan was coming down the ley line. Now his fellows in the shadow fight against King Mezentio thought he could work magic twice when he hadn't really done it once. *I'll try. I have to try.*

"Come on, then," the irregular told him. "Let's get moving. We have no time to waste. If the redheads get them to a captives' camp, we've lost."

Skarnu paused only to pull on his boots. "I'm ready," he said, and bowed to the farmer. "Thanks for putting me up. Now forget you ever saw me."

"Saw who?" the farmer said with a dry chuckle. "I never saw nobody."

A carriage waited outside the barn. Skarnu climbed up into it, picking bits of straw off himself and yawning again and again. "Zarasai" took the reins. He drove with practiced assurance. Skarnu asked, "Which ley line will the redheads be using?"

Sounding slightly embarrassed, the other man replied, "We don't quite know. They've been acting busy at three or four different places down along the coast, running a caravan to this one, then another to that one, and so on. They're getting sneakier than they used to be, the miserable, stinking whoresons."

"We've caused 'em enough trouble to make 'em realize they have to be sneaky," Skarnu observed. "It's a compliment, if you like." He yawned again, trying to flog his sleepy wits to work. "Whatever they're doing with this sacrifice, they think it's important. They've never put this much work into trying to fool us before."

"Zarasai" grunted. "I'm glad I came for you. I hadn't thought of it like that. I don't think anybody's thought of it like that." He flicked the reins to make the horse move a little faster. "Doesn't mean I think you're wrong, on account of I think you're right. Powers below eat the Algarvians."

"Maybe they already have," Skarnu said, which kept his companion thoughtfully silent for quite a while.

Had an Algarvian patrol come across the carriage, it would have gone hard for the two irregulars, who were traveling far past the curfew hour. But Mezentio's men, and even the Valmierans who helped them run the occupied kingdom, were spread thin. Dawn was making the eastern sky blush when "Zarasai" drove into a village that made Pavilosta look like a city beside it: three or four houses, a tavern, and a blacksmith's shop. He tied the horse in front of one of the houses and got down from the carriage. Skarnu followed him to the front door.

It opened even before "Zarasai" knocked. "Come in," a woman hissed. "Quick. Don't waste any time. We'll get the carriage out of sight."

Fancier than a farmhouse, the place boasted a parlor. The furniture would have been stylish in the capital just before the Six Years' War. Maybe it was still stylish here in the middle of nowhere. Skarnu didn't know about that. He didn't have much of a chance to wonder, either, for his eye was drawn like iron to a lodestone in the direction of the half dozen crystals on the elaborately carven table in the middle of that parlor.

"We can talk almost anywhere in the kingdom," the woman said, not without pride.

"Good," Skarnu said. "Just don't do too much of it, or you'll have the Algarvians listening in." The woman nodded. Despite his words, Skarnu was impressed. Down on the farm near Pavilosta, he'd often wondered if his pinpricks meant anything to the Algarvians, and if anyone else in Valmiera was doing anything against them. Seeing with his own eyes how resistance spread across the whole kingdom felt very fine indeed.

"Zarasai" went back into the kitchen and returned with a couple of steaming mugs of tea. He passed one on to Skarnu, waited till he'd sipped, and then said, "All right—you're in charge. Tell us what to do, and we'll do it."

Maybe having served as a captain fitted Skarnu to the role thrust on him. Having wrecked the one caravan didn't, as he knew too well. Doing his best to think like a soldier, he said, "Have you got a map with ley lines marked? I want to see the possibilities."

"Aye," the woman said matter-of-factly, and pulled one from the bureau drawer.

Skarnu studied it. "If they're after Setubal again, they'll send the captives to the camp by Dukstas, the one they used before when the Lagoans raided them."

The irregular from Zarasai nodded. "We figure that one's the most likely. They'd dearly love to serve Setubal as they served Yliharma. All these other camps are smaller and farther east. Setubal's the best target they've got. I don't see that they'd want to hit Kuusamo again and leave Lagoas untouched."

"No, I wouldn't think so, either," Skarnu agreed. But he frowned. "Dukstas is the obvious place to send the captives."

"Of course it is," "Zarasai" said. "That's why they're doing all these dances, isn't it?—to keep us from seeing what's obvious, I mean."

"Maybe." Skarnu shrugged. "It could be, aye. But I just don't know. . . ." He cursed under his breath. "Can we try to sabotage the ley lines into all of these camps?"

"We can *try* doing them all." The other irregular sounded dubious, and explained why: "Odds are, some of the people we send in will get caught. They've got lots of soldiers and lots of cursed Valmieran traitors guarding the ley lines. They want to get these captives through, that's plain."

"That means something really big," Skarnu said. "Setubal or . . . something else." His frown turned into a scowl. "What could be bigger than Setubal, if they can bring it off? But Setubal doesn't *feel* right to me—do you know what I mean?"

"It's your call," the man from Zarasai answered. "That's why you're here."

"All right." Skarnu nodded to the woman who did duty for a crystallomancer. "As much in the way of sabotage on every ley line we can reach that leads to one of those camps. I'm not convinced the captives are going to Dukstas. Maybe we'll see where they *are* going when we seen which ley lines the redheads defend hardest."

"Sabotage all the ley lines we can," the woman repeated. "I shall pass the word." Pass it she did, one crystal at a time.

Having given his orders, Skarnu could only wait to see how things far away turned out. That was new for him: he'd been a captain before, aye, but never a general.

Reports started coming back around midday, some from raiders who had planted eggs, others from bands that failed because their stretch of ley line was too strongly protected. A couple of bands never reported back at all. Skarnu worried about that. Eyeing the map, "Zarasai" said, "Well, the buggers won't ship 'em into Dukstas, and that's flat."

"So it is." Skarnu felt a certain satisfaction himself. A few hours later, word came that the Algarvians had succeeded in moving the Kaunian captives into a seaside camp, but one far, far to the east. He cursed, but made the best of things: "They may manage something, but we kept them from doing their worst."

Four

From the dining room of the hostel that had been run up in the wilderness of southeastern Kuusamo, Pekka looked out on bright sunlight shining off snow. She took another bite of a grilled and salted mackerel. "Finally," she said in classical Kaunian. "Decent weather for more experiments."

"I've seen *bad* weather," Ilmarinen said. "I don't know that I've ever seen *indecent* weather. Might be interesting." Even in the classical language, he liked to twist words back on themselves to see what happened.

Pekka gave him a sweet smile. "Any weather with you out in it, Master, would soon become indecent."

Siuntio coughed. Fernao chuckled. Ilmarinen guffawed. "That all depends on whether the experiment goes up or down," he said.

Siuntio coughed again, more sharply this time. "Let us please remember the high seriousness of the work in which we are engaged," he said.

"Why?" Ilmarinen asked. "The work will go on just the same either way. We'll have more fun if we have more fun, though."

"We are also more likely to make a mistake if we take things lightly," Siuntio said. "Considering the forces we are trying to manipulate, a mistake would be something less than desirable."

"Enough," Pekka said before the elderly and distinguished mages could get any further into their schoolboy bickering. "One of the mistakes we make is arguing among ourselves."

"Quite right." Siuntio nodded, then shook a finger in Ilmarinen's direction. "You should pay attention to Mistress Pekka's wisdom, for she—"

Now Fernao coughed. "It pains me to tell you this, Master Siuntio," he said in his careful Kaunian, "but you are still arguing."

"I am?" Siuntio sounded astonished. Then he seemed to consider. "Why, so I am." He dipped his head to Fernao. "My thanks for pointing it out; I confess I hadn't noticed."

Pekka believed him. He was just the sort of man who might do such a thing without paying much attention to what he was doing. She said, "When we go out today—or tomorrow, if we do not get the chance to do it today—we have to remind the secondary sorcerers to bend every effort to keeping all the animals hale while we perform the primary incantations. Having one of the rats in the younger group die before the spell was complete ruined a day's work and more."

"As opposed to ruining a good part of the landscape," Ilmarinen said.

"We have already done that," Pekka said. "Even after the blizzards come and pour snow over the latest hole in the ground, you can still see the scars of what we have done." She shook her head. "And to think all this started with an acorn disappearing."

"More than an acorn disappearing nowadays," Fernao said, "but that will be the experiment the textbooks of the future mention."

"Textbooks," Ilmarinen said with the scorn of a man who'd written a good many. "The permanent written record of what the world doesn't remember quite the right way."

"I want to go out to the site," Pekka said. "I want to go into the blockhouse and cast the spells. We have come so far now. We need to go on."

"We need to pluck more fresh, green grass from the latest crater," Ilmarinen said, throwing oil on the fire. "We need to see what we can do about that, and we need to see if anything smarter than a blade of grass can come through unchanged." He eyed Fernao, then shook his head. "No, you wouldn't make a proper experimental subject there."

"True," Fernao agreed imperturbably. "I am not green."

Ilmarinen looked wounded at having provoked no warmer response. Pekka pushed her plate toward the center of the table and stood up. "Let us go out to the blockhouse," she said. "Let us see if we can keep from snapping one another's heads off while we go."

As usual, she rode in the sleigh with Fernao. Part of that was deference to the two senior sorcerers. Part of it was that the two younger mages had more in common with each other than either did with Siuntio or Ilmarinen. Some small part of it was slowly growing pleasure in each other's company.

The blockhouse had had new work done on it since the experiments began, to make it stronger and better able to withstand the energies the mages released. Even so, the secondary sorcerers set up the rows of animal cages more than twice as far from the little reinforced hut as they had when the series of spells started.

"Well, let's get on with it," Ilmarinen said when they were assembled in the blockhouse. "With any luck at all, we can drop this whole corner of the island into the sea. In a few weeks, who knows? Maybe we'll manage the whole island."

One of the secondary sorcerers said, "May it please you, Masters, Mistress, the animals are ready."

He spoke in Kuusaman. When he started to repeat himself in classical Kaunian for Fernao's benefit, the Lagoan mage said, "Never mind. I understand."

In Kaunian, Pekka said, "Your Kuusaman has a noticeable Kajaani accent."

"Does it?" Fernao said. "I wonder why that would be." They smiled at each other.

"To business, if you please," Siuntio said.

"Aye. To business," Pekka agreed. She took a deep breath, then intoned the words with which a mage of her blood prefaced every major sorcerous operation: "Before the Kaunians came, we of Kuusamo were here. Before the Lagoans came, we of Kuusamo were here. After the Kaunians departed, we of Kuusamo were here. We of Kuusamo are here. After the Lagoans depart, we of Kuusamo shall be here."

Siuntio and Ilmarinen both nodded; they'd used that ritual far longer than she'd been alive. One of Fernao's eyebrows rose. He had to know what the words were, what they meant. Did he believe them, as the Kuusaman sorcerers did? That was bound to be a different question.

Ritual complete, Pekka glanced to the secondary sorcerers. They nodded: they were ready to support the experimental animals and to transmit the magecraft so it had its proper effect. Pekka took another deep breath. "I begin."

She had not got more than half a dozen lines into the newly revised and strengthened spell—not nearly far enough to land in serious trouble for stopping—when her head suddenly came up and she looked away from the text she'd been reading. "Something's wrong," she said, first in her own language, then in classical Kaunian.

Siuntio and Fernao both frowned; whatever it was that had disturbed her, they didn't sense it. But Ilmarinen's head was up and swinging this way and that, too, the expression on his face one that might have been a wolf's when it feared a hunter close by.

And then, as that wary old wolf might have, he took a scent. "The Algarvians!" he said harshly. "Another slaughter."

This time, Siuntio nodded. His eyes went very wide, wider

than Pekka had ever seen them, wider than she'd thought a
Kuusaman's eyes could get. White showed all around his
irises. He said the three worst words Pekka could imagine
just then: "Aimed at us."

Pekka gasped. She felt it, too, the horrid sense of potent
murder-powered magic not so far away. She and Siuntio and
Ilmarinen had been in Yliharma when Mezentio's mages attacked the capital of Kuusamo. That had been bad, very bad.
She hadn't thought anything could be much worse. But she'd
been wrong. Now she found out how wrong.

As he usually did, Siuntio had the right of it: this time, the
stolen life energy of those Kaunian captives was hurled
straight at the blockhouse, a deadly dart of sorcerous force.
The lamps flickered in a strange, rhythmic pattern. Then the
walls started to shake in the same rhythm, and then the floor
beneath Pekka's feet. The air felt hot and thick in her lungs. It
tasted of blood.

The paper on which her cantrip was written burst into
flames. One of the secondary sorcerers screamed. Her hair
had burst into flames, too. A comrade swaddled her head
with a blanket, but the flames did not want to go out.

"No!" Siuntio shouted, a battle cry that might have burst
from the throat of a man half his age. "By the powers above,
no! You shall not have us! You shall not!" He began what had
to be a counterspell. Pekka had never imagined such a
thing—one determined mage, all alone, trying to withstand
the massed might of many, a might magnified by murder.

Ilmarinen's voice joined Siuntio's a moment later. They
were the finest sorcerers of their generation. For an instant,
just for an instant, Pekka, marshaling in her mind what she
could do to aid their magecraft, thought they might have
fought the Algarvians to a standstill. But then the lamps went
out altogether, plunging the blockhouse into darkness. With a
shriek of bursting timbers, the roof fell in. Something hit
Pekka in the side of the head. The dark went black, shot with
scarlet.

She couldn't have stayed senseless long. When she woke,
she was lying in the snow outside the blockhouse—the burn-

ing blockhouse, for flames crackled and smoke poured from it. She tried to sit up, but the pounding pain in her head got worse. Her eyes didn't want to focus. The world seemed to spin. So did her guts. She leaned over and was violently sick in the snow.

Somewhere not far away, Ilmarinen let out a string of horrible curses in Kuusaman, Kaunian, and Lagoan all mixed together. "Go after him, you fools!" he bellowed. "Go after him! Go on, powers below eat you all! He's worth more than the lot of you put together. Get him out of there!"

Pekka tried again to sit. This time, moving ever so slowly and carefully, she managed it. Ilmarinen and Fernao both stood by the blockhouse. Fernao was shouting, too, in Kaunian when he remembered and in incomprehensible Lagoan when he didn't.

Ilmarinen tried to run into the burning building. One of the secondary sorcerers grabbed him and pulled him back. He stuck an elbow into the man's belly and broke free. But two other men seized him before he could do what he so plainly wanted to.

Fernao turned to him and said something Pekka didn't catch. Ilmarinen's shoulders sagged. He seemed to shrink in on himself. In that moment, for the very first time, he looked his age, with another twenty years tacked on besides.

Pekka grubbed up some snow well away from where she'd vomited and used it to rinse the vile taste from her mouth. The motion drew the notice of the other two theoretical sorcerers. They both came over to her, Fernao making slow going of it with the one stick he'd managed to bring out into the open.

"What—what happened?" The banality of the question shamed Pekka, but it was the best she could do.

"The Algarvians must have noticed the sorcerous energy we were releasing in our experiments," Fernao answered. "They decided to put a stop to them." He had a cut above one eye, a shiner, and another cut on his cheek, and appeared to notice none of them.

Ilmarinen added, "Rather like stepping on a cockroach with a mountain. Powers above, they're strong when they

want to be. Curse them all. Curse them forever." Tears froze
halfway down his cheeks.

Trying to make her battered brains think at all, Pekka
asked, "Where's Master Siuntio?" Neither mage answered.
Fernao looked back toward the burning blockhouse. Ilmarinen started cursing again. More tears flowed and froze.
Pekka gulped, a heartsickness far worse than the pounding
her body had taken. Siuntio—gone? Now, when they needed
him more than ever?

Grimly, Ilmarinen said, "There shall be a reckoning. Aye,
by the powers above, there shall be a reckoning indeed."

Fernao sat in the dining room of the small hostel in the Kuusaman wilderness. When he lifted a finger, a serving woman
brought him a new glass of brandy. Glasses he'd already emptied crowded the table in front of him. No one said a word
about it. Kuusamans often mourned their dead with spirits. If
a foreigner wanted to do likewise, they would let him.

Presently, I shall fall asleep. Fernao thought with the false
clarity of a man already drunk and getting drunker. *Then they
will carry me upstairs, the way they carried Ilmarinen upstairs half an hour ago.*

He was surprised and proud he'd outlasted the Kuusaman
mage. But Ilmarinen had thrown himself into his binge with a
frightening enthusiasm, as if he didn't care whether he came
out the other side. He'd known Siuntio for more than fifty
years. In their minds, they'd both gone places no one else in
the world could reach till they showed the way. No wonder Ilmarinen drank as if he'd lost a brother, maybe a twin.

Fernao reached for the new glass—reached for it and
missed. "Hold still," he told it, and tried again. This time, he
not only captured it, he raised it to his mouth.

Even if his body didn't want to obey him, his wits still
worked after a fashion. *What will I be like tomorrow morning?* he wondered—a truly frightening thought. He drank
some more to drown it. Part of him knew that wouldn't help.
He drank anyway.

He'd almost emptied the glass when Pekka stepped into

the dining room. Seeing him, she came his way. She walked slowly and carefully. She'd taken a nasty whack when the blockhouse came down in ruin, and her head had to hurt even more now than his would come morning.

"May I join you?" she asked.

"Aye. Please do. I am honored." Fernao remembered to answer in classical Kaunian, not Lagoan, which she didn't speak. He stopped just before he ran through the whole passive conjugation of the verb *to honor: you are honored, he/she/it is honored, we . . .*

"I wondered if I would see Master Ilmarinen here," Pekka said.

"He went belly-up a while ago," Fernao answered.

"Ah." Pekka nodded. "They understood each other, those two. I wonder if anyone else did."

That so closely paralleled Fernao's thought, he tried to tell her of it. His tongue tripped over itself and wouldn't let him. "I am sorry, milady," he said. "You see me . . . not at my best." He knocked back his brandy and signaled for another.

"You need not apologize, not here, not now," Pekka said. "I would drink to the dead, too, but the healers gave me a decoction of poppy juice and told me I must not take spirits with it."

The serving woman brought Fernao a fresh brandy, then glanced a question at Pekka. Ever so slightly, the Kuusaman mage shook her head. The serving woman went away. "Which decoction?" Fernao asked. What with his injuries down in the land of the Ice People, he'd become something of an expert on the anodynes made from poppy sap.

"It was yellow and tasted nasty," Pekka answered.

"Ah, the yellow one." Part of Fernao's nod was drunken gravity, part remembering. "Aye. Compared to some of the others, it leaves your wits fairly clear."

"Then the others must be ferocious," Pekka said. "I thought my head would float away. Considering how it felt, I hoped my head would float away. Some of the drug has worn off since." Her grimace showed she wished it hadn't. She brightened when she added, "I can take more soon."

For Fernao, the yellow decoction had been a long and welcome step back toward the real world; he'd been taking more potent mixtures before. For Pekka, plainly, it was a long and welcome step out of the real world.

After a little while, she said, "One of the secondary sorcerers told me you dragged me out of the blockhouse. Thank you."

"I wish I could have carried you." Abrupt fury filled Fernao's voice. "If I could have moved faster, I might have got you out and then gone back in and got Siuntio, too, before the fire spread too badly. If . . ." He knocked back the brandy. In spite of it, his hand shook as he set down the empty glass.

Pekka said, "Had you been standing closer to him than to me, you would have taken him first, and then you would have tried to come back for me." She reached into her belt pouch and took out a bottle full of the yellow decoction and a spoon. "It is not quite time for my dose yet, but I do not care. I do not wish to think about that." Fernao would have taken more, but he was bigger than she.

The serving woman appeared at his elbow. He hadn't noticed her come up. There were a good many things he wasn't noticing right now. "Will I get you another, sir?" she asked.

"No, thank you," he said, and she went away again.

"How badly are we set back?" Pekka said.

Fernao shrugged. "I think they are still sorting things out. Sooner or later, we shall have answers."

"Answers of a sort," Pekka said. "But we shall never again have Master Siuntio's answers, and there are none better." She sighed, but then her pain- and grief-lined face softened. "The decoction works quickly. I can forget for a little while that my head belongs to me."

"I know about that," Fernao said. "Believe me, I know about that." He also knew he would wish for some of the yellow liquid—or maybe one of the stronger ones—in the morning. He would wish for it, but he wouldn't borrow any from Pekka. After so long taking decoctions of one color or another, he'd had to get over a craving for poppy juice. He didn't want to bring it back to life. He hoped he would remember that when he went from drunk to hung over.

Pekka said, "What will we do without Siuntio? How can we go on without him? He made this field what it is today. Everyone else walks in his footsteps—except Ilmarinen, who walks around them and pisses in them whenever he sees the chance."

Fernao would have laughed at that even sober. Drunk, he thought it the funniest thing he'd ever heard. He laughed and laughed. He laughed so hard, he had to put his head down on the table. That proved a mistake, or at least the end of his evening. He never heard himself starting to snore.

He never knew how he got into his bed, either. Most likely, the servitors carried him up, as they'd carried up Ilmarinen. Fernao couldn't have proved it. For all he could prove, it might as readily have been cockroaches or dragons.

Whoever had done it, he wished they'd thrown him on the rubbish heap instead. His head pounded even worse than he'd thought it would. The wan sunshine of winter in southern Kuusamo seemed as bright as the Zuwayzi desert; he had to squint to see at all. By the taste in his mouth, he'd been sleeping in a latrine trench.

He felt of himself, and made at least one happy discovery. "Powers above be praised, I didn't piss the bed," he said. Then he winced again. His voice might have been a raven's, a very loud raven's, harsh croak.

Holding his head with his free hand, he limped into the commode with one crutch. Along with a water closet, it also boasted a cold-water tap. He splashed water on his face. He cleaned his teeth. After rinsing his mouth, he took a couple of sips of water. Even that was almost too much for his poor, abused stomach. He thought he'd be sick right there. Somehow, he wasn't.

Groaning—and trying not to groan, because the noise hurt his head—he limped back to bed. He felt better than he had before he got up, which meant he was no longer actively wishing he were dead. He lay there for a while. Quiet and with his eyes closed, he did his best to wait out the hangover.

Again, he didn't notice drifting off. This time, he fell into something close to real sleep, not sodden unconsciousness. He would have slept longer, but someone tapped on his door. The taps weren't very loud—except to his ears. He sat up, and winced. "Who is it?" he asked, and winced again.

"I." Pekka's voice came through the door. "May I come in?"

"I suppose so," Fernao answered.

The door opened. Pekka carried a tray to his bedside. "Here," she said briskly. "Half a raw cabbage, chopped. And a mug of cranberry juice with a slug—a small slug—of spirits mixed in. Eat. Drink. You will be better for it."

"Will I?" Fernao said dubiously. His own countrymen used fruit juice laced with spirits to fight the morning after, but cabbage was a remedy new to him. He didn't much feel like eating or drinking anything, but had to admit himself improved after he did.

Pekka saw as much. "You will do," she said. "Ilmarinen is worse, but he will do, too."

In an odd way, Fernao found himself agreeing with her. He *would* do. "How are *you?*" he asked, knowing sudden shame that he'd let her serve him. "You are the one who is truly hurt. This"—he patted his own forehead—"this will be nothing at all in a few hours. But you have real injuries."

"My head hurts," Pekka said matter-of-factly. "I have a little trouble remembering things. I would not want to try to work magic right now. I do not think it is the yellow decoction. I think you are right. I think it is the blow to the head. As with you, time will set it right. With the yellow liquid, it is not too bad."

He suspected she was making light of what had happened to her. If she wanted to do that, he wouldn't challenge her; he honored her courage. There was something he'd meant to tell her the night before. He was surprised he recalled it. He was surprised he recalled anything from the night before. But he realized now that it didn't matter. He couldn't say what he'd meant to, anyhow.

Pekka went on, "Alkio and Raahe and Piilis will be coming here now. You will know of them, if you do not know them."

"I met them in Yliharma," Fernao said. "Good theoretical sorcerers, all three."

"Aye." Pekka nodded carefully. "And the first two, husband and wife, work very well together. Add up the three of them and they are . . . not too far from Siuntio."

"May it be so." Fernao wondered if three good mages could match one towering genius.

"And now, the Seven Princes will give us everything we need or might need or imagine we need," Pekka said. "If we have done enough to alarm the Algarvians, to make them strike at us, we must be doing something worthwhile—or so the Princes think. This assault may prove the greatest mistake Mezentio's mages ever made."

"May it be so," Fernao repeated.

"And Siuntio saved us," Pekka said. "He and Ilmarinen—had they not resisted as best they could, we would all have died in the blockhouse." Fernao could only nod at that. Pekka rose and picked up the tray. "I will not disturb you anymore. I hope you feel better soon."

"And you," he called as she left the room. No, he couldn't very well tell her she'd made one small mistake. When the Algarvians assailed the blockhouse out in the wilderness, he'd been several strides closer to Siuntio than to her. But he'd turned one way, done one thing, and not the other . . . and now he and everyone else, everyone save poor Siuntio, would have to live with the consequences of that.

Before he'd got blazed, Major Spinello had served in southern Unkerlant. Now he'd been sent to the north of King Swemmel's realm. He found he loathed this part of the kingdom at least as much as he'd despised the other.

Blizzards seemed less common here, but cold, driving rain went a long way toward making up for them. Most of his regiment was holed up in a little town called Wriezen, with the rest on a picket line west of the place. Nothing would be coming at them quickly, not today—and not tomorrow or the next day, either. Here in the north, the muddy season lasted most of the winter.

Naturally, Spinello had commandeered the finest house in Wriezen as his own. It had probably belonged to the firstman of the place, but he'd long since fled. Spinello turned to his seniormost company commander, a dour captain named Turpino, and said, "How do we give the Unkerlanters a good boot in the balls?"

"We wait till the ground dries out, and then we outmaneuver them," Turpino answered. "Sir."

Spinello hopped in the air in annoyance. "No, no, no!" he exclaimed. "That isn't what I meant. How do we boot 'em in the balls *now?*"

Turpino, who was several inches taller than he, looked down his nose at him. "We don't," he said. "Sir."

Spinello carefully didn't notice how slow Turpino was with the title of respect. "Do Swemmel's men think we can't do anything in this mess, too?" he demanded.

"Of course they do," Turpino answered. "They're no fools." By his tone, he wasn't sure the same applied to his superior officer.

"If they think it can't be done, that's the best argument in the world for doing it," Spinello said. "Now we have to consider ways and means."

"Excellent." Turpino gave him a stiff bow. "If you transform our soldiers into worms, they can crawl through the mud and take the Unkerlanters by surprise coming at them from behind."

If I transform my troopers into worms, you'll be a bloodsucking leech, Spinello thought resentfully. "With the south in chaos, we ought to keep moving forward here in the north."

"If the moves serve some strategic purpose, certainly," Turpino said.

Spinello snapped his fingers to show what he thought of strategic purpose. Part of him knew the gloomy captain had a point of sorts. The rest, the bigger part, craved action, especially after so long flat on his back. He said, "Anything that throws the foe into confusion and either forces him back or forces him to shift troops here serves a strategic purpose, would you not agree?"

Captain Turpino's face was a closed book. "I would rather answer a specific question than a hypothetical one."

It was as polite a way of saying, *You won't ask me a specific question, because you haven't got a real plan,* as any Spinello had heard. If Turpino hadn't irked him, he might have admired the other officer. Instead, snapping his fingers again, he said, "What are the dominant features of the terrain at the present time, Captain?"

"Rain," Turpino answered at once. "Mud."

"Very good." Spinello bowed and made as if to applaud. "And how do we get around in the mud, pray?"

"Mostly we don't." Turpino's responses were getting shorter and shorter.

With another bow—sooner or later, Turpino would have to lose his temper—Spinello said, "Let me try a different question. How do the Unkerlanters get around in the rain?" He held up a forefinger. "You needn't answer—I already know. They have those high-wheeled wagons with the round bottoms that might almost be boats. If anything moves, those wagons do."

"Miserable little things." Turpino's lip curled. "They don't hold much."

"But what they do hold moves," Spinello said. "If we can get our hands on a hundred of them, Captain, we can move, too. And the Unkerlanters will never expect us to use those miserable little things." He didn't quite mimic Turpino's tone, but he came close. "What do you think?"

Turpino grunted. "Aye, we might move," he said at last. "If we could lay hold of a hundred of them. Sir."

By the way he sounded, he didn't think the regiment could do it. Spinello grinned at him. "You will provide the wagons for the regiment, Captain. You have four days. Gather them here, and we shall go west. Otherwise, we hold in place."

This time, Turpino didn't say anything. Of course he didn't. Spinello had given him an order he disliked. If he failed to carry it out, nothing much would happen to the regiment or to him.

Spinello's grin got wider. "If that attack goes in, my dear fellow, I intend to lead it in person. If I fall, the regiment is yours, at least for the time being. I can't promise you a pretty blond Kaunian popsy like the one I enjoyed back in Forthweg, but isn't that the next best thing?"

Turpino still didn't smile. He was far more staid than most of his countrymen. All he said was, "I'll see what I can do."

Four days later, 131 wagons clogged the muddy streets of Wriezen. "Commendable initiative, Captain," Spinello remarked.

"Incentive," Turpino replied. "Sir."

"Now, lads"—Spinello raised his voice to be heard through the rain—"Swemmel's men don't expect us to do a thing in this weather. And when we do things the Unkerlanters don't expect, they break. You've seen it, I've seen it, we've all seen it. So let's go give them a surprise, shall we?" He blew his whistle. "Forward!"

Where anything else would have bogged down in the thick mud, the wagons did go forward. Along with commandeering them from the countryside, Captain Turpino had also made sure the regiment had plenty of horses and mules to draw them. He wanted the attack to go in after all. If it failed, and maybe even if it succeeded, the regiment would be his.

The rain hadn't eased. That cut Spinello's visibility down to yards, but he didn't mind. If anything, it cheered him. He knew where the Unkerlanters were. This way, they wouldn't be able to see his men and him coming.

A few eggs, not many, burst out in front of the wagons. Here in the north, not enough egg-tossers were stretched too thin along too many miles of battle line. Spinello hadn't even tried to get Turpino to gather them as he'd gathered the wagons. No one cared about funny-looking Unkerlanter wagons, but every Algarvian officer jealously clutched to his bosom all the egg-tossers he had.

One slow step after another, the horse pulled Spinello's wagon forward. The rest of the wagons churned their way west along the road and through the fields to either side. With their tall wheels, they found bottom where any Algarvian vehicle this side of a ley-line caravan would have bogged down. Mucky wakes streamed out behind those wheels and sometimes behind the wagons, too, as if they were on a river rather than what was supposed to be dry land.

Somebody up ahead shouted something at Spinello in a language he didn't understand. If it wasn't Unkerlanter, he would have been mightily surprised. He shouted back, not in Algarvian but in classical Kaunian, in which he was quite fluent. The odd sounds confused the fellow who'd challenged him. The stranger shouted again, this time with a questioning note in his voice.

By then, Spinello's wagon had got close enough to let him see the other man: an Unkerlanter, sure enough. It had also got close enough to let him blaze the fellow in spite of the way the driving rain degraded his beam's performance. His stick went to his shoulder; his finger found the touch-hole. The Unkerlanter had been about to blaze at him, too. Instead, he crumpled back into his hole in the ground.

Spinello whooped with glee. He blew his whistle again, a long, piercing blast. "Forward!" he shouted.

Forward they went. They knocked over a few more pickets and then rolled toward a peasant village about a quarter the size of Wriezen. A couple of Unkerlanter soldiers came out of the thatch-roofed huts and waved to them as they came up. Spinello laughed out loud. Swemmel's men thought they were the only ones who knew what those wagons were good for.

They soon discovered their mistake. The Algarvians swarmed out of the wagons and through the village, making short work of the little Unkerlanter garrison there. Before long, some high-pitched screams rang out. That meant they'd found women, and were making a different sort of short work of them.

Spinello let them have their fun for a little while, but only for a little while. Then he started blowing his whistle again. "Come on, my dears," he shouted. "Finish them off and let's get back to work. They're only ugly Unkerlanters, after all—they're not worth keeping."

Once his men, or most of them, were back in the wagons, the advance slashed forward again. Not far west of the village, they came upon three batteries of Unkerlanter egg-tossers. Again, they overran them without much trouble. The enemy didn't realize he was in danger till too late.

"Turn them around, boys, turn them around," Spinello said, and his soldiers fell to work with a will. "Let's drop some eggs on the heads of our dear friends farther west."

Captain Turpino squelched up to him. "You're not advancing any more?" he asked.

"I hadn't planned to," Spinello answered. "We've done what we came to do, after all. Go too far and Swemmel's men will bite back."

To his surprise, Turpino swept off his hat and bowed low. "Command me, sir!" he exclaimed, his voice more friendly, more respectful, than Spinello had ever heard it. "You've proved you know what you're doing."

"Have I?" Spinello said, and Turpino, still bareheaded, nodded. Spinello went on, "Well then, put your hat back on before you drown." Turpino laughed—another first—and obeyed. Spinello asked him, "Do you know anything about serving egg-tossers?"

"Aye, somewhat," the other officer replied.

"Good—you take charge of that business," Spinello said. "I'll make sure the Unkerlanters won't have an easy time throwing us back. I was down in Sulingen. I know all about field fortifications, by the powers above."

"Mm." Turpino grunted again. "Aye, you would, down there. How'd you get out?" Before Spinello could answer, the captain pointed to the wound badge on his chest. "Is that when you picked up your trinket?"

Spinello nodded. "Sniper got me a month or so before the Unkerlanters cut us off, so they were able to fly me out and patch me up." His wave encompassed the ground the regiment had taken. "Now we'll patch this place up and hold onto it as long as we can—or else move forward again if we see the chance." Would Turpino argue again? No. The senior captain just saluted. If he was happy, the rest of the officers in the regiment would be. To Spinello, that mattered almost as much as taking a worthless village and some egg-tossers away from King Swemmel's men. He'd made the regiment *his*. From here on out, it would follow wherever he led.

Cockroaches scuttled across the floor of Talsu's cell. He'd given up stomping them not long after his captors put him in there. He could have stomped night and day and not killed them all. This one prison probably held as many of them as Jelgava held people.

His stomach growled. These past few days, he'd started getting tempted to kill them again rather than doing his best to ignore them. They were food, or they could be food if a man were desperate enough.

Talsu didn't want to think he was that desperate. But the bowls of mush his captors doled out didn't come close to keeping him fed. His body was consuming itself. He didn't want to take off his tunic: his cell was anything but warm. But when he ran a hand along his ribs, he found them easier to feel every day as the flesh melted off him. More and more, he found himself wondering what the roaches tasted like and whether he could get them down without heaving them up again a moment later.

One day, the door to his cell came open at an hour when it usually stayed closed. Three guards stood outside, all of them with their sticks pointed at him. "Come along with us," one of them said.

"Why?" Talsu asked. Moving at all seemed more trouble than it was worth.

But the guard strode in and backhanded him across the face. "Because I say so, you stinking turd," he said. "You don't ask questions here, curse you. *We* ask questions." He slapped Talsu again. "Now come along."

Tasting blood from a split lip, Talsu came. He feared he knew where they were going. After they'd taken two turns, he knew he was right. The Jelgavan constabulary captain hadn't grilled him for a while. He wondered what sort of torments he would have to go through this time, and whether he would be able to endure them without starting to name names for the Algarvians' hound.

He was still half a corridor away from the captain's office when his nose twitched. His head came up. It had been a long time since he'd smelled roast mutton rather than the usual prison stinks. Spit flooded into his mouth. He muttered under his breath, being careful not to say anything loud enough to draw the notice—and anger—of the guards. He'd only thought he knew how hungry he was.

"Here he is, sir." The guards shoved him into the office.

"Talsu son of Traku!" the constabulary captain exclaimed, as if greeting an old friend. "How are you today? Sit down, why don't you?"

Astonishingly, a chair waited for Talsu in front of the captain's desk. He hadn't noticed it till the captain invited him to sit. He hadn't noticed it because all his attention focused on the desk itself, and on the lovely leg of mutton sitting there along with olives and white bread and butter and green beans cooked with little bits of bacon and a big carafe of wine red as blood.

"How are you today?" the constabulary captain asked again as Talsu, like a man in a dream, took his seat.

"Hungry," Talsu murmured. He could hardly talk—powers above, he could hardly think—staring at all that wonderful food. "So hungry."

"Isn't that interesting?" the Jelgavan in Algarvian service replied. "And here I was just sitting down to supper." He gestured to the guard who'd slapped Talsu around. "Pour this fellow some wine, will you? And some for me, too, while you're at it."

Sure enough, two glasses stood by that carafe. The guard

filled them both. Talsu waited till he saw the constabulary captain drink before raising his own glass to his lips. He realized that might not help. If the wine was drugged, the captain might already have taken an antidote. But Talsu couldn't resist the temptation. He took a long pull at the glass.

"Ahh," he said when he set it down. He might almost have been sighing with longing for Gailisa, his wife. He smacked his lips, savoring the sweetness of the grape cut with the juices of lemon and lime and orange in the usual Jelgavan fashion.

Slowly, deliberately, the constabulary captain cut a slice from the leg of mutton and set the meat on his plate. He took a bite, chewed with appetite, and swallowed. Then he looked up. His blue eyes, mild and frank, met Talsu's. "Would you . . . like to join me for supper?" he asked.

"Aye!" The word was out of Talsu's mouth before he could call it back. He wished he hadn't said it, but the constable would have known he was thinking it even so.

"Pour him some more wine," the captain said. As the guard obeyed, the officer helped himself to green beans, ate an olive and spat the pit into the wastepaper basket, and tore off a chunk of that lovely white loaf and spread butter over it. He smiled at Talsu. "It's all very good."

Talsu didn't dare speak. He also didn't dare hurl himself at the food on the constabulary captain's desk without permission. No matter how hungry he was, he feared what the guards would do to him. But he had permission to drink the wine. After the stale, musty water he'd been getting, how fine it tasted!

Half starved as he was, it mounted straight to his head. Back in Skrun-da, a couple of glasses of wine wouldn't have mattered much. Back in Skrunda, though, he would have had enough to eat; he wouldn't have poured them down on an empty, an ever so empty, stomach.

"Now then," the constabulary captain said, "suppose you tell me the names of the others who conspired with you against King Mainardo back in Skrunda." He took another bite of pink, juicy mutton. "If you want us to cooperate with you, after all, you have to cooperate with us, my friend." He swallowed the bite. He'd never missed a meal. Constabulary captains never did.

"Cooperate." Talsu could hear how his own voice slurred. Instead of naming names, he said what was uppermost in his mind: "Feed me!"

"All in good time, my friend; all in good time." The constable took a bit of bread. Butter left his lips greasy, shiny, till he gently blotted them on a snowy linen napkin. At his gesture, the guard put an identical napkin on Talsu's lap. Then the fellow poured Talsu's wineglass full once more.

"I don't want . . ." But Talsu couldn't say that. He couldn't come close to saying that. He did want the wine. He wanted it with all his soul. Even it made him feel less empty inside. He drank quickly, fearful lest the guard snatch the glass from his hand. When the glass was empty again, he stared owlishly at the food.

"It's very good," the constabulary captain remarked. "Tell us a few names. What's so hard about that? Once you've done it, you can eat your fill."

"Feed me first," Talsu whispered. It wasn't bargaining. At least, he didn't think of it as bargaining. It was much more like pleading.

The captain nodded to the guard. But it wasn't the sort of nod Talsu had hoped for. The guard slapped him again, hard enough to make his head ring. He dropped the wineglass. It fell on the floor and broke. "You don't tell us what to do," the captain said in a voice like iron. "We tell you what to do. Have you got that?" The guard belted him again.

Through swollen lips now bleeding freely, Talsu mumbled, "Aye."

"Well, good." The interrogator's tone softened. "I try to give you something you might want, and what thanks do I get? What cooperation do I get? I must say, you've disappointed me, Talsu son of Traku."

"I'm sure you don't disappoint the Algarvians," Talsu said. He hurt already. He didn't think they'd make him hurt too much worse.

They were about to do their best. The guards who'd brought him from the cell growled and raised their arms to strike. But the constabulary captain raised his arm, too, hand open, palm out. "Wait," he said, and the guards stopped. His gaze swung back to Talsu. "I do my duty. I serve my king, whoever he may be. I served King Donalitu. Now I serve King Mainardo. Should King Donalitu return—which I do not expect—I would serve him again. And he would want my services, for I am good at what I do."

"I don't understand," Talsu muttered. His notion of duty was loyalty to the kingdom. His interrogator seemed to think it meant going on with his job no matter whom it benefited: that the work was an end in itself, not a means to serving Jelgava. Talsu wished he thought the captain a hypocrite. Unfortunately, he was convinced the man meant every word he said.

"You don't need to understand," the constabulary captain told him. "All you need to do is give me the names of others in Skrunda who are not favorably inclined to the present authorities."

"I've told you before—Kugu the silversmith is the only one who ever said anything like that to me," Talsu answered. "I'll gladly denounce him."

"That, I fear, is not an adequate offer." The interrogator cut a bite of mutton and offered it to Talsu on the tip of his knife. "Here. Maybe this will make you change your mind."

Talsu leaned forward. He more than half expected the officer to withdraw the meat as he did so, but the man held it steady. He took the bite off the knife. It was as good as he'd thought it would be. He chewed it as long as he could, and then a little longer than that, but at last he had to swallow.

When he did, the constabulary captain handed him an olive. He ate it with the same loving care he'd given the mutton. To show his thanks, he didn't spit the pit back at the interrogator, but down on the floor by his chair. "Now," the officer said, with the air of a man getting down to business, "do you suppose you can come up with any more names for me? It would be a shame to make me eat this whole lovely supper by myself."

Talsu's belly screamed for food—screamed all the louder now that it had a tiny bit inside it. Wine made his tongue freer, as the constabulary captain must have planned. But the wine didn't make his tongue run along the ley line for which the interrogator had hoped. He said, "When the Algarvians ship you west to cut your throat, do you think they'll care what you did for them?"

That blaze got home. Just for a moment, Talsu saw fury in the constable's eyes, fury and—fear? Whatever it was didn't stay there long. The interrogator nodded to the guards. "You may as well go ahead, boys. It seems I've kept you waiting too long already."

The guards did go ahead, and with a will. They had to man-handle Talsu back to his cell: by the time they'd finished, he couldn't put one foot in front of the other. When they let go of him, he lay on the floor while the door slammed shut behind him. Only later did he find the strength to crawl to his cot.

A cockroach scuttled over him, and then another. He lacked the energy to try to mash them or to catch them. *Maybe I should have made up some names,* he thought. They hadn't beat him up so badly the time before.

But then they'd own you, the way they own Kugu. That was doubtless true. The way he hurt now, he had a hard time caring.

Durrwangen was less battered than Sulingen had been. That was about as much as Marshal Rathar would say for the city. Down in Sulingen, the Algarvians had fought till they couldn't fight anymore. Here, they'd pulled out just before his armies surrounded them. That meant some buildings remained intact.

He made his headquarters in one of those. It had been a bank. By the time he took possession of it, though, the vaults were empty. Someone, Algarvian or Unkerlanter, was richer than he had been . . . if he'd lived to enjoy his wealth.

Along with General Vatran, Rathar studied a map tacked to the wall. Vatran was in high spirits, as high as Rathar had ever seen him show. "We've got the whoresons," Vatran boomed. "By the powers above, they're on the run now. I never thought I'd see the day, but I believe I do."

"It could be," Rathar said. "Aye, it could be." That was as large a display of high spirits as he would allow himself. No, not quite: when he reached out and touched the map, he might have been caressing the soft, warm flesh of his beloved.

And he had reason to caress that map. Three Unkerlanter columns pushed out from Durrwangen, one to the east, one to the northeast toward the border of the Duchy of Grelz, and one due north. The Algarvians weren't managing much more than a rear-guard fight against any of them.

"Did I hear right?" Vatran asked. "Did the redheads cashier the general who pulled their soldiers out of here without orders?"

"That's what captives say," Rathar answered. "I'd be amazed if they were wrong."

Vatran's chuckle was wheezy. "Oh, aye, lord Marshal, so would I." His bushy white eyebrows flew upwards. "If one of our generals had done such a thing . . . If one of our generals had done such a thing, he'd count himself lucky to get cashiered. He'd count himself lucky just to lose his head, he would. Sure as sure, King Swemmel'd be pouring the water into a great big pot and stoking the fire underneath it."

Rathar nodded. A good many officers who'd failed to meet King Swemmel's exacting requirements were no longer among those present. Rathar had come close to seeing the inside of a stew pot a couple of times himself.

But when he looked at the map, he made a discontented noise. "That was a stupid order: the one to hold Durrwangen at all costs, I mean. The redhead may have paid with his job, but he saved an army the Algarvians will be able to use against us somewhere else."

"Would *you* have disobeyed?" Vatran's voice was sly.

"Don't ask me things like that," Rathar said irritably. "*I'm* not an Algarvian, and I'm cursed glad I'm not, too."

But he kept worrying at the question, as he might have at a

bit of gristle stuck between two back teeth. Mezentio gave his officers more freedom to use their judgment than did Swemmel, who trusted no one's judgment but his own. Not even the Algarvians, though, tolerated direct disobedience: the man who'd retreat from Durrwangen had got the sack. And yet . . . Rathar studied the map one more time, trying to remember how things had been a few weeks before. He couldn't make himself believe that redhead had been wrong.

A commotion in the street outside the plundered bank distracted him—or rather, he let it distract him, not something he usually did. Vatran, now, Vatran liked excitement. "Let's see what's going on," he said, and Rathar followed him out.

Men and women pointed and hooted at three men led up the street by soldiers carrying sticks. "You're going to get it!" somebody shouted at the glum-looking men. Somebody else added, "Aye, and you'll deserve it, too!"

"Oh. Is this all?" Vatran looked and sounded disappointed.

"Aye. Collaborators." The word left a sour, nasty taste in Rathar's mouth. He'd seen and heard of too many men and women willing—even eager—to go along with the Algarvian invaders. Things weren't so bad here as they were over in Grelz, but they were bad enough. But when the Unkerlanters retook a town, people sometimes settled scores with enemies by calling them collaborators. He'd seen and heard of too much of that, too.

None of these men was crying out that he'd been wrongly accused. Even the guilty often did that. The silence here said these fellows had no hope of being believed, which meant they must have been in bed with the redheads.

Vatran must have been thinking along similar lines, for he said, "Good riddance to bad rubbish. We might as well get back to work."

"Fair enough." No one ever had to urge Rathar back to work twice.

When they returned, Vatran pointed to the map and said, "The more I look at it, the worse the trouble Mezentio's men are in."

"Here's hoping you're right." Rathar tapped the pins that showed how far the columns advancing out of Durrwangen had got. "What we have to do is, we have to make sure we push the Algarvians back as far as we can before the spring thaw gets this far south. Then we'll be properly set up for the battles this summer."

For two summers in a row, King Swemmel had wanted to hit the Algarvians before they hit him. The first year, he'd flat-out failed; King Mezentio beat him to the punch. The second year, Vatran had launched an attack against the red-heads south of Aspang—right into the teeth of their own building force. Attack all too soon became retreat.

This coming summer . . . Rathar dared look ahead to the battles of this coming summer with something approaching optimism.

And then Vatran said, "The other thing I wonder is what new sorceries the Algarvian mages will come up with."

That sank Rathar's optimism as if it were an egg bursting on a fishing boat. With an angry grunt, the marshal answered, "Those whoresons'll fight the war to the very last Kaunian. There will be a reckoning for that. By the powers above, there will be."

Vatran grunted, too. "Oh, there's a reckoning, all right. Every time they slaughter their Kaunian captives to power magecraft against us, we have to reckon how many of our own peasants we've got to kill to block their sorcery and to make matching magics of our own."

"Aye." A lot of kingdoms, Rathar suspected, would have folded up and yielded when the Algarvians started aiming murder-powered magecraft at them. He'd been horrified himself; no one had fought wars like that for centuries. The Twinkings War had been as savage a struggle as any in the world, but neither Swemmel nor Kyot had started massacring people for the sake of potent sorcery.

But Swemmel hadn't hesitated here, not for a heartbeat. As soon as he'd learned what the Algarvians were doing, he'd ordered his own archmage to match Mezentio's men murder for murder. He'd come right out and said that he didn't care if he ended up with only one subject . . . so long as no Algarvians were left by then.

In a way, Marshal Rathar had to admire such ruthless determination. Without it, the Algarvians probably would have taken Cottbus, and who could guess whether Unkerlant would have been able to continue the fight without its capital? Cottbus had held, Sulingen had held, and now Rathar's men were moving forward.

In another way, though, Swemmel's complete indifference to what happened to his kingdom as long as he held the throne chilled the marshal to the marrow. If Rathar failed, he might end up in a camp with his throat slit to fuel the magic backing the attack some other marshal would make.

Before he could go on with that gloomy thought, a dowser rushed into the headquarters and cried, "Dragons! Dragons heading this way out of the north!"

"How many?" Rathar rapped out. "How soon?"

"I don't know, lord Marshal," the man answered. "They're throwing out those cursed strips of paper again." Dowsers had a sorcerous gift—sometimes the only sorcerous gift they had—for sensing motion: water through ground, ships on water, dragons through the air. But Algarvian dragonfliers had taken to throwing out bits of paper as they flew. The motion of those scraps helped mask the motion of the dragons themselves.

"Won't be long," Vatran predicted gloomily. Rathar could only nod, because he thought the general was right. Vatran went on, "Well, what'll it be when they do get here? Will they go after the ley lines again, or will they try and drop those eggs on our heads? Place your bets, folks."

"If they have any sense, they'll go after the ley lines," Rathar replied. "If their eggs can smash up the depot or hit a line itself and overload it with energy, that really hurts us. But if they knock headquarters flat, so what? Swemmel chooses a couple of new generals, and the war goes on the same as it would have."

Vatran chuckled. "You don't give yourself enough credit, Marshal—or me, either, come to that."

Before Rathar could answer, eggs started bursting not far away. "Maybe the redheads are being stupid," the marshal said. "In any case, I move we adjourn."

"I've heard worse ideas," Vatran admitted.

They both went down into what had been the vault. A faint metallic smell lingered in the air, a monument of coins now vanished. In the meanwhile, artisans attached to the Unkerlanter army had further shored up the ceiling with crisscrossing timbers. If an egg burst directly on top of it, those timbers might not—probably wouldn't—hold out all the sorcerous energy. Otherwise, the men down there were safe enough.

Rathar cursed in a mild sort of way. "What's eating you now?" Vatran asked.

"When I'm down here, I can't tell where the eggs are bursting," Rathar complained. "They all just sound like they're up there somewhere."

"You couldn't do much about them right this minute, except maybe get caught by one," Vatran pointed out. He was right, too, however little Rathar cared to admit it. After a while, Vatran went on, "I don't know where all those eggs are bursting, but sounds like there's a lot of them."

"Aye, it does." Rathar didn't like that, either. "The Algarvians shouldn't be able to put so many dragons in the air against Durrwangen."

"The Algarvians shouldn't be able to do all sorts of things they end up doing," Vatran said. He was right about that, too, however little Rathar cared to acknowledge it.

"We haven't routed out as many of their dragon farms as we thought we had," Rathar said. As if to underscore his words, an egg burst somewhere close to the headquarters building, close enough that plaster pattered down through the rows of crisscrossed timbers and into the cellar.

"If we'd wanted easy work, we would have been headsmen, not soldiers," Vatran observed. "The fellows we'd deal with then wouldn't fight back."

Another near miss shook the vault and sent more plaster down into it. Coughing a little at the dust in the air, Rathar said, "Every now and again, you know, that doesn't sound so bad."

"We've got the redheads on the run, remember," Vatran said. "We were both sure of it just a little while ago."

"Oh, aye," Rathar said. "You know it, and I know it. But do the redheads know it?"

Bembo was feeling more like a spy than a constable these days. Turning to Oraste, he said, "I told you that Kaunian robber you blazed earlier this winter would turn out to be somebody important."

"Why, you lying sack of guts!" Oraste exclaimed. "You didn't think anything at all about him till I wondered why his pals and him knocked over that jeweler's shop and what they'd do with the loot."

"Oh." Bembo had the grace to look shamefaced. "Now that I think on it, you may be right."

"May I shit in my hat if I'm not," Oraste said.

"Took us long enough to get any leads to the dead whoreson's pals," Bembo said. "That's suspicious all by itself, you ask me."

"Well, we've got 'em now. Only question is how much good they'll do us." Oraste spat on the sidewalk of Gromheort. "Cursed Kaunian sorcery. If a blond looks like a Forthwegian all the time these days, how do we go about hauling him in?"

"By figuring out *which* Forthwegian he looks like," Bembo answered. "Or by remembering that the magic doesn't change his voice. That's how I bagged that longwinded foof of a Brivibas, if you'll recall." He strutted a couple of paces. That had been his coup, not Oraste's.

His partner grunted. "Aye, but you'd heard that old cocksucker's voice before. We don't know what these buggers sound like."

Since Bembo didn't feel like answering that, he kept quiet. The address they'd been given wasn't anywhere near Gromheort's Kaunian quarter, even though both men they wanted were—or, before hair dye and sorcery, would have been—blonds. "Powers below eat the Kaunians," Bembo growled. "They make us work too cursed hard."

"Powers below eat the Kaunians," Oraste said. "Period." He needed no special reason to hate them. He just did. After another half a block, he snapped his fingers. "You know what we ought to do?"

"Stop in a tavern and have some wine?" Bembo suggested. "I'm thirsty."

Oraste ignored him. "What we ought to do is, we ought to go into the Kaunian quarter and grab everybody who's got dark hair. Ship all those fornicators west. We wouldn't even have to make up any new rules to let us do it. Owning black hair dye's already against the law."

After some thought, Bembo nodded. "That's not too bad. But the real trouble is all the Kaunians who've already snuck out of the quarter here and the one in Eoforwic. Once they're out, they look like ordinary Forthwegians as long as they can keep the magic up. Then they can go anywhere. And do you know what else I've heard?"

"Tell me." Oraste was a stolid specimen of an Algarvian, but not altogether immune to the lodestone of gossip.

"Some of the blonds are even dyeing their bushes to make it harder for us to tell who's what," Bembo said.

"That's disgusting," Oraste said. "It's also pretty sneaky." A lot of Algarvian constables would have spoken with a certain grudging admiration. They admired clever criminals— and admired them all the more when they didn't have to try to run them down. But Oraste wasted neither admiration nor sympathy on Kaunians.

The two constables rounded the last corner and started toward the block of flats in which the robber Gippias' pals were alleged to be holed up. Bembo whistled. "Well, we've got company. A good thing, too, if you ask me."

"Plenty of company," Oraste added. "See? The powers that be don't like Kaunians who knock over jewelers' shops. Jewels mean money, and blonds with real money are liable to mean real trouble."

"You were right," Bembo admitted. "Do you want a medal? If we catch these buggers, they'll pin one on you."

"I'd rather have some leave or a pass to a brothel, but I'll take a medal if they give me one." Oraste was a relentless pragmatist.

"I hope they've got a mage here," Bembo said as they walked up to the other constables already assembled outside the building. "That'd make it a lot easier to tell who's a Kaunian and who's nothing but a stupid Forthwegian."

"What other kind is there?" asked Oraste, who loved none of his kingdom's neighboring peoples. He went on, "I almost hope there *isn't* a mage."

"Why?" Bembo said in surprise.

"Because if there is, he won't be any bloody good, that's why," Oraste said. "The ones who know what they're doing are either home ensorceling weapons or fighting the stinking Unkerlanters. The kind we'd get here, they'd be the whoresons who couldn't count to twenty-one without reaching under their kilts."

That jerked a laugh out of Bembo. When he saw that the constables did have a mage with them, and what sort of mage he was, it stopped being funny. Bembo knew a drunk when he saw one. He'd dragged plenty of them out of the gutter—aye, and beaten a few who'd provoked him, too. This fellow was standing up, but looked as if he'd fall over in a stiff breeze. He also looked like a man with a monster hangover, an expression with which Bembo was intimately familiar.

"Listen to me, you people!" shouted the Algarvian constabulary captain who looked to be in charge of things. "We are going to get everybody out of this here building. Men, women, children—everybody. We'll clip 'em all, top and bottom."

"See?" Bembo whispered to Oraste. His partner nodded.

The captain went on, "On account of that still might not tell us what we want—these Kaunians are demon sly, they are—we've got Master Gastable here with us." He pointed to the mage, who still seemed less than steady. "He can sniff out a blond like a dog can sniff out—"

"Another dog's backside," Bembo said, and missed whatever simile the officer used.

"So we'll root 'em out if they're in there," the constabulary captain finished. "And if they're not, odds are we'll dig up some other nasty Kaunians even so. Our soldiers'll be able to use their life energy—you'd best believe that."

Use their life energy. That was a nice phrase. Bembo contemplated it and nodded. You could say something like that and not have to think at all about actually killing people. Bembo approved. He didn't like to think about killing people, even Kaunians. Sometimes it needed doing—he knew that—but he didn't like to think about it.

"Let's go!" the captain cried. The constables swarmed into the block of flats and started pounding on doors. The captain stayed out on the sidewalk. It wasn't as if he'd do any of the hard work himself. He took a flask from his belt, swigged, and passed it to Gastable the mage.

"Open up!" Bembo shouted in front of the first door he and Oraste came to. The two of them waited a few heartbeats. Then Oraste kicked in the door. The constables burst into the flat, sticks aimed and ready to blaze. But there was nobody to blaze; the place appeared to stand empty. They quickly turned it upside down, poking their noses everywhere someone might hide. They found nobody.

"Whoever lives there'll get a surprise when he comes home tonight," Oraste said cheerfully. He and Bembo didn't bother closing the door after themselves. "I wonder if he'll have any stuff left by then. No skin off my nose either way."

He pounded on the next door. A Forthwegian woman opened it. Bembo eyed her appreciatively. She had a pretty face; he thought it a pity she followed her country's fashion by wearing such a long, baggy tunic. "Out!" he said, and jerked a thumb toward the stairs leading down to the street. "Anybody else in here with you?"

She yammered at him in Forthwegian, which he didn't speak. He tried again, this time in his halting classical Kaunian. She understood that, and turned out to speak Kaunian a lot better and a lot more angrily than he did. But when Oraste pointed his stick at her face, she quieted down and got moving in a hurry.

"See?" Oraste said. "You just have to know which language to use."

They went through the flat and found an old woman snoring in bed, sound asleep despite the commotion. When they shook her awake, she cursed in Forthwegian and Kaunian. "Oh, shut up, you horrible hag," Bembo said, not bothering to waste politeness on anybody who wasn't good-looking. "Go downstairs." He managed to put that into Kaunian, and the old woman, still fuming, went.

"I hope she turns out to be a blond," Oraste said. "Serve the noisy sow right."

"She'll be steamed enough when they flip up her tunic and trim her bush." Bembo shuddered. "Checking her daughter would be fun, but her? I'm glad somebody else'll get stuck doing that."

Along with the rest of the constables, they went through the building like a dose of salts. A few coins left too visible ended up in Bembo's belt pouch. He didn't notice Oraste making up for low pay, but he wouldn't have been surprised. Once the constables had got up to the top floor, a sergeant said, "All right, let's go back down and make sure the whoresons we rousted don't give anybody any trouble."

When Bembo got down to the sidewalk again, women were screeching about getting clipped anywhere but on their heads. A man and woman who hadn't thought to dye the hair on their private parts had been separated from their neighbors. Their faces were masks of dismay; four or five Algarvian constables pointed sticks at them.

Gastable was making sorcerous passes and muttering to himself in front of a pair of men who looked like Forthwegians. They kept on looking like Forthwegians once he finished his passes, too. Did that mean they weren't disguised, or was he inept? Bembo had no answers. He suspected Gastable had no answers, either.

He wasn't the only one with such suspicions. Oraste said, "I don't think this mage could tell a turd from a tulip."

"I wouldn't be surprised if you were right," Bembo agreed. "Of course, who knows if those Kaunian bandits were here to begin with?"

No sooner had the words come from his lips than the next pair of men fetched before Gastable suddenly seemed to writhe and change shape. They weren't Forthwegians—they were Kaunians with dyed hair. The constabulary captain spoke to Bembo and Oraste: "Are these the men you saw with the perpetrator Gippias?"

The two constables looked at each other. They both shrugged. "We don't know, sir," Bembo said. "When we saw 'em, they were in their sorcerous disguise and running like blazes around a corner."

"How are we supposed to identify them, if you bloody well can't?" the captain asked.

"Don't you still have hold of that Forthwegian who told us the name of the one Kaunian whoreson?" Bembo asked.

By the way the captain set his hands on his hips, he didn't. By the way he glared at Bembo and Oraste, he was ready—even eager—to blame them for what was obviously his failing. But he seemed to realize he couldn't quite get away with that. Scowling, he tried to make the best of it: "Well, we'll just have to see what we can squeeze out of them."

"Aye, sir," Bembo said—that actually made sense. He pointed to the two discovered Kaunians and spoke to Oraste in a low voice: "By the time we're through with them, they'll wish they'd just been shipped west."

Oraste considered. After a moment, he said, "Good."

"And the two of us are off the hook," Bembo added. As far as he was concerned, that was pretty good, too.

Five

When Ealstan came into the flat he shared with Vanai, she handed him an envelope. "Here," she said. "This came in the morning's post. The rest was just advertising circulars. I threw them away."

He kissed his wife, then said, "All right—what have we got here?" He thought he knew; the hand that had addressed the envelope looked familiar. When he opened it and extracted the note inside, he nodded. "Ethelhelm is back in Eoforwic," he told Vanai.

"And he'll want you to reckon up the accounts for the band's tour in the provinces?" she asked.

"That's right." Ealstan sighed. "I wonder if he'll have any money left, what with the squeeze the redheads take from him." Ethelhelm was half Kaunian. If he hadn't been the most popular singer and band leader in Forthweg, he might well have been shipped west. As things were, the Algarvians preferred to let him go on playing, but to make him pay heavily for the privilege of staying free. It was a highly unofficial form of taxation, but that didn't mean it wasn't lucrative.

Ethelhelm played Forthwegian-style music. Ealstan knew Vanai didn't much care for it; her tastes along those lines were purely Kaunian, which meant she liked a thumping beat to every song. And her thoughts here weren't strictly on the music anyhow. She said, "As long as the Algarvians leave him enough money to keep paying you."

"If they don't, he'll bloody well have to find himself another bookkeeper, that's all." Ealstan sighed again. "He used to be my friend, you know, not just my client. He used to write bold songs, strong songs, songs that'd make even a

lackwit sit up and think about what Mezentio's men were doing to us. Then they got their hooks into him."

"If he hadn't gone to sing for the men of Plegmund's
Brigade when they were training outside of town here . . ."
Vanai's voice trailed away.

"Aye, he might have stayed free," Ealstan said. "Of course,
the redheads might have flung him into a ley-line caravan car
and cut his throat, too. You can't know." Ethelhelm hadn't had
the nerve to find out. Ealstan wondered what he would have
done in the band leader's place. He was glad he didn't know.

"You can worry about Ethelhelm later," Vanai said. "For
now, you can sit down to supper. I found some nice sausage
at the butcher's."

"Probably half horsemeat and half dog," Ealstan said.
Vanai made a horrible face at him. Shrugging, he went on, "I
don't care. I'll eat it anyway, as long as it doesn't bark when
I stick a fork in it."

Enough garlic and pepper and oregano and mint spiced the
sausage to make it impossible to tell what the meat had been
before it was ground up and stuffed into a casing. Whatever it
was, it went well with salted olives and crumbly white cheese
and bread and honey, and filled the hole in Ealstan's belly.

Walking over to Ethelhelm's block of flats the next morning reminded Ealstan of the distance between the wealthy en-
tertainer and the fellow who kept books for him. Actually,
Ealstan could have afforded a better flat for himself, but
clung to the neighborhood into which he'd moved when he
first came to Eoforwic because it let him—and, more important, Vanai—stay nearly invisible to the Algarvian occupiers.

Ethelhelm's building boasted a doorman. Ealstan was glad
his building boasted a sturdy front door. The doorman
opened the door from inside the lobby. Nodding to Ealstan,
he said, "Master Ethelhelm told me I was to expect you, sir.
Go right on up."

"Thanks," Ealstan said, and did. Ethelhelm's building also
boasted carpeting on the stairs. Nobody'd pissed in the stairwell, either.

138   HARRY TURTLEDOVE

And yet, when Ealstan rapped on Ethelhelm's door, he knew he would rather have worn his own shoes than the band leader's. Ethelhelm looked worn to a nub. Ealstan had seen that before on his face when he came back from a tour. But Ethelhelm had never seemed quite so frazzled till now. "Hard trip?" Ealstan asked, hoping that accounted for the musician's state.

"You might say so," Ethelhelm answered. "Aye, you just might say so." A glass of brandy rested on the arm of a chair. Pointing to it, Ethelhelm asked, "Will you join me?" He didn't bother to wait for an answer, but went into the kitchen to pour another glass, brought it back, and thrust it into Ealstan's hand. He pointed to another chair. "Sit, if you care to."

Ealstan sat. The chair, at a guess, was worth more than all the furniture in his flat. He raised the glass Ethelhelm had given him and asked, "To what shall we drink?"

"I've been drinking for a while," the band leader said. "I've been drinking to being able to drink. Will that do for you, or do I have to come up with something fancier?" He knocked back his glass of brandy at a gulp.

More cautiously, Ealstan drank, too. "As bad as that?" he asked.

"Worse," Ethelhelm said. "Eventually, you can go through all the receipts and see how much money I lost. It could have been worse. I could have stayed here and lost even more. Aye, as bad as that."

"Why did they let you go, then, if all they were going to do was steal from you?" Ealstan didn't usually drink brandy in the morning, but made an exception today. He thought he would need lubricating to hear the band leader's story.

"Why?" Ethelhelm's laugh had nothing to do with honest mirth; it seemed more a howl of pain. "I'll tell you why: so they would have more to steal, that's why." He disappeared into the kitchen again, and returned with his glass newly full. "But I never thought when I set out that they'd steal so bloody much."

"They're Algarvians," Ealstan said, as if that explained everything.

But Ethelhelm only laughed that raw, wounded laugh again. "Even Algarvians have limits—most of the time. They don't have any limits with me. None at all. Look."

He rose again. Ealstan had hardly any choice but to look at him. The band leader was swarthy like a proper Forthwegian, but he overtopped Ealstan (who was of good size by Forthwegian standards) by half a head. His face was longer than a Forthwegian's should have been, too. Kaunian blood, sure as sure.

"If I don't do what they tell me, if I don't pay whatever they ask of me . . ." His voice faded out. "They'd just as soon kill me as waste their time dickering. You can't pick your ancestors. That's what everybody says, and it's not a lie, but oh, by the powers above, how I wish it were."

"Maybe you ought to quit singing and find quiet work where they won't pay any attention to you," Ealstan said slowly.

Ethelhelm glared. "Why don't you ask me to cut my leg off, too, while I'm at it?"

"If it's in a trap, sometimes you have to," Ealstan answered. He knew all about that. He'd had to flee Gromheort after stunning his cousin Sidroc when Sidroc found out he'd been seeing Vanai. At the time, he hadn't known whether Sidroc would live or die. He'd lived, lived and gone on to kill Ealstan's brother Leofsig, so Ealstan wished he'd killed him.

Ethelhelm was shaking his head back and forth. He looked trapped. "I can't, curse it," he said. "Ask me to live without my music and you might as well ask me not to live at all."

Patiently, Ealstan said, "I'm not asking you to live without your music. Make all you want, for yourself and for whatever friends you make after you disappear from Eoforwic. Just don't make a big enough splash with it to draw the redheads' notice."

"It's not just making the music." The band leader shook his head. "I think I'm trying to explain color to a blind man. You don't know what it's like to get up there on a stage and have thousands of people clapping and yelling out your name." He waved at the elegant flat. "You don't know what it's like to have all this stuff, either."

Ethelhelm didn't know that Ealstan's father was well-to-do. Ealstan didn't know how much like his father he sounded when he said, "If these things are more important to you than staying alive, you haven't got them. They've got you. Same goes for getting up on stage."

Now Ethelhelm stared at him. "You're not my mother, you know. You can't tell me what to do."

"I'm not telling you what to do," Ealstan said. "I'm just a bookkeeper, so I can't. But I can't help seeing how things add up, either, and that's what I'm telling you. You don't have to listen to me."

Ethelhelm kept shaking his head. "You don't have any idea how hard I've worked to get where I am."

"And where is that, exactly?" Ealstan returned. "Under the Algarvians' eye, that's where. Under their thumb, too."

"Curse you," the band leader snarled. "Who told you you could come here and mock me?"

Ealstan got to his feet and gave Ethelhelm a courteous bow: almost an Algarvian-style bow. "Good day," he said politely. "I'm sure you'll have no trouble finding someone else to keep your books in order for you—or you can always do it yourself." He had a good deal of his father's quiet but touchy pride, too.

"Wait!" Ethelhelm said, as if he were a superior entitled to give orders. Ealstan kept walking toward the door. "Wait!" Ethelhelm said again, this time with a different kind of urgency. "Do you know any people who could help me disappear out from under the redheads' noses?"

"No," Ealstan said, and set his hand on the latch. It was true. He wished he did know people of that sort. He would gladly have joined their ranks. Even if he had known them, though, he wouldn't have admitted it to Ethelhelm. The musician might have used their services. But he might also have betrayed them to Mezentio's men to buy favor for himself. Ealstan opened the door, then turned back and bowed again. "Good luck. Powers above keep you safe."

Walking home, he wondered how he'd make up the hole in his income he'd just created for himself. He thought he would be able to manage it. He'd been in Eoforwic a year and a half now. People who needed their accounts reckoned up were getting to know he was in business, and that he was good.

Men were pasting up new broadsheets in his neighborhood. They showed a dragon with King Swemmel's face flaming eastern Derlavai, the slogan beneath reading, SLAY THE BEAST! The Algarvians used good artists. Ealstan still wondered if anyone took the broadsheets seriously.

The postman was putting mail in boxes when he went into his building. "One for you here," the fellow said, and thrust an envelope into his hand.

"Thanks," Ealstan replied, and then said, "Thanks!" again in a different tone of voice when he recognized his father's handwriting. He didn't hear from Gromheort nearly often enough, though he understood why: he might still be sought, and writing carried risk. He was smiling when he opened the envelope and stepped into the stairwell—he'd read the letter on the way up.

By the time he got to the top, he wasn't smiling anymore. When Vanai opened the door to let him in, he thrust the letter into her hand. She quickly read it, then let out a long sigh. "I wish I were sorrier to hear they'd caught my grandfather," she said at last. "He was a fine scholar."

"Is that all you have to say?" Ealstan asked.

"It's bad luck to speak ill of the dead," she answered, "so I said what good I could." Brivibas had raised Vanai from the time she was small; Ealstan knew as much. He didn't know what had estranged them, and wondered if he ever would. Later that evening, he found his father's letter, a balled-up wad of paper, in the wastebasket. Whatever her reasons, Vanai meant them.

Lieutenant Recared's whistle squealed. "Forward!" the young officer shouted.

"Forward!" Sergeant Leudast echoed, though without the accompaniment of the whistle.

"Urra!" the Unkerlanter soldiers shouted, and forward they went. They'd been going forward ever since they cut off the redheads down in Sulingen, and Leudast saw no reason they shouldn't keep right on going forward till they ran King Mezentio out of his palace in Trapani.

He had no sure notion of where Trapani was. Until Swemmel's impressers hauled him into the army, he'd known only his own village not too far west of the border with Forthweg and the nearby market town. He'd seen a lot more of the world since, but few pleasant places in it.

The village ahead didn't look very pleasant. It did have one thing in common with Trapani, wherever Trapani was: it was full of Algarvians. Mezentio's soldiers had never quit fighting through their long, hard retreat from southern Unkerlant; they simply hadn't had the manpower to hold back the Unkerlanters over a broad front. In any one skirmish, though, there was no guarantee Leudast and his countrymen would come out on top.

That thought crossed Leudast's mind even before eggs started bursting among the advancing Unkerlanters. He threw himself down in the snow, cursing as he dove: nobody had told him the Algarvians had a couple of egg-tossers in the village. Some of his men dove for cover, too. Some—the new recruits, mostly—kept running forward in spite of the eggs. A lot of them went down, too, as if a scythe had sliced through them at harvest time. Their shrieks and wails rose above the roar of the bursting eggs.

Algarvian pickets in carefully chosen hidey-holes in front of the village blazed at Leudast and his comrades. "Sir," he shouted to Lieutenant Recared, who sprawled behind a rock not far away, "I don't know if we can pry them out of there by ourselves."

At the start of the winter campaign, Recared would have called him a coward and might have had him blazed. They'd been ordered to take the village, and orders, to Recared, might have been handed down by the powers above. But action had taught the company commander a couple of things. He pointed off to the left, to the west. "We don't have to do it by ourselves. We've got behemoths for company."

Leudast yelled himself hoarse as the big beasts lumbered

forward. He'd hated it when the Algarvians threw behemoths at him, and loved Unkerlanter revenge in equal measure. Eggs from the tossers mounted on the behemoths' back started bursting in the village. The redheads there stopped pounding the Unkerlanter footsoldiers and swung their egg-tossers toward the behemoths.

"Forward!" Recared yelled again, to take advantage of the enemy's distraction.

But, even though the tossers weren't aimed at the footsoldiers, eggs kept bursting under them anyhow as they got closer to the village. "They've buried them under the snow!" Leudast shouted. "We burst them as we run over them." He'd seen the Algarvians do that before, but not since the fighting in the ruins of Sulingen, where they'd had plenty of time to dig in.

No sooner had that thought crossed his mind than an Unkerlanter behemoth trod on a buried egg. The burst of sorcerous energy killed the beast at once. Its body shielded the crew who rode it from the worst of the energies, but as it toppled over onto its side, it crushed a couple of men beneath it.

Recared's whistle squealed again—the shrill squeak reminded Leudast of the noise a pig made in the moment it was castrated. "Forward!" the young lieutenant yelled once more. "Look behind you—we're not in this alone. We've got reinforcements coming up to give us a hand, too."

Leudast risked a quick glance over his shoulder. Sure enough, a fresh wave of soldiers in white smocks worn over long gray tunics stormed toward the village on the heels of Recared's regiment. That was plenty to make him shout, "Urra!" and scramble toward the huts himself. This winter, for the first time, his kingdom seemed able to put men where they were needed when they were needed there. Up till very recently, far too many attacks had gone in either late or in the wrong place.

An Algarvian picket popped up out of his hole to blaze at the onrushing Unkerlanters. Leudast raised his own stick to his shoulder and blazed the redhead. The enemy soldier went down with a screech. An Unkerlanter closer to that hole than Leudast was jumped down into it. A moment later, he scrambled out again and ran on toward the village. The Algarvian didn't come up again.

As King Swemmel's men pushed forward, a couple of enemy pickets tried to run back into the village themselves. One fell before he could take half a dozen steps. The other might have blazed Leudast if he hadn't been more interested in trying to get away.

"Surrender!" Leudast shouted in Algarvian. "Hands high!" That was about all of the language he knew: all a soldier needed to know.

The soldier took a couple more steps. Leudast raised his stick, ready and more than ready to blaze. Then the redhead seemed to realize he couldn't get away. He threw his stick down in the snow and raised his hands over his head. The smile he aimed at Leudast was was half cheerful, half fearful. He loosed a torrent of speech in his own language.

"Shut up," barked Leudast, who understood not a word. He strode forward and relieved the Algarvian of money and rations, then gestured with his stick: go to the rear. Hands still high, the redhead obeyed. Maybe he'd end up in a captives' camp; maybe the other Unkerlanters would kill him before he got off the battlefield. Leudast didn't look back to find out.

Sticks or bursting eggs had started fires in a couple of the peasant huts at the southern end of the village. Leudast welcomed the smoke. It made the Algarvians have a tougher time seeing him, and it might attenuate their beams, too. More eggs churned up the ground in front of him as the behemoth crews did all they could to help the footsoldiers.

Getting through the houses in the southern half of the village proved easier than Leudast had expected. Once the Unkerlanters reached those houses, the enemy fought only a rear-guard action against them. That surprised Leudast till he got to the edge of the market square.

As in most Unkerlanter peasant villages, the square was good and wide. In happier times, people would buy and sell things there, or else just stand around and gossip. Now . . . Now the Algarvians had dug themselves in on the far side of the square. If the Unkerlanters wanted to come at them, they would have to charge across that open space. It might be possible. It wouldn't be easy, or cheap.

An Algarvian beam seared the timbers of the hut behind which Leudast crouched. He pulled back in a hurry; smoke scraped his throat as he breathed in. He hoped the hut wouldn't catch.

A couple of men, both new recruits, tried to rush across the square. Almost contemptuously, the Algarvians let them run for four or five strides before knocking them over. One crumpled and lay still. The other, moaning and dragging a useless leg, crawled back toward cover. Beams boiled snow into puffs of steam all around him. He'd nearly made it to safety when one struck home. His moans turned to shrieks. A moment later, another beam bit. He fell silent.

"Can we do it, Sergeant?" a soldier asked Leudast.

He shook his head. He wouldn't order a charge across the square. If Recared did, he'd try to talk the regimental commander out of it. If he couldn't, he'd sprint across the square along with his comrades—and see how far he got.

Somewhere a few houses over, Lieutenant Recared was speaking to some other soldiers: "We'll have to be quick, aye, and we'll have to be bold, too. The Algarvians can't have *that* many men on the other side of the square." Leudast's heart sank. He saw no reason why the redheads couldn't have that many men and more in the northern part of the village.

But it turned out not to matter. He didn't know where the dragons came from. Maybe they were returning from another raid when some of their dragonfliers looked down and saw the fighting, or maybe the other regiment had a crystallomancer with better connections than Recared's. The Algarvians in the village were surely ready for an attack on the ground. They were just as surely not ready for the death that swooped on them from the sky.

When Leudast heard the thunder of great wings overhead, he threw himself flat in the muddy snow—not that that was likely to save him. But the attacking dragons were painted rock-gray, and they flamed the half of the village Mezentio's men still held. Even from across the market square, he could feel the heat as houses and barricades—and soldiers—caught fire. Soldiers burned not quite to death screamed. A couple of minutes later, the Unkerlanter dragons flamed the Algarvians again. Then they flew off toward the south.

Even before Lieutenant Recared blew his precious officer's whistle, Unkerlanters started rushing across the square. A few of them fell; the dragons hadn't killed all the redheads. But they had flamed the heart out of the enemy's position. Some of the Algarvians fought on anyhow, and made Swemmel's men pay a price for killing them. The rest—more than usual in this kind of fight—surrendered. They seemed dazed, astonished to be alive.

"Another village down," Recared said proudly. "Little by little, we take back our kingdom."

"A village down is right, sir," Leudast answered, coughing a little and then more than a little. "It'll be a while before the peasants move back here."

Recared opened his mouth in surprise, as if the people who'd once lived in the village hadn't crossed his mind. They probably hadn't; he was, Leudast knew, a city man. After a moment, he did find a reply: "They weren't serving the kingdom with the Algarvians holding this place." Since that was true, Leudast nodded. He couldn't prove Recared had missed the point.

With what light remained to the day, the Unkerlanters pushed north again. Leudast approved of that without reservation. He approved of it even more because it didn't involve fighting. Somewhere up ahead, Algarvians would be holed up in the next village. When he came to them, he'd do whatever he had to do. Till then, he enjoyed the respite.

He didn't enjoy having Recared shake him awake in the middle of the night. "What's gone wrong, sir?" he asked, assuming something had.

Only faint glowing embers illuminated the young lieutenant's face. In that dim, bloody light, Recared looked, for once, far older than his years. "Our crystallomancer just got the order," he said. "We have to countermarch, head back south."

"What?" Leudast exclaimed. "Powers above, why?"

"*I* don't know, curse it. The order didn't explain." Recared sounded as harassed as an ordinary soldier. "But you're bound to be right, Sergeant: something's gone wrong somewhere."

Hajjaj hoped no one knew he'd left Bishah. He did manage to sneak out of the capital every now and again. So far, he'd managed to keep the secret from those who would have been most interested in learning it: chief among them Marquis Balastro, the Algarvian minister to Zuwayza. Balastro knew Zuwayza was imperfectly happy in her role as Algarve's ally; Hajjaj worked hard to keep him from knowing just how unhappy his kingdom was, not least since Zuwayza would have been even unhappier without Algarve.

As the ley-line caravan glided east out of the Zuwayzi capital, Hajjaj smiled at his secretary and said, "Isn't it astonishing how quickly I've recovered from the indisposition everyone thinks I have?"

Qutuz smiled, too. "Astonishing indeed, your Excellency. And I am very glad to see you looking so well."

"I thank you, my dear fellow, though I think I ought to ask whether you need new spectacles," Hajjaj said. "I don't look particularly well. What I look is old." He paused a moment in thought. "Of course, a man my age who does not look well is liable to look dead."

"May you live to a hundred and twenty," Qutuz replied, a polite commonplace among the Zuwayzin.

"I've been over halfway there for a while now, but I don't think my private ley line will stretch quite so far," Hajjaj said. "Tewfik, now, Tewfik seems bound and determined to take the proverb literally. I hope he makes it."

"Someone does every now and then, or so they say," his secretary answered.

"They say all sorts of things," Hajjaj observed. "Every now and then, what they say is even true—but don't count on it." As foreign minister of a kingdom with a large, unfriendly neighbor and an arrogant cobelligerent, Hajjaj didn't see the advisability of counting on much of anything.

Qutuz leaned back in his seat—King Shazli had laid on a first-class caravan car for Hajjaj and his secretary—and remarked, "The scenery is prettier than usual, anyhow."

"Well, so it is," Hajjaj agreed. "It was high summer the last time I traveled to Najran, and the sun had baked the life out of everything. Gray rock, yellow rock, brown thornbushes—you know what it's like most of the year."

"Don't we all?" Qutuz spoke with a certain somber pride. In high summer, the sun of northern Zuwayza stood right at the zenith or even a little south of it, something seen nowhere else on the mainland of Derlavai. Except at oases and along the banks of the few streams that flowed down from the mountains the year around, life seemed to cease. Qutuz's wave urged Hajjaj to look out the window. "Certainly not like that now, your Excellency."

"No, it isn't." As his secretary had said, Hajjaj could for once enjoy peering through the glass. Late winter was the time for that in Zuwayza, if ever there was such a time: some years, there wasn't. But, by Zuwayzi standards, this had been a wet winter. The thornbushes were green now. Flowers of all sorts carpeted the usually barren hills and splashed them with crimson and gold and azure.

Had the ley-line caravan halted, Hajjaj would have been able to spy butterflies, moving bits of color. Toads would be croaking and creeping in the wadis, the dry riverbeds, that weren't quite dry now. Had Hajjaj been lucky, he might have spotted a small herd of antelope grazing on greenery whose like they wouldn't see again for months.

He sighed. "It won't last. It never does." With another sigh, he added, "And if that's not a lesson for anyone daft enough to want to be a diplomat, curse me if I know what would be."

The ley-line caravan got into Najran late in the afternoon, gliding up over a last little rise before revealing the almost painfully blue sea ahead. The ley line that ran from Bishah to Najran continued on out into the Bay of Ajlun. If it hadn't, Najran would have had no reason for being. As things were, its harbor was too small and too open to the elements to let it become a great port, or even a moderately important one. It was nondescript, isolated—a perfect home for the Kaunian refugees who'd fled west across the sea from Forthweg.

Their tents, these days, considerably outnumbered the ramshackle houses of the fishermen and boatbuilders and netmakers and the handful of merchants who called Najran home. Without the ley line, the Zuwayzin could never have kept them fed. Pale-skinned men and women in tunics and trousers were more common on the streets than naked, dark brown locals. But the Kaunians had universally adapted the wide-brimmed straw hats the Zuwayzin wore. If they hadn't, their brains would have baked in their skulls.

Hajjaj had thought about putting on tunic and trousers himself when he came to visit the refugees. In the end, he'd decided not to. They were guests in his kingdom, after all, so he didn't feel the need to go against his own usages, as he did when meeting diplomats from other, chillier lands.

A carriage waited for him at the caravan depot: much the largest building in Najran. As he and Qutuz climbed in, he told the driver, "The tent city."

"Aye, your Excellency," the man said, touching the brim of his own big hat. He flicked the reins and clucked to the horses. They were sad, skinny beasts, and didn't seem in a hurry to get anywhere—they would pause to graze whenever they passed anything green and growing.

"Fellow ought to take a whip to them," Qutuz grumbled.

"Never mind," Hajjaj said. "We're not going far, and I'm not in that big a hurry." The truth was, he didn't have the heart to watch the horses beaten.

Blond men and women, a lot of them sunburned despite their hats, greeted the carriage as it approached. Hajjaj heard his own name spoken; some of the people in the growing crowd recognized him from his earlier visit. They started taking off their hats and bowing—not theatrically, as Algarvians would have, but with great sincerity. "Powers above bless you, sir!" someone called to Hajjaj, and a moment later everyone took up the cry.

Irony smote: he'd learned classical Kaunian in Algarve before the Six Years' War. He stood up in the carriage and bowed to the refugees in return. Letting them stay in Zuwayza sometimes felt like the single most worthwhile thing he'd done in the war. Had he given them to the Algarvians, they would surely be dead now.

A couple of blond men pushed their way through the cheering crowd. They, too, bowed to Hajjaj, who returned the courtesy. "Thank you for coming, your Excellency," one of them said. "We're grateful to you once more."

"Which of you is Nemunas, and which Vitols?" Hajjaj asked.

"I'm Vitols," said the man who'd spoken before.

"And I'm Nemunas," the other one added. He was a couple of years older than Vitols, and had a nasty scar on the back of one hand. They'd both been sergeants in King Penda's army before the Algarvians crushed Forthweg. Now they led the Kaunian refugees in Zuwayza.

Vitols pointed to a tent not far away. "We can talk there, if that suits you."

"As good a place as any," Hajjaj said. "This gentlemen with me is my secretary, Qutuz. He knows what we'll be discussing." The Kaunians bowed to Qutuz, too. He bowed back.

In the tent waited tea and wine and cakes. Hajjaj was touched again that the blonds favored him with a Zuwayzi ritual. He and Qutuz sipped and ate and made small talk; as hosts, Vitols and Nemunas were the ones to say when to get down to serious business. Nemunas didn't wait long. "*Will* you let us sail back to Forthweg, like we asked in our letter?" he said. "Now that there's a magic to let us look like Forthwegians, we can go back there and take proper revenge on the redheads."

He and Vitols leaned toward Hajjaj, waiting on his reply. He didn't leave them waiting long. "No," he said. "I will not permit it. I will not encourage it. If Zuwayzi ships see Kaunians sailing east, they will sink them if they can."

"But—why, your Excellency?" Nemunas sounded astonished. "You know what the Algarvians are doing to our people there. You'd never have let us stay here if you didn't."

"Every word of that is true." Hajjaj clamped his jaws shut tight after he finished speaking. He'd known this would be hard, brutally hard, and it was.

"Well, then," Vitols said, as if he expected the Zuwayzi foreign minister to change his mind on the instant and give his blessing to the Kaunians who wanted to go back to Forthweg and cause trouble for Algarve there.

But Hajjaj did not intend to change his mind. "No," he repeated.

"Why?" Vitols and Nemunas spoke together. Neither sounded as if he believed his ears.

"I will tell you why," Hajjaj replied. "Because, if you go back to your homeland and harass my cobelligerents, you make them more likely to lose the war."

Both Kaunian refugee leaders spoke several pungent phrases of a sort Hajjaj's language master had never taught him. He understood the sentiment if not the precise meaning of those phrases. At last, the Kaunians grew more coherent. "Of course we want to make them lose the war," Vitols said.

"Why wouldn't we?" Nemunas added. "They're murdering us."

"Why won't you let us strike back at them?" Vitols demanded. "Why don't you want them to lose the war? Why don't you curse them the way we curse them?"

"Because if Algarve loses the war, Zuwayza loses the war, too," Hajjaj said. "And if Zuwayza loses the war, King Swemmel is all too likely to serve my people as King Mezentio is serving yours."

"He wouldn't," Vitols said. "You might lose, you might even have to go back under Unkerlanter rule again, but you wouldn't get slaughtered."

"It is possible that you are right," Hajjaj admitted. "On the other hand, it is also possible that you are wrong. Knowing Swemmel, knowing the affront Zuwayza has given him, I must tell you that I do not care to take the chance. The things my cobelligerents have done horrify me. The things my foes could do if they get the chance horrify me more. I am sorry, gentlemen, but you cannot ask me to risk my people for the sake of yours."

Nemunas and Vitols put their heads together for a couple of minutes, muttering in low voices. When they were done, they both bowed to Hajjaj. Vitols spoke for them: "Very well, your Excellency. We understand your reasons. We don't agree, mind, but we understand. We'll obey. We wouldn't endanger your folk after you saved ours."

"I thank you." Hajjaj bowed in return. "I also require that obedience."

"You'll have it," Vitols said, and Nemunas nodded. The meeting ended a few minutes later.

On the way back to the ley-line caravan depot, Qutuz remarked, "They're lying."

"I know," Hajjaj said calmly.

"But . . ." his secretary said.

"I've done what I had to do," Hajjaj said. "I've warned them. Our ships will sink some of them. That will make the Algarvians happy. And if some do get back to Forthweg and raise trouble . . . that won't make me altogether unhappy." He smiled at Qutuz. The carriage rolled on toward Najran.

Krasta had been to a good many entertainments since joining herself with Colonel Lurcanio. Having a companion from among the victorious Algarvians with whom to go to entertainments had been one of the reasons, and not, perhaps, the least of them, why she'd let Lurcanio into her bed. But this one, at a wealthy cheese merchant's house in Priekule, struck her as the strangest of any of them.

After looking around at the other guests, she stuck her nose in the air, ostentatiously enough for Lurcanio to notice. "Is something troubling you, my sweet?" he asked, concern mostly masking the faint scorn in his voice.

"Something? Aye, something." Krasta struggled to put what she felt into words. Except when inspired by spite, she wasn't usually very articulate. What she came up with now was a horrified four-word outburst: "Who *are* these people?"

"Friends of Algarve, of course," Lurcanio said.

"Powers above help you, in that case." As soon as she spoke, Krasta realized she might have gone too far. She cared—Lurcanio, when annoyed, made life unpleasant for her—but only to a point. The trouble was, she'd spoken altogether too much truth.

Most gatherings since the redheads overran Valmiera featured mixed crowds. Krasta had grown to accept that. Some nobles, like her, made the best of things; others chose not to appear with the occupiers. Not all the female companions the Algarvians found for themselves were noblewomen, or even ladies. And a lot of the Valmieran men who worked hand in glove with Algarve conspicuously lacked noble blood.

But tonight's crowd . . . Except for Lurcanio—*possibly except for Lurcanio,* Krasta thought with a sweet dash of spite—the Algarvian officers were boors, busy getting drunk as fast as they could. The women with them were sluts; half of them were making plays for men of higher rank than the ones who'd brought them.

One of them, in too much powder and paint and not enough clothes, sidled up to Lurcanio, who didn't bother pretending he didn't notice her. "Go away," Krasta hissed at her. "You'll give him a disease."

"He already has one," the tart retorted. "You're here."

"What's your name?" Krasta asked sweetly. "Do you dare tell it? If they look in the constabulary records, how many solicitation charges will they find?"

She hadn't meant to be anything but bitchy, but the other woman, instead of going on with the row, turned pale under her thick makeup and found something else to do in a hurry.

"I have better taste than that, I assure you," Lurcanio said.

"Maybe you do." Krasta's eyes left her Algarvian lover's face and slid down to the front of his kilt. "I'm not so sure about *him.*" Lurcanio threw back his head and laughed, for all the world as if she were joking.

She didn't enjoy her little triumph long. It oozed away as

she went back to contemplating the company she was keeping. The Algarvian officers were bad. The Valmieran women were worse. But the Valmieran men were worst of all.

Even the handful of nobles depressed her. Backwoods counts and viscounts, they'd never shown their faces in Priekule before the Algarvians came—and there were good reasons why they hadn't. Krasta knew a couple of them by reputation. The Valmieran nobility was and always had been reactionary. Krasta despised commoners and was proud of it. But, even by her standards, that count over there—the one who belted his trousers with a short, nasty whip—went too far.

She had little use for the commoners in the crowd, either. Some people came from families that had been prominent for generations, even if they weren't noble. You could rely on folk like that. The ones here at the cheese merchant's . . . Krasta hadn't heard of any of them before the Algarvians took Priekule, and wished she hadn't heard of most of them since.

"We *shall* prevail," one of them told another not far away.

"Oh, aye, of course we shall," the other man answered. "We'll grind Swemmel into the dust. Plenty of time after that to settle with treacherous Lagoas."

Both men wore kilts and tunics not merely Algarvian in style but modeled after those of Algarvian soldiers. They'd grown side whiskers and little strips of chin beard, too; one of them waxed his mustaches so that they stuck out like horns. But for being blond and speaking Valmieran, they might have been born in Mezentio's kingdom.

Krasta nudged Lurcanio and pointed to the two men. "Buy them some hair dye and you could have a couple of new Algarvians to throw into the fighting against Unkerlant."

He surprised her by taking her seriously. "We've thought about that. But in Forthweg and in Algarve, hair dye has caused us more problems than it's solved, so we probably won't."

"What kind of trouble?" Krasta asked.

"People masquerading as things they aren't," the Algarvian colonel said. "We've pretty much put a stop to that by now—and about time, too, if you ask me."

"People masquerading," Krasta echoed. "The folk here are masquerading as things they aren't—as important people, I mean."

"Oh, but they are important," Lurcanio said. "They are very important indeed. Without them, how could we run Valmiera?"

"With your own men, of course," Krasta answered. "If you don't run Valmiera with your own men, why have you taken half my mansion?"

"Do you know what the Algarvians in your mansion do?" Lurcanio asked. "Have you any idea?"

Krasta didn't like his sardonic tone. She returned it, with venomous interest: "You mean, besides seducing the serving women? They run Priekule for your king." Spoken baldly like that, it seemed less shameful that Algarve should run a city that had never been hers.

Lurcanio clicked his heels and bowed. "You are correct. We run Priekule. And do you know how we run Priekule? Nine times out of ten, we go to some Valmieran and say, 'Do thus and so.' And he will bow and say, 'Aye, your Excellency.' And lo and behold, thus and so will be done. We have not the men to do all the thus and sos ourselves. We never did. With the war in the west drawing so many thither, having so many Algarvians here grows more impossible by the day. And so, as I say, we rule this kingdom and your countrymen run it for us."

Valmieran constables. Valmieran caravan conductors. Valmieran tax collectors. Even, Krasta supposed, Valmieran mages. And every one of them in the service, not of poor drunken King Gainibu, but of redheaded King Mezentio and the Algarvian occupiers.

She shuddered. Before she thought—nothing new for her—she said, "It reminds me of sheep leading other sheep to the slaughter."

Lurcanio started to reply, then checked himself. "There are times when I do believe that, given education and application, you could be formidable." He bowed to Krasta, who wasn't sure whether that constituted praise or dismissal.

When she didn't say anything, he went on, "As for your metaphor, well, what do you think a bell wether is sometimes called upon to do? And what do you think happens to a ram when he is made into a wether?"

"I don't know," Krasta said, irritable again. "All I know is, you're confusing me."

"Am I?" Lurcanio's smile turned smug again. "Well, this isn't the first time, and I doubt it will be the last."

Krasta found one question more—one question too many, probably: "What will happen to all these people if Algarve loses the war?"

The smug smile slipped. "You may rest assured, my poppet, that will not happen. Life is not so easy as we wished it would be, but it is not so hard as our enemies wish it were, either. We struck Kuusamo a heavy blow not long ago—struck it from here in Valmiera, in fact." Lurcanio seemed on the point of saying more, but turned the subject instead: "But I will answer you, in a hypothetical sense. What would happen to them? Not what will, mind you, but what would? It should be obvious even to you: whatever the victors wanted."

If Algarve somehow lost the war, what *would* the victors do with those who had taken her side? Krasta couldn't stay on that high philosophical plane for long. As usual, her thoughts descended to the personal: if Algarve somehow lost, what would the victors do to *her?*

She shuddered again. That might have some distinctly nasty answers. She'd made her bed, made it and lain down in it and invited Lurcanio into it to keep her warm. Clasping his arm in sudden fright, she said, "Take me home."

"You listened to a ghost story and frightened yourself," Lurcanio said.

That was likely to be true. Krasta hoped it was. She would have held that hope even more strongly were Lurcanio not pursuing her brother, and had Skarnu not penned that sheet claiming all sorts of horrors in the west. But she'd chosen her side, and she had no idea how to unchoose it. "Take me home," she repeated.

Lurcanio sighed. "Oh, very well," he said. "Let me apologize to our gracious host"—he couldn't say that with a straight face, try as he would—"for leaving the festivities so early."

A chilly rain had begun to fall. They both put up the hoods to their cloaks as they hurried out to Lurcanio's carriage. He spoke to his driver in Algarvian. The driver, already hooded against the rain, nodded and got the horses moving. The carriage rolled away from the cheese merchant's house.

"I hope he can find his way back," Krasta said. "It's very dark. I can hardly see across the street."

"I expect he will manage," Lurcanio answered. "He used to have trouble, I know, but by now he has been here long enough to learn his way around." That was another way of saying Valmiera had been in Algarvian hands for quite a while. Krasta sighed and snuggled against Lurcanio, partly for warmth, partly to keep from thinking about the choices she'd made and the choices she might have made.

They hadn't gone far before a dull roar sounded off to the north, and then another and another. "The Lagoans," Krasta said. "They're dropping eggs on us again." Yet another burst of sorcerous energy echoed through Priekule, this one quite a bit closer.

"Well, so they are," Lurcanio answered. "Dropping them at random, too, in this weather. Charming people, there on the other side of the Strait." If he knew he was in danger, he gave no sign of it. He'd never lacked for courage.

"Should we find a shelter?" Krasta asked.

She felt rather than seeing Lurcanio shrug. "If you like," he said. "I think the odds favor us, though. He spoke in Algarvian to the driver, who laughed and replied in the same language. Lurcanio also laughed, and translated: "He says he is fated to be blazed by an outraged husband at the age of a hundred and three, and so he is not worried about Lagoan eggs."

That made Krasta laugh, too. Then an egg burst close enough for her to see its flash, close enough that a piece of its thin metal casing whined through the air past the carriage. It had certainly come down on somebody's head. Krasta knew she could have been that somebody. And she, unlike Lurcanio and his driver, had no Algarvian bravado to sustain her. She cursed the Lagoans all the way back to her mansion. Did they care about the Valmierans one bit more than Mezentio's men did? If so, she wished they would have found a different way to show it.

Things could have been worse. A few weeks before, watching Algarvian soldiers stream out of Durrwangen without orders, against orders, Colonel Sabrino would have had a hard time saying that. Now . . . Now it looked as if something might be salvaged in the southwest after all.

The colonel of dragonfliers wasn't the only one with that thought. At supper one evening at the wing's dragon farm, Captain Domiziano raised a glass of ferocious Unkerlanter spirits in salute and said, "Here's to General Solino. Looks like he really did know what he was doing."

He knocked back the spirits, coughing a little as he did so. Along with the rest of the officers, Sabrino also drank to the toast. Captain Orosio said, "Aye. Turns out we're better off with that army loose and able to hit back than we would have been if we'd pissed it away like the one down in Sulingen."

"Pity Solino's head had to roll," Domiziano said. "Doesn't seem fair."

Orosio shrugged. "The price you pay for being right."

"Aye, that's how things work," Sabrino agreed. "If you advance against orders to hold and something good comes of it, you're a hero. If you retreat against orders to hold, they'll reckon you a coward no matter what happens. Even if you were right, they'll figure you're liable to run away the next time, too." He pointed to the big plate of pork ribs in the middle of the table. "Pass me a couple more of those, somebody, if you please."

Once he had the ribs, he smeared them with horseradish sauce and gnawed all the meat off the bones. Like his own glass of spirits, the sauce gave the illusion of warmth. In an Unkerlanter winter, even the illusion was not to be despised.

Domiziano also spread the sauce over another rib. In between bites, he sighed and said, "This cursed war is jading my palate so I'll never properly appreciate a delicate sauce again."

Sabrino chuckled at that. "There are worse problems to have. I was in the trenches in the Six Years' War, and I know." Domiziano had been making messes in his drawers during the Six Years' War, if he'd been born at all. He looked at Sabrino as if he'd started speaking Gyongyosian. Orosio was only a little older, but he understood such things. His nod and, even more, his knowing expression said as much.

A dragon handler stuck his head into Sabrino's tent and said, "Sir, that new wing is starting to land at the farm."

"The one that had been flying against Lagoas?" Sabrino asked, and the handler nodded. Mischief glinting in his eyes, Sabrino turned back to his squadron commanders. "Well, gentlemen, shall we help them settle in? I'm sure they'll be delighted at the accommodations they find waiting for them here."

Even Domiziano recognized the irony there well enough to chuckle. Orosio laughed out loud. Sabrino got to his feet. His subordinates followed him out.

Cold bit at his nose and cheeks. He ignored it; he'd known worse. Sure enough, dragons spiraled down out of the cloudy sky along with the occasional snowflake. Many, many dragons . . . "Powers above," Sabrino said softly. "If that's not a full-strength wing, then I'm a naked black Zuwayzi." Wings with their full complement of sixty-four dragons and dragonfliers simply didn't exist in the war against Unkerlant. Whenever he got his up over half strength, he counted himself lucky.

Accompanied by a dragon handler, an officer he'd never seen before came up. "You are Colonel Sabrino?" the newcomer asked, and Sabrino admitted he was. After bows and an embrace and kisses on both cheeks, the other officer continued, "I am Colonel Ambaldo, and I was told you would arrange for the well-being of my dragons and my men."

"My handlers will do what they can, and we'll see what we

can scrounge up in the way of extra tents and extra rations," Sabrino answered. "Anything you brought and anything you can steal will help a lot, though."

Ambaldo stared at him. "Is that a joke, my dear sir?"

"Not even close to one," Sabrino answered. "Let me guess. You've spent the whole war up till now in Valmiera? At some pretty little peasant village? With pretty blond women to darn your socks and warm your beds? It's not like that here."

"My dear sir, I have been fighting, too," Ambaldo said stiffly, "fighting against the vile air pirates of Lagoas and Kuusamo. You will please remember this fact."

Sabrino bowed again. "I didn't say you haven't been fighting. But I meant what I did say. It's not like that here. It's nothing like that here. The Unkerlanters really and truly hate us, or most of them do, anyway. We haven't got enough of anything to go around: not enough men, not enough dragons, not enough supplies, nothing. The current strength of my wing is thirty-one—I've just been reinforced."

"Thirty-one?" Ambaldo's eyes looked as if they'd pop out of his head. "Where are the rest, by the powers above?"

"Where do you think?" Sabrino said. "Dead or wounded. And a lot of the replacements that could have got sent to me went to some other wing instead."

"Do your superiors hate you so?" Ambaldo asked.

"No, no, no." Sabrino wondered if he could ever get through to this poor, naive soul. "They went to other wings because those were even further under strength than mine."

Orosio spoke up: "Colonel Ambaldo, sir, if you want to look good in your uniform, you can do that anywhere. If you want to fight a war and hurt the kingdom's enemies, this is the place."

"Who is this insolent man?" Ambaldo demanded of Sabrino. "I ask, you understand, so that my friends may speak to him."

"We don't duel on this front," Sabrino said. "Oh, there's no law or king's command against it, but we don't. The Unkerlanters kill too many of us; we don't make things easier for them by killing each other."

Ambaldo's eyebrows shot upwards. "Truly I have come to

a barbarous country." Some of his officers walked up behind him. They were staring around in amazement at the landscape in which they found themselves.

Sabrino had a hard time blaming them. Had he been jerked out of a pleasant billet in Valmiera and plopped down in the wilds of Unkerlant, he would have been amazed, too, and not with delight. "Come on, gentlemen," he said. "We'll do what we can for you. We have to work together, after all."

The newcomers had brought some tents. Sabrino shoehorned the rest of their dragonfliers in with his men; he shoehorned Colonel Ambaldo in with himself. Getting enough meat for the new dragons would have been impossible if his dragon handlers hadn't come across the bodies of a couple of behemoths. Brimstone was not a problem. Brimstone had never been a problem. Quicksilver . . . He didn't have and couldn't get enough quicksilver to give his own dragons all they needed. He shared what he had with the new arrived wing.

Horseradish and raw Unkerlanter spirits did nothing to improve Ambaldo's mood. He kept muttering things like, "What did we do to deserve this?" Since Sabrino didn't know whom Ambaldo might have offended, he couldn't very well answer that. At last, to his relief, the other wing commander pulled himself together and asked, "What is to be done?"

"Here." Sabrino pointed to a map. "The Unkerlanters have failed to concentrate their forces as they should have. Instead of one large attack advancing from Durrwangen to some other point that could anchor their whole line, they've sent columns out in several directions, none of them with its far end secured by a river or mountains or anything we can't maneuver around. And so, we're going to cut those columns off and then cut them up." He showed what he meant with several quick gestures.

Ambaldo studied the map. "Do we have the force here to bring this off?"

Good. Sabrino thought with more relief. *He's not a fool.* "On paper, the Unkerlanters always have more than we do," he answered. "But, for one thing, we're better than they are, no matter how much Swemmel babbles about efficiency. And, for another"—he grimaced—"our mages work stronger magic killing Kaunians than theirs do, slaughtering their own peasants."

Ambaldo didn't just grimace. He reached for the jar of spirits, poured his mug full, and gulped it down. "They really do those things here, then?" he said. "Nobody in Valmiera much wanted to talk about them—we were living among blonds, after all."

"They do them," Sabrino answered grimly. "So do we. By the end of this fight, only one side will be left standing. It's as simple as that." He hated that truth with all his soul, but hating it made it no less a truth. Colonel Ambaldo drank more spirits.

But Ambaldo was ready to fly again the next day, and so were his dragons. In spite of their long journey from Valmiera, Sabrino envied them their condition. They'd eaten better and fought less than any wing here in the west.

And they proved professionally competent; they plastered an Unkerlanter strongpoint northeast of Durrwangen with eggs and swooped low to attack a ley-line caravan surely loaded with enemy soldiers. They left the caravan a flaming wreck. Sabrino, whose smaller, more depleted wing accompanied and guided them on their attacks, found nothing about which he could complain.

Ambaldo's image appeared in his crystal. "Why didn't we win the war here long ago, if this is the best the Unkerlanters can do?" demanded the wing commander from out of the west.

Before Sabrino could reply, the Unkerlanters gave Ambaldo an answer of their own. Dragons painted rock-gray hurled themselves at the Algarvians in the air. As usual, Swemmel's men flew with less skill than the Algarvians they attacked—and Ambaldo's dragonfliers showed they had as much skill aboard their mounts as any other Algarvians. But there were, also as usual, a demon of a lot of Unkerlanters. Ambaldo's wing had holes torn in it, even though it gave better than it got.

So did Sabrino's. He was, by now, long since used to scraping by and making do with whatever replacements he happened to get—if he happened to get any. He wondered how Ambaldo's men would fare in a place where, without scrounging and improvising, they couldn't hope to keep going. They hadn't had to do such things in Valmiera—that was plain from the abundance they'd brought west.

Down on the ground, Algarvian troopers and behemoths were moving toward the places the dragons had pounded. Sabrino wondered if they included regiments and brigades plucked from occupation duty in Valmiera or Jelgava and carried across a good stretch of Derlavai by ley-line caravan so they could get into this fight. He rather hoped so. He'd gone on peacetime holiday to the beaches of northern Jelgava. Occupation duty there had to be a true hardship—he rolled his eyes, thinking of how dreadful patrolling beaches full of nearly naked bathers had to be. A little frostbite would go a long way toward fixing the sunburn from which those troopers might be suffering.

And then the ground shook down below: literally, for he could see the ripples as it writhed like an animal in pain. Here and there, purple flames shot up through the snow and stabbed toward the heavens. What had been Unkerlanter strongpoints were wrecked, ruined, ravaged.

Sabrino's sardonic smile slipped. How many Kaunians had died to power that magecraft? However many it was, even troops plucked from pleasant occupation duty should have been able to exploit the holes it tore in the Unkerlanter line.

Garivald was on sentry-go when the Grelzer company strode into the forest Munderic's band of irregulars reckoned all their own. He didn't see the Grelzers till they were quite close; snow was falling fairly heavily, cloaking things in the middle and far distance from his eyes.

When he did spy them, he pulled the hood of his white snow smock down low on his forehead, making sure it covered his dark hair. Then he slipped back through the barebranched woods toward the clearing where the irregulars had their headquarters. He moved far faster than the soldiers who'd chosen Raniero the Algarvian puppet rather than Swemmel of Unkerlant. He knew where he was going, while the Grelzers couldn't be sure—he hoped they couldn't be sure—just where in the woods the irregulars lurked.

He'd got about halfway to the clearing when a soft, clear voice called a challenge: "Who goes?"

"It's me, Obilot—Garivald," he answered.

She slid out from behind a birch, her snow smock hardly lighter than its pale bark. Her stick didn't quite point at him, but wouldn't have to move far to do so. After she recognized that it was indeed he, she demanded, "Why aren't you at your post?"

"Because there's a great mob of Grelzers not very far behind me," he answered. "We'd better get ready to beat them back if we can, or to make sure they don't find us if we can't."

Her mouth twisted. "Fair enough," she said, and then, "*Can* we make sure they don't find us? It's not like they're Algarvians or those mercenaries from up in Forthweg."

"I know," Garivald said unhappily. Except in their choice of a king, the Grelzers who favored Raniero weren't much different from the ones who still carried on the fight against him and against Algarve. Some of them would have hunted in this forest in peacetime, hunted or come here to gather mushrooms or honey. They might not *know* where the irregulars denned, but they would have some idea.

"Go on, then," Obilot said. "You haven't got time to waste." Garivald nodded and plunged on through the woods.

He got challenged once more before reaching the clearing: Munderic was not about to be taken by surprise. The other irregular also passed him through after only a few words. Raniero's troopers hadn't come into the forest in force for quite a while.

When he trotted, panting, into the clearing, he wanted to shout out his warning. He didn't, not knowing how far behind him the Grelzer troopers were, he didn't want to risk their hearing a wild cry of alarm. Instead, he called out the news urgently but without panic or excitement in his voice.

That did what wanted doing. The irregulars came boiling out of their makeshift shelters, almost all of them clutching sticks. "What do we do?" Garivald asked Munderic. "Do we fight them, or do we try to get away?"

Munderic gnawed on his lower lip. "I don't know," he answered. "I just don't know. What *kind* of soldiers are they? That's the rub. If they just go forward till they bump into something and then run away, that's one thing. But if they're like that bunch we ran into on the way to the ley line . . ." He scowled and shook his head. "Those whoresons meant it, powers below eat them."

"Let's fight 'em!" Sadoc boomed. If the makeshift mage favored fighting, that in itself was to Garivald a strong argument against it.

Munderic had more confidence in Sadoc's sorcerous abilities than Garivald thought wise. *Any* confidence in Sadoc's sorcerous abilities was more than Garivald thought wise. But the leader of the irregulars never had believed Sadoc made much of a general. Munderic said, "No, I think we'd do better to pick the fight ourselves and not let those bastards do it for us. Let's slide into the woods off to the west and see if we can't give 'em the slip."

Another irregular hurried into the clearing with word of the advancing Grelzers. That seemed to decide the men and the handful of women there against arguing with Munderic. They left the clearing by ones and twos, slipping deeper into the woods. Munderic gestured to Garivald, who nodded. They hurried out together.

"We've played these games before," Munderic said. "Remember the fun we had when the Algarvians tried to chase us out of here?"

"Oh, aye," Garivald answered. "I'm not likely to forget—I was part of it, after all."

But befooling the Algarvians in summer, when trees in full

leaf gave extra cover and when dirt didn't hold tracks so well, was a business different from confusing Grelzer soldiers here in winter, where the trees were bare and when snow on the ground told trackers too much. Maybe Munderic didn't want to think about that. Maybe he just didn't believe the irregulars could make a standup fight. And maybe he was right not to believe that, too.

If he was, though, what did that say about how much good the irregulars were doing in their fight against Algarve and her puppets? Maybe Garivald didn't want to think about that.

Munderic pointed to a snow-covered boulder. "Shall we flop down behind that and pot ourselves a couple of those Grelzer traitors if they try and come after us?"

"Aye. Why not?" Garivald said. "I wondered if you intended to do any fighting."

"Oh, I'll fight . . . now and again," Munderic answered, not much put out. "I'll fight when I can hurt the enemy and he can't do much to hurt me. Or I'll fight when I haven't got any other choice. Otherwise, I'll run like a rabbit. I'm not doing this for the glory of it."

There he sounded very much like an Unkerlanter peasant—or perhaps like a soldier who'd been in enough fights to realize he didn't want to be in a whole lot more. Garivald stretched out behind the boulder. Munderic had certainly been in enough fights to know good cover when he saw it. Garivald barely had to lift his head to have a perfect view of the route by which the pursuers would likely come—and they would have a demon of a time spotting him.

By the happy grunt Munderic let out from the other side of the boulder, his position was just as good. "We'll sting them here, so we will," he said.

"You could have Sadoc make a great magic and sweep the Grelzers to destruction," Garivald said, unable to resist the gibe.

"Oh, shut up," the leader of the irregulars muttered. He turned his head to glare at Garivald. "All right, curse you, I'll admit it: he's a menace when he tries to do magecraft. There. Are you happy?"

"Happier, anyhow." But Garivald didn't have long to celebrate his tiny triumph—he spied motion through the dancing snow and flattened himself behind the rock. "They're coming."

"Aye." Munderic must have seen it, too: his voice dropped to a thin thread of whisper. "We'll make them pay."

The Grelzers advanced as confidently as if they'd taken lessons in arrogance from their Algarvian overlords. Garivald thought Munderic would tell him to wait, not to hurry, to let the enemy come close before he started blazing. But Munderic kept his mouth shut. It wasn't because the Grelzers were already so close, he'd give himself away; they weren't. It was, Garivald realized after a long moment's silence, because he himself had turned into a veteran, and could be trusted to do the right thing without being told.

He waited. Then he waited some more. *We'll know what kind of soldiers they are as soon as the blazing starts,* he thought. That made him want to wait even longer. Not knowing, he could imagine that the men who followed the Algarvian-imposed King of Grelz were a pack of cowards who'd run right away. The last thing he cared to do was discover he was wrong.

At last, he couldn't wait anymore. A couple of soldiers with white smocks over the dark green of Grelz were within ten or twelve paces of the boulder. They were looking off into the trees farther west; if they hadn't been, they surely would have spotted Munderic or him.

Garivald slipped his finger out through the hole in his mitten and into the blazing hole on his stick. The beam leaped forth. It caught a Grelzer square in the chest. He stopped as abruptly as if he'd walked into a stone wall, then crumpled. Munderic blazed his companion, not so neatly—the second Grelzer started howling like a dog a wagon had run over and tried to drag himself away. Munderic blazed him again. He shuddered and lay still.

"Urra!" the irregulars in the rear guard shouted as they started blazing down the men who'd invaded their forest.

"King Swemmel! Urra!" If they made as much noise as they could, the Grelzers might think they had more men than they really did.

They were blazing from ambush, every one of them, and took their foes by surprise. A good many Grelzers went down. But the others dashed for cover with a speed that warned they had a good notion of what they were doing. They raised shouts of their own: "Raniero of Grelz!" "Death to Swemmel the tyrant!" "Grelz and freedom!"

"Grelz and the Algarvians' cock up your arse!" Garivald yelled back—not a splendid song lyric, but a fine insult. A Grelzer, shouting with fury, hopped up from behind the bush where he crouched. Garivald blazed him. He'd never been trained in the proper response to literary criticism, but had considerable natural talent.

A beam sizzled snow not far from Garivald's head: one of the critic's comrades, protesting his sudden abridgement. Garivald blazed back, making the Grelzer keep his head down. Then he glanced over at Munderic. "Most of the band will have slid off to some other hidey-holes. Don't you think it's about time we did the same?"

"Aye, we'd better," Munderic agreed. "Otherwise they'll flank us out and rip us to pieces. The redheads would, and these whoresons have been taking lessons."

Garivald scrambled back toward a pine. More beams sent up gouts of steam as the Grelzers tried to make sure he'd sing no more songs. But he made it to the tree, scuttled behind it, and started blazing at Raniero's men again.

Munderic had waited till Garivald could cover him before retreating himself. The leader of the irregulars dashed off toward a bush thickly covered with snow. He never made it. A beam caught him in the flank as he ran. He let out a horrible scream and fell in the snow. He crawled on for another few feet, leaving a long trail of scarlet behind him. Then, as if very tired, he let his hands slip out from under him and sprawled at full length. He might have been lying down to sleep, but from this sleep he would not awaken.

Cursing, Garivald blundered west through the forest, blazing now and then but also doing his best to shake off the Grelzers. He finally did; they weren't cowards, but the irregulars knew the routes they'd made through these woods better than they did. Munderic's men had made false trails, too, and punished the Grelzers from ambush when they came charging down them.

Every time he came on some of his fellows, Garivald had to tell them Munderic was dead. It tore at him; he hadn't had such a hard time speaking of a death since his own father's. At least, near sundown, the irregulars—those who survived—gathered in a clearing well to the west of the one they'd called their own. Garivald started to say something. Then he saw all of them looking straight at him. "Not me!" he exclaimed, but his comrades nodded as one man. He never would have joined a band of irregulars on his own, but now he led one.

Six

C ome on!" Sergeant Werferth shouted. "Keep moving. That's what we've got to do, keep moving. We're calling the tune now, not those Unkerlanter barbarians. Shake a leg, boys, or you'll be sorry."

"Slave driver," Sidroc muttered to Ceorl as they tramped south and west over a field in southern Unkerlant. "All he needs is a whip."

"Shut up, boy," the ruffian answered. "Don't give him ideas." But he didn't sound so sour as usual. Plegmund's Brigade was moving forward for the first time in weeks, and that made up for a multitude of failings.

"There." Werferth pointed to a couple of troops of Algarvian behemoths up ahead. "We'll form up with them."

"If they don't try and blaze us or toss eggs at us first, we will," Ceorl said, and spat in the snow. "Half the time, these fornicating idiots think we're Unkerlanters our own selves." He spat again, as offended as any Forthwegian would be to get mistaken for his cousins to the west.

Sidroc made such excuses for the Algarvians as he could: "Some of these fellows we're seeing here at the front don't look like they ever set eyes on an Unkerlanter before, let alone a Forthwegian. They've been doing occupation duty somewhere off in the east."

"Powers below eat 'em for it, too," Ceorl said. "They've been eating and drinking and screwing themselves silly, and we've been doing their fighting and dying for them. About time they started earning their cursed keep."

"Aye, that's so," Sidroc admitted. "It won't do us much good if they do decide we're Unkerlanters, though."

For a moment, it looked as if the behemoth crews *would* think the men shouting and waving and advancing on them belonged to the enemy. Only when the Algarvian officers leading the Forthwegians came out in front of them did the redheads on the behemoths relax . . . a little.

"Plegmund's Brigade?" one of them said as Sidroc and his comrades approached. "What in the futtering blazes is Plegmund's Brigade? Sounds like a futtering disease, that's what." A couple of the other troopers on the behemoth laughed and nodded.

Not bothering to keep his voice down, Sidroc asked Werferth, "Sergeant, can we whale the stuffing out of these redheaded fools before we go on and deal with the Unkerlanters?"

With what looked like real regret, Werferth shook his head. Since Sidroc had spoken in Forthwegian, the Algarvians aboard the behemoth didn't know what he'd said. But one of the redheaded officers with the Brigade said what amounted to the same thing—"We'll show you what we are, by the powers above!"—and said it in unmistakable Algarvian.

Sidroc stood very straight, his chest swelling with pride. But Ceorl only grunted. "That means they'll spend us the way a rich whore spends coppers. They'll throw us away to prove we're brave."

"Bite your tongue, curse it!" Werferth exclaimed. Sidroc was scowling, too; Ceorl's words had a horrid feel of probability to them.

The soldiers of Plegmund's Brigade had to march hard to keep up with the advancing behemoths. "Bastards would slow down a little for their own kind," Sidroc grumbled.

"Maybe," Werferth said. "But maybe not, too. Getting there fast counts in this business."

War had already swept its red-hot rake over the countryside, swept it coming and going. All the villages had been fought over, most of them twice, some, by their look, more often than that. The Unkerlanter soldiers based in the ruined villages seemed astonished to find King Mezentio's men moving forward once more.

Astonished or not, the Unkerlanters fought hard. From everything Sidroc had seen, they always did. But footsoldiers without behemoths were at a great disadvantage facing footsoldiers with them. Sidroc had already had his nose rubbed in that lesson. Before long, and at small cost, they cleared several villages, one after the other.

"Forward!" shouted the Algarvian officers attached to Plegmund's Brigade. "Forward!" shouted the officers who led the behemoths. Across the snowy fields, Sidroc saw Algarvian footsoldiers moving forward, too.

"We've doubled back around the Unkerlanters," he said in considerable excitement. "If we can cut them off, we'll give 'em a good kick in the arse."

"Thanks, Marshal Sidroc," Ceorl said. "I'm sure you'll be telling King Mezentio where to go and what to do one fine day."

"I'll tell you where to go and what to do when the powers below drag you down there," Sidroc retorted.

And that was plenty to set Ceorl off. "Don't you talk to me like that, you son of a whore," he snarled. "You talk to me like that, I'll cut your fornicating heart out and eat it with onions."

Back in the Brigade's training camp, Ceorl had frightened the whey out of Sidroc. He was a robber, likely a murderer, and Sidroc had led a quiet, prosperous life till the war turned everything on its head. But a lot had changed since the Brigade came to Unkerlant. Sidroc had seen and done things every bit as dreadful as anything Ceorl had done. He looked at the ruffian and said, "Come ahead. I'll give you all you want."

Ceorl snarled again and grabbed for his knife. "Stop that, you stupid buggers, or you'll answer to the redheads," Sergeant Werferth growled. "After we win the war, you two can do whatever you want to each other, and I won't care a fart's worth. Till then, you're stuck with each other."

Sidroc kept his hand on his own knife hilt till he saw Ceorl lower his. As the Forthwegians marched on, he kept watching his countryman. In spite of Werferth's order, he didn't trust Ceorl. Ceorl was watching him, too. The way he watched reassured Sidroc—it wasn't contemptuous, but a look that said Ceorl had something to worry about, and knew it.

Werferth was watching both of them. "Powers above, you lackwits, show some sense," he said after about half a mile. "What's the point in going after each other when the Unkerlanters are liable to do worse to you than either one of you could dream of?"

That held an unpleasant amount of sense. Sidroc saw as much at once. For a wonder, Ceorl saw it, too. The frozen, twisted corpses lying in the snow they passed made it easier for Werferth to get his point across.

Someone up ahead shouted and pointed. There were more Unkerlanters, tramping south across the plains. They had a few behemoths with them, but only a few. Officers' whistles squealed in Plegmund's Brigade and among the Algarvians. The same order rang out among them all: "Forward!"

Swemmel's men, intent on their retreat, didn't notice the attack developing against their flank till too late. Sidroc soon discovered why: they were falling back under pursuit from the north. Eggs burst among them, kicking up puffs of snow and knocking over footsoldiers and a couple of behemoths. One of the behemoths, to his disappointment, scrambled back to its feet, though without most of its crew.

His comrades and he flopped down in the snow and started blazing at the Unkerlanters. The Algarvian behemoths plastered them with more eggs. Beams from heavy sticks seared three Algarvian behemoths in quick succession. They also sent up great gouts of steam when they bit into the snow.

"Forward!" the officers cried, and the men of Plegmund's Brigade, along with their Algarvian allies, got up again and rushed toward the enemy.

We're going to get killed, Sidroc thought, even as he slogged through the snow. He'd seen Unkerlanter troops fierce in attack and stubborn in defense. Now, for once, he saw them taken by surprise and panic-stricken. A few of the men in rock-gray tunics stood their ground and blazed at the Algarvians and Forthwegians, but more simply fled. Quite a few threw their hands in the air and surrendered.

"You're a Grelzer?" one of those asked Sidroc as Sidroc stole his weapon and money and food. Unkerlanter and Forthwegian were cousins; Sidroc had no great trouble understanding the question.

"No. Plegmund's Brigade," he answered. That didn't seem to mean anything to the captive. *Well, we'll make it mean something to these whoresons,* Sidroc thought. He gestured with his stick. The Unkerlanter, hands still high, headed north, away from the fighting. Sooner or later, someone would take charge of him. He was far from the only captive who needed to be gathered in.

King Swemmel's soldiers kept running. A few tried to make a stand in a little village in the path of Plegmund's Brigade, but the Forthwegians were so close behind them, they got in among the houses at almost the same time as the Unkerlanters did.

Shrieks from a couple of peasant huts brought howls of delight from the men of the Brigade. "Women!" somebody yelled, as if those screams needed to be identified. Either the local peasants had never left this place or they'd returned, thinking men who fought for Mezentio would never come so far again. If that was what they'd thought, they'd miscalculated.

They'd also given the Forthwegians one more reason to finish off the enemy soldiers in the village as fast as they could. The Unkerlanters wouldn't have lasted long anyhow, not when they were badly outnumbered and unable to form a defensive line. As things were, they vanished as if they had never been.

And then the other hunt was on. By twos and threes, the men of Plegmund's Brigade hammered down the door to every hut in the village.

Only an ancient woman and an even more ancient man stared in horror as Sidroc and Ceorl and another trooper burst into the hut where they'd lived for most if not all of their lives. Ceorl stared in disgust. "You're no cursed good!" he exclaimed, and blazed them both.

But screams and excited shouts from next door sent the men from Plegmund's Brigade rushing over there. Two of their comrades were holding a woman down while a third pumped between her legs. One of the men holding her looked up and said, "Wait your turn, boys. Won't be long—we've all gone without for a long time."

Sidroc took his turn when it came. Back in Gromheort, there were laws against such things. No law here, only winners and losers. The Unkerlanter peasant woman had stopped screaming. Sidroc knelt and thrust and grunted as pleasure shot through him. Then he got to his feet, fixed his drawers, and picked up his stick, which he'd set down for a little while.

Ceorl took his place. He was glad he'd gone before the ruffian; it made him less likely to need a physician's services later on.

Outside, whistles were screeching. Algarvian officers were yelling: "Forward! Come on, you filthy cockhounds!"

Regretfully, Sidroc left the hut. The chilly wind smote him. Sergeant Werferth waved him south and west. "Did you get any?" Sidroc asked.

Werferth nodded. "Wouldn't let it go to waste."

With a nod of his own, Sidroc fell in behind the squad leader. The army was advancing. He'd enjoyed the fruits of victory. War didn't look so bad.

"Another big Algarvian victory near Durrwangen!" a news-sheet vendor shouted to Vanai. "Unkerlanters falling back in disorder!" He waved the sheet, doing his best to tempt her.

"No," she said, and hurried past him toward her block of flats. She had to hurry. She'd been out longer than she'd planned to be. Somehow, time had got away from her. She didn't know how long she would go on looking like a Forthwegian.

Worse, she wouldn't know when she stopped looking like a Forthwegian. She couldn't see the spell that kept her safe. It was for others, not for herself.

She was almost running now. She kept waiting for the cry of, "Kaunian!" to ring out behind her. Oh, her hair was dyed black, but that wouldn't save her once her features shifted.

Only a few more blocks to go—a few more crowded blocks, a few more blocks full of Forthwegians, full of people all too many of whom hated Kaunians. If the Forthwegians hadn't hated Kaunians, how could the Algarvians have done what they'd done to Vanai's people? They couldn't. She knew it only too well.

She imagined she felt the enchantment slipping away. Of course it was imagination; she couldn't feel the enchantment at all, any more than she could see it. But she could feel the fright welling up inside her. If she couldn't renew the spell— if she couldn't renew it *now*—she thought she would go mad. Wait till she got to the flat? It might be too late. Powers above, it might be too late!

And then she let out what was almost a sob of relief. Not the block of flats—not even her street, not yet—but the next best thing: the Forthwegian apothecary's shop whose propri-etor had given her medicine for Ealstan even though, in those days, she'd not only been a Kaunian but looked like one, and who'd passed her spell on to the other Kaunians in Eoforwic.

She had a length of yellow yarn and a length of dark brown in her handbag. She always kept them there against emergencies—but she hadn't thought today would turn out to be an emergency, not when she went outside she hadn't. If the apothecary would let her use a back room for a few minutes, she'd be safe again for hours on end.

When she walked in, he was molding pills in a little metal press. "Good day," he said from behind the high counter. "And how may I help you?"

"Could I please go into some quiet little room?" she asked. "When I come out again, I'll feel much better, much . . . safer." She was pretty sure he already knew she was a Kaunian—who else but a Kaunian would have given him such a spell? Even so, fear made her stop short of coming out and saying it.

But he only smiled and nodded and said, "Of course. Come around behind here and right on into my storeroom. Take as much time as you need. I'm sure you'll look the same when you come out as you do now."

The spell hadn't slipped yet, then. "Powers above bless you!" Vanai exclaimed, and hurried into the room. The apothecary shut the door behind her and, she supposed, went back to grinding pills.

Only a small, dim lamp lit the room. It was full of jars and vials and pots that crowded shelves and one little table set into a back corner. Vanai breathed in a heady mixture of poppy juice and mint and licorice and laurel and camphor and at least half a dozen other odors she couldn't name right away. She took a couple of long, deep breaths and smiled. If she had anything wrong with her lungs, she wouldn't when she came out.

She fished through her handbag—far less convenient than a belt pouch, but Forthwegian women didn't belt their tunics, using them to conceal their figures—till she found the lengths of yarn. She set them on the table, twisting them together, and began her chant.

Because it was in classical Kaunian, a forbidden language in Forthweg these days, she kept her voice very low: she didn't want to endanger the apothecary who'd done so much for her and for Kaunians all over the kingdom. She would have been amazed if he were able to hear her through the door.

Just as she was finishing the cantrip, she distinctly heard him say, "Good day. And how may I help you gentlemen?" Maybe he spoke a little louder than usual to warn her someone else had come into the shop; maybe the wood of the door just wasn't very thick. Either way, she was glad she'd incanted quietly. She waited in the little storeroom, sure the apothecary would let her know when it was safe to come out.

And then one of the newcomers said, "You are someone who knows of the filthy magics the Kaunian scum make to disguise themselves." He spoke fluent Forthwegian, but with a trilling Algarvian accent.

"I don't know what you're talking about," the apothecary answered calmly. "Can I interest you in a horehound-and-honey cough elixir? You sound stuffy, and I've just mixed up a new batch."

In the little storeroom, Vanai shivered with terror. She hadn't wanted to bring the man danger by casting her spell too loudly, but she'd brought him worse danger, deadly danger, by asking him to pass it on to her fellow Kaunians. And now the redheads were here, and one jump away from her.

She wanted to jump out from the storeroom and attack them, as if she were the heroine of one of the trashy Forthwegian romances of which she'd read so many while cooped up in the flat. Common sense told her that would only ruin her along with the apothecary. She stayed where she was, hating herself for it.

"You are a whorehound, and a son of a whorehound besides," the Algarvian said. He and his comrade both laughed loudly at his wit. "You are also a lying son of a whorehound, and you are going to pay for it. Come with us right now, and we shall have the truth from you."

"I have given you the truth," the apothecary said.

"You have given us dung, and told us it is perfume," the Algarvian retorted. "Now you come with us, or we blaze you where you stand. Here! Hold! What are you doing?"

"Taking a pill," the apothecary said, his voice easy and relaxed. "I've been getting over the grippe. Let me swallow it down, and I am yours."

"You are ours, all right. Now we have you in our grip." Mezentio's man, along with his other depravities, fancied himself a punster.

"I go with you under protest, for you are seizing an innocent man," the apothecary said.

That sent both Algarvians into gales of laughter. Vanai leaned forward and ever so cautiously pressed her ear to the door. Receding footsteps told her of the redheads' departure with their captive. She didn't hear the front door slam behind them. The Algarvians wouldn't care who plundered the shop, while the apothecary, bless him, was giving her a way to slip off without drawing notice to herself.

She waited. Then she opened the door the tiniest crack and peered out. Not seeing anyone, she darted out from behind the counter and into the front part of the shop, as if she were an ordinary customer. Then, as casually as she could, she left the place and strode out onto the street.

Nobody asked her what she was doing coming out of the shop bare minutes after a couple of Algarvians had hauled away the proprietor. Nobody paid her any heed at all, in fact. A good-sized crowd had gathered down at the end of the block.

Confident now that she would keep on looking Forthwegian, Vanai hurried over to find out what was going on. She saw two redheads in the middle of the crowd: they overtopped the Forthwegians around them by several inches. One of them said, "We did not touch him, by the powers above! He just fell over."

She'd heard that voice in the apothecary's shop. The Algarvian wasn't punning now. His partner bent down, disappearing from Vanai's view. A moment later, he spoke in his own language: "He's dead."

The day was cool and gloomy, but sunshine burst in Vanai. She didn't know, but she would have bet her life what the apothecary had taken had nothing to do with the grippe. The Algarvians reached the same conclusion a heartbeat later.

They both started cursing in their own language. "He cheated us, the stinking bugger!" cried the one who'd done all the talking in Forthwegian.

"If he weren't already dead, I'd kill him for that," the other one answered.

The one who did the talking in Forthwegian started waving his arms. That got him attention, not least because he held a short, deadly looking stick in his right hand. "Go away!" he shouted. "This criminal, this dog who hid Kaunians, has escaped our justice, but the fight against the menace of the blonds goes on."

Vanai wondered how many in the crowd were sorcerously disguised Kaunians like herself. Because the Forthwegian majority left without a word of protest, she couldn't stay. She had to act as it she were a person who despised her own kind. It left her sick inside, even as she realized she had no choice.

She had to walk past the apothecary's shop on the way back to her block of flats. People were already going in and starting to clean the place out. Vanai wanted to scream at them, but would good would that do? Again, none at all. It would only draw the Algarvians' notice, the one thing she couldn't afford, the thing the apothecary had kept from happening.

"He's dead because of what I did," she said to Ealstan when he came home that evening. "How do I live with that?"

"He'd want you to," Ealstan answered. "He killed himself so Mezentio's men couldn't pry anything about you out of him—and so they couldn't torment him, of course."

"But they wouldn't have had anything to torment him about if it weren't for me," Vanai said.

"And if it weren't for you and it weren't for him, how many Kaunians who are still alive would be dead now?" her husband returned.

It was a good question. It had no good answer. No matter how obvious its truth, Vanai still felt terrible. And she had an argument of her own: "He shouldn't have died for what he did. He should be a hero. He *is* a hero."

"Not to the Algarvians," Ealstan said.

"A pestilence take the Algarvians!" Vanai glared at him, starting to get really angry. "They're evil, nothing else."

"They would say the same about Kaunians. A lot of Forthwegians would say the same about Kaunians," Ealstan replied. "They really believe it. I used to think they knew they were doing wrong. I'm not so sure anymore."

"That doesn't make it any better," Vanai snapped. "If anything, that makes it worse. If they can't tell the difference between right and wrong . . ."

"It makes it more complicated," Ealstan said. "The more I look at things, the more complicated they get." His mouth twisted. "I wonder if your magic would work on Ethelhelm."

"If it did, maybe he wouldn't have to sell himself to the Algarvians any more." Vanai drummed her fingers on the table. "I suppose you're going to tell me that's complicated, too."

"I sometimes have some sympathy for him," Ealstan answered. "He tried to make a little bargain with the redheads, and—"

Vanai pounced. "And he found out you can't make a little bargain with evil."

Ealstan thought about that. Slowly, he nodded. "Maybe you're right. Ethelhelm would say you were."

"I should hope so," Vanai said. "When you're a mouse, there's nothing complicated about a hawk." She stared a challenge at Ealstan. He didn't argue with her, which was one of the wiser things he'd done, or hadn't done, since they were married.

Cornelu thought no one could possibly hate the Algarvians more than he did. They'd invaded and occupied his kingdom. Powers above, they'd invaded and occupied his wife. But the two men who met him at the leviathan pen in Setubal harbor gave him pause.

They stared at him out of chilly, gray-blue eyes. "You look too much like one of Mezentio's men," one of them said in Lagoan spoken with a rather mushy Valmieran accent.

He drew himself up with all the dignity he had. "I am of

Sibiu," he replied. "This for Mezentio's men." He spat on the timbers of the pier.

"Some Sibians fight side by side with Algarve," the other Valmieran said. "Some Sibians . . ." He spoke too rapidly for Cornelu to follow.

Whatever it was, the tone made him bristle. Switching to classical Kaunian, he said, "Perhaps you will explain yourself, sir, in a language with which I am more familiar than that of this kingdom. Or perhaps you will apologize for what certainly sounded as if it might be a slur against my own homeland."

"I apologize for nothing," the second Valmieran said in the language of his imperial ancestors. "I spoke nothing but the truth: some of your countrymen, in Algarvian service, go forward because some of my fellow Kaunians were murdered to make magic against the Unkerlanters."

Cornelu started to let his temper slip. But then he checked himself. Sibiu was occupied, aye. The kingdom was sad and hungry and grim. He'd seen it for himself after his leviathan was killed off his home island of Tirgoviste, seen it till he could escape again. He had no doubt that a good many Sibians known to be unfriendly to King Mezentio no longer remained among the living. But the Valmieran was right: Mezentio's minions hadn't started massacring Sibians, as they had Kaunians from Forthweg.

He bowed and spoke one word: "Algarve." Then he spat again.

The Valmierans looked at each other. Grudgingly, the one who'd accused Cornelu of looking too much like one of Mezentio's men said, "It could be that even men with red hair can hate Algarve."

Lagoas was a land of mostly redhaired folk. Somehow, the Valmieran exiles seemed not to have noticed that. Still speaking classical Kaunian—his Lagoan remained bad, and Sibian, being so close to Algarvian, would have set their teeth on edge if they understood it—Cornelu said, "I shall take you across the Strait of Valmiera. Help your countrymen resist."

That last was a barb of its own. A lot of Valmierans, nobles and commoners alike, *weren't* resisting but acquiescing in Algarvian rule. By the way the two exiles flinched, they knew it too well. Jelgava was the same way; Cornelu had brought home a sorcerously disguised Kuusaman who was stirring up trouble there.

"Let us be off," the first Valmieran said. "Enough talk back and forth."

"That is well said," Cornelu answered. It was, as far as he was concerned, the first thing these supercilious blonds had said well. One could see why the Algarvians . . . He shook his head. He didn't want his thoughts gliding down that ley line, even in annoyance.

He slapped the surface of the water in the leviathan pen. That let the beast know who he was and that he was allowed, even required, to be here. Had he got into the water without the slaps, the leviathan might have recognized him; they'd been working together for a while now. Had the arrogant Valmierans got into the water without the recognition signal, their end would have been swift and unpleasant.

Up to the surface came the leviathan. It pointed its long, toothy snout at Cornelu and let out a surprisingly shrill squeak. He patted the slick, smooth skin, then reached into a bucket on the pier and tossed it a couple of fish. They disappeared as if they had never been, fast enough to make anyone watching glad the leviathan was tame and well trained.

Smiling an unpleasant smile, Cornelu threw the beast another mackerel. As its great teeth closed on the tidbit, he turned that smile on the Valmierans he was to ferry across the strait and back to their own kingdom. "Shall we go, gentlemen?" he asked as he slid down into the water.

They looked at each other before answering. At last, one of them said, "Aye," and they both got in.

They weren't leviathan-riders; if Cornelu had to guess, he would have said they'd never done this before, not even once. He had to show them how to secure themselves in harness, and how to lie still along the leviathan's back and not give the beast even inadvertent signals. "It would be unfortunate if you did that," he remarked.

"How unfortunate?" one of the Valmierans asked.

"That depends," Cornelu replied. "You might live. On the other hand . . ." He was exaggerating, but he didn't want his passengers annoying or confusing the leviathan.

When he was sure everything was ready, he waved to the Lagoans who handled the nets that formed the pen. They waved back and let down one side; the leviathan swam out of the pen and into the harbor channel that led to the sea.

Cornelu wasn't quite so happy as usual to be leaving Setubal. The reason for that was simple: he wasn't alone with his thoughts, as he so often was on leviathanback, and as he craved to be. He had company, and not the best of company, either.

They weren't seamen, despite the rubber suits and spells that kept them from freezing or drowning in the chilly waters of the Strait of Valmiera. And they *were* Valmieran nobles, which meant that to them even a minor noble of Algarvic blood like Cornelu wasn't far removed from a savage hunting wild boar in the forest. They kept talking about him in Valmieran. He didn't speak it, but enough words were recognizably similar to their classical Kaunian ancestors for him to have no trouble figuring out they weren't paying him compliments.

By the powers above, Valmiera deserved to have the Algarvians run over it, Cornelu thought. If Mezentio's men were only a little smarter, they might have slaughtered all the nobles there—and even more so in Jelgava—and won the commoners to them forever. But they hadn't. They'd worked through the nobles who would work with them and replaced others with men more cooperative but no less nasty. And so both kingdoms still had rebellions simmering against the occupiers.

Maybe these fellows would help bring the rebellion in Valmiera from simmer to boil. That would be good; it would distract the Algarvians from their even bigger troubles elsewhere. But Cornelu wouldn't have bet much above a copper on it. He didn't want anything to do with them. Why would anyone with a dram of sense in their own kingdom think any different?

He knew nothing but relief when he saw the coast of the Derlavaian mainland crawl up over the horizon. It had been an easy trip across the Strait: no enemy ley-line ships, no leviathans, only a couple of dragons off in the distance—and neither of their dragonfliers had spotted the leviathan.

"Is this the place where you are to land us?" one of the Valmierans demanded. "Are you sure this is the place where you are to land us?" He sounded as if he didn't think Cornelu could find his way across the street, let alone across a hundred miles of ocean.

"By the landmarks, by the configuration of the ley lines, this is the place where I am to land you," the leviathan-rider answered with such patience as he could muster. "Swim to shore and twist the Algarvians' tails for them."

The two blonds struck out awkwardly toward the land a couple of hundred yards away. Cornelu would go no closer, for fear of beaching his leviathan. The Valmierans couldn't drown, no matter how hard they tried, not with the spells laid on them. If they had to, they would walk across the seabottom to the shore, breathing as if they were fish. Cornelu felt a little guilty about not wishing them good luck, but only a little.

They didn't bring him any luck, not on the way back to Setubal. An Algarvian dragonflier spotted his leviathan and dropped a couple of eggs close enough to it to panic the beast—and very nearly close enough to hurt or kill it. The leviathan swam at random, deep underwater, till at last it had to surface once more.

That might have been the best thing it could have done. When it did spout, the dragon was far away; the Algarvian aboard it must have assumed that Cornelu would run straight south for Setubal. And so he might have, but he hadn't anything to do with it. The leviathan had swum almost due west—in the direction of Algarve itself. Cornelu would have loved to attack Mezentio's land, but he had no weapons with which to do it, not this time.

He regained control over the leviathan during its next dive, and did manage to lead it away from the Algarvian dragon. The search spirals the dragon flew worked against it this time, carrying it farther and farther from Cornelu. At last, when he was sure the dragonflier couldn't possibly see him, he waved a courteous good-bye. It was a relieved good-bye, too. He hesitated to admit that, even to himself.

About halfway across the Strait, he spied a great many dragons ahead. That meant only one thing: the Lagoans and Algarvians were fighting at sea. On a leviathan not carrying eggs, Cornelu should have stayed away. He knew that. He could do nothing. But the spectacle of the fight would be riveting in itself. He steered the leviathan toward it.

A Lagoan ley-line cruiser was engaging two lighter, swifter Algarvian vessels. They tossed eggs at one another and blazed away with sticks that drew their sorcerous energy from the world's grid over which the ships traveled: sticks far larger and heavier and more powerful than any that could have been made mobile on land.

More eggs fell from the dragons overhead. But they couldn't swoop to drop them with deadly accuracy, as they might have against footsoldiers. Those potent sticks would have blazed them out of the sky had they dared. And so the dragons wheeled and fought among themselves high above the bigger fray on the surface of the sea. The eggs their dragonfliers dropped churned the Strait, but few struck home.

Someone aboard the Lagoan cruiser spotted Cornelu atop his leviathan. A stick swung his way with terrifying speed. "No, you fools, I'm a friend!" he shouted, which of course did no good at all.

The beam missed, but not by much. A patch of ocean perhaps fifty yards from the leviathan turned all at once to steam, with a noise as of a red-hot iron behemoth suddenly falling into the sea. The leviathan didn't know that was dangerous. Cornelu did. He urged the beast into a dive and took it away from the fight he shouldn't have approached.

When he got back to Setubal, he learned the cruiser had sunk, as had one of its Algarvian foes. The other, badly damaged, was limping toward home with more Lagoan ships in pursuit. No one really owned the Strait. Cornelu doubted anyone would, not till the Derlavaian War was as good as won. Till then, both sides would keep struggling over it.

A new man in Istvan's squad, a fellow named Hevesi, came up to the front from regimental headquarters with orders to be alert because of a possible Unkerlanter attack and with gossip that had his hazel eyes bugging out of his head. "You'll never guess, Sergeant," he said to Istvan after relaying the order. "By the stars, you couldn't guess if you tried for the next five years."

"Well, you'd better tell me, then," Istvan said reasonably.

"Aye, speak up," Szonyi agreed. Safe behind a timber rampart, he stood up to show that he towered over Hevesi, as he did over most people. "Speak up before somebody decides to tear the words out of you."

"Anything new would be welcome in this dreary wilderness," Corporal Kun added. The rest of the soldiers crowded toward Hevesi so they could hear, too.

He grinned, pleased at the effect he'd created. "No need to get pushy," he said. "I'll talk. I'm glad to talk, to spit it out." He spoke with the accent of the northeastern mountain provinces of Gyongyos, an accent so much like Istvan's that he might have come from only a few valleys away.

When he still didn't start talking right away, Szonyi loomed over him and rumbled, "Out with it, little man."

Hevesi wasn't so little as all that. But he was a good-natured fellow, and didn't get angry, as many Gyongyosians might have. "All right." For dramatic effect, he lowered his voice to not much more than a whisper: "I hear that, up a couple of regiments north of us, they burned three men for—goat-eating."

Everyone who heard him exclaimed in horror. But Hevesi didn't know his comrades were expressing two different kinds of horror. Istvan hoped he never found out, either. Eating goat's flesh was the worst abomination Gyongyos recognized. Istvan and several of his comrades knew the sin from the inside out. If anyone but Captain Tivadar ever discovered that they knew, they were doomed. Some of their horror was disgust at themselves, some a fear others might learn what they'd done.

"How did they come to do that?" asked Lajos, who'd already shown more interest in goats and goat's flesh than Istvan was comfortable with.

"They overran one of those little forest villages you stumble across every once in a while," Hevesi answered. Istvan nodded. He and his squad had overrun such a village himself, and doubted if any mountain valley in all of Gyongyos were so isolated. Hevesi went on, "The accursed Unkerlanters keep goats, of course. And these three just slaughtered one and roasted it and ate of the flesh." He shuddered.

"Of their own free will?" Kun asked. "Knowingly?"

"By the stars, they did," Hevesi said.

Kun bared his teeth in what was anything but a smile. In the tones of a man passing sentence, he said, "I expect they deserved it, then."

"Aye." Istvan could speak with conviction, too. "If they did it and they knew what they were doing, that sets them beyond the pale. There might be some excuse for letting them live if they didn't." He wouldn't look at the scar on his hand, but he could feel the blood pulsing through it.

"I don't know that it really much matters, Sergeant. If they ate goat . . ." Hevesi drew his thumb across his throat.

"By the stars, that's right," Lajos said. "No excuse for that sort of filthy business. None." He spoke with great certainty.

"Well, there are those who would tell you you're right, and plenty of 'em," Istvan said, wishing with all his heart that Hevesi had come back to his squad with any other gossip but that. The way things looked, he would never be able to escape from goat-eating and stories about goat-eating as long as he lived.

"What was that?" Szonyi suddenly pointed east. "Did you hear something from the Unkerlanters?"

The question made soldiers separate as fast as Hevesi's gossip had brought them together. Men snatched up their sticks and scrambled off to loopholes and good blazing positions. Istvan wouldn't have thought that standing on the defensive came naturally to the warrior race the Gyongyosians prided themselves on being. But they'd seemed willing enough to give the Unkerlanters the initiative; by all the signs, they'd never quite known what to do with it themselves.

After an anxious pause here, they relaxed. "Looks like you were wrong," Istvan told Szonyi.

"Aye. Looks like I was. Doesn't break my heart." Szonyi's broad shoulders went up and down in a shrug.

Kun said, "Better to be alert about something that isn't there than to miss something that is."

"That's right," Istvan said gravely. The three veterans, and a couple of other men in the squad, nodded with more solemnity than the remark might have deserved. Istvan suspected Szonyi hadn't heard anything whatsoever out of the ordinary. He had managed to get Hevesi and the rest of the squad to stop talking about—more important, to stop thinking about—the abomination of goat-eating, though, and that, as far as Istvan was concerned, was all to the good.

Kun might have been thinking along with him. Behind the lenses of his spectacles, his eyes slid toward Szonyi. "Sometimes you're not as foolish as you look," he remarked, and then spoiled it by adding, "Sometimes, of course, you bloody well are."

"Thanks," Szonyi said. "Thanks ever so much. I'll remember you in my nightmares."

"Enough," Istvan said. "I've had enough of saying, 'Enough,' to the two of you."

And then he made a sharp chopping motion with his right hand, urging Szonyi and Kun and the rest of the squad to silence. Somewhere in the woods out in front of them, a twig had snapped—not an imaginary one like Szonyi's, but unquestionably real. There was plenty of snow and ice out there; its weight sometimes broke great boughs. Those sharp reports could panic a regiment. This one might have been something like that, but smaller. Or it might have been an Unkerlanter making a mistake.

"What do you think, Sergeant?" Kun's voice was a thin thread of whisper.

Istvan's shrug barely moved one shoulder. "I think we'd better find out." He made a little gesture that could be seen from the side but not from ahead. "Szonyi, with me."

"Aye, Sergeant," Szonyi said. Istvan could hear the answer. He didn't think any of Swemmel's men would be able to, even if they were just on the other side of the redoubt.

Kun looked offended. Istvan didn't care. Kun was a good soldier. Szonyi was a better one, especially moving forward. But then, instead of getting angry, Kun said something sensible: "Let me use my little sorcery. That will tell you if anyone's out there before you go."

After a couple of heartbeats' thought, Istvan nodded. "Aye. Go ahead. Do it."

The charm was very simple. If it hadn't been very simple, the former mage's apprentice wouldn't have been able to use it. When he was done, he said one word: "Somebody."

"There would be." Istvan gestured to Szonyi. "Let's go find out. The idea is to come back, understand, not just to disappear out there."

"I'm not stupid," Szonyi answered. Istvan wasn't altogether sure that was true, but he didn't argue.

They left the redoubt to the rear, shielded from the enemy's sight—and from his sticks—by the snow-covered logs piled up in front. Istvan gestured to the left. Szonyi nodded. Both the gesture and the nod were small, all but unnoticeable. In their white smocks, Istvan and Szonyi might have been a couple of moving drifts of snow. Istvan felt cold as a snowdrift.

But, even as he muttered inaudibly to himself about that, he also felt like a proper warrior again. He wondered about that. It perplexed him. Saying it alarmed him wouldn't have been far shy of the mark, either. He'd seen enough fighting to last him a lifetime, probably two. Why go looking for more?

Because that's what I've been trained to do, he thought, but that wasn't the whole answer, or even any great part of it.

Because if I don't go looking for it, it'll come looking for me. At that, he nodded again, though he was careful to keep the hood of his smock low and expose none of his face to an enemy's beam.

He knew what he was doing in the snow. He'd had enough practice in it, after all; his home valley was worse in winter than these woods ever dreamt of being. He got within five or six feet of an ermine before it realized he was there. He'd spotted it by the triangle of black dots that marked its eyes and nose and the black spot at the very tip of its tail that never went white in winter. It drew back in sudden horror when it spied or scented him, baring a pink mouth full of needle teeth. Then it scurried behind a tree trunk and vanished.

Istvan followed it, not in any real pursuit but because that beech also gave him cover from the east. The ermine, by then, was gone, only tiny tracks in the snow showing where it had run.

Szonyi had found cover behind a pine not far away. He glanced toward Istvan, who paused for a moment, taking his bearings. Then Istvan pointed in the direction from which he thought the suspicious noise had come. Szonyi considered, then nodded. They both crawled forward again.

Now they advanced separately, each one taking his own path to the target. *If something happens to me, Szonyi will get back with the word,* Istvan thought. He hoped the converse was in Szonyi's mind. He hoped even more that the two of them were right.

Have to be close now, went through his mind a few minutes later. He looked around for Szonyi, but didn't see him. He refused to let that worry him. Despite the stories told, silently killing a man wasn't that easy. Had something gone wrong, he would have heard the struggle. So he told himself, at any rate.

He started to come out from behind a birch, then froze in the sense of not moving as opposed to the sense of being cold. In the snow in front of the tree were tracks—not the little marks of an ermine, but those of a man on snowshoes. The

Unkerlanters were very fond of snowshoes, and Istvan didn't think any of his own folk had come this way lately.

A scout, he thought. *Doesn't look like more than one man. Just a scout, snooping around to see what we're up to.* That wasn't so bad. He vastly preferred it to coming across the forerunners of a brigade about to sweep down on him. Maybe the rumor of attack Hevesi had brought was nothing but a rumor. *The Unkerlanters have as much trouble putting enough men into this fight as we do. Different reasons, but as much trouble.*

No sooner had that thought crossed his mind than the Unkerlanter soldier came out from behind a tree a couple of hundred yards away. Istvan got only a glimpse—other trees blocked his view and gave him hardly any chance for a good blaze.

He wasn't too inclined to take one anyhow; he had more sympathy for Swemmel's men than he'd had when the war was new. But, a moment later, the Unkerlanter crumpled with a yowl of pain—Szonyi, evidently, had a better spot and less sympathy. "Back now!" Istvan called, and headed off toward the redoubt. If Swemmel's men had hoped to catch the Gyongyosians hereabouts napping, they'd just been disappointed.

Captured by the Algarvians the summer before, retaken by Unkerlant only a couple of months earlier, the starting point from which Marshal Rathar had sent out his attacking columns to ravage the redheads further, Durrwangen was under Algarvian attack again.

Now that it was too late to do him any good, Rathar understood the lesson Mezentio's men had taught him. "We just pushed them back here and there," he said to General Vatran. "We didn't pinch in behind them and destroy them, the way they did to us so many times."

"You wanted to make them fight in front of rivers and such," Vatran said. "We thought they were panicked, or else turning coward, when they wouldn't stand and fight, but fell back instead."

"Never trust an Algarvian retreat," Rathar said solemnly—mournfully, when you got down to it. "They saved their men, they concentrated them—and then they went and hit us with them."

"Disgraceful, deceitful thing to go and do," Vatran said, as if the Algarvians had pulled off some underhanded trick instead of one of the more brilliant counterattacks Rathar had ever seen. He would have appreciated it even more had it not been aimed at him.

"We were almost up to Hagenow," he said, pointing to the map. His voice grew more mournful still. "We'd driven east all the way up to the border of Grelz. And then, curse them, the redheads bit back." He kicked at the floor of the battered bank that housed his headquarters. "I knew they'd try. I didn't think they could bite so hard, or with such sharp teeth."

As if to underscore that, more eggs burst in Durrwangen, some of them close to the headquarters. He didn't have to worry about splinters of glass flying through the air like shining knives to pierce him; by now, he doubted whether any building in Durrwangen kept glazed windows. He knew perfectly well that the headquarters didn't.

"Shall we go down to the vault?" Vatran asked.

"Oh, very well." Rathar's voice was testy. He seldom suggested such a thing himself; he was too proud for that. But he wasn't too proud to acknowledge common sense when he heard it.

Down in the vault, everyone—commanders, subordinate officers, runners, crystallomancers, secretaries, cooks, what have you—was crowded together as tightly as sardines in a tin. People didn't even have oil to lubricate the spaces between them. They elbowed one another, trod on one another's toes, breathed in one another's faces, and, without intending to at all, generally made themselves as unpleasant for one another as they could.

Above them, around them, the ground shuddered as if in torment. And that was only from the sorcerous energy the Algarvian eggs released when they burst. If Mezentio's mages decided to start killing Kaunians ... Turning to Vatran,

Rathar asked, "Are our special sorcerous countermeasures in place?"

Special sorcerous countermeasures was a euphemism for the peasants and condemned criminals Unkerlanters had available and ready to slay to blunt Algarvian magics and to power spells against the redheads. Rathar was no more comfortable than anyone else—always excluding King Swemmel, whose many vices did not include hypocrisy—about calling murder by its right name.

Vatran nodded. "Aye, lord Marshal. If they try and bring the roof down around our ears with magecraft, we can try to hold it up the same way."

"Good," Rathar said, though he was anything but sure it was. He wished the Algarvians hadn't turned loose the demon of slaughter. It might have won them the war if Swemmel hadn't been so quick to adopt it for his own, but Swemmel, as he'd proved in the Twinkings War, would do anything survival called for. Now both sides slaughtered, and neither gained much by it.

More eggs fell, these closer still. Ysolt the cook, who'd been steady as a rock in the cave by the Wolter River even when the fighting for Sulingen was at its worst, let out a shriek that tore at Rathar's eardrums. "We'll all be killed," she blubbered. "Every last one of us killed." Rathar wished he were convinced she was wrong.

And then Vatran asked him a truly unwelcome question: "If they try to throw us out of Durrwangen, can we stop 'em?"

"If they come straight at us out of the north, aye, we can," Rathar replied. But that wasn't exactly what the general had asked. "If they try to flank us out . . . I just don't know."

Vatran replied with what the whole Derlavaian War had proved: "They're cursed good at flanking maneuvers."

Before Rathar could say anything to that, Ysolt started screaming again. "Be silent!" he roared in a parade-ground voice, and the cook, for a wonder, *was* silent. He wished once more, this time that he could control the Algarvians so easily. Since he couldn't, he answered Vatran, "Up until a few days ago, I was hoping for a late thaw this spring, so we could grab all we could before everything slowed to a crawl. Now I'm hoping for an early one, to do half—powers above, more than half—our fighting for us."

Vatran's chuckle was wheezy. "Oh, aye, Marshal Mud's an even stronger master than Marshal Winter."

"*Curse* the Algarvians," Rathar ground out. "We had them on the run. I never dreamt I was fighting circus acrobats who could turn a somersault and then come forward as fast as they'd gone back."

"Life is full of surprises," Vatran said dryly. An egg burst close enough to the headquarters to add a deafening emphasis to that. Chunks of plaster slid between the boards that shored up the ceiling and came down on people's heads. Ysolt started screaming again, and she wasn't the only one. Some of the cries were contralto, others bass.

And, at that most inauspicious moment, a crystallomancer shouted, "Lord Marshal, sir! His Majesty would speak to you from Cottbus!"

Rathar had a long list of people to whom he would sooner have spoken than Swemmel just then. Having such a list did him no good whatever, of course. "I'm coming," he said, and then had to elbow his way through the insanely crowded vault to get to the crystal.

When he did, the crystallomancer murmured into it, presumably to his colleague back in Cottbus. A moment later, Swemmel's long, pale face appeared in the crystal. He glared out at Rathar. Without preamble, he said, "Lord Marshal, we are not pleased. We are, in fact, far from pleased."

"Your Majesty, I am far from pleased, too," Rathar said. Another handful of eggs burst on Durrwangen, surely close enough to the headquarters for Swemmel to hear them through the crystal. In case he didn't recognize them for what they were, Rathar added, "I'm under attack here."

"Aye. That is why we are not pleased," Swemmel answered. Rather's safety meant nothing to him. The disruption of his plans counted for far more. "We ordered you to attack, not to be attacked."

"You ordered me to attack in every direction at once, your

Majesty," Rathar said. "I obeyed you. Now do you see that an attack in every direction is in fact an attack in no direction at all?"

Swemmel's eyebrows rose in surprise, then came down in anger. "Do you presume to tell us how to conduct our war?"

"Isn't that why you pay me, your Majesty?" Rathar returned. "If you want a cake, you hire the best cook you can."

"And what sort of sour, burnt thing do you set on the table before us?" Swemmel demanded.

"The kind you ordered," Rathar said, and waited. Swemmel was more likely to make the roof cave in on him than were Algarvian eggs.

"You blame us for the debacle of Unkerlant's arms?" the king said. "How dare you? We did not send the armies out to defeat. You did."

"Aye, so I did," Rathar agreed. "I sent them out according to your plan, at your order, and against my better judgment—the Algarvians were not so weak as you supposed, and they have proved it. If you put sour milk, rancid butter, and moldy flour into a cake, it will not be fit to eat. If you joggle an officer's elbow when he tries to fight an army, the fighting it gives you will not be what you had in mind, either."

Swemmel's eyes opened very wide. He wasn't used to frank speech from those who served him, not least because of the horrible things that often happened after someone was rash enough to speak his mind. In most of the things that went on at court, whether Swemmel heard the truth or a pleasing lie mattered little in the grand scheme of things. But in matters military, that wasn't so. Bad advice and bad decisions in the war against Algarve could—and nearly had—cost him his kingdom.

For years, then, Rathar had used frankness as a weapon and a shield. He knew the weapon might burst in his hand one day, and wondered if this would be that day. Vatran would handle things reasonably well if he got the sack. There were some other promising officers. He hoped Swemmel would grant him the quick mercy of the axe and not be so angry as to boil him alive.

It had got very quiet inside the vault. Everyone was staring at the small image of the king. Rathar realized, more slowly than he should have, that King Swemmel might not be satisfied with his head alone. He might destroy everyone at the headquarters. Who was there to tell him he could not, he should not? No one at all.

Next to Swemmel's wrath, the eggs bursting all around were indeed small tubers. Swemmel could, if he chose, wreck his realm in a moment of fury. The Algarvians couldn't come close to that, no matter how hard they tried.

Rathar couldn't help feeling fear. He stolidly refused to show it: in that, too, he differed from most of the king's courtiers. After a long, long pause, Swemmel said, "We suppose you will tell us now that, if we give you your head, you will reverse all this at the snap of a finger and swear by the powers above to preserve Durrwangen against the building Algarvian attack?"

"No, your Majesty," Rathar said at once. "I'll fight for this town. I'll fight hard. But we stretched ourselves too thin, and Mezentio's men are the ones on the move right now. They can't just break into Durrwangen, but they may be able to flank us out of it."

"Curse them," Swemmel snarled. "Curse them all. We live for the day we can hurl their sovereign into the soup pot."

At least he wasn't talking about hurling Rathar into the soup pot. The marshal said, "They may retake Durrwangen. Or, as I told you, we may yet hold them out of it till spring comes, and the spring thaw with it. But even if they do take it, your Majesty, they can't possibly hope to do anything more till summer."

"So you say." But the king didn't call Rathar a liar. Swemmel had called Rathar a great many things, but never that. Maybe a reputation for frankness was worth something after all. After muttering something about traitors Rathar was probably lucky not to hear, King Swemmel went on, "Hold Durrwangen if you can. We shall give you the wherewithal to do it, so far as that may be in our power."

"What I can do, I will," Rather promised. Swemmel's image winked out. The crystal flared, then went dark. Rather sighed. He'd survived again.

"Sir?" Leudast came up to Lieutenant Recared as his company commander sat hunched in front of a little fire, toasting a gobbet of unicorn meat over the flames.

"Eh?" Recared turned. His face and voice were still very young, but he moved like an old man these days. Leudast could hardly blame his superior; he felt like an old man himself these days. The lieutenant let out a weary sigh. "What is it, Sergeant?"

"Sir, I was just wondering," Leudast answered. "Have you got any notion of where in blazes we are? We've done so much marching and countermarching, hopping onto this leyline caravan car and off of that one—I wouldn't be sure I'd brought my arsehole along if it weren't attached, if you know what I mean."

That got him a wan smile from Lieutenant Recared, who said, "I wouldn't put it quite that way, but I do know what you mean, aye. And I can even tell you where we are—more or less. We're somewhere south and a little west of Durrwangen. Does it make you happy to know that?"

"Happy? No, sir." Leudast shook his head. One of the earflaps on his far cap flipped up for a moment; he grabbed it and shoved it back into place. The spring thaw was coming. It hadn't got here yet, and nights remained bitterly cold. "We came through this part of the country a while ago. I didn't ever want to see it again. It was ugly to start with, and it hasn't got better since."

Recared smiled again, and added a couple of syllables' worth of chuckle. "There are other reasons for not wanting to see it again, too," he said, "as in, if we had the bit between our teeth instead of the Algarvians, they wouldn't have forced us into defensive positions to try to save Durrwangen again." He cut a piece from the chunk of unicorn meat with his knife and popped it into his mouth. "Powers above, that's good! I don't remember the last time I had anything to eat."

He didn't offer to share, but Leudast wasn't particularly

offended—Recared was an officer, after all. And Leudast wasn't particularly hungry, either; he made a better forager than Recared would be if he lived to be a hundred. The very idea of living to a hundred made Leudast snort. He didn't expect to live through the war, and was amazed he'd been wounded only once.

A few eggs burst, several hundred yards off to the west. "Those are ours, I think," Leudast said. "Anything we can do to make the redheads keep their heads down is fine by me."

"They have to be almost at the end of their tether," Recared said. "Who would have thought they could counterattack at all, the way we drove them north and east through the winter?" His face set in unhappy lines. "They're a formidable people."

He spoke with regret and with genuine if grudging respect. There might have been Unkerlanters who didn't respect Algarvian soldiers after seeing them in action. Leudast hadn't met any, though. He suspected that most of his countrymen who couldn't see what was in front of their noses didn't live long enough to spread their opinions very far.

Felt boots crunched on crusted snow. Leudast whirled, snatching his stick off his back and swinging it in the direction of the sound. "Don't blaze, Sergeant!" an unmistakable Unkerlanter voice called. A trooper—a man of Recared's regiment—came into the small circle of firelight. "I'm looking for the lieutenant."

Recared raised his head. "I'm here, Sindold. What do you need from me?"

"Sir, I've got Captain Gundioc with me here," Sindold answered. "He's commanding a regiment that's just come up out of the west through Sulingen. They'll be going into the line alongside of us, and he wants to know what they'll be up against."

"That's about the size of it," Captain Gundioc agreed, coming forward into the light with Sindold. "I'm new to this business, and so are the soldiers I'm commanding. You've been through the fire; I'll be grateful for anything you can tell me."

He looked like a man who hadn't yet seen combat. His face—strong and serious, with a jutting chin—was well shaven. He wore a thick, clean cloak over his equally clean uniform tunic. Even his boots had only a couple of mud stains on them, and those looked new. He might have been running a foundry or teaching school only a few days before.

"I'll be glad to tell you what I know, sir," Recared answered. "And this is Sergeant Leudast, who has a lot more experience than I do. If you don't mind his sitting in, you can learn from him. I have."

Leudast hid a grin. He knew he'd taught Recared a thing or two; he hadn't been so sure the lieutenant also knew it. Gundioc nodded, saying, "Aye, I'll gladly hear the sergeant. If he's fought and he's alive, he knows things worth knowing."

He may be raw, but he's no fool, Leudast thought. After coughing a couple of times, he said, "The thing to remember about the redheads, sir, is, they think lefthanded a lot of the time. They'll do things we'd never imagine, and they'll make them work. They love to feint and to make flank attacks. They'll look like they're going to hit you one place and then drive it home somewhere else—up your arse, usually."

"All that's true," Recared agreed. "Every word of it. It's also wise not to go right at them. A charge straight for their lines will slaughter the men who make it. Use the ground as best you can. Use feints, too. If it's obvious, they'll wreck it. If it's not, you have a better chance."

"I understand," Gundioc said. "This all strikes me as good advice. But if I'm ordered to go forward and I have inspectors with sticks standing behind my line to make sure I obey, what am I to do?"

Blaze those buggers, Leudast thought. But he couldn't say that aloud, not unless he wanted an inspector blazing him. He glanced over to Recared. If the officer had the privileges of his rank, he also had the obligations, which included answering nasty questions like that. Answer he did, saying, "If you are ordered, you must obey. But men who give such orders often don't live very long in the field. The Algarvians seem to kill them quickly."

Or we can blame it on the Algarvians, anyhow, Leudast thought. He didn't know exactly how many Unkerlanter officers had met with unfortunate accidents from the men they were supposed to be leading. Not enough, probably. One reason the Unkerlanters had suffered such gruesome casualties was that their officers weren't trained so well as their counterparts in Mezentio's service. Another was that, with plenty of men to spend, the Unkerlanters put out fires by throwing bodies on them till they smothered.

Did Gundioc understand what Recared had just told him? If he didn't, maybe he was the sort of officer who'd meet with an accident one fine day. But he did. His eyes narrowed. The lines running down from his nose to his mouth deepened and darkened and filled with shadow. "I . . . see," he said slowly. "That sounds . . . unofficial."

"I haven't the faintest idea what you're talking about, sir," Recared answered.

"Which is probably just as well." Gundioc got to his feet. "Thank you for your time. You've given me a thing or two to think about." He trudged across the snow toward his own regiment.

Leudast went up to his company, not far behind the fighting front. His nose guided him to a pot sizzling above a little fire. A cook ladled bits of turnip and parsnip and chunks of meat into his mess tin. He didn't ask what the meat was. Had he found out, he might have decided he didn't want to eat it, and he was too hungry to take the chance.

"What are the redheads doing?" he asked—the first question anyone with any sense asked on getting near the Algarvians.

"Nothing much, Sergeant, doesn't look like," one of his troopers answered. "Real quiet-like over there."

Suspicion flowered in Leudast. "That's not good," he said. "They're up to something. But what? Will it land on our heads, or will it come down on somebody else?"

"Here's hoping it's somebody else," the soldier said.

"Oh, aye, here's hoping." Leudast's voice was dry. "But hope doesn't milk the cow. We'll send extra pickets forward. If the redheads have got something nasty under their kilts, they'll have to work hard to bring it off."

Even with extra men out in front of the main line, he had trouble going to sleep. He didn't like having raw troops to his left. Their commander seemed smart enough, but how good were his men? What would they do if the Algarvians tested them? He dozed off dreaming about it.

When he woke, he thought he was still in the dream: a soldier shook him awake, shouting, "Sergeant, everything's gone south on the left!"

"What do you mean?" Leudast demanded. Somebody had been saying much the same thing to him in his nightmare.

"The redheads hit that new regiment and broke through, Sergeant," the soldier answered, alarm in his voice. "Now they're trying to swing over and attack us from the flank."

"Aye, that sounds like them." After two sentences, Leudast was fully awake. He started shouting orders: "First squad, third squad, fall back and form a front to the left. Runner! I need a runner!" For a wonder, he got one. "Go back to brigade headquarters and tell them we're under attack from the left."

"Aye, Sergeant!" The runner dashed off.

A couple of squads of Leudast's company weren't the only Unkerlanters trying to stem the Algarvian breakthrough. Recared's other company commanders also used some of their men as a firewall against the redheads. Like him, they were all sergeants who'd seen a lot of fighting; they knew what having Mezentio's men on their flank meant, and how much danger it put them in.

The trouble was, telling who was who in the dark wasn't easy. Some of the men running toward the line Leudast and his comrades desperately tried to form were Unkerlanters from Gundioc's shattered regiment, fleeing the Algarvian onslaught. Others were authentic redheads. They didn't yell "Mezentio!" as they came forward, not now—silence helped them sow confusion.

"If it moves, blaze it!" Leudast shouted to his men. "We'll sort it out later, but we can't let the Algarvians get in among us." That was all the more true—and urgent—because the men he'd pulled out to face left didn't have enough holes in which to hide, and the ones they did have weren't deep enough. If it meant some of his countrymen got blazed, it did, that was all. *And how are you different from the officers you warned Gundioc about?* Leudast wondered. He had no answer, except that he wanted to stay alive.

Someone blazed at him out of the night. The beam hissed as it boiled snow into steam a few feet to his right. He blazed back, and was rewarded with a cry of pain: more to the point, a cry of pain whose words he didn't understand but whose language was undeniably Algarvian. He didn't have to feel personally guilty, not yet.

His runner, or another one from the regiment, must have got through. Eggs started falling where the Algarvians had broken the line. A fresh regiment of Unkerlanter soldiers— all of them shouting, "Urra!" and "Swemmel!"—rushed up to push the redheads back. A couple of troops of behemoths came forward with the reinforcements. Sullenly, the Algarvians withdrew.

After the sun came up, Leudast saw Captain Gundioc's body. He sprawled in the snow with some of his own men and some redheads. Leudast sighed. Gundioc might well have made a good officer with some seasoning. He'd never get it now.

Seven

Wind whipped past Colonel Sabrino's face as his dragon dove on a ley-line caravan coming up into Durrwangen from the south. He didn't know whether the caravan was carrying Unkerlanter soldiers or horses and unicorns or simply sacks of barley and dried peas. He didn't much care, either. Whatever it was carrying would help King Swemmel's men inside Durrwangen—if it got there.

As the dragon stooped like a striking falcon, the caravan swelled from a worm on the ground to a toy to its real size with astonishing speed. "Mezentio!" Sabrino shouted, loosing the eggs slung under his mount's belly. Then he whacked the dragon with his goad to make it pull up. If he hadn't, the stupid thing might have flown itself straight into the ground.

Without the weight of the eggs, it gained height more readily. Behind it, twin flashes of light marked bursts of sorcerous energy. Sabrino looked back over his shoulder. He whooped with glee. He'd knocked the caravan right off the ley line. Whatever it was carrying wouldn't get to Durrwangen any time soon. Flames leaped up from a shattered caravan car. Sabrino whooped again. Some of what that caravan was carrying wouldn't get to Durrwangen at all.

Captain Domiziano's image appeared in the crystal Sabrino carried. "Nicely struck, Colonel!" he cried.

Sabrino bowed in his harness. "I thank you." He looked around. "Now let's see what else we can do to make King Swemmel's boys love us."

No immediately obvious answer sprang to mind. A nice pillar of smoke was rising from the wrecked ley-line caravan now. More smoke, much more, rose from Durrwangen itself. Algarvian egg-tossers and dragons had been pounding the city ever since the late-winter counterattacks pushed this far south. Sabrino hoped his countrymen would be able to break into Durrwangen before the spring thaw glued everything in place for a month or a month and a half. If they didn't, the Unkerlanters would have all that time to fortify the town, and then it would be twice as expensive to take . . . if it could be done at all.

That wasn't anything about which he could do much. He couldn't even drop any more eggs till he flew back to the dragon farm and loaded up again.

"Sir!" That was Domiziano again, his voice cracking with excitement like a youth's. "Look over to the west, sir. A column of behemoths, and curse me if they aren't stuck in a snowdrift."

After looking, Sabrino said, "You have sharp eyes, Captain. I didn't spot those buggers at all. Well, since you did see them, would you like to give your squadron the honor of the first pass against them?"

"My honor, sir, and my pleasure," Domiziano replied. Not all the rank-and-file dragonfliers had crystals; he used hand signals to point them toward the new target. Off they flew, the rest of Sabrino's battered wing trailing them to ward against Unkerlanter dragons and to finish whatever behemoths they might miss.

Sabrino sang a tune that had been popular on the stage in Trapani the year before the Derlavaian War broke out. It was called "Just Routine," and sung by one longtime lover to another. Smashing up columns of Unkerlanter behemoths was just routine for him these days. He'd been doing it ever since Algarve and Unkerlant first collided, more than a year and a half ago now.

Great wingbeats quickly ate up the distance to the behemoths. Sabrino laughed aloud, saying, "So your snowshoes didn't help you this time, eh?" The first winter here in the trackless west had been a nightmare, with the Unkerlanters able to move through snow that stymied Algarvian men and behemoths. Those odds were more even now: experience was a harsh schoolmaster, but an undeniably effective one.

The snow down there didn't seem all that deep. Sabrino had seen drifts that looked like young mountain ranges, drifts into which you could drop a palace, let alone a behemoth. Of course, gauging the ground from above was always risky business. Maybe snow filled a gully, and the behemoths had discovered it the hard way. Still, although they'd halted, they didn't seem to be in any enormous distress.

He frowned. That thought sent suspicion blazing through him. He peered through his goggles, trying to see if anything else about the behemoths looked out of the ordinary. He didn't note anything, not at first.

But then he did. "Domiziano!" he shouted into the crystal. "Pull up, Domiziano! They've all got heavy sticks, and they're waiting for us!"

Usually, dragons took behemoths by surprise, and the men

aboard those behemoths had scant seconds to swing their sticks toward the dragonfliers diving on them. Usually, too, more behemoths carried egg-tossers—useless against dragons—than heavy sticks. Not this column. Swemmel's men had set a trap for Algarvian dragonfliers, and Sabrino's wing was flying right into it.

Before Domiziano and his dragonfliers could even begin to obey Sabrino's orders, the Unkerlanters started blazing at them. The behemoth crews had seen the dragons coming, and had had the time to swing their heavy sticks toward the leaders of the attack. The beams that burst forth from those sticks were bright and hot as the sun.

They struck dragon after dragon out of the sky, almost as a man might swat flies that annoyed him. A heavy stick could burn through the silver paint that shielded dragons' bellies from weapons a footsoldier might carry, or could sear a wing and send a dragon and the man who rode it tumbling to the ground so far below.

Domiziano's dragon seemed to stumble in midair. Sabrino cried out in horror; Domiziano had led a squadron in his wing since the war was new. He would lead it no more. His dragon took another couple of halfhearted flaps, then plummeted. A cloud of snow briefly rose when it smashed to earth: the only memorial Domiziano would ever have.

"Pull up! Pull back!" Sabrino called to his surviving squadron commanders. "Gain height. Even their sticks won't bite if we're high enough—and we can still drop our eggs on them. Vengeance!"

A poor, mean vengeance it would be, with half a dozen dragons hacked down. How many Unkerlanter behemoths made a fair exchange for one dragon, for one highly trained dragonflier? More than were in this column: of that Sabrino was sure.

Another dragon fell as one of his own men proved less cautious than he should have. Sabrino's curses went flat and harsh with despair. Some of his dragonfliers started dropping their eggs too soon, so they burst in front of the Unkerlanters without coming particularly close to them.

But others had more patience, and before long the bursts came among the behemoths, as nicely placed as Sabrino could have wished. When the snow cleared down below, some of the beasts lay on their sides, while others lumbered off in all directions. That was how behemoths should have behaved when attacked by dragons. Even so, Sabrino ordered no pursuit. The Unkerlanters had already done too much damage to his wing, and who could say what other tricks they had waiting?

"Back to the dragon farm," he commanded. No one protested. The Algarvians were all in shock. Not till they'd turned and been flying northeast for some little while did he realize that, for perhaps the first time in the war, the Unkerlanters had succeeded in intimidating him.

Because of that weight of gloom, the flight back to the dragon farm seemed against the wind all the way. When he finally got his dragon down on the ground, Sabrino discovered he *had* been flying against the wind. Instead of endlessly blowing out of the west, it came from the north, and carried warmth and an odor of growing things with it.

"Spring any day now," a dragon handler said as he chained Sabrino's mount to a crowbar driven into the ground. He looked around. "Where's the rest of the beasts, Colonel? Off to a different farm?"

"Dead." Whatever the wind said, Sabrino's voice held nothing but winter. "The Unkerlanters set a snare, and we blundered right into it. And now I have to write Domiziano's kin and tell them how their son died a hero for Algarve. Which he did, but I'd sooner he went on living as a hero instead."

He was writing that letter, and having a tough go of it, when Colonel Ambaldo stuck his head into the tent. Ambaldo was beaming. "We smashed them!" he told Sabrino, who could smell brandy fumes on his breath. With a scornful snap of his fingers, the newcomer from the east went on, "These Unkerlanters, they are not so much of a much. The Lagoans and Kuusamans are ten times the dragonfliers you see here in Unkerlant. We smashed up a couple of squadrons over Durrwangen, and dropped any number of eggs on the town."

"Good for you," Sabrino said tonelessly. "And now, good

my sir, if you will excuse me, I am trying to send my condolences to a fallen flier's family."

"Ah. I see. Of course," Ambaldo said. Had he left the tent then, everything would have been . . . if not fine, then at least tolerably well. But, perhaps elevated by the brandy, he added, "Though how anyone could easily lose men to these Unkerlanter clods is beyond me."

Sabrino rose to his feet. Fixing Ambaldo with a deadly glare, he spoke in a voice chillier than any Unkerlanter winter: "A great many things appear to be beyond you, sir, sense among them. Kindly take your possessions and get them out of this, my tent. You are no longer welcome here. Lodge yourself elsewhere or let the powers below eat you—it's all one to me. But get out."

Colonel Ambaldo's eyes widened. "Sir, you may not speak to me so. Regardless of what you claim to be the rules of the front, I shall seek satisfaction."

"If you want satisfaction, go find a whore." Sabrino gave Ambaldo a mocking bow. "I told you, we do not duel here. Let me say this, then: if you ever seek to inflict your presence upon me here in this tent again, I will not duel. I will simply kill you on sight."

"You joke," Ambaldo exclaimed.

Sabrino shrugged. "You are welcome to make the experiment. And after you do, somebody will have to write to your kin, assuming anyone has any idea who your father is."

"Sir, I know you are overwrought, but you try my patience," Ambaldo said. "I warn you, I will call you out regardless of these so-called rules if provoked too far."

"Good," Sabrino said. "If your friends—in the unlikely event you have any—speak to mine, they need not inquire as to weapons. I shall choose knives."

Sticks were common in duels. They got things over with quickly and decisively. Swords were also common, especially among those with an antiquarian bent. Knives . . . A man who chose knives didn't just want to kill his opponent. He wanted to make sure the foe suffered before dying.

Ambaldo licked his lips. He wasn't a coward; no Algarvian

colonel of dragonfliers was likely to be a coward. But he saw that Sabrino meant what he said and, at the moment, didn't much care whether he lived or died. With such dignity as he could muster, Ambaldo said, "I hope to speak to you again someday, sir, when you are more nearly yourself." He turned and left.

With a last soft curse, Sabrino sat down again. He re-inked his pen, hoping the fury that had coursed through him would make the words come easier. But it didn't. He'd had to write far too many of these letters, and they never came easy. And, as he wrote, he couldn't help wondering who would write a letter for him one day, and what the man would say.

Sidroc took off his fur hat and stowed it in his pack. "Not so cold these days," he remarked.

Sergeant Werferth made silent clapping motions. "You're a sly one, you are, to notice that. I bet it was all the stinking snow melting that gave you the clue."

"Heh," Sidroc said; Werferth being a sergeant, he couldn't say any more than that without landing in trouble. He could and did turn away from the sergeant and walk off down one of the lengths of trench north of Durrwangen Plegmund's Brigade was holding. His boots made squelching, sucking noises at every step. Werferth had been rude, but he hadn't been wrong. The snow was melting—indeed, had all but melted. When it melted, it didn't just disappear, either. Things would have been simpler and more convenient if it had. But it didn't: it soaked into the ground and turned everything to a dreadful morass of mud.

A couple of eggs came whizzing out from Durrwangen to burst close by, throwing up fountains of muck. It splatted down with a noise that reminded Sidroc of a latrine, only louder. He threw his hands in the air, as if that would do any good. "How are we supposed to go forward in this?" he demanded, and then answered his own question: "We can't. Nobody could."

"Doesn't mean we won't," Ceorl said. The ruffian spat; his

spittle was but one more bit of moisture in the mire. "Haven't you noticed?—the redheads would sooner spend our lives than theirs."

"That's so." Sidroc didn't think anyone in Plegmund's Brigade hadn't noticed it. "But they spend plenty of their own men, too."

Ceorl spat again. "Aye, they do, and for what? This lousy stretch of Unkerlant isn't worth shitting in, let alone anything else."

Sidroc would have argued with that if only he could. Since he agreed with it, he just grunted and squelched along the trench till he came to a brass pot bubbling over a little fire. The stew was oats and rhubarb and something that had been dead long enough to get gamy but not long enough to become altogether inedible. He filled his mess tin and ate with good appetite. Only after he was done, while he was rinsing the mess tin with water from his canteen, did he pause to wonder what he would have thought of the meal were he still living soft back in Gromheort. He laughed. He would have thrown the mess tin at anyone who tried to give it to him. Here and now, with a full belly, he was happy enough.

He was also happy that none of the Brigade's Algarvian officers looked to be around. As long as they weren't there, nothing much would happen. He'd seen that they didn't trust the Forthwegian sergeants to do anything much. Forthwegians were good enough to fight for Algarve, but not to think or to lead.

The Unkerlanters launched more eggs from the outskirts of Durrwangen. These burst closer than the others had, one of them close enough to make Sidroc throw himself down in the cold, clammy mud. "Powers below eat them," he muttered as bits of the thin metal shell that had housed the egg's sorcerous energy hissed through the air. "Why don't they just run off and make things easy on us for once?"

But, despite the pounding the Algarvians had given Durrwangen, Swemmel's men showed no inclination whatever to run off. If the Algarvians wanted them gone, they would have to drive them out. After the eggs stopped falling, Sidroc stuck his head up over the parapet and peered south. "Get down, you fool!" somebody called to him. "You want a beam in the face?"

He got down, unblazed. The outskirts of Durrwangen lay a mile or so away. The Unkerlanters held on to the city, from the outskirts to its heart, like grim death. He couldn't see all the fortifications they'd put up, but that proved nothing; he'd already discovered the gift they had for making fieldworks that didn't look like much—till you attacked them. Whatever they had waiting in Durrwangen, he wasn't eager to find out.

Whether he was eager or not, of course, didn't matter to the Algarvian officers commanding Plegmund's Brigade. They came back from wherever they'd been with smiles as broad as if they'd just heard King Swemmel had surrendered. Sidroc's company commander was a captain named Zerbino. He gathered his men together and declared, "Tomorrow, we shall have the high honor and privilege of being among the first to break into Durrwangen."

He spoke Algarvian, of course; the Forthwegians in the Brigade were expected to understand him rather than the other way round. But, no matter what language he used, none of his troopers was eager to go forward against the heavily defended city. Even Sergeant Werferth, who loved fighting for its own sake, said, "Why am I not surprised they chose us?"

Captain Zerbino fixed him with a malignant stare. "And what, pray tell, do you mean by this, Sergeant?" he asked in his haughtiest manner.

Werferth knew better than to be openly insubordinate. But, from behind the Algarvian officer, somebody—Sidroc thought it was Ceorl, but he wasn't sure—spoke up: "He means we aren't redheads, that's what. So who gives a fornicating futter what happens to us?"

Zerbino whirled. He drew himself up to his full height; being an Algarvian, he had several inches on most of the men in his company. After a crisp, sardonic bow, he answered, "*I* am a redhead, and I assure that, when the order to attack is given, I shall be at the fore. Where I go, will you dare to follow?"

Nobody had anything to say to that. Sidroc wished he could have found something, but his wits were empty, too. Like all the officers assigned to Plegmund's Brigade, Zerbino had shown himself to be recklessly brave. Where he went, the company *would* follow. And if that was straight into the meat grinder . . . then it was, and nobody could do anything about it.

Sidroc slapped his canteen. It held nothing but water. He sighed, wishing for spirits. Somebody would have some, but would anybody be willing to give him any? All he could do was try to find out.

He ended up paying some silver for a short knock. "I can't spare any more," said the soldier who let him have it. "I'm going to drink the rest myself before we go at 'em tomorrow."

Sidroc wished he could get drunk for the assault, too. He wrapped himself in his blanket and tried to sleep. Bursting eggs didn't bother him; he had their measure. But thinking about what he'd go through come morning . . . He tried not to think about it, which only made things worse.

Eventually, he must have slept, for Sergeant Werferth shook him awake. "Come on," Werferth said. "It's just about time."

Egg-tossers and dragons were pounding the forwardmost Unkerlanter positions. "More will come when we go forward," Captain Zerbino promised. "We are not breaking into Durrwangen alone, after all; Algarvian brigades will be moving forward, too."

Which is why they'll do something more to help us along, Sidroc thought. Before he could say it aloud—not that it needed saying, not when most of the men in the company were doubtless thinking the same thing—Zerbino raised his long, tubular brass whistle to his lips and blew a blast that pierced the din of battle like a needle piercing thin, shabby cloth. And, as Zerbino had promised, he was the first one out of the muddy holes in which the men of Plegmund's Brigade sheltered, the first one moving toward the enemy.

The ground ahead was also muddy, muddy and churned to chaos by the bursts of endless eggs. It sucked, leechlike, at

Sidroc's boots, trying to pull them off his feet. The mud stank, too, stank with the odor of all the men and animals already killed in it. There would be more before the day was through. Sidroc hoped he wouldn't be part of the *more*.

A barrage of eggs flew through the air, arcing up from the south toward the soldiers of Plegmund's Brigade and the Algarvians who advanced on either side of them. Try as they would, the Algarvians' egg-tossers and dragons hadn't wrecked the Unkerlanters' ability to hit back.

Sidroc would have been angrier had he expected more. As things were, he threw himself down into the noisome mud and hoped no egg burst right on top of him. Captain Zerbino kept blowing his whistle for all he was worth. That pulled Sidroc up and got him squelching toward Durrwangen again.

An egg burst just in front of Zerbino. It flung him high in the air. Limp and broken, he fell to the soggy ground. *No more whistles,* Sidroc thought. He trudged on anyhow. Someone, he was all too certain, would blaze him if he turned back.

The ground shook under his feet. Up ahead, some of the rubble in which the Unkerlanters sheltered slid into ruin. Only when Sidroc saw purple flames shooting up from the ground among those ruins did he fully understand. Then he whooped and cheered. "Aye, kill those Kaunians!" he yelled. "They don't deserve anything better, by the powers above!" Had his superiors asked it of him, he would cheerfully have set about killing blonds himself.

As things were, he rushed toward the defenses battered by Algarvian sorcery—rushed as best he could with great globs of mud clinging to his boots and more sticking on at every stride. Even the strongest sorcery didn't take out all the defenders. Here and there amidst the wreckage ahead, beams winked to life. A Forthwegian not far from Sidroc dropped his stick, threw up his hands, and fell face forward into the muck.

But Plegmund's Brigade and the Algarvians moving forward with it pressed on toward Durrwangen. With the city battered by murderous magecraft, Sidroc didn't see how they could fail to break in.

And then the ground shook beneath him, hard enough to knock him off his feet. As he sprawled in the mire, a great crack opened ahead. It sucked down a couple of Forthwegian troopers and slammed shut again, smashing them before they could even scream.

Sidroc felt like screaming himself. He did scream—he screamed curses at the Algarvian wizards safe behind the line: "Them, you crackbrained whoreson arseholes! Them, not us!"

"Crackbrain yourself!" Ceorl yelled. "That's not the redheads. That's Swemmel's mages killing peasants and hitting back."

"Oh." Sidroc felt like a fool, not for the first time since joining Plegmund's Brigade. That didn't even count the times he felt like a fool *for* joining Plegmund's Brigade. He looked to his right and left gain. The Algarvian troops to either side of the Brigade had been hit at least as hard as his Forthwegian countrymen. "How are we supposed to go forward, then?"

Ceorl didn't answer. Swarms of Unkerlanter dragons painted rock-gray flew up from the south, dropping eggs on the attackers and flaming those incautious enough to bunch together. The Algarvians' magecraft hadn't reached far enough to do anything to King Swemmel's dragon farms.

And then the ground shook and opened and closed again, almost under Sidroc's feet. More purple flames shot up from it. One incinerated an Algarvian behemoth and its crew not far away. King Swemmel didn't seem to care how many of his own folk his mages killed, so long as they halted their foes. And they'd done that. Sidroc was no general and never would be, but he could tell at a glance that the Algarvians hadn't the least chance of taking Durrwangen till after the mud of southern Unkerlant turned hard again.

Spring was coming to the Valmieran countryside. The first shoots of new green grass were springing up from the ground. Leaf buds sprouted on apple and plum and cherry trees. Early birds were returning from their winter homes in northern Jelgava and Algarve and on the tropical continent of Siaulia.

Pretty soon, Skarnu thought, *it'll be time to plant the year's barley and wheat and turn the cattle and sheep out to pasture instead of feeding them on hay and silage.* He laughed at himself. Before the war, he'd never thought about where food came from or how it was produced. For all he knew or cared, it might have appeared by sorcery in grocers' or butchers' shops.

He knew better now. He knew enough to make himself more than a little useful on a farm out in the country. He'd helped one farmer who hid him, and now he was doing the same for another. This fellow was as surprised as the other had been. He said, "I heard tell you were a city man. You talk like a city man, that's a fact. But you know what to do with a pitchfork, and that's a fact, too."

"I know what to do with a pitchfork," Skarnu agreed, and let it go at that. The less people knew about him, the better.

Again, he wasn't too far from Ventspils, and wanted to get farther away. The Algarvians had come too close to nabbing him—to nabbing the whole underground organization—there. Somebody'd been made to talk somewhere, or trusted someone he shouldn't have—the risks irregulars inevitably took when fighting an occupying army more powerful than they.

When fighting an occupying army and a whole great swarm of traitors, Skarnu thought sourly. As always, the first traitor whose face came to mind was his sister, Krasta. Right behind her, though, were all the Valmieran constables who served the Algarvians as steadily as they'd ever served King Gainibu. If they hadn't, he didn't see how the redheads could have held on to his kingdom and held it down.

But the fellow who came to the farm a couple of days later was neither an Algarvian nor a constable in the redheads' pay. The painter who headed up the irregulars in Ventspils found Skarnu weeding the vegetable plot by the farmhouse. Amusement in his voice, he said, "Hello, Pavilosta. Anybody would think you'd been doing that all your born days."

"Hello yourself." Skarnu got to his feet and swiped at the mud on the knees of his trousers. "Good to see Mezentio's men didn't manage to grab you, either."

"I worry more about our own," the painter said, echoing Skarnu's earlier thought. "But I came out here to talk about you, not me. What are we going to do with you, anyhow?"

"I don't know." Skarnu pointed to the plants he'd been weeding. "The scallions and leeks look to be doing nicely."

"Heh," the underground leader said: not a laugh, but the appearance of one. "You're too good a man with your hands to waste them on produce. You need to go someplace where you can give the redheads a hard time. I wish we could send you into Priekule. You'd do good things, the way you know the city."

"Trouble is, the city knows me, too," Skarnu said. "I wouldn't last long before somebody fingered me to the Algarvians." He thought of Krasta again, but she wasn't the only one—far from it. How many Valmieran nobles in the capital were in bed with the occupiers, literally or metaphorically? Too many. He sighed. "I wish I could go back to the farm by Pavilosta. I was doing fine there."

"Not safe." The painter spoke with great authority. He rubbed his chin as he thought. "I know of a couple of fellows you might want to meet. They've been away for a while— you could show 'em how things have changed."

"Why me? What in blazes do I know about anything?" Skarnu didn't try to hide his bitterness. "I couldn't even guess where the redheads were shipping those poor cursed Kaunians from Forthweg. They must have aimed their magic at Kuusamo, but it wouldn't have gone at Yliharma, or we would have heard about it." He stared down at his hands. They had mud on them, too, but in his eyes it looked like blood.

"No, not at Yliharma," the man from Ventspils agreed.

"They did something nasty with the life energy they stole, something that helped them and hurt us. I don't know any more about it than that. I don't think anybody in Valmiera knows much more about it than that."

He'd succeeded in making Skarnu curious. He'd also let him know his curiosity wouldn't be satisfied. Scowling, Skarnu said, "Who are these two fellows, and how will you bring them here without bringing Mezentio's men, too?"

"I won't," the painter said. "You'll go to them. You know that little village you visited once before? Tomorrow, about noon, a wagon will stop here. The man driving it will say, 'The Column of Victory.' You answer, 'Will rise again.' He'll take you where you're going."

"What if he doesn't say that?" Skarnu asked.

"Run like blazes," the other irregular leader answered. As if he'd said everything he'd come to say, he turned on his heel and ambled back toward Ventspils.

Sure enough, the wagon turned up the next day. Skarnu warily approached. The driver said what he was supposed to say. Skarnu gave the countersign. The driver nodded. Skarnu climbed aboard. The driver flicked the reins and clucked to the horses.

They got to the village a day and a half later. By then, Skarnu thought his fundament was turning to stone. The driver seemed undisturbed. He even chuckled at the old man's hobble with which Skarnu made for the house that served as the underground's nerve center.

The woman he'd met there at his last visit let him in. She gave him bread and beer, which were both welcome, and let him sit down on a soft chair, which at the moment seemed almost as fine as falling into Merkela's arms. He let out a long sigh of pleasure before asking, "I'm to meet someone?"

"So you are," she said. "Let me go upstairs and get them. I'll be back directly." Skarnu was perfectly content for her to take as much time as she wanted. He could have sat in that chair forever without minding in the least. But she came back, far too soon to suit him fully, with a couple of men

dressed in the shabby homespun of farmers—dressed much
as he was, as a matter of fact.

He had to heave himself to his feet to greet them. His back
groaned when he rose. But then, to his astonishment, he discovered he recognized both newcomers. "Amatu! Lauzdonu!
I thought you were dead."

"No such luck," said Lauzdonu, the taller of the two. He
grinned and pumped Skarnu's hand.

"We were both flying dragons down in the south when the
collapse came," Amatu added.

"I knew that," Skarnu said. "That's why I thought you'd
bought a plot."

"Came close a few times," Lauzdonu said in the offhand
way of a man who had indeed had death brush his sleeve a
time or two. "The Algarvians had too many dragons down
there—nothing like a fair fight."

"They had too much of everything all over the place,"
Skarnu said bitterly.

"That they did," Amatu agreed. "But when the surrender
order came, neither one of us could stomach it. We climbed
on our dragons and flew across the Strait of Valmiera to
Lagoas, and we've been in Setubal ever since." His lip
curled. "They're Algarvic over there, too, but at least they're
on our side."

Skarnu remembered that Amatu had always been a snob.
Lauzdonu, who had somewhat more charity in him, put in,
"Aye, they kept fighting even when things looked blackest."

"Well, so did you two," Skarnu said. "And so did I." *And if
more Valmieran nobles had, we'd have given Mezentio's men
a harder time*, he thought. But most of them, and a lot of the
kingdom's commoners, had made their accommodations. Inevitably, his sister sprang to mind yet again. To force the
thought of Krasta down, he asked, "And what are you doing
here on the right side of the Strait again?"

Their faces, which had been smiling and excited, closed
down again. Skarnu knew what that meant: they had orders
they couldn't talk about. Lauzdonu tried to make light of it,

saying, "How's that pretty sister of yours, my lord Marquis?"

"My lord Count, she's sleeping with a redhead." Skarnu's voice went flat and harsh.

Lauzdonu and Amatu both exclaimed then, the one in surprise, the other in outrage. Lauzdonu strode forward to lay a sympathetic hand on Skarnu's shoulder. Skarnu wanted to shake it off, but made himself endure it. Amatu said, "Something ought to happen to her, and to her lover, too."

"I wouldn't mind," Skarnu said. "I wouldn't mind at all." He eyed the two nobles he'd known in Priekule. "You may have to talk to me sooner or later. They brought me here to go with you, wherever it is you're going."

"Better you than that leviathan-rider who fetched us from Lagoas," Amatu said. "He told us he was a Sib, but he could have passed for an Algarvian any day."

"It'll be good to have you along," Lauzdonu said. "After all, it's been going on three years since we left. We don't know who's alive, who's dead ... who chose the wrong bloody side." He patted Skarnu again.

"Where are you going?" Skarnu asked. "I won't ask what you'll do when you get there, but I do need to know that."

"Zarasai," Lauzdonu answered. Amatu's lip curled again. To him, any town that wasn't the capital really wasn't worth visiting. Lauzdonu seemed to have a clearer understanding of the way things worked: "If we go to Priekule, somebody will betray us to the Algarvians."

"That's why I haven't gone back," Skarnu agreed. He nodded to the two of them. Priekule, then Setubal—they'd been spoiled, and they didn't even know it. "You'll find the rest of the countryside isn't so bad. And"—he turned serious—"you'll find you do better if you don't let on that you've got noble blood."

"Commoners getting out of hand, are they?" Amatu said. "Well, we'll tend to that once we've beaten the Algarvians, by the powers above."

"I'm surprised you didn't take your dragons up to Jelgava," Skarnu murmured. "You'd have felt right at home there." Amatu stared at him in annoyed incomprehension.

Lauzdonu snickered and then tried to pretend he hadn't. Jel-gavan nobles had long since given themselves a name for re-action. That Amatu couldn't hear how he sounded warned that he would indeed have fit right in.

Lauzdonu said, "Skarnu knows how things work these days, better than we do."

"I suppose so," Amatu spoke grudgingly.

"Zarasai." Skarnu spoke in musing tones. "Well, among other things, that's a good place to monitor the ley lines com-ing down toward the coast from the north and west."

"What *are* you talking about?" Amatu sounded impatient, in a way that reminded Skarnu achingly of Krasta. Lauzdonu murmured in the other returned exile's ear. "Oh." Amatu's nod was reluctant, too, even after he got the point. Skarnu wondered what he'd done to make the irregulars hate him enough to saddle himself with these two. *Maybe it's their re-venge on me for being of noble blood myself.* He sighed. The Algarvians were the only people on whom he wanted that much revenge.

A Valmieran waiter fawned on Colonel Lurcanio—and, inci-dentally, on Krasta, too. Krasta expected servile deference from commoners. So did Lurcanio: servile deference of a slightly different sort, the deference of the conquered to their conquerors. Since he got it here, he seemed happy enough. In fact, he seemed happier than he had for quite some time.

"The war news must be good," Krasta ventured.

"Better, at any rate," Lurcanio allowed. "Even if the cursed Unkerlanters did keep us from retaking Durrwangen, they won't be doing anything much for some weeks. General Mud has replaced General Winter over there, you see."

"No, I don't see." Krasta's voice had an edge in it. "What are you talking about? Why do you always talk in riddles?"

"No riddle," he said, and then paused while the waiter brought him white wine and Krasta ale. When the fellow scurried off again, Lurcanio resumed: "No riddle, I say, merely mud, a great, gluey sea of it. And when the fighting

starts again, it will be on our terms, not King Swemmel's."
He raised his wineglass. "To victory!"

"To victory!" Krasta sipped her ale. Part of her—she
wasn't sure how much, and it varied from day to day, sometimes from minute to minute—even meant it. An Algarvian
triumph in the west would justify everything she'd done here,
and the Unkerlanters were surely uncultured barbarians who
deserved whatever happened to them. The other things an Algarvian triumph in the west would mean . . .

This time, Krasta gulped at the ale. She didn't want to
think about that.

She was relieved when the waiter brought the dinners
they'd ordered: beef ribs in a creamy gravy with spinach in
cheese sauce and boiled beans for her, a trout sautéed in wine
and a green salad for Lurcanio. He stared at her plate in
some bemusement, remarking, "I have never understood
why Valmierans aren't round as footballs, considering what
you eat."

"You complain about things like that almost every time we
go out," Krasta said. "I like the way my kingdom cooks.
Why aren't Algarvians all skin and bones, if they eat the way
you do?"

Lurcanio laughed and mimed taking a sword in the chest.
Like so many of his countrymen, he had a gift for pan-
tomime. Even though Krasta had been feeling gloomy, his
antics made her smile. He had charm when he chose to use it.
And he also had frightful severity when he chose to use that.
The combination kept Krasta off balance, never quite sure
where she stood.

Before long, he'd reduced his trout to nothing but a skeleton with head and tail still attached. "It's looking at you,"
Krasta said with more than a little distaste. "Those boiled
eyes staring up . . ."

"You, milady, have never seen combat," Lurcanio answered. "If you had, you would not let something so small as
a fish head get in the way of your appetite." Under the table,
his hand found her leg, well above the knee. "Of any of your
appetites," he added.

Krasta sighed. She knew what that meant. Lurcanio never raised a fuss if she kept him out of her bed of an evening. But she didn't dare do it very often. If she did, he was liable to find someone else who wouldn't. That would leave her without an Algarvian protector. Spring was in the air, but the thought filled her with winter. The occupiers answered to themselves, and to themselves alone. Without an Algarvian by her side, what was she? *Fair game,* she thought, and shivered.

"Are you cold, milady?" Colonel Lurcanio asked. Startled, Krasta shook her head. Lurcanio's smile put her in mind of that of a beast of prey. "Good. You are well advised not to be cold." She sighed again.

After supper, Lurcanio's driver threaded his way through the dark streets of Priekule to a theater not far from the palace. The play, like so many showing these days, was a comedy of manners from a couple of centuries before: nothing in it that could offend anyone, Valmieran or Algarvian. Nothing political, at any rate; the manners it featured were mostly bad, including an inordinate number of cuckoldings. Lurcanio laughed his head off.

"Do you think infidelity is funny?" Krasta asked, not without malice aforethought, as they headed for the exit.

"That depends," Lurcanio replied with a splendid Algarvian shrug. "If it happens to someone else, most certainly. If I give the horns, all the more so. If I have to wear them—and if I have to notice I am wearing them—that is another business altogether. Do you understand me?"

"Aye," Krasta said coldly. He'd made her very unhappy when he caught her kissing Viscount Valnu. She didn't want that to happen again. If she decided to stray once more, she knew she dared not get caught.

She was moodily silent on the ride back to the mansion on the edge of town. Lurcanio affected not to notice. That, Krasta knew, was an act. It was a good act, and would have been better had he not been so conscious of how good it was.

When they got there, Lurcanio went up the stairs to Krasta's bedchamber with the easy familiarity of a man who had visited it many times before. His manner in the bedchamber sometimes struck her as a good act, too, again slightly marred by his being aware of how good it was. But he succeeded in giving her pleasure as well as taking his own. Things could have been worse. Lurcanio occasionally made it plain that they could have been worse. What he'd done with her, to her, after catching her with Valnu ... Such things had been against the law in Valmiera, and still were, she'd heard, in Jelgava.

Afterwards, Lurcanio dressed quickly. "Sleep well, my sweet," he said. "I know I shall." Even his yawn was as calculated, as theatrical, as anything she'd seen on the stage earlier in the evening.

But Krasta, full and sated, did sleep well—until, some time after midnight, a noisy commotion at the front entrance woke her. Someone was pounding on the door and shouting, "Let me in! By the powers above, let me in!" at the same time as the Algarvian sentries out there yelled, "Silence! Stopping! Stopping or blazing!"

Krasta threw open her window and cried, "No! No blazing! I know this man." Then, in a lower voice, she went on, "This is most unseemly, Viscount Valnu. What in blazes are you doing here at whatever hour this is?"

"Marchioness, I am here to save my life, if I can," Valnu answered. "If I don't do it here, I won't do it anywhere."

"I can't imagine what you're talking about," Krasta said.

"Let me in and I'll tell you." Valnu's voice rose with urgency once more: "Oh, by the powers above, let me in!"

"Shutting up, noisy maniac," one of the sentries said. "Waking everyone inside, making everyone to hating you."

"*I* don't hate him," Krasta said sharply, which was, most of the time, true. As if to prove it, she added, "I'll be right down."

Her night tunic and trousers were thin and filmy; she threw on a cloak over them. By the time she got downstairs, several servants had gathered in the front hall. Krasta sent them back to bed with angry gestures and opened the front door herself. Valnu darted in and fell at her feet, as if prostrating himself before the king of Unkerlant. "Save me!" he cried, as melodramatically as an Algarvian.

"Oh, get up." Krasta's voice turned irritable. "I let you into my house. If this is some mad scheme to get me to let you into my bed, you're wasting your time." Anything she said here would get back to Lurcanio, as she was uneasily aware. She hated having to be uneasy about anything.

But Valnu answered, "I did not come here for that. I did not come here to see you at all, milady, though I bless you for letting me in. I came here to see your protector, the eminent Count and Colonel Lurcanio. He can truly save me, where you cannot."

"And why should I save you, Viscount Valnu?" Lurcanio strode into the front hall from the west wing. "Why should I not order you blazed for disturbing my rest, if not for any of a large number of other good reasons?"

"Because, except in this particular instance, perhaps, you would be blazing an innocent man," Valnu said.

"My dear fellow, you have not been an innocent for a great many years," Lurcanio said with sardonic glee. "Not even in your left ear."

Valnu bowed very low. "That you pick the left rather than the right proves how closely you listen to your fellow officers who know me well—know me intimately, one might even say. But I am an innocent in matters concerning your bold Algarvian hounds. By the powers above, your Excellency, I *am*!"

"And what matters are those?" Sure enough, Lurcanio had a purr in his voice, almost as if he were talking to Krasta after bedding her.

"They think I am playing some sort of stupid—some sort of idiotic—double game, looking to tear down everything Algarve's done," Valnu answered. "It's a lie! By the powers above, a *lie*!" He did not draw attention to the kilt he was wearing. At first, Krasta thought that might be a mistake. Then she decided Valnu was making Lurcanio notice it for himself—not a bad ploy.

She saw the Algarvian eyeing Valnu's bare, knobby knees. But her lover was first and foremost an officer of his kingdom. "You've called on the powers above twice now, Viscount," he said. "By the powers above, sir, why should I believe you and not my kingdom's hounds? Their task, after all, is to sniff out treason and rebellion wherever they find them. If they turn their noses your way..."

"If they turn them my way, they turn them in the wrong direction," Valnu insisted. "Ask your lady, if you doubt me."

That made Colonel Lurcanio laugh out loud. "Considering the embrace the two of you were enjoying when I was so inconsiderate as to interrupt you, I might be inclined to doubt her objectivity." But his eyes swung toward Krasta nonetheless. "Well, milady? What say you?"

Krasta could have said a good deal. Valnu must have known she could have said a good deal. He was betting his life that she didn't want him dead, no matter how much he'd irked her in days gone by—and he'd irked her a great deal indeed.

If she spoke against him, he was dead. If she spoke for him too fulsomely, Lurcanio wouldn't believe her. What she did say was, "Whatever his problem may be, I wish he wouldn't bring it here at this ridiculous hour of the morning. And that, Colonel, is nothing but the truth."

"I wish the same thing." Lurcanio fixed Valnu with a hard stare. "To a certain degree, I admire your nerve—but only to a certain degree. Go back to your home. If the hounds come for you, then they come—but I will have them explain themselves to me before they do anything too drastic. That is the most I intend to give you."

Valnu bowed low again. "I thank you, your Excellency. It is more than I deserve."

"I am afraid you may be right," Lurcanio answered. "Now get out."

"Aye, get out," Krasta said. "Let decent people sleep, if you'd be so kind." For reasons she absolutely could not fathom, both Valnu and Lurcanio started laughing at her.

*   *   *

Pekka wished things were as they had been before the Algarvians struck at her comrades and her. Without Siuntio, though, they would never be the same. First and foremost, she missed the master mage more with every passing day. She hadn't realized how much she'd relied on his good sense, his resolute optimism, and his capacity for moral outrage till they were gone.

Second, and as important in a less personal, less intimate way, Siuntio had been the one mage who could keep Ilmarinen under something vaguely resembling control. Ilmarinen was wild for revenge against Algarve, aye, but he was also wild for experimenting with the nature of time and wild for one of the serving women at the hostel (a passion apparently not returned, which somehow didn't seem to bother him in the least) and wild for the birds flocking into the area with the return of spring and wild for . . .

"Anything! Everything!" Pekka complained to Fernao in the dining room one morning. "He is supposed to be in charge. He is supposed to be leading us in our work against Mezentio's men. And what is he doing? Running around in all directions at once, like a puppy in a park full of interesting smells."

The Lagoan mage quirked up a gingery eyebrow. "If you can make similes like that in classical Kaunian, maybe you ought to try writing along with magecraft."

"I do not want to try writing," Pekka said. "I want to get on with the work we are supposed to be doing. Have we done that under Ilmarinen? He is not the leader I hoped he would be. I hate to say that, but it is the truth."

"Some people are not made to be either leaders or followers," Fernao observed. "Some people listen only to themselves."

"That may be so," Pekka replied, reflecting that with Ilmarinen it certainly seemed so. "But leading is the job he has been given."

Fernao sipped from his mug of tea and looked at her over the top of it with his disconcertingly Kuusaman eyes. "If he is not doing it, maybe you should have it instead."

"Me?" Pekka's voice rose to a startled squeak, one that made Raahe and Alkio, sitting a couple of tables away, turn and stare at her. She fought for quiet, fought and won it. "How could I take it? By what right? Without Siuntio and Il-marinen, this project would not exist. The Seven Princes would not have supported it."

"As may be." Fernao shrugged. "But now that they are supporting it, do you not think they expect success to follow from that support?"

"I couldn't," Pekka muttered in Kuusaman, more to herself than to him. "It would be like throwing my father out onto the street."

But the Lagoan mage's grasp of her language got better day by day. "Not to do with family," he said in Kuusaman, and then returned to classical Kaunian: "This is not even the business of the kingdom. This is the business of the world."

"I couldn't," Pekka repeated.

Now Fernao eyed her with the first open disapproval she'd seen from him. "Why not?" he asked pointedly. "If not you, who? I am an ignorant foreigner. The newcomers?" He low-ered his voice a little further. "They are all a step below you and two steps behind you. If it is not to be Ilmarinen . . ."

He had confidence in her where she had none in herself. Pekka had never known that from anyone but her husband before. She wished Leino were here now. He would know how to gauge things. In the aftermath of the Algarvians' sor-cerous assault, she'd lost her feel.

And then, when she was hoping Fernao would leave her alone, he found one more question: "How long do you sup-pose it will be before Mezentio's mages strike us again? If they do, can we withstand them?"

"Why should they strike us again?" Pekka asked. "Since they hit us the last time, what have we done that would draw their notice?" She rose from the table and left in a hurry. If she hadn't just made Fernao's point for him, what had she done? He called after her, but she kept walking.

Going up to her room didn't help. She looked out and saw mud and rock where snow had lain, mud and rock with grass and bushes growing furiously. Here, almost as in the land of the Ice People, everything had to grow furiously, for winter came early and left late, giving life little time to burgeon.

Buntings and pipits chirped. Insects buzzed. Before long, Pekka knew, there was liable to be a plague of gnats and mosquitoes, again as happened on the austral continent. The bog the countryside became after the snow melted made a perfect breeding ground for all sorts of bugs.

But the signs of spring did nothing to cheer Pekka. Instead, they reminded her how time was running out, slipping away through her fingers. Experiments should have resumed. They should have been strengthened. They hadn't. The landscape by the blockhouse should have had new craters. It didn't.

"Curse me if Fernao isn't right," Pekka exclaimed, though no one was there to hear her. "If I don't do something, who will?"

She left her room and walked down the hall to Ilmarinen's. Her knock was sharp and peremptory. Ilmarinen opened the door. When he saw her, he smiled in something that looked like relief and said, "Oh, good. I thought you were Linna." That was the serving woman with whom he was infatuated. "If she knocked like that, she'd want to knock my block off next thing."

"*I* want to knock your block off," Pekka said. "Why aren't we working more? When Mezentio's mages attacked us, you promised vengeance for Siuntio. Where is it? How far away is it? How long does his shade have to wait?"

"Well, well," Ilmarinen said, and then again: "Well, well. Who's been feeding you raw meat, my dear?"

"I am not your dear," Pekka snapped, "not when you sit there and twiddle your thumbs instead of doing what needs doing. If you don't move this project forward, Master Ilmarinen, who will?"

"I *am* moving it forward," Ilmarinen answered, a little uneasily, "and we will get back in the field very soon."

"When *is* soon?" Pekka asked. "We should have been back weeks ago, and you know it as well as I do. What are the Al-

garvians doing while we do nothing? How are we remembering Master Siuntio?"

Ilmarinen fell back a step in the face of that barrage of
questions. Uneasiness gave way to anger on his face. "If you
think going forward is so very easy, Mistress, if you think it
can be done just like that"—he snapped his fingers—"maybe
you ought to try running this mess yourself."

Fernao had told Pekka that. She'd told herself that. Now Ilmarinen was telling her that, too? With a crisp nod, she said,
"Aye, I think you're right. I ought to. Let's go to the crystallomancer so we can let Prince Juhainen know we're making
the change. Come on."

"You're serious." Ilmarinen spoke in tones of wonder.

"By the powers above, I am," Pekka said. "We've been
frozen while the ground was melting. Time to let Juhainen
know we're going to thaw out." She sighed. Juhainen wasn't
quite so solidly behind the research project as his predecessor
and uncle, Prince Joroinen, had been. But Joroinen was dead,
buried in the rubble of the princely palace when Algarvian
magic smote Yliharma. Still, since Juhainen's princely domain included her home town of Kajaani, she expected he
would take her more seriously than any of the other Seven.

Ilmarinen followed her down the hall. "If you're trying to
cast me out like an Algarvian bandit overthrowing his chief-
tain, why do you suppose I'd want to work with you—work
under you—afterwards?"

"Why?" Pekka spun on her heel and glared at the older
mage. "I'll tell you why, Master Ilmarinen: because I will
break you in half with my own hands if you try to leave. Now,
have you got that? At the moment, it would be a pleasure."

Pekka waited. If Ilmarinen's temper, always uncertain, did
burst like an egg, what could she do about it? Nothing that
she could see. And if the senior theoretical sorcerer did decide to abandon the project, could she really stop him? She
feared she couldn't.

Sometimes, though, just showing you were ready to face a
question meant you didn't have to. As her son Uto usually

did when she took a firm stand, Ilmarinen yielded. "Take it, then, and welcome," he growled. "May you have more joy of it than I did when it landed in my lap."

"Joy?" Pekka shook her head. "Not likely. But, by the powers above, I am going to have my revenge if it's there to have. Now let's get along to the crystallomancer and let Prince Juhainen know." She didn't intend to give Ilmarinen any chance to change his mind once the shock of being confronted wore off.

And he not only came with her, he spoke in favor of the change when Juhainen's image appeared in the crystal. "For some reason or other—probably doing as I please all these years—I appear to make a better sorcerer than administrator," he told the prince. "Putting Mistress Pekka in charge of things here will move us ahead faster than we could go if I tried to steer us down the ley line."

Juhainen said, "If you both think this is for the best, I will not quarrel with it. Moving down the ley line is what matters. I don't care how you do it, and I don't think any of my colleagues will, either."

"Thank you, your Highness," Pekka said with considerable relief. Juhainen was a young man, hardly more than a youth, but he looked to be showing the common sense that had marked his uncle, Prince Joroinen.

His answer displayed more of that common sense: "I don't know why you are thanking me. You've just had a lot more hard work land on your head."

"It needs doing," Pekka said. "With the help of everyone here"—she let her eyes flick toward Ilmarinen—"I think I can get it done."

"Let it be so, then," Prince Juhainen said, and turned back to whatever he'd been doing when the call came in. The crystal into which Pekka had been speaking flared briefly before returning to quiescence.

Ilmarinen gave Pekka a bow half mocking, half respectful. "Let it be so, then," he echoed. "But you can't just let it be so, you know. You have to make it be so. Lucky you."

"For now, what I have to do is let the others know it is so," Pekka said. "Will you come down with me, or would you rather I did that myself?"

"Oh, I'll come," Ilmarinen said. "Some of them may care to see that you haven't murdered me. Of course, some of them may not, too."

When Pekka got down to the dining hall, she was surprised to find Fernao and Raahe and Alkio still there. Piilis had come down to eat, too. Her rebellion—*my successful rebellion,* she thought dizzily—hadn't taken long. Fernao's eyes widened when he saw Ilmarinen behind her. Pekka said, "Ah, good. Now I can tell everyone at once. With the agreement of Prince Juhainen, I am now responsible for taking our work forward. If the weather lets us do it, I want us experimenting again within three days."

She'd spoken Kuusaman. She started to turn her words into classical Kaunian for Fernao, but the Lagoan mage waved to show her she needn't bother. Her eyes darted to the other theoretical sorcerers. No one burst into applause—that would have been cruel to Ilmarinen—but everyone looked pleased. *It's mine now,* Pekka thought, and responsibility, heavy as the weight of the world, came pressing down on her shoulders.

Qutuz came into Hajjaj's office. "Your Excellency, the Marquis Balastro is here to see you," the Zuwayzi foreign minister's secretary said.

"I thank you," Hajjaj answered. "Show him in—as you see, I am ready to receive him." He wore an Algarvian-style tunic and pleated kilt. With every day that spring advanced, clothes grew less comfortable for him, but discomfort was part of the price he paid for diplomacy.

Qutuz, being a mere secretary, did not have to drape himself in cloth that clung and held the heat. After bowing to Hajjaj, he went out to the antechamber and returned with Algarve's minister to Zuwayza. Balastro wore tunic and kilt, too, and was sweating in them even more than Hajjaj.

The Algarvian minister offered his hand. Hajjaj clasped it. Balastro said, "You look very well, your Excellency. And you are the picture of sartorial splendor—for the year after the end of the Six Years' War."

Hajjaj laughed. "What I usually wear never goes out of style—another advantage to skin, if you care what I think."

"As much as I ever do." Balastro's grin showed teeth white but slightly crooked. He was a bluff, blocky, middle-aged man with sandy-red hair streaked with gray. He wasn't subtle, but he wasn't stupid, either. On the whole, Hajjaj liked him—not that he let that get in the way of doing what he needed to do for his kingdom.

"And how can I help you today, your Excellency?" Hajjaj inquired. "Besides amusing you with my wardrobe, I mean. Would you care for some refreshments?"

Before answering, Balastro lowered himself to the carpeted floor and piled up cushions till he'd made a comfortable nest. More than most foreign envoys who came to Zuwayza, he imitated local customs. Once he was reclining, he grinned at Hajjaj and shook his head. "Since you give me the choice, I'll decline. How many hours over the years have you kept me simmering while we sip and nibble?"

"As many as I thought were needed," Hajjaj answered imperturbably, which made Balastro laugh out loud. Hajjaj piled up pillows, too, by his low desk. "If, today, I claim I am simply aiming to get out of these unpleasantly warm garments before too long, I doubt you will be able to contradict me."

"If you like, I'll take off my clothes so you can shed yours," Balastro said. He'd done that a few times, which made him unique in the annals of diplomacy in Zuwayza. With his pale body and his circumcision, though, he did not make an inconspicuous nude in this kingdom—on the contrary.

And so Hajjaj said, "Never mind. By all means do say on, though. I listen with great attention." He had to listen with great attention, Algarve being Zuwayza's cobelligerent against King Swemmel of Unkerlant and much the bigger power of the two.

"Things are looking up," Balastro said. "It's been a hard winter, aye, but things are looking up. I can, I think, say that truthfully now, looking at the way things down in the south have gone."

"Considering how things were there a few weeks ago, Algarve does seem to have managed a revival," Hajjaj agreed. "After Sulingen fell, there was some small concern lest your entire position in the south unravel." A lifetime of diplomacy had taught him to minimize things. Zuwayza and Yanina and even neutral, landlocked Ortah had all been terrified of the prospect of swarms of Unkerlanters rolling down on their kingdoms without any Algarvian armies left to throw them back.

"Well, it didn't. It didn't, and it won't." Balastro always spoke confidently. Here, his confidence seemed justified. He went on, "We've stabilized the battle line, and we're deeper into Algarve than we were a year ago." That was all true, even if mildly obscene. Of course, it said nothing of the debacle at Sulingen. But then, Balastro did not pretend to be objective.

"I am pleased to hear it," Hajjaj said. "General Ikhshid has been full of admiration for the way you let the Unkerlanters overextended themselves and then struck them in the flanks and rear."

"For which I think him," Balastro, as if the generalship were his. He continued, "Pity we couldn't drive them out of Durrwangen again, too, but the mud got too thick too fast. When it dries out again, we'll deal with them there."

"May it be so," Hajjaj said, on the whole sincerely. He knew of Unkerlanter mud, of course, but it didn't seem quite real to him, any more than the savage summer heat of Bishah would seem real to a man from Durrwangen hearing about it without having experienced it.

"Oh, it will." Balastro might have been talking about tomorrow's sunrise. "We've pushed well past the place to both east and west, even if we couldn't quite break in. A couple of attacks to pinch off the neck of the salient"—he gestured—"and the head falls into the basket."

"A vivid image." Deadpan, Hajjaj asked, "Are you sure you will have enough Kaunians to make it real?"

"You need have no fear on that score," the Algarvian minister replied. He impaled Hajjaj with a cold green stare. "We would have even more if you weren't harboring those cursed refugees."

"Since they are here in my kingdom, King Shazli's kingdom, they are no concern of yours," Hajjaj said: the position Zuwayza had held ever since Kaunians from Forthweg began sailing to her eastern shore. "And I have repeatedly ordered them to stay here in Zuwayza and under no circumstances to return to Forthweg."

"You are the soul of virtue," Balastro said sourly. "You know as well as I, your Excellency, that any order you have to give repeatedly is an order that is not working."

"Would you rather I gave no such order at all?" Hajjaj returned.

"I would rather that you put some teeth in the order you have given," Balastro said. "String up a few blonds and the rest will get the point."

"I shall consider it." Hajjaj wondered if he would have to do more than consider it. If the Algarvian minister insisted boisterously enough, he might have to follow through.

Balastro grunted. "That's more than I thought I'd get out of you. You're a stubborn old crow, Hajjaj—you know that?"

"Why, no, your Excellency." Hajjaj's eyes widened in almost convincing surprise. "I had no idea."

"Prevaricating old porcupine, too," Balastro said. "Your father was a tortoise and your mother was a thornbush."

"Have you got any more compliments to pay me, or are we through till the next session of teeth-pulling?" Hajjaj asked, but less gruffly than he would have liked—on the whole, he took Balastro's words for compliment rather than insult.

"Not quite through," the Algarvian minister answered. "My military attaché has asked me to ask you if Zuwayza can do without a good many of the behemoths and dragons we've sent you over the past couple of years."

"I am not the one to respond to questions on matters military," Hajjaj said, trying to hide the alarm he couldn't help feeling. "If your attaché does not care to do so himself, I shall raise the issue with General Ikhshid and pass on to you his reply." *Assuming he doesn't have an apoplexy and fall down frothing on the floor.* "May I tell him why you would consider withdrawing this aid?" *You can't be* that *angry about our harboring the Kaunians . . . can you?*

"I'm no soldier, either," Balastro said, "but what it amounts to is this: we aim to force a decision in Unkerlant, and we'll need everything we can scrape together when we do it. We don't aim to lose a fight because we didn't strike a blow with all our strength."

"I . . . see," said Hajjaj, who was not altogether sure he did. "Well, would you have me inquire of Ikhshid, or would your attaché sooner do it directly?"

"If you'd be so kind, I'd be grateful," Balastro answered, suave and smooth as if he'd never called Hajjaj a porcupine in all his born days.

"As you wish, of course," the Zuwayzi foreign minister said.

"Good." Balastro heaved himself to his feet, which meant Hajjaj had to rise, too. The Algarvian made his farewells and departed with the air of a man well pleased with himself.

Hajjaj was pleased to be able to shed the clothes he despised. He was much less pleased when he called Qutuz and said, "Would you be so kind as to inquire of General Ikhshid if he would give me the pleasure of his company for a few minutes as soon as he conveniently can?"

What that meant in plain language was, *Get Ikhshid here this instant.* Qutuz, a good secretary, recognized as much. "Of course, your Excellency," he said, and hurried away.

As Hajjaj had hoped he would, he had General Ikhshid with him when he returned. Ikhshid was not far from Hajjaj's age: a stocky, white-haired soldier who'd served in the Unkerlanter army during the Six Years' War and, rare for a Zuwayzi, had gained captain's rank there. After bows and handclasps, Ikhshid spoke with almost Unkerlanter bluntness: "All right, what's gone and got buggered up now?"

"Nothing yet," Hajjaj said. "Marquis Balastro asked me to

inquire of you how the buggering might go forward at some future date." He relayed the Algarvian minister's remarks to the general.

Ikhshid's shining eyebrows were like signal flags, astonishingly visible against his dark skin. They twitched now, twitched and then descended and came together. "Sounds like they're thinking of staking everything on one throw of the dice. You don't really want to do that, not if you're fighting a war."

"I wouldn't want to do it no matter what I'm doing," Hajjaj said. "Why would King Mezentio?"

"Algarvians are better soldiers than Unkerlanters," Ikhshid remarked, not quite responsively. "Put a company of redheads up against a company of Swemmel's men and the Algarvians will come out on top. Put a company of Algarvians against two companies of Unkerlanters and they still might come out on top. Put them up against three . . ." He shook his head.

"Ah." Hajjaj inclined his head. "There's always the third Unkerlanter."

"Aye, there is. There is indeed," Ikhshid agreed. "The Algarvians didn't take Cottbus. They didn't take Sulingen. They don't have that many more chances left. It's not just men, either, your Excellency. It's horses and unicorns and behemoths and dragons, too. Skill counts, or the redheads wouldn't have got as far as they did. But weight counts, too, or they'd've got farther."

"And so the Algarvians are aiming to put all their weight into whatever blow they choose to strike next," Hajjaj said slowly. "Balastro said as much."

Ikhshid nodded. "That's how it looks to me, and it'd look that way even if Balastro hadn't said so."

"Can we afford to let them take dragons and behemoths out of Zuwayza to strike this blow?" the foreign minister asked.

"That comes down to two questions," Ikhshid answered. "First, can we stop 'em if they choose to do it? I doubt it. And second, of course—when they strike this blow, will it finally go to the heart?"

"Aye." Hajjaj let out a long, slow sigh. "We have to hope for the best, then." He wondered what the best was, and if, in this cursed war, it even existed.

Eight

Fernao found his Kuusaman getting better day by day. More Kuusaman mages had come to the hostel: not just Piilis and Raahe and Alkio, all of whom spoke excellent classical Kaunian, but several others who didn't know so much. Those less fluent newcomers weren't directly involved in the experiments the theoretical sorcerers were making, but were important even so. Their duty was to repel, or at least to weaken, any new assaults Algarvian mages might launch against the experiments.

"Can you do it?" Fernao asked one of them, a woman named Vihti. "Much force. Many killings."

"We can try," Vihti answered. "We can fight hard. They are not close. Distance—" She used a word Fernao didn't know.

"Distance does what?" he asked.

"At-ten-u-ates," Vihti repeated, as to a child, and then used a synonym: "Weakens. If you had been working in the north of Kuusamo and not down here in the south, the last attack would have done you all in."

"You need not sound so happy," Fernao said.

"I am not happy," Vihti said. "I am telling you what is." That was something Kuusamans were in the habit of doing. Vihti went off muttering under her breath, probably about flighty, overimaginative Lagoans.

When Fernao went out to the blockhouse with Pekka and Ilmarinen and the three newly arrived theoretical sorcerers, he didn't think he was the overimaginative one. The Kuusamans had done things that no one else would have dreamt of for years.

The blockhouse was new, and stronger than the one the Algarvians had wrecked. But a few of the timbers were charred ones salvaged from the old blockhouse. Pointing to them, Pekka spoke in classical Kaunian: "They help remind us why we continue our work."

Where nothing else lately seemed to have, that got Ilmarinen's notice. "Aye," he growled with something of the fire he'd had before the Algarvian attack. "Every one of those boards has Siuntio's blood on it."

"We shall have our revenge." Piilis was a careful man who spoke careful Kaunian. "That is what Siuntio would have wanted."

Pekka shook her head. "I doubt it. He saw what needed doing against Algarve, but vengeance was never any great part of his style." Her eyes flashed. "I do not care. Regardless of whether he would have wanted me to take revenge, I want it for my own sake. I do not think he would have approved. Again, I do not care."

"Aye." Hot eagerness filled Fernao's voice. He believed in vengeance, too, probably more so than any of the Kuusamans. Elaborate revenge was part of the Algarvic tradition Lagoas shared with Sibiu and Algarve herself. Kuusamans were generally calmer and more restrained. Siuntio had been. But calm and restraint, however valuable in peacetime, grew less so after war began.

Fewer secondary sorcerers had accompanied Fernao and his colleagues to the blockhouse this time. With the coming of spring, the experimental animals shouldn't freeze unless magecraft kept them warm. But the secondary sorcerers still did have to transfer the spell Pekka would recite to the racks of cages that held the rats and rabbits.

"Remember, we are trying something new this time," Pekka said. "If all goes as planned, most of the sorcerous energy we unleash today will strike at a point well removed from the animals. We have to learn to do this if we are to turn our magecraft into a proper weapon. The Algarvians can do it with their murderous magic. We must be able to match them."

"And if things don't go quite right, we'll bring it down on our own heads, and that will put paid to this project once for all," Ilmarinen said.

Oddly, his gloom didn't bother Fernao so much. The master mage had been making cracks like that for as long as Fernao had been in Kuusamo ... and undoubtedly for a lot of decades before that. Getting him back to sounding like his sardonic self was if anything an improvement.

"Are we ready?" Pekka's voice had steel in it, warning that anyone who wasn't ready would face her wrath. She didn't even come up to the top of Fernao's shoulder, but he wouldn't have wanted to have to do that. No one admitted he wasn't ready. Pekka's gaze flicked around the blockhouse. After a sharp, abrupt nod, she quietly recited the ritual sentences with which Kuusamans began any sorcerous operation.

Raahe and Alkio and Piilis spoke the words with her. So did the secondary sorcerers and Vihti and the other protective mages. And so did Ilmarinen, who had about as little concern for most forms of ritual correctness as any wizard Fernao had ever known. Fernao himself stood mute. Pretending he shared the Kuusamans' belief would have been useless, perhaps even dangerous, hypocrisy.

No one insisted that he join the recitation. But when it was through, Pekka glanced toward him. "In my class at Kajaani City College, you would have had to say the words," she remarked.

"We are all learning here," Fernao answered.

That seemed to please her. She nodded again, more relaxed, less jerky, than she had been. Then, after a couple of deep breaths, she turned to the secondary sorcerers and asked again in Kuusaman if they were ready. Fernao knew a certain amount of pride at understanding the question. He understood the answer, too—they confirmed they were. Pekka inhaled once more, then spoke first in her language and afterwards in classical Kaunian: "I begin."

And begin she did, with the same quiet authority Fernao had seen again and again in her incanting. She was rougher at her work than a mage who spent day after day refurbishing rest crates would have been at his, but such a mage barely touched the surface of sorcery, while Pekka understood it down to the very roots, down deeper, in fact, than anyone before her had imagined those roots ran. Watching her, listening to her attack the spell, Fernao could have loved her not for who she was but for what she knew, a distinction of a sort he'd never imagined making.

He felt rather less proud of the spell she was using. All the Kuusamans had joined together in crafting it, and it had the smoothed corners and shapelessness characteristic of a work formed by committee. Even with his imperfect grasp of Kuusaman, he could tell as much from the feel of the air in the blockhouse as she worked. He did not doubt the spell would do what it was designed to do. But it had no elegance to it. Had Siuntio drafted it, it would have been half as long and twice as strong; Fernao was sure of it. He had no proof, though. He would never have proof, not anymore, not with Siuntio dead.

Force built—not the blood-tasting force the Algarvians had brought down on their heads, but potent nonetheless. Potent enough to confront Mezentio's murder-powered magic? Fernao wouldn't have thought so, not from what was in the air, but he'd seen what this energy release could do. Transferring it from one site to another seemed far easier than finding out how to elicit it had been.

And then, as matter approached a climax, Pekka made the sort of mistake that could befall any mage working through a long, complex, difficult spell: she dropped a line. Ilmarinen jumped. Piilis exclaimed in horror. Raahe and Alkio seized each other's hands as if they never expected to touch anything else again.

Fernao knew a certain amount of pride at recognizing the problem as fast as any of the Kuusamans. He also knew the same fear that gripped them: Ilmarinen's joke about bringing the sorcerous energy down on their own heads wasn't funny anymore. When things went wrong at this stage . . .

"Counterspells!" Ilmarinen rapped out, and began to chant with sudden harsh urgency. So did Raahe and Alkio, their two voices merging into one. So did Pekka, trying to reverse what she'd unleashed. Dismay still seemed to freeze Piilis.

Not so Fernao. For a long time, he'd had nothing to do but draft and refine counterspells. Because he wasn't fluent in Kuusaman, he'd been only an emergency backstop, a firewall. The spell he raced through now wasn't in Kuusaman, or even classical Kaunian. It was in Lagoan: his birthspeech, he'd long since decided, would be best for such magic, for he could use it faster and more accurately than any other.

And he, like the rest of the mages, was incanting for his life now. He knew as much. The sorcerous energies that would have torn a new hole in the landscape were poised now to do the same to the mages who had unleashed them. If the mages couldn't divert those energies, weaken them, spread them fast enough, they wouldn't get a second chance.

Past, present, and future seemed to stretch very thin—all too fitting for the sort of sorcery they'd been using. Fernao felt an odd rush of memories: from his youth, from his childhood, from what he would have taken oath were his father's and grandfather's childhoods as well—but all recalled or perhaps relived with as much immediacy, as much reality, as his own. And, at the same time (if *time* had any meaning here), he knew also memories from years he hadn't yet experienced: from himself as an old man; from one of the children he did not at this moment have, also old; and from that child's child.

He wished he could have held those memories instead of just being aware that he'd had them. All the Kuusaman mages around him were exclaiming in awe and dread as they used their counterspells, so he supposed they were going through the same thing he was. And then, at last, when he thought the chaos in the timestream would cast them adrift in duration—or perhaps cast them out of it altogether—the counterspells began to bite.

Now suddenly took on meaning again. His consciousness, which had been spread over what felt like a century or more,

contracted back to a single sharp point that advanced heartbeat by heartbeat. He remembered things that had happened
to him before that point, but nothing more. No, not quite
nothing more: he remembered remembering other things, but
he could not have said what they were.

"Well, well," Ilmarinen said. Sweat beaded his face and
soaked the armpits of his tunic. Even so, he didn't forget to
use classical Kaunian: "Wasn't that *interesting,* my friends?"
He didn't forget his ironic tone, either.

Pekka, who had been standing while she cast the spell that
went awry, slumped down onto a stool and began to weep, her
face hidden in her hands. "I could have . . . us all," she said in a
broken voice. Fernao didn't know the Kuusaman verb, but he
would have been astonished if it didn't mean *killed.*

He limped over to her and put a hand on her shoulder. "It is
all right," he said, cursing the classical tongue for not letting
him sound colloquial. "We are safe. We can try again. We
shall try again."

"Aye, no harm done," Ilmarinen agreed. "Any spell you
live through is a spell you learn something from."

"Learn what?" Pekka said with a laugh that sounded more
like hysterics than mirth. "Not to miss a line at the key moment of the incantation? I was already supposed to know
that, Master Ilmarinen, thank you very kindly."

Fernao said, "No, I think there is more to learn here than
that. Now we know from the inside out what our spell does,
or some of what it does. If our next version is not better on
account of that, I shall be surprised. The method was drastic,
but the lesson is worthwhile."

"Aye," Ilmarinen repeated. "The Lagoan mage has the
right of it." He glanced over at Fernao. "Accidents will happen." Fernao smiled and nodded, as if at a compliment. Ilmarinen glared at him, which was exactly what he wanted.

Every time a peasant sneaked into the woods and sought out
the battered band of irregulars Garivald was leading these
days, he almost wished the newcomer would go away. He'd
heard a great many tales of woe, some of them horrible

enough to move him close to tears. How could he resist bringing such people into the band? He couldn't. But what if one of them was lying?

"What do I do?" he asked Obilot. "Let in the wrong man— or woman—and the Grelzers will know everything about us a day later."

"If we don't get new blood, they won't care about us one way or the other," she answered. "If we didn't take chances, none of us would be irregulars in the first place."

Garivald grunted. That held an unpleasant amount of truth. But he said, "It's not on your shoulders. It's on my shoulders. And you're one of the people who helped dump it there." He glowered at her with none of the interest, none of the liking—why lie? none of the desire—he usually felt.

Obilot met the glare with a shrug. "Munderic got killed. Somebody had to lead us. Why not you? Thanks to your songs, people have heard your name. They want to join Garivald the Songmaker's band."

"But I don't want to lead them!" Garivald said in a sort of whispered scream. "I never wanted to lead anybody. All I ever wanted to do was raise a decent crop and stay drunk through the winter and—lately—make songs. That's all, curse it!"

"I wanted this and that, too," Obilot said. "The Algarvians made sure I wouldn't have any of that." She'd never said just why she'd joined the irregulars, but she hated the redheads with a passion that made what her male comrades felt toward them seem mere mild distaste by comparison. "And now you can't have the things you always wanted, either. Isn't that one more reason to want to do everything you can to make them suffer?"

"I suppose so," he admitted. "But it doesn't mean I want to lead. Besides, we aren't strong enough to do anything much right now."

"We will be." Obilot sounded more confident than Garivald felt.

He didn't have to answer. Rain had been falling steadily for a while. Now lightning flashed and thunder bellowed, drowning out anything he might have said. Nobody could do anything much in such weather: the Grelzers couldn't push into the woods, as they had when snow lay on the ground, but the band of irregulars couldn't very well sally forth by squelching through the mud.

After another peal of thunder rumbled and subsided, Obilot said, "Would you rather be taking orders from Sadoc?"

"That's not fair," Garivald answered, though he couldn't have said why it wasn't. As a matter of fact, he had no desire whatever to take orders from Sadoc; the idea scared him worse than going up against the Algarvians in battle. But no one had proposed the inept would-be mage to succeed Munderic. No one had proposed Garivald, either, or not exactly. People had just looked at him. They hadn't looked at anyone else, and so the job ended up his.

But the irregulars couldn't very well stay holed up in the woods forever, either. A fellow named Razalic came up to Garivald while the rain was still falling and said, "You know, boss, we're almost out of food."

"Aye," Garivald agreed, not altogether happily. "We'd better pay a call on one of those villages outside the forest—maybe on more than one of them." Some of the peasant villages in these parts collaborated with the irregulars and gave them grain and meat. Others had firstmen who worked hand in glove with the Grelzer authorities and with their Algarvian puppet masters.

But when Garivald led a couple of dozen men out of the woods, he found the peasants from even the friendliest villages imperfectly delighted to see him. He'd expected nothing better. Early spring was the hungry time of year for everybody. Living on the end of the supplies that had brought them through the winter, the peasants had little left over to share with anyone.

"What do you want us to do?" he asked the firstman of a hamlet named Dargun. "Dry up and blow away and leave you at the mercy of the redheads and the Grelzer dogs who sniff their arses?"

"Well, no," the firstman answered, but he didn't sound pleased. "Don't want the brats here to starve, either, though."

Garivald set his hands on his hips. He knew a trimmer when he heard one. "You can't have it both ways," he said. "We can't farm and fight the Algarvians at the same time. That means we've got to get food from somewhere. This is somewhere." Even to him, though, it looked like nowhere. Next to Dargun, Zossen—nothing out of the ordinary as villages went—looked like a metropolis.

The firstman's sigh was close to a wail. "What I really wish is, things were back the way they were before the war started. Then I wouldn't have to . . . worry all the time."

Then I wouldn't have to make hard choices. That, or something close to it, had to be what he meant. And what hard choices was he contemplating? Feeding the irregulars or betraying them to the soldiers who followed false King Raniero? That was one obvious possibility.

"Everything gets remembered," Garivald remarked, keeping his tone casual. "Aye, that's so—*everything* gets remembered. When King Swemmel's inspectors come back to this part of the realm, they'll know who did what, even if something goes wrong with us. *Somebody* will tell them. Or do you think I'm wrong?"

By the look the firstman gave him, he was certainly loathsome, regardless of whether he was right or wrong. "*If* the inspectors ever get this far again," the fellow said.

Munderic would have blustered and bellowed. Garivald pulled a knife from his belt and started cleaning dirt from under his fingernails with the point. "Chance you take," he agreed, doing his best to stay mild. "But if you think the inspectors aren't ever coming back, you never should have started feeding us in the first place."

The firstman bit his lip. "Curse you!" he muttered. "You don't make things easy, do you? Aye, I want the Algarvians out, but—"

"But you don't want to do anything to make that happen," Garivald finished, and the firstman bit his lip again. Garivald went on, "You're not fighting. Fair enough—not everybody can fight. But if you won't fight and you won't help the folk who are fighting, what good are you?"

"Curse you," the firstman repeated, his voice weary, hopeless. "It almost doesn't matter who wins the stinking war. Whoever it is, we lose. Take what you need. You would anyhow." Back before the Algarvians had hauled him out of Zossen, Garivald hadn't felt much different. He'd just wished the war would go away and leave him and his alone. But it hadn't worked like that. It wouldn't work like that here in Dargun, either.

Along with his irregulars and several pack mules borrowed from the village, he trudged toward the woods. One peasant from Dargun came along, too, to lead the mules back after they weren't needed anymore. The mules were heavily laden with sacks of beans and barley and rye. So were the men—as heavily laden as they could manage and still walk through the mud. Garivald, his back bent and creaking, didn't want to think about what would happen if a Grelzer patrol came across them. Because he didn't want to think about it, he had trouble thinking about anything else.

More irregulars met them at the edge of the woods and took the sacks the mules carried. The peasant headed off to Dargun. Garivald wondered if he should have kept him behind. Munderic might have. But Garivald didn't see much point to it. Everybody knew the irregulars denned somewhere in this forest. The peasant wouldn't find out where. As far as Garivald could see, that meant he was no great risk.

When he got back to the clearing the irregulars had reclaimed after the Grelzer raiders left the wood, he expected applause from the men and women who hadn't gone along to bring in the supplies. After all, he'd done what he set out to do. If anything, he'd done better than he expected. They wouldn't have to worry about food again for two or three weeks, maybe even a month.

And, indeed, people were staring at him and the men he led as they came into the clearing. Among the people staring were a couple of men Garivald had never seen before.

He wondered if he ought to shrug the beans off his back and grab for his stick. But the irregulars who hadn't gone out to Dargun seemed to take the newcomers for granted. They wouldn't have if they'd thought the strangers meant trouble.

Obilot came up to one of those strangers and pointed toward Garivald. "That's our leader," she said, her voice not loud but very clear. A couple of the other irregulars nodded. Garivald straightened with pride despite the weight he carried.

Both newcomers strode toward him. They had on rock-gray tunics. At first, that meant little to him; a lot of the men in his band still wore the ever more threadbare clothes they'd used while serving in King Swemmel's army. But these tunics weren't threadbare. They weren't particularly clean, but they were new. Garivald didn't need long to realize what that meant. He let the sacks of beans down to the ground and stuck out his hand. "You must be real soldiers!" he exclaimed.

The two men looked at each other. "He's quick," one of them said.

"Aye, he is," the other agreed. "That's efficient." But, by the way one of his thick eyebrows rose, he might have thought Garivald too quick for his own good.

"Wonderful to see real soldiers here," Garivald said. He knew the real fighting still lay far to the west, which led to an obvious question: "What are you doing here?"

"Being efficient." The Unkerlanter soldiers spoke together. The one who might have thought Garivald too efficient continued, "We've brought you a crystal."

"Have you, now?" Garivald wondered how efficient that was. "Can I keep it activated without have to sacrifice somebody every month or two, the way a mage had to do back in my home village?"

Before the soldiers could answer, Sadoc's big head bobbed up and down. "Aye, you can," he said. "There's a power point in these woods—not a very big one, but it's there. If it wasn't, I couldn't work any magecraft at all."

In Garivald's view, that would have been an improvement, but he didn't say so. Instead, he gave a sharp, quick nod and turned back to the soldiers. "All right. I guess I can run a crystal. Now what will I do with it?"

"Whatever his Majesty's officers tell you to do, by the powers above," answered the one who'd mentioned the crystal. "We're getting these things out to as many bands behind the Algarvian line as we can. The more you people work with the regular army, the more efficient the fight against the redheads becomes."

That made a certain amount of sense. It also fit in with everything Garivald knew about King Swemmel: he wanted control as firmly in his fists as he could make it. The other Unkerlanter soldier said, "We'll also bring you weapons and medicines whenever we can."

"Good. I'm glad to hear it. We can use them." Garivald eyed the two regulars. "And you'll tell us what to do whenever you can."

They looked at each other for a moment. Then they both nodded. "Well, of course," they said together.

Bembo walked up to Sergeant Pesaro in the constabulary barracks and said, "Sergeant, I want some leave time."

Pesaro looked him up and down. "I want all sorts of things I'm not going to get," the fat sergeant said. "After a while, I get over it and go about my business. You'd better do the same, or you'll be sorry."

"Have a heart!" Bembo exclaimed—not a plea likely to win success when aimed at a superior. "I haven't been back to Tricarico in forever. Nobody's got out of Forthweg in a demon of a long time. It's not fair. It's not right."

Pesaro opened a drawer of the desk behind which he sat. "Here." He handed Bembo a form—a form for requesting leave, Bembo saw. "Fill this out, give it back to me, and I'll pass it on up the line . . . and it'll bloody well get ignored, the way every other leave-request form gets ignored."

"It's not fair!" Bembo repeated.

"Life's not fair," Pesaro answered. "If you don't believe me, go dye your hair blond and see what looking like a Kaunian gets you. They aren't taking many leave requests from soldiers, and they aren't taking any from constables. But if you want to volunteer to go fight in Unkerlant so you have a little chance of getting leave, I've got a form for that, too." He made as if to reach into the desk drawer again.

"Never mind," Bembo said hastily. "I feel better about things already." Compared to leave in Tricarico, patrolling the streets of Gromheort wasn't so good. Compared to fighting bloodthirsty Unkerlanter maniacs, it wasn't so bad.

"There, you see?" Pesaro's round, jowly face radiated as much goodwill as a sergeant's face was ever likely to show. But he didn't keep on beaming for long. The scowl that spread over his countenance was much more in character. "What in blazes are you doing now?"

"Filling out the leave form," Bembo answered, doing just that. "You never can tell. Lightning might strike."

"Lightning'll strike you," Pesaro rumbled. But he waited till Bembo finished checking boxes, and he didn't throw the form in the wastebasket by the desk. In fact, he read through it. "What's this?" His coppery eyebrows leaped up. " 'I want to start a family'? You son of a whore, you're not married!"

"Sergeant, you don't have to be married to do what it takes to start a family." Bembo was the picture—the implausible picture, but the picture nonetheless—of innocence.

Pesaro snorted. "If you think his Majesty is going to ship you back to Tricarico so you can get your ashes hauled, you've been chewing on Zuwayzi hashish. You know where the brothels are in town."

"It's not the same in a brothel," Bembo complained.

"No—you have to pay for it." Pesaro looked down at the form again. His shoulders shook with silent laughter. "Beside, how do you know you'd get laid if you did go back to Tricarico? It's not like you even had a girlfriend there or anything."

That really hurt, not least because it was true. "Sergeant!" Bembo said reproachfully.

But Sergeant Pesaro lost patience—not something of which he'd ever had any great supply. "Enough!" he growled. "Too fornicating much! Get your arse out on the street. I'll send the stinking form up the line. Just don't hold your breath waiting for a ley-line caravan ticket back to Tricarico, that's all." To add insult to injury, he started eating one of the flaky, many-layered pastries full of honey and nuts in which Forthweg specialized. He didn't offer Bembo any.

Stomach gurgling, head full of a sense of injustice that would have been worse still if he hadn't paused to contemplate the idea of going to Unkerlant, Bembo stomped out of the barracks. He couldn't even complain to Oraste; his partner was nursing a sprained ankle, and couldn't walk his beat for a few days. On reflection, Bembo decided that wasn't so bad. He'd met a lot of people more sympathetic than Oraste. Had he met anybody *less* sympathetic? He wasn't so sure about that.

Even early in the morning, the day was fine and mild. He didn't mind Gromheort's weather, which wasn't much different from Tricarico's. Now that winter had given way to spring, the rain had pretty much stopped. Before long, he would be sweating and glad of his broad-brimmed hat to keep his face from burning.

Forthwegians on their way to work and to Gromheort's market square crowded the streets. Men wore knee-length tunics, women garments that reached almost to their ankles. Bembo wondered how many of them were Kaunians in sorcerous disguise. He couldn't do anything about that, not by himself, not unless somebody's features changed right before his eyes.

Just before he rounded a corner, he heard raucous hoots and jeers. When he did round it, he spied a bright blond head coming his way. As the woman drew closer, he realized the Forthwegians weren't raising an uproar only because she was a Kaunian. Seeing her made him want to raise an uproar himself. She was young and pretty, and wore a tunic of transparent green silk, while her trousers might have been painted onto her hips and haunches, display all the more startling in a land where most—almost all—women didn't try to show off their shapes.

She stopped in front of Bembo, letting him look her up and down. The way she looked at him was half respectful, half as if he were something nasty she'd found on the sole of her shoe. He tried to keep his voice brisk, but couldn't help coughing a couple of times before saying, "You'll have a pass, I expect."

"Aye, Constable, of course I do," she answered in good Algarvian—he'd expected that, too. She opened out her belt pouch, took out a folded sheet of paper, and handed it to him.

"Doldasai daughter of Daukantis," he read, and the Kaunian woman nodded. The pass did indeed allow her out of the Kaunian quarter when and as she chose: for all practical purposes, it made her an honorary Forthwegian. The price she'd paid to get it was obvious enough. "Aye, I've seen you before," Bembo said, handing the paper back to her. He smiled. "I've always been glad when I have, too."

Doldasai made sure of the precious pass before answering him: "I am a woman for officers, you know." Her voice also held that mixture of respect and contempt. He was an Algarvian, so she couldn't ignore him as she had the jeering Forthwegians, but the pass proved she had powerful protectors. And, he realized a moment later, he was a man—like a lot of courtesans, she likely despised his whole sex.

He said, "I'm keeping my hands to myself." To prove as much, he clasped them behind his back. "Dressed the way you are, though, you can't expect me not to look."

"I am a Kaunian in Forthweg," Doldasai said. "How can I possibly expect anything?" She didn't even sound bitter— just very tired.

Bembo said, "Powers above, if you don't like the life you're living, why don't you get your hands on the charm that makes you people look like Forthwegians? Then you could just disappear."

Doldasai stared at him, perhaps for the first time noticing the person inside the uniform. "You say this?" she asked. "You say this, a constable of Algarve? You tell me to break the law your own people made?" She dug a finger in one ear, as if to be sure she heard correctly. Her nails were carefully trimmed and painted the color of blood.

"I did say it, didn't I?" Bembo spoke in some surprise. Maybe, by doing something like that for her, he could take a tiny step toward making up for all the Kaunians he'd forced into their tiny district or simply sent west. Maybe, too, he'd just been staring at the pink-tipped breasts so plainly visible through the thin silk of her tunic. He shrugged. Now that the words were out of his mouth, he made the best of them: "You could do it, you know. Who'd be the wiser?"

"Curse you," she muttered in classical Kaunian before going back to Bembo's language. "Every time I steel myself to see you Algarvians as nothing but pricks with legs, one of you has to go and remind me you're people, too." She set a hand on his arm, not provocatively but in a friendly way. "Kind of you to say that. Kind of you to think that. But I can't."

"Why not?" Bembo asked. "Seems like about every third Kaunian around has already done it. More, for all I know."

Doldasai nodded. "True. But your folk don't hold hostage the parents of most Kaunians in Gromheort. They have way to make sure of my . . . good behavior. And so, you see, I can't just disappear."

"That's . . ." Bembo didn't want to say what he thought it was. He could hardly denounce his own officers to a woman whose looks proclaimed her an enemy of Algarve. What he did say was, "Tell me where they're at and I'll see if I can't get 'em moved into the regular Kaunian district. After that— well, if you look like everybody else around these parts, who's going to ask any questions?"

Now the Kaunian courtesan frankly gaped. "You would do that . . . for a blond?" She didn't make him answer; she might have been afraid of the result. She might have been wise to be afraid, too. Instead, she hurried on, "If you do that—if you can do that—I'll give you anything you want." She shrugged. Bembo watched, entranced. She said, "What difference would one more time make, especially if it was the last?"

"If you think I'll go all noble and say, 'You don't have to do that, sweetheart,' you're daft," Bembo said. Doldasai nodded; she understood such deals. Bembo went on, "Now, where are they?"

"They're quartered in Count Brorda's castle—the place where your governor rules now," she answered. "Their names are Daukantis and Feliksai."

Bembo started to say he didn't care what their names were, but then realized knowing might be useful. Instead, he asked, "Do you know whereabouts they are in the castle?"

"Aye." Doldasai told him. He made her repeat it so he had it straight. She did, and then said, "Powers above bless you. For you to do such a thing—"

He reached out and caressed her. She let him do it. "Believe me, sweetheart, I know why," he told her. *And I'm not going to risk my neck for theirs, either,* he thought. *If it's easy, fine. If it's not . . . I copped a feel, anyhow.* Aloud, he went on, "There are rooms above a tavern called the Imperial Unicorn, a couple of blocks inside the Kaunian district. You know the place?" Her eyes showed she did. Bembo said, "Wait for me there. We'll see what I can do, and we'll see what you can do."

Back in Algarve, the great stone pile that lay at the center of Gromheort would have been labeled quaint. Here in Forthweg, the adjectives chilly, ugly, and gloomy more readily sprang to mind. Soldiers and bureaucrats bustled this way and that. Nobody bothered noticing a plump, redheaded constable. To Bembo's vast relief, the sentry in front of Daukantis and Feliksai's door was a soldier he'd never seen before, not a fellow constable. With a nasty smile, he said, "I've come for these Kaunian buggers. They're going straight back in with the rest of their stinking kind."

Very possibly, nobody'd told the sentry why the blonds were being held. He didn't argue. He didn't make Bembo sign anything or ask his name and authority. He just grinned wolfishly, opened the door, and said, "They're all yours. Good riddance to 'em."

No one paid any attention to a constable marching a couple of Kaunians along in front of his stick, either. Once Bembo got them out of the castle, he murmured, "Now they don't have a hold on your daughter any more." They gaped and then started to weep. That was nothing out of the ordinary, either.

At the edge of the Kaunian quarter, another constable waved to Bembo and called "Caught a couple, did you? You lucky whoreson!" Bembo waved his hat with typical Algarvian braggadocio.

Like the ancient Kaunian Empire, the tavern called the Imperial Unicorn was a sad shadow of its former self. Bembo took Doldasai's father and mother upstairs. She was pacing the narrow hallway there. She looked from Bembo to Feliksai and Daukantis and back again in astonished disbelief. "You really did it," she whispered, and then flew into her parents' arms.

"Bargain," Bembo said pointedly.

"Bargain," Doldasai agreed. She took her mother and father into one of the little rooms, then came out and took Bembo into another one. "For what you just did, you deserve the best," she said, and proceeded to give it to him. If she didn't enjoy it herself, too, she was a better actress than any courtesan he'd known. Her pleasure might have been set off more by her parents' rescue than his charms, but he thought it real even so.

And his own pleasure, as he left the Kaunian district, was more than merely physical. He hadn't quite done a good deed for the sake of doing a good deed, but he'd come a lot closer than usual, close enough to leave his conscience as happy as the rest of him, which was saying a great deal.

"Come on, boys, get yourselves ready," Major Spinello told the troopers in his regiment. "We've been kicking the Unkerlanters' arses for almost two years now. We'll go right on doing it, too, won't we?"

The Algarvian soldiers cheered. Some of them waved their sticks in the air. *What a liar I'm turning into*, Spinello thought. He hadn't told a lie, or not exactly. If his countrymen hadn't won victory after victory, he and the regiment wouldn't have been here deep in northern Unkerlant.

But Swemmel's men could kick, too. Every time he took off his tunic to bathe, the puckered scar on the right side of his chest reminded him of the truth there. Had that beam caught him in the left side of the chest, it wouldn't have left a scar. It would have killed him outright. And the Unkerlanter campaign against Sulingen had come too close to killing all the Algarvian armies in the southern part of King Swemmel's domain. It hadn't, though. Like Spinello, they'd been badly scarred. Like him, too, they kept battling.

"All right, then," he told his men. "We'll go forward for King Mezentio, powers above bless him. And we'll go forward because there aren't any Unkerlanters on the face of the earth who can stop us."

He got more cheers from the men. Even some of his officers applauded. Captain Turpino didn't look altogether convinced. Turpino, in fact, looked about to be ill. He didn't lead with speeches. He was always at the head of his company when an attack went in, and that seemed to be enough for him. Spinello led from the front, too, but he remained convinced that getting the most from his soldiers was also a sorcery of the sort the universities didn't teach to mages.

Just before Spinello could give the command that would send his men forward, a rider on a lathered horse came up calling his name. "I am Spinello," he said, drawing himself up to his full if not very impressive height. "What would you? Be quick—we are about to attack."

"I have orders for you, sir, and for your regiment." The messenger opened a leather tube he wore on his belt and took out a roll of paper bound with a ribbon and a wax seal. "From army headquarters."

"I see that," Spinello said. Brigade headquarters would have been much less formal. He took the orders and used his thumbnail to crack the seal, then unrolled the paper and quickly read it. Even before he'd finished, he started to curse.

"What's wrong, sir?" Turpino asked.

"We are *not* going to stamp the Unkerlanters into the dust today," Spinello answered.

"What?" His men howled furious protests: "Don't they think we're good enough?" "We'll lick 'em!" "A plague on the Unkerlanters, and another one on our generals!"

"You have your men very ready for action," the messenger observed.

"What's gone wrong, sir?" Captain Turpino had. He assumed something had, and Spinello could hardly blame him for that. Spinello had thought something was wrong, too, till he'd gone all the way through the orders.

As things were, he said, "Nothing, Captain. It is, if you like, even a compliment." He passed the paper to Turpino so the senior company commander could see for himself. Spinello addressed the regiment as a whole: "We are withdrawn from the line for rest, refit, and reinforcements—this because of our outstanding fighting qualities, as the general heading up the army says in so many words. They want us in very top shape before they throw us into battle again, so we can do the enemy as much harm as possible."

"Aye, that's what it says," Turpino agreed. "It also says we're going to get sent south when the refit's done."

Spinello nodded. "That looks to be where the war will be won or lost. I say that because, having fought there, I see the difference between that part of the front and this one. Here, we go forward or we go back, and not a whole lot changes either way. There . . . There they take whole armies off the board when things go wrong. They've gone wrong for us and the Unkerlanters both. Next time, by the powers above, I want 'em going wrong for Swemmel's men, and we can help make that happen."

His men clapped their hands. A few of them tossed their hats in the air. The messenger saluted Spinello. "Sir, you've got them eating out of the palm of his hand."

"Do I?" Spinello looked at the palm in question. Grinning, he wiped it on his kilt. "I've been wondering why it was wet." The messenger snorted. Spinello turned back to his troops. "Form up, you lugs. Some other lucky fellows get the joy of fighting Unkerlanters here. Poor us—we have to face baths and barbers and beds and brothels. I don't know how we'll be able to manage it, but for the sake of the kingdom we have to try."

"You *are* a mountebank," Turpino said as Spinello led his soldiers out of the line. "Sir." His voice held nothing but admiration.

A new regiment came up the dirt road to replace Spinello's. It looked to be a very new regiment, with plump, well-fed men wearing clean uniforms. "Do your mothers know you're here?" one of Spinello's scrawny veterans called. That set off an avalanche of jeering. The raw troops smiled nervously and kept marching. They didn't jeer back, which only proved they didn't know what they were getting into.

"Stay awake," Spinello told his men. "Keep an eye skinned for dragons. I think we've got enough holes in the ground to dive into if we have to." That drew more laughter from the veterans. The landscape, like most landscapes that had seen a lot of fighting, was a jumble of craters and old, half-collapsed trenches and foxholes. Spinello bunched his fingertips and kissed them. "Aye, Unkerlant is beautiful in the springtime."

He'd hoped for a ley-line caravan ride back to Goldap, the Unkerlanter town the Algarvians used for a rest center and replacement depot. But Swemmel's men had sabotaged the ley line, and the Algarvian mages were still working to repair the damage. That meant three days of marching through mud for the regiment.

Once they got into Goldap, soldiers exclaimed at how large and fine it was. Maybe they were from little farms and had no idea what a city was supposed to be like. Maybe, and more likely, they'd been out in the field too long, so that any place with several streets' worth of buildings standing seemed impressive.

Spinello got them billeted and queued up at a bathhouse next door to the barracks before seeking army headquarters to report his presence. Though normally fastidious—indeed, more than a bit of a dandy—he didn't bother cleaning up first.

If he brought the smell of the front with him, then he did, that was all. And if he brought a few fleas and lice with him, too, well, the officers here had a better chance of getting rid of them than somebody who spent all his time fighting.

As Spinello had expected, the lieutenant to whom he first announced his presence wrinkled his nose and did his best not to breathe. But the colonel to whom the lieutenant conducted him only smiled and said, "Major, about every third officer who visits me tries to show me how dreadful things are up at the front. I know it for myself, believe me."

Spinello eyed the decorations the colonel wore. They included a couple of medals for gallantry, a pair of wound badges, and what the troops called the frozen-meat medal marking service in Unkerlant the first winter of the war against Swemmel. "Perhaps you do, sir," Spinello admitted. "But you might have been someone just in from Trapani, too."

"In which case, you'd've made me feel guilty for being clean and safe, eh?" the colonel said. "I'd be angrier at you if I hadn't played those games every now and again, too. As things are, I'm trying to arrange another field command for myself."

"I hope you get one, sir," Spinello said. "Anybody can be a hero back here. You've shown you can do it where it counts."

The colonel rose from his chair so he could bow. "You are too kind," he murmured. "And you have made a respectable name for yourself as a combat soldier, I might add. If you hadn't, we would have left you here in a sector where nothing much ever happens. As things are, you'll serve the kingdom where it really matters."

"Good." Hearing himself sound so fierce, Spinello started to laugh. "Can you believe, sir, that before this war started I was more interested in the archaeology and literature of the Kaunian Empire than in how to outflank a fortified position?"

"Life is to live. Life is to enjoy—till duty calls," the colonel answered. "Me, I was a beekeeper. Some of the honeys my hives turned out won prizes at agricultural shows all over Algarve. Now, though, I have to pay attention to behemoths, not bees."

"I understand," Spinello said. "If they're sending us south, does that mean we aim to have another go at Durrwangen once the ground really gets hard?"

"I can't tell you for a fact, Major, because I don't know," the colonel said. "But if you can read a map, I expect you'll draw certain conclusions. I would."

Now Major Spinello bowed. "I think you've answered me, sir. Where am I to pick up the drafts of men who will bring my regiment to full strength?"

"We've taken over a couple of what used to be hostels down the street from the caravan depot," the colonel replied. "At the moment, we've got a brigade just in from occupation duty in Jelgava. Three companies have your name on them. Speak with one of the officers there; they'll take care of you. If they don't, send them on to me and I'll take care of them." He sounded as if he relished the prospect.

Spinello laughed again. "From Jelgava, eh? Poor bastards. They'll be wondering what in blazes hit 'em. And then they go down south? Powers above, they won't enjoy that much. I hope they'll be able to fight."

"They'll manage," the other Algarvian officer said. "This past winter, we had a brigade from Valmiera get out of its caravan in a blizzard in a depot the Unkerlanters were attacking right that minute. They gave Swemmel's men a prime boot in the balls."

"Good for them!" Spinello clapped his hands together. "May we do the same."

"Aye, may you indeed," the colonel agreed. "Meanwhile, though, go collar your new men. Make sure the ones you already have are able to climb into their caravan cars day after tomorrow. We'll try not to halt 'em at a depot where they have to fight their way off."

"Generous of you, sir," Spinello said, saluting. "I'll do everything you told me, just as you said. I won't be sorry to go down south again." He reached up and touched his own wound badge. "I owe the Unkerlanters down there a little something, that I do."

"And you believe in paying your debts?" the colonel asked.

"Every one of them, sir," Spinello answered solemnly. "Every single one—with interest."

"Hello, there," Ealstan said to the doorman at Ethelhelm's block of flats. "I got a message he wanted to see me." He didn't bother hiding his distaste. He wished he hadn't come at all, but had ignored the band leader and singer who couldn't break with the Algarvians.

And then the doorman said, "You got a message from whom, sir?"

Ealstan stared. This fellow had been letting him into the building for months so he could cast the singer's accounts. Had he suddenly gone soft in the head? "Why, from Ethelhelm, of course," he answered.

"Ah." The doorman nodded and looked wise. "I thought that might be whom you meant, sir. But I must tell you, that gentleman no longer resides here."

"Oh, really?" Ealstan said, and the doorman nodded again. Ealstan asked, "Did he leave a forwarding address?"

"No, sir." Now the doorman shook his head. His cultured veneer slipped. "Why do you want to know? Did he skip out owing you money, too?"

Too? Ealstan thought. But he also shook his head. "No. As a matter of fact, we were square. But why did he ask me to come here if he knew he was going to disappear?"

"Maybe he didn't know," the doorman said. "He just up and left a couple of days ago. All kinds of people have been looking for him." He sighed. "Powers above, you should see some of the women who've been looking for him. If they were looking for me, I'd make cursed sure they found me, I would."

"I believe that." Ealstan decided to risk a somewhat more dangerous question: "Have the Algarvians come looking for him, too?"

"Haven't they just!" the doorman exclaimed. "More of those buggers than you can shake a stick at. And this one red-headed piece . . ." His hands described an hourglass in the air. "Her kilt was so short, I don't hardly know why she bothered wearing it at all." He made a chopping motion at his own knee-length tunic, just below crotch level, to show what he meant.

Vanai had talked about seeing Algarvian women in the baths. Ealstan had no interest in them. He wondered what Ethelhelm had wanted, and what the musician was doing now. Whatever it was, he hoped Ethelhelm would manage to do it far from the Algarvians' eyes.

Aloud, he said, "Well, the crows take him for making me come halfway across town for nothing. If he ever wants me again, I expect he knows where to find me." He turned and left the block of flats. *With a little luck, I'll never see it again,* he thought.

Someone had scrawled PENDA AND FREEDOM! on a wall not far from Ethelhelm's building. Ealstan nodded when he saw that. He hadn't felt particularly free when Penda still ruled Forthweg, but he hadn't had standards of comparison then, either. King Mezentio's men had given him some.

He saw the slogan again half a block later. That made him nod even more. New graffiti always pleased him; they were signs he wasn't the only one who despised the Algarvian occupiers. He hadn't seen so many since the spate of scribbles crowing about Sulingen. The redheads, curse them, had proved they weren't going to fold up and die in Unkerlant after all.

When an Algarvian constable came round the corner, Ealstan picked up his pace and walked past the new scribble without turning his head toward it. He must have succeeded in keeping his face straight, too, because the constable didn't reach for his club or growl at him.

I'm well rid of Ethelhelm anyhow, Ealstan thought. He'd found a couple of new clients who between them paid almost as much as the musician had and who didn't threaten to disappoint him with a friendship that would turn sour. His father had been friendly with his clients, but hadn't made friends with them. Now Ealstan saw the difference between those two, and the reason for it.

Not far from the ley-line caravan depot, a work gang was clearing rubble where an Unkerlanter egg had burst. Some of the laborers, the Forthwegians among them, looked like pickpockets and petty thieves let out of gaol so the Algarvians could get some work from them. The rest were trousered Kaunians taken out of their district.

Ealstan hadn't seen so many blond heads all together for a long time. He wondered why the Kaunian men hadn't dyed their hair and used Vanai's spell to help themselves disappear into the Forthwegian majority. Maybe they just hadn't got the chance. He hoped that was it. Or maybe they didn't want to believe what the Algarvians were doing with and to their people, as if not believing it made it less true.

The Forthwegians weren't working any harder than they had to. Every so often, one of the redheads overseeing the job would yell at them. Sometimes they picked up a little, sometimes they didn't. Once, an Algarvian whacked one of them in the seat of his tunic with a club. That produced a yelp, a few curses, and a little more work. The Kaunians in the gang, though, labored like men possessed. Ealstan understood that, and wished he didn't. The Forthwegians would sooner have been sitting in a cell. But if the Kaunians didn't work hard, they'd go west and never, ever come back. Their lives depended on convincing the Algarvians they were worth their keep.

A Forthwegian passing by called, "Hey, you Kaunians!" When a couple of the blonds looked up, he drew his finger across his throat and made horrible gurgling noises. Then he threw back his head and laughed. So did the Algarvian strawbosses. So did about half the Forthwegian laborers. The Kaunians, for some reason, didn't seem to find the joke so funny.

And Ealstan had to walk on by without even cursing his loutish countryman. He didn't dare do anything that would draw the occupiers' notice. His own fate was of no great concern to him. Without him, though, how would Vanai manage? He didn't want her to have to find out.

At the doorway to the flat, he gave the coded knock he always used. Vanai opened the door to let him in. After they kissed, they both said the same thing at the same time: "I've got news." Laughing, they pointed to each other and said the same thing at the same time again: "You first."

"All right," Ealstan said, and told Vanai of Ethelhelm's disappearance. He finished, "I don't know where he's gone, I don't know what he's doing, and I don't much care, not anymore. Maybe he even listened to me—maybe he's gone off to find some quiet little place in the country where nobody will care where he came from or what he used to do as long as he pulls his weight."

"Maybe," Vanai said. "That would be easier for him if he didn't look as if he had Kaunian blood, of course. Maybe someone got my spell to him."

"Maybe somebody did," Ealstan said. "For his sake, I hope somebody did. It would make things easier." He paused, then remembered he wasn't the only one with something on his mind. He pointed at Vanai and asked, "What's your news?"

"I'm going to have a baby," she answered.

Ealstan gaped. He didn't know what he'd expected her to say. Whatever it was, that wasn't it. For a couple of seconds, he couldn't think of anything to say. What did come out was a foolish question: "Are you sure?"

Vanai laughed in his face. "Of course I am," she answered. "I have a perfectly good way to tell, you know. I was pretty sure a month ago. There's no room for doubt now, not anymore."

"All right," he mumbled. His cheeks and ears heated. Talk of such intimate details embarrassed him. "You surprised me."

"Did I?" Vanai raised an eyebrow. "*I'm* not surprised, not really. Or rather, the only thing I am surprised about is that it took so long to happen. We've been busy."

He heard her, but he wasn't really paying much attention to what she said. "A baby. I don't know anything about taking care of babies. Do you?"

"Not really," she said. "We can learn, though. People do. If they didn't, there wouldn't be any more people."

"We'll have to think of a name," Ealstan said, and then added, "Two names," remembering it might be either boy or girl. "We'll have to do . . . all sorts of things." He had no idea what most of them were, but Vanai was right—he could learn. He'd have to learn. "A baby."

He walked past his wife into the kitchen, opened a jar of red wine, and poured two cups full. Then he went out to Vanai, handed her one, and raised the other in salute. They both drank. Vanai yawned. "I'm sleepy all the time. That's another thing that's supposed to be a sign."

"Is it?" Ealstan shrugged a shrug meant to show ignorance. "I'd noticed you were, but I didn't think it meant anything."

"Well, it does," she said. "You sleep as much as you can beforehand, because you won't sleep once the baby's born."

"That makes sense," Ealstan agreed. "A baby." He kept saying the words. He believed them, but in a different sense he had trouble believing them. "My mother and father will be grandparents. My sister will be an aunt." He started to mention his brother also, started and then stopped. Leofsig was dead. He still had trouble believing that, too.

Vanai's mind was going down the same ley line. "My grandfather would be a great-grandfather," she said, and sighed. "And he would grumble about miscegenation and halfbreeds as long as he lived."

Ealstan hadn't cared about that. He didn't think his family would, either. Oh, there was Uncle Hengist, Sidroc's father, but Ealstan wasn't going to waste any worry on him. "The baby will be fine," he said, "as long as—"

He didn't break off quite soon enough. Vanai thought along with him again. "As long as Algarve loses the war," she said, and Ealstan had to nod. She went on, "But what if Algarve doesn't lose? What if the baby's looks show it has Kaunian blood? Will we have to make magic over it two or three times a day till it can make magic for itself? Will it have to make magic for itself for the rest of its life?"

"Algarve can't win," Ealstan declared, though he knew no certain reason why not. The redheads seemed convinced they could.

But Vanai didn't contradict him. She wanted to believe that as much as he did—more than he did. "Let me get supper ready," she said. "It won't be anything fancy—just bread and cheese and olives."

"That will be fine," Ealstan said. "The way the redheads

are stealing from us, we're lucky to have that. We're lucky we can afford it."

"That's not luck," Vanai answered. "That's because you do good work."

"You're sweet." Ealstan hurried over to her and gave her another kiss.

"I love you," she said. They'd both been speaking Forthwegian; they almost always did these days. Suddenly, though, she switched to Kaunian: "I want the child to learn this language, too, to know both sides of its family."

"All right," Ealstan replied, also in Kaunian. "I think that would be very good." He was pleased he could bring the words out quickly. He pulled out a chair for Vanai. "If it is cheese and olives and bread, you sit down. I can fix that for us."

More often than not, she didn't want him messing about in the kitchen. Now, with a yawn, she said, "Thank you." After a moment, she added, "You speak Kaunian well. I'm glad."

Ealstan, of course, hadn't learned it as his birthspeech. He'd acquired it from schoolmasters who'd stimulated his memory with a switch. Even so, he told the truth when he answered, "I am glad, too."

Cornelu's leviathan heartily approved of swimming south and west toward the outlet of the Narrow Sea, to the waters just off the coast of the land of the Ice People. He'd expected nothing different; Eforiel, the leviathan he'd ridden for King Burebistu of Sibiu, had also liked to make this journey. The tiny plants and animals that fed bigger ones flourished in the cold water off the austral continent.

The leviathan cared nothing for tiny plants and animals. Whales fed on those, sieving them up with baleen. But the squid and mackerel and tunny that swarmed where food was so thick delighted the leviathan, delighted it so much that Cornelu sometimes had trouble persuading it to go where he wanted.

"Come on, you stubborn thing!" he exclaimed in exasperation more affectionate than otherwise. "Plenty of nice fish for you to eat over here, too." Despite taps and prods, the beast didn't want to obey him. If it decided to go off on its own and eat itself fat, what could he do? Every so often, a leviathan-rider went out on a mission that looked easy and was never seen again. . . .

Eventually—and, in fact, well before he could go from exasperated to alarmed—the leviathan decided there might be good eating in the direction he chose, too. That didn't mean Cornelu could take it easy and not worry on the ride. Algarvian warships prowled the ley lines that ran south from occupied Sibiu. Algarvian leviathans swam in these seas, too. And Algarvian dragons flew overhead.

Every day was longer than the one that had gone before. And, the farther south the leviathan swam, the longer the sun stayed in the heavens. At high summer, daylight never ceased on the austral continent. The season hadn't come to that yet, but it wasn't far away.

Ice floating in the sea foretold the presence of the austral continent: first relatively small, relatively scattered chunks, then bergs that loomed up out of the water like sculpted mountains of blue and green and white and bulked ever so much larger below the surface of the ocean. Somehow, leviathans could sense those great masses of underwater ice without seeing them, and never collided with them. Cornelu wished he knew how his beast managed that, but the finest veterinary mages were as baffled as he.

In winter, the sea itself froze solid for miles out from the shore of the land of the Ice People. The icebergs Cornelu passed broke off from the main mass as sea and air warmed when the sun swung south in the sky once more.

He and his leviathan had to thread their way through channels in the ice to the little settlement Kuusaman and Lagoan sorcerers had established east of Mizpah, on the long headland that jutted out toward the island the two kingdoms shared. A Kuusaman mage in a rowboat came out to bring Cornelu the last couple of hundred yards to shore.

"Very good to see you," the Kuusaman said in classical Kaunian, the only language they proved to have in common.

He introduced himself as Leino. "Very good to see anyone who is not a familiar face, as a matter of fact. All the familiar faces have become much too familiar, if you know what I mean."

"I think I do," Cornelu answered. "I suspect you would be even happier to see me if I were a good-looking woman."

"Especially if you were my wife," the Kuusaman said. "But Pekka has her own sorcerous work, and I know as little about what she is doing as she knows about what goes on here."

"What *does* go on here?" Cornelu looked at the miserable collection of huts and camel-hide tents on the mainland. "Why would anyone in his right mind want to come here?"

Leino grinned at him. "You make assumptions that may not be justified, you know." The mage might smile and joke, but didn't answer the question.

Cornelu knew he wasn't going to get much of an answer, but he did want some. "Why on earth did they have my leviathan bring you two large egg casings filled with sawdust?"

"No trees around these parts," Leino replied as the rowboat ran aground on a pebbly beach. "Hard to get a ship through all these icebergs. A leviathan can carry more than a dragon. And so—here you are."

"Here I am," Cornelu agreed in hollow tones. "Here I may stay, too, unless you get me back to my leviathan before it swims off after food."

"No worry there." Leino scrambled out of the boat. "We have a good binding spell on the sea hereabouts. You are not the first leviathan-rider to come here, but not a one of them has been stranded."

"Fair enough." Cornelu got out of the boat, too. With rubber flippers still on his feet, he was as awkward as a duck on land. He persisted: "Why sawdust?"

"Why, to mix with the ice, of course," Leino replied, as if that were the most obvious thing in the world. "We have plenty of ice here."

Cornelu gave up. He might hope for a straight answer, but

he could tell he wasn't going to get one. He asked a different sort of question: "How do you keep yourselves fed?"

Leino seemed willing enough to answer that. "We buy reindeer and camel meat from the Ice People." His flat, swarthy features twisted into a horrible grimace. "Camel meat is pretty bad, but at least the camel it comes from is dead. Live camels—believe me, Commander, you do not want to know about live camels. And we blaze seals and sea birds every now and then. They are not very good, either. To keep us from dying of scurvy, the Lagoans are generous enough to send us plenty of pickled cabbage." By his expression, he also didn't care for that.

"Cranberries fight scurvy, too," Cornelu said. "Do cranberries grow on this part of the austral continent?"

"Nothing has grown on this part of the austral continent since I got here," Leino replied. He looked around at the green sprouting up here and there. "I must admit, I cannot be quite so sure about what will grow now. See? Even these sorry things yield up a crop."

He pointed to the shelters, from which emerged a couple of dozen other mages. Most were easy to type as either Kuusamans or Lagoans, but six or eight could have been either and were in fact partly both. Such untidiness bothered Cornelu. In Sibiu, everyone was recognizably Sibian. He shrugged. He couldn't do anything about it here.

Whatever their blood, the mages were friendly. They gave Cornelu smoked meat and sour cabbage and potent spirits Leino hadn't mentioned. Some of them spoke Algarvian, in which he was more fluent than classical Kaunian. Waving a slice of meat, he said, "This stuff isn't so bad. It's got a flavor all its own."

"That's one way to put it," said a mage who looked like a Kuusaman but spoke Lagoan when he wasn't using Algarvian or classical Kaunian. "And do you know why it's got that flavor? Because it was smoked over burning camel dung, that's why."

"You're joking." But Cornelu saw that the wizard wasn't.

He set down the meat and took a big swig of spirits. Once he had the spirits in his mouth, he swished them around before swallowing, as if cleaning his teeth. In fact, that was exactly what he was doing.

The mage laughed. "You've got to get used to eating things cooked with it if you're going to try and live in the land of the Ice People. There isn't much in the way of wood here. If there were, would you be bringing sawdust from Lagoas?"

"You never can tell," Cornelu answered, which made the mage laugh again.

"Well, maybe not," the fellow said. "Some of those blockheads in Setubal ought to be ground up for sawdust themselves, if anybody wants to know what I think."

Cornelu tried again: "Now that you have all this sawdust, what will you do with it?"

"Mix it with ice," the Lagoan mage answered, as Leino had. "We're trying to make cold drinks for termites, you see."

"Thank you so very much," the Sibian exile said. All that got him was still more laughter from the wizard.

"Are you feeling refreshed after your long journey here?" Leino asked in classical Kaunian. When Cornelu admitted he was, the Kuusaman mage asked, "Then you will not mind if I row you out to sea again so you can summon your leviathan and so we can bring these casings full of sawdust to the shore?"

Whatever the mages wanted to do with the sawdust, they were eager to get at it. With a sigh, Cornelu got to his feet again. "After tasting the delicacies of the countryside here, I suppose I can," he answered. The sooner he left the land of the Ice People and its delicacies, the happier he would be. He didn't say anything about that. The mages who were stuck down here at the bottom of the world couldn't leave no matter how much they wanted to.

Leino handled the oars with ease a fisherman might have envied. As he rowed, he asked, "When you go back to Setubal, Commander, you will take letters with you?"

"Aye, if you and your comrades give them to me," Cornelu answered.

"We will." The Kuusaman sighed. "The cursed censors will probably have to use their black ink and knives on them. They have taken too many bites out of the letters my wife sends to me."

"I can do nothing about that." Cornelu's wife didn't write him letters. The most he could say about her was that she hadn't betrayed him to the Algarvians even after she started giving herself to them. It wasn't enough. It wasn't nearly enough.

Leino let the rowboat drift to a stop. "This was about where I picked you up, was it not?"

"I think so, aye." Cornelu leaned out over the gunwale and slapped the water in the pattern that would summon his leviathan if it was anywhere close by. He waited a couple of minutes, then slapped again.

He got only a brief glimpse of the leviathan's sinuously muscled shape before its snout broke the surface by the boat and sent water splashing up onto the two men in it. Still in his rubber suit, Cornelu didn't mind. Leino spluttered and said something in Kuusaman that sounded pungent before returning to classical Kaunian: "I think the beast did that on purpose."

"I would not be a bit surprised if you were right," Cornelu answered. "Leviathans seem to think people were made for their amusement." He slid down into the sea and swam over to the leviathan. After patting it and praising it for coming, he undid the egg casings it carried under its belly and brought the two ropes over to Leino. "The cases are of neutral buoyancy," he said as he got back into the boat. "They will not pull you under." Leino made the ropes fast to the stern of the boat.

When the Kuusaman mage started to row again, he grunted. "They may not sink me, but they are not light. The shore looks a good deal farther away than it did when you were here before."

"I gather you and your colleagues wanted a good deal of sawdust," Cornelu replied. "I still do not understand why you wanted it, but you did, and now you have it. I hope you use it to confound Algarve."

"With the help of the powers above, I think we may be able to oblige you." Leino took another stroke and grunted again. "Assuming my arms do not fall out of their sockets between here and the beach, that is."

"Would the work not go on either way?" Cornelu asked, as innocently as he could.

Leino started to say something—perhaps something sharp—then checked himself and chuckled. "Commander, you are more dangerous than you look."

Cornelu courteously inclined his head. "I hope so."

Nine

Tears ran down Vanai's face. She'd just finished chopping up a particularly potent onion when someone knocked on the door to the flat. As she hurried out of the kitchen, whoever it was knocked again, louder and more insistently. Fear blazed through her. This wasn't just a knock. This was liable to be *the* knock, the one she'd dreaded ever since coming to Eoforwic.

"Opening up!" The call came in Algarvian-accented Forthwegian. "Opening up or breaking down, by powers above!"

Vanai wondered if she ought to leap out the window and hope she could end everything quickly. The redheads wouldn't get the use of her life energy that way, anyhow. But she'd just renewed the spell that disguised her Kaunianity—and she was carrying a child. If that wasn't an expression of hope, what was?

She unbarred the door and worked the latch. The kilted Algarvian in the hall had his fist upraised to knock again. A couple of burly Forthwegian constables flanked him like bookends. He looked Vanai up and down, then said, "You are being Thelberge, wife to Ealstan?"

"Aye. That's right." More hope flowered in Vanai. If the Algarvian called her by her Forthwegian name, he probably wasn't going to seize her for being a Kaunian. Gathering courage, she asked, "What do you want?"

"Your husband is keeping books for Ethelhelm, the singing and drumming man?"

Ah. Vanai wouldn't let her knees shake with relief. If that was why the redhead was here, she could even tell the truth. "Ealstan did keep books for Ethelhelm, aye. But Ethelhelm hasn't been his client since late winter."

"But Ealstan is going—*was* going—to seeing Ethelhelm only a few days ago."

It wasn't a question. Maybe the Algarvian had talked to the doorman at Ethelhelm's block of flats. Again, Vanai could tell the truth, and did: "Ethelhelm did send Ealstan a note asking him to visit. But when he went to Ethelhelm's block of flats, he found Ethelhelm had left the building."

"He is knowing where the singing and drumming man is going—has going?"

"No," Vanai said. "He was surprised when he found Ethelhelm had gone. From what he told me, everyone was surprised when Ethelhelm left."

"*That's* the truth," one of the Forthwegian constables muttered.

"You husband Ealstan not hearing from Ethelhelm since?" the Algarvian asked.

"No," Vanai repeated. "He doesn't want to hear from him, either. They'd fallen out. I don't know what Ethelhelm wanted with him, and I don't want to find out, either." That was also true. She recognized how craven it was, but she didn't care. She only wanted that Algarvian to go away, and to take his Forthwegian henchmen with him.

And she got what she wanted. The redhead swept off his hat and bowed to her. "All right, pretty lady. We going. You seeing this Ethelhelm item, you hearing him, you telling us. We wanting him. Oh, aye. We wanting him. You telling?"

"Of course," Vanai answered: a lie, this time. The Algarvian and the two Forthwegians tramped down the hall to the odorous stairwell. Vanai stood in the doorway and watched till they disappeared. Then she shut the door, leaned against it, and slid halfway to the ground as her knees did weaken with relief.

As she put the bar back on the door, she realized what a narrow escape that had been. Ealstan and Ethelhelm might have fallen out at any time. If they had, and if Ethelhelm had disappeared not long afterwards, Mezentio's men would have come around asking questions. If they'd done it while she still looked like the Kaunian she was . . .

She went back to the onion and threw it in the stew pot. It still stung her eyes, but she didn't feel like crying anymore, not after she'd had her disguise tested and she'd won through to safety.

When Ealstan got back that evening, she told him about her adventure. He held her and squeezed her and didn't say anything for a long time. Then he set the palm of his hand on her belly and murmured, "You are all right. You are both all right."

Vanai needed a moment to realize he'd spoken Kaunian. She smiled and snuggled against him. Speaking Forthwegian had always seemed safer, and more and more lately. It wasn't that Ealstan was more at home in it than in Kaunian; that had always been true. But when Vanai wore Thelberge's seeming, she put on all the trappings that went with being Thelberge, including her language.

As he had when she told him she would have a baby, he went into the kitchen and came back with two cups of wine. "To freedom!" he said, also in classical Kaunian, and she happily drank to that.

He probably assumed they would make love after supper. Vanai assumed the same thing; they'd spent a lot of evenings doing that, both back in the days before she could leave the flat and afterwards. Her own left hand went to her belly as she spooned up more bean-and-barley soup with grated cheese and a couple of marrow bones. If they hadn't, she wouldn't have had a baby growing in there. She yawned. She wouldn't have been so tired all the time, either.

When they were done eating, she went out to the sofa and lay down. The next thing she knew, Ealstan was shaking her awake. "Come on," he said. "Time and past time to go on into the bedchamber. I've washed the dishes and put them away."

"You have?" Vanai said, astonished. "Why? What time is it?"

By way of answer, Ealstan pointed to their windows, which faced toward the southwest. They framed the first-quarter moon, now sinking down toward the horizon. He spelled out what that meant: "Getting on toward midnight."

"But it can't be!" Vanai exclaimed, as if he'd somehow tricked her, cheated her. "I just came out here to rest for a few minutes, and—"

"And you started to snore," Ealstan said. "I wasn't going to bother you, but I didn't think you'd want to spend the whole night here."

"Oh." Now Vanai sounded sheepish. "It caught me again." She yawned again, too. "Am I going to stay asleep till the baby's born?"

Ealstan grinned at her. "Maybe you ought to hope you will. I don't know much about what women do while they're expecting, but you were the one who said you wouldn't get much sleep after the baby's here."

That was indeed all too likely to be true. Vanai got up, cleaned her teeth, changed into a light linen tunic, and lay down in bed beside Ealstan. He went to sleep right away. She tossed and turned for a while. She was used to sleeping on her belly, but her breasts were too tender for that to be comfortable. She curled up on her side and . . .

It was morning. She rolled over. Ealstan wasn't there. Noise from the kitchen told where he'd gone. She went out there herself. He was dipping bread into olive oil and sipping from a cup of wine. "Hello, there," he said cheerfully, and got up and gave her a quick kiss. "Shall I fix you some?"

"Would you, please?" Vanai laughed a small, nervous laugh. "I didn't have any trouble keeping supper down. Let's hope I do all right with this, too."

"You haven't been too bad that way," Ealstan said, cutting her a chunk of bread, adding oil to the dipping bowl, and pouring wine.

"That's easy for you to say," Vanai answered. Some women, she'd heard, got morning sickness right away and kept on having it till their babies were born. She didn't know how long she'd keep having hers, of course, but she didn't have it all the time. Ealstan was right about that. Even a couple of meals disastrously lost, though, were plenty to make her wary about food.

This morning, everything seemed willing to stay down. She'd almost finished when Ealstan said, "Your spell just slipped."

"Did it?" Vanai raised a hand to her face. That was foolish; she couldn't feel any change in her looks, any more than she could see one.

Ealstan reached across the table and stroked her cheek, too. "Aye, it did," he answered, eyeing her. "That's the face I fell in love with, you know."

"You're sweet," Vanai said. "It's also the face that could ruin everything if anybody but you saw it." She got the yellow and dark brown lengths of yarn out of her handbag, twisted them together, and chanted in classical Kaunian: one use for her own first language that would not go away. When she finished, she looked a question to Ealstan.

He nodded. "Now you look like my sister again."

"I wish you'd stop saying that," Vanai told him. It was the wrong sort of family connection to have, especially now that she was pregnant.

"I'm sorry." Ealstan finished his wine. "If this cursed war ever ends, if you and Conberge ever get the chance to meet, I think you'll like each other."

"I hope so," Vanai said. She hoped with all her heart that his family would like her; so far as she knew, none of her own family was left alive. After a moment, she went on, "The one I truly want to meet is your father. He made you what you are. That first time we met in the woods, you said, 'Kaunians are people, too,' and that he'd taught you that. If more Forthwegians thought that way, I wouldn't have to worry about my magecraft."

"I know he'll like you," Ealstan told her. "He's bound to like you. You're difficult."

"Am I?" Vanai wasn't sure how to take that. It sounded as if it wanted to be a compliment.

Ealstan nodded. "Don't you suppose the Algarvians think you're difficult?"

"I never even learned that apothecary's name," Vanai said. It didn't sound like a responsive answer, but it was. Mezentio's hounds had been one man away from learning who'd devised the magic that let Kaunians look like their Forthwegian neighbors. If the apothecary hadn't had a lethal dose ready to hand, they might have torn the knowledge out of him. She wondered what they would do to someone who'd caused them so much trouble. She shivered. She was glad she didn't have to find out.

Ealstan poured his cup half full of wine once more, gulped it down, and said, "I'm off. I've got a couple of people whose accounts need casting, and another fellow, a friend of one of theirs, might want to take me on, at least to give his regular bookkeeper a hand. Pybba heads up one of the biggest pottery outfits in town, which means one of the biggest ones in the kingdom. He'd pay well. He'd better, or I won't work for him."

"Good," Vanai said. "I approve of money."

"Aye, my father would like you—will like you—just fine," Ealstan said. "That you're mother to his grandchild won't hurt, either." He got up and brushed her lips with his. She tasted the wine on them.

She stood, too, to give him a quick hug. "I'll do what I can around the house," she said. "And what I can't . . ." She shrugged and yawned. "I'll curl up like a dormouse and sleep the day away."

"Why not?" Ealstan said. "If Ethelhelm comes knocking, don't let him in."

"You don't need to worry about that," Vanai said. One of the reasons she approved of money was that it would let her bribe Algarvians at need. She never wanted to have to bribe them about her Kaunianity; that would leave her enslaved to them. But some silver might make them stop asking her questions about the singer. She hoped she wouldn't have to find out, but she could try it if she had to.

Through the winter, the woods in the west of Unkerlant had been quiet save for the sounds of men and men's magic. With the coming of spring, birdsongs burst out everywhere. The very air took on a fresh, green smell as the sap rose in untold millions of trees. Even some of the logs in front of the Gyongyosian army's redoubts sprouted little leafy shoots. But the Gyongyosians stayed on the defensive.

One day, Szonyi came up to Istvan and said, "Sergeant, the stars only know what kind of horrible scheme the Unkerlanters are hatching over there." He pointed east. "We ought to give 'em a good prod, knock 'em back on their heels."

Istvan shrugged. "We haven't got any orders." He shook his head. "No, I take that back. We have got orders—to sit tight."

"It's foolishness," Szonyi insisted. "It's worse than foolishness. It's going to get a lot of us killed." He waved his arms in disgust.

The motion drew Corporal Kun's notice. "What's eating him?" he asked Istvan, as if Szonyi weren't there.

"He wants to go out and kill things again," Istvan answered.

"Ah." Spectacles glinting in a shaft of sunlight, Kun turned to Szonyi. "When was the last time we saw anything that looked like reinforcements?"

"*I* don't know," Szonyi said impatiently. "What's that got to do with anything?"

"If we attack and use up our men and don't get any new ones, how long will it be before we haven't got any men left at all?" Kun asked, as if to an idiot child.

"I don't know that, either," Szonyi said. "But if we sit here and don't do anything and let the Unkerlanters build up and roll over us, how long will it be before we haven't got any men left that way?"

"He has a point," Istvan said.

"He should wear a hat on it," Kun said. Istvan laughed at the former mage's apprentice. Kun hated admitting that Szonyi could score off him.

Lajos, who was on sentry duty, called, "Who comes?" That sent Istvan and Kun and Szonyi and everybody else in the squad grabbing for sticks.

But the answer was immediate: "I—Captain Tivadar."

"Come ahead, sir!" Lajos said, and the men in the redoubt relaxed.

Tivadar did, sliding down into the trench behind the log barricade. Istvan hurried over to salute him. "What can we do for you today, sir?" he asked.

"Not a thing. Carry on as you were," his company commander replied. "I just came up to see how things were going."

"We're all right, sir," Istvan said. "Nothing much going on in front of us right now." Szonyi stirred, but didn't say anything. Seeing him stir made Istvan remark, "Been a while since we've seen any new men up here, sir. We could use some."

"This whole line could use some," Tivadar agreed. "Don't hold your breath till we get them, though, or we'll have one more casualty to replace."

"Something's gone wrong somewhere," Istvan spoke with the assurance of a man who had seen a great many things go wrong. "Up till not very long ago, we got—well, not everything we needed, but enough to keep us going from day to day. Now . . . Stars above know I mean no disrespect to Ekrekek Arpad or anybody else, but it's like people have forgotten we're here."

"You're not far wrong," Tivadar answered. "Things aren't going so well out in the islands in the Bothnian Ocean. I'm not giving away any great secrets when I tell you that. The Kuusamans keep biting them off one after another, and we're putting more and more soldiers into the ones we still hold. We don't really have enough men to fight that campaign to the fullest and this one to the fullest at the same time."

"By the stars, a couple of years ago the Kuusamans couldn't even throw us off Obuda," Istvan exclaimed. "What have they done since, and why haven't we done anything about it?"

Kun asked a different but related question: "Kuusamo is fighting us and Algarve, the same as we're fighting them and Unkerlant. How is it that they can divide up their forces but we can't?"

"Because, Corporal, their fight with Algarve is only a sham." Tivadar chose to answer Kun. "They face our allies with ships and dragons, but not with many men. What soldiers they have in the fight, they throw at us. Both our fronts are real."

"That's true," Kun said. "And if the Unkerlanters hit us hard here, we'll fall down like a stone-block house in an earthquake."

"Unkerlant's got two fronts, too," Istvan said, "and this is the one that's their sham."

Tivadar nodded. "That's about the size of it, Sergeant. We can grab chunks of their land here, but that's the most we can do. We can't take Cottbus away from them, and the Algarvians might."

Cottbus was only a name to Istvan, and not a name that seemed particularly real. Once, when the fight in western Unkerlant was new, Kun had calculated how long the Gyongyosians would need to get to Cottbus at the rate of advance they'd had then. It had been years; Istvan remembered that. How many? Three? Five? He couldn't recall. One thing seemed certain: if his countrymen weren't advancing toward Cottbus at all, they'd never get there.

That led to the next interesting question: "Sir, do you think we'll be able to hold what we've already taken from Unkerlant? The way things are now, I mean."

"Well, we're still going to try, Sergeant, sure as blazes," Tivadar replied. "The last time we talked about this, I was pretty sure we could do it. Now . . . It'll be harder. I'd be a liar if I said otherwise. It'll get harder still if we have to pull men out of the woods here so we can send them to fight on the islands. But the Unkerlanters have their troubles, too. We'll do our best."

"The stars favor us," Szonyi said. "With the heavens smiling, how can we lose?"

Tivadar walked over and slapped him on the back. "You're a good man. With men like you in our army, how can we lose?" Just for a moment, Szonyi held out his left hand, palm up, and looked at the scar on it. Tivadar thumped him on the back again. "You heard what I said, soldier. I meant it." Szonyi stood straight and looked proud.

Kun said, "How can we lose? That's why people fight wars—to find out how one side can lose."

Szonyi started to get angry. Istvan took a deep breath, casting about for the words that would put Kun in his place. But Captain Tivadar just laughed and said, "We need a few city men in the ranks, too. Otherwise, the rest of us would take too much for granted."

"He can't take it for granted that his—" Szonyi started.

"Enough!" Now Istvan's voice cracked sharp as a whip.

"Aye, enough." Tivadar looked from Kun to Szonyi and back again. His eye fell on Istvan, too, as his gaze passed from one soldiers to the other. "You are brothers, blooded together . . . in battle." The slight pause reminded them how they'd been blooded together for a different reason, too. But no one who didn't know about that other, darker, reason could have guessed it from the company commander's words. Tivadar continued, "Let no quarrel come between you now."

Kun nodded at once. City men didn't cling to feuds the way folk from the mountain valleys did. Szonyi took longer. Tivadar and Istvan both glared at him. At last, reluctantly, his big, shaggy head bobbed up and down, too.

"That's a strong fellow," Tivadar said. He turned and started to climb out of the redoubt.

"Sir? One more question?" Istvan asked. Tivadar paused, then nodded. Istvan asked, "Have we got enough mages forward to warn us if Swemmel's whoresons are going to turn that horrible magic loose on us again? You know the one I mean."

"I know the one you mean," the company commander agreed grimly. "What I don't know is the answer to your question. I'm not even sure mages can detect that spell before the Unkerlanters start slaughtering people to power it. We might do better to slide forward to find out if they're bringing peasants up toward the front."

"That's not a bad notion, sir," Kun said. "I don't mean just for us. I mean all along the line of these cursed woods."

"I'm no general. I can't give an order for the whole line. I can't even give an order for the whole regiment," Tivadar said. "But if you boys want to poke men out to the east to see what's going on, you won't make me unhappy. And now I will be on my way." He climbed the sandbagged steps at the rear of the redoubt and hurried off through the forest.

"He had a good idea there, Sergeant," Kun said. "If we could get some warning before the Unkerlanters started slaying . . ." He shuddered. "When they loosed that magic the last time, it was so vile I thought my head would burst like an egg. By the stars, I *hoped* my head would burst like an egg."

"All right, we'll do it," Istvan said, "though it'd only be luck if Swemmel's buggers had their victims in our sector. We *ought* to have scouts pushing forward all along the line. The Unkerlanters do, may the stars go black for them."

Before he could order anyone to go out and scout around in the woods to the east, an egg burst about fifty yards in front of the redoubt. A moment later, another burst less than half as far away. Before the third egg could land, Istvan was flat on his belly, his face pressed against the black earth. He breathed in a moist lungful of air smelling of mold and old leaves.

That third egg burst behind the redoubt, close enough that the blast of sorcerous energy made the ground shudder beneath Istvan's prostrate form. A couple of trees crashed in noisy ruin. Earth and twigs rained down on Istvan. He'd been through such pummelings before. Unless an egg burst right on top of the redoubt, he knew he was safe enough.

He was. His squad was. As more eggs burst all around, he exclaimed in dismay: "Captain Tivadar!" He didn't dare raise his head very far, no matter how dismayed he was.

"He has a good chance," Kun said, his head not an inch farther from the ground than Istvan's was. "He'd have gone flat when the first egg flew, and started digging himself a hole before the second one burst. You would. I would. The captain, too. He's no fool." From Kun, that was highest praise.

"We ought to go out after him," Szonyi said. "If it was one of us stuck in a storm like that, *he'd* go out and bring us back."

"We don't even know which way he went," Istvan said. But that sounded hollow even to him. Szonyi didn't answer. His silence sounded more reproachful than shouted curses would have.

Cursing on his own, Istvan heaved himself to his feet and left the redoubt. As soon as he was out in the woods, he went down on his belly again; eggs were still bursting all around. "Captain Tivadar!" he shouted, though his voice seemed tiny and lost through those shattering roars of suddenly released sorcerous energy. "Captain Tivadar, sir!"

Even if Tivadar did answer, how was Istvan supposed to hear him? His ears were bruised, overwhelmed, battered. An egg burst nearby, very close. A pine that might have stood for a hundred years swayed, toppled, and crashed down. Had it fallen at a slightly different, an ever so slightly different, angle, it would have crushed the life out of him.

Was that someone's tawny hair or a bit of dead, yellowed fern? Istvan crawled toward it, then wished he hadn't. There lay Tivadar, broken like a jointed doll some thoughtless child had stepped on. But dolls didn't bleed. A bursting egg must have flung him full force into a tree trunk.

At least he can't have known what hit him, Istvan thought. "Stars above preserve and guide his spirit," he murmured, and hurried back to the redoubt. He hoped his own end, if it came, when it came, would be as quick.

As winter gave way to spring, so Talsu accommodated himself to life in prison. He hadn't intended to do any such thing. But, as he'd found in the Jelgavan army, routine had a force of its own. Even when the routine was horrid, as it was here, he got used to it. His belly anticipated almost to the minute the times the guards fed him his nasty, sadly inadequate bowls of gruel. Afterwards, for half an hour, sometimes even for an hour, he felt as nearly content as he could in a small, stinking, vermin-infested cell.

Nearly. His best time in the prison was the exercise period, when, along with other captives from his hall, he got to tramp back and forth in the yard. Even whispers among them could bring the wrath of the guards down on their heads. The gray stone of the prison was as unlovely in the yard as anywhere else. But Talsu saw it by sunlight, a light that grew brighter almost ever day. He saw blue sky. He breathed fresh air. He began to hear birds sing. He wasn't free. He knew that all too well. But the exercise period let him remember freedom.

And then, like a drowning man sinking beneath the surface of the sea, he would have to go back into the gloom and the reek. Even that came to be part of the routine. He would put a lot of himself away, deaden himself, till the next time he got to go out and see the sun once more.

Whenever routine broke, he dreaded it. He had reason to dread it: routine never broke for anything good. The Jelgavan constabulary captain hadn't summoned him for several weeks now. Talsu hoped that meant the fellow had given up. He didn't believe it, though. If the authorities decided he was innocent—or at least harmless—wouldn't they let him go?

One morning, not long after what passed for his breakfast, the door to his cell came open at an unaccustomed time. "What is it?" Talsu demanded, alarm in his an voice. Any change in routine meant something that could—that was about to—go wrong.

"Shut up," the lead guard said. "Stand up." Talsu sprang off his cot to his feet. He said not another word. The guards punished without mercy anything that smacked of disobedience or insubordination. "Come along," the man at their head commanded, and Talsu came.

To his relief, he discovered he was not going down the corridors that led to the constabulary captain's lair. Instead, he was installed in another cell, even smaller and darker than the one from which he'd been taken. Light from the corridor leaked in only through a couple of tiny peepholes.

The guards stayed in there with him, which convinced him this change wasn't permanent. Their leader said, "All right, boys—gag him." With rough efficiency, the other guards did. Talsu wanted to struggle, but the sticks they aimed at him persuaded him not to. He wanted to protest, too, but the gag kept him from doing that.

"Here," said one of the men who'd bound the leather-and-cloth contraption over his mouth. "Now you get to look out." The guards shoved him up to one of the peepholes.

Doing his best to be contrary, Talsu closed his eyes tight. Whatever they wanted him to see, he would do his best not to see it. Then he felt the business end of a stick pressed against the back of his head. "If you make even the smallest sound now, I will blaze you," the lead guard whispered. "And that will not be the worst thing that happens—not even close to the worst. I almost hope you do sing out."

They were playing games with him. Talsu knew they were playing games with him. But that didn't mean he could keep from opening his eyes. What was so important that he had to see it but also had to keep silent about it?

There was the corridor, as uninteresting as the stretch of hallway in front of his own cell. What sort of foolish game were the gaolers making him join? A guard walked along the hall, into and out of Talsu's limited field of vision. Even if he'd looked full at Talsu, all he could have seen of him through the peephole were a couple of staring eyes. But he walked past the closed door as if it didn't exist.

"Not a word," the lead guard whispered again. Talsu nodded, but only a little. He kept his eyes to the peephole, he surely did. The guards had him going. Aye, he knew it, but he couldn't do anything about it.

Here came another guard, this one as indifferent to the door to Talsu's new cell as the first fellow had been. Behind him walked a woman. She wasn't a prisoner—her person and clothes were clean. At first, that was all Talsu noticed. Then he recognized his wife. He started to scream, "Gailisa!" in spite of the guard's warning. But he almost blessed the gag, which reminded him he must not make a sound.

Another guard followed Gailisa, but Talsu hardly saw him. His eyes were only on his wife, and he couldn't have seen her for more than two heartbeats, three at the outside. Then she was gone. The corridor was just a corridor again.

"You see?" the lead guard said with complacency that was almost obscene. "We have her, too. It won't get any better for you, and oh, how easy it can get worse."

He didn't bother ordering his henchmen to ungag Talsu before they took him back to his own cell. If any other captives were looking out and saw a gagged man marched down a corridor, what would that do except make them more likely to submit to escape a similar fate?

After they took Talsu back, after they released him from the gag, they let him stew in his own juice for a couple of days. Only then did they haul him out again and bring him before the constabulary captain who served King Mainardo as ready as he had served King Donalitu.

"Talsu son of Traku." The captain sounded reproachful. "Do you see what your stubbornness has got you? We had no choice but to bring in your wife for interrogation, too. And what she told us . . . I wouldn't say it looks good. No, by the powers above, I wouldn't say that at all."

I don't believe you, Talsu started to say. But he bit that back almost in the same way he'd bitten back Gailisa's name there in the cell with the peephole. Anything he said gave them a greater hold on him. He stood there and waited.

"Aye, she's turned on you," the constabulary captain said. "And she's given us enough denunciations to keep us busy for quite a while, that she has." He eyed Talsu. "What have you got to say about that?"

"Nothing, sir," Talsu answered. Eventually, this would end.

"Nothing?" Now disbelief filled the officer's voice. "Nothing? I can't believe my ears. Well, that's not what your pretty little Gailisa had to say. She sang like a redbreast—and she sang about *you*." He pointed a forefinger at Talsu as if it were a stick.

That bit of overacting convinced Talsu of what he'd only hoped before: that the captain was lying. He was sure Gailisa would never betray him, not like that, not for anything. He said, "Well, sir, you've already got me."

"And we'll have all the rebels in Skrunda before long," the constabulary captain said. "Make it easy on yourself like your wife did. Help us."

"But I have no names to give you," Talsu said, more than a little desperation in his voice. "We've cut these trousers before." He knew what would come at the end of such protestations, too: another beating. If that was the routine for interrogations, he wouldn't be sorry to disrupt it.

Sure enough, the guards behind him growled in eager anticipation. They knew what would come, too, and they looked forward to it. So much in life depended on whether one did or was done to.

"Here." The captain picked up a sheet of paper with writing on it and waved it in Talsu's face. "Your wife has given us a list of names. You see? She's not so shy, not so shy at all. And now, for both your sakes, I'd better have a list of names from *you*. And a good many of the names on it had better match the ones on this list here, or you'll be even sorrier than you are already. You may take that to the bank, Talsu son of Traku."

Seeing the list did rock Talsu. Was the constable lying? Or had Gailisa given him names? Would she do that, in the hope of freeing Talsu? She might. Talsu knew only too well that she might. She'd never betray him, but she might betray others to save him. He might have done the same for her.

What names would she give, though? She wouldn't know anyone who really was involved in fighting the Algarvian occupiers. Such people did not advertise. Talsu had gone looking for them when he started learning classical Kaunian, and whom had he found? Kugu the silversmith, Kugu the traitor. Which meant . . .

"Curse you," Talsu said, and the guards behind him

growled again. But, before they could do anything more than growl, he went on, "Let me have some paper and a pen. I'll give you what you want. Just leave my wife alone."

"I knew we would find a key to pick your lock." The constabulary captain smiled broadly. With an almost Algarvian flourish, he passed Talsu the writing tools. "Remember what I told you."

"I'm not likely to forget," Talsu mumbled as he started to write.

He still didn't know for a fact that Gailisa had given the constabulary captain any names at all. The fellow hadn't let him get a good enough look at the list to recognize her writing. But if she had written down names, whose names would they be?

Most likely, Talsu judged, the names of people who liked the Algarvians well enough but weren't out-and-out lickspittles—using those would have made what she was up to only too clear. Talsu knew a good many people of that sort. And the redheads and their Jelgavan hounds wouldn't be able to trust people like that: after all, such folk might just be putting up a good front.

And so, wishing the worst to those who seemed happy under an Algarvian puppet king, Talsu set down a dozen names and then, after a little thought, three or four more. He passed his list back to the constabulary captain. "These are the ones I can think of."

"Let's see what we've got." The captain compared the sheet he'd got from Talsu to the one he'd waved. Maybe Gailisa really had given him a list. Maybe he wasn't such a dreadful actor after all. He clicked his tongue between his teeth. "Isn't that interesting?" he murmured. "There *are* some matches. I must admit I'm a little surprised. You took a long time coming to your senses, Talsu son of Traku, but I'm glad you've finally seen who has the strength in this new and greater Jelgava."

"That's pretty plain," Talsu said, which wasn't altogether untrue: had things been the other way round, men who served redheaded King Mainardo could never had laid hands on Gailisa.

"We shall have to do some more investigating—aye, indeed we shall," the captain said, at least half to himself. "Powers above only know what may have been going on right under our noses. Well, if it was, we'll put a stop to it. Aye, we will."

"What about me?" Talsu demanded. "I've given you what you wanted." He sounded like a girl who'd just let a seducer have his way with her. He felt like that, too. He'd yielded, but the constabulary captain wasn't doing anything for him.

The captain tapped the list with a fingernail. "What about you? I don't know yet. We'll find out. If you've done us some good, we'll do you some good. If you haven't . . ." He tapped it again. "If you haven't, you'll be sorry you tried to get clever with us." He nodded to the guards. "Take him back to his cell."

Back Talsu went. The guards didn't work him over. That was something. He returned to his place in time for supper. That was something, too. Routine returned. He wondered when it would end again . . . when, and how.

Pybba the pottery magnate was about fifty, with energy enough to wear down any three men half his age. He certainly left Ealstan panting. "Don't complain," he boomed. "Don't carp. Just do the work, young fellow. As long as you do the work, everything will be fine. That's why I sacked the bookkeeper I had before you: he couldn't keep up. Couldn't come close to keeping up. I need someone who *will* attend. If you will, I'll pay you. If you won't, I'll boot you out on your arse. Is that plain enough?"

He'd been standing much too close to Ealstan, and all but bellowing in his ear. With his most innocent expression, Ealstan looked up from the accounts he'd been casting and said, "No, sir. I'm sorry, but I don't know what you're talking about."

Pybba stared. "Wha-at?" he rumbled. Then he realized Ealstan was pulling his leg. He rumbled again, this time with laughter. "You've got spunk, young fellow, I'll say that for you. But have you got staying power?—and I don't want to hear what your wife thinks."

That made Ealstan laugh, too, if a little uncomfortably. "I'm managing so far. And you pay well enough."

"Do the work and you earn the money. That's only fair," Pybba said. "Do the work. If you don't do the work, the powers below are welcome to you—and I'll give 'em horseradish and capers to eat you with."

Ealstan could have done the work better and faster if Pybba hadn't hovered there haranguing him. But Pybba, as best he could see, harangued everybody about everything. He also worked harder than any of his employees. As far as Ealstan was concerned, his example was a lot more persuasive than his lectures.

Eventually, Pybba went off to yell at someone else: the kilnmaster, as Ealstan—and everyone else within earshot—soon realized. Not paying attention to Pybba when he wasn't talking to them was a skill a lot of people who worked for him had acquired. Ealstan hadn't, not yet, but he was learning.

He was also learning a demon of a lot about bookkeeping. Nobody back in Gromheort ran a business a quarter the size of Pybba's. Ethelhelm had made almost as much money, but his accounts were straightforward by comparison. With Pybba, it wasn't just the right hand not knowing what the left was doing. A lot of his fingers hadn't been introduced to one another.

"Well, what do you think this is?" he demanded when Ealstan asked him about an incidental expense.

"It looks like a bribe to keep the Algarvians sweet," Ealstan answered.

Pybba beamed at him. "Ah, good. You're not a blind man. Have to stay in business, you know."

"Aye," Ealstan said. Pybba was a full-blooded Forthwegian; he had to pay out less than Ethelhelm had to stay in business. The Algarvians couldn't seize him merely for existing, as they could with the half-breed band leader. After some thought, Ealstan shook his head. The Algarvians *could* do that if they wanted to badly enough; they could do anything if they wanted to badly enough. But they had far less reason to want to than they did with Ethelhelm.

Because the Algarvians didn't force his bribes to rise out

of the range of ordinary thievery, Pybba was making money almost faster than he knew what to do with it. "And he should be making even more than he is," Ealstan said to Vanai one evening over supper. "I don't quite know where some of it's going."

"Well, you said he pays his people well," she answered around one of a long series of yawns. "He's paying you well, that's certain. And he hired you just about full-time soon enough."

"Oh, he does," Ealstan agreed. "And he is, and he did. But that's all in the open—all in the books. Somewhere, money's leaking out of things. Not a whole lot, mind you, but it is."

"Is somebody stealing from Pybba?" Vanai asked. "Or is that what he's paying Mezentio's men so they won't bother him?" She knew how the redheads operated.

"It's not bribes," Ealstan said. "Those are on the books, too, though that's not what they're called. Someone stealing? I don't know. It wouldn't be easy, and you're right—he pays well enough, you'd have to be a greedy fool to want more."

"Plenty of people *are* greedy fools," Vanai pointed out. Ealstan couldn't disagree with that.

He still had clients other than Pybba, though the pottery magnate swallowed more and more of his hours. He kept trying to find out how and why Pybba wasn't making quite so much money as he should have. He kept trying, and kept failing. He imagined his father looking over his shoulder and making disapproving noises. As far as Hestan was concerned, numbers were as transparent as glass. Ealstan had thought they were, too, but all he found here was opacity.

At last, baffled, he brought the matter to Pybba's notice, saying, "I think you have a thief, but I'm cursed if I can see where. Whoever's doing this is more clever than I am. Maybe you ought to have him casting your accounts instead of me."

"A thief?" Pybba's hard face darkened with anger. "You'd better show me what you've found, lad. If I can figure out who the son of a whore is, I'll break him in half." He didn't sound as if he were joking.

"I hope you can figure it out, because I can't," Ealstan answered. "And I have to tell you, I haven't really *found* anything. All I've noticed is that something is lost, and I'm not even sure where."

"Let me have a look," Pybba said.

Ealstan guided him through it, showing how things didn't quite add up. He said, "I've been looking back through the books, too, trying to find out how long this has been going on. I'm sure it was happening while your last bookkeeper before me was here. The other thing I'm sure of is that he didn't even notice."

"Him? He wouldn't have noticed a naked woman if she got into bed with him, he wouldn't." Pybba snorted in fine contempt. The finger he used to mark his place darted now here, now there, as he followed the track Ealstan set out for him. He clicked his tongue between his teeth. "Well, well, young fellow. Isn't that interesting?"

"That's not the word I'd use," Ealstan answered. "The word I'd use is *larcenous*." He hated cooked books. They offended his sense of order. In that as in so many things, he was very much his father's son.

Then Pybba astonished him. Instead of furiously bursting like an egg and blasting his bookkeeper—and maybe the office, too—to smithereens, he set a hand on Ealstan's shoulder and said, "I'm going to pay you a bonus for finding this. You've earned it; I don't think one man in ten would have noticed any of it, let alone all of it. But it's not so much of a much. You don't need to fret yourself over it, the way you've been doing."

"Are you sure?" Ealstan asked, in lieu of, *Are you out of your mind?* "Somebody's stealing from you. If he's stealing not so much from you now, he's liable to steal a lot more later. And even a little hurts. And it's wrong." He spoke that last with great conviction.

Pybba said, "All sorts of things are wrong. You can start with the redheads and go on from there. I'm not going to get excited about this. It's not big enough to get excited about. And if you've got any sense, you won't get excited about it, either."

He phrased that as a request but plainly meant it as an order. Ealstan didn't see how he could disobey it, however much he might want to. But he did speak up, in plaintive tones: "I don't understand."

"I know that. I noticed." Pybba let out a gruff chuckle. "But you don't get silver for understanding. You get silver for keeping my books. You're good at that. You've proved it. You'll get your bonus, too, like I said. But if I'm not worried about this, nobody else needs to be."

That made the third time he'd said pretty much the same thing. Ealstan was—had to be—convinced he meant it, which brought him no closer to following Pybba's mind. He slammed the ledgers shut one after another, to show without words what he thought. Pybba only chuckled again, which irked him further.

But the pottery magnate, though he could be as sharp-tongued as the sherds that sprang from his trade, was a man of his word. When he gave Ealstan his next week's pay, he included the promised bonus. The size of it made Ealstan's eyes go big. "This is too much," he blurted.

Pybba threw back his head and roared laughter. "By the powers above, I've heard plenty whine that they got too little, but never till now the other way round. Go on, go home; spend it. You've said your wife is big with child, haven't you? Aye, I know you have. With a brat on the way, there's no such thing as too much money."

Coins heavy and jingling in his belt pouch, Ealstan went back to his flat in something of a daze. Vanai clapped her hands together in delight when she saw how much Pybba had given him. "He knows you're good," she said proudly.

Ealstan shook his head. He separated the silver into two gleaming piles. Pointing to the smaller one, he said, "This is what he pays me for being good." Then he pointed to the bigger one. "And this is what he paid me for . . . powers above only know what."

"For being good at what you do," Vanai repeated, showing more faith in him than he had in himself. "If you weren't good, you wouldn't have seen what you saw, and you wouldn't have got this."

Her logic was as good as a geometry master's—up to a point. Ealstan said, "I still don't know what in blazes I saw. And he's not paying me because I saw it. He'd be pushing hard after whoever was stealing from him if that were so. No. He's paying me—" He broke off. When he spoke again, it was with sudden new certainty: "He's paying me to keep my mouth shut, that's what he's doing. It can't be anything else."

"Keep your mouth shut about what?" Vanai asked.

"About seeing this—whatever it is," Ealstan answered. "He was surprised when I did. His last bookkeeper hadn't. I'm sure of that. He's bribing me, the same way he's bribing the Algarvians."

Vanai found the next question: "Are you going to let him bribe you?"

"I don't know." Ealstan scratched his head. "If he's hiring robbers or murderers with that missing money, then I don't want anything to do with him, either. If he's got a lady friend somewhere, that's his wife's worry. But if he's doing something to the redheads with the money . . . If he's doing something like that, by the powers above, the only thing I'd want to do was join him."

He wondered how he could tell Pybba that. He wondered if he ought to tell Pybba that. He couldn't prove the pottery magnate wasn't working *for* the Algarvians. Plenty of Forthwegians were. And Ealstan, with a Kaunian wife—and with a baby on the way—had even more to lose from a wrong guess than most of his countrymen would have.

With a regretful sigh, he said, "I don't dare try to find out. Too many bad things could happen."

"You're probably right." But Vanai sighed, too. "I wish you had the chance."

"So do I." Ealstan plucked a hair from his beard, looked at it, and let it fall to the floor. "If I ever find out where that money's going—find out for sure, I mean, not just that it's going missing somewhere—then I'll know what to do."

But Pybba had no intention of making that easy for him. When Ealstan came into the office the next day, his employer said, "Remember why you got your extra silver. No more snooping around, or you'll be sorry."

"I remember," Ealstan assured him.

That wasn't the same as promising he wouldn't snoop anymore. Most people wouldn't have noticed. Pybba did. "No getting cute with me, either, or your arse'll be out on the sidewalk before you've got time to fart. Do you understand me? Do you believe me? I won't just give you the boot, either. I'll blacken your name all over town. Don't you even think about doubting me."

"I wouldn't," Ealstan answered, thinking of nothing else.

Like most educated folk in the eastern regions of Derlavai and the islands lying near the mainland, the Kuusaman physician spoke classical Kaunian along with her own language. Nodding to Fernao, she said, "You will have to strengthen that leg a good deal more, you know."

The Lagoan mage looked down at the limb in question. It was only about half as thick as its mate. "Really?" he said in pretty convincing astonishment. "And here I was planning a fifty-mile hike tomorrow morning. What shall I do now?"

For a moment, the physician took him seriously. Then she exhaled in loud exasperation. "People who cannot take even their own health seriously do not deserve to keep it," she said.

Fernao said, "I'm sorry," in Kuusaman. That mollified the physician, who smiled at him instead of wearing that severe frown. He went on his way with nothing but a cane to help him walk. *I'll probably limp all my days,* he thought as he walked toward the dining room of the isolated hostel in the Naantali district. *I'll probably limp, but I'll be able to walk.*

Pekka was already in there, sitting alone at a table drinking a mug of ale. A couple of secondary sorcerers sat at another table, arguing about the best way to focus a spell at a distance from where it was cast. Not so long before, Fernao wouldn't have known what they were talking about. His Kuusaman got a little better every day.

Seeing him, Pekka set down the mug and clapped her

hands together. "You really are making progress," she said in her own language. And, because he was making progress in that, too, he understood her.

With a nod, he said, "Aye, a bit," also in her tongue. He lifted the cane into the air and stood on his own two feet and nothing else for a few heartbeats. Pekka clapped again. Reveling in his Kuusaman, Fernao asked, "May I join you?"

That was what he thought he asked, anyhow. Pekka giggled. Switching to classical Kaunian, she said, "Several words in Kuusaman may be translated as *to join*. You might be wiser not to use that one to a woman married to another man."

"Oh." Fernao's cheeks got hot. "I'm sorry," he said, as he had to the physician.

Pekka returned to Kuusaman. "I'm not angry. And aye, you may join me." She used a verb different from the one he'd tried.

"Thank you," Fernao said, and asked a server for a mug of ale of his own. He had that request quite well memorized.

When his mug came, Pekka raised hers in salute. "To your full recovery," she said, and drank.

Fernao drank to that toast, too—who wouldn't? If he doubted the wish would be fully granted . . . then he did, that was all. And he enjoyed what he drank; the Kuusamans were good brewers. Then he said, "I hope you are well."

"Well enough, anyhow." Pekka said something in Kuusaman he didn't catch. Seeing as much, she translated it: "Overworked." She hesitated a moment, then asked, "Does the name Habakkuk mean anything to you?"

"It sounds as if it ought to come from the land of the Ice People," he replied in the classical tongue. "Other than that, no. Why? What is it?"

"Something I heard somewhere," Pekka answered, and Fernao hardly needed to be a mage to realize she wasn't telling him everything she knew. But when she went on, "I do not know what it is, either," he thought she might be telling the truth.

"Habakkuk." He tasted the word again. Sure enough, it put him in mind of a caravanmaster hairy all over and stinking because he'd never had a bath in all the days of his life. Fernao's opinion of the nomadic natives of the austral continent was not high. He'd seen enough of them for familiarity to breed contempt.

He wasn't altogether surprised when Pekka changed the subject. "In a few days, I will be going away for a week or two," she said. "I have got leave."

"You will put Ilmarinen in charge again?" Fernao asked.

"For a little while," she answered. "Only for a little while. I have got leave to see my husband and my son. And I have got leave to see my sister, too. Elimaki is expecting her first child. Her husband got leave not so long ago, you see."

Fernao smiled. "So I do. Or maybe I do." He wondered if Pekka would come back from leave expecting her second child. If she didn't, it probably wouldn't be from lack of effort. He said, "I wonder whom I would have to kill to get leave for myself."

As the physician had before, Pekka took him literally. "You would not have to kill anyone," she said. "You would have to ask me. You would ask, and I would say aye. How could I refuse you leave? How could I refuse you anything, after you have saved the project—saved me?"

Be careful, he thought. *You don't know what I might ask for, and it wouldn't be leave.* He rather suspected she *did* know. He hadn't tried to push things. He hadn't used the wrong verb on purpose. He saw no point to pushing, not when she was so obviously eager to go home to her husband. But the notion wouldn't leave his mind.

He said, "Whatever we do, the project needs to go forward. After you come back here, I can think about leave. I wonder if I speak Lagoan anymore, or if I will go through the streets of Setubal trying to use classical Kaunian with everyone I meet."

"Many people would understand you," Pekka said, "though you might surprise them—or, with your eyes, they might take you for a Kuusaman with a lot of Lagoan blood. When I return, you tell me what you want, and I shall give it to you."

To keep from saying anything he would regret later, Fernao

took a long pull at his ale. Having the mug in front of his face also kept Pekka from seeing him go red again. Maybe a few passages with a friendly woman, or even a mercenary one, would let him keep his mind on business when he got back.

Ilmarinen came into the dining hall and walked over to the table where Fernao and Pekka were sitting. Nodding to Pekka, he said, "Do I hear right? I'm going to be in charge again?" He spoke Kuusaman, but Fernao followed well enough.

Pekka nodded. "Aye, for a little while," she answered in courteous classical Kaunian. "Try not to destroy the place while I am gone."

"I thought destroying as much of Naantali as we could was the reason we came here," Ilmarinen said, also in the classical language. Then he switched back to Kuusaman and called to the serving woman: "Another mug of ale over here, Linna!"

"Aye, Master Ilmarinen," Linna said. "You can have anything you want from me, as long as you just want ale."

Ilmarinen winced. "Heartless bitch," he muttered in Kaunian. His pursuit of the serving girl had gone exactly nowhere. Fernao winced, too, in sympathy. He was glad—he supposed he was glad—he hadn't tried pursuing Pekka anywhere except inside his mind.

As Linna brought the mug, Pekka told Ilmarinen, "If you want to carry out the experiments while I am away, please do. The more we get done, the sooner we can take it into battle."

"We have a ways to go before we manage that." Ilmarinen swigged at the ale, then wiped his wispy mustache on his sleeve. "And we've been hitting the Gongs pretty hard just in the ordinary way of doing things."

"Gyongyos is one kind of fight," Pekka said. "When we go onto the Derlavaian mainland against Algarve, that will be another kind. Tell me I am wrong, Master." She stuck out her chin and looked a challenge at Ilmarinen.

He only grunted and drank more ale by way of reply. Gyongyos was far away, and her soldiers being driven back one island at a time. Algarve had already proved she could strike across the Strait of Valmiera. All the mages who'd been in the blockhouse were lucky to be alive.

Fernao said, "Unkerlant will be glad to have more company in the fight on the ground when we do cross to the mainland."

"Unkerlant." Ilmarinen spoke the name of the kingdom as if it were the name of a loathsome disease. "The measure of Unkerlant's accursedness is that King Swemmel's subjects fight by the tens of thousands for murderous Mezentio against their own sovereign." He held up a hand before either Fernao or Pekka could speak. "And the measure of Algarve's accursedness is that practically every other kingdom in the world has lined up with Swemmel and against Mezentio."

"That is not a very happy way of looking at the world," Fernao said: as much protest as he was prepared to make.

"The world is not a happy place to look at nowadays," Pekka said.

"Too right it's not," Ilmarinen said. "Do you know the state we're reduced to? We're reduced to hoping the Algarvians and the Unkerlanters do a right and proper job of slaughtering each other so we can pick up the pieces without getting too badly mauled ourselves. Aren't you glad to be living in a great kingdom?" He drained his ale and shouted for a refill.

Fernao said, "I would rather live in a kingdom still fighting the Algarvians than in one that had yielded to them."

"And so would I," Ilmarinen agreed. "What we have here isn't the best of things, but it's a long way from the worst of things."

"Oh, indeed," Pekka said. "We could be Kaunians in Forthweg. That's one of the reasons we're fighting, of course: to keep Mezentio's men from having the chance to use us as they use those Kaunians, I mean."

Ilmarinen shook his head. "No. That's not right. Or it's not quite right, anyhow. We're fighting to keep anybody from using anybody else the way the Algarvians are using those poor cursed Kaunians." He held up his hand again. "Aye, I see the irony of our being allied to Unkerlant in that fight."

Linna brought him a full mug and took away the empty. "You people would be happier if you stuck to Kuusaman all the time," she declared. "All this chatter in foreign languages never did anybody any good."

With almost clinical curiosity, Pekka asked Ilmarinen, "What on earth *do* you see in her?" She made a point of using classical Kaunian.

After coughing a couple of times, the master mage answered, "Well, she *is* a pretty little thing." He glanced toward Fernao, perhaps hoping for support. Fernao only shrugged; the serving girl wasn't ugly, but she didn't do anything for him. With a sigh, Ilmarinen went on, "And besides, there's something cursed attractive about such invincible stupidity."

"I do not understand that at all," Pekka said.

"I do not, either," Fernao knew he would have been much less interested in Pekka if he hadn't thought at least as much of her mind as he did of her body.

"Sometimes things should be simple," Ilmarinen insisted. "No competition, no quarrels, no—"

"No interest in you whatever," Pekka put in.

"Besides which," Fernao said, "while you would not quarrel about your work with an invincibly stupid woman"—he used Ilmarinen's words even though he was far from sure Linna deserved them—"you would be likely to quarrel with her over everything else. Or do you think I am wrong?"

Ilmarinen gulped down his ale, sprang up from his seat, and hurried away without answering. "You frightened him off," Pekka said.

"Only from us. Not from Linna," Fernao predicted.

"Unless he decides he would rather go after some other girl," Pekka said. "As for me, I am glad my heart points in only one direction." Because of his cane, Fernao couldn't spring up and hurry away. He didn't shout for more ale—or, better, spirits—to make him forget he'd heard that, either. He hoped Pekka never realized how close he came to doing both.

* * *

When Krasta went into the west wing of her mansion to ask something of Colonel Lurcanio, she noticed more empty desks there than she'd ever seen before. It didn't take much to knock a thought right out of her head, and that was plenty. Among the empty desks was that of Captain Gradasso, Lurcanio's adjutant. Captain Mosco, Gradasso's predecessor, had already been sent off to fight in Unkerlant. Krasta wouldn't have been broken-hearted to see the same fate befall Gradasso, who embarrassed her by speaking far better classical Kaunian than she did.

But, with Gradasso's desk empty, there was no one to keep her from barging right into Lurcanio's office. Rather to her disappointment, she found Gradasso in there. He and her Al-garvian lover were standing in front of a large map of eastern Derlavai tacked to the wall, and were arguing volubly in their own language.

They both jumped a little when Krasta came in. Lurcanio recovered first. "Later, Captain," he told Gradasso, switching to Valmieran so Krasta could follow.

"Aye, later, an it be your pleasure," Gradasso replied in what he thought was Valmieran. He hadn't known the mod-ern language till being assigned to Priekule, and mixed in a lot of classical constructions and vocabulary when he spoke it. With a bow to Lurcanio, he strode past Krasta to his usual station as the colonel's watchdog.

"What was that all about?" Krasta asked.

"We don't see eye to eye about what Algarve ought to do in Unkerlant once the mud dries up," Lurcanio answered.

"Whatever it is, does it account for all those desks with no people sitting at them?" Krasta asked.

"As a matter of fact, it does," Lurcanio said. "When we strike Swemmel's soldiers this year, we shall strike them with all our strength. On that Gradasso and I agree—we can do nothing less, not if we intend to win the war, and we do. But on what to do with our strength once mustered . . ." He shook his head. "There we differ."

Interested in spite of herself, Krasta asked, "What does he want? And why do you think he's wrong?"

Lurcanio didn't answer directly. Krasta often thought Lurcanio incapable of answering directly. Instead, the Algarvian colonel said, "Here, come look at the way things are for yourself." Not without trepidation, Krasta walked to the map. Geography had never been a strong subject for her, not that many subjects in her brief and checkered academic career had been strong ones. Lurcanio pointed. "Here is Durrwangen, in southern Unkerlant. The Unkerlanters took it away from us this winter, and we could not quite get it back before the spring thaw down there turned the landscape to soup and stopped both sides from doing much."

Krasta nodded. "Aye, I remember you complaining about that."

"Do you?" Lurcanio bowed. "Will marvels never cease?" Before Krasta could even wonder if that was sardonic, he pointed to the map again. "You see, though, that to both the east and west of Durrwangen, we have pushed some distance south of the city."

He waited. Krasta realized she was supposed to say something. She nodded again. "That's plain from where the green pins are, and the gray ones." Her tone sharpened. "It's also plain this wall will need replastering when your precious map comes down."

Lurcanio ignored that. He was good at ignoring things he didn't want to hear. In that, he resembled Krasta herself, though she didn't realize it. He waved at the map. "You are quite the most charming military cadet I have ever seen. If Algarve's fate lay in your pretty hands, how would you take Durrwangen when the fighting starts anew?"

The day was mild and cool, but sweat burst out on Krasta's forehead. She hated questions. She always had. And she particularly hated questions from Lurcanio. He could be—he delighted in being—rude when her answers didn't satisfy him. But she saw she had to answer. After examining the map, she drew two hesitant lines with her forefinger. "If you move your armies here so they meet behind this Durrwangen place—it doesn't look like you'd have to move them very far—you could come at it from every which way at once. I don't see how the Unkerlanters could keep you out of it then."

To her astonishment, Lurcanio took her in his arms and did a good, thorough job of kissing her. "Nicely reasoned, my sweet," he said, and pinched her on the backside. She squeaked and leaped into the air. "You have reached exactly the same solution as Captain Gradasso, exactly the same solution as King Mezentio himself."

"You're teasing me!" Krasta said, wondering what kind of foolish, obvious blunder she'd made. Whatever it was, Lurcanio would enjoy pointing it out. He always did.

But he solemnly shook his head. "By the powers above, milady, I am not. You have seen the very thing that caught the eye of some of the ablest officers in the kingdom."

Krasta studied him. He remained solemn. When he felt like slapping her down, he didn't usually wait so long. But his voice had had an edge to it, even if not one aimed at her. "You were arguing with Gradasso," she said slowly. "Does that mean you didn't see this move? If I saw it, couldn't anyone—any soldier, I mean—see it?"

Lurcanio kissed her again, which left her more confused than ever. "Oh, I saw it," he said. "I would have to be far gone in my second childhood not to have seen it." Sure enough, the sarcastic sparkle was back in his voice. "But if the king saw it, if I saw it, if Captain Gradasso saw it, if even you saw it, would you not suspect the Unkerlanters might see it, too?"

"*I* wouldn't know." Krasta tossed her head. "I've never had anything to do with Unkerlanter barbarians, nor wanted to, either. Who can say what they'd see and what they wouldn't?"

"There is something to that," Colonel Lurcanio admitted. "Something—but how much? When we went into Unkerlant, we did not think Swemmel's men could see the sun when it was shining in their eyes. We have discovered, to our sorrow, that we were mistaken."

Which is why you started killing Kaunians from Forthweg, Krasta thought. She almost blurted that aloud. But Lurcanio would be on her like a hawk if she did. The Kaunians of

Valmiera weren't supposed to know anything about that. Discretion didn't come easy, but she managed it. She asked, "What will happen if the Unkerlanters do see this?"

"What looks easy on the map will get much harder," Lurcanio replied. "That is why I wish we were doing something else, anything else."

"Have you told anybody?" Krasta asked. "You are an important man. What you think carries weight."

"I am an important man in Priekule," Lurcanio said. "In Trapani, where these decisions are made, I am nothing in particular. Only a colonel. Only a military bureaucrat. What could I know about actual fighting? I have sent my superiors a memorial, aye. Much good it will do me. Either they will read it and ignore it or they will not bother reading it before they ignore it."

Krasta gaped. Lurcanio often mocked her. He mocked other Valmierans, too. She'd even heard him mock his countrymen here in Priekule. But never till now had she known him to sound so bitter about his superiors. Slowly, she asked, "What will you do if they turn out to be right?"

"Take off my hat and bow to them." Lurcanio suited action to word, which made Krasta laugh.

But then she asked, "And what will you do if you turn out to be right and the generals back in Trapani are wrong? They won't take off their hats and bow to you."

"Of course they won't." With a lifted eyebrow, Colonel Lurcanio cast scorn on the idea. "What will I do if things come to such a pass? Most likely, my dear, I will get my marching orders, I will pick up a stick, and I will go where my colleagues have gone before me: off to the west, to do my best to throw back the Unkerlanter hordes with my body." He looked Krasta up and down, undressing her with his eyes. "There are, I confess, other things I would sooner do with my body."

"Right here? With Gradasso outside?" Krasta giggled. Being outrageous, being risky, often excited her. She'd flipped up Lurcanio's kilt in here before. "Do you want to?"

Rather to her disappointment, her Algarvian lover shook

his head. "No, not now. Tonight, perhaps, but I have not the time now." He sighed. "I really have not the time to argue with my adjutant, either. With more and more of the men who have been aiding me gone, more and more of the work falls on my shoulders. For the work must be done, regardless of who does it."

To Krasta, those who occupied Valmiera had always seemed to have it easy. They lived well when even Valmieran nobles often had trouble making ends meet. They had their choice of bed partners—she knew that all too well. That they, or some of them, also worked themselves to exhaustion hadn't crossed her mind.

Lurcanio asked, "Did you come down here to pick my brains over strategy or to molest me? The one was interesting, the other would be enjoyable, but I really am too busy for either."

Being twitted worked a minor miracle: it made Krasta remember why she had come down to see Lurcanio, something that had gone clean out of her mind even before she got to his office. She said, "What did your hounds end up deciding about Viscount Valnu? He made more entertaining company at most festivities than almost anyone else who was likely to come."

"Oh, aye, indeed—Valnu has charmed any number of people, of all genders and preferences." Lurcanio didn't bother hiding his contempt. "He does very little for me, in which I seem to be almost unique in the city. But you asked about the hounds. They must not have found anything worth mentioning, for I am given to understand he is at liberty once more."

"Is he?" Krasta breathed.

She must have sounded more excited than she'd intended to, for Lurcanio laughed at her. "Aye, he is. Why? Does it mean so much to you? Will you rush right out and make him the same offer you just made me? I would advise against that; I suspect he owes his freedom not least to the, ah, enthusiasm of certain handsome Algarvian officers."

That wouldn't have particularly surprised Krasta. Valnu

did what he felt like, with whomever he felt like. But she heard the edge in Lurcanio's voice, and knew she would have to soften him. "Oh, no," she said, making her eyes go wide with little-girl innocence. "I wouldn't think of doing such a thing, not after the lesson you taught me the last time."

To her chagrin, that only made Lurcanio laugh again. "You wouldn't think of doing such a thing if you might get caught. Isn't that what you mean?"

"I don't know what you're talking about," Krasta said with such dignity as she could muster. Lurcanio laughed harder than ever. She stuck out her tongue at him. She hated being transparent, and disliked the Algarvian for showing her she was. When he wouldn't stop laughing, she flounced out of his office, slamming the door behind her. But she knew that, when he came to her bedchamber that evening, she wouldn't slam the door in his face.

Ten

Sergeant Pesaro glared at the Algarvian constables drawn up at attention in front of the barracks in Gromheort. "Listen up, you lugs," he growled. "You'd better listen up, on account of this is important."

As imperceptibly as he could, Bembo shifted from foot to foot. "How many times have we heard speeches like this?" he whispered to Oraste, who stood next to him.

Oraste might have been carved from stone. Even his lips hardly stirred as he answered, "Too cursed many."

"Shut up, the lot of you!" Pesaro roared. His jowls wobbled when he opened his mouth very wide. "You'd better shut up, or you'll bloody well be sorry. Have you got that?" He looked so fierce, even Bembo, who'd known him since dirt, decided he had to take him seriously. After one more glare, Pesaro went on, "All right. That's better. Our kingdom needs us, by the powers above, and we're going to come through."

Alarm blazed up Bembo's back. One of the things he'd always feared was that the meat grinder of war might decide to take constables and turn them into soldiers. By the horrified expressions some of his comrades were wearing, the same thing had occurred to them, too.

Pesaro's chuckle was anything but pleasant. "There. Have I got your attention? I cursed well better have. What we're going to do is, we're going to go into the Kaunian quarter here, we're going to grab as many blonds as we can, and we're going to ship 'em west. The men in the trenches there'll need all the sorcerous help they can get. We're the boys who can give 'em what they need."

"As long as we're not going into the trenches ourselves," somebody behind Bembo muttered. Bembo had all he could do to keep from nodding like a fool, because that was exactly how he felt himself.

A constable in front of him stuck up a hand. When Pesaro nodded, the fellow asked, "What do we do if we run into people who look like Forthwegians?"

"Grab 'em anyhow," Pesaro answered promptly. "We'll throw the buggers into holding cells. If they still look like Forthwegians a day later, we'll turn 'em loose. And if they don't—which, you ask me, is a lot more likely—then off they go. If they're in the Kaunian quarter, we figure they're blonds till they show us different."

Another constable, a young fellow named Almonio, raised his hand. "Permission to fall out, Sergeant?" He never had had the stomach for seizing Kaunians who would be doomed to massacre.

But Pesaro shook his head, which made his jowls wobble again, this time from side to side. "No." His voice was flat and hard. "You can come along, or you can go to the guardhouse. Those are your choices."

"I'll come," Almonio said miserably. "It's not right, but I'll come." Bembo knew the youngster would drink himself into a stupor the first chance he got.

"You bet your arse you'll come." Pesaro wasn't just going to have his way; he was going to rub the other constable's nose in it, so that Almonio wouldn't pester him again with second thoughts. "This war we're fighting with Unkerlant touches everybody now. We're all fighting it, irregardless of whether we're in the front line or not." A smile spread over his broad, fleshy face—he plainly thought that rather fine.

Elsewhere on the parade ground in front of the barracks, other sergeants were haranguing other squads of constables. That fit in with what Bembo knew, or thought he knew, of how soldiers and their leaders behaved before a battle. All the sergeants finished at about the same time. That, Bembo suspected, was no accident.

The captain who'd led the raid on the block of flats where the Kaunian robber Gippias' pals had been hiding out was in charge of this assault on the Kaunian quarter. Bembo still didn't know his name. He did know the fellow was from Trapani, and had a vast contempt not only for Kaunians but also for Forthwegians and for his own countrymen who had the misfortune to come from provincial towns.

"We'll get them," the captain declared as the constables marched toward the little district into which the blonds had been shoehorned. "We'll get them, and we'll teach them what it means to be Algarve's enemies."

"He sees what needs doing, anyhow," Oraste said. But then the captain repeated himself, and then he said the same thing over again for a third and soon for a fourth time. Oraste rolled his eyes. "All right. We've got the fornicating idea."

Forthwegians who saw a company's worth of constables bearing down on them sensibly got out of the way as fast as they could. Pride made Bembo suck in his belly, throw back his shoulders, and march as if marching really mattered. Like any Algarvian, he reckoned being part of a parade the only thing better than watching one.

But that thought had hardly crossed his mind before the constables had to halt. It wasn't Forthwegians or Kaunians who stopped them, either: it was their own countrymen. A couple of regiments of soldiers were marching through the city toward the ley-line caravan depot. They didn't swagger, as the constables did; they just tramped along, intent on getting where they were going—probably back to the front in Unkerlant. The ones who weren't lean were downright skinny. Their tunics and kilts were faded and patched. And they all had a knowing look in their eyes, a look that said they'd been places and done things the constables couldn't—and wouldn't want to—imagine.

"Aren't they cute?" one soldier said to another, pointing at the constables. "Aren't they sweet?"

"Oh, aye, they're just the most precious dears I ever saw," his friend answered. Both men guffawed. Bembo's ears heated in dull embarrassment.

Another Algarvian trooper was blunter. "Slackers!" he yelled. "Whose prong did you suck to stay out of the real fight?" His pals growled and shook their fists at the constables. One of them flipped up his kilt and showed his bare buttocks—he wasn't wearing drawers.

"Get that man's name! Discipline him!" the constabulary captain shouted to the sergeants and lieutenants and captains marching past. But, in spite of his fury, the military officers paid him no attention. The more they ignored him, the angrier and louder he got. It did him no good at all.

He was still steaming when the last footsoldier finally walked past. Some of the other constables had got angry, too. More, like Bembo, were just resigned. "Soldiers never have any use for us," he said. "They're jealous that they have to go forward and we get to stay back here."

"Wouldn't you be?" Oraste returned.

"Of course I would. You think I'm daft?" Bembo said. "But I don't have to be jealous of me, on account of I'm a constable, not a soldier."

Oraste might have had further opinion on just what Bembo

was. If he did, he kept his mouth shut about them. The two constables were partners, after all. They marched on till they came to the edge of the Kaunian quarter. There the captain divided them into two groups: a larger one that would go into houses and shops and bring out the blonds, and a smaller one that would guard them and keep them from slipping away in the confusion. Bembo and Oraste were both in the first group.

"This is for Algarve!" the captain declared. "This is for victory! Go in there and do your duty."

Had the constables been rookies, they might have charged into the Kaunian district with cheers ringing from their lips. But almost all of them had been through roundups before, both in Gromheort and in the surrounding villages. They had a hard time getting excited about another one.

Oraste might not have been excited, but he enjoyed kicking in a door when no one responded after he yelled, "Kaunians, come forth!" He liked breaking things and knocking things down. Roundups gave him the chance to have fun.

But he went from gloating to cursing when he and Bembo found nobody in the flat once he had kicked in the door. They went next door. This time, Bembo shouted, "Kaunians, come forth!" Again, no one came forth. No one responded at all. With a snarl, Oraste put a boot to the door near the latch. It flew open. The constables swarmed in, sticks in hand and ready to blaze. Once more, though, they found only a deserted flat.

"Powers above!" Oraste exclaimed. "Did *all* the stinking blonds magic themselves dark and sneak out when nobody was looking?"

"They couldn't have," Bembo said, though without much conviction. "Somebody would have noticed."

"Then where are they?" Oraste asked, and Bembo had no good answer for him. He did hope Doldasai and her family had managed to get out of the Kaunian quarter. If they hadn't, he wouldn't be able to do a thing about it if they got seized again.

They both shouted, "Kaunians, come forth!" in front of the

doorway to the next flat. Once more, no one inside came out or said a word. Yet again, Oraste kicked in the door—not only was he better at it than Bembo, he enjoyed it more. This time, though, they found a man and a woman hiding in a closet under some cloaks. Both of them might have been Forthwegian by their looks.

"We were just visiting," the man quavered in Algarvian, "and your shout frightened us, so—"

"Shut up!" Oraste said, and hit him in the head with his bludgeon. The woman screamed. He hit her, too. "For one thing, I know you're lying. For another thing, I don't give a fart. Orders are to grab everybody, and I don't care what you look like. Get moving, or else I'll wallop you again."

As the unhappy couple stumbled toward the door, blood ran down their faces and dripped on the shabby carpeting. Desperation in his voice, the man said, "I'll give you anything you want to pretend you never saw us."

"Forget it," Oraste said. Bembo couldn't do anything but nod. Oraste continued. "Go on, curse you. It's not like anybody'll miss you once you're gone."

The man said something in classical Kaunian. Oraste didn't know a word of the language. Bembo knew just enough to recognize a curse when he heard one. He hit the man again, on the off chance that the fellow was mage enough to make the curse stick if he got to finish it. "None of that," he snapped. "We're warded against wizardry anyhow." He hoped the wards worked well.

He and Oraste led the couple they'd captured back to the constables in charge of holding Kaunians once caught. Other constables were leading more Kaunians and presumed Kaunians out of the cramped district. "Powers above, a lot of these buggers look like Forthwegians and wear tunics," Oraste said.

Bembo could only nod. Close to half the captives looked swarthy and dressed like their Forthwegian countrymen. Genuine blonds wearing genuine trousers had become scarce even in the Kaunian quarter. "I do wonder how many have slipped away to someplace where nobody knows what in blazes they are," Bembo said.

"Too cursed many, I'll tell you that," Oraste said.

The captain in charge of the operation plainly agreed with him. "You'll have to do better than this," he shouted to his men. "Algarve's going to need bodies for the fight ahead. You've got to go in there and get 'em."

"There aren't that many bodies to get, not anymore," Bembo said. "We've already nabbed a good many, and likely even more have slipped through our fingers with their sorcerous disguises." Again, he hoped Doldasai had. He wouldn't have wanted to put his neck on the block like that for nothing.

"Too right they have," Oraste agreed. "But the ones that are left, we've bloody well got to dig out. Come on." Back into the Kaunian quarter he went, intent on doing all he could. Bembo couldn't come close to matching such zeal, and didn't much want to, but he followed nonetheless. *What choice have I got?* he wondered. He knew the answer all too well: none whatever.

Smooth as velvet, the ley-line caravan glided to a stop at the depot. "Skrunda!" the conductor yelled, going from car to car. "All out for Skrunda!"

"Your pardon," Talsu said as he got to his feet. The man sitting next to him swung his legs into the aisle so Talsu, who'd been by the window, could get past and walk to the doorway that would let him return to his own town.

He had to snatch at his trousers as he went up the aisle. They'd fit fine when the Algarvians first captured him. After months in prison, though, they threatened to fall down with every stride he took. He was willing to hang on to them. When he got home, he or his father could alter his clothes so they'd fit his present scrawny state. And he could start eating properly again, to start making himself fit the clothes.

"Watch your step, sir," the conductor said as Talsu got down from the caravan car by way of the little set of stairs that led to the platform. His voice was an emotionless drone. How many thousands of times, how many tens of thousands of times, had he said exactly the same thing? Enough to drive a man easily bored mad, surely. But he said, "Watch your step, sir," to the man behind Talsu, too, in just the same way.

Talsu had no baggage to reclaim. He counted himself lucky that his captors had given him back the clothes he was wearing when they'd seized him. He hurried out of the depot and onto the streets of the town where he'd lived all his life till conscripted into King Donalitu's army. That hadn't turned out well, not for him and not for Jelgava, either. Next to months in a dungeon, though . . .

He went through the market square at close to a trot. Part of him said the bread and onions and olives and almonds and olive oil on display there were shadows of what had been for sale before the war. The rest, the part that had thought hard about eating cockroaches, wanted to stop right there and stuff himself till he couldn't walk anymore.

He did stop when someone called his name. "Talsu!" his friend repeated, coming up to pump his hand. "I thought you were . . . you know."

"Hello, Stikliu," Talsu said. "I was, as a matter of fact. But they finally let me go."

"Did they?" Something in Stikliu's face changed. It wasn't a pleasant sort of change, either. "How . . . lucky for you. I'll see you later. I have some other things to do. So long." He left as fast as he'd come forward.

What was that all about? Talsu wondered. But he didn't need to wonder for long. Stikliu thought he'd sold his soul to the Algarvians. Talsu scowled. A lot of people were liable to think that. For what other reason would he have come out of the dungeon? What would he have thought if someone imprisoned were suddenly freed? Nothing good. Stikliu hadn't thought anything good, either.

A couple of other people who knew Talsu saw him on the way to the tailor's shop and the dwelling over it. They didn't come rushing over to find out how he was. They did their best to pretend they'd never set eyes on him. His scowl got deeper. Maybe the gaolers hadn't done him such an enormous favor by turning him loose.

He walked into the tailor's shop. There behind the counter sat his father, doing the necessary hand stitching on an Algarvian kilt before chanting the spell that would use the laws of similarity and contagion to bind the whole garment together. Traku looked up from his work. "Good morn—" he began, and then threw down the kilt and ran out to take Talsu in his arms. "Talsu!" he said, and his voice broke. He rumpled his son's hair, as he had when Talsu was a little boy. "Powers above be praised, you've come home!" He didn't care how that might have happened; he just rejoiced that it had.

"Aye, Father." Tears ran down Talsu's face, too. "I'm home."

Traku all but squeezed the breath out of Talsu. Then Talsu's father hurried to the stairway and called, "Laitsina! Ausra! Come quick!"

"What on earth?" Talsu's mother said. But she and his sister Ausra both hurried downstairs. They both squealed—shrieked, actually—when they saw Talsu standing there, and then smothered him in hugs and kisses. After a couple of minutes, coherent speech and coherent thought returned. Laitsina asked, "Does Gailisa know you're free?"

"No, Mother." Talsu shook his head. "I came here first."

"All right." Laitsina took charge, as she had a way of doing. "Ausra, go to the grocer's and bring her back. Don't name any names, not out loud." She rounded on her husband. "Don't just stand there, Traku. Run upstairs and bring down the wine."

"Aye." Ausra and Traku said the same thing at the same time, as if to their commander. Ausra dashed out the door. Traku dashed up the stairs. In his army days, Talsu had had only one officer who'd got that instant obedience from his men. Poor Colonel Adomu hadn't lasted long; the Algarvians had killed him.

Traku came down with the wine. He poured cups for himself, his wife, and Talsu, and set the jar on the counter to wait for Ausra and Gailisa. Then he raised his own cup high. "To freedom!" he said, and drank.

"To freedom!" Talsu echoed. But when he sipped, the red wine—made tangy in the usual Jelgavan style with the juices of limes and oranges and lemons—put him in mind of the prison and of the Jelgavan constabulary captain who'd given him all the wine he wanted to get him to denounce his friends and neighbors.

"What finally made them let you go, son?" Traku asked.

"You must know how they took Gailisa away," Talsu said, and his father and mother both nodded. He went on, "They brought her to my prison and made her write out a list of names. Then they told me she'd done it, and that my names had better match hers. I knew she'd never denounce anyone who really hated Algarvians, so I wrote down people who liked them but weren't real showy about it—you know the kind I mean. And I must have been thinking along with her, because they turned me loose."

"Clever lad!" Traku burst out, and hit him in the shoulder. "You can say a lot of things about my line, but we don't raise fools." Laitsina contented herself with kissing Talsu, which probably amounted to the same thing.

His parents were pleased with him. They thought him a clever fellow. But what would other people in Skrunda think of him? He'd already had a taste of the answer: they'd think he'd sold himself to the redheads. Would they have anything to do with him now that he'd been released? The only ones likely to were men and women of the sort he'd named as anti-Algarvian activists. That was funny, if you looked at it the right way. It would have been even funnier if he'd wanted to have anything to do with those people.

The problem seemed urgent . . . for a moment. Then the bell rang as the door opened again. There was Ausra, with Gailisa right behind her. Talsu's wife gaped at him, then let out exactly the squeal a seven-year-old might have used at getting a new doll. She threw herself into Traku's arms. "I don't believe it," she said, over and over again. "I can't believe it."

Talsu had trouble believing the feel of a woman pressed against him. He'd thought his imagination and memory had held onto what that feeling was like, but he'd been wrong, wrong. "I saw you once," he said, in between kisses.

"Did you?" Gailisa answered. "When they took me to that horrible prison? I wondered if you would, if that was why. I didn't see you."

"No, they wouldn't let you," Talsu said. "But I was looking out through a peephole when they took you down the hallway. And when they told me you'd written a denunciation, I had to figure out what kind of names you'd put in it so mine would match. I guess I did it right, on account of they let me go."

"I named all the fat, smug whoresons I could think of, is what I did," Gailisa said.

"Me, too," Talsu said. "And it worked."

Somebody—he didn't notice who—had brought down and filled another pair of cups. His mother gave one to Ausra; his father gave the other to Gailisa. They both drank. Gailisa turned an accusing stare on his sister. "You didn't tell me why I had to come back here," she said. "You just told me it was important."

"Well, was I right or was I wrong?" Ausra asked.

"You were wrong, because you didn't come close to saying enough," Gailisa answered. "You didn't come close." She seized Talsu's arm and stared up into his face in such a marked manner that at any other time he would have been embarrassed. Not now. Now he drank in the warmth of her affection like a plant long in darkness drinking in the sun.

Not very much later, still holding him by the arm, she took him upstairs. Ausra started to follow them. Traku contrived to get in her way. In a low voice—but not quite low enough to keep Talsu from overhearing—he said, "No. Wait. Whatever you want up there, it will keep for a while."

Talsu's ears got hot. His parents and his sister had to know what he and Gailisa would be doing in the little bedchamber that had been his alone before he got married. Then he shrugged. If it didn't bother them—and it didn't seem to—he wasn't about to let it bother him, either.

Gailisa closed and barred the door to the bedchamber. Then she undid the toggles on Talsu's tunic. "How skinny you've got!" she said, running the palm of her hand along his ribs. "Didn't they feed you anything?"

"Not much," Talsu answered. The ease with which his trousers came down proved that.

"Don't you worry," Gailisa said. "I'll take care of things. Aye, I will." She let her hand linger for a moment, then planted it in the middle of his chest. He went over on his back onto the bed. "Stay there," she told him, busy with the fastenings of her own clothes. Once she was out of them, Talsu stared and stared. No, memory and imagination were only shadows when set beside reality.

She lay down beside him. Their lips met. Their hands wandered. Before long, Gailisa straddled him and impaled herself upon him. "Ohhh," he said—one long exhalation. How could he have misremembered so much?

"You hush," Gailisa said. "Just let me . . ." And she did, slowly, carefully, lovingly. Having gone without so long, Talsu didn't think he'd be able to last now, but she took care of that, too. When he finally did groan and shudder, it was as if he were making up for all the lost time at once. Gailisa leaned forward and brushed his lips with hers. "There," she murmured, almost as if to a child. "Is that better?"

"Better, aye," he said. But he was still a young man, even if poorly fed, and his spear retained its temper. This time, he began to move, slowly at first but then with more insistence. Gailisa threw her head back. Her breath came short. So did his. She clenched him, as with a hand. He groaned again. This time, so did she.

Sweat made their skins slide against each other as they separated. Talsu hoped for a third round, but not urgently. He caressed Gailisa, marveling all over again at how soft she was.

A heavily laden wagon rattled by outside, turning his mind away from lovemaking and toward less delightful things. "People are going to think I sold out to the redheads," he said.

"They already think I did," Gailisa answered. "Powers below eat them."

"Aye." Talsu's hand closed on her bare left breast. Somehow, talking of such things while they sprawled naked and sated was an exorcism of sorts, even if modern thaumaturgy had proved precious few demons really existed. He went on,

"Do you know who betrayed me?" He waited for her to shake her head, then spoke three more words: "Kugu the silversmith."

"The classical Kaunian master?" Gailisa exclaimed in horror.

"The very same fellow," Talsu said.

"Something ought to happen to him." His wife spoke with great conviction.

"Maybe something will," Talsu said. "But if anything does, it won't be something anybody can blame me for." Gailisa accepted that as naturally as if he'd said the sun rose in the east.

Pekka lay beside Leino in the big bed where they'd spent so much happy time together. He'd be ready again pretty soon, she judged, and then they would start another round of what they'd both been too long without. "So good to be here," her husband murmured.

"So good to be here with you," Pekka said.

Leino laughed. "So good to be here at all. Compared to the land of the Ice People . . ." His voice trailed off. "I've said too much."

"Habakkuk," Pekka said.

Her husband nodded. "Aye, Habakkuk. I never should have said anything about that, either. And if I did say something about it, the censor never should have passed it. But I did and he did, and now we've got to live with it."

"Fer . . . one of the other mages who's working with me said the name sounded as if it came from the land of the Ice People." Pekka didn't want to—very strongly didn't want to—mention Fernao's name while she was in bed with her husband. She'd worry about what that meant, and if it meant anything, another time.

"He was right." If Leino noticed her hesitation, he didn't make a big thing of it. Forbearance was one of the reasons she loved him. He sighed and went on, "I think you've got the more interesting job, working with people like Ilmarinen and Siuntio. . . . What's the matter now?"

"Siuntio's dead." Pekka knew she shouldn't have been so startled, but she couldn't help it. Her husband couldn't have known. She hadn't written about it to him; even if she had, one of the censors probably would have kept the news from getting out. The harder the time Mezentio's men had of learning what they'd done, the better.

"Is he?" Leino clicked his tongue between his teeth. "That's a pity, but he wasn't a young man to begin with."

"No, not dead like that." Pekka would have staked her life that the redheads couldn't possibly be listening to what went on in her bedchamber. "Dead in an Algarvian attack. If he hadn't fought it off, or at least fought part of it off, the whole team might have died with him."

"By the powers above," Leino said. "You never told me anything about this before. You couldn't, could you?" Pekka shook her head. With a sigh, Leino went on, "I think I'm working on a sideshow. You're doing what really matters."

"Am I? I hope so." Pekka clung to him. She didn't want to have to think about the work she'd finally escaped. She was more interested in thinking about the two of them, what they had been doing, and what they'd soon do again.

But Leino couldn't do it again quite yet. Had he been able to, he would have been stirring against her thigh. Because he couldn't quite yet, he was interested in what Pekka had been up to. "The Algarvians must think so," he said. "If they didn't, they wouldn't have bothered attacking you. How did they do it? Dragons?"

Pekka shook her head. She didn't want to think about that, either, but the question gave her no choice. "No. Another Kaunian sacrifice. I don't know whether they just grabbed the first however many Valmierans they saw, or if they brought Kaunians east out of Forthweg. Whichever, it was very bad." She shuddered, recalling just how bad it had been.

Leino held her and stroked her. She could tell he was bursting with curiosity. She'd known him a good many years now; if she couldn't tell such things, who could? But he did his best not to let any of it show, because he knew that would bother her. And if a mage's suppressing his curiosity wasn't love, what was it? As much in gratitude as for any other reason, she slid down and took him in her mouth, trying to hurry things along. That wasn't magic, but it worked as if it were. Before long, they both stopped worrying about what Habakkuk was or why Mezentio's mages chose to assail Pekka and her colleagues.

But lovemaking never resolved things; it only put them off for a while. After they'd gasped their way to completion, Pekka knew Leino wouldn't be trying yet another round any time soon. That meant his thought would turn elsewhere. And sure enough, he said, "You must be working on something truly big, if the Algarvians used that spell against you."

"Something, aye." Pekka still didn't want to talk about it.

Leino said, "They tried to use that same spell to drive us off the austral continent, you know." Pekka nodded; she'd heard something about that. Her husband continued, "It went wrong. It went horribly wrong, and came down on their heads instead of ours and the Lagoans'. Magecraft that works fine here or on the mainland of Derlavai has a way of going wrong down in the land of the Ice People."

"That's what they say." Pekka nodded again, then laughed. "Whoever *they* are." Because she found worrying about her husband's problems easier than worrying about her own, she quickly found another question to ask: "Will that cause trouble for Habakkuk?"

"It shouldn't." Leino used an extravagant gesture. "Habakkuk is . . . something else." He chuckled ruefully. "I can't talk about it, any more than you can say much about whatever it is you're working on."

"I know. I understand." Pekka wanted to tell him everything. Just for a moment, she wished Fernao were there so she could talk shop. Then she shook her hair, and had to brush hair out of her eyes. He was part of what she'd come here, come away from the project, to escape.

"I love you," Leino said, and Pekka reminded herself he'd come a long way to escape hard, dangerous work, too. She clung to him as he clung to her. They didn't make love again; Leino wasn't so young that he could do it whenever he wanted. But the feel of him pressed against her was about as good as the real thing for Pekka, especially when they'd been apart so long. She hoped holding her was as good for him, but had her doubts. Men were different that way.

The next morning, Uto woke both of them at an improbably early hour. With Kajaani so far south, spring days lengthened quickly: the sun rose early and set late. Even so, Pekka's sleep-gummed eyelids told just how beastly early it was. "You don't treat Aunt Elimaki this way, do you?" she asked, wishing either for tea, which she could get, or another couple of hours' sleep, which she wouldn't.

"Of course not," her son said virtuously.

That, as Pekka knew, might mean anything or nothing. "You'd better not," she warned. "Aunt Elimaki is going to have a baby of her own, and she needs all the sleep she can get."

"She won't get it later, that's for sure." Leino sounded as sandbagged as Pekka.

"All right, Mother. All right, Father." Uto, by contrast, might have been the soul of virtue. He patted Pekka on the arm. "Are you going to have another baby, too, Mother?"

"I don't think so," Pekka answered. She and Leino smiled at each other; if she wasn't, it was in spite of last night's exertions. She yawned and sat up in bed, somewhat resigned to being awake. "What would the two of you like for breakfast?"

"Anything," Leino said before his son could speak. "Almost anything at all. Down in the land of the Ice People, *I* counted for a good cook, if you can believe it."

"I'm so sorry for you," Pekka exclaimed. The horror of that idea was plenty to rout her out of bed and into the kitchen. She got the teakettle going, then folded fat, fresh shrimp into an omelette. Along with fried mashed turnips and bread and butter (olive oil was an imported luxury in Kuusamo, not a staple), it made a fine breakfast.

Uto inhaled everything. He wasn't picky in what he ate; he chose other ways to make himself difficult. Leino ate hugely, too, and put down cup after cup of tea. "That's *so* much better," he said.

"Will you be able to sleep at all tonight?" Pekka asked him.

He nodded and opened his eyes very wide, which made Uto laugh. "Oh, aye," he said. "I won't have any trouble. I may have to eat seal every now and again down in the land of the Ice People, but there's plenty of tea. The Lagoans drink even more of it than we do. They say it lubricates the brain, and I can't argue with them."

"Seal?" Uto sounded horrified, but looked interested. "What does it taste like?"

"Greasy. Fishy," his father answered. "We eat camel, too, sometimes. That's better, at least for a while. It sort of tastes like beef, but it's fatter meat. The Ice People live on camel and reindeer almost all the time."

"Are they as ugly as everybody says?" Uto asked.

"No," Leino said, which obviously disappointed his son. Then he added, "They're uglier," and everything was right with the world as far as Uto was concerned.

"Hurry up and get ready for school," Pekka told him. He greeted that with moans and groans. Now that his parents were back in Kajaani, he wanted to spend as much time as he could with them. Pekka was inflexible. "You'll be back this afternoon, and you need to learn things. Besides, you're the one who got us up early." That produced as many more groans as she'd thought it would, but Uto, wearing a martyred expression, eventually went out the door and headed for school.

"Privacy," Leino said when he was gone. "I'd almost forgotten what it means. There in the little sorcerers' colony east of Mizpah, everybody lives in everybody else's belt pouch all the time."

"It's not quite so bad over in the Naantali district." Pekka started to laugh. "And now we've both said more than we should have."

Leino nodded. He took keeping secrets seriously. His voice was thoughtful, musing, as he said, "The Naantali district, eh? Nothing but empty space in those parts—I can't think of anybody who'd want to go there or need to go there—which probably makes it perfect for whatever you're doing." He held up a hand. "I'm not asking any questions. And even if I did, I know you couldn't give me any answers."

"That's right." Pekka sent him a challenging stare. "Well, now that we've got this privacy, what shall we do with it?"

"Oh, maybe we'll think of something." Leino pulled his tunic off over his head.

Pekka didn't know if either of them had been so ardent even on their honeymoon. They'd spent that at a small hostel in Priekule, and had alternated making love and sightseeing. Now they just had each other, and they were intent on making the most of it before they both had to return to the war.

"I'm not quite so young as I used to be," Leino said at some point that morning when, after several days of horizontal exercises, he failed to rise to the occasion.

"Don't worry about it," Pekka said. "You've done fine, believe me." Her body felt all aglow, so that it seemed they would hardly need the bedchamber lamp that evening.

"I wasn't worried," Leino said. "The people who worry about things like that are the ones who think there's only one way to get from hither to yon. Mages know better—or if they don't, they ought to." With fingers and tongue, he showed her what he meant. He was right, too—that road worked as well as the other one.

When Pekka's breathing and heartbeat had slowed to something close to normal, she said, "They talk about women wearing men out. This is the other way round." She ran a hand down his smooth chest—Kuusamans weren't a very hairy people. "Not that I'm complaining, mind you."

"I hope not," Leino said. "This is like putting money in Olavin's bank." Elimaki's husband, these days, was keeping the finances of the Kuusaman army and navy straight, but Pekka understood what her own husband meant. He went on, "We don't get many chances now, so we have to make the most of them, put them away in our memory bank. They may not earn interest, but they're interesting."

"That's one word," Pekka remarked. Leino's hands had started wandering again, too. But when one of them found its way between her legs, she said, "Wait a bit. I really have done everything I can right now. Let's see what I can do for you."

She crouched beside him, her head bobbing up and down.

Rather sooner than she'd expected, she pulled away, taking a couple of deep breaths and choking a little. "Well, well," Leino said. "I didn't think I had it in me."

"You certainly did." Pekka went over to the sink and washed off her chin.

"You'll have to excuse me now," her husband said, curling up on the bed. "I'm going to sleep for about a week." He offered a theatrical snore.

It made Pekka smile, but it didn't convince her. "A likely story," she said. "You'll be feeling me up again before Uto gets home."

"Who was just doing what to whom?" Leino asked, and Pekka had no good answer. He stretched out again, then said, "I love you, you know."

"I love you, too," she said. "That's probably why we've been doing all this."

"Can you think of a better reason?" Leino said. "This is a lot more fun than being lonely and jumping on the first halfway decent-looking person you find."

"Aye," Pekka said, and wished Fernao hadn't chosen that moment to cross her mind again.

Vanai poured out wine and listened to Ealstan pour out excitement. "He is! Pybba *is,* by the powers above," her husband said. "Sure as I'm sitting here, he's funneling money into things that hurt the Algarvians."

"Good for him," Vanai said. "Do you want some sausage? It's the first time in a while the butcher had some that looked even halfway decent."

"Sausage? Oh, aye." Ealstan's voice was far away; he'd heard what she said, but he hadn't paid much attention to it. His mind was on Pybba's accounts: "If he's fighting the Algarvians, maybe I'll finally get the chance to fight them, too. I mean, really fight them."

"And maybe you'll get in trouble, too," Vanai said. "For all you know, his accounts are like a spiderweb, set up to catch somebody who's not quite as smart as he thinks he is." She put a length of sausage on Ealstan's plate and then set a hand on her own belly. "Please be careful."

"Of course I'll be careful." But Ealstan didn't sound as if that were the first thing on his mind, or even the fourth or fifth. He sounded annoyed at Vanai for reminding him he might need to have a care.

You're a man, sure enough, Vanai thought. *You'll do whatever you please and then blame me if it doesn't work out the way you want.* She sighed. "How is the sausage?" she asked.

Ealstan suddenly seemed to notice what he'd been devouring for supper. "Oh! It's very good," he said. Vanai sighed again. As soon as Ealstan finished eating, he started going on about Pybba some more. Short of clouting him in the head with a rock, Vanai didn't know how to make him shut up. But when he declared, "It's practically my patriotic duty to see what's going on," she lost patience with him.

"You are going to do this thing," she said. "I can tell you're going to do it, and you won't listen to me no matter what I say. But I am going to say this: don't go charging straight ahead, as if you had four legs and two big horns and no brains at all. If you do that, I have the bad feeling you'll disappear one day, and I'll never see you again."

"Don't be silly," he answered, which really made her want to clout him in the head with a rock. But he went on, "I'm my father's son, after all. I don't go blindly charging into things."

That held enough truth to give her pause, but not enough fully to reassure her. Ealstan was his father's son, but he was also a red-blooded Forthwegian. Vanai knew that without fully understanding it; Forthweg was her homeland, but she didn't love it the way Forthwegians did. Why should she? A good part of the overwhelming Forthwegian majority would have been just as well pleased if she and all the Kaunians in the kingdom disappeared. And now a lot of the Kaunians in the kingdom were disappearing, thanks to the Algarvians—and thanks to Forthwegians not sorry to see them go.

Those thoughts flashed through her mind in a moment.

She hardly missed a beat in answering, "I hope you don't. You'd better not."

"I won't. Truly." Ealstan sounded perfectly confident. He also sounded perfectly blockheaded.

Vanai couldn't tell him that. It wouldn't have made him pay attention to her, and would have made her angry. What she did say was, "Remember, you've got a lot to live for here at the flat."

She wondered if she ought to pull off her tunic and skin out of her drawers. That would remind him of what he had to live for if nothing else did. Patriot or no, he was wild for lovemaking—a good deal wilder than she was at the moment, with pregnancy making her desire fitful. But she shook her head, as if he'd asked her to strip herself naked. She had too much pride, too much dignity, for that. She'd been Major Spinello's plaything. She wouldn't make herself anyone else's, not that way.

Ealstan pointed to her. For a moment, she thought he was going to ask her to do what she'd just rejected. She took a deep breath: she was ready to scorch him. But he said, "Your sorcery's slipped. You need to set it right. You especially need to keep it strong now. Mezentio's men have been taking a demon of a lot of people out of the Kaunian quarter lately."

"Oh." Vanai's anger evaporated. "All right. Thank you." She always kept the golden yarn and the dark brown in her handbag. She got them, twisted them together, and chanted the spell she'd devised. When she was done, she turned to Ealstan and said, "Is it good?"

"It's fine." Ealstan's smile was suddenly shy. "I'm sorry you can't look like yourself—the way you're supposed to look, I mean—all the time. You're very pretty when you look like a Forthwegian—don't get me wrong—but I think you're beautiful when you look like a Kaunian. I always have, from the day I first saw you."

"Have you?" Vanai said. Ealstan's nod was shy, too. As few things did, that little show of embarrassment reminded her she was a year older than he. He'd been fifteen when they first met in the oak wood between Oyngestun and Gromheort, his beard only darkening fuzz on his cheeks. He looked like a man now, and acted like a man . . . and he wanted to fight like a man. Vanai didn't know what to do about that. She feared she couldn't do anything about it.

She let him make love to her when they went to bed. It made him happy, and that made her happy, though she didn't kindle. *One thing,* she thought as she drifted toward sleep, *I don't need to worry about whether I'm going to have a baby. Now I know.*

Her spell had slipped again by the time she woke the next morning. She hastily repaired it while Ealstan ate barley porridge and gulped a morning cup of wine. As it had the night before, his smile reassured her. She could cast the spell with no one checking her, but she'd find out the hard way if she made a mistake.

Ealstan gave her an absentminded kiss and hurried out the door. By the way he hurried, Vanai was sure he was heading to Pybba's pottery works, though he didn't say so. She shook her head. She'd done everything she could to keep him safe. He would have to do something for himself, too.

She also had to go out, to the market square. While she'd kept her Kaunian looks, Ealstan had done the shopping. Getting out of the flat still seemed a miracle: so much so that she didn't mind lugging food back. Beans? Olives? Cabbages? So what? Just the chance to be out on the streets of Eoforwic, to see more than she could from her grimy window, made up for the work she had to do.

The apothecary's shop where she'd almost been caught out as a Kaunian, where the proprietor had killed himself rather than letting the Algarvians try to torment answers out of him, was open again. UNDER NEW OWNERSHIP, a sign in one window said. NEW LOWER PRICES, cried another sign, a bigger one, in the other window. *I might get medicines there,* Vanai thought. *I'd never trust this new owner, whoever he is, with anything more. He might be in the redheads' belt pouch.*

For all she knew, the new owner might be a relative of the dead apothecary. She still wouldn't trust him, and he still might be in the Algarvians' pay.

She didn't trust the butcher, either, but for different reasons: suspicion that he called mutton lamb, that he put grain in his sausages when he swore he didn't, that his scales worked in his favor. Writers had complained about such tricks in the days of the Kaunian Empire. Brivibas, no doubt, could have cited half a dozen examples, with appropriate citations. Vanai bit her lip. Her grandfather wouldn't be citing any more classical authors. Half the distress she felt was at not feeling more distress now that he was dead.

Marrow bones would flavor soup. The butcher said they were beef. They might have been horse or donkey. Vanai couldn't have proved otherwise; there, for once, the lie, if it was one, was reassuring. The gizzards he sold her probably did come from chickens—they were too big to belong to crows or pigeons. "I wouldn't have had 'em by this afternoon," he told her.

"I know that," she answered, and took them away.

When she got out on the street, people were nudging one another and pointing. "Look at him," somebody said. "Who does he think he is?" somebody else, a woman, added. "What does he think he is?" another woman said.

Vanai didn't want to look. She was too afraid of what she'd see: a Kaunian whose magic had run out, most likely. If the fellow had dyed hair, he wouldn't look exactly like a Kaunian, but he wouldn't look like a Forthwegian, either. Before long, the cry for Algarvian constables would go up.

Horrid fascination didn't take long to turn Vanai's eyes in the direction of the pointing fingers. The man at whom people were pointing didn't look just like a Forthwegian, but he wasn't an obvious Kaunian, either. *Halfbreed*, Vanai thought. Eoforwic held more than the rest of Forthweg put together. Her hand flattened on her belly. She held one herself.

Then she gasped, because she recognized the man. "Ethelhelm!"

The name slipped from her lips almost by accident. In a moment, it was in everyone's mouth. And the singer and drummer grinned at the crowd that had been so hostile and now paused, uncertain, waiting to hear what he would say. "Hello, folks." His voice was relaxed, easy. "I often use a little magic so I can go out and about without people bothering me. It must've worn off. Can I give you a song to make up for startling you?"

He'd told a great, thumping lie, and Vanai knew it. The redheads were hungry for Ethelhelm. But the crowd didn't know that. With one voice, they shouted, "Aye!" They might have mobbed an ordinary Kaunian or halfbreed whose luck had run out with his magic. Ethelhelm wasn't ordinary. He might have lost his magic, but he still had some luck.

And he still had his voice. He grabbed a wooden bucket from someone, turned it upside down, and used it to beat out a rhythm as he sang. After one song—he carefully picked one that said nothing about the Algarvians—the crowd howled for another. The impromptu concert was still going on when Vanai left.

He'll get away, she thought. *He'll keep playing till he satisfies them, then get off somewhere by himself and renew his spell. And then he'll be an ordinary Forthwegian . . . the same way I'm an ordinary Forthwegian.* But that wasn't quite right. The Algarvians wanted Ethelhelm because of who he was, not what he was. Vanai shook her head in slow wonder. She'd finally found somebody worse off than she was.

When Skarnu had visited Zarasai by himself, he hadn't been much impressed: it was a southern provincial town without much going for it that a man from Priekule could see. Returning to it with Amatu and Lauzdonu was unpleasantly like torture. The two Valmieran nobles who'd come back from Lagoas seemed to him to be doing their best to get caught.

His temper didn't take long to kindle. When he got them alone in the flat the underground had found for them, he snapped, "Why don't you just carry signs that say WE HATE KING MEZENTIO? Then the constables would nab you and the people who really know what they're doing could get back to doing it instead of spending half their time saving you.

Whenever you go outside, you risk yourselves and everybody who helped you get here in one piece."

"Sorry," said Lauzdonu, who had some vestiges of sense. "The kingdom's changed a lot more than we thought it had since we flew our dragons south instead of giving up."

"Aye." Amatu had a sharp, rather shrill voice that would have irritated Skarnu no matter what he said. When he said things like, "It's changed for the worse, that's what it's done," he irritated Skarnu all the more. And then he went on, "It looks like nine people out of every ten are stinking traitors, that's what it looks like. And I'm not so bloody sure about the tenth chap, either." He looked Skarnu full in the face as he made that—perhaps impolitic—remark.

I'm not supposed to bash him in the head, Skarnu reminded himself. *We're on the same side. We're supposed to be, anyhow.* "People are trying to live their lives," he said. "You can't blame them for that. What's a waiter to do if an Algarvian comes into his eatery? Throw him out? The poor whoreson'd get arrested, or more likely blazed."

"And who'd arrest him?" Lauzdonu put in. "Not the redheads, most likely. It'd be a Valmieran constable. You bet it would."

"They're the real traitors," Amatu snarled. "They all need shortening by a head, powers below eat 'em." He was quick to condemn. "And the waiters, too. If an Algarvian comes into their eatery, the redhead ought to go out with a case of the runs or the pukes. That'd teach him a lesson."

"So it would," Skarnu agreed, "the lesson being that something dreadful ought to happen to the waiter who messed with his stew or his chop. You haven't got any sense, Amatu."

"You haven't got any balls, Skarnu," retorted the noble returned from exile.

Lauzdonu had to step between them. "Stop!" he said. "Stop! If we quarrel, who laughs? Mezentio, that's who."

That was enough to halt Skarnu in his tracks. Amatu still seethed. "I ought to call you out," he snarled.

"Aye, go ahead—imitate the Algarvians," Skarnu said. That brought the other noble up short, where nothing else had done the job. Pushing his edge, Skarnu went on, "Can we look for ways to hurt the enemy instead of each other?"

"You don't seem to know who the enemy is." But now Amatu only sounded sulky, not incandescent.

"We do what we can," Skarnu answered. "We came here, remember, because a lot of ley lines run south through Zarasai. We want to keep the redheads from sending Kaunians to the seashore and slaughtering them to strike at Lagoas and Kuusamo."

Amatu's lip curled. "Maybe you came here for that. I came here to strike at the Algarvians and their lickspittle lapdogs. Who cares what happens to the kingdoms on the far side of the Strait of Valmiera?"

Doing his best to be reasonable, Lauzdonu said, "Except for Unkerlant, they're the only two kingdoms still in the fight against Algarve. That counts for something." All he got was another sneer from Amatu.

Skarnu said, "My lord, if you're not interested in doing the job you were sent here to do, if you'd sooner do what you think best, you can do that. But you'll have to move out of this flat and find one on your own, and you'll have to strike at the redheads on your own, too. No one from the underground will help you."

"Find a flat on my own?" Amatu looked horrified. Without a doubt, he'd never had to look for lodgings in his whole life. Skarnu wondered if he had any idea how to go about it. By his expression, probably not.

"The fight against Algarve is bigger than any one man." Skarnu knew he sounded like a particularly gooey kind of recruiting poster, but he didn't much care. Anything to get some use out of Amatu.

"All right. All *right!*" The returned exile threw his hands in the air. "I'm yours. Do with me as you will. And once you're done, once I have time of my own, have I got your gracious leave to go after the Algarvians in my own way?" He bowed himself almost double.

He really did want to go after the redheads. Skarnu recognized as much. The trouble was, he made almost every

Valmieran commoner and a lot of nobles want to go after him. When betrayal was as simple as a word whispered in the ear of a Valmieran constable, that wouldn't do. Skarnu had to remember to bow back, lest Amatu think he was offering a deadly insult. "Of course you may, as long as you try not to do anything that'll get us killed or captured and tortured. Betraying our friends isn't what we've got in mind, either."

"I understand that. I'm not an idiot," Amatu said testily, though Skarnu might not have agreed with him. The noble went on, "I'll haunt the caravan depot, if that's what you need from me. If I could sleep upside down in the rafters like a bat, I'd do that. Are you satisfied?"

"No," Skarnu said at once, which made Amatu glare at him all over again. He went on, "You and Lauzdonu and a lot of other people we don't even know will wander through the depot every so often—not often enough to make the Algarvians or their Valmieran hunting dogs notice us. If we see anything—powers above, if we smell anything, because those cars stink—there's a little eatery where we can go. In the back of that eatery, there's a crystal. Here's hoping we don't have to use it."

"Aye," Lauzdonu said. "That would mean trouble for us, and trouble for the poor Kaunians in the caravan car, too." He had some basic sense of reality.

Amatu? Skarnu wasn't so sure about him. He might have forgotten what he'd promised a moment before. Now he said, "Hang around in the depot? Oh, very well." He gave a martyred sigh. "But if I were a woman or Viscount Valnu, I might get arrested for soliciting."

"No, not like that," Skarnu said again. "Don't hang around. Wander through. Pause on a platform when a caravan comes in from the north or east. Wander off again. Buy yourself a mug of ale or a news sheet. Kill time."

"Beastly lies in the news sheets," Amatu said.

"Of course there are," Skarnu agreed. "But knowing how the enemy is lying is military information, too." That seemed to startle the other noble, who thought for a bit before nod-

ding. Amatu had probably been fine fighting on dragonback—his headlong aggressiveness matched his mount's.
Skarnu's opinion was that his brainpower also matched his
mount's, but that was nothing he could say.

He decided not to trust Amatu alone in the ley-line caravan
depot, at least at first. To his relief, the returned exile seemed
glad for company, not irate because Skarnu was coming with
him. *He probably hasn't realized why I'm coming along,*
Skarnu thought. *I'm not going to tell him, either.*

"Bloody ugly building," Amatu remarked as they walked
up to the red-brick depot. Skarnu agreed with him, but he
hadn't come as an architecture critic. Once they got inside,
he studied the board, then pointed. Amatu nodded. "Aye.
Platform three," he said. Skarnu didn't stomp on his toes to
make him shut up, but couldn't have said why he didn't. He
was more merciful than he'd suspected, that was all.

On the way to platform three, he bought some ale and a
news sheet. Amatu refused to buy a news sheet and made a
horrible face when he tasted his ale. Skarnu wondered if his
comrade were trying to get them both caught, if he were in
Algarvian pay. Skarnu didn't think so, but stupidity and arrogance could be as deadly as treason.

The caravan that stopped at the depot seemed ordinary. It
had no passenger cars with wooden shutters nailed over the
windows, no baggage cars from which came the stench of
crowded, filthy people. "Well, this was a waste of time,
wasn't it?" Amatu said.

"Aye, it was, but we didn't know ahead of time that it
would be," Skarnu answered in a much lower voice. "That's
why we keep an eye on the depot: because we don't know
ahead of time, I mean."

Amatu accepted that, even if reluctantly. He was glad to
leave the depot, though. Alone, Skarnu would have hung
around for a while longer. With Amatu for a comrade, he was
delighted to get away unscathed. He let out a silent sigh of relief when they got past the pair of Valmieran constables
standing at the entranceway.

Once they reached their street, Amatu started toward their block of flats without the least hesitation. "Wait," Skarnu murmured, and took him by the arm. "Let's walk past. Let's not go inside."

"Why not?" For a wonder, Amatu kept his voice down.

"I've never seen those fellows lounging by the stairway," Skarnu answered. "Beggars usually have their own turfs. Those fellows are new. Their rags look too clean, and so do they. They've never missed a meal. I think they're constables. . . . No, curse you, don't stare at them."

"Lauzdonu—" Amatu began.

Skarnu had become a better actor than he would have imagined in his carefree days in Priekule. Without seeming to break stride, he contrived to step on Amatu's foot and make the noble hop and curse. For good measure, he stuck an elbow in the pit of Amatu's stomach, too. "Shut up, you cursed fool," he hissed. "They may have him already. Odds are, they do."

For another wonder, Amatu heeded him and said not another word till they'd turned the corner. Then, in tones more subdued than he usually used, he asked, "What do we do now?"

"We go to that eatery," Skarnu answered patiently. "We talk on the crystal—just long enough to let people know there's trouble here. After that, we disappear again. This isn't my town, you know."

"Nor mine, powers above be praised for that," Amatu said. "All right—the eatery."

No suspiciously well-fed tramps lingered outside. But when Skarnu casually asked after the waiter's health, the fellow answered that he was fine, and didn't use the words he was supposed to. Skarnu ordered ale and a plate of smoked beef tongue for himself and Amatu. They ate and drank, paid the scot, and left.

"No good?" Amatu asked.

"No good," Skarnu agreed. "They're waiting for people in the underground to come in and show themselves. If we'd done it, we wouldn't have walked out again."

"What do we do now?" Amatu asked again.

"Walk around for a while," Skarnu answered. "They can't have grabbed everybody in Zarasai. Somebody will give us a hand." *I hope,* he thought. *Oh, by the powers above, how I hope. Otherwise I'm stuck here with the worst excuse for an underground man the world has ever known, and no way to get free of him.*

The bigger of the two Unkerlanter soldiers who'd come east into the Duchy of Grelz was named Gandiluz. The smaller one was Tantris. They were both back with Garivald's band of irregulars these days. Tantris did most of the talking for them. "Now that the trees are in full leaf again, things favor you," he declared. "You've got to strike the Algarvians and their Grelzer puppets one stinging blow after another."

"We'll do what we can, of course," Garivald answered, "but look around. We're not a big band."

Tantris waved that aside, as if of no account. "And you've got a mage."

"Where?" Garivald asked in real perplexity.

"There." The Unkerlanter regular pointed at Sadoc.

Garivald threw his hands in the air. "Oh, by the powers above!" he howled. "Munderic thought the same bloody thing. Every time Sadoc tried a spell, something would go wrong. Every stinking time. Sometimes it'd be something big, sometimes just something little. But *something* would always happen." He turned his furious glare on Sadoc. "Tell 'em yourself. Am I right, or am I wrong?"

"Well, aye, you're right," Sadoc said. "But that's only so far. I think I know what I've been doing wrong. I'll be better from here on out."

"A likely story," Garivald growled. He turned back to the pair of Unkerlanter regulars. "Are you both daft? Do you want to get the lot of us killed before you can squeeze any kind of proper use out of us?"

"Of course not," Gandiluz said.

"Shut up," Tantris told him, and shut up he did. Tantris returned his attention to Garivald. "What we want to do should be as plain as the nose on my face." He had a formidable Unkerlanter beak. "We want to do the most harm we can to the Algarvians with this band of irregulars. It stands to reason that we can do more using magecraft than we can without it. If we've got a mage here, we ought to get what we can out of him."

"If we had a mage here, that would be a good idea," Obilot put in. "What we've got is Sadoc, so you can forget about it." Garivald sent her a grateful glance.

"I'm sure he's not a first-rank mage like the ones they've got in Cottbus. . . ." Tantris began.

"He's not even a fifth-rank mage like the worthless drunk they sent to Zossen, my home village," Garivald said. "What he is is a disaster waiting to happen."

"I won't be that bad from now on," Sadoc insisted. "I truly won't. I can do just about anything now. I know I can."

That was one of the more frightening things Garivald had heard. Sadoc scared him almost as much as had the Algarvian officer who'd told him he'd be boiled alive in Herborn, the capital of Grelz. The Algarvian had turned out to be wrong. Garivald was sure Sadoc was wrong, too.

He scowled at the Unkerlanter irregulars who'd encouraged the would-be mage to new dreams of glory. "If you want to get the most out of us, why don't you just cut our throats and use our life energy against the redheads?"

Tantris didn't turn a hair. "We've thought about that. If we have to, we'll do it."

He and Gandiluz were King Swemmel's only formal representatives within the clearing. The irregulars could have blazed them down and buried them with no one outside the woods the wiser. But they didn't. They'd been too accustomed for too long to doing what Unkerlanter inspectors and impressers said—when they couldn't get around it, that is.

Garivald hoped he could get around it here. "You've been in Grelz for a few weeks. We've been doing this ever since the Algarvians came through." He hadn't, not quite, but Swemmel's men didn't need to hear that. "Don't you think we know whether we've got a mage here or not?"

"What we think is, you haven't been using him the right way," Tantris said, and Gandiluz nodded to show he was part of that *we*. Tantris went on, "It's especially important to hit the Algarvians now, to make it hard for them to bring men and beasts to the fighting front southwest of here."

From behind Tantris, somebody said, "We've heard nothing but how this is especially important and that's especially important and the other thing is especially important, too. When it's all especially important, none of it's especially important."

"Well, this truly is," Tantris said. "If the Algarvians win the summer's fight, we're almost as bad off as we were last year. They might even have another go at Sulingen, curse 'em. But if we win it, then they're the ones who have to worry."

"How is Sadoc's magecraft going to make a copper's worth of difference?" Garivald demanded. "I mean, how would it make any difference if he had any magecraft?"

"He will disguise us as we charge down on the enemy," Tantris declared. Sadoc nodded. He thought he could do it. But Garivald had seen how Sadoc had thought he could do any number of things he couldn't do.

Here, Garivald didn't have to do any complaining. The other irregulars did it for him. The woods were alive with the sound of outrage. Obilot proved most articulate: "If you use us to charge down on the enemy, you use us once. I thought the point of a band of irregulars was stinging the enemy again and again. We've done that. We can keep doing it, too—if you leave any of us alive *to* do it."

"Saving the kingdom comes first," Gandiluz said, for once speaking ahead of his comrade. "Saving the band comes only after that."

Garivald nodded. "Fine. You show me how charging down on a bunch of Grelzers—or even redheads—will save the kingdom, and we'll do it. Till you show us that, we'll hit the foe and run away, the way we've been doing for almost two years now. That's what efficiency is all about, isn't it?"

Tantris gave him a dirty look. "You're not cooperating. His Majesty will hear of this."

"I'm doing my best," Garivald said. "Tell me what you want. Let's see if we can't do it without magecraft."

"A company of Grelzers will march past these woods day after tomorrow," Tantris said. "You ought to attack them."

He didn't say how he knew. That was supposed to make him seem knowledgeable and impressive. But Garivald had a good idea of all the ways he might know. Magic was one. Getting the news from a Grelzer soldier was another, a Grelzer clerk a third. Gossip would work about as well as patriotism (or treason, from a Grelzer point of view). Or, of course, it could have been a trap.

But none of that mattered. A certain amount of common sense did. Garivald waved. "Look at us. It's been a hard winter. I don't care if you disguise us as behemoths or butterflies—how likely are we to take out a company of soldiers?"

"Say, that ferocious company of Grelzers, though—Algarve wouldn't have a chance of winning the war without them," Obilot said.

Her sarcasm finally got under Tantris' hide. He snapped, "Be silent, woman," as if he were her husband back in a peasant village.

She was carrying her stick, of course. She was hardly ever without it. As if by magic, the business end suddenly pointed at Tantris' belly. "If you want to come here and make me, come right ahead," she said pleasantly.

Gandiluz started to move to flank her. "Not you," Garivald told him, also pleasantly. Talking back to the regulars got easier the more he did it. He aimed his stick at Gandiluz's midriff. Gandiluz stopped moving. He didn't stop weighing his chances, though. Neither did Tantris. King Swemmel might have sent out petty tyrants, but he hadn't chosen cowards.

In the confrontation, everyone had forgotten about Sadoc. The peasant who'd struggled so hard to become a mage was dark with fury. "There is a power point in these woods, and I'm going to use it," he growled, his hands moving in swift passes that certainly looked confident and competent. "Garivald, you'll pay for mocking me."

Garivald knew a certain amount of alarm—but less than

he had going into combat against the Grelzers. They'd made it plain they knew what they were doing when they tried to kill him; Sadoc hadn't proved any such thing. "Don't be a bigger jackass than you can help," Garivald suggested.

"And you'll pay for that, too," Sadoc said. "I can call down lightnings out of a clear blue sky—I can, and I will!" He raised his hands to the heavens and cried out words of power—or they might have been nonsense syllables, for all Garivald knew.

But power gathered in the air. Garivald could feel it. He'd felt it before when Sadoc tried to do this, that, or the other thing. The would-be wizard could prepare for a spell. What came after the preparations, though . . .

"Sadoc, stop it this instant!" Now Obilot's voice came sharp as a whipcrack. Garivald wasn't the only one who felt that building power, then.

As a matter of fact, Gandiluz felt it, too. "You see?" he said to Garivald. "He *can* be what we need against Algarve."

"My arse," Garivald said succinctly.

"No, my arse," Sadoc said. "You can kiss it, Garivald!" He brought down his hands in a gesture filled with hate—and lightning followed.

Garivald fell to the ground, stunned and blinded by the blue-white stroke. Thunder roared around him. For a couple of heartbeats, he thought he really was dead. But then, like the rest of the irregulars, he staggered to his feet. Sadoc was still upright, looking in astonishment at what he'd done. Like everybody else's, Garivald's gaze followed his.

"Oh, you idiot," Garivald said, astonished at how few shakes his voice held. He blinked, but it would be a while before he stopped seeing the world through green and purple snakes. "You big, clumsy, futtering idiot."

There stood Tantris. He was shaking, shaking like a leaf. And there beside him lay the charred, smoking ruins of Gandiluz—one Unkerlanter regular who would never report back to King Swemmel again. Sadoc had called down the lightning, all right, but not on the target he'd had in mind.

"I-I'm sorry," he stammered. "I really am. I aimed to hit

you with that, Garivald. I probably shouldn't have done that either, should I?"

"No, you bloody clot," Garivald snapped. He rounded on Tantris again. "Well?" he demanded. "Are you going to tell me some more about how Sadoc is the unicorn you're going to ride to victory, and he'll gore everything that gets in front of you out of the way?"

Tantris was still gaping at the remains of his comrade. The stench of burnt meat filled the clearing. Garivald had to repeat himself to get his attention. When he did, Tantris shuddered. He leaned over and was noisily sick. Garivald nodded to the irregular closest to him. The man gave Tantris a canteen. After he'd rinsed his mouth and spat, he violently shook his head. "I'm not going to tell anybody anything, not for a while," he answered.

"That's the first sensible thing you've said since you got here," Garivald told him.

But Tantris shook his head. "No. We really do need to do everything we can to keep the redheads from moving supplies through Grelz. However we do it."

"However we do it—aye," Garivald said. "Suppose you let us find our way instead of telling us yours." Tantris looked at Gandiluz's corpse again. He gulped. He said not another word.

Eleven

No one could have come near the fighting line through the great woods of western Unkerlant without knowing two armies grappled there. The ignorant traveler's nose would have told him if nothing else did. Istvan was no ignorant traveler, but he smelled the reek of unwashed bodies, the

fouler stench of imperfectly covered latrines, and the sharp
tang of woodsmoke, too.

And yet, at this season of the year, those stinks were almost afterthoughts in the air. Everything was green and
growing. Broad-leafed trees, bare through the winter, had
cloaked themselves anew. So had the bushes and ferns that
grew under them. Pines and firs and balsams stayed in leaf
the year around, but the sap rising in them put out spicy notes
Istvan's nostrils appreciated.

He also appreciated the lull in the fighting. "We're on the
defensive," he told Captain Frigyes when the new company
commander came forward to inspect the redoubt, "and
they're on the defensive, too. Put it all together and it means
there's not a whole lot of action."

"Sometimes the stars shine on us," Frigyes said. He was a
big man, burly even by Gyongyosian standards, with a scar
on his right cheek. "We have troubles out in the islands, the
Unkerlanters have troubles off in the east. Put it all together
and they don't want to be fighting here and neither do we."

Captain Tivadar might have said the same thing. Istvan
missed his longtime superior, but Frigyes looked to be a solid
officer—and he knew nothing of why Istvan and several of
his squadmates bore scars on their left hands. Istvan looked
around. All of his troopers were busy with other things. He
could bring out a question perhaps improper for a man of a
warrior race: "Why don't we go ahead and make peace,
then?"

"Because we would betray our Algarvian allies if we did,
and they've struck some heavy blows at the accursed Kuusamans," Frigyes answered. "Also, because King Swemmel
hasn't shown any interest in making peace, may the stars
withhold their light from him."

Anyone would reckon Swemmel the warrior, Istvan
thought uncomfortably. *But he's just a madman. Everybody
knows that. Even his own soldiers know it. But why do they
fight so hard for a madman?*

"Enjoy this while it lasts," Frigyes told him. "It won't last forever. Sooner or later, the Algarvians will strike their blow, as they do every spring. Then, odds are, they'll drive the Unkerlanters back again, and then the Unkerlanters will hit us again here."

"I'm sorry, sir." Istvan frowned. "I don't follow that."

"How likely is Swemmel to get summer victories against Algarve?" Frigyes asked. "Not very, not if you look at what's happened the past two years. So if the Unkerlanters want wins to keep their own people happy, they'll try to get them against us."

"Oh." That made an unpleasant amount of sense. It was also an insult of sorts. "We're easier than the Algarvians, are we? We shouldn't be easier than anyone."

"We're easier than the Algarvians, aye." Frigyes didn't seem insulted. "They can bring their whole apparatus of war with them. We can't. All we've got here in these woods are some of the best footsoldiers in the world." He slapped Istvan on the back, climbed out of the redoubt, and went on his way."

Istvan turned to his squad. "The captain says Gyongyos has some of the best footsoldiers in the world. He hasn't seen you lazy buggers in action yet, that's what *I* think."

"There hasn't *been* any action for a while," Szonyi said, which was also true.

"Do you really want much?" Kun asked. Even if he did wear spectacles, he could ask a question like that: he'd seen as much desperate fighting as any man in the woods, Istvan possibly excepted.

Had one of the newer men put the question, Szonyi would have felt compelled to puff out his chest and act manly. As things were, he shrugged and answered, "It'll probably come whether I want it or not, so what's the point of worrying?"

A red squirrel was rash enough to show its head around the trunk of a birch. Istvan's stick, ready for Unkerlanters, was ready for a squirrel, too. It fell into the bushes under the trees. "Nice blazing, Sergeant," Lajos said. "Something good for the pot."

Kun sighed. "By the time you skin it and gut it, there's hardly enough meat on a squirrel to be worth bothering about."

"That's not why you're complaining," Istvan said as he left the redoubt to collect the squirrel. "I know why you're complaining. You're a born city man, and you never had to worry about eating things like squirrels before they sucked you into the army." In the bushes, the squirrel was still feebly thrashing. Istvan found a rock and smashed its head a couple of times. Then he carried it back by the tail, pausing once or twice to brush away fleas. He hoped he got them all. If he didn't, he'd do some extra scratching.

"Doesn't seem natural, eating something like that," Kun said as Istvan's knife slit the squirrel's belly.

"What's not natural is going hungry when there's good food around," Istvan said. His squadmates spoke up in loud agreement. They came off farms or out of little villages. Gyongyos was a kingdom of smallholdings. Towns were market centers, administrative points. They weren't the heart of the land, as he'd heard they were elsewhere on Derlavai. And stewed squirrel, no matter what Kun thought of it, was tasty.

Kun didn't complain when it was ladled out to him. By then, it had got mixed up with everything else in the pot, mixed to where you couldn't point at any one chunk of meat and say, *This is squirrel.* Off to the south, somebody started lobbing eggs at somebody else. Istvan had no idea whether it was the Unkerlanters or his own countrymen. Whoever it was, he hoped they'd stop it.

Captain Frigyes came back the next day with a mage in tow. That made Kun perk up; it always did. "Men," the new company commander said, "this is Major Borsos. He's going to be—"

"Well, by the stars, so it is!" Istvan exclaimed. "No offense, sir, but I figured you'd be dead by now." He saw blank expressions all around him, including the one on Borsos' face. He explained: "Sir, I fetched and carried for you on Obuda, when you were dousing out where the Kuusaman ships were."

"Oh." Major Borsos' face cleared. He was a major by courtesy, so ordinary troopers *would* fetch and carry for him. He'd been a captain by courtesy out on the island in the Both-

nian Ocean, so he'd come up a bit in the world. Istvan had
been a common soldier then, so he had, too. "Good to see
you again," Borsos said, a beat slower than he might have.

Istvan suspected the mage didn't really remember him. He
shrugged. Borsos had seen a lot since then, as he had himself.
And Kun looked as green with envy as the tarnished bronze
dowsing rods Borsos had used on Obuda. Istvan smiled. That
was worth something.

Frigyes said, "I didn't expect it to be old home week here.
But Major Borsos is going to do what he can to spy out the
Unkerlanters."

"Ah," Istvan said. "How will your dowsing sort through all
the moving beasts and especially the moving leaves to find
the moving Unkerlanters, eh, Major?"

Borsos beamed. "Aye, by the stars, you did assist me,
Sergeant, or some dowser, anyhow, and he listened when he
ran on at the mouth." Kun was standing behind his back, and
behind Frigyes', and looked to be on the point of retching.
Istvan wanted to make a face back at him, but couldn't. Borsos went on, "The answer is, just as I have a dowsing rod attuned to the sea, so I've also got one attuned to soldiers. It
hardly cares about leaves, and it isn't much interested in
beasts, either, though mountain apes might confuse it. Here,
I'll show you." He set down the leather satchel he was carrying. It clanked. He opened it and went through the rods, finally grunting when he found the one he wanted. "Doesn't
look like much, does it?"

"No, sir," Istvan answered. The dowsing rod wasn't of
fresh, shiny bronze, or of the green, patinaed sort, either. It
looked like a thin length of rusty iron—if those stains on it
were rust. Kun was about to speak. Again, Istvan beat him to
the punch, pointing and asking, "Unkerlanter blood?"

Borsos beamed again. Frigyes said, "My, what a clever
chap you turn out to be." Kun looked about ready to burst like
an egg from rage and jealousy. That made Istvan happier than
either officer's reaction. He had to live with Kun all the time.

"Even so, Sergeant. Even so," Borsos answered, beaming
still. "By the law of similarity, when I dowse with this rod,

I'll sense motion from Unkerlanters, and very little from any other source." He waved the rod as if it were a sword, then thwacked it into the palm of his hand. "It's not perfect—dowsing isn't—but it's pretty good."

"Go ahead, Major," Captain Frigyes said. He wouldn't have talked like that to a real soldier of rank higher than his own. "Let's see what's going on out there."

Major Borsos didn't take offense. He'd probably had officers—real officers, men of noble blood—treat him a good deal worse. He said, "Aye, Captain, just as you please." Holding the handle of the dowsing rod in both hands, he swung it to the east, murmuring as he did so. He hadn't gone far before it dipped sharply. "Something in that direction—not far away, unless I miss my guess."

"Oh, that's where their scouts always hide, sir," Szonyi said. "Nothing much to worry about unless you feel a whole lot of the buggers."

"No," Borsos said, looking down at his hands as if asking them to speak more clearly. After some thought, he nodded. "No, it doesn't feel like a lot of men. One, not far away—that could well be so."

Kun worked his little magic and said, "He's not moving toward us."

"No?" Borsos said. "What charm were you using there, soldier?" He shrugged. "Whatever it is, it won't matter to me. I never have been able to do much in the way of magecraft save for dowsing. The art is in the blood, or else it's not. With me, it's not, unless I have a dowsing rod in my hand."

"It's very easy, sir," Kun said, and ran through it.

Borsos tried the charm, then shrugged again. "I can't tell if anyone is moving or not. You have your gift; I have mine. And now, I had better finish doing what I can do." He started working the dowsing rod again.

Kun looked proud that he could do something the dowser couldn't. He didn't bother remembering that Borsos could do something he couldn't—something a great deal larger. People, Istvan had noticed, were often like that.

After sweeping through the entire half-circle, Borsos

turned to Frigyes and said, "I see no vast hordes of Unkerlanters set to sweep down on this redoubt. Of course, if
they're more than a mile or so away, I probably *won't* see
them. That's the range I can get out of this rod." With a shrug,
he put it back into his valise.

"Thanks, Major," Captain Frigyes said. "I didn't really expect an attack, but it's nice to know we haven't got one building . . . here." He corrected himself before Borsos could do it
for him.

"Sir, you could sense Kuusaman ships out beyond the
horizon," Istvan said. "Why can't you see that far with your
Unkerlanter rod?"

"Mainly because a big moving warship creates a lot more
disturbance than even a whole lot of moving men," the
dowser answered. "Men aren't all moving in just the same direction. Some of them might even move away on purpose to
confuse people like me. This is a funny business I'm in, no
two ways about it."

Istvan started to say that he'd trade in a flash, but checked
himself. Borsos' job brought him up to the front lines, too,
and he was no great shakes at fighting back. *Each sheep has
its own pasture,* Istvan thought. He looked up and laughed a
little. His pasture came with altogether too many trees.

When Hajjaj walked into General Ikhshid's office, the portly
officer started to get to his feet so he could bow. "Don't
bother, General, I pray you—don't bother," Hajjaj said. "I am
willing—indeed, I am eager—to take the thought for the act."

"You're kind, your Excellency, very kind," Ikhshid
wheezed. "Since you say I may, I'm more than content to
stay down here on my arse, believe me I am."

"Are you well, General?" the Zuwayzi foreign minister
asked in some anxiety—if Ikhshid went down, he didn't
know who could replace him. As a soldier, Ikhshid was better
than competent, but no more than that. But he had the respect
of every clanfather in Zuwayza. Hajjaj couldn't think of any
other officer who did.

With another wheeze, the general answered, "I'll last as long as I can—and a little longer than that, with any luck at all. But I didn't ask you to drag your own set of old bones over here for that. I wanted you to take a look at the map and tell me what you see." He gestured toward the map of Derlavai that took up most of one office wall.

"No tea and wine and cakes?" Hajjaj asked mildly.

"If you want to waste time on frivolities, I'll send for 'em," Ikhshid answered. "Otherwise, I'd sooner talk about what's what."

"From your charm, anyone could guess you'd served in the Unkerlanter army," Hajjaj murmured. That squeezed a breathy snort out of Ikhshid. Hajjaj said, "I suppose we can dispense with ritual." He studied the map. "I am pleased to note the advances our bold Zuwayzi forces have made here in the north."

Ikhshid snorted again, this time in derision. "Cut to the chase, your Excellency. By the powers above, cut to the chase. You see that big ugly bulge down around Durrwangen the same as I do. There can't be a soldier on Derlavai—or on the island, either—who looks at the map and doesn't see that bulge."

"Not just soldiers," Hajjaj said. "Some weeks ago, Marquis Balastro assured me the Algarvians would cut it off as soon as the ground dried." He shook his head. "What a strange notion—ground getting too wet for armies to move across it, I mean."

"I've seen it myself, matter of fact," Ikhshid said. "It'd be like trying to fight in a tin of cake batter. That's what the muddy season's all about down there. But never mind that. The ground's been dry enough to hold armies for a while now, and the Algarvians still haven't moved. How come?"

"You would do better to ask Marquis Balastro or his military attaché," Hajjaj replied. "I fear I cannot tell you."

"I suppose not. But *I* can tell *you*, and I'm not an Algarvian," Ikhshid said. "The thing of it is, you think Marshal Rathar doesn't know what's coming next? They might have come close to a surprise if they'd moved as soon as ever they could, but now?" He shook his head. "Now it's a slugging match."

"Ah." Hajjaj studied the map. "If they strike there, they won't have much of an advantage of maneuver, will they?"

Ikhshid beamed so widely, his face showed a net of wrinkles that didn't usually appear. "Your Excellency, when I fall over dead, they can paint stars on your arm and you can take over for me."

"May you live to a hundred and twenty years, then," Hajjaj exclaimed. "The only thing I want to do less than command a few soldiers in the field is command a lot of soldiers in the field. And that is nothing but the truth."

"As may be," Ikhshid said. "But you can see it, too. If Rather can't, he's dumber than I know he is."

"Why are Mezentio's men waiting, then?" Hajjaj asked.

"Only reason I can think of is to get everyone and everything into the fight," Ikhshid answered. "Moving soldiers from every other part of the line, pulling animals off the breeding farms young and half trained . . . They've hit Unkerlant as hard as they could two summers in a row, and King Swemmel wouldn't fall over. If they hit him again, they'll try to hold a rock in their fist."

"But finding the rock takes time," Hajjaj said.

Ikhshid nodded. "We'll know more about how things look once they finally get around to fighting the battle."

"When Marquis Balastro speaks of this, he'll guarantee Algarvian victory," Hajjaj predicted.

"Of course he will. That's his job," Hajjaj said. "Your job, though, your job is to keep King Shazli from listening to a pack of lies."

Hajjaj bowed where he sat. "I have seldom met a Zuwayzi with such a delicate understanding of what I do and what I'm supposed to do."

"Delicate, my arse," Ikhshid said. "If my men tell me they've seen thus and so in the Unkerlanter lines and it turns out not to be thus and so at all, I look like a fool and some good men end up dead. If you tell King Shazli what isn't so, you can kill more Zuwayzin than I'd ever dream of doing."

"That, unfortunately, is true." Hajjaj got to his feet. He knees and back and ankles creaked. "Seriously, Ikhshid, I hope you stay well. The kingdom needs you—and I would enjoy harassing a new commander, a serious commander, much less than I like bothering you."

"Well, you're a wizened old thornbush, but Zuwayza's got used to having you around," Ikhshid said. Once more, he didn't get up. He sat on his hams, his eyes turned to the map.

"Your Excellency," Qutuz said when Hajjaj returned to his own office, "the Algarvian minister would confer with you."

"Why am I not surprised?" Hajjaj murmured, and then, "I will see him."

"He says he will be here in half an hour," Qutuz said.

"Time enough for me to get dressed." Hajjaj let out a heartfelt sigh. "With the weather warmer than it was, I'm starting to feel that I'm martyring myself for the sake of diplomacy again."

"What if he comes naked?" Qutuz asked. "What if he comes showing off his circumcision?" He sounded as queasy talking about that as a prim and proper Sibian would have sounded while taking about going naked.

"I don't expect it," the Zuwayzi foreign minister replied. "He's only done it a couple of times, and then as much to startle us, I think, as to conform to our customs. If he does . . . if he docs, I'll get out of my own clothes again, and I'll spend the time he's in my office *not* looking between his legs." The idea of mutilating oneself, and especially of mutilating oneself *there,* left him queasy, too. He went on, "Make sure you fetch in the tray of tea and wine and cakes. With Balastro, I may want to spin things out as long as I can."

His secretary bowed. "Everything shall be just as you say, your Excellency."

"I doubt it," Hajjaj answered bleakly. "Not even a first-rank mage can make that claim. But we do what we can, so we do."

He'd started quietly baking in his Algarvian-style clothes when Marquis Balastro came strutting into his office. The Algarvian minister, to Hajjaj's relief, was himself clothed. After the handshake and bows and protestations of esteem—some of which approached sincerity—Hajjaj said, "You look extraordinarily dapper today, your Excellency."

Balastro chortled. "How in blazes would you know?"

Hajjaj shrugged. "So much for diplomacy. Take a seat, if you'd be so kind. Qutuz will be here with tea and wine and cakes in a moment."

"Will he?" The Algarvian minister sent him a sour look. "Which means there are things about which you don't care to talk to me. Why am I not surprised?" But even as Balastro grumbled, he made a nest for himself in the pillows that took the place of chairs in Hajjaj's office. "Tell me, my friend, since you can't very well say a bare-naked man is looking dapper, what *do* you say for polite chitchat along those lines? 'Hello, old fellow. Your wen's no bigger than it was the last time I saw you'?"

"If it's not," Hajjaj answered, which made Balastro laugh. "Or you can talk about sandals or jewelry or hats. Hats do well."

"Aye, I suppose they would, with so little competition." Balastro nodded to Qutuz, who fetched in the traditional Zuwayzi refreshments. "Good to see you. Nice hat you're not wearing."

Qutuz stooped to set the tray on Hajjaj's low desk. Then he bowed to Balastro. "I thank you very kindly, your Excellency," he replied in good Algarvian. "I hope you like it just as much the next time you don't see it." He bowed again and departed.

Balastro stared after him, then chortled again. "That one's dangerous, Hajjaj. He'll succeed you one of these days."

"It could be." Hajjaj poured wine. It was, he saw, date wine, which meant Qutuz hadn't been so diplomatic as all that; Zuwayzin were the only folk with a real taste for the stuff. "Most people, however, prefer *not* to think of their successors, and in this I must confess to following the vulgar majority."

At last, as the tea and wine and cakes failed, so did the small talk. Leaning forward a little, Hajjaj asked, "And how may I serve you today, your Excellency?"

"It appears likely that Kaunian marauders have made their way back to Forthweg from the refuge places Zuwayza had unfortunately granted them," Balastro said. "I will have you know that King Mezentio formally protests this outrage."

"His protest is noted," Hajjaj replied. "Be it also noted that Zuwayza has done everything possible to prevent such unfortunate incidents. Our navy has sunk several boats sailing east toward Forthweg for unknown but suspicious purposes." How many more had slipped past Zuwayza's small, not very energetic navy, he couldn't begin to guess.

Balastro's snort said he couldn't begin to guess, either, but assumed the number was large. Hajjaj didn't worry overmuch about that snort. If the Forthwegian Kaunians were all that Balastro had on his mind, the Zuwayzi foreign minister would be well content.

But, snort aside, Balastro still had reasons to confer with Hajjaj. Hajjaj had been mournfully certain he would, and even on which topic. Sure enough, Balastro said, "You are doubtless wondering why we have not struck at the Unkerlanters."

"I?" Hajjaj contrived to look innocent. "Even if such a thought were in my mind—"

Balastro cut him off with a sharp gesture, more the sort an Unkerlanter might have used than anything he would have expected from an Algarvian. "We're getting ready, that's all. We're not leaving anything to chance this time. When we hit them, we're going to hit them with everything we've got. And we're going to smash them flat."

"May it be so." On the whole, Hajjaj meant it. Algarve was a nasty cobelligerent. Unkerlant was a nasty neighbor, which was worse. King Swemmel rampant in triumph . . . His mind shied away, like a horse from a snake.

"Believe it!" Balastro said fervently. "Only believe it, and it becomes that much likelier to be true. He whose will fails first fails altogether."

"It's rather harder than that, I fear," Hajjaj said. "If it weren't, you would not have needed to pause to gather all your forces in the south." Balastro stared at him, as if astonished to be called on the inconsistency. Hajjaj didn't care, not about that; part of the diplomatist's art was knowing when not to be diplomatic.

As Cornelu urged the leviathan west, islands rose up out of the sea. He couldn't see all of them, even if the leviathan stood on its tail, but he knew how many lay ahead of him: five good-sized ones, one for each crown on the breast of the rubber suit he wore.

"Sibiu," he whispered. "My Sibiu."

The last time he'd gone back to his Sibiu, the Algarvian occupiers had killed his leviathan out from under him. But the Algarvians had done worse than that; they'd killed his family out from under him, even though Costache and Brindza remained alive.

He was glad this scouting mission didn't take him to Tirgoviste town, didn't take him to Tirgoviste island. How alert were Mezentio's men around Facaceni island, the westernmost of the main five? If they were too alert, of course, he wouldn't bring the leviathan back to Setubal, but that would tell the Lagoan naval officers something worth knowing, too.

He kept an eye peeled for dragons, another for ley-line warships. So far, no sign of either. The Algarvians, these days, had a lot of coast to watch: Sibiu's, of course, but also their own and Valmiera's and Jelgava's and Forthweg's and, Cornelu supposed, Zuwayza's and Yanina's as well. The Algarvian navy hadn't been enormous before the war began. It also had to hold off Unkerlant's, to try to keep an eye on the land of the Ice People, and to help colonial forces keep the sputtering war going in tropical Siaulia. Looked at that way, was it any wonder Cornelu saw no warships?

Maybe the Lagoans and Kuusamans could send a fleet into Sibiu and snatch it out from under the Algarvians' noses. Maybe. That was one of the reasons Cornelu and his leviathan were here. If they didn't spot any patrollers, maybe Mezentio's minions were sending everything west for the big fight, the fight that couldn't be ignored, the fight against Unkerlant.

What sort of garrison stayed in Facaceni town? Real soldiers? Or beardless boys and gray-haired veterans of the Six Years' War? Cornelu couldn't tell that, not from the sea, but Lagoas and Kuusamo were bound to have spies in the town, too. What were they telling the spymasters in Setubal and Yliharma? And how much of what they were telling those spymasters could be believed?

On swam the leviathan, pausing or turning aside now and again to snap up a fish. Somewhere along the coastline, the Algarvians would have men with spyglasses or perhaps mages watching for the approach of foes from the west. Cornelu and his leviathan would not draw the mages' notice, for he pulled no energy from the ley lines that powered fleets. And to a man with a spyglass, one spouting leviathan looked much like another. For that matter, from farther than a few hundred yards, a spouting leviathan looked much like a spouting whale.

As he rounded the headland and neared Facaceni town, Cornelu saw several sailboats bobbing in the water. They wouldn't draw the notice of any mages, either. Cornelu grimaced. The Algarvians had conquered Sibiu through a daring reversion to the days before ley lines were known: with a fleet of sailing ships that reached Cornelu's kingdom unseen and undetected in dead of night. In a world of ever-growing complexity, the simple approach had proved overwhelmingly successful.

He thought about going up to one of the boats and asking the fishermen for local news. Most Sibians despised their Algarvian overlords. Most . . . but not all. Mezentio's men recruited Sibians to fight in Unkerlant. Sibian constables helped the Algarvians rule their countrymen. A few folk genuinely believed in the notion of a union of Algarvic peoples, not pausing to think that such a union meant the Algarvians would stay on top forever.

One of the fishermen saw Cornelu atop his leviathan when the great beast surfaced. He sent an obscene gesture Cornelu's way. That probably meant—Cornelu hoped it meant—he thought Cornelu an Algarvian. But Cornelu didn't find out by experiment.

When he got to Facaceni town, he spied a couple of dragons on patrol above it, wheeling in the clear blue sky. He noted them with grease pencil on a slate. What he could not note was how many more dragons might rise into the sky on a moment's notice if dragonfliers or mages spied something amiss.

Facaceni town, of course, faced the Derlavaian mainland—faced toward Algarve, in fact. All the major Sibian towns did; only the lesser ones turned toward Lagoas and Kuusamo. Part of that was because Sibiu lay closer to the mainland than to the big island. The rest was due to the way the ley lines ran. In olden days, before ley lines mattered so much, Sibiu had long contended with Lagoas for control of the sea between them. She'd lost—Lagoas outweighed her—but she'd fought hard.

As an officer of the Sibian navy, Cornelu knew the ley lines around his kingdom the way he knew the pattern of red-gold hairs on the back of his right arm. If anything, he knew the ley lines better; they mattered more to him. He knew just when he could peer into the harbor of Facaceni to see ley-line warships, if any were there to be seen.

And some were. He cursed softly under his breath to spot the unmistakable bulk of a ley-line cruiser and three or four smaller craft. They were Algarvian vessels, too, with lines slightly different from those of the warships the Sibian navy had used. A civilian spy might not have noticed the differences. To Cornelu, once more, they were obvious.

He saw no Sibian vessels. He didn't know where they'd gone; he couldn't very well urge his leviathan into the harbor and ask. He made more grease-pencil notes. He had a crystal with him. If he'd spotted something urgent, he could have let the Admiralty back in Setubal know. As things were, he scribbled. No Algarvian mage, no matter how formidable, could possibly detect the emanations from a grease pencil.

Some Lagoan was probably peering into the harbor of Tirgoviste town. Cornelu cursed softly again. He didn't even know why he was cursing. Did he really want to lacerate himself by seeing his home town again? Did he really want to stare up the hills of Tirgoviste town to see if he could catch a glimpse of his old home? Did he really want to wonder if the Algarvians had put a cuckoo's egg in his nest?

The trouble was, part of him did: the part that liked to pick scabs off scrapes and watch them bleed again. Most of the time, he could keep that part in check. Every so often, it welled up and got loose.

You're going back to Janira, he reminded himself. That didn't stop him from wanting to see what Costache was up to at this very moment, but it helped him fight the craving down to the bottom of his mind again.

"Come on," he told the leviathan. "We've done what we've come to do. Now let's go . . . back to Setubal." He'd almost said, *Let's go home.* But Setubal wasn't home, and never would be. Tirgoviste town was home. He'd just come up with all the good reasons he didn't want to go there. Even so, he knew the place would draw him like a lodestone till the day he died.

Absently, he wondered why a lodestone drew little bits of iron to it. No mage had ever come up with a satisfactory explanation for that. He shrugged. In a way, it was nice to know the world still held mysteries.

His leviathan, of course, made nothing of human speech. He wondered what it thought he was doing. Playing some elaborate game, he supposed, more elaborate than it could have devised on its own. He tapped its smooth skin. That got it moving where words could not have. It turned away from Facaceni town and swam back in the direction from which it had come.

Cornelu kept it underwater as much as he could. He didn't want to draw the notice of those dragons over Facaceni town, and of whatever friends they had down on the ground. Again, the leviathan didn't mind. All sorts of interesting fish and squid swam just below the surface.

He took his bearing whenever it had to surface to blow. That was enough to let him know when he rounded Facaceni island's eastern headland. Someone there spotted him and flashed a mirror at him in an intricate pattern. Since he had no idea whether it was an Algarvian signal or one from local rebels, he kept his leviathan on the course it was swimming and didn't try to answer. Whoever was using it, the mirror was a clever idea. It involved no magic and, if well aimed, could be seen only near its target.

He found out in short order to whom the mirror belonged. An egg flew through the air and burst in the sea about half a mile short of his leviathan. Another one followed a minute later. It threw up a plume of water a little closer than the first had, but not much.

"Nyah!" Cornelu thumbed his nose at the Algarvians on the headland. "Can't hit me! You couldn't hit your mother if you swung right at her face! Nyah!"

That was bravado, and he knew it. Facaceni lay farthest west of Sibiu's main islands. He expected to run a gauntlet before he could escape into the open ocean. The Algarvians would be after him like hounds after a rabbit. He'd had to run from them enough times before. No, not like hounds alone—like hounds and hawks. They'd surely put dragons in the air, too.

And so they did—a couple. They flew search spirals, but didn't happen to spot him. And Mezentio's men sent out a couple of swift little ley-line patrol boats after him, but again, only a couple. He had no trouble making good his escape. It was, in fact, so easy it worried him. He kept anxiously looking around, wondering what he'd missed, wondering what was about to drop on his head.

But nothing did. After a while, the pursuit, never more than halfhearted, simply gave up. He had an easy time returning to the harbor at Setubal.

He almost got killed before he could enter it, though. Lagoan patrol boats were thick as fleas on a dog. They could go almost anywhere in those waters; more ley lines converged on Setubal than on any other city of the world. He got challenged three different times in the course of an hour, and peremptorily ordered off his leviathan when the third captain decided he sounded like an Algarvian. To his surprise, the fellow had a rider on his ship, a man who examined the leviathan, made sure it was carrying no eggs, and took it into the port himself.

"What happened?" Cornelu asked, over and over, but no one on the patrol boat would tell him. Only after Admiralty officials vouched for him was he allowed to learn: the Algarvians on Sibiu had been quiet, but the ones in Valmiera hadn't. They'd sneaked a couple of leviathan-riders across the Strait, and the men had planted eggs on half a dozen warships, including two ley-line cruisers.

"Most embarrassing," a sour-faced Lagoan captain said in what he imagined was Sibian but was in fact only Algarvian slightly mispronounced. Most of the time, that playing fast and loose with his language offended Cornelu. Not today—he wanted facts. Instead, the captain gave him an opinion: "Worst thing that's happened to our navy since you Sibs beat it right outside of Setubal here two hundred and fifty years ago."

It was, at least, an opinion calculated to put a smile on Cornelu's long, dour face. He asked, "What will you do now?"

"Build more ships, train more men, give back better than we got," the captain replied without hesitation. "We did that against Sibiu, too."

He was, unfortunately, correct. Here, at least, he and Cornelu had the same enemy. "Where do I make my report?" the Sibian exile asked.

"Third door on your left," the sour-faced captain answered. "We'll get our own back—you wait and see." Cornelu didn't want to wait. He hurried to the third door on his left.

"In the summertime," Marshal Rathar said, "Durrwangen can get quite respectably warm."

"Oh, aye, I think so, too," General Vatran agreed. "Of course, the naked black Zuwayzin would laugh themselves to death to hear us go on like this."

"I won't say you're wrong." Rathar shuddered. "I was up in the north for the end of our war against them, you know." He waited for Vatran to nod, then went on, "Ghastly place. Sand and rocks and dry riverbeds and thornbushes and camels and poisoned wells and the sun blazing down—and the Zuwayzin fought like demons, too, till we broke 'em by weight of numbers."

"And drove 'em straight into King Mezentio's arms," Vatran said mournfully.

"And drove 'em straight into King Mezentio's arms," Rathar agreed. He stared north across the battered ruins of Durrwangen toward the Algarvian lines not far outside of town. Then he turned to Vatran. "You know, if the redheads wanted to come straight at us, they could push us out of here."

Vatran's nod was stolid. "Oh, aye, they could. But they won't."

"And how do you know that?" Rathar asked with a smile.

"How do I know?" Vatran's shaggy white eyebrows rose. "I'll tell you how, by the powers above. Three different ways." As he spoke, he ticked off points on his gnarled fingers. "For one thing, they learned at Sulingen that coming straight at us doesn't pay, and they haven't had the chance to forget it yet. For another, they're Algarvians—they never like doing anything simple if they can do it fancy and tie a big bow and red ribbons around it besides."

"Huh!" Rathar said. "If that's not the truth, curse me if I know what is."

"You hush, lord Marshal. I wasn't done." Vatran overacted reproach. "For a third, all the signs show that they're going to try to bite off the salient and trap us here, and all the captives we take say the same thing."

"I can't argue with any of that," Rathar said. "It's your second reason that worries me a little, though. Doing it fancy might mean setting us up for an enormous surprise." But he shook his head. "They're Algarvians, and that means they think they're smarter than everybody else." He sighed. "Sometimes they're right, too—but not always. I don't think they're right here."

"They'd better not be," Vatran said. "If they are, it'll mean we've wasted a cursed lot of work in the salient."

"We've done what we can," Rather said. "Anybody who tries to break through there will have a rough time of it." He sighed again. "Of course, the Algarvians have done things I would've sworn were flat-out impossible. How they got into Sulingen last summer . . ."

"They got in, but they didn't get out again." Vatran sounded cheerful, as he usually did. Rathar had a good soldier's confidence, even a good soldier's arrogance, but he was not by nature a cheerful man. Nobody who'd served so long directly under King Swemmel had an easy time being cheerful.

"We beat them in the wintertime, the same as we held them out of Cottbus the winter before," Rathar said. "It's summer now. Whenever they attack in the summer, they drive us before them."

"Nobody's driving us out of this salient," Vatran said, "Nobody. And just because you're talking about what they have done, what's that got to do with what they're going to do? Not a fornicating thing, says I."

Rathar slapped him on the shoulder, not so much for being right as for trying to raise both their spirits. But if the Algarvians had gone forward by great leaps in the two earlier summers of their war against Unkerlant, what was to keep them from going forward by great leaps in this third summer of the war?

Unkerlanter soldiers, that's what, he thought. *Unkerlanter behemoths, Unkerlanter dragons, Unkerlanter cavalry. We've learned a lot from these redheaded whoresons the past two years. Now we'll find out if we've got our lessons right.*

If they hadn't learned, they would have gone under. He knew no stronger incentive than that. They might still go under, if King Mezentio's men did break through what Unkerlant had built here to hold them back. But the Algarvians would know they'd been in a fight. They already knew they'd been in a fight, a harder fight than they'd had anywhere in the east of Derlavai.

Vatran had been thinking with him. "Invade our kingdom, will they? We'll teach them what we think of people who do things like that, powers below eat me if we don't."

"If we don't, the powers below will eat both of us," Rathar said, and Vatran nodded. They trudged through rubble-strewn streets—or perhaps across what had been yards from which most of the rubble had been blown—back toward the battered bank building where Rather had made his headquarters. A lot of eggs had fallen on Durrwangen since, but the building still stood. Banks had to be strong places; that was one of the reasons Rathar had chosen this one.

No sentries stood outside to snap to attention and salute as he and General Vatran came up. King Swemmel would have had sentries out there; Swemmel insisted on show. Maybe because his sovereign did, Rathar didn't. Also, of course, sentries outside the building would have been likely to get killed when the Algarvians tossed in some more of their endless eggs. Rathar had sent uncounted tens of thousands of soldiers to their deaths, but he wasn't deliberately wasteful. He hoped the war never made him so hard or simply so indifferent as that.

A horned lark hopped out of his way, then leaped into the air to catch a fly. The golden-bellied lark was svelte, even plump. It probably had a great brood of svelte, even plump, nestlings somewhere amid the ruins. With so much dead but unburied flesh in Durrwangen, there were a great many flies to catch.

Inside the headquarters building, a sentry did salute the marshal and his general. Rathar nodded to the youngster. Then he spoke to Vatran: "Let's go look at the map." He wondered how many times he'd said that. Whenever he was worried, undoubtedly. He'd been worried a lot.

Vatran walked over to the map table with him. Algarvian-held bulges overlapped Durrwangen to either side. "They're good, curse them," Vatran said. "Who would've thought they had that counterattack in 'em?"

"We didn't, that's certain." Rathar ruefully shook his head. "And we've paid for it. And we're liable to pay more." He pointed to the map. "Are these the best sites we could have picked for the centers?"

"Archmage Addanz thinks so." Vatran scowled. "Are you ready to argue with him? He'd likely turn you into a frog." He chuckled, but the laughter sounded strained. "War would be easier without magecraft."

"Maybe it would." Rathar shrugged. "But I'll argue with Addanz if I have to. I've asked him to come up to Durrwangen; he should be here soon. I'll argue with anyone and do anything I have to to win this war."

"I don't like arguing with mages," Vatran said. "Too many things they can do to you if you rub 'em the wrong way."

"A soldier can generally slay a mage faster than a mage can get rid of a soldier," Rathar said serenely. "And magecraft, even the simple stuff, isn't easy. If it were, we'd have mages running the world. And we don't."

"And a good thing, too, says I," Vatran exclaimed.

"Excuse me, lord Marshal." The sentry came back to the map table. "Sorry to bother you, but the archmage is here."

"Good," Rathar said. Vatran looked as if he thought it was anything but. The marshal continued, "Send him right on back here. We've got things to talk about, he and I." The sentry saluted and hurried up to the entrance. He didn't just send the archmage back: he brought him. Rathar nodded approval. He rarely found fault with a man who exceeded his orders.

Addanz was a well-groomed man of middle years, perhaps a little younger than Rathar. Few old men served King Swemmel; Vatran was an exception. A lot of leaders of the generation ahead of Rathar's had chosen the wrong side in the Twinkings War. Most of the others had managed to displease the king in the intervening years—or he'd killed them anyway, to make others thoughtful or simply on a whim. Swemmel did as he chose. That was what being King of Unkerlant meant, as long as a king lived. Swemmel had lived a surprisingly long time.

"I greet you, lord Marshal." Addanz's voice was rich and smooth, like strong tea with milk. Rathar was a long way from sure he was the best mage in Unkerlant. What he was, without a doubt, was the prominent mage with the fewest enemies.

"Hello, Archmage." Set beside Addanz, Rathar felt himself to be all harsh stone and rough edges. The archmage was a courtier; Rathar wasn't, or was as little as he could get away with. But regardless of what he wasn't, he cursed well was a soldier, and he'd summoned Addanz on soldiers' business. His index finger stabbed down at the map. "This center here, the western one—are you sure it's where you want it? If they break through past this line of low hills, they may overrun it."

"The closer, the stronger—so we have shown," Addanz answered. "With soldiers and magecraft to defend it, it should serve well enough. Besides, given how soon Mezentio's minions may strike at us, have we got the time to move it and set it up again farther from the front?"

Rathar gnawed his lower lip. "Mm—you're likely right. If I thought we had more time, I'd still have you move it a bit. You're liable to take a pounding from dragons, too, you know."

"That would be so even if we did move it," Addanz answered. Rathar gnawed his lip some more. The archmage went on, "And we have masked it as best we can, both with magecraft and with such tricks as soldiers use." He didn't sound patronizing; he seemed to make a point of not sounding patronizing. That only made Rathar feel twice as patronized.

He shook his head. Addanz had won this round. "All right. I'll never complain about anyone who wants to get close to the enemy. I just don't want the enemy getting too close to you too fast."

"I rely on your valiant men and officers to keep such a calamity from happening," Addanz said. *I'll blame them to Swemmel if it does.* He didn't say that, but he might have.

"Your mages know exactly what they have to do?" Rathar persisted.

"Aye." Addanz nodded. A year and a half before, the notion had so rocked him, he couldn't even think of it for himself.

How Swemmel had laughed! Nothing rocked Swemmel, not if it meant holding on to his throne. And now Addanz took it for granted, too. The war against Algarve had coarsened him, as it had everybody else. That was what war did.

Distant thunder rumbled, off to the south. But there should have been no thunder, not on a fine, warm early summer day. Eggs. Thousands of eggs, bursting at once. Rathar looked to Vatran. Vatran was already looking to him. "It's begun," the marshal said. Vatran nodded. Rathar went on, "Now we'll know. One way or the other, we'll know."

"What?" Addanz needed a moment to recognize the sound. When the archmage did, he blanched a little. "How shall I go back to the center now?"

"Carefully," Rathar answered, and threw back his head and laughed. Addanz looked most offended. Rathar hardly cared. At last, after longer than he'd expected, the waiting was over.

Even Sergeant Werferth, who had been a soldier for a long time, first in Forthweg's army and then in Plegmund's Brigade, was impressed. "Look at 'em, boys, he said. "Just look at 'em. You ever see so fornicating many behemoths in one place in all your born days?"

Sirdoc wrinkled his nose. "Smell 'em, boys," he said, doing his best to imitate his sergeant. "Just smell 'em. You ever smell so fornicating many behemoths in one place in all your born days?"

Everybody in the squad laughed—even Ceorl, who was about as eager to fight Sidroc as the Unkerlanters; even Werferth, who seldom took kindly to being lampooned. They all had to laugh. Sidroc's joke held altogether too much truth. Algarve had indeed assembled a great host of behemoths to hurl against the western flank of the Unkerlanter salient around Durrwangen. And those behemoths did indeed stink. They'd been moving up toward the front for days now, and the air was thick with the rotten-grass reek of their droppings.

It was also thick with flies, which buzzed around the behemoths and their droppings, and which weren't too proud to visit the waiting men and their latrines as well. Like the other soldiers in Plegmund's Brigade, like the Algarvians with them, Sidroc slapped all the time.

Like everybody else, he also did his best to be careful where he put his feet. He knew all about stepping in horse turds. Who didn't, by smelly experience? But a horse turd dirtied the bottom of a shoe, and maybe a bit of the upper. Behemoths were a lot bigger than horses. Their droppings were in proportion. Those who didn't notice them in the weeds and rank grassland and unattended fields had enormous reason to regret it.

An Algarvian senior lieutenant named Ercole had replaced the late Captain Zerbino as company commander. Sidroc wondered how Ercole had got to be senior to anybody; he doubted the redhead had as many years as his own eighteen. Ercole's mustache, far from the splendid waxed spikes his countrymen adored, was hardly more than copper fuzz. But he sounded calm and confident as he said, "Once the eggs stop falling, we go in alongside the behemoths. We protect them, they protect us. We all go forward together. The cry is, 'Mezentio and victory!'"

He waited expectantly. "Mezentio and victory!" shouted the Forthwegians of Plegmund's Brigade. The Brigade might have been named after their own great king, but it served Algarve's.

Were any Unkerlanters close enough to hear? Sidroc didn't suppose it mattered. They'd soon hear a lot of that cry. With the help of the powers above, it would be the last cry a lot of them heard.

Algarvian egg-tossers began to fling then. Sidroc whooped at the great roar of bursts to the east of him. And it went on and on, seemingly without end. "There won't be anything left alive by the time they're through!" He had to shout even to hear himself through the din.

"Oh, yes, there will." Sergeant Werferth was shouting, too. His shout held grim certainty: "There always is, curse it."

As if to prove him right on the spot, Unkerlanter egg-tossers began hurling sorcerous energy back at the Algarvians. There didn't seem to be so many of them, and they flung fewer eggs, but they hadn't gone away, either. Sidroc wished they would have. He crouched in a hole scraped in the ground and hoped for the best. Not a lot of Unkerlanter eggs were falling close by. He approved of that, and hoped it would go on.

Algarvian dragons flew by overhead at what would have been treetop height had any trees grown close by. They had eggs slung under their bellies to add to those the tossers were flinging. Not long after they struck Swemmel's men, fewer eggs flew back toward the Algarvian army of which Plegmund's Brigade was a part.

The pounding from the Algarvian side kept on. "They've put everything they've got into this, haven't they?" Sidroc shouted.

This time, Ceorl answered him: "Aye, they have. Including us."

Sidroc grunted. He wished Ceorl wouldn't have put it quite like that. He also wished he could have found some way to disagree with the ruffian.

At last, after what seemed like forever but was probably a couple of hours, the Algarvian egg-tossers stopped as abruptly as they'd begun. All up and down the line, officers' whistles shrilled. They didn't seem so much of a much, not to Sidroc's battered ears. But they were enough to send men and behemoths trotting forward against the foe.

Lieutenant Ercole blew his whistle as lustily as anyone else. "Forward!" he shouted. "Mezentio and victory!"

"Mezentio and victory!" Sidroc shouted as he scrambled out of his hole. He kept shouting it as he went forward, too. So did the rest of the Forthwegians in Plegmund's Brigade. They wore tunics. They had dark hair and proud hooked noses. Even though they wore beards, they didn't want ex- citable Algarvians—and what other kind were there?—tak- ing them for Unkerlanters and blazing them by mistake.

If anything or anyone had stayed alive in the tormented landscape ahead, Sidroc had trouble understanding how. After a good part of a year in action, he reckoned himself a connoisseur of ruined terrain, and this churned, smoking, cratered ground was as bad as any he'd ever seen.

And then, off to his right, a new crater opened. A flash of sorcerous energy and a brief shriek marked the passage of an Algarvian soldier. Someone shouted an altogether unnecessary warning: "They've buried eggs in the ground!"

All at once, Sidroc wanted to tippytoe forward. Then, a little farther away, an egg burst under a behemoth. That one blast of sorcerous energy touched off all the eggs the behemoth was carrying. Its crew had no chance. Sidroc wondered if any pieces would come down, or if the men were altogether destroyed.

And he couldn't tippytoe despite the buried eggs, another of which blew up a soldier not too far from him. However many eggs the tossers had rained down on the ground ahead, they hadn't got rid of all the Unkerlanters. Sidroc hadn't really expected they would, but he had hoped. No such luck. Swemmel's men popped up out of holes and started blazing at the soldiers struggling through the belt of buried eggs. Going fast meant you might miss whatever signs there were on the ground to warn you an egg lay concealed beneath it. Going slow meant the Unkerlanters had a better chance to blaze you.

Shouting, "Mezentio and victory!" at the top of his lungs, Sidroc dashed ahead. He might get through to unblighted ground. If he stayed where he was, he would get blazed. Lieutenant Ercole was shouting and waving all his men on, so Sidroc supposed he'd done the right thing.

When the crews of the Algarvian behemoths saw targets, they lobbed eggs at them or blazed at them with heavy sticks. Fewer beams tore at the advancing soldiers. Men ahead of Sidroc were battling Unkerlanters in their holes. He saw a man in a rock-gray tunic show his head and shoulders as he looked for a target. That was enough—too much, in fact. Sidroc blazed the Unkerlanter down.

"Keep moving!" Ercole screamed. "You've got to keep moving. This is how we beat them—with speed and movement!" By all the news sheets Sidroc had read back in

Gromheort before joining Plegmund's Brigade, by all the training he'd had, by all the fighting he'd seen, the company commander was right.

But it wouldn't be easy, not here it wouldn't. The Unkerlanters had known they were coming—had probably known for a long time. They'd fortified this ground as best they could. It didn't look like much, but obstacles—tree trunks, ditches, mud—made the going slower than it would have been otherwise. Those obstacles also channeled the advancing men and behemoths in certain directions—right into more waiting Unkerlanters.

As soon as the Algarvians and the men of Plegmund's Brigade got in among the first belt of Unkerlanter defenders, others farther back began blazing at them from long range. More obstacles slowed their efforts to get at the Unkerlanters who now revealed themselves. Men on both sides fell as if winnowed. Algarvian behemoths went down, too, here and there, though few Unkerlanter behemoths were yet in the fight.

At last, around noon, Mezentio's men cleared that first stubborn belt of defenders. Ercole was almost beside himself. "We aren't keeping up with the plan!" he cried. "We're falling behind!"

"Sir, we've done everything we could," Sergeant Werferth said. "We're still here. We're still moving."

"Not fast enough." Ercole stuck his whistle in his mouth and blew a long, piercing blast. "Onward!"

For a furlong or so, the going was easy. Sidroc's spirits began to rise. Then he heard the sharp, flat roar of an egg bursting under another Algarvian soldier. He realized why no Unkerlanters infested this stretch of ground—they'd sown it with more eggs to slow up his advancing comrades.

What had been woods ahead had taken a demon of a beating, but still offered some shelter: enough that the Unkerlanter behemoths emerging from it were an unwelcome surprise. "Powers above!" Sidroc exclaimed in dismay. "Look at how many of the whoresons there are!"

The behemoths started tossing eggs at Plegmund's Brigade

and at the Algarvian footsoldiers to either side of the Forthwegians. Sidroc jumped into a hole in the ground. He had plenty from which to choose. So did Ceorl, but he jumped down in with Sidroc anyhow. Sidroc wondered whether he wouldn't be safer facing the Unkerlanter behemoths.

"Hard work today," Ceorl remarked, as if he'd been hauling sacks of grain or chopping wood.

"Aye," Sidroc agreed. An egg burst close by, shaking the ground and showering them with clods of dirt.

"But we'll do it," Ceorl went on. "We go east, the redheads on the other side come west, and we meet in the middle. Be a whole great fornicating kettle full of dead Unkerlanters by the time we're through, too." He sounded as if he enjoyed the idea.

"A lot of us dead, too," Sidroc said. "A lot of us dead already."

Ceorl shrugged. "Can't make an omelette without breaking eggs." He brought out the cliché as if he were the first one ever to use it. Maybe he thought he was.

An officer's whistle squealed. "Onward!" That was Lieutenant Ercole, who'd had the sense to jump in a hole. Now, sooner than he might have been, he was out again. The Algarvians hadn't given Plegmund's Brigade any officers who weren't recklessly brave—that Sidroc had to admit. "Come on!" Ercole shouted again. "We won't win anything if we stay here all day!"

Sidroc surged up out of the hole. The Algarvian behemoths had taken care of a lot of their Unkerlanter counterparts, but they'd had holes torn in their ranks, too. A dragon fell from the sky and thrashed out its death throes a couple of hundred yards from Sidroc. It was painted rock-gray. A moment later, an Algarvian dragon smashed down even closer.

By the time night came, they'd almost cleared that second belt of defenders.

"We've got to be efficient." Lieutenant Recared sounded serious and earnest. "The Algarvians will throw everything they've got at us. We've got to make every blaze count, and to *use* the positions we've spent so long building up." He turned to Leudast. "Anything you want to add to that, Sergeant?"

Leudast looked at the men in his company. They knew the Algarvians would be coming any day, maybe any minute. They were serious, even somber, but, if they were afraid, they didn't let it show. Leudast knew he was afraid, and did his best not to let that show.

He thought Recared wanted him to say something, so he did: "Just don't do anything stupid, boys. This'll be a hard enough fight even if we're smart."

"That's right." Recared nodded vigorously. "Being smart is being efficient. The sergeant said the same thing I did, only with different words."

I guess I did, Leudast thought, a little surprised. That hadn't occurred to him. He peered east, toward the rising sun. If the Algarvians attacked now, they'd be silhouetted against the bright sky every time they came over a rise. He judged they would wait till the sun was well up before moving. He was in no great hurry to risk getting killed or maimed. They could wait forever, for all of him.

Light built, grew. Leudast studied the landscape. He couldn't see most of the defensive positions the Unkerlanters had built. If he couldn't see them, that meant Mezentio's men wouldn't be able to, either. He hoped that was what it meant, anyhow.

The sun climbed in the sky. The day grew warm, even hot. Leudast slapped at bugs. There weren't so many as there had been right after the snow melted, when the endless swampy puddles in the mud bred hordes of mosquitoes and gnats. But they hadn't all gone away. They wouldn't have wanted to, not with so many latrines and animals to keep them happy.

Leudast was pissing in a slit trench when the Algarvians started flinging eggs. He almost jumped right into that latrine trench; combat had taught him how important taking cover was, and diving into the closest available hole was almost as automatic as breathing. But he hadn't wanted to breathe by the noisome, nearly full trench, and he didn't jump into it, either. Not quite. He ran back toward the hole in the ground from which he'd come.

Such sensibilities almost cost him his neck. An egg burst not far behind him just as he started sliding into his hole. It flung him in instead, flung him hard enough to make him wonder if he'd cracked his ribs. Only when he'd sucked in a couple of breaths without having knives stab did he decide he hadn't.

He'd been through a lot fighting the Algarvians. He'd helped hold them out of Cottbus. He'd been wounded down in Sulingen. He'd thought he knew everything the redheads could do. Now he discovered he'd been wrong. In all that time, with everything he'd seen, he'd never had to endure such a concentrated rain of eggs as they threw at him, threw at all the Unkerlanters.

The first thing he did was dig himself deeper. He wondered if he were digging his own grave, but the shallow scrape he'd had before didn't seem nearly enough. He flung dirt out with his short-handled spade, wishing all the while that he had broad, clawed hands like a mole's so he wouldn't need a tool. Sometimes he thought bursts all around him threw as much dirt back into the hole as he was throwing out.

After the hole was deep enough, he lay down at full length in it, his face pressed into the rich, dark loam. He needed a while to realize he was screaming; the din of those bursting eggs was so continuous, he could hardly even hear himself. Realizing what he was doing didn't make him stop. He'd known fear. He'd known terror. This went past those and out the other side. It was so immense, so irresistible, it carried him along as a wave might carry a small boat.

And, after a little while, it washed him ashore. If he was beyond fear, beyond terror, what else was there to do but go on? He got up onto his knees—he wasn't ready to expose his body to blasts of sorcerous energy and to flying metal shards of egg casing—and looked at the sky instead of the dirt.

He had plenty to watch up there. Dragons wheeled and dueled and flamed, some painted in Unkerlant's concealing rock-gray, others wearing Algarve's gaudy colors. It was a dance in the air, as intricate and lovely as a springtime figure dance in the square of the peasant village where he'd grown up.

But this dance was deadly, too. An Algarvian dragon flamed one from his kingdom, flamed its wing and flank. Across who could say how much air, he heard the great furious bellow of agony the Unkerlanter dragon let out. Surely the dragonflier screamed, too, but his voice was lost, lost. The dragon frantically beat the air with its one good wing. That only made it twist in the other direction. And then it twisted no more, but fell, writhing. It smashed to the unyielding ground not far in front of Leudast.

As abruptly as they'd started, the Algarvians stopped tossing eggs. Leudast knew what that meant. He snatched up his stick and did peer out from his hole. "They're coming!" he shouted. His own voice sounded strange in his ears because of the pounding they'd taken.

Dimly, as if from far away, he heard others shouting the same thing. Footsoldiers loped ahead of Algarvian behemoths. The men in kilts looked tiny. Even the behemoths looked small. The redheads would have to fight their way through a couple of defensive lines before they reached the position Lieutenant Recared's regiment held. By the way they came on, Mezentio's men thought they could fight their way through anything. After what they'd done two summers in a row in Unkerlant, who could say they were wrong?

Then the first redhead stepped on a buried egg and abruptly ceased to be. "Good riddance, you son of a whore!" Leudast shouted. Soldiers had spent weeks burying eggs. Soldiers and conscripted peasants had spent those same weeks fortifying the ground between the belts. Some of those peasants might have gone back to their farms. Others, Leudast was sure, remained in the salient. He wondered how many of them would come out once more.

Now that the Algarvians were out in the open, Unkerlanter egg-tossers began flinging death their way. Unkerlanter dragons swooped low on Mezentio's men. Some of them dropped eggs, too. Others flamed footsoldiers and behemoths, too. Leudast cheered again.

More Algarvian behemoths than usual seemed to be carrying heavy sticks. Those were less useful than egg-tossers against targets on the ground, but ever so much more useful against dragons. Their thick, strong beams seared the air. Several dragons fell. One, though, smashed into two behemoths as it struck the ground, killing them in its own destruction.

Leudast stopped cheering. He was too awed to see how many of his countrymen had survived the ferocious Algarvian bombardment. But the Algarvians showed no awe. They went about their business with the air of men who'd done it many times before. A charge of behemoths tore an opening in the first defensive line. Footsoldiers swarmed through the gap. Then some of them wheeled and attacked the line from the rear. Others pushed on toward Leudast.

"They did that too fast, curse them," Lieutenant Recared said from a hole not far from Leudast's. "They should have been hung up there longer."

"They're good at what they do, sir," Leudast answered. "They wouldn't be here in our kingdom if they weren't."

"Powers below eat them," Recared said, and then, "Ha! They've just found the second belt of eggs." He shouted toward the redheads: "Enjoy it, you whoresons!"

But the Algarvians kept coming. In two years of war against them, Leudast had rarely known them to be less than game. They were game here, sure enough. After a few minutes, he started to curse. "Will you look at what those buggers have done? They're using that dry wash to get up toward our second line."

"That's not good," Recared said. "They weren't supposed to go that way. They were supposed to be drawn toward the places where we have more men."

"I wish it would rain," Leudast said savagely. "They'd drown then."

"I wish our dragons would come and flame them to ruins and drop eggs on the ones left alive," Recared said.

"Aye." Leudast nodded. "The redheads' dragons would do that to us, down in Sulingen."

Recared sounded worried. "I don't think our men up there in the second line can see what the Algarvians are doing." He shouted, "Crystallomancer!" When no one answered, he shouted again, louder.

This time, he did get a reply. "He's dead, sir, and his crystal smashed," a trooper said.

"Sergeant." Recared turned to Leudast. "Go down there and let them know. With everything else that's going on, I really don't think they have any idea what Mezentio's men are up to. If a regiment of redheads erupts into the middle of that line, it won't hold. Get moving."

"Aye, sir." Leudast scrambled out of his hole, got to his feet, and started trotting toward the line ahead. If he hadn't, Recared would have blazed him on the spot. As things were, all he had to do was run across perhaps half a mile of field and grassland full of buried eggs. If he went up like a torch in a blaze of sorcerous energy, the second line wouldn't know its danger till too late.

He looked back over his shoulder. Three or four more Unkerlanter soldiers came trotting after him. He nodded to himself. Recared was minimizing the risk. The pup made a pretty fair officer.

Leudast trotted on. One foot in front of the other. Don't think about what happens if a foot comes down in the wrong place. Odds are, it won't happen. Don't think about it. Odds are, it won't. And the insistent, rising scream in his mind— *Oh, but what if it does?*

It didn't. He still had trouble finding the Unkerlanter field fortifications. Then a nervous soldier in a rock-gray tunic popped up and almost blazed him. Panting, he stammered out his message. The soldier lowered his stick. "Come on, pal," he said. "You'd better tell my captain."

Tell him Leudast did. The captain's crystallomancer was still alive. He got the word to soldiers nearer the dry wash. An attack went in. It didn't stop the Algarvians, but it slowed them, rocked them back on their heels.

"Your lieutenant did well to send you," the captain told Leudast. He handed him a flask. "Here. Have a taste of this. You've earned it."

"Thanks, sir." Leudast swigged. Spirits ran hot down his throat. He wiped his mouth on his sleeve. "Are we winning?"

The captain answered with a broad-shouldered shrug. "We're just getting started."

Twelve

Major Spinello had thought the fighting in Sulingen the worst warfare possible. Now, as his regiment fought its way east toward other, far-off, Algarvian forces fighting their way west, he saw Sulingen re-created across miles of rolling plains. The Unkerlanters had been waiting for this assault. There didn't seem to be an inch of their salient where they hadn't either built a redoubt or buried an egg. By now, most of the dowsers who'd picked out paths through those buried eggs were dead or wounded, either from their own mistakes or from Unkerlanter beams or eggs.

Five days into the fighting, the Algarvians on the western edge of the bulge around Durrwangen had advanced perhaps half a dozen miles. They were far behind where they should have been. Spinello knew as much. Every Algarvian officer—and probably every Algarvian common soldier, too—knew as much. Spinello counted it a minor miracle that his countrymen were still moving forward at all.

He lay behind a dead Unkerlanter behemoth that was starting to stink under the hot summer sun. Captain Turpino lay at the other end of the dead beast. Turpino turned a filthy, haggard, smoke-blackened face to Spinello and asked, "What now . . . sir?"

"We're supposed to take that hill up ahead." Spinello's hand shook as he pointed. He was every bit as filthy and haggard as his senior company commander. He couldn't remember the last time he'd slept.

Cautious, Turpino peered up over the carcass. "What, the regiment by itself?" he demanded. "That hill's got Unkerlanter behemoths—live ones—the way a dog has fleas."

"No, not the regiment by itself. Our army. However much of it we can aim at the high ground." Spinello yawned. Powers above, he was tired. It was like being drunk; he didn't care what came out of his mouth. "I don't think our regiment's in any shape to take a gumdrop away from a three-year-old."

Turpino stared at him, then laughed as cautiously as he'd looked at the hill ahead. Spinello's answering grimace might have been a smile. Along with the rest of the great force the Algarvians had mustered, the regiment had hammered its way through five successive Unkerlanter lines—and, in the hammering, had burned away like wood in the fire.

He wondered if he still had half the men who'd gone forward when he first blew the whistle. He doubted it. The three companies plucked from occupation duty in Jelgava had suffered particularly hard. It wasn't that they weren't brave. They were, to a fault. They went forward when they should have hesitated, and had got themselves and their comrades into a couple of desperate pickles simply because they'd lacked the experience to see traps they should have. Well, they had that experience now—the survivors, anyhow.

Turpino turned his head. "More of our behemoths coming up, and—" He stiffened. "Who're those buggers in the wrong-colored tunics? Are the Unkerlanters trying to pull another fast one?"

After looking back toward the footsoldiers, Spinello shook his head. "That's Plegmund's Brigade. They're on our side—Forthwegians in Algarvian service."

"Forthwegians." Turpino's lip curled. "We *are* throwing everything we've got left into this fight, aren't we?"

"Actually, they're supposed to be brave," Spinello said. Turpino looked anything but convinced.

On came the behemoths. They started tossing eggs at the Unkerlanter beasts on the hill the Algarvians needed to take. The Unkerlanters answered, but they still didn't handle their beasts or their gear as well as Mezentio's men. Spinello cheered when an Algarvian behemoth crew used the heavy stick mounted on their beast to burst the eggs an Unkerlanter behemoth carried, and then, a moment later, repeated the feat and took out another behemoth and crew.

But the Unkerlanters' eggs and beams knocked down Algarvian behemoths, too. And more beasts with Unkerlanters aboard trotted over the crest of the hill. Captain Turpino cursed. "How many fornicating behemoths do Swemmel's fornicators have?" he demanded, or words to that effect.

"Too many," Spinello answered, looking from the beasts on the hill to the Algarvian behemoths moving against them. He sighed. "Well, we'll just have to get them off of there, won't we?" He blew his whistle as he got to his feet. "Forward!" he shouted, waving his arm to urge on his troops—what was left of them.

Turpino stayed beside him as they advanced. Turpino still wanted the regiment if Spinello fell, and he also wanted to show he was at least as brave as the man who held it now. Spinello grinned as he ran past craters and corpses and dead beasts. He'd expected nothing less. Algarvians were like that.

The Unkerlanters not only had behemoths on that hill, they had footsoldiers there, too. Spinello watched beams flash from places where he would have sworn no squirrel, let alone a man, could have hidden. Beams burned brown lines in the green grass, some very near him. Here and there, little grass fires sprang up. He almost welcomed them. The smokier the air, the more it spread beams and the more trouble they had biting. But bite they still did; men fell all around him.

He dove into a hole in the ground. It was big enough to hold two, and Spinello's dour shadow dove in right behind him. Turpino said, "They're going to make us pay a demon of a price for that high ground."

"I know," Spinello answered. "We've got to have it, though."

"The army's melting the way the snow did this spring," Turpino said.

"I know that, too" Spinello said. "I'm not blind." He raised his voice to a shout again: "Crystallomancer!" A moment later, he shouted it once more, and louder: *"Crystallomancer!"*

"Aye, sir?" The Algarvian who scrambled over to Spinello didn't belong to his regiment. He'd never seen the fellow before. But he had a crystal with him, and that was good enough.

"Get me the mages at Special Camp Four," Spinello said: the fourth special camp was attached to his division.

"Aye, sir," the crystallomancer repeated, and went to work. In bright daylight, Spinello could hardly see the flash of light that showed the crystal's activation, but he couldn't miss the image of the mage that formed in it. The crystallomancer said, "Go ahead, sir."

"Right." Spinello spoke into the crystal: "Major Spinello here. My regiment and a good part of this army, footsoldiers and behemoths both, are pinned down in front of the hill at map grid Green-Seven. We need that hill if we're going to go on, and we need the special sorceries if we're going to take it."

"Are you certain?" the mage asked. "Demand for the special sorceries has been very high, far higher than anyone expected when we began this campaign. I am not sure we'll have enough to sustain us if we keep using up our resources at this rate."

Spinello abruptly dropped the language of euphemism: "If you don't start killing Kaunians pretty cursed quick, there won't be any campaign left to worry about. Have you got that, sorcerous sir? If the Unkerlanters halt us here, what's to stop *them* from rolling forward? What's to stop them from rolling over you and all the precious Kaunians you're hoarding?"

"Very well, Major. The point is taken." The Algarvian mage looked and sounded affronted. Spinello didn't care, so long as he got results. The mage said, "I shall consult my colleagues. Stand by to await developments."

His image winked out. The crystallomancer said, "That's it, sir."

Turpino said, "You made him angry when you reminded him what he was really doing back there."

"What a pity," Spinello growled. "If he's unhappy about it, let him come to the front and see what we're really doing up here." That earned him one of the few looks of unreserved approval he'd ever had from Turpino. He went on, "Besides, if he's not getting screams from every other officer on this field, I'm a poached egg."

Regardless of whether he was a poached egg, the mages back at the special camp must have decided the Algarvian army did need help. Spinello knew to the moment when the sacrifices began. A great cloud of dust rose from the hillside as the ground shook there. Cracks opened, then slammed shut. Flames shot up from the ground.

"*Now* we're in business," Turpino said happily. "Cursed Kaunians are good for something, anyhow." This time, he rose and ran forward first, leaving Spinello to hurry after him. Spinello did. So did the crystallomancer, evidently glad to have someone giving him orders even if it wasn't his proper commander.

But they hadn't gone far before the ground trembled under their feet. A huge crack opened under the crystallomancer. He had time for a terrified shriek before it smashed him as it closed. Violet flame engulfed two behemoths and their crews not far from Spinello, and more men and beasts elsewhere on the field.

Spinello fell. He clutched the ground, trying to make it hold still. "Powers below eat the Unkerlanters," cried Turpino, who had also fallen. "Their mages are hitting back harder and faster than they ever did before."

"Can they spend more peasants than we can spend Kaunians?" Spinello asked—a question on which the fate of the battle might turn. He gave the only answer he had for it: "We'll find out."

Even before the mage-made earthquake ended, he fought his way back onto his feet. He hauled Turpino up, too. "Thanks," the company commander said.

"My pleasure," Spinello said, and bowed. He looked behind him. "I think we've got more still standing than the Unkerlanters do." After blowing his whistle, he yelled, "Come

on! Aye, all of you—you Forthwegians, too! We can take that
hill!"

Take it they did, though the Unkerlanters who hadn't been
overwhelmed by Algarvian magecraft sold themselves dear
and weren't finally driven back or killed till after sunset. By
then, nobody on the blood-soaked field had any doubts left
about whether the men of Plegmund's Brigade could fight.
Algarvians and bearded Forthwegians sat down together and
shared food and wine and water and lay down side by side to
rest and ready themselves for the next day's horrors.

Spinello found himself trading barley bread he'd taken
from a dead Unkerlanter for the sausages a couple of men
from Plegmund's Brigade had. One of them looked more like
a bandit than a soldier. The other was younger, but might
have been grimmer. Speaking pretty good Algarvian, he said,
"I hope they get rid of all the Kaunians. It's the only thing
they're good for."

"Oh, not the only thing." Tired as he was, Spinello still
laughed. "I was posted in Forthweg before I came here, in a
little pisspot village named Oyngestun."

"I know it," the man from Plegmund's Brigade said. "I am
from Gromheort."

"All right, then," Spinello said. "I found this Kaunian tart
there named Vanai, who . . ." He'd been telling stories about
her since coming to Unkerlant.

Tonight, to his astonishment, he was interrupted. "Vanai!
By the powers above! I remember now," the Forthwegian exclaimed. "My cousin, the cursed fool, was sweet on a Kaunian bitch named Vanai, and she was from Oyngestun. Could
it be . . . ?"

"Don't ask me, for I don't know," Spinello said. "But I do
know this: I was in there first." And he got to tell his bawdy
stories after all, there in the brooding night filled with the
stink of fire and the far worse stink of death.

Even in his dreams, Count Sabrino flew his dragon against
the Unkerlanters. He had few dreams. He had little time for
sleep. He and the men of his wing and Colonel Ambaldo's

wing and all the other Algarvian dragonfliers on the eastern side of the Unkerlanter salient around Durrwangen had been flying as often as their flesh and that of their mounts would stand, or perhaps rather more than that.

But Sabrino was dreaming now. He'd blazed an Unkerlanter dragonflier and made the man's beast fly wild when suddenly his own beast was flamed from behind. It stumbled in midair, trying to right itself, but could not. It stumbled, it staggered, it shook. It shook . . .

Sabrino's eyes came open. He discovered a dragon handler shaking him awake. Sabrino groaned and tried to roll away. The handler was inexorable. "Colonel, you've got to get up," he said urgently. "The wing's got to fly. You've got to fly now."

"Powers below eat you," Sabrino said.

"Dowsers have spotted a great swarm of Unkerlanter dragons flying our way," the dragon handler said. "They'll want to catch us on the ground, drop their eggs all over the dragon farms hereabouts. But if we get into the air first . . ."

Sleep, and the need for sleep, fell away from Sabrino like an abandoned kilt. "Get out of the way," he growled, springing off his cot. He checked himself, but only for an instant. "No. Run and sound the alarm."

Before the dragon handler could ever begin to turn, horns blared in the predawn darkness. Sabrino grunted in satisfaction. He pulled on his boots, donned the heavy coat he'd been using as a blanket, and put his goggles on his head. Then he ran past the dragon handler and toward his own stupid, evil-tempered mount.

Other dragonfliers, from his wing and Ambaldo's, were dashing to their dragons, too. Sabrino grudged a quarter of a minute to cry out, "If we get into the air, we slaughter the Unkerlanters who are coming to call. If they catch us on the ground, the way they want to, we're dead. Come on. *Mezentio!*"

"Mezentio!" the dragonfliers shouted.

Behind them, in the east, the sky was going pink. Off to the west, the direction from which those rock-gray dragons would be coming, stars still shone and night still ruled. But not securely, not even there. Purple-black had lightened to deep blue, and the dimmer stars winked out one by one. Day was coming. By all the signs, trouble would get here first.

A handler released the chain that held Sabrino's dragon to the spike driven deep into the black soil of southern Unkerlant. Sabrino whacked the dragon with his goad. It screamed at him. He'd known it would. He whacked it again, and it bounded into the air as much from sheer rage as for any other reason.

Sabrino didn't care why the dragon flew. He only cared that it flew. As the ground fell away below them, he spoke into his crystal to his squadron commanders: "Get as high as you can. We don't want Swemmel's boys to know we're up here till we drop on them."

"Aye, Colonel." That was gloomy Captain Orosio. He was the senior squadron commander left alive. He'd been juniormost when the war started—or had he even had a squadron then? After close to four years, Sabrino couldn't remember anymore. He marveled that he himself still survived. *If fighting on the ground in the Six Years' War didn't kill me, nothing here will,* he thought.

Light spread in the sky as he urged his dragon ever higher. Before long, he spied the sun, low and red in the east. Its rays hadn't yet reached the ground, and wouldn't for some little time to come. He might have been on a mountaintop, looking down into some still-dark valley.

And then, as he'd hoped he would, he saw things moving in the air below his squadron. He whooped with glee. "There they are!" he shouted into the crystal, and pointed for good measure.

"Aye, Colonel." That was Orosio again. "I saw 'em a little while ago." Dour, laconic—he hardly seemed like an Algarvian, but he was a good officer. Had he come from a more prominent family, he would have had a better chance to prove it. No matter how fierce the casualties among dragonfliers, he wasn't likely to rise above his present rank.

Flashes of light from the ground said the Unkerlanters

were plastering the dragon farm with eggs, no doubt thinking they were wreaking havoc on the Algarvian beasts. Sabrino hoped the handlers had found holes. King Swemmel's drag-onfliers would do some·damage down below, but they hadn't yet awakened to the realization that they were about to take damage, too.

With astonishing speed, the Unkerlanter dragons swelled beneath Sabrino. He had his pick of targets; sure enough, the enemy had no idea he and his comrades were above them. This time, the dowsers had been right on the money. "And now the Unkerlanters will pay," Sabrino muttered. "How they will pay."

The wind from his dive swept the words away. For once, it mattered not at all. Sabrino blazed not just one Unkerlanter dragonflier, as he had dreamt, but two in quick succession. Even as the beasts they'd ridden went wild and useless, his own dragon flamed another Unkerlanter's mount. Sabrino brought his dragon in as close as he dared before letting it flame. Quicksilver was in short supply, and without it a dragon's flame grew short, too. But his mount had enough. The dragon painted rock-gray fell out of the air.

Sabrino looked around the brightening sky, looked around and howled with savage glee. Almost every Algarvian drag-onflier was having luck to match his. The Unkerlanters had hoped to catch them by surprise, but ended up caught them-selves. In hardly more than the twinkling of an eye, the air was free of them. The ones left alive flew back toward the salient as fast as their dragons' wings would take them.

"Pursuit, sir?" Captain Orosio's voice came from the crystal.

Reluctantly, Sabrino said, "No. We take the dragons down, we get them fed—we get ourselves fed, too, while we're at it—and then we go back to hammering the Unkerlanter posi-tions on the ground. I wish we could rest them more, but we haven't got the time. We land." He emphasized the words with hand signals, so all the dragonfliers could see what he meant.

They obeyed him. He would have been astonished—horrified—if they hadn't. Down they went. Now the sun had reached the Unkerlanter plains. Dead dragons, almost all of them painted rock-gray, cast long shadows across those plains. Sabrino whistled softly to see how many he and his comrades had knocked out of the sky.

"A good morning's work," he said to the handler who started tossing his dragon gobbets of meat. "The dowsers gave us a hand today."

"Aye," the handler agreed. "Wouldn't have been much fun if those buggers had caught us unawares."

"No." Sabrino shuddered at the thought of it. As he freed himself from his harness and slid to the ground, he asked the handler, "How's the cinnabar holding out?"

"All right so far," the fellow told him. "We'll get through this fight without any trouble, I think. Don't know what we'll do about the next one, though."

"Worry about it later. What else can we do?" Sabrino hurried off toward the mess tent. He would rather have gone back to his cot, but that wouldn't do. He yawned enormously. Falling asleep aboard his dragon wouldn't do, either. He gulped hot, strong tea, gulped it and gulped it till it pried his eyelids open. Breakfast was more of the stew that had been in the pot for supper the night before. He recognized barley, buckwheat, carrots, celery, onions, and bits of meat. He couldn't tell what the meat was. Maybe that was for the best.

Colonel Ambaldo raised his mug of tea in salute, as if it held wine. "Here's to the Unkerlanters outsmarting themselves," he said.

"I'll gladly drink to that," Sabrino said. "This morning's ours. Till they can bring more dragons forward, we'll pound 'em to our hearts' content."

"Sounds good to me, by the powers above," Ambaldo said. "The lads down on the ground need all the help they can get."

In Sabrino's eyes, Ambaldo wasn't too much more than a lad himself. That didn't make him wrong. Sabrino said, "Swemmel's men have been waiting for us too cursed long in these parts. Row on row of fieldworks, and they fight to hold every miserable, stinking little village as if it were Sulingen."

"Too right they do," Ambaldo agreed. "Brigades go into those places and companies come out. It's butchery, is what it is."

"Never saw anything like this in Valmiera, did you?" Sabrino couldn't resist the jab.

Colonel Ambaldo shook his head. "Never once. Not even close. They're madmen, these Unkerlanters. They fight like madmen, anyhow. No wonder we started killing Kaunians to shift 'em. Though from what I hear, we're using up the blonds so fast, we're liable to run short."

"Swemmel won't ever run short on people to kill to power his magecraft," Sabrino said gloomily. "Unkerlant has more peasants than it knows what to do with." He scowled. "That's not quite right. Swemmel knows too bloody well what to do with them—and to them."

Both wing commanders slammed down their empty mugs at the same time. They hurried out of the mess tent, shouting for their men to join them. Sabrino spent a little while cursing because the dragon handlers hadn't finished securing the eggs under all the dragons in his wing.

But the delay was only short. It might even have worked to the dragonfliers' advantage, though Sabrino wouldn't have admitted that to the handlers. Feeling how his dragon labored under him, Sabrino knew it needed rest, rest it couldn't have. A few more quiet minutes on the ground had surely done it some good.

Not having many fresh Unkerlanter dragons to face did the Algarvians a lot of good, too. Most of Swemmel's dragon-fliers wouldn't have been allowed to mount an Algarvian beast, but they had more dragons than did Sabrino and his countrymen. A bad dragonflier on a fresh beast could match a master aboard a worn, overworked dragon.

A fresh Algarvian attack was just going in against the village of Eylau. The wreckage of a couple of previous assaults still lay outside the place: dead men and behemoths. By all the signs, the new brigades assailing the Unkerlanter strong-point would have had no easier time of it. But, after two wings of Algarvian dragons delivered an all but unopposed attack on Eylau, the strongpoint wasn't so strong anymore. The footsoldiers and behemoths battled their way into the village.

They fought their way in, but would they fight their way out? Already, more Unkerlanter soldiers were moving forward to try to hold them there. Even if the Algarvians did advance, how much good would it do them? Eylau was less than ten miles west of the point from which the assault had begun. At that rate, how long would this army take to join the one pushing east toward it? And would either of them have any men left alive by the time they joined?

Sabrino had no answers. All he could do was command his wing as best he could and hope those set over him knew what they were about. He ordered his dragonfliers back to the farm. More meat for the dragons, more eggs loaded under them, a little food and a lot of tea for the men, and back into the fight once more.

Sidroc wondered why he still breathed. Everything he'd been through before this great fight on the flank of the Durrwangen bulge, however horrid and terrifying it seemed at the time, was as nothing beside reality here. He'd always thought a fight would start, and then it would end. This one had started, aye, but it showed no sign of ever wanting to end.

"A week and a half," he said to Sergeant Werferth, who by some miracle also had not been blazed or gone up in a burst of sorcerous energy or been butchered by a flying fragment of egg casing or flamed by a dragon or had any other lethal or disabling accident befall him. "Have we won? Are we winning?"

"Futter me if I know. Futter me if I know anything any more." Werferth scratched his hairy chin. "I've got lice in my beard. I know that."

"So do I," Sidroc said, and scratched like a Siaulian monkey.

Smoke stained the sky above them. Somewhere not far away, eggs burst: Unkerlanter eggs, pounding the Algarvians, pounding the men of Plegmund's Brigade who fought at their side. Werferth said, "Every time we think we've knocked those buggers flat, they pop up again."

"If we kill enough Kaunians—" Sidroc began.

But Werferth shook his head. "What good would it do us? They'd just kill some more of their own, and we'd be back where we started. We've seen that happen too cursed often already."

Sidroc wanted to argue. He wanted Kaunians dead. What else were they good for?—except the enjoyment that Algarvian major had taken from the one his cousin was sweet on. "Vanai," Sidroc muttered under his breath. It had gone clean out of his head till the Algarvian spoke—knocked out when Cousin Ealstan slammed his head against the wall while they were fighting. But he remembered now. Aye, the pieces fit together again.

He laughed, a sound not far from honest mirth. He wondered what had happened, up there in Forthweg. Had the Algarvians gone in and cleaned the Kaunians out of Oyngestun, the way they should have? Or was dear old Ealstan still getting that redhead's sloppy seconds?

"We might as well kill some more Kaunians," he said, thinking of a new argument. "You think the Unkerlanters'll stop slaying their own if we quit? Not bloody likely, you ask me. They'll keep right at it, they will. Even if we don't kill blonds to strike, we'll need to do it to shield ourselves." He stuck out his chin. "Go on. Tell me I'm wrong."

Werferth grunted. "I'll tell you you talk too cursed much, that's what I'll do." He yawned so wide, the hinge at the back of his jaw cracked like a knuckle. "I want to sleep for a year. Two years, with any luck at all."

"I'm with you there." Sidroc had never known a man could be so worn. "I don't think I've slept more than a couple of hours at a stretch since this cursed fight started. I feel drunk half the time."

"I wish I were drunk," Werferth said. "Haven't even had a nip since I found that one dead Unkerlanter with a canteen half full of spirits." He stretched himself out on the torn ground. A couple of minutes later, he was snoring.

A couple of minutes after that, Sidroc was probably snoring, too. His comrades said he did. Since he'd never heard himself, he couldn't have proved it one way or the other. Snoring or not, he was certainly asleep, the deep, almost deathlike sleep that comes from complete exhaustion.

And, a couple of minutes after *that*, he and Werferth were both awake and both digging like men possessed as Unkerlanter eggs burst all around them. Sidroc felt as if he were moving underwater. He kept dropping the little short-handled shovel. "Cursed thing," he muttered, as if his clumsiness were its fault.

The Algarvians finally started tossing eggs back at King Swemmel's men. "Took 'em long enough," Werferth growled. "I figured they'd wait till we were all dead and then give back a little something."

"I'm not all dead," Sidroc said. "I'm just mostly dead." He and the sergeant both found that very funny, a telling measure of how tired they were. They laughed without restraint, till tears rolled down their faces. And then, in spite of the eggs that kept bursting all around them, they lay down in the hole they'd dug and went back to sleep.

An officer's whistle woke Sidroc a little before dawn. Lieutenant Ercole looked as grimy and beat as any of the Forthwegians he commanded; not even Algarvian vanity let him steal a few minutes for primping, not on this field. But he sounded far livelier than Sidroc felt. "Up, you lugs!" he cried. "Up! Up and forward! We've got a long way to go before we can be lazy again."

"What does he mean, again?" Werferth mumbled, staggering to his feet as if he'd suddenly aged forty or fifty years. "We've never once been lazy. Powers above, when have we had the time for it?"

"I'd like to have the time to be lazy," Sidroc said. He reached into his belt pouch and pulled out a chunk of stale barley bread. He gnawed it as he listened to Ercole.

The company commander pointed ahead. "You see that wedge of behemoths in front of us?" Sure enough, a couple of dozen of the great shapes were silhouetted against the lightening sky. Lieutenant Ercole went on, "We are going to form up behind them. They will pound a breach in the next Unkerlanter line for us. We will go in behind them. We will go into the enemy line. We will go through the enemy line. We will go on toward our brothers who are fighting their way west toward us. Mezentio and victory!"

"Mezentio and victory!" The men of Plegmund's Brigade tried their best, but couldn't raise much of a cheer. Too many of them were dead, too many wounded, too many of the un-hurt survivors shambling in an exhausted daze like Sidroc and Werferth.

Dazed or not, exhausted or not, Sidroc trudged forward to find his place behind the behemoths. Not only Forthwegians from Plegmund's Brigade were assembled there, but also Al-garvian footsoldiers. The redheads didn't sneer at the Forth-wegians anymore; ties of blood bound them together.

Other wedges of behemoths were coming together along the Algarvian line. "They've thought of something new," Sidroc remarked.

"Good for them," Werferth said. "And we get to be the ones who find out whether it works." He kicked at the dirt. "If we live, we're heroes." He kicked again, then shrugged. "And if we don't live, who gives a futter what we are?"

At shouts from the men who crewed them, the behemoths tramped off toward the rising sun. They didn't advance at a full, thunderous gallop, which would have left the footsol-diers far behind, but did move with an implacability that sug-gested nothing would stop them. Sidroc hoped the suggestion held truth.

From on high, Algarvian dragons dropped eggs on the Un-kerlanter trenches and redoubts ahead. The crews of the behe-moths with egg-tossers also began pounding the enemy position as soon as they drew within range. The Unkerlanters had dug ditches to keep behemoths away from their trench line, but the rain of eggs caved in the edges to a lot of those ditches. And behemoths, even armored, even carrying men and egg-tossers or heavy sticks, were surprisingly nimble beasts. They had little trouble finding ways to go forward.

Just before the behemoths reached the first trench line, both Algarvian and Unkerlanter wizards used sacrifices to get the life energy they needed for their potent spells. Lieutenant Ercole wasn't twenty feet from Sidroc when violet flame shot up from the ground and consumed him. He had time for one brief, agonized shriek before falling silent forever. Sidroc smelled burnt meat. Absurdly, dreadfully, the smoke-sweet scent made his mouth flood with spit.

As soon as the ground stopped shaking beneath him, he got up and moved on. From not far away, Ceorl called to Werferth, "You're in charge of the company now."

"Aye, so I am." Werferth sounded surprised, as if he hadn't thought of that.

"The redheads won't let you keep it," Sidroc predicted. "After all, you're just a lousy Forthwegian."

"I've got it now, though," Werferth said. "Don't see anything to do but keep on going forward. Do you?"

Sidroc stared at him. "You're not supposed to ask me what to do. You're supposed to tell me what to do. You're supposed to tell all of us what to do."

"Aye," Sergeant Werferth said again. He pointed ahead. "There's a little rise. Let's take it, and then we'll figure out what to do next."

Like any high ground on this field, the little rise had Unkerlanters on it. The men of Plegmund's Brigade were able to get closer to the foe than Algarvians would have before the Unkerlanters started blazing. For once, being Forthwegians helped them—King Swemmel's men thought for a little too long that they were on the same side. By the time they realized their mistake, Sidroc and his countrymen were already on top of them.

From the crest of the rise, they could see more high ground farther east. Pointing again, Werferth said, "If we can get up there, I think we can tear this whole position open."

"We?" Sidroc echoed. "Do you mean this company? Do you mean Plegmund's Brigade, whatever's left of it?"

Wearily, Werferth shook his head. "No and no. I mean the whole army. The behemoths will have to do most of the work. I can't see footsoldiers making it all that way without help. Must be another five, six miles."

In ordinary marching, that would have taken the soldiers a couple of hours—a good deal less than that, if they were in a hurry. Sidroc wondered how long it would take with what had to be all the Unkerlanters in the world between his army and that precious ground.

Swemmel's soldiers weren't inclined to let Plegmund's Brigade move another inch forward, let alone five or six miles. As soon as the Unkerlanters realized they'd lost the rise, they started tossing eggs at it. Sidroc and his comrades huddled in the holes from which they'd driven the enemy.

"Here they come!" Ceorl shouted. Sure enough, Unkerlanters in rock-gray tunics swarmed up the eastern slope of the rise, intent on retaking it. Sidroc blazed down several of them. The other Forthwegians did as well, but the Unkerlanters kept coming.

Then eggs started bursting among Swemmel's soldiers. A beam from a heavy stick blazed down two Unkerlanters unlucky enough to be in line with it. "Behemoths!" Sidroc yelled, his throat raw with excitement and smoke. "Our behemoths!"

Caught by surprise, the Unkerlanters ran away. They would sometimes do that when facing the unexpected, though not often enough for anyone ever to count on it. Sidroc waited for Werferth to order a pursuit. The order didn't come. Instead, Werferth said, "Let's wait till we get some more troops up here. Then we'll go after the whoresons."

Sidroc couldn't very well argue with that. More eggs began falling on the men from Plegmund's Brigade. Sidroc looked out toward the high ground in the distance. How could they hope to advance when it was all they could do not to retreat?

Once upon a time, probably, the village of Braunau hadn't been much different from any other Unkerlanter peasant village.

That was before the Algarvians pushing west collided here with the Unkerlanters who had no intention of letting them go any farther. Now whatever was left of the village once the fighting finally went somewhere else would be remembered forever. How it would be remembered . . . The answer to that question was being written in blood in and around the place.

Again, Leudast thought of Sulingen. The Unkerlanters defending Braunau fought with the same determination their countrymen farther south had shown. Every hut, every barn, every well was defended as if it were the gateway to King Swemmel's palace in Cottbus. No one counted the cost. The determination was there: the Algarvians would not get past the village.

For their part, King Mezentio's soldiers remained stubborn and resourceful. No sooner would the defenders of Braunau chew up one brigade than another went into the fight. As always, the redheads were brave. Here, that ended up hurting them at least as much as it helped.

"They can't get at Braunau any other way than from straight ahead, do you see?" Recared said. "The ground won't let them try any of their fancy Algarvian tricks and come up our backside."

"That's the way it looks, anyhow," Leudast agreed. He wasn't so sure about what Mezentio's men could or couldn't do. He'd been wrong too many times.

Recared had fewer doubts—but then, he hadn't been in the fight as long as Leudast had. "Do they play the game called 'last man standing' in your village?" he asked.

"Aye, sir," Leudast answered. "They play it everywhere, I think. It helps if you're drunk." Two men stood toe to toe, taking turns hitting each other as hard as they could. Eventually, one of them wouldn't be able to get up any more, and the other fellow was the winner.

"Well, that's what we've got here," Recared said. "Either we end up on our feet here in Braunau, or the Algarvians do."

"Something to that," Leudast said. "But whether we're standing or the redheads are, Braunau won't be."

Not much of Braunau was standing at the moment. Leudast and Recared both peered out of a trench between a couple of ruined houses on the eastern edge of the village. A dead Algarvian lay in front of them; a couple more lay behind them. The redheads had twice got into Braunau, but they hadn't been able to stay. Their trenches, right this minute, lay a couple of hundred yards outside it.

From behind Leudast, Unkerlanter egg-tossers on the ridge in back of Braunau began pounding the Algarvian positions. Algarvian egg-tossers answered. Leudast said, "Better to have the redheads aiming at them than at us."

"Oh, they'll get to us, never fear," Recared said. "They always do." Leudast wished he thought the regimental commander were wrong.

Algarvian dragons flew by. They also dropped eggs on the Unkerlanter tossers. Some of them dropped eggs on Braunau, too. "Where are our dragons?" Leudast demanded. "Haven't seen many of them since this fight was new."

"Something went wrong," Recared answered. "I don't quite know what, but something did. We were supposed to hit the Algarvians a hard blow, but they did it to us instead."

Leudast sighed. "How many times have we heard that sort of story before?" he said. "How many of us are going to end up dead on account of it? They ought to blaze whoever fouled things up for us."

"Odds are, the Algarvians killed him, whoever he was," Recared said.

But Leudast said, "No. Somebody behind the line will have forgotten something or overlooked something. That's how it is with us. He's the one who deserves to get boiled alive."

"Maybe you're right," Recared said. "But even if you are, we can't do anything about it. All we can do is hold on here and not let the redheads through."

"No, sir." Leudast shook his head. "There's one other thing we can do. We can pay the price for that cursed fool's mistake. We can. And it looks like we will."

Lieutenant Recared scowled at him. "Sergeant, if you'd

said something like that to me this past winter, I'd have given you up to the inspectors without a qualm."

He might not have had any qualms; the idea was plenty—more than plenty—to send a chill through Leudast. Leudast had the feeling that anybody turned over to the inspectors today would be sacrificed tomorrow, or the day after at the latest, and his life energy turned against the Algarvians. But Recared wasn't proposing to give him up now. Cautiously, he asked, "What makes you think different these days?"

"Well, a couple of things," the young regimental commander answered. "For one, I've seen that you're a brave man and a good soldier. And . . ." He sighed. "I've also seen that not all our higher officers are everything they might be."

With that, Recared had just put his own life in Leudast's hands. If Leudast chose to denounce him, the regiment would have a new leader immediately thereafter. That it was in the middle of a desperate battle, a battle where the future of Unkerlant hung in the balance, would not matter at all. After saluting, Leudast spoke with great solemnity: "Sir, I didn't hear a word you said there."

"No, eh?" Recared wasn't a fool. He knew what he'd done, too. "Well, that's probably for the best."

Leudast shrugged. "You never can tell. It might not have mattered any which way. I mean, what are the odds that either one of us is going to come out of Braunau in one piece? Let alone both of us?"

"If it's all the same to you, I'm not going to answer that question," Recared said. "And if you've got any sense, you won't spend much time thinking about it, either."

He was right. Leudast knew as much. Most of the time, he didn't worry about getting wounded or killed. Worrying wouldn't help, and it was liable to hurt. You had to do what you had to do. If you spent too much time thinking and worrying, that might make you slow when you most needed to be fast. But here in Braunau, as in Sulingen, you were only too likely to get hurt or killed regardless of whether you were a good soldier. Too many eggs, too many beams, too many Algarvian dragons overhead.

Recared pulled out a spyglass and peered down the charred slopes toward the redheads' positions. "Careful, sir," Leudast warned. "That's a good way to get yourself blazed. They've got plenty of snipers who could put a beam right through your ear at that range."

"We have to see what's going on," Recared said peevishly. "If we fight blind, we're bound to lose. Or will you tell me I'm wrong there, too?"

Since Leudast couldn't tell him any such thing, he kept his mouth shut. Going into the fight, about half the regiment's companies had been commanded by lieutenants junior to Recared, the other half by sergeants like Leudast. He didn't know how many of those junior lieutenants were left alive. He did know he didn't want to have to try commanding a regiment himself if an Algarvian sniper did pick off Recared.

Recared stiffened, though not because he'd taken a beam. "Uh-oh," he said, and pointed out beyond the redheads' front line. "They're bringing blonds forward."

"Powers above," Leudast said hoarsely. "That means they're going to aim that filthy magecraft of theirs right at us, from as close as they can."

"That's just what it means." Recared's voice was grim. It got grimmer: "And we haven't got much in the way of dragons to stop them, either—we've seen that. They'll keep out of range of our egg-tossers, too. By now, they'll have that measured to the yard. So they'll turn Braunau inside out with their magic, and we can't do a thing to stop 'em. All we can do is take it."

That's what Unkerlanters do best anyhow, Leudast thought. But then he had another thought, one that appalled him with its monstrous cold-bloodedness but might keep him breathing. He grabbed Recared by the arm, an unheard-of-liberty for a sergeant to take with an officer. "Sir, if our own mages send some of that same kind of magic at those poor Kaunian buggers, Mezentio's men won't be able to use their life energy against us."

By *send some of that same kind of magic*, he meant, of course, having Unkerlanter mages kill some of their own countrymen for their life energy. He couldn't stomach saying it in so many words, even if killing was part of his line of work, too.

Recared stared at him, then shouted, "Crystallomancer!"

The regiment had a new one, replacing the minor mage slain in the first day of the battle for the Durrwangen salient. "Aye, sir?" he said, making his way up through the maze of trenches to Recared's side. When Recared told him what he wanted, the crystallomancer hesitated. "Are you sure, sir?" His eyes were round and fearful.

Mind made up, Recared didn't hesitate. "Aye," he said. "And hurry, curse you. If we don't do what we have to do, and if we don't do it fast, the Algarvians will work their magic on us. Would you sooner sit still for that?"

"No, sir," the crystallomancer said, and activated his crystal. When a face appeared in it, he passed it to Recared. "Go ahead, sir."

Recared spoke quickly and to the point. The mage on the other end of the etheric connection listened, then said, "I cannot decide this. Wait." He disappeared.

A moment later, another face appeared in the crystal. "I am Addanz, archmage of Unkerlant. Say your say." Recared did, as concisely as he had before. He even gave Leudast credit, not that Leudast much wanted any such thing. Leudast had met the archmage once before, in trenches not far outside of Cottbus. Perhaps fortunately, Addanz didn't seem to remember that. He said, "Tell me how far east of Braunau the Kaunians are."

"Just outside of egg-tosser range, sir," Recared replied.

"Very well," Addanz said, and then shook his head. "No, not very well—very ill. But no help for it. You'll have your magecraft, Lieutenant."

"Quickly then, sir, or you waste it," Recared said.

"You'll have it," Addanz repeated, and his image vanished like a blown-out candle flame.

Leudast imagined Unkerlanter mages lining up Unkerlanter peasants and miscreants so Unkerlanter soldiers could slay them. He wished he hadn't; the picture in his mind was all too vivid. And here, for once, Swemmel's endless talk of efficiency proved true. Hardly five minute passed before the ground shuddered under those luckless Kaunians, before fissures opened and flames shot forth.

Recared pounded Leudast on the back. "Well done, Sergeant, by the powers above!" he shouted. "Let's see the redheads make their cursed magic now. If we live, you'll get a decoration for this."

All Leudast said was, "I feel like a murderer." He'd caused his own countrymen—for all he knew, maybe his own kinsmen—to die so their life energy could go into killing Kaunians so the Algarvians couldn't kill the Kaunians to kill him. That wasn't war, or it shouldn't have been. He stared east, toward the Algarvian trenches. If he knew Mezentio's men, they wouldn't let a setback stop them for long. They never had yet.

Colonel Sabrino had rarely seen an army brigadier so furious. The Algarvian officer looked about ready to leap out of the crystal and strangle somebody—King Swemmel by choice, no doubt, but Sabrino thought he might do himself at a pinch.

"Do you know what those fornicating Unkerlanters did?" the brigadier howled. "Have you got any idea?"

"No, sir," Sabrino said around a yawn—he grabbed what sleep he could between flight, and didn't take kindly to interruptions. "But you're going to tell me, I expect."

The brigadier went on as if he hadn't spoken, which might have been lucky for him: "We had our Kaunians all ready to slay, to rout Swemmel's buggers out of that stinking Braunau place, and the Unkerlanter whoresons killed most of 'em by magic before we got to use their life energy. The attack went in anyhow, and we got thrown back again. We've got to get past there if we're ever going to join hands with our men on the other side of the enemy salient."

"Aye, sir, I know that," Sabrino said, wondering if the Algarvians on the western flank of the bulge were doing any better than the eastern army to which he was attached. He wished his countrymen hadn't started using murder-powered magecraft. Now both sides used it ever more freely, which added to the death toll without changing much else. He also suspected the brigadier shouldn't have attacked Braunau once the sorcerous backing for the assault collapsed. Suggesting such things to a superior was a tricky business. He didn't try; he knew he was too worn to be tactful. Instead, he asked, "What would you have me do, sir?"

"If we can't knock Braunau out from under those buggers with dead Kaunians, next best thing is to pound it flat—flatter—with dragons," the brigadier answered. "You've got the edge on 'em there in this side of the salient."

"For now, anyway," Sabrino said. "They've put more dragons in the air today than they did yesterday, and still more than the day before. They've got more dragons than we thought they did."

"They've got more of everything than we thought they did," the brigadier said. "But we can still lick 'em. We *can*, curse it." He sounded as if Sabrino were arguing with him.

"We'd better," was all Sabrino did say about that. He went on, "Tell me when you want us there, sir, and we'll be there." *Colonel Ambaldo is probably sleeping, too,* he thought. *That means I get to wake him up.* There were prospects he might have enjoyed less. Ambaldo, after all, had spent a lot of the war in the comfortable east. He hadn't had his full share of the delights of Unkerlant—or any share at all in the different delights of the land of the Ice People.

"An hour," the brigadier said. When Sabrino nodded, the army officer's image vanished from the crystal. It flared, then went back to being a simple globe of glass.

Sabrino strode out of his tent and shouted for dragon handlers. The men came running, their kilts flapping at each long stride. He said, "Get the dragons ready, and start kicking the men awake. We're going after Braunau again."

"Just your wing, sir, or both of them at this farm?" a handler asked.

"Both," Sabrino answered. "But I'll wake Ambaldo myself." His face must have worn an evil grin, because several of the handlers snickered.

Colonel Ambaldo awoke with several loud, fervent curses. He also woke grabbing for the stick by his cot. Sabrino got it first. Grabbing and missing seemed to restore something like reason to Ambaldo. He glowered at Sabrino and asked, "All right, your Excellency, who's gone and pissed in the soup pot this time?"

"King Swemmel's little friends, who else?" Sabrino said. "Not that it doesn't sound like some hamfisted generalship from us went into the mix, too." He quickly explained what had gone wrong in front of Braunau.

Ambaldo grunted and rubbed his eyes. "This whole business of killing Kaunians is filthy, if anybody wants to know what I think," he said as he sat up. He looked defiance at Sabrino. "And I don't care what you may believe about it."

"No?" Sabrino said mildly. "I told King Mezentio the same thing before we really started doing it. His Majesty didn't care what I believed about it."

"Really? You said that to Mezentio? To his face?" Ambaldo asked. Sabrino nodded. Ambaldo let out a soft whistle. "I will be dipped in dung. I knew you for a brave man, your Excellency, but still, you surprise me."

"If I weren't a brave man, I wouldn't have come in here to get you," Sabrino said. "Shall we be at it?"

Ambaldo got to his feet and bowed. "I wouldn't miss it for the world."

When Sabrino went out to his dragon, he found it loaded with eggs. The handler was tossing chunks of meat to it. The dragon caught them out of the air one after another. "How's the cinnabar holding out?" Sabrino asked the handler.

He got no more reassuring answers, as he had earlier in the fight. The fellow spread his hands and said, "If they'd known this stinking battle was going to last so bloody long, they should've given us more." Before Sabrino could say anything to that, the dragon handler added, "Of course, maybe they didn't have any more to give." On that cheerful note, he went back to feeding the dragon.

Sabrino climbed aboard the great scaly beast and fastened himself into his harness at the base of its neck. Distracted by raw meat, the dragon didn't even raise a fuss. Then the handler stopped feeding it and undid its chain from the iron spike driven deep into the soil of Unkerlant. Sabrino whacked the dragon with his goad, urging it into the air.

The dragon bellowed in fury at the idea that it should work for a living. As far as it was concerned, it had been hatched to sit on the ground so people could feed it to the bursting point. No matter how often Sabrino tried to give it other ideas with the goad, it was surprised and outraged every time.

It sprang into the air as much from fury as for any other reason. As usual, Sabrino didn't care why. As long as the dragon rose, he'd take that. The other dragons in his wing were every bit as offended at having to earn their keep as was his. They all screeched as they spiraled upward.

Colonel Ambaldo's dragons were flying, too. Sabrino, of necessity his own crystallomancer while on dragonback, murmured the charm that attuned the emanations of his crystal with that of the other wing commander. When Ambaldo's image appeared in his crystal, Sabrino said, "Now that you're awake, your Excellency, how do you want to handle the strike at Braunau? If you like, we'll go in first and then fly cover for your wing."

"Aye, good enough," Ambaldo said, and Sabrino cursed under his breath. He'd made the offer for form's sake, no more. Ambaldo's dragons had been worked hard in this fight, but were still fresher than Sabrino's. They would have made a better covering flight than Sabrino's wing. Ambaldo should have been able to see that for himself. If he couldn't, though, Sabrino had too much pride to point it out to him. Ambaldo did say, "We'll cover you on the way in."

"Thank you so much." Sabrino knew how little he meant that. Ambaldo was brave, but bravery didn't matter much, not here on the western front. The Unkerlanters were brave, too.

What really set the Algarvians apart from them was brains. Without a guiding wit behind the fighting, it turned into nothing but a slugging match. King Swemmel's men could afford that better than Algarve could.

Sabrino's mouth turned down in discontent as he steered the dragon east toward Braunau. By the look of the battlefield far below, it had already turned into a slugging match. No more lightning thrusts around Unkerlanter positions to flank them out. The Algarvian attack had gone straight into the heart of the toughest and deepest set of field fortifications Sabrino had ever seen—on the eastern side of the Durrwangen salient and, by all the signs, on the western side as well.

No wonder progress was so painfully slow. No wonder so many dead men and horses and unicorns and behemoths lay on the ground. Where, Sabrino wondered, would their replacements come from? One thought ran through his mind. *We'd better win here. If we don't, if we've thrown all this away with nothing to show for it, how are we going to carry the war to the Unkerlanters from here on out?*

"Powers above," he muttered as his wing flew over what would have been the place where the Kaunians were sacrificed in front of Braunau, "we're even running out of blonds." King Swemmel's mages had helped there, too. Sabrino cursed softly, and the wind blew his words away. All things considered, maybe he should have called on the powers below instead.

And then he had no more time for such worries, for there lay battered Braunau, corking the Algarvians' advance. He spoke into his crystal again, this time to his own squadron leaders: "We'll dive to drop our eggs on the village, then climb quick as we can and cover Ambaldo's wing while they do the same."

"Here's hoping the Unkerlanters don't hit us," Captain Orosio said. "We've got tired beasts. We'll have trouble giving our best."

Because Sabrino knew that, too, he made his voice harsh as he answered, "It's what we're going to do." He never asked his dragonfliers to do anything he wouldn't do himself, so he was the first to urge his own mount into a dive over Braunau. Footsoldiers down there blazed at him. So did the crew of heavy sticks. If one of those hit his dragon, the beast wouldn't gain height again, and Sabrino's mistress and his wife might miss him. Just above rooftop height, he loosed his eggs, then beat his dragon as hard as he could to make it pull up.

He cursed again when a couple of dragonfliers didn't follow him back up into the sky. Maybe Ambaldo's fresher, faster dragons would have made the men at the heavy sticks miss. No way to know. Sabrino looked back over his shoulder. Ambaldo's dragons were delivering their load of death over Braunau, going in with as much indifference to danger as any Algarvian could want to show.

Sabrino thought he was the first one to spot the swarm of rock-gray Unkerlanter dragons racing toward Braunau from the southwest. He hadn't even the time to grab for his crystal and shout out a warning before the Unkerlanters swooped down on Ambaldo's wing, slicing through his own almost as if it didn't exist.

The Unkerlanters treated Ambaldo and his dragonfliers about as rudely as the Algarvians had treated the Unkerlanter attack on their dragon farms earlier in the battle. Dragon after dragon painted in green and red and white tumbled out of the sky, beset from above. Sabrino wasted no time ordering his own men back into the fray. But the enemy, having struck hard and fast, flew off. Sabrino's dragons were too weary to make much of a pursuit.

Worse, he feared flying into another Unkerlanter trap. With the tired beasts his men were flying, that would be the end of them. Ambaldo's dragons, or those of them that were left, aligned on his. When he shouted the other wing commander's name through the crystal, he got no answer. He didn't think anyone would get answers from Ambaldo again.

"Back to our dragon farm," he told his own squadron leaders. "We'll put the pieces back together as best we can and go on." He didn't know where more dragons—or, for that matter, more dragonfliers—would come from. He didn't know how long the wing could keep going without them, either. All at once, without warning, he felt old.

*   *   *

"Come on!" Major Spinello shouted as he led his troopers east. "We can still do it. By the powers above, we can! But we've got to keep moving."

He wasn't commanding his own regiment anymore. The battered formation he headed was about as big as his regiment had been at the start of the battle of Durrwangen, but it consisted of the mixed-up remnants of three or four different regiments. As cooks threw leftovers together to get another meal out of them, so Algarvian generals stirred together broken units to get one more fight from them. Battle Group Spinello, they called this one. Spinello would have been prouder if he hadn't been so tired.

He pointed ahead. "If we get over that ridge line and onto the flat land up there, we can tear Swemmel's whole position open. It's only a couple of miles now. We *can* do it!"

Was anybody listening to him? Was anybody paying any attention at all? He looked around to see. What he saw were men as filthy and unshaven and weary as he was. He looked ahead. Even the Algarvian behemoths seemed worn unto death. A couple of wedges of them led Battle Group Spinello ahead. Without them, every footsoldiers would have been wounded or killed by now.

More behemoths led more Algarvian footsoldiers toward that ridge line. Here and there, they dueled at long range with Unkerlanter behemoths. Spinello had never imagined that Unkerlant had bred so many behemoths. He'd never imagined that Swemmel's men would handle them so well, either.

When a well-placed Algarvian egg knocked over one of those behemoths, he let out a cheer. "See, boys?" he said. "We can still lick 'em. No point in running if you see a couple of enemy beasts and you haven't got any of your own close by."

That had happened a few times in this battle. The Algarvians were used to sending their foes fleeing in panic with their behemoths. They were anything but used to being on the receiving end of panic. But any army's nerve wore thin if its men were fought as hard as they could be and then three steps more besides. Every so often, troops would scream,

"Behemoths!" and run the other way when a couple of Unkerlanter beasts showed themselves over the top of a rise.

Captain Turpino limped up to Spinello. His left calf was bandaged; he'd taken a blaze between the top of his boot and the bottom of his kilt. But he refused to leave the field. Spinello was glad to have him here. Turpino was about as far from lovable as a man could get, but he knew his business.

Now he said, "Sir, looks like that little tiny rise there"—he pointed—"will screen us from the worst of what the Unkerlanters can throw at us and still let us move east toward the real high ground."

Spinello considered. His nod, when he gave it, was hesitant. "Aye, unless the Unkerlanters see that, too, and they've got a brigade lying in wait for us."

With a shrug, Turpino answered, "Sir, they've been lying in wait for us ever since we started this attack. You want to know what I think, somebody's head ought to roll for that."

"I'm not saying you're wrong, but you ought to have a care there," Spinello told him. "People I believe tell me this attack went in at the orders of his Majesty himself."

"Mezentio's a good king. That doesn't necessarily make him a good general," Turpino said. "And what's he going to do to me? Boil me alive the way Swemmel might? Not likely! Besides, what can he do to me that's worse than what we've gone through these past two weeks?"

"Good question," Spinello admitted. "The sort of question, though, where you may not want to find out the answer."

"I'll worry later," Turpino said. "Right now, the only thing I'm going to worry about is staying alive through this cursed fight. If I manage that, King Mezentio is welcome to whatever's left of my carcass afterwards."

Nodding, Spinello shouted for a crystallomancer. When an officer-by-courtesy with a crystal trotted over to him, he said, "Can you get hold of the fellow commanding the behemoths in front of us?"

"I can try, sir," the crystallomancer said. "You've got to remember, though, in a field as crowded as this, that Swemmel's men are liable to pick up some of our emanations, the same way we steal theirs every chance we get."

"I'll keep it in mind," Spinello said. "Now get him."

"Aye, sir." The crystallomancer murmured the charm. After his crystal flared with light, an officer on a behemoth appeared in it. Actually, Spinello couldn't see much of him, for the brim of his iron helmet almost covered his eyes, while cheekpieces hid most of the rest of his face. Spinello knew he'd be wearing chain and plate on his body, too. He didn't have to haul the weight around; his behemoth did.

He listened to Spinello, then eyed the ground ahead himself. After a moment, he nodded. "All right, Major, we'll go that way. Once we make it up to the top of the big rise, then we'll see what we see."

"How do you like our chances?" Spinello asked.

"We're short a few behemoths, or maybe more than a few, down in the southeast," the other officer answered. "Swemmel's whoresons held 'em up longer than we expected. But we ought to be able to do the job just the same."

"Good," Spinello said.

"It'll have to do," said the fellow on the behemoth. "And now—farewell." He vanished from the crystal. The crystallomancer put it back into his pack.

The behemoths turned to use the track Captain Turpino had suggested. Spinello blew his whistle. "Follow me!" he shouted—a cry that made Algarvian footsoldiers respect and obey the men who led them. Then he added another cry that was more likely to keep the men of Battle Group Spinello alive: pointing to the behemoths, he yelled, "Follow them!"

For half a mile or so, everything went very well—so well, in fact, that Spinello started to get suspicious. His eyes went back and forth, back and forth. He kept expecting hordes of drunken Unkerlanters to leap from trenches on either flank and rush toward his men with shouts of, "Urra!"

But the trouble, when it came, came from the front. The Unkerlanters crouched in their holes and waited till the wedges of behemoths were almost upon them. Some of those holes were so hard to spot, Spinello guessed they had sorcery covering them. When Swemmel's men did pop up and start blazing, even they weren't so rash—or so drunk—as to charge. Instead, they ducked down again and waited for the Algarvian onslaught.

They didn't have long to wait. The behemoths tossed eggs into their trenches. "Forward!" Spinello shouted again. "Loose order!" The men he led probably could have done the job without commands. They'd done it before, some of them countless times. Having behemoths along to help was, if anything, an unusual luxury. They advanced by rushes, some soldiers blazing while others moved ahead. The Unkerlanters had an unpleasant choice: keep their heads down till they were slaughtered in their holes or come out and try to get away.

More often than not, most of them would have died in place. Here, rather to Spinello's surprise, most of them fled. *Maybe it's the behemoths,* he thought. *If we can be twitchy about theirs, no reason they shouldn't be twitchy about ours.*

Whatever the reason, running did the Unkerlanters little good. More eggs from the Algarvian behemoths burst among them, flinging them this way and that like broken toys. When the beam from a heavy stick caught a man in the back, he didn't just go down. He also went up—in flames.

"Forward!" Spinello shouted. Every step took Battle Group Spinello—and the behemoths with it—closer to the high ground at the heart of the salient. If the Algarvians could get up there in numbers, if they could move quickly once they did, this great, bloody grapple might yet turn out to have been worthwhile.

But one of the Unkerlanter officers must have had a crystal, and must have used it before he fell. The Algarvians hadn't gone far past the Unkerlanter trench line before eggs began dropping among them. Spinello curled himself into a ball behind a boulder. The big gray rock shielded him from the energies of eggs bursting in front of it. It would do him no good if eggs burst in back of it. He preferred not to dwell on that.

Somewhere not far away, an Unkerlanter was down and

shrieking for his mother in a high, shrill voice. His cries went on and on, then cut off abruptly. Somebody, Spinello supposed, had put him out of his agony. He hoped someone would do the same for him if the need arose. Even more, he hoped it never would. He aimed to die in bed, preferably with company.

Despite the eggs falling among its men and behemoths, Battle Group Spinello fought its way forward. Spinello noticed the ground rising more sharply under his feet than it had before. "We're getting where we need to go," he called, pointing ahead. "If we can get up there in strength, if we can drive the Unkerlanters back once we do it, nothing we've been through will have mattered. We'll rip Swemmel's boys a new arsehole, and then we'll go on and win this war. Mezentio and victory!"

"Mezentio and victory!" the soldiers shouted. They were veterans. They knew he was telling them the truth. As long as they could keep going forward, they would finally battle their way past the last Unkerlanter defensive line. Then it would be fighting in open country, and Swemmel's soldiers had never been able to match them in that. Destroy the Durrwangen bulge, destroy the Unkerlanter armies here, and who could say what might happen after that?

The Unkerlanters might have drawn the same conclusion. If they had, they liked it less than Spinello had. More eggs fell on the advancing Algarvians, forcing footsoldiers to go to earth and separating them from the behemoths, which made life more difficult for all of Mezentio's men. Algarvian egg-tossers and Algarvian dragons went hunting the enemy's tossers.

But Algarvian dragons didn't have everything their own way, not here. Dragons painted rock-gray swooped down on Battle Group Spinello. Unkerlanter dragons had contested the sky west of here ever since this battle began. Some of them tried to flame behemoths. Others dropped still more eggs on the Algarvian footsoldiers.

Spinello was running toward the crater one egg had blown in the ground when another burst close by. All at once, he wasn't running anymore, but flying through the air. He landed in a thornbush, which tore at him but probably saved him from the worse damage he would have got slamming into the ground.

Not till he freed himself, tried to go on, and put weight on his right leg did he realize a chunk of metal egg casing had wounded him. He went down in a heap. Unlike Turpino's, his leg wouldn't support him anymore. Blood poured from a gash above the knee. Pain poured from the gash, too, now that he knew he had it.

"Stretcher-bearers!" he bawled, hoping some of them would hear him. "Stretcher-bearers!" He took a bandage from his belt pouch and bound up the wound as best he could. He also gulped down a little jar of poppy juice. That made the pain retreat, but couldn't rout it. *Battle Group Turpino now*, he thought.

"Here we are, pal," an Algarvian said. He and his comrade lifted Spinello and set him on their stretcher. "We'll get you out of here—that or die trying." It wasn't a joke, even if it sounded like one.

"I wanted to see the fight on the high ground," Spinello grumbled. But he wouldn't, not now.

Thirteen

Marshal Rathar had stayed in Durrwangen to direct the twin fights on each flank of the salient from his headquarters for as long as he could stand—and, indeed, for a little longer than that. As long as both battles were going furiously, he didn't see much point to directly overseeing one or the other. He might have guessed wrong as to which would prove the more important, and would have no one but himself to blame. King Swemmel would have no one but him to blame, either.

Now, though, the Algarvians plainly wouldn't break through in the east. They'd thrown everything they had at Braunau. They'd broken into the village several times. They'd never gone past it, and they didn't hold it at the moment. Rathar had a good notion of the reserves the redheads had left on that side of the bulge, and of his own forces over there. Braunau and that whole side of the salient would stand.

Here in the west, though . . . Here on the western side of the bulge, the Unkerlanters had badly hurt Mezentio's men. They'd killed a lot of enemy behemoths, and they'd cost the Algarvians a lot of time fighting their way through one heavily defended line after another.

But on this flank, unlike the other, the Algarvians hadn't had to halt. They were still coming, they'd gained the high ground he'd hoped to deny them, and they might yet break through and race to cut off the salient in the style they'd shown the past two summers.

"We'll just have to stop them, that's all," he said to General Vatran.

"Oh, aye, as easy as boiling water for tea," Vatran said, and took a sip from the mug in front of him. His grimace filled his face with so many wrinkles, it might almost have belonged to an aging gargoyle. "Don't I wish! Don't we all wish!"

"We have to do it," Rathar repeated. He got up from the folding table at which he'd been sitting with Vatran and paced back and forth under the plum trees that shielded his new field headquarters from the prying eyes of dragonfliers. The plateau up here sloped down toward the ground the Algarvians had already won. Gullies, some of them dry, more with streams at their bottom, cut up the flat land. Most of it was given over to fields and meadows, but orchards like this one and little clumps of forest varied the landscape. Rathar sat his jaw. "We have to do it, and we cursed well will." He raised his voice: "Crystallomancer!"

"Aye, lord Marshal?" The young mage came running, his crystal ready to hand.

"Get me General Gurmun, in charge of the reserve force of behemoths," Rathar said.

"Aye, sir." The crystallomancer murmured the charm he needed. Light flared from the crystal. A face appeared in it: another crystallomancer's face. Rathar's man spoke to the other fellow, who hurried away. Less than a minute later, General Gurmun's hard visage appeared in the sphere of glass. Rathar's crystallomancer nodded. "Go ahead, lord Marshal."

Without preamble, Rathar said, "General, I want all your behemoths moving to me and to the advancing Algarvians in an hour. Can you do it?"

If Gurmun said no, Rathar intended to sack him on the spot. Gurmun had first won command of an army in the war against the Zuwayzin, when his then-superior proved too drunk to deliver an attack when Rathar wanted it. Drunkenness wasn't Gurmun's vice. He hadn't shown many vices in the three and a half years since, but now would be the worst possible moment for one to make itself known.

"Sir, we can," Gurmun said. "Inside half an hour, in fact. We'll hit the redheads an hour after that. By the powers above, we'll hit 'em hard, too."

"Good enough." Rathar gestured to his crystallomancer, who broke the etheric link. Gurmun's image vanished as abruptly as it had appeared.

Vatran whistled, a low, soft note. "The whole reserve of behemoths, lord Marshal?" He pointed west, toward Mezentio's own oncoming horde of behemoths. "The field won't be big enough to hold all the beasts battling on it."

Rathar didn't answer. He walked to the edge of the plum orchard and swung a spyglass in the direction Vatran had pointed. Advancing wedges of Algarvian behemoths leaped toward his eye. The redheads weren't having things all their own way—Unkerlanter behemoths and footsoldiers and dragons made them pay for every yard they gained. But Mezentio's men had the bit between their teeth. Like any good troops, they could feel it. On they came. If the reserves couldn't stop them . . .

If the reserves couldn't stop them, odds were Vatran or Gurmun or some other general would get the big stars on his collar, the green sash, and the ceremonial sword that went with being Marshal of Unkerlant. Swemmel had been more forgiving of Rathar than of any other officer in his command, perhaps—but only perhaps—because he truly believed Rathar wouldn't try to steal the throne. But he was unlikely to tolerate failure here. Sitting on the throne, Rathar knew he too would have been unlikely to tolerate failure here.

Unkerlanter dragons struck at the Algarvian behemoths. Algarvian dragons promptly struck at the Unkerlanters, keeping them too busy to deliver the blows they should have. Rathar cursed under his breath. He'd hoped to have gained control of the air by this point in the fighting. No such luck. As far as he could tell, neither side dominated the air above the Durrwangen bulge.

He turned to the southeast, looking for some sign of the arrival of Gurmun's behemoths. No such luck there, either. The plum trees screened him away from a good view in that direction. He looked back toward the Algarvians and scowled. If Gurmun didn't get here when he'd said he would, this headquarters would come under attack before long.

Even though Rathar couldn't see much to the southeast, he knew to the minute when the behemoth reserve began to draw near. Half, maybe more than half, of the Algarvian dragons broke off their fight with their Unkerlanter counterparts and flew off to the southeast as fast as they could go. He might not have seen Gurmun coming, but they had.

Rathar ran back to the table where Vatran still stat. As he ran, he shouted for the crystallomancer again. "The commanders of the dragon wings," he ordered when the minor mage hurried up to him. Then he spoke urgently into the crystal: "The redheads kept you from savaging their behemoths too badly. By the powers above, you've got to keep them from punishing ours before they reach the field. If you fail there, we're liable to be ruined."

One after another, the wing commander promised to obey. Rathar hurried back to the edge of the orchard. This time, Vatran came with him. Fewer Unkerlanter dragons were attacking the Algarvian behemoths. He supposed that meant—he hoped it meant—the Unkerlanters were holding the Algarvian dragons away from their behemoths. "Curse the redheads," he growled. "They're altogether too good at what they do."

Vatran set a hand on his arm. "Lord Marshal, you've done everything you could do here," he said. "Now it's time to let the men do what they can do."

"I want to grab a stick and fight alongside them," Rathar said. "I want to be everywhere at once, and fighting in all those different places."

"You are," Vatran told him. "Everybody out there"—he waved—"is doing what he's doing because your orders told him to do it."

"Not everybody," Rathar said. Vatran raised a shaggy white eyebrow. The marshal explained: "The Algarvians, powers below eat 'em, don't want to listen to me at all."

Vatran laughed, though Rathar hadn't meant it as a joke. Then, at the same time, he and Vatran both cocked their heads to one side, listening hard to a low but building rumble to the southeast. Or was it listening? Vatran said, "I'm not sure I hear that with my ears or feel it through the soles of my feet, you know what I mean?" Rathar nodded; that said it better than he could have.

He stepped out from the cover of the plum trees and looked in the direction of the rumble again. A couple of Algarvian behemoths had drawn close enough for their crews to spy him. Eggs flew toward him, but burst a couple of hundred yards short.

And then he whooped like a schoolboy unexpectedly dismissed early. "Here they come!" he shouted. "Gurmun's on time after all."

Now that their crewmen had seen the Algarvian enemy, the behemoths from Gurmun's reserve—several hundred of them, a whole army's worth—broke into a furious gallop, to get into the fight quick as they could. They cut in behind the leading Algarvian behemoths, moving so fast that the redheads didn't have time to deploy against them.

"Look at that!" Hardly aware he was doing it, Rathar

pounded Vatran on the back. "Will you look at that? There hasn't been a charge like that this whole bloody war. Some of them are even using their horns to fight with."

If the field had seemed too small with only the Algarvian behemoths moving forward on it, it suddenly got more than twice as crowded. Rathar knew a moment's pity for the foot-soldiers on that field. Neither side's behemoths were likely to. Their crews tossed eggs and blazed at one another from ridiculously short ranges. As Rathar had said, some gored others right through their armor, as if they were unicorns back in the days before mages learned how to make sticks.

Grass fires sprang up in a dozen places at once, making it harder for Rathar to tell what was going on even with his spy-glass. But he could see that the Algarvians, as was their way, didn't stay surprised long. They fought back furiously against Gurmun's behemoths. Wedges of Algarvian beasts would pop out from behind orchards and copses, toss eggs and blaze at the foe, and then take cover again. Gurmun didn't need long to adopt the same tactics.

Overhead, both sides' dragons battled to something close to a draw. The Algarvians sacrificed Kaunians. Addanz and the other Unkerlanter mages sacrificed their own luckless people to answer. The sorcerous duel, the duel of horrors, was also as near even as made no difference.

That left it up to the behemoths. They surged back and forth over the plain as the sun crawled across the sky. If the redheads had enough beasts left after shattering Gurmun's re-serve, their own attack might go on. But Rathar knew that part of their force of behemoths remained some miles to the southwest. It wouldn't get here while today's fight lasted. Gurmun had the advantage of numbers, the Algarvians, in spite of everything, the advantage of skill. With two heavy weights flung into the pans of the scale, they jounced up and down, now one higher, now the other.

An Unkerlanter behemoth crew blazed down an Algarvian beast. The other Algarvian behemoths in that part of the field attacked the Unkerlanters, badly wounding their behemoth. The driver, the only crewman left on it, charged the Algarvians. He blazed down one and gored another in the flank before his own behemoth finally toppled.

By then, the sun had sunk low in the southwest. Seen through thick smoke, it was red as blood. Rathar wondered where the day had gone. He turned to Vatran. "We haven't broken them, but we've held them," he said. "They aren't going to come pouring through in a great tide, the way we feared they would."

Wearily, Vatran nodded. "No doubt you're right, lord Marshal. They can't hit us another blow like this one—they've left too many men and beasts dead on the field."

"Aye." Marshal Rathar preferred not to dwell on how many Unkerlanter men and beasts lay dead on the fields of the Durrwangen bulge. Whatever the cost, though, he and the soldiers of his kingdom *had* stopped the Algarvians here. Which meant . . . He called for the crystallomancer. When the man came up to him, he said, "Connect me to the general commanding our army east and south of the Algarvian forces on the eastern flank of the salient." And when that officer's image appeared in the crystal, Rathar spoke four words: "Let the counterattack begin."

Like the rest of the Algarvian constables in Gromheort, Bembo avidly followed news of the big battles down in the south of Unkerlant. News sheets from across the nearby border with Algarve were brought into town daily, so the constables didn't have to go to the trouble of learning to read Forthwegian.

For the first several days of the fight near Durrwangen, everything seemed to go well. The news sheets reported victories on the ground and in the air, and their maps showed King Mezentio's armies advancing. The news sheets in Forthwegian must have said the same thing, for the locals, who didn't love their Algarvian occupiers, strode through Gromheort with long faces.

And then, little by little, the news sheets stopped talking about the battle. They didn't proclaim the great, crushing triumph all the Algarvians had looked for. "I want to know what's going on," Constable Almonio complained one morning while he and his comrades were queued up for breakfast.

Bembo stood right behind him. Sergeant Pesaro stood behind Bembo. Turning to Pesaro, Bembo said, "Touching to see such innocence in this age of the world, isn't it?"

"It is indeed," Pesaro said, as if Almonio weren't there. "But then, he's the tender-headed one, remember? Almonio wouldn't hurt a fly, or even a Kaunian."

That made Bembo laugh. It made Almonio furious. "I keep trying to behave like a human being, in spite of what the war is doing to all of us," he snapped.

"Like a drunken human being, a lot of the time," Bembo said. Almonio really didn't have the stomach for rounding up Kaunians. He poured down the spirits whenever he had to do it, to keep from dwelling on what he'd done.

But he was sober now, sober and angry. "I still don't know what the two of you are talking about," he said, that edge still in his voice.

"Like a stupid human being," Pesaro said, which only made Almonio angrier. Pesaro, though, was a sergeant, so Almonio couldn't show that anger so readily, not if he had the slightest notion of what was good for him. With a sigh both sad and sarcastic, Pesaro went on, "He really doesn't get it."

Almonio threw his hands in the air. He just missed knocking another constable's mess tin out of his hands, which would have given the other fellow reason to be angry at him. "What is there to get?" he demanded. "All I want to know is how the battle turned out, and the miserable news sheets won't tell me."

"A natural-born innocent," Bembo said again, to Pesaro. Then he gave his attention back to Almonio. "My dear fellow, if you really need it spelled out for you, I'll do the job: if the news sheets don't give us any news, it's because there's no good news to give. There. Is that simple enough, or shall I draw pictures?"

"Oh," Almonio said, in a very small voice. "But if the Unkerlanters have beaten us down at Durrwangen, if they've beaten us in the summertime . . ." His voice trailed away altogether.

"We're constables," Sergeant Pesaro said, perhaps as much to reassure himself as to make Almonio (and, incidentally, Bembo) feel better. "We've got a job to do here, and an important job it is, too. Whatever happens hundreds of miles away doesn't matter a bit to us. Not a bit, do you hear me?"

Almonio nodded. So did Bembo. He wasn't so sure his sergeant was right, but he wanted to think so. Anything else was too depressing to contemplate. The wine the refectory served with breakfast was nasty, sour stuff, but he had an extra mug anyhow. Almonio had an extra two or three; Bembo wasn't keeping close track.

When he went out on patrol with Oraste, he found his partner in a dour mood. Oraste was often dour, but more so than usual today. At last, Bembo asked him, "What's gnawing at you?"

Oraste walked on for several paces without answering. Bembo thought he wouldn't answer, but after a bit he did: "How in blazes are we supposed to win the war now?"

"What do you think I am?" Bembo demanded, so fiercely that even rugged Oraste gave back a pace. "A general? King Mezentio? I don't know anything about that business. All I know is, the bigwigs in Trapani will come up with something. They always have. What's one more time?"

"They'd better," Oraste growled, as if he'd hold Bembo responsible if they didn't. "That was what should have happened in this big battle. It didn't. How many more chances do we get?"

"As long as they're fighting way inside Unkerlant, I'm not going to worry about it," Bembo said. "If you've got any sense, you won't worry about it, either. You're the one who was always saying that if I didn't like it here, I could get a stick and go fight the Unkerlanters. Now I'll tell you the same cursed thing."

"Powers below eat you, Bembo," Oraste said, surprisingly little rancor in his voice. "You were supposed to say something funny and stupid, so I could stop brooding about the way things are going. But you don't like it any more than I do, do you?"

Instead of answering that straight out, Bembo said, "I had to explain the facts of life to Almonio this morning. He couldn't figure them out for himself."

"Why am I not surprised? That one . . ." Oraste grimaced. "The other question is, how come I'm jealous of him?"

Bembo didn't answer that at all.

Shouts from around a corner made them both yank out their sticks and start to run. Bembo was amazed at the relief with which he ran. Catching thieves and robbers was why he was here in Gromheort. As long as he was doing his job, he wouldn't have to worry about anything else.

"What's going on here?" he yelled when he got to the two shouting Forthwegians.

Of necessity, he spoke Algarvian. Both Forthwegians looked as if they understood the language. They were middle-aged, and had probably had to learn it in school back in the days before the Six Years' War; this part of Forthweg had belonged to Algarve then. After glancing at each other, they spoke together: "Why, nothing."

"Don't get wise with us," Oraste said. "You'll be sorry if you do." If he could pummel or blaze a Forthwegian or two, he wouldn't have to think about the way things looked in Unkerlant.

One of the Forthwegians said, "It *was* nothing, really."

"We were just having a bit of a disagreement," the other one said. "Sorry we got so loud."

Bembo put away his stick, but drew his bludgeon from its loop on his belt and thwacked it into the palm of his left hand. "You heard my partner. Don't get wise with us. We're not in any mood to waste time with Forthwegians who want to act cute. Have you got that?" On reflection, Bembo wondered if he should have put it that way. What it meant was, *We're jumpy as cats because the war against Unkerlant isn't going the way we'd like.* The Forthwegians didn't have to be theoretical sorcerers to figure that out, either.

But Bembo and Oraste had clubs. They had sticks. They had the power of the occupying authority behind them. Even if the Forthwegians were privately contemptuous, they didn't dare show what they were thinking. One of them said, "Sorry, sir." The other one nodded to show he was sorry, too.

"That's better," Bembo said. "Now, I'm going to try this one more time, and I want a straight answer. What in blazes is going on here?"

"We're both oil merchants," one of the Forthwegians said. "Olive, almond, walnut, flax-seed, you name it. Oil. And we were arguing about which way prices were going to go on account of . . ." He paused. The pause stretched. He'd just admitted knowing things weren't going so well for Algarve. That wasn't very smart. Lamely, he finished, ". . . on account of the way things are."

"I'll tell you what you were doing," Bembo said. "You were disturbing the peace, that's what you were doing. Creating a disturbance. That happens to be a crime. We'll have to haul you up before a judge."

Both Forthwegians looked appalled, as he'd known they would. "Isn't there some other arrangement we might make?" asked the oil merchant who'd done most of the talking.

"Aye," Oraste rumbled. "We might not bother with a fornicating judge. We might whale the stuffing out of you ourselves instead." He sounded as if he'd enjoy pounding on the Forthwegians. The reason he sounded that way, as Bembo knew perfectly well, was that he *would* enjoy it.

Unlike Oraste, Bembo didn't usually beat people for the sport of it. He said, "Maybe you boys might find some reason why we wouldn't want to do that."

The oil merchants found several interesting reasons. Those reasons clinked in the constables' belt pouches as they went back to walking their beat. Oraste reached out and hit Bembo in the belly—not much of a punch, but the flesh gave a good deal under his fist. "You're soft," he remarked. "Soft in more ways than one."

"You just want to smash everything flat," Bembo answered. "They're oil merchants. They greased our palms. That's what they're for, right?"

"Funny," Oraste said. "Funny like a man with a wooden leg."

Bembo sent him an injured look. "When we get back to Tricarico, we'll be rich, or close to it, anyway. It's not like we've got a lot to spend our money on here. The wine and the spirits are cheap, and nobody wants to go to the brothel every night."

"Speak for yourself," Oraste said—like any Algarvian, he was vain about his manhood. "The whores here aren't as expensive as they are back home." His lip curled. "Of course, they aren't as pretty as they are back home, either."

Oh, I don't know. Bembo almost said it, remembering his steamy passage with Doldasai. He was vain about his manhood, too. But then he remembered he couldn't talk about that. Nobody'd grabbed her or her mother and father when the Algarvians raided the Kaunian quarter in Gromheort. From that, Bembo figured the blonds had got and used the sorcery that let them look like Forthwegians and slipped out of the quarter before the raids. Nobody'd ever said anything about their disappearance where he could hear, but some high-ranking officers wouldn't be happy that they weren't enjoying what he'd had once. Keeping his mouth shut came no easier for him than for any other boastful Algarvian, but a keen sense of self-preservation made him do it.

Their remaining time on the beat passed easily enough. When they got back to the constabulary barracks, Bembo pounced on the latest edition of the news sheet. "Ha!" he said. "Here's news of the fighting, or of some fighting, anyway."

"What's it say?" Oraste asked.

"I'll read it." Bembo did, in a deep, artificial, portentous voice: " 'In severe defensive struggles southeast of Durrwangen, Algarvian forces inflicted severe casualties on the foe. Despite heavy bombardment by egg-tossers and fierce attacks from Unkerlanter dragons and behemoths, his Majesty's forces withdrew to already prepared rearward positions, yielding only about a mile of ground and shortening their lines in the process.' " He returned to his normal tones to ask Oraste, "What do you make of that?"

His partner pondered, but not for long. "Sounds like a de-mon of a lot of dead soldiers to me."

"Ours or theirs?"

"Both," Oraste said.

Bembo gave forth with a theatrical sigh. "I was hoping you'd tell me something different, because that's what it sounds like to me, too."

"Where is everyone?" Krasta demanded of Colonel Lurcanio as the carriage pulled up in front of Viscount Valnu's house. She gave her Algarvian lover a peeved look. "Are you sure you got the date right?" She hoped—oh, how she hoped—Lurcanio had got it wrong. If he had, she'd never let him live it down.

But he nodded and pointed through the gloom. "A few car-riages are there—do you see?" Even so, his voice was doubt-ful as he added, "I admit, I expected a good many more."

"Is someone else giving another entertainment?" Krasta asked.

Lurcanio shook his head. In dark night, with no street lamps, Krasta could barely see the motion. He said, "No. I would have heard of that. And if by some chance I did not, you would have."

He was right; Krasta realized as much at once. "We'll just have to find out, then, won't we?" she said as the carriage pulled to a stop. "Where everyone else has gone, I mean."

"Aye. So we will." Now Lurcanio's voice had an edge to it. "Perhaps people have not gone anywhere. Perhaps they have simply chosen not to come."

"Don't be ridiculous." Krasta didn't wait for him to hand her down, but descended from the carriage herself and hur-ried toward Valnu's house. Over her shoulder, she added, "Why would anybody be as stupid as that?"

Lurcanio caught up with her faster than she might have wanted. "There are times when you can be quite refreshingly naive," he remarked.

"I don't know what you're talking about," she said in some annoyance.

"I know. It's part of your charm," Lurcanio answered. Krasta would have snapped at him some more, but he'd already rung the bell. A moment later, the door swung open. One of Valnu's servants let them into the front hall. He closed the door behind them before opening the dark curtains at the end of the hallway that kept light from leaking out.

Krasta blinked at the bright lights the curtains revealed. She also blinked at Viscount Valnu, who stood just beyond the curtains. His tunic and kilt were of cloth-of-gold that caught the lamplight and glittered. She wouldn't have wanted to wear such material herself—too gaudy. But Valnu brought it off, not least by appearing to reject the possibility that he might do anything else.

"My lady!" he cried when he saw Krasta. He took her in his arms and kissed her on the cheek. "So good to see you here."

"Spare me your embraces," Lurcanio said dryly as Valnu turned to him. Valnu had been known to kiss him on the cheek, too: Valnu was never one who did anything by halves.

"I obey," he said now, and bowed himself almost double. Krasta had to blink again because of the reflections coruscating from his costume. Then he bowed again, as if intent on showing himself to be even more ceremonious than the average Algarvian. Speaking with unwonted seriousness, he went on, "I am in your debt, your Excellency, and I am not ashamed to own it. Were it not for your good offices, I would probably be languishing in some nasty cell."

"I had little to do with it," Lurcanio answered. "Some of your *friends*"—he put a certain ironic emphasis on the word—"undoubtedly helped you more."

Valnu didn't pretend to misunderstand him. "But you, sir, unlike they, were known to be disinterested."

"Disinterested? No." Lurcanio shook his head. "Uninterested? There I must say aye. A nice show of the difference in meaning between the two words, eh?"

"Your Excellency, you speak my language with a scholar's precision," Valnu said.

"I beg leave to doubt it," Lurcanio replied. But he didn't sound displeased. He took Krasta's arm and led her past their host. Krasta gave Valnu a bright, even a glowing, smile. She kept trying to forget about the trouble in which she'd landed herself for trifling with him and letting him trifle with her. She probably would have succeeded, too, had Lurcanio not found such a fitting way to punish her. Few lessons stuck with her for long, but that one, at least, had left her cautious.

As for Valnu, his long, lean face stayed sober. Maybe he really did think he owed Lurcanio a debt. Or maybe he didn't feel like taking the chance of getting caught again, either.

His cook and his cellarer had set out an elegant and lavish display, as they always did. Krasta hadn't eaten supper. Even so, she hesitated to go over and get anything. The guests already here left her dismayed. Oh, not the Algarvian officers and their Valmieran mistresses: she was used to them. But the few Valmieran nobles who'd come were either of the fierce and brutal sort or else were those who fawned on the Algarvians the most extravagantly.

"Where are all the *interesting* people?" Krasta murmured to Lurcanio.

Her Algarvian lover had also been surveying the crowd—not that it unduly crowded Valnu's reception hall. Lurcanio sighed. "Fair-weather friends, most of them."

"What do you mean?" Krasta asked.

"What do I mean? I mean that too many of them are wondering about their choices." Lurcanio let out a scornful sniff. "Mark my words, my dear: no one can recover his virginity as easily as that."

He was being obscure again. Krasta hated it when he wouldn't come out and say what he meant. *Powers above,* she thought. *I always say what I mean.* But she'd already asked what he meant once. She had too much pride—and too much dread of his sharp tongue—to embarrass herself by asking again.

With another sigh, Colonel Lurcanio said, "We might as well drink. After a while at the bar, things may look better."

"Why, so they may." Krasta had improved plenty of gatherings with enough porter or wine or, for severe cases, wormwood-laced brandy. This festivity, if that was what it was, looked like a severe case. Even so, she started with red wine, reasoning she could always move up to something stronger later on.

Lurcanio raised an eyebrow when she gave the tapman her order. Maybe he'd expected her to drink herself blind in short order. She smiled at him over the top of her goblet. She didn't want to be too predictable. Smiling himself, a little quizzically, Lurcanio asked for red wine, too. "To what shall we drink?" he asked.

That startled Krasta; he usually proposed toasts himself rather than asking her for them. She raised her goblet. "To good company!" she said, and then, under her breath, "May we find some soon." She drank.

With a laugh, so did Lurcanio. Then the laughter slipped from his face. "I think we are about to have company, whether good or otherwise." He bowed to the Valmieran nobleman approaching him. "Good evening sir. I do not believe we have met. I am Lurcanio. I present to you also my companion here, the Marchioness Krasta."

"Right pleased to meet you, Colonel," the Valmieran said in a backwoods dialect. "I'm Viscount Terbatu." He held out his hand. Lurcanio, in Algarvian fashion, clasped his wrist. Except for a brief nod, Terbatu ignored Krasta. That suited her fine. He looked more like a tavern brawler than a viscount: his nose bent sideways, and one of his ears was missing half the lobe. She drank more wine, content to let Lurcanio deal with him.

"I am pleased to make your acquaintance, your Excellency," Lurcanio said, polite as a cat. "And what can I do for you?" By his tone, he assumed Terbatu would want him to do something.

"Fight," Terbatu growled.

"I beg your pardon?" Lurcanio said. And then, though he remained a polished gentleman, he showed he was polished steel. Drawing himself a little straighter, he asked, "Do we need to continue this conversation through friends? If so, I shall make every effort to give satisfaction."

By that, even Krasta understood him to mean, *I'll kill you.* She thought he could do it, too, and without breaking a sweat. Terbatu put her in mind of a bad-tempered hound barking at a viper. He was liable to be dead before he knew it.

But he shook his close-cropped head. "No, no, no. Not fight you, sir—not that at all. Fight for you, I meant. Valmierans fighting for Algarve. I've tried to get your people to let me raise a regiment and go hunting Unkerlanters, but nobody wants to pay any attention to me. Who do I have to kill to make you wake up?"

Lurcanio rocked back on his heels. To Krasta, who knew him well, that showed astonishment. To Terbatu, it might have shown nothing at all. Krasta was astonished, too, and not so good at hiding it as Lurcanio. "You want to fight for the redheads?" she blurted, careless of her lover beside her. How could any man of Kaunian blood want to do that when Mezentio's men were murdering the Kaunians from Forthweg for the sake of their life energy?

Terbatu said, "I'm not wild about the notion of fighting for Algarve." He nodded to Lurcanio. "No offense, your Excellency." Turning back to Krasta, he went on, "But the Unkerlanters, now, the Unkerlanters deserve smashing up. If ever a kingdom was a boil on the arse of mankind, Unkerlant's the one. Bloody big boil, too," he added, looking to Lurcanio again.

"It certainly is," the Algarvian colonel agreed. After a moment, he bowed to Terbatu. "You must understand, sir, that I appreciate the spirit in which you offer yourself and whatever countrymen who might fight under your banner. There are, however, certain practical difficulties of which I doubt you are aware."

You're a Kaunian, and we're already killing Kaunians to fight Unkerlant. That was what Lurcanio meant. Krasta knew it. Again, she had all she could do not to shout it at the top of her lungs.

And then Terbatu said, "Wouldn't you sooner have live men fighting on your side than dead ones, Colonel?"

Krasta stared at him. So did Lurcanio. After a long, long pause, Lurcanio said, "I have no idea what you are talking about, my lord Viscount."

The backwoods noble started to get angry. Then, grudgingly, he checked himself and nodded. "I suppose I see why you have to say such things, your Excellency. But we're men of the world, eh, you and I?"

Lurcanio certainly was. He didn't look as if he wanted to admit any such thing about Terbatu. Krasta didn't blame him there. He let another pause stretch longer than it should have, then said, "In any case, your Excellency, I am not the man to hear such proposals. You must put them to Grand Duke Ivone, my sovereign's military governor for Valmiera. If you will excuse me—" Rather pointedly, he took Krasta by the elbow and steered her away.

He also left Valnu's mansion earlier than he might have. "I trust you enjoyed yourself, your Excellency, milady?" Valnu said.

Krasta was willing to keep silent for politeness' sake. Lurcanio said, "I am glad to find you such a trusting soul." Once out of the mansion and into his carriage, he asked Krasta, "Do you know what that Terbatu fellow was talking about back there?"

Cautiously—ever so cautiously—she answered, "I think a lot of people have heard things. Nobody knows how much to believe." The first sentence was true, the second anything but: she, at least, knew exactly how much to believe.

"A good working rule," Lurcanio said, "is to believe as little as one possibly can." Krasta laughed a nervous laugh, but he was plainly serious. And if a crack like that didn't mark him as a man of the world, what would?

King Shazli of Zuwayza leaned toward his foreign minister. "The question, I gather, is no longer whether Algarve can go forward against Unkerlant, but whether she can keep Unkerlant from going forward against her."

"No, your Majesty." Hajjaj solemnly shook his head.

"No?" Shazli frowned. "This is what I have understood

from everything you and General Ikhshid have been telling me. Am I mistaken?"

"I'm afraid you are, your Majesty." Hajjaj wondered how he would have been able to say such a thing to King Swemmel. Well, no: actually, he didn't wonder. He knew it would have been impossible. As things were, he had no trouble continuing, "Unkerlant *will* go forward against Algarve this summer. This question is, how far?"

"Oh," King Shazli said, in the tones of a man who might have expected better but who saw the difference between what he'd expected and what lay before him. "As bad as that?"

"I would be lying if I told you otherwise," Hajjaj said. "Down in the south, our ally's attack did not do everything the Algarvians had hoped it would. Now it's Swemmel's turn, and we'll have to see what he can do. One hopes for the best while preparing for the worst."

"A good way to go about things generally, wouldn't you say?" Shazli remarked. Hajjaj nodded. He had to work hard to keep his face straight, but he managed. He'd been saying such things to his young sovereign for many years. Now the king was repeating them back to him. Few things gave a man more satisfaction than knowing someone had listened to him. But then, with the air of someone grasping for straws, Shazli went on, "Things are quiet here in the north."

"So they are—for now," Hajjaj agreed. "For the past two summers, the greatest fight in Unkerlant has been down in the south. But I would say that, at the moment, the Algarvians don't know how long that will last, and neither do we. The only people who know are King Swemmel and perhaps Marshal Rathar."

Shazli poured more date wine into his goblet. He gulped it down. "If the blow falls here, can the Algarvians withstand it? By the powers above, your Excellency, if the blow falls here, can *we* withstand it?"

"From my conversations with General Ikhshid, he is reasonably confident the blow will not fall on us any time soon," Hajjaj replied.

"Well, that's something of a relief, anyhow," the king said.

"So it is." Hajjaj didn't think he needed to tell Shazli Ikhshid's reason for holding that opinion: that Zuwayza was only a distraction to Unkerlant, and Algarve the real fight. Hajjaj did say, "The Algarvians are the ones who will best know their situation in this part of the world."

"How much do you suppose Balastro would tell you?" King Shazli asked.

"As little as he could," Hajjaj said with a smile. Shazli smiled, too, though neither of them seemed much amused. Hajjaj added, "Sometimes, of course, what he doesn't say is as illuminating as what he does. Shall I consult with him, then?"

"Use your own best judgment," Shazli answered. "By the nature of things, you will be seeing him before too long. So long as the blow has not fallen, when you do will probably be time enough." He gnawed at the inside of his lower lip. "And if the blow does fall, it will tell us what we need to know." He softly clapped his hands together, a gesture of dismissal.

Hajjaj rose and bowed and left his sovereign's presence. Even the thick mud-brick walls of Shazli's palace couldn't hold out all the savage heat, not at this season of the year. Servitors strolled rather than bustling; sweat streamed down their bare hides. Hajjaj was not immune to sweat. Indeed, he was sweating as much from what he knew as from the weather.

When he got back to his own office, his secretary bowed and asked, "And how are things, your Excellency?"

"You know at least as well as I do," Hajjaj said.

"Maybe I do," Qutuz answered. "I was hoping they would be rather better than that, though."

"Heh," Hajjaj said, and then, "What have we here?" He pointed to an envelope on his desk.

"One of Minister Horthy's aides brought it by a few minutes ago," Qutuz said.

"Horthy, eh?" Hajjaj said. Qutuz nodded. What went through Hajjaj's mind was, *It could be worse.* It could have been an invitation from Marquis Balastro. Or it could have come from Minister Iskakis of Yanina. Horthy of Gyongyos was a large, solid man not given to displays of temper—he made a good host.

Like any diplomat, Horthy wrote in classical Kaunian, saying, *Your company at a reception at the ministry at sunset day after tomorrow would be greatly appreciated.* Hajjaj studied the note in some bemusement. In the days of the Kaunian Empire, his ancestors had traded with the blonds, but that was all. In far-off Gyongyos, the Kaunian Empire had been the stuff of myth and legend, as Gyongyos had been to the ancient Kaunians. Yet he and Horthy, who had no other tongue in common, shared that one.

There was one irony. Another, of course, was that Zuwayza and Gyongyos shared Algarve as an ally. Considering what King Mezentio's soldiers and mages were doing to the Kaunians of Forthweg, Hajjaj sometimes felt guilty for using their language.

"May I see, your Excellency?" Qutuz asked, and Hajjaj passed him the leaf of paper. His secretary read it, then found the next logical question: "When I reply for you, what shall I say?"

"Tell him I accept with pleasure, and look forward to seeing him," Hajjaj said. His secretary nodded and went off to draft the note for his signature.

Hajjaj sighed. Balastro would be at Horthy's reception. So would Iskakis. The diplomatic community in Bishah was shrunken these days. The ministers for Unkerlant and Forthweg, Valmiera and Jelgava, Sibiu and Lagoas and Kuusamo stood empty these days. Little Ortah, the only neutral kingdom left in the world, looked after the buildings and after the interests of the kingdoms.

From his office in the anteroom to Hajjaj's, Qutuz asked, "Do you suppose Iskakis will bring his wife?"

"I'm sure I don't know, though he often does," Hajjaj replied. "He likes to show her off."

"That's true," his secretary said. "As far as anyone can tell, though, showing her off is all he likes to do with her." He sighed. "It's a pity, really. I don't care how pale she is—she's a lovely woman."

"She certainly is," Hajjaj agreed. "Iskakis wears a mask and wants everyone to take it for his face." No matter how lovely his wife was, Iskakis preferred boys. That didn't particularly bother Hajjaj. The Yaninan minister's hypocrisy did.

"What sort of clothes will you wear?" Qutuz asked.

"Oh, by the powers above!" the Zuwayzi foreign minister exclaimed. That problem wouldn't arise at a Zuwayzi feast, where no one would wear anything between hat and sandals. "Algarvian-style will do," Hajjaj said at last. "We are all friends of Algarve's, however . . . exciting the prospect is these days."

Thus it was that, two days later, he rolled through the streets of Bishah in a royal carriage while wearing one of his unstylish Algarvian outfits. His own countrymen stared at him. A few of them sent him pitying looks—even though the sun had sunk low, the day remained viciously hot. And someone sent up a thoroughly disrespectful shout: "Go home, you old fool! Have you lost all of your mind?" Patting his sweaty face with a linen handkerchief, Hajjaj wondered about that himself.

The Gyongyosian guards outside the ministry were sweating, too. No one shouted at them. With their fierce, leonine faces—even more to the point, with the sticks slung on their backs—they looked ready to blaze anyone who gave them a hard time. What with Gyongyosians' reputation as a warrior race, they might have done it.

But they bowed to Hajjaj. One of them spoke in their twittering language. The other proved to know at least a few words of Zuwayzi, for he said, "Welcome, your Excellency," and stood aside to let the foreign minister pass.

Inside the Gyongyosian ministry, Horthy clasped Hajjaj's hand and said the same thing in classical Kaunian. With his thick, gray-streaked tawny beard, he too put Hajjaj in mind of a lion. He was a cultured lion, though, for he continued in the same language: "Choose anything under the stars here that makes you happy."

"You are too kind," Hajjaj murmured, looking around in fascination. He didn't come here very often. Whenever he did, he thought himself transported to the exotic lands of the uttermost west. The squared-off, heavy furniture, the pictures of snowy mountains on the walls with their captions in an angular script he could not read, the crossed axes that formed so large a part of the decoration, all reminded him how different these folk were from his own.

Even Horthy's invitation felt strange. Alone among civilized folk, the Gyongyosians cared nothing for the powers above and the powers below. They measured their life in this world and the world to come by the stars. Hajjaj had never understood that, but there were a great many more urgent things in the world that he didn't understand, either.

He got himself a glass of wine: grape wine, for date wine was as alien to Gyongyos as swearing by the stars was to him. He took a chicken leg roasted with Gyongyosian spices, chief among them a reddish powder that reminded him a little of pepper. Nothing quite like it grew in Zuwayza.

One of the Gyongyosians was an excellent fiddler. He strolled through the reception hall, coaxing fiery music from his instrument as he went. Hajjaj had never imagined going to war behind a fiddle—drums and blaring horns were Zuwayza's martial instruments—but this fellow showed him a different way might be as good as his own.

There was Iskakis of Yanina, in earnest conversation with a handsome junior military attaché from Gyongyos. And there, over in a corner, stood Balastro of Algarve, in earnest conversation with Iskakis' lovely young wife. Hajjaj strolled over to them. He had not the slightest intention of asking about the military situation in southern Unkerlant, not at the moment. Instead, he hoped to head off trouble before it started. Iskakis might not be passionately devoted to her as a lover, but he did have a certain pride of possession. And Balastro . . . Balastro was an Algarvian, which meant, where women were concerned, he was trouble waiting to happen.

Seeing Hajjaj approach, he bowed. "Good evening, your Excellency," he said. "Coming to save me from myself?"

"By all appearances, someone should," Hajjaj replied.

"And what would you save me from, your Excellency?"

Iskakis' wife asked in fair Algarvian. "The marquis, at least, seeks to save me from boredom."

"Is that what they call it these days?" Hajjaj murmured. Rather louder, he added, "Milady, I might hope to help save you from yourself."

Not caring in the least who heard her, she answered, "I would like you better if you looked to save me from my husband." With a sigh, Hajjaj went off to find himself another goblet of wine. Diplomacy had failed here, as it had all over Derlavai.

Part of Pekka wished she'd never gone home to Kajaani, never spent most of her leave in her husband's arms. It made coming back to the Naantali district and the rigors of theoretical sorcery all the harder. Another part of her, though, quite simply wished she hadn't come back. The wilderness seemed doubly desolate after seeing a city, even a moderate-sized one like Kajaani.

And she had trouble returning to the narrow world that centered on the newly built hostel and the blockhouse and the journey between them. Everything felt tiny, artificial. People rubbed her raw without intending to do it. Or, as in the case of Ilmarinen, they meant every bit of it.

"No, we are not going to do that," she told the elderly theoretical sorcerer. She sounded sharper than she'd intended. "I've told you why not before—we're trying to make a weapon here. We can investigate the theoretical aspects that haven't got anything to do with weapons when we have more time. Till then, we have to concentrate on what needs doing most."

"How can we be sure of what that is unless we investigate widely?" Ilmarinen demanded.

"We don't have the people to investigate as widely as you want," Pekka answered. "We barely have the people to investigate all the ley lines we're on right now. There aren't enough theoretical sorcerers in the whole land of the Seven Princes to do everything you want done."

"You're a professor yourself," Ilmarinen said. "On whom

do you blame that?" Sure enough, he was being as difficult as he could.

Pekka refused to rise to the bait. "I don't blame anyone. It's just the way things are." She smiled an unpleasant smile. If Ilmarinen felt like being difficult, she could be difficult, too. "Or would you like us to bring in more mages from Lagoas? That might give us the manpower we'd need."

"And it might give Lagoas the edge against us in any trouble we have with them," Ilmarinen answered. Then he paused and scowled at Pekka. "It might give you the chance to poke pins in me to see me jump, too."

"Master Ilmarinen, when you are contrary with numbers, wonderful things happen," Pekka said. "You see things no one else can—you see things where no one else would think to look. But when you are contrary with people, you drive everyone around you mad. I know you do at least some of it for your amusement, but we haven't got time for that, either. Who knows what the Algarvians are doing?"

"I do," he answered at once. "They're retreating. I wonder how good they'll be at it. They haven't had much practice."

That wasn't what she'd meant. Ilmarinen doubtless knew as much, too. He hated the Algarvians' murderous magecraft perhaps even more than she did. But she thought—she hoped—he'd made the crack as a sort of peace offering. She answered in that spirit, saying, "May they learn it, and learn it well."

"No." Ilmarinen shook his head. "May they learn it, and learn it badly. That will cost them more." He called down imaginative curses on the heads of King Mezentio and all his ancestors. Before long, in spite of everything, he had Pekka giggling. Then, making her gladder still, he left without arguing anymore for abstract research at the expense of military research.

"He has lost his sense of proportion," Pekka told Fernao at breakfast the next morning. The Lagoan mage probably would have understood had she spoken Kuusaman; he'd made new strides in her language even in the short time she'd been away. But she spoke classical Kaunian anyhow—using the international language of scholarship helped give her some distance from what had gone on.

Fernao spooned up more barley porridge seasoned with butter and salt. His answer also came in classical Kaunian: "That is why you head this project and he does not, or does not anymore. You can supply that sense of proportion, even if he has lost it."

"I suppose so." Pekka sighed. "But I wish he would remember that, too. Of course, if he remembered such things, I would not have to lead the way here now. I rather wish I did not."

"Someone must," Fernao said. "You are the best suited."

"Maybe." Pekka had a little bone from her grilled smoked herring stuck between two teeth. After worrying it free with her tongue, she said, "I had hoped more would be done while I was away."

"I am sorry," Fernao said, as if the failure were his fault.

Pekka didn't think that was true. She knew, however, that Fernao was the only theoretical sorcerer who showed any sign of taking responsibility for the lull. She said, "Maybe you should have been in charge while I went to Kajaani."

"I doubt it," he answered. "I would not care to take orders from a Kuusaman in Lagoas. No wonder the reverse holds true here."

"Why would you not want to take orders from one of my countrymen in your kingdom?" Pekka asked. "If the Kuusaman were best suited to lead the job, whatever it was . . ."

Fernao laughed, which bewildered Pekka. He said, "I think you may be too sane for your own good."

That made her laugh in turn. Before she could say anything, a crystallomancer came into the dining hall calling her name. "I'm here," she said, getting to her feet. "What is it?"

"A message for you," the young woman answered stolidly.

"I suspected that, aye," Pekka said. "But from whom? My son? My husband? My laundryman back in Kajaani?" That was a bit of sarcasm of which she thought even Ilmarinen might have approved.

"It's Prince Juhainen, Mistress Pekka," the crystallo-mancer said.

"What?" Pekka squeaked. "Powers above, why didn't you say so?" She rushed out of the dining hall past the crystallo-mancer, not bothering to wait for her. The woman hurried after her, stammering apologies. Pekka ignored those, but dashed into the room where the crystals were kept. Sure enough, Prince Juhainen's image waited in one of them. She went down to a knee for a moment before asking, "How may I serve you, your Highness?"

"Along with two of my colleagues, I propose visiting your establishment soon," the young prince answered. "We have spent a good deal of money over in Naantali, and we want to discover what we are getting for it."

"I see," Pekka said. "It shall be as you say, of course."

"For which I thank you," Juhainen said. "We expect to be there day after tomorrow, and hope to see something interest-ing."

"Very well, your Highness. Thank you for letting me know you are coming," Pekka said. "We shall try our best to show you what we've been doing, and, if you like, we can also dis-cuss where we hope to go from here."

Juhainen smiled. "Good. You have taken the words out of my mouth. I look forward to seeing you in two days' time, then." He nodded to someone whose image Pekka couldn't see—probably his own crystallomancer. A moment later, his image vanished.

"A princely visit!" the crystallomancer at Naantali ex-claimed. "How exciting!"

"A princely visit!" Pekka echoed. "How appalling!" Per-forming under the eyes of Siuntio and Ilmarinen had been in-timidating in one way: if she blundered, she would humiliate herself in front of the mages she admired most. She didn't ad-mire Juhainen and his fellow princes nearly so much as she did her peers. But performing in front of them would be in-timidating, too. If they didn't like what they saw, they could end the project with a snap of the fingers. The power of the purse wasn't sorcerous, but was potent nonetheless.

She hurried out of the chamber with the crystals and started telling every mage she knew. Her colleagues reacted with the same mixture of surprise, anticipation, and dread that she felt. When Ilmarinen said, "With any luck at all, once they see what we're up to, we can all go home," Pekka laughed, too. Ilmarinen sardonic was far preferable to Ilmarinen whining and nagging.

Fernao asked a truly relevant question: "Can they get here by day after tomorrow, with this hostel out in the middle of nowhere?"

"I do not know," Pekka admitted. "But we are going to assume they can. If we are ready and they are not here, that is one thing. If they are here and we are not ready, that is something else again—something I do not intend to let happen."

They readied the animals they would use in the experiment. The secondary sorcerers practiced their projection spells. All the theoretical sorcerers but Pekka prepared more counterspells in case something went wrong with her incantation. She went over the charm again and again. *I will not drop a line this time,* she thought fiercely. *By the powers above, I will not.*

The princes did arrive on the appointed day, though late. They brought with them a fresh squad of protective mages. That, to Pekka, made excellent sense. The Algarvians hadn't struck here since their first heavy blow, but there was no guarantee that they wouldn't.

With Juhainen came Parainen of Kihlanki in the far east and Renavall, in whose domain the district of Naantali lay. Pekka went to one knee before each of them. She said, "By your leave, your Highnesses, we shall demonstrate our work tomorrow. For tonight, you are welcome to share our hostel here and see how we live."

Prince Renavall chuckled and remarked, "This is probably an effort to extort finer quarters from us." Pekka and the other mages laughed. So did Juhainen. Prince Parainen only nodded, as if his colleague had said what he was already thinking.

Ilmarinen said, "If we can survive here for months on end,

even princes are a good bet to last the night." In a lot of kingdoms, such a crack would have made him a good bet not to last the night. In easygoing Kuusamo, Juhainen and Renavall laughed again. Even Parainen, who worried more about Gyongyos than the Algarvian threat against which the mages were so concerned, managed a smile.

Sure enough, all three princes came down to breakfast the next morning and accompanied the team of sorcerers to the blockhouse. They and their protective mages badly crowded it, and they suffered most because of that, since Pekka insisted on stationing them against the walls where they wouldn't be in the way. "You came to see the sorcery succeed—is that not so, your Highnesses?" she said with her sweetest smile. "And so you could not possibly want to interfere with those who perform it, could you?" Juhainen shrugged. Renavall smiled. Parainen gave back only stony silence.

We had better succeed now, Pekka thought. She recited the Kuusaman ritual that marked the beginning of any sorcerous enterprise in her land. As always, it helped steady her. "I begin," she said abruptly, and did.

For a demonstration for three of the Seven, they broke no new ground. She used a spell they had tested before, and gave it every ounce of concentration she had. The rumbling roar of suddenly released energies shook the blockhouse. Stones and clods of dirt thudded down on the roof, even though the secondary sorcerers had transferred the effect of the spell to the animal cages a couple of miles away.

"May we see what you wrought?" Parainen asked when silence and steadiness returned.

Glad he was the one who'd asked and even gladder he sounded less sure of himself now, Pekka said, "By all means." Ilmarinen caught her eye. She shook her head. This was not the time or place for him to expound on his hypothesis of what they were really doing. To her relief, he subsided.

To her even greater relief, the princes gaped in undisguised wonder at the new crater gouged from the soil of Naantali. Parainen said the two words Pekka most wanted to hear from him: "Carry on."

*　*　*

Numbers had always been Ealstan's friends. He was, after all, a bookkeeper's son, and now a bookkeeper of growing experience himself. He saw patterns in what looked like chaos to most people, as mages did when they developed spells. And when he found chaos in what should have been order, he wanted to root it out.

Pybba's books drove him mad. Money kept right on leaking out of the pottery magnate's business. Ealstan was morally certain it went to resist the Algarvians, but Pybba had paid him a hefty sum not to notice. Vanai didn't want him poking his nose into things, either.

And so, when he probed the mystery, he had to be most discreet. He told neither his boss nor his wife what he was doing. He just quietly kept doing it. *My father would act the same way,* he thought. *He'd want to get to the bottom of things, even if somebody told him not to. Maybe especially if somebody told him not to.*

More of the money vanished in the invoices at one of Pybba's warehouses than from any other place in the magnate's business. Ealstan had never been to that warehouse, which lay on the outskirts of Eoforwic. He thought about asking Pybba if he might go look things over there, thought about it and shook his head. His boss would see right through him if he did.

When he went to look the place over, then, he went on his day off. He wore a grimy old tunic and a battered straw hat against the sun. As he headed out the door, Vanai said, "You look like you're ready for a day of tavern crawling."

He nodded. "That's right. I'm going to come home drunk and beat you, the way Forthwegian husbands do."

Even in sorcerous disguise as a swarthy Forthwegian, Vanai blushed. Kaunians often perceived Forthwegians as drunks. In modern Kaunian literature in Forthweg, the drunken Forthwegian was as much a cliché as the sly or aloof Kaunian was in Forthwegian romances. Vanai said, "You're the only Forthwegian husband I know, and I like the things you do."

"That's good." A wide, foolish grin spread over Ealstan's face. He couldn't get enough praise from his wife. "I'm off," he said, and headed out the door.

To get to that warehouse, he could either walk for an hour or ride most of the way on a ley-line caravan. Without hesitation, he chose the caravan. He tossed a small silver bit into the fare box—everything was outrageously expensive under the Algarvians—and took his seat.

Because the fare was high, the caravan wasn't close to full. As best he could tell, the car hadn't been cleaned since the Algarvians took Eoforwic, or maybe since the Unkerlanters took it a year and a half before that. Someone had slit the upholstery of the seat on which Ealstan sat. Someone else had pulled out most of the stuffing. What was left protruded from the gashes in the fabric in pathetic tufts. The seat next to Ealstan's had no padding at all, and no upholstery left, either. None of the windows in the car would open, but several had no glass, so that evened out.

Getting out of the car was something of a relief, at least till Ealstan saw what sort of neighborhood it was. He marveled that Pybba would put a warehouse here; it seemed the sort of place where breaking crockery was the favorite local sport. No matter how shabby Ealstan looked, he had the feeling he'd overdressed.

A drunk came up and whined for money. Ealstan walked past as if the beggar didn't exist, a technique he'd had to perfect since coming to Eoforwic. The drunk cursed him, but only halfheartedly—a lot of people must have walked past him over the last few years. Down an alley, a dog barked and then snarled, a sound like ripping canvas. Ealstan bent down and grabbed a stout olive branch. To his relief, the dog didn't come out after him. He held on to the branch anyhow, and methodically pulled twigs from it. It was better than nothing against beasts with four or two legs.

He had no trouble finding the warehouse. PYBBA'S POT-TERY, shouted a tall sign with red letters on a yellow ground. Pybba never did anything by halves, which was part of what made him so successful. People all over western Forthweg knew who he was. His pots and cups and basins and plates might not have been better than anyone else's, but they were better known. That counted for at least as much as quality.

Now that Ealstan had got here, he wondered what the demon to do next. How in blazes could he hope to find out why the money from Pybba's booming business looked to be leaking here? He doubted the clerks would say, if they even knew. Maybe he should have gone out and got drunk instead. He would have had more fun, even if beating his wife wasn't part of it. He could hardly have had less.

As he walked up to the warehouse entrance, he was surprised to see a couple of guards there. He shouldn't have been; he remembered the line item for their salary. But a line item was one thing. A couple of burly men carrying bludgeons was something else again. Ealstan made a point of setting down his olive branch before he got close to them.

"Hello, friend," one of them said with a polite nod and a smile that didn't quite reach his eyes. "What can we do for you today?"

"Want to buy some dishes," Ealstan answered. "My wife keeps throwing 'em at me, and we're running out."

The guards relaxed and laughed. The one who'd spoken before said, "This is the place, all right. I used to hang around with a woman like that. Aye, she was good in bed, but after a while she got to be more trouble than she was worth, you know what I mean?"

Ealstan nodded. "I hear what you're saying, but you know how it is." His shrug suggested a man who was putting up with a lot for the sake of a woman. Laughing again, the guards stepped aside to let him into the warehouse.

After the bright sunshine outside, Ealstan's eyes needed a moment to adjust to the gloom within. When they did, he gaped at aisle on aisle of crockery, every one with a sign that said SALE! or MARKED DOWN! or PYBBA'S LOW PRICES! As best Ealstan could tell, his boss didn't miss a trick.

He couldn't stand there gaping very long. A woman said, "Get out of the way," and pushed past him before he could.

She made a beeline for a display of cups and saucers with a mustard-yellow glaze. Ealstan thought them very ugly, but Pybba was going to rack up a sale no matter what he thought.

Ealstan ambled up one aisle and down the next, making as if to examine more different kinds of pottery than he'd ever seen under one roof. Nothing he spotted on the floor of the main room gave him the slightest hint about where Pybba's money was going. He hadn't really thought anything would. Anything obvious to him would be obvious to other people, too—to the Algarvians, if Pybba really was trying to fight them.

Several doors led into back rooms. Ealstan eyed those as he pretended to examine dishes. Going through one of them might tell him what he wanted to know. It also might land him in more trouble than he could afford. Whatever he did, he wouldn't get the chance to go through more than one. He was sure of that.

Which one, then? From this side, they all looked alike. He chose the one in the middle of the back wall, for not better reason than its being in the middle. After fidgeting in front of it for a minute or two, he opened it and walked into the back room. A man sitting at a desk looked up at him. Ealstan scowled and said, "That fellow out there said this was where the jakes were at."

"Well, they bloody well aren't," the man replied in some annoyance.

"You don't have to bite my head off," Ealstan said, and closed the door behind him. He chose four dinner plates in a flowered pattern, paid for them, and left. The guards nodded to him as he went. He walked away from the ley-line caravan stop, not toward it. Once he was around the corner from the warehouse, he doubled back and found his way to the stop.

To his relief, a caravan car glided up a few minutes after he got to that corner. He put another small silver coin in the fare box and sat down for the ride back to the heart of Eoforwic. The plates rattled against one another in his lap.

A man sitting across the aisle pointed to them and said, "Powers below eat me if you didn't get those at Pybba's."

"Best prices in town," Ealstan answered—one of the many slogans Pybba used to promote himself and his business.

"That's the truth," the other passenger said. "I've bought plenty from him myself."

"Who hasn't?" Ealstan said. Nobody gave him any trouble the rest of the way home, though a couple more people asked if he'd got his plates from Pybba. By the time he got off at the stop closest to his flat, he'd started to think his boss could have occupied all of Forthweg if the Algarvians hadn't beaten him to it.

Vanai wasn't deceived when he brought the plates home. She asked, "Did you learn anything while you were snooping around?"

"Well, no," Ealstan admitted, "but I didn't know I wouldn't before I started out." He was ready to do a more thorough job of defending himself than that, but Vanai only sighed and dropped the subject. That left him feeling bloated: he had what he thought a pretty good argument trapped inside him, but it couldn't get out.

As he went off to cast accounts for Pybba the next morning, he decided that argument could stay right where it was. It would have done him no good had he had to use it to sweeten his boss. Pybba was not a man arguments could sweeten. The only arguments he listened to were his own.

"About time you got here," he shouted when Ealstan walked into his office. Ealstan wasn't late. He was, if anything, early. But Pybba was there before him. Pybba was there before everybody. He had a wife and family, but Ealstan wondered if they ever saw him.

That, though, was Pybba's worry. Ealstan settled down and got to work. Before long, Pybba started shouting at somebody else. He had to shout at someone. The louder he yelled, the more certain he seemed that he was alive.

Halfway through the day, somebody said, "Oh, hello," to Ealstan. He looked up from endless columns of numbers and saw the man who'd been behind the desk in that back room at the potter warehouse. The fellow went on, "I didn't know you worked for Pybba, too."

Pybba overheard. Despite the racket he always made, he overheard a lot. Pointing to Ealstan, he asked the other man, "You know him?"

"I don't really know him, no," the man replied. "Saw him at the warehouse yesterday, though. He was looking for the jakes."

"*Was* he?" Pybba rumbled. He shook his head in what looked like real regret, then jerked his thumb from Ealstan toward the door. The gesture was unmistakable, but he added two words anyhow: "You're fired."

Fourteen

Skarnu had no trouble ambling along a road in southern Valmiera as a peasant would have done. He didn't look to be in much of a hurry, but mile after mile disappeared behind him. That wasn't so bad. He wished even more, though, that Amatu would disappear behind him.

No such luck there. The noble who'd come back from Lagoan exile stuck like a burr, and was just about as irritating. Not only that—Skarnu feared that Amatu would get both of them caught by the Algarvians or by the Valmieran constables who did their bidding. Amatu couldn't walk like a peasant, not—literally—to save his life. The concept of ambling seemed alien to him. He marched, and if he didn't march, he strutted. He might almost have been an Algarvian himself, as far as swagger went.

"Maybe we ought to put some pebbles in your shoes," Skarnu said in something close to despair.

Amatu looked down his nose at him—not easy, when Skarnu stood several inches taller. "Maybe you ought to let me be what I am, and not carp so much about it," he replied, his voice dripping aristocratic hauteur.

He risked giving himself away every time he opened his mouth, too. Skarnu had trouble putting on a rustic accent. But by not saying much, and by speaking in understatements when he did talk, he got by. Amatu, on the other hand, always overacted. He might have been the foolish, foppish noble in a bad play.

Back before the war, Skarnu hadn't thought such people really existed. He supposed Amatu had acted the same way then. Powers above, he'd probably acted the same way himself. But it hadn't mattered in those days, not among the aristocracy of Priekule. Now it did. Skarnu had adapted. As far as Amatu was concerned, adapting meant betraying his class.

"Being what you are is one thing," Skarnu said. "Getting me caught because you won't see reason is something else again."

"You haven't got caught yet, have you?" Amatu said.

"No thanks to you," Skarnu retorted. "You keep trying to stick your neck—and mine—in the noose."

"You keep saying that," Amatu answered. "If there's so bloody much truth to it, how come I'm still running around loose when the Algarvians grabbed everybody in the underground in Ventspils—everybody who knew *just* what he was doing?"

"How come? I'll tell you how come," Skarnu said savagely. "Because you were with me when we came back to our building, that's how come. If you hadn't been, you would have strolled right up to the flat where we were staying—and right into the redheads' arms, too. Or had you forgotten that, your Excellency?"

He used Amatu's title of respect with as much scorn as an angry commoner might have. And he succeeded in angering the returned exile, too. "I'd have done fine without you," Amatu snarled. "For that matter, I can still do fine without you. If you want me to go off on my own, I'm ready. I'm more than ready."

Part of Skarnu—a large, selfish part of Skarnu—wanted nothing more. But the rest made him answer, "You wouldn't last an hour on your own. And when the Algarvians nailed you—and they would—they'd squeeze out everything you knew, and then they'd come after me."

"You're not my mother," Amatu said. "I'm telling you they wouldn't catch me."

"And I'm telling you—" Skarnu broke off. Two Algarvians on unicorns came around a bend in the road a couple hundred yards ahead. Skarnu lowered his voice: "I'm telling you to walk soft now, by the powers above, if you want to keep breathing."

He wondered if Amatu would have the least idea what he was talking about. But the returned exile had spotted Mezentio's men, too. Amatu hunched his shoulders forward and pulled his head down. That didn't make him walk like a peasant. It made him walk like somebody who hated Algarvians and was trying not to show it.

And, sure as sunrise following morning twilight, it made the redheads notice him. They reined in as they came up to the two Valmierans walking along the road. Both of them had their hands on their sticks. One spoke to Amatu in pretty good Valmieran: "What's chewing on you, pal?"

Before Amatu could speak, Skarnu did it for him. "We just came from a cockfight," he said. "My cousin here lost more silver than he's got." He sadly shook his head at Amatu. "I told you that bird wasn't good for anything but chicken stew. Would you listen? Not likely."

Amatu glared at him. But then, given what he'd said, Amatu had plausible reason to glare at him. The Algarvian who spoke Valmieran translated for his companion, who evidently didn't. They both laughed. Skarnu laughed, too, as he would have at the folly of a silly cousin. The redhead who knew Valmieran said, "Never bet on cockfights. You can't tell what a cock will do, any more than you can with a woman." He laughed again, on a different note. "I know what I want my cock to do."

He tried to translate that into Algarvian, too, but the pun

must not have worked in his own language, because his pal looked blank. Skarnu managed a laugh, too, to show he appreciated the trooper's wit. Then he asked, "Can we go on now, sir?"

"Aye, go, but keep your cocks out of mischief." Like a lot of people, the Algarvian ran what had been a good joke into the ground. He laughed again, louder than ever. Skarnu smiled. Amatu kept on looking mutinous. The Algarvian cavalrymen dug their knees into their mounts' barrels and flicked the reins. The unicorns trotted on down the road.

"Cocks!" Amatu snarled when the redheads were out of earshot. "I ought to put a curse on theirs."

"Go ahead and try, if you want to waste your time," Skarnu answered. "You're no trained mage, and they're warded against all the little nuisance spells, same as we were. You want to kill a soldier, you have to blaze him or cut him."

That wasn't strictly true. Sacrifice enough men and women—Kaunians from Forthweg, say, or Unkerlanter peasants—and you could power a spell that would kill plenty of soldiers. Skarnu knew as much. He preferred not to think about it.

Amatu's mind traveled along a different ley line, one that ran straight toward the sewers. "The way you talked to those fornicating whoresons, anybody would think you wanted to suck their—"

Skarnu knocked him down. When Amatu surged to his feet, murder blazed in his eyes. He rushed at Skarnu, fists flailing. He had courage. Skarnu had never doubted that. But, as a dragonflier, Amatu had never learned to fight in the hard and ruthless school of ground combat. Skarnu didn't waste time on fisticuffs. He kicked Amatu in the belly instead.

"Oof!" Amatu folded up like a concertina. Skarnu did hit him then, with an uppercut that straightened him again. Amatu had grit. He didn't go down even after that. But he was in no condition to fight anymore. As he stood swaying, Skarnu hit him once more, a blow he could measure carefully. Now Amatu crumpled.

He tried to get up again. Skarnu kicked him in the ribs, not quite hard enough to break them. So he gauged it, anyhow. If he was wrong, he wouldn't lose any sleep over it. Amatu still tried to get up. Skarnu kicked him yet again, rather harder this time. Amatu groaned and flattened out.

Skarnu kicked him once more, for good measure, and got another groan. Then he bent down and took away Amatu's knife. "We're through," he said evenly. "I'm going my way. You find yours. If you come after me from now on, I'll kill you. Have you got that?"

By way of reply, Amatu tried to hook an arm around Skarnu's ankle and bring him down. Skarnu stamped on his hand. Amatu howled like a wolf. When the howl turned into words, he cursed Skarnu as vilely as he could.

"Save it for the Algarvians," Skarnu told him. "You came back across the Strait to fight them, remember? All you've done since you got here was make trouble for everybody else who's fighting them. Now you're on your own. Do whatever you bloody well please."

Amatu answered with a fresh flurry of obscenities. He aimed more of them at Krasta than at Skarnu. Maybe he thought that would make Skarnu angrier. If he did, he was wrong. In Skarnu's mind, he'd been calling his sister worse things than any Amatu came up with ever since he found out she was sleeping with an Algarvian.

"I'm leaving you your silver," Skarnu said when Amatu finally flagged. "As far as I'm concerned, you can buy a rope and hang yourself with it. It's the best thing you could do for the kingdom."

He walked away from Amatu even as the returned exile reviled him again. However much Amatu cursed, though, he didn't get up and come after Skarnu. Maybe he was too battered. Maybe he believed Skarnu's warning. If he did, he was wise, for Skarnu meant every word of it.

When Skarnu went round the bend in the road from which the Algarvian cavalrymen had come, he looked back over his shoulder one last time. Amatu was on his feet by then, but going in the opposite direction, the direction the men on unicornback had taken. Skarnu nodded in somber satisfaction. With any luck at all, he would never see Amatu again.

He also tried to make sure luck wouldn't be the only factor involved. Whenever he came to a crossroads, he went right or left or straight ahead at random. By the time evening approached, he was confident Amatu would have no idea where he was. For that matter, he had no sure idea where he was himself.

A couple of big, rough-coated dogs ran out from a farmhouse and barked at him. His hand went to one of the knives on his belt. He didn't like farm dogs, which would often try to bite strangers. Here, though, they subsided when the farmer came after them and shouted, "Down!"

"Thanks, friend," Skarnu said from the roadway. He glanced at the sun. No, he couldn't go much farther before darkness overtook him. He turned back to the farmer. "Will you let me chop wood or do some other chores for supper and a night in your barn?" He hadn't intended to end up here, nor anywhere very close to here.

The farmer hesitated. Skarnu did his best to look innocent and appealing. A lot of people didn't trust anyone these days. If the fellow said, "No," he'd have to lie up under a tree or wherever else he could find makeshift shelter. But the farmer pointed. "There's the woodpile. There's the axe. Let's see what you can do while the light lasts."

He didn't promise anything. *Clever or just tight-fisted?* Skarnu wondered. Aloud, he said, "Fair enough," and got to work. By the time the sun went down, he'd turned a lot of lumber into firewood.

"Not bad," the farmer allowed. "You've done it before, I'd wager." He brought Skarnu bread and sausage and plums and a mug of what was obviously home-brewed ale, then said, "You can stay in the barn tonight, too."

"Thanks." Skarnu chopped more wood in the morning, and the farmer fed him again. Never once, though, did Skarnu set eyes on the man's wife and whatever children he had. That saddened him but left him unsurprised. Things worked so these days.

He grimaced. Over by Pavilosta—not so far away—he had

a child himself, or would soon. He wondered if he'd ever get to see it.

"Setubal!" the conductor shouted as the ley-line caravan slid into the depot at the heart of Lagoas capital. "All out for Setubal, folks! This is the end of the line."

To Fernao, newly arrived in the great city after months in the wilds of southeastern Kuusamo, that was true in more ways than one. He'd been staring out the window in astonished wonder ever since the caravan began gliding through the outskirts of Setubal. Were there really so many people, so many buildings, in the whole world, let alone in one city? It seemed incredible.

Leaning on his cane and carrying a carpetbag in his other hand, he made his way out of the caravan car. He knew no little pride in managing so well. His bad leg would never be what it had been before he was injured down in the austral continent, but he could use it. Aye, he limped. He would always limp. But he could get around.

Noise smote him like a bursting egg when he got down on the platform. "Powers above!" he muttered. Had Setubal always been like this? It probably had. No, it surely had. He'd lost his immunity to the racket by going away. He wondered how—and how fast—he could get it back. Soon, he hoped.

Through the din, he heard someone calling his name. His head turned this way and that as he tried to spot the man. He looked for someone waving, but half—more than half—the people on the platform were waving.

And then he did spy Brinco, the secretary to the Lagoan Guild of Mages. They fought their way toward each other through the crowd, and clasped each other's wrists in the traditional style of all Algarvic peoples when they finally came face-to-face. "Good to see you moving so well," Brinco said. A grin stretched across his plump face. More often then not, Fernao knew, the jolly fat man was a myth. In Brinco, the cliché lived.

"Good to be moving so well, believe me," Fernao told him.

"Let me take your bag," Brinco said, and did. "Let me clear a path. You follow along behind. A cab is waiting. We'll get you to the guild hall, and—"

"And Grandmaster Pinhiero will grill me like a bloater," Fernao said. Brinco laughed at that, but didn't deny it. The secretary shouldered a man out of the way. Fernao was perfectly content to follow him. He got the feeling Brinco could have cleared a path through the icebergs that swelled from the shores of the austral continent every winter.

Absently, he asked, "Do you know the name Habakkuk?"

"Aye," Brinco answered over his shoulder. "I also know you shouldn't, and that you shouldn't throw it around where others might hear it."

"Since I do know of it, will you tell me more?"

"Not here. Not now," Brinco said. "Later, perhaps, should the Grandmaster judge that wise." A skinny little fellow caromed off his chest. "I'm so sorry," he told the man, his voice oozing false sympathy. When Fernao tried to bring up Habakkuk again, Brinco didn't seem to hear him. His deafness was patently false, too, but Fernao couldn't do anything about it.

The cab had a closed body, but Fernao gritted his teeth at the racket that came through. He peered out the windows. Every so often, he noticed missing buildings or, a couple of times, blocks of buildings that had been standing when he left for the wilds of the Naantali district. "I see the Algarvians still keep paying us calls," he remarked.

"Aye, every now and again," Brinco agreed. "Not so much lately; they've sent a lot of the dragons they did have up in Valmiera west to fight the Unkerlanters." He was some years older than Fernao, but his grin made him look like a boy. "By all accounts, the dragons aren't helping them much there."

"Too bad," Fernao said.

"It *is* a pity, isn't it?" Brinco said, grinning still. But the grin slipped. "By what I hear, we were lucky they didn't get the chance to serve us as they served Yliharma."

"Not just Yliharma," Fernao said grimly. "They used that cursed magecraft against us, too, you know. That's why we haven't got Siuntio working with us anymore. If it hadn't been for him, I wouldn't be here talking to you now. None of the mages over there would be here talking to anybody now."

"How did he—how did the lot of you—withstand that vicious spell, even in so far as you did?" Brinco asked.

"Siuntio and Ilmarinen rallied us," Fernao answered. "Siuntio . . . seemed to carry the whole world on his shoulders for just long enough to give the rest of us a chance. I don't know another mage who could have done it."

Brinco grunted and gave him a sidelong look. For a moment, Fernao had trouble understanding why. Then he realized how he'd miffed the Guild Secretary: Siuntio, of course, wasn't a Lagoan. Fernao shrugged. For a long time now, he'd been the only Lagoan working on the largely Kuusaman project. They hadn't sneered at his blood, and he didn't care to sneer at theirs.

"Here y'are, gents," the hackman, reining in in front of the great neoclassical hall that housed the Lagoan Guild of Mages. Still looking unhappy, Brinco paid the fare; Fernao had wondered if he'd be stuck with it. But Brinco carried his carpetbag up the white marble steps to the colonnaded entranceway, and seemed in good spirits as he led Fernao back toward Grandmaster Pinhiero's office.

The trip took longer than it might have. Fernao kept greeting and getting greetings from colleagues he knew. Once past greetings, though, conversations flagged. Fernao wasn't the only one who said, "I wish I could tell you what I'm working on these days." He'd heard half a dozen variations on the theme by the time Brinco ushered him in to see Pinhiero.

"Welcome home," the Grandmaster said, rising and coming out from behind his desk to clasp Fernao's wrist. Pinhiero was in his sixties, his once-red hair and mustache mostly gray now. He wasn't a great mage; his name would never go into the reference books, as Siuntio's already had. But he had gifts of his own, not least among them political astuteness. After he poured wine for Fernao and helped him ease down into a chair, he asked, "Well, is it what we thought it was?"

"No," Fernao answered, which made Pinhiero blink. Fernao sipped the wine, enjoying the Grandmaster's discomfiture. Then he said, "It's more—or it can be more, if we ever learn to control it."

Pinhiero leaned forward, as a falcon might on catching sight of a mouse. "I thought so," he breathed. "If it were less, they would have said more." He blazed out a question as if it were the beam from a stick: "Will it match Mezentio's foul magics?"

"In force, aye," Fernao said. "Again, though, the question is control. That will take time. I don't know how long, but it won't happen tomorrow, or the day after tomorrow, either."

"And meanwhile, of course, the war grinds on," Pinhiero said. "Sooner or later, Lagoas and Kuusamo will be fighting on the mainland of Derlavai. Will these spells be ready when that day comes?"

"Grandmaster, I haven't the faintest idea," Fernao answered. "For one thing, I don't know when that day will come. Maybe you know more about that than I do. I hope so—you could hardly know less."

"I know what I know," Pinhiero said. "If you don't know, I daresay there are reasons why you don't."

Arrogant old thornbush, Fernao thought. But he'd already known that. Aloud, he said, "No doubt you're right, sir. The other trouble, of course, is that no one has any sure knowledge of when the cantrips will be ready to use in war and not as an exercise in theoretical sorcery."

"You had better hurry up," the Grandmaster warned, as if it were Fernao's fault and no one else's that the project wasn't advancing fast enough to suit him. "While you play with your acorns and rats and rabbits, the world around you moves on—aye, and at an ever faster clip, too."

Fernao did his best to look wise and innocent at the same time. "That's what Habakkuk is all about, eh?"

"One of the things," Pinhiero said, and then, too late, "And how do you happen to know of Habakkuk?"

"I would have trouble telling you that, sir," Fernao answered, more innocently than ever. "The world has moved on so fast since I heard about it that I've forgotten."

Pinhiero's green eyes flashed. He wasn't used to being on the receiving end of sarcasm, and didn't seem to like it much. His lips drew back from his teeth in what was as much snarl as smile. "You would have done better to forget the thing itself. But I don't suppose we could expect that of you."

"Not likely," Fernao agreed. "Will Habakkuk be ready when we need to go back to the mainland?"

"Oh, sooner than that," Pinhiero said. "Or it had better be—if not, some fancy sorcerous talent will find itself shorter by a head." He hadn't told Fernao anything about what Habakkuk actually was, merely that it was important, which the mage already knew. And now he continued, "Whether it is or it isn't, though, it's got nothing to do with you. This project you *are* working on is rather different, wouldn't you say? You do have some idea of what you're doing there? You'd bloody well better."

"I think I may," Fernao said tightly.

"Good," the Grandmaster told him. "Here's what we'll do: we'll put you up in a room in the guild hall here—with a cot and everything, mind—and you can draft a report for us, let us know what the Kuusamans are doing and how they're doing it. Start at the beginning and don't leave anything out."

"That isn't why I came back to Setubal," Fernao said in something approaching horror. "It's not the only reason I came back, anyhow."

Grandmaster Pinhiero was implacable. "Your kingdom needs you."

It came close to a kidnapping. Pinhiero didn't actually have four burly mages drag Fernao off to the room, but he made it plain that he would unless Fernao went there on his own. When Fernao stuck his head out a little later, he discovered one of those burly mages standing in the hallway. He nodded to the fellow and withdrew again. He couldn't sneak away, then. And he couldn't very well magic his way free, either, not with so much of the sorcerous talent in the world right here. Master Ilmarinen might have tried—and, being Master Ilmarinen, might have succeeded. Fernao knew his own talents weren't up to such sorcery. Having no other choice, he settled down and wrote.

As long as he was doing what Pinhiero wanted, the Grand-master took care of him. Whatever he wanted in the way of food and drink came up from the kitchens in the blink of an eye. Mages fetched sorcerous tomes from the guildhall li-brary whenever he needed to check a point. If he felt like soaking for an hour in a tub full of steaming water, he could. And once, even though he hadn't made any such request, a very friendly young woman visited the room.

She shook her head when he tried to give her something. "It's all arranged," she said. "The Grandmaster told me he'd turn me into a vole if I took even a copper from you." By the melodramatic way she shivered as she put her kilt back on, she believed Pinhiero would do just as he'd said.

"Pinhiero would never waste an important natural resource like that," Fernao said, which made the girl smile as she left. Fernao went to sleep that night with a smile on his face, too. But in the morning, after breakfast, he had to go back to writ-ing. He started to look forward to returning to the Naantali district. He hadn't had to work nearly so hard there.

Sooner or later, Talsu knew, he would run into Kugu the sil-versmith again. Skrunda wasn't a big city, where they might easily have avoided each other. And, sure enough, one day in the market square Talsu came face-to-face with the man who'd betrayed him to the Algarvians.

Talsu was haggling with a farmer selling salted olives, and paid little attention to the man buying raisins at the next stall till the fellow turned around. He and Kugu recognized each other at the same instant.

Kugu might have been a treacherous whoreson and an Al-garvian puppet, but he had his share of nerve and more. "Good morning," he said to Talsu, as coolly as if he hadn't had him flung into a dungeon. "It's good to see you here again."

"It's good to be here again," Talsu answered, all the while thinking, *I can't wring his neck here in the middle of the mar-*

ket square. People would talk. He couldn't even glare so
fiercely as he wanted to. If he roused Kugu's suspicions, the
Algarvians would seize him again.

"I'm glad you've seen the light of day in the metaphorical
as well as the literal sense of the words," Kugu said.

Before studying classical Kaunian with Kugu, Talsu would
have had no idea what a metaphor was. But he'd learned
more than metaphors from the small, precise silversmith. He
just nodded now. If Kugu wanted to think him a traitor to Jelgava, too—well, so what? A lot of people thought that. What
difference could one more make?

Kugu nodded, too, as if he'd passed a test. Maybe he had.
The silversmith said, "One of these days, we'll have to have a
talk."

"I'd like that," Talsu said. "I'd like to learn some more of
the old language, too."

"Would you?" Kugu said. "Well, perhaps it can be
arranged. But now, if you will excuse me . . ." He went back
to looking at raisins.

*I know what he'll want. He'll want me to help him trap
other people who don't think Jelgava ought to have an Algarvian king.* Talsu wondered how many of the people who'd
been studying classical Kaunian with Kugu remained outside
of Algarvian dungeons. Some still would; he was sure of that.
If people Kugu taught started disappearing every week or so,
the ones who remained at large wouldn't take long to realize
what was going wrong.

"You going to buy those olives, pal, or are you just going
to gawk at them?" asked the farmer by whose cart Talsu
stood.

Talsu did end up buying the olives. Running into Kugu left
him too distracted to haggle as hard as he should have. The
farmer didn't bother hiding a self-satisfied smirk as Talsu
gave him silver. When Talsu's wife and mother found out
what he'd paid, they would have something sharp to say to
him. He was mournfully certain of that.

And he proved right in short order, too. Laitsina said, "Do
you think your father mints the coins himself?"

"No. He wouldn't put Mainardo's face on them," Talsu answered, giving his mother a better comeback than he'd had for the farmer.

"You could have got a better price than that at my father's shop," Gailisa said reproachfully after she came back from working there.

"I have an excuse, anyhow," Talsu said. His wife raised an eyebrow. By her expression, no excuse for spending too much on food could possibly be good enough. But then Talsu explained: "I ran into Kugu in the market square."

"Oh," Gailisa said. A moment later, she repeated the word in an altogether different tone of voice: *"Oh."* Kugu wouldn't have wanted to hear the way it sounded the second time. Gailisa went on, "Did you leave him dead and bleeding there?"

Regretfully, Talsu shook his head. "I had to be polite. If I'd done what I wanted to do, I'd be back in the dungeons now, not here."

"I suppose so." His wife sighed. "I wish you could have. I'm surprised he didn't try to talk you into trapping people along with him—he must think you're safe."

"As a matter of fact, he did drop a hint or two," Talsu said. At that, Gailisa let out such a furious squawk, everyone else hurried up to find out what was wrong. Talsu had to explain all over again, which led to more furious squawks.

Traku said, "Don't go back and study the old language with him again. Don't have anything to do with him, if you can help it."

"I would like to learn more classical Kaunian," Talsu said. "If the redheads think it's worth knowing—and they do—we ought to know it, too."

"Fair enough." His father nodded. "But don't study with that son of a whore of a silversmith. Find somebody else who knows it or find yourself a book and learn from that."

"I was thinking that if I got close to him . . ." Talsu's voice trailed away.

"No. No, no, and no," Traku said. "If you hang around him and something happens to him, what will the Algarvians do?

Blame you, that's what. That's not what you want, is it? It had better not be."

"Ah," Talsu murmured. His father made an uncomfortable amount of sense. He did want something to happen to Kugu, and he didn't want Mezentio's men to pin it on him. But after a little thought, he said, "I may not have as much choice as I'd like. If I act like I can't stand the bugger, that's liable to be enough to get him to give me to the Algarvians all over again."

Gailisa spoke up: "Just tell him you're too busy working to go out of nights. He won't be able to say a word about that. The way the Algarvians squeeze us these days, everybody has to run as fast as he can to stay in one place."

"That's not bad," Talsu said. "It's not even a lie, either."

"Maybe you won't see him at all," his mother said. "I'll send Ausra to the market instead of you for a while. And I don't suppose Master Kugu would have the crust to stick his nose through this door after the trouble he caused you—the trouble he caused every one of us."

Ausra stuck out her tongue at Talsu. "See? Now I'm going to have to do your work," she said. "You'd better find a way to make that up to me."

"I will," he said, which looked to astonish his sister. In fact, he only half heard her. He was thinking about ways to make things up to Kugu, ways to make something dreadful happen to the silversmith without drawing suspicion to himself.

Gailisa must have seen as much. That night, while they lay crowded together in their narrow bed, she said, "Don't do anything foolish."

"I won't." Talsu hugged her to him. "The only really foolish thing I ever did was trust him in the first place. I won't make *that* mistake again any time soon."

The next morning, his father remarked, "You don't want to do anything right away, you know."

"Who says I don't want to?" Talsu answered. They sat side by side in the tailor's shop, working on heavy wool quilts for a couple of Algarvians who would be going from warm, sunny Jelgava to Unkerlant, a land that was anything but.

Traku looked at him in some alarm. He went on, "I won't, because it would give me away, but that doesn't say anything about what I want to do."

"All right," Traku said, and then, a moment later, "No, curse it, it isn't all right. Look what you made me do. You frightened me so there, my finishing spell went all awry." The pleat he'd sewn by hand was perfectly straight. The spell should have made all the others match it. Instead, they twisted every which way, as jagged as the skyline of the Bratanu Mountains on the border between Jelgava and Algarve.

"I'm sorry," Talsu said.

"Sorry? Sorry doesn't cut any cloth. I ought to box your ears," Traku grumbled. "Now I'm going to have to remember that spell of undoing. Powers above, I hope I can; I haven't had to use it in a while. I ought to make you rip all these seams out by hand, is what I ought to do."

Still fuming, Talsu's father muttered to himself, trying to make sure he had the words to the spell of undoing right. Talsu would have offered to help, but wasn't sure he could. No good tailor needed the spell of undoing very often. When Traku did begin his new chant, Talsu listened intently. No, he hadn't had all the words straight. He would now, though.

After calling out the last command, Traku grunted in relief. "There. That's taken care of, anyhow. No thanks to you, either." He glared at Talsu. "Now I get to do the finishing spell over again. You're going to cost me an hour's work with your foolishness. I hope you're happy."

"Happy? No." But Talsu glanced over to his father. "D'you suppose we could build the spell of undoing into some of the clothes we make for the redheads, so their tunics and kilts would fall to pieces, say, six months after they got to Unkerlant?"

"We could, maybe, but I wouldn't." Traku shook his head. "You don't shit where you eat, and we eat with the clothes we make."

Talsu sighed. "All right. That makes sense. I wish it didn't. We have to be able to do *something* about the Algarvians."

"Doing something about our own people who suck up to

them would be even better," Traku said. "Algarvians can't help being Algarvians, any more than vultures can help being vultures. But when people in your own town, people you've known for years, suck up to Mezentio's men, that's cursed hard to take."

With a nod, Talsu went back to the kilt he was working on. Thinking about the Jelgavans who sucked up to the redheads inevitably brought him back to thinking about Kugu. His hands folded into fists. He wanted to ruin the silversmith—more, he wanted to humiliate him. But he wanted to do it in a way that wouldn't put him back inside a dungeon an hour later.

He came up with nothing that suited him then, nor in the couple of days that followed. He was walking home from taking a cloak to a customer—an actual Jelgavan customer, not one of the occupiers—when he ran into Kugu on the street.

As they had in the market square, they eyed each other warily. Kugu said, "I gave my lessons last night. I wondered if you would come by. When you didn't, I missed you."

"My wife and family took things the wrong way," Talsu answered. "They don't understand how things are in the bigger world. So I'm having to be quiet about my change of heart, if you know what I mean. I don't want to stir anybody up, and so I think I'd be smarter to stay home for a while."

Kugu nodded, swallowing the lie as smoothly as if it were truth. "Aye, that can prove troublesome," he agreed. "Perhaps you could arrange to have something happen to one of them."

Perhaps I could arrange to have something happen to you, you son of a whore, Talsu thought. But all he said was, "People would wonder about it, you know."

"Well, so they would," the silversmith admitted, "and that kind of gossip would make you less useful. We'll think of something sooner or later, I'm sure."

Useful, am I? went through Talsu's mind. *We'll see about that, by the powers above.* He smiled at Kugu. "So we will."

Vanai hated it when Ealstan was gloomy. She did her best to cheer him up, saying, "You're bound to find more work soon."

"Am I?" He sounded anything but cheered. "Pybba wasn't joking, curse him. After he gave me the sack, he slandered me to everybody he knew. Finding anybody who'll trust me not to steal hasn't been easy."

"Powers below eat Pybba," Vanai said, in lieu of saying something like, *Why didn't you keep your nose out of his business when he told you to?* The good sense in a question like that was plain to see, but it didn't help her now. She'd said the same thing before, and Ealstan hadn't wanted to listen.

"The powers below will eat us if I don't start bringing in more money again." His voice was raw with worry.

"We're all right for a while yet," Vanai said, which was true. "We got ahead of the game when you did so well there for a while, and I spent a lot of time being poor. I know how not to spend very much."

Her husband drained his breakfast cup of wine. He made a face. Vanai understood that; it was about as cheap as it could be while staying this side of vinegar. She'd already started economizing. With a sigh, he said, "I'll go out and see what I can scrape up. I'll give it another few days. After that, if nobody wants me to cast books for him anymore . . ." He shrugged. "My brother spent the last couple of years of his life building roads. There's always work for somebody with a strong back." He got up, gave Vanai a quick kiss, and went out the door.

As she washed bowls and mugs, she remembered her grandfather after Major Spinello set him to work building roads outside Oyngestun. A few days of that had almost killed Brivibas. A few weeks of it surely would have, and so she'd started giving herself to Spinello to save Brivibas from the road crew.

Because of all that, the notion of Ealstan building roads filled her with irrational dread. *At least I know it's irrational,* she thought: small consolation, but consolation nonetheless. Ealstan was young and strong, not an aging scholar. And he was Forthwegian, not Kaunian—an overseer wouldn't be tempted to work him to death for the sport of it.

She looked in the pantry and sighed. She hadn't wanted to

go shopping today, but she couldn't very well cook without olive oil, and only a little was left in the bottom of the jar. A yawn followed the sigh. More than a little ruefully, she looked down at her belly. The baby didn't show yet, but it did still leave her tired all the time.

Before she left the flat, she renewed the spell that kept her looking like a Forthwegian. She wished she'd done that while Ealstan was still there. Aye, the spell had become second nature to her, but she liked to be reassured that she'd done it right. If she ever did make a mistake, she wouldn't know till too late.

Silver clinked sweetly as Vanai put coins in her handbag. She nodded to herself. She'd told Ealstan the truth; money wasn't a worry yet, and wouldn't be for a while. She still found the handbag a minor annoyance. Trouser pockets were more convenient for carrying things. But Forthwegian women didn't wear trousers. If she wanted to look like a Forthwegian, she had to dress like one, too.

She'd just lifted the bar from the door when someone knocked on it. She jerked back in surprise and alarm. She hadn't expected visitors. She never expected visitors. Visitors meant trouble. "Who is it?" she asked, hating the quaver in her voice but unable to hold it out.

"Mistress Thelberge?" A man's voice, deep and gruff. Unquestionably Forthwegian—no Algarvian trill.

"Aye?" Cautiously, Vanai opened the door. The fellow standing in the hallway was a vigorous fifty, with shoulders like a bull's. She'd never seen him before. "Who are you? What do you want?"

He drew himself up straight. "Pybba's the name," he rumbled. "Now where in blazes is your husband?" He spoke as if Vanai might have had Ealstan in her handbag.

"He's not here," she said coldly. "He's out looking for work. Thanks to you, he'll probably have a hard time finding any. What more do you want to do to him?"

"I want to talk to him, that's what," the pottery magnate answered.

Vanai set a hand on the door, as if to slam it in his face. "Why should he want to talk to you?"

Pybba reached into his belt pouch. He pulled out a coin and tossed it to her. "Here. This'll give him a reason," he said as she caught it. She stared at the coin in her hand. It was gold.

Vanai couldn't remember the last time she'd seen a gold-piece, let along held one. Silver circulated far more freely in Forthweg than gold, and Brivibas, back in Oyngestun, had not been the sort of man who attracted any of the few gold-pieces the kingdom did mint. "I don't understand," Vanai said. "You just sacked Ealstan. Why—this?" She held up the gold coin. It lay heavier in her hand than silver would have.

"Because I've learned some things I didn't know when I gave him the boot, that's why," Pybba replied. "For instance, he's got—he had—a brother named Leofsig. Isn't that so?" Vanai stood mute. She didn't know where the pottery mag-nate was going with his questions or why he was asking them. Pybba seemed to take her silence for agreement, for he went on, "And some son of a whore from Plegmund's Brigade killed his brother. Isn't *that* right?"

He didn't know everything; he didn't know that the fellow from Plegmund's Brigade who'd killed Leofsig was Eal-stan's—and poor Leofsig's—first cousin. But he knew enough. Vanai asked, "What's this to you?"

"It's worth gold to me to see him, that's what it is. You tell him so," Pybba said. "Aye, tell him just that. And keep the money whether he decides he wants to see me or not. He'll be stubborn. I know cursed well he will. Some ways, he reminds me of the way I was back in my puppy days." He laughed. "Don't tell him that. It'll just put his back up. So long, sweet-heart. I've got work to do." Without another word, he hurried toward the stairs. Vanai got the idea he always hurried.

She went through the rest of the day in a daze. She didn't want to take the goldpiece with her when she went down to the market square to buy oil, but she didn't want to leave it back in the flat, either. She knew that was foolish; aye, it was worth six-teen times its weight in silver, but the flat already held a good deal more than sixteen times as much silver as there was gold in that one coin. The nervousness persisted even so.

When she got back with the olive oil, the first thing she did was make sure the gold coin was where she'd left it. Then she had to wait for Ealstan to come home. The sun seemed to crawl across the sky. It was sinking down behind the block of flats across the street when he finally used the familiar coded knock.

One glance at his face told Vanai he'd had no luck. "About time for me to start paving roads, looks like," he said glumly. "Pour me some wine, will you? If I get drunk, I won't have to think about what a mess I'm in."

Instead of pouring wine, Vanai brought back the goldpiece and displayed it in the palm of her hand. As Ealstan's eyes widened, she said, "Things may not be quite so bad."

"Where—?" Ealstan coughed. He had to break off and try again. Speaking carefully, he asked, "Where did that come from?"

"From Pybba," Vanai answered, and her husband's eyes got wider still. Handing him the goldpiece, she went on, "He wants to talk with you."

Ealstan tossed the coin up into the air. "That means this is probably brass," he said as he caught it. Vanai shook her head. Ealstan didn't push it; he knew the heft of gold when he felt it, too. He scowled in bewilderment. "What does he want? What *can* he want? For me to come in so he can gloat?"

"I don't think so," Vanai said. "He knows about Leofsig." She explained what Pybba had said, finishing, "He said that whole business with your family was why he wanted to see you again."

"I don't understand," Ealstan muttered, as if he didn't want to admit that even to himself. He gave the goldpiece back to Vanai. "What do you think I ought to do?" he asked her.

"You'd better go see him," she replied; she'd been thinking about that ever since Pybba left. "I don't think you have any choice, not after this." Before he could indignantly deny that and insist that he could do as he pleased, she forestalled him by choosing that moment to get the wine after all, leaving him by himself to think for a minute or two. When she brought it back, she asked, "Can you tell me I'm wrong?"

"No," he said darkly, and gulped down half the cup at once. "But powers above, how I wish I could."

"Let me get supper ready." Vanai chopped cabbage and onions and radishes and dried mushrooms, adding crumbly white cheese and shaved bits of smoked pork for flavor. She dressed the salad with spiced vinegar and some of the olive oil she'd bought. Along with bread and more oil and some apricots, it made a quick, reasonably filling meal.

Her own appetite was pretty good, and everything looked like staying down. She still had occasional days when she gave back as much as she ate, but they were getting rarer. Ealstan seemed so distracted, she might have set anything at all before him. Halfway through supper, he burst out, "But how am I supposed to trust him after this?"

Vanai had no trouble figuring out who *him* was. "Don't," she answered. "Do what business you have to or you think you should with him, but that hasn't got anything to do with trust. Even if you go back to work for him, he's just your boss. He's not your father."

"Aye," Ealstan said, as if that hadn't occurred to him. Maybe it hadn't. He'd looked for great things from Pybba. He'd looked too hard for great things from Pybba, in fact. Maybe now he would see the pottery magnate as a man, not a hero.

When they made love later that evening, Ealstan didn't show quite the desperate urgency he'd had lately. He seemed a little more able to relax and enjoy himself. Because he did, Vanai did, too. And she slept well afterwards. Of course, she would have slept well afterwards even if she hadn't enjoyed herself making love. Carrying a child was the next best thing to getting hit with a brickbat for ensuring sound sleep.

In the morning, after more bread and oil and a cup of wine, Ealstan said, "I'm off to see Pybba. Wish me luck."

"I always do," Vanai answered.

Then she had nothing to do but wait. She'd done so much of that since coming to Eoforwic. She should have been good at it. Sometimes she even was. But sometimes waiting came hard. This was one of those days. Too many things could go very wrong or very right. She had no control over any of them. She hated that.

The longer she waited for Ealstan, the more worried she got. Waiting all the way into the early evening left her something close to a nervous wreck. When at last he knocked, she all but flew to the door. She threw it open. "Well?" she said.

"Well," he answered grandly, breathing wine fumes into her face, "well, sweetheart, I think we're back in business. Back in business, aye." He savored the phrase. "And what a business it is, too."

The summer before, the fight in the forests of western Unkerlant had been as grand as the attacking Gyongyosians could make it. They'd driven the goat-eating Unkerlanters before them, almost breaking through into the open country beyond the woods. Now . . . Now Istvan counted himself lucky that the Unkerlanters weren't driving his own countrymen west in disorder. King Swemmel's men seemed content to harass the Gyongyosians without doing much more.

"I'll tell you what I think it is," Corporal Kun said one evening.

"Of course you will," Istvan said. "You've always got answers, you do, whether you know the question or not."

"Here, the question's simple," Kun said.

Szonyi boomed laughter. "Then it's just right for you, by the stars." He hugged himself with glee, proud of his own wit.

Kun ignored him and went on talking to Istvan: "Remember how people were saying the Unkerlanters would hit us hard if they got into trouble with Algarve?" He waited for his sergeant to nod before going on, "Since they haven't hit us, doesn't it follow that they didn't get into trouble against the Algarvians?"

Istvan plucked at his beard. "That sounds like it ought to make sense. But our allies have hammered Unkerlant two summers in a row. Why shouldn't they be able to do it again?"

"If you hit a man but you don't knock him down and kick him till he quits, pretty soon he's going to start hitting you, too," Kun said. "That's what the Algarvians did. Now we're going to see how well they stand getting hit. That's my guess, anyhow."

Before Istvan could reply, a sentry called a challenge: "Halt! Who comes?" Everybody in the redoubt grabbed for his stick.

"I, Captain Frigyes," came the answer, and the Gyongyosian soldiers relaxed.

"Advance and be recognized," the sentry said, and then, a moment later, "Come ahead, sir."

Frigyes scrambled down into the redoubt. Nodding to Istvan, he asked, "All quiet in front of you, Sergeant?"

"Aye, sir," Istvan answered. "Swemmel's whoresons are sitting tight. And so are we. But you know about that. I guess everything worth having is heading for the islands, to fight the stinking Kuusamans."

The company commander nodded. His every motion was sharp, abrupt. So was the way he thought. He was a good soldier, but Istvan often missed the more easygoing Captain Tivadar—and he didn't want to think what would have happened had Frigyes been the officer who discovered he'd inadvertently eaten goat.

"Everything worth having is heading for the islands," Frigyes agreed. "That includes us. We pull out of line here tomorrow, after sundown, the whole regiment. No, the whole brigade."

For a moment, none of the soldiers in the redoubt spoke. Several of them stood there with their mouths hanging open. Istvan didn't realize he was one of those till he had to shut his before he could start talking: "Where will we go, sir? And who'll take our places here?"

Frigyes' broad shoulders moved up and down in a shrug. "We'll go where they send us. And I don't know who's coming in to deal with Swemmel's goat-eaters. I don't care. They're not my worry anymore. Somebody else will kill them; that's all I need to know. Anybody here ever fight against the Kuusamans?"

Istvan stuck up his hand. So did Kun and Szonyi. "Aye, sir," they chorused. "On Obuda," Istvan added.

"I'll pick your brains as we head west, then," Frigyes said. "I know the Unkerlanters, but those scrawny little slanteyes who follow the Seven Princes are a closed book to me." He turned and went up the sandbag steps and out of the redoubt. Over his shoulder, he added, "Have to let the rest of the squads know." Then he was gone.

His footsteps were still receding when all the soldiers in Istvan's squad started talking at once. He let them babble for a little while, but only for a little while. Then he made a sharp chopping motion with his right hand. "Enough!" he said. "The captain told us to be ready to move out tomorrow after sunset, and that's what we're going to do. Anybody who can't get ready by then"—he smiled his nastiest smile, all teeth and flashing eyes—"we'll leave behind for the Unkerlanters to eat."

"They're pulling the whole brigade out of the line," Kun said in wondering tones. "They can't be putting another brigade in. There'd be no point to that—if they had another brigade to put in, they'd have sent that one to the islands instead of us."

"The Unkerlanters are quiet," Szonyi said. "We've been talking about how quiet they are."

"But how long will they stay quiet once we're gone?" the youngster named Lajos asked, undoubtedly beating Kun to the punch.

"Like the captain said, that's not our worry anymore," Istvan said. "One way or another, the generals will deal with it. We've got to start thinking about the Kuusamans." He didn't care for that notion. They'd come unpleasantly close to killing him a couple of times on Obuda. Now they'd get more chances.

When Istvan thought of the Kuusamans, he thought of going into action against them as soon as he left the redoubt. Reality proved more complex, as reality had a way of doing. Along with the rest of the brigade, Istvan's regiment pulled out of the line when ordered. He didn't see any inexperienced young men trudging forward wide-eyed and eager, as befitted a warrior race, to take their places. It was nighttime, of course. Maybe that made a difference. Maybe. He tried to make himself believe it.

Having left their positions at night—presumably to keep the Unkerlanters from realizing they were going—they got no sleep. They got no sleep the next day, either, but kept tramping west through woods that seemed to go on forever. By the time Istvan finally was allowed to stop and rest, he was readier to fight his own officers than he ever had been to fight the Kuusamans.

The brigade had to march through the woods for most of a week before they got to a ley line. There might have been others closer, but they hadn't been charted. This whole stretch of the world was far, far off the beaten track. And then the weary men had to wait till enough caravan cars accumulated to carry them all west.

"It could be worse," Kun said as the squad did at last climb aboard one. "They could have decided to make us march the whole way, across the Ilszung Mountains and all. Why not? We fought our way across 'em coming east."

"Shut up, curse you," Istvan said. "Don't let any officers hear you saying something like that, or they're liable to take you up on it."

He didn't see the ley-line caravan leave the forest; by then he was asleep, his chin on his chest. When he woke again, the mountains were near. And then the caravan traveled over mountains and through mountain valleys for the next couple of days. Much of the terrain reminded Istvan achingly of his own home valley; many of the villages, with their walls and their fortresslike, steep-roofed houses of gray stone, could have been Kunhegyes, where he'd grown up. But Kunhegyes lay far from any ley line.

Some of the men from the mountains of eastern Gyongyos had never seen the plains that led down to the Bothnian Ocean. The only flat ground they'd ever known was that of the great woods of western Unkerlant, and they exclaimed in wonder to see farmland stretching from one horizon to the other.

Kun looked at Istvan over the tops of his spectacles. "I thought you'd be oohing and ahhing with the rest of the back-country lads," he remarked.

"Then you're not as smart as you like to think you are," Istvan retorted. "Didn't I come this way before, when they threw me onto a ship and sent me to Obuda?"

Kun thumped his forehead with the heel of his hand. "Aye, of course you did, and I'm a natural-born idiot. I must be."

Down in the flatlands, towns got bigger and closer together. Istvan had all he could do not to marvel at the sight of so many buildings all in the same place, and at the sight of tall towers climbing toward the stars. "How do so many clans live together in one place without feuds tearing them to pieces?" he asked Kun. "You're a city man, so you ought to know."

"What you have to understand is, a lot of people move to the cities from out of the countryside," the former mage's apprentice answered. "Some of them are younger sons and the like—men who won't get a fair share from their family plots. And others are the men who want to find out if they can get rich. The odds are slim in town, stars above know that's so, but it'll never, ever happen on a farm."

"I suppose you're going somewhere with this, but I'm not following you, not yet," Istvan said.

"Bear with me," Kun told him. "In your valley, your clan's been living next to its neighbors for hundreds of years. Everybody remembers who did what to whom, and why, since the stars first shone. Some of the clan quarrels are that old, too. Am I right, or am I wrong?"

"Oh, you're right, of course," Istvan said. "That's how things are."

"Ha!" Kun pounced. "But it's not how things are in the cities, or not so much. If you move away from most of the people in your clan, you move away from most of the old squabbles, too. You get to know a man for what he is himself, not for whether his grandfather's great-uncle stole three hens from your cousin's great-grandma. Do you see what I'm saying?"

"What it sounds like is the army, except without the discipline in the army," Istvan said. "Here, I do what I do because the officers tell me to, and you do what you do because I tell you to, and the troopers do what they do because you tell them to. Back in my valley, my place in the clan tells me what to do. I always know what's expected, if you understand what I'm saying." He waited for Kun to nod, then went on, "But if you're living in the city away from your clan, how do you know what to do or how to act? Who tells you?"

"I tell myself," Kun answered. "That's what cities are all about: making your own choices, I mean. They're changing the face of Gyongyos, too."

Istvan disapproved of change on general principles. In that, he reckoned himself a typical Gyongyosian. His eyes slid over to Kun, who smiled as if knowing what he was thinking. As far as Istvan was concerned, Kun was no typical Gyongyosian—*and a good thing, too,* he thought. What Kun might be thinking of him never entered his mind.

They slid through Gyorvar the next morning, heading down to the docks. All the chief rivers watering the Gyongyosian plain came together at Gyorvar and went down as one to the not far distant sea. Istvan didn't think about that. He craned his neck to get a glimpse of Ekrekek Arpad's palace. Before his first trip through the capital, he'd imagined it as a tower taller than any mountains, a tower from which the Ekrekek could reach out and touch the sacred stars if he so desired. It was nothing of the sort, being pavilions of gleaming marble scattered across parkland, but lovely nonetheless. He'd remembered that.

And then, after Istvan got his glimpse, the ley-line caravan stopped at the docks, which were anything but lovely. He'd remembered that, too. The battered transports waiting to take his comrades and him across the sea were even more unlovely than the ones he remembered from his last trip through Gyorvar. He didn't know what that meant. Nothing good, probably.

* * *

Little by little, Cornelu was learning to read Lagoan. He'd never thought he would do that, but he turned out to have a powerful incentive: the better he read, the more readily he could learn of Unkerlant's advances in the west. Anything that told him of Algarve's troubles was worth investigating in detail. He might not have liked Lagoas' language, but he liked what was being said in it.

When he took Janira out to a band concert, though, he stuck to Sibian, saying, "Mezentio's men are finally starting to pay for their folly."

"Good," she answered in the same language. She had an odd accent—part lower-class, part Lagoan. Her father, Balio, was a Sibian fisherman who'd settled in Setubal after the Six Years' War, married a local woman, and started an eatery. Janira was in fact more fluent in Lagoan. That she spoke Sibian at all helped endear her to Cornelu.

"Aye," he said fiercely, and squeezed her hand. "May they be driven back on every front. May they be driven from Sibiu."

"May they stop dropping eggs on Setubal," Janira said. "Father's only just starting to get back on his feet." An Algarvian egg had wrecked the eatery where Balio had cooked and Janira served. She went on, "Everything is more expensive in the new place."

"I'm sorry," Cornelu said. And he was: that meant she had to work even more than she had before, which meant she had fewer chances to see him. Since his own duties often kept him from seeing her, their romance, if that was the name for it, had advanced only by fits and starts.

Of course, Cornelu was also a married man, at least technically. He hoped his little daughter Brindza was doing well back in Tirgoviste town. He hoped no such thing for his wife, not after Costache had taken up with at least one of the Algarvian officers who'd been billeted on her.

Standing in line with Janira, Cornelu tried to put all that out of his mind. The line snaked forward in the darkness. He passed through a couple of black curtains before emerging into light and paying the fee for himself and Janira. They both held out their hands. One of the fee-takers stamped them with red ink to show they'd paid. Then they hurried into the concert hall.

It was filling fast. Cornelu spotted a couple of seats. He went for them as ferociously as if charging on leviathanback. "There!" he said in something like triumph as he and Janira reached them just ahead of a Lagoan couple.

Janira smiled. "I can see why all your enemies must fear you," she said, sitting down beside him.

Cornelu smiled, too. "The main reason my enemies fear me is that they do not know my leviathan and I are there till too late. Sometimes they never find out what happened to them. Sometimes they do realize, and it is the last thing they ever know."

"You sound so . . . happy about it," Janira said with a small shiver.

"I am happy about it," he replied. "They are Algarvians. They are the enemies, the occupiers, of my kingdom. They are the enemies of this kingdom, too."

"I know. I understand all that." She hesitated, then went on, "It's only that . . . I haven't heard you sound really happy very often. It's . . . strange when you sound that way and it has to do with killing."

"Oh." Cornelu contemplated that for a moment. "I should probably be ashamed. But, aside from that, I have not had much to be happy about lately." Just before he turned the evening into a disaster even as it began, he redeemed himself with a handful of words: "Present company excepted, of course." Janira, who had started to cloud up, relaxed and leaned her head on his shoulder.

They both applauded when the musicians came out on stage. Lagoan music was on the whole delicate, like that of the other Algarvic kingdoms. It didn't thump and harangue, the way Kaunian music did. A couple of things set it apart, though. For one, it was generally more cheerful than anything Cornelu would have been likely to hear in Sibiu. Of course, the Lagoans had more reason to be cheerful—they lived farther away from Algarve. And, for another, they'd borrowed triangles and bells from their Kuusaman neighbors, which gave their pieces an almost fantastical feel to Cornelu's ears.

Janira enjoyed the music; that was plain. Cornelu applauded a little more than dutifully when the concert ended. Seeing his companion having a good time let him have a good time at one remove. That was almost as good as the real thing.

Even in the darkness imposed on it to keep from offering targets to Algarvian dragons, Setubal remained a busy place after dark. The Lagoans seemed to think they could use noise to make up for the lack of light. Everybody shouted at the top of his lungs. Carriages carried little bells to warn other carriages they were there. Ley-line caravan cars moved slowly and clanged big, deep-toned bells, as ships would during thick fog. From what the news sheets said, people walked in front of them every so often anyhow. Walking in front of even a slow-moving caravan car usually produced a funeral. But the alternative to going out in pitch darkness was staying at home, and the folk of Setubal didn't fancy that.

As far as Cornelu was concerned, the cacophony of shouts and most unmusical bells of all sizes and tones might as well have canceled the concert. "Powers above," he muttered. "I wouldn't be surprised if Algarvian dragonfliers could hear Setubal, even if they can't see it."

Janira had a Sibian father, aye. She spoke the language of the island kingdom, aye. But she proved herself a true Lagoan by the way she navigated the dark streets back to the flat she shared with Balio. "Here we are," she said at last.

"If you say so," Cornelu answered. "For all that I can tell by looking, we might be going into King Vitor's palace."

Janira laughed. "No," she said. "That's down the street. And it's not half so fine a place as this." She laughed again. "Why, you can see for yourself."

To Cornelu, a sober, literal-minded man not much given to whimsy, that meant nothing for a moment. Then he got the joke and laughed, too. He took her in his arms. Their lips had no trouble finding each other in the darkness. His hands slid

along the length of her. She let him lift her kilt and stroke her
there, but then she twisted away. "Janira—" he said hoarsely.
They could have done anything at all right there, and no one
but the two of them would ever have known.

"Not now," she said. "Not yet. I'm not ready, Cornelu.
Good night." He heard her footsteps on the stairs. The door to
her block of flats opened. Then it closed.

He kicked at the slates of the sidewalk. She wasn't teasing
him, leading him on. He was sure of that. One of these days,
when she was ready, they would go further. "But why not
tonight?" he muttered, kicking at the sidewalk again. In the
blackness, he could have reached under his own kilt and relieved some of his agitation, too, but he didn't. Instead, he set
out for his dockside barracks.

Not being a native of Setubal, he didn't unerringly find his
way to them. He did manage to get aboard one of the many
ley-line caravans gliding through the streets of the city. It
wasn't any of those that went down to the harbor district, but
it took him to a stop where he could catch a caravan that
would carry him where he needed to go. He felt pretty good
about that.

He didn't feel so good when reveille pried him out of his
cot the next morning. Yawning, he staggered to the galley and
gulped cup after cup of strong tea. One of his fellow exiles
teased him: "You'll be pissing all day long."

"I probably will," Cornelu agreed, yawning again. "At
least all the running to the jakes and back will keep me
awake."

"Must have been quite a night last night." His countryman
sounded jealous.

"Not so bad," Cornelu said. Janira, had she heard that,
would have been irate; it implied he'd had his way with her,
which he hadn't. But she wasn't there and the other Sibian
was, and so Cornelu boasted a little.

He was going back for yet another mug of tea when a
Lagoan officer he'd never seen before strode briskly into the
mess hall. Suspicion flamed in Cornelu; an unfamiliar
Lagoan with something on his mind was the last thing he

wanted to see early in the morning—or any other time of day, either.

Sure enough, the Lagoan spoke up in his own language: "How many of you understand me?" About half the Sibians raised their hands. Cornelu followed well enough, but kept his down. The Lagoan switched to Algarvian: "How many of you understand me now?"

This time, Cornelu raised his hand. So did most of his countrymen. One of them called out in his own language: "Why don't you speak Sibian, if you want to talk to us?"

The Lagoan ignored that. Lagoans were generally good at ignoring anything they didn't want to hear. In Algarvian, the fellow continued, "You will all report to the Admiralty offices after breakfast for an important briefing."

"What's it about?" Cornelu called.

He got no answer. He hadn't really expected one. Having delivered his message, the Lagoan officer turned on his heel and marched away. Muffled curses followed him—and some that weren't so muffled. "High-handed son of a whore," one of the exiles said, and everybody else nodded. Lagoans were like that.

But the Sibians all tramped over to the Admiralty offices at the required time, too. Cornelu wondered what sort of orders—or lies—they would hear from the Lagoan officers in charge of getting the most out of them. Cornelu sometimes thought the Lagoans were as intent on using up the Sibians as they were on using them. He shrugged. He couldn't do anything about that.

At the Admiralty, a grizzled Lagoan petty officer whose ribbons and medals declared that he'd fought bravely during the Six Years' War spoke to the Sibians: "Down the hallway to the conference room." Unlike a lot of his countrymen—including plenty with fancier ranks and fancier educations—he spoke Sibian, not Algarvian. He even had a Facaceni accent.

"Where did you learn my language?" Cornelu asked him.

"Always a bit of dealing going on," the Lagoan answered, and said no more. *Smuggler,* Cornelu guessed. Whether he was right or wrong, he couldn't do anything about it now.

Gold letters over the entrance to the conference room proclaimed that it was named for Admiral Velho, one of Lagoas' heroes in the last naval war against Sibiu a couple of hundred years before. Assembling Sibians here to listen to whatever the Lagoans had to say struck Cornelu as less than tactful, but the Lagoans had been less than tactful ever since the Sibian exiles arrived.

Cornelu turned to complain to one of his countrymen as he started into the conference room, but stopped with the words unuttered. One look at the map on the far wall swept them out of his head. The other Sibians were pointing and staring, too. Their talk rose to an excited buzz.

A Lagoan officer in tunic and kilt darker than the Sibian sea-green stood beside the map. "Have we got your attention?" he asked the exiles—in Algarvian. For once, Cornelu didn't care. With that map in front of him, he would listen to anything.

Fifteen

"To sing a song of victory." Words bubbled inside Garivald like stew bubbling in a pot over a hot fire. "The day they thought they'd never see." He paused, waiting for the next couplet to form. "They thought they'd hit us hard in summer. But now we know their days are numbered." He shook his head. That wouldn't do, not even with music to make the bad rhyme and scansion less obvious.

He cast about for a better line. Before he could find one, the Unkerlanter regular named Tantris came up to him. Whatever line might have taken shape flew away instead. He gave Tantris a dirty look.

The regular ignored it. He said, "We need to strike the followers of Raniero the pretender, to show them they aren't safe even though his Majesty's troops haven't yet started taking Grelz back from the invaders. Can we do it?"

"You're asking me now?" Garivald said, intrigued. Tantris nodded. Garivald persisted: "You're not giving orders? You're not saying you know everything and I don't know anything, the way you did before?"

"I never said *that*," Tantris protested.

"No?" Garivald glowered at him. "Where's Gandiluz, then? Dead, that's where. Dead because you wouldn't listen to me when I told you Sadoc could no more work magic than a bullfrog can fly. You had it all planned, the two of you. But you weren't quite as efficient as you thought, were you?"

Tantris gave him a long, expressionless look. "You do want to have some care in how you speak to me."

Garivald wanted nothing of the sort. Tantris put him in mind of all the inspectors and impressers he'd had to obey his whole life long. But he didn't have to obey this whoreson. The band of irregulars in the woods west of Herborn was *his*, not Tantris'. One word from him and the regular soldier would meet with an unfortunate accident. Garivald smiled. Power was heady stuff.

Tantris nodded as if Garivald had spoken his thoughts aloud. "Everything gets remembered, you know," Tantris said. "Everything. With his Majesty's armies moving forward again, debts will be paid, every single one of them. Before very long, Grelz will find out exactly what that means."

Birds chirped. Leaves were green. The sun shone brightly. But, just for a moment, winter lived in Garivald. He held the whip hand right now. But behind him stood only his irregulars. Behind Tantris stood the whole great apparatus of Unkerlanter intimidation, reaching all the way back to the throne room in Cottbus and to King Swemmel himself. Which carried more weight in the end? Garivald knew too mournfully well. With a sigh, he said, "We hate the redheads and the traitors worse than we hate each other. We'd better, anyhow."

"Aye. We'd better." Tantris' smile was crooked. "And we'd better show the traitors that we're still in business around these parts. Their hearts will be down in their boots anyhow, with the Algarvians falling back toward the borders of Grelz. A lot of them will be looking for ways out of the fight. Their hearts won't be in it anymore."

"Maybe," Garivald said. "Some of them follow King Raniero—"

"False King Raniero," Tantris broke in.

"False King Raniero," Garivald agreed dutifully. "Some of them follow him for the sake of a full belly or a place to sleep at night. But some of them . . ." He paused, wondering how to say what needed saying without putting his own head in the noose. "Some of them, you know, really mean it."

Tantris nodded. "Those are the ones who really need killing. We can't let people think they can side with the redheads and against our kingdom and get away with it. This isn't a game we're playing here. They'd get rid of every one of us if they could, and we have to treat them the same way."

Garivald nodded. Every word of that was true, however much he wished it weren't. "What have you got in mind?" he asked. "If it's something we can do, we'll do it." He couldn't resist a last jab: "If it's more of Sadoc's magic, maybe you'd better think again."

Tantris winced. The lightning Sadoc had called down could have seared him instead of Gandiluz. It could have seared Garivald, too. Garivald knew what had saved him, though: Sadoc had aimed the lightning his way. And Sadoc had proved he couldn't hit what he was aiming at.

"No more magic," Tantris said with another shudder. "What I have in mind is hitting one of the villages around the woods that the Grelzers garrison. If we kill a few Algarvians in the fighting, all the better."

"All right," Garivald said. "As long as you don't want to make us stand and fight if they turn out to be stronger than we expect going in." King Swemmel was liable to reckon it efficient to get rid of men bold enough to be irregulars at the same time as he was fighting the Grelzers.

If that had occurred to Tantris, he didn't show it. He said, "Whatever you think best, as long as we strike the blow."

Garivald scratched his chin. Whiskers rasped under his fingers; he still shaved every now and then, but only every now and then, and he had the fair—or rather, the dark—beginnings of a beard. After some thought, he said, "Lohr. That'll be the place we'll have the easiest time hitting. It's not very far from the woods, and the garrison there isn't very big. Aye, Lohr."

"Suits me well enough," Tantris said.

"I was blooded in this band between Lohr and Pirmasens," Garivald said. "We ambushed a squad of Algarvian footsoldiers marching from one to the other. I don't think there are any redheads down there these days—they've mostly gone west, and they leave it to the traitors to hold down the countryside."

"Our job is to show 'em that won't work," Tantris said.

Two nights later, the irregulars left the shelter of the woods and marched on Lohr. Actually, it was more of a straggle than a march. They ambled along in a column, tramping down the dirt road toward the village. Garivald posted a couple of men who'd grown up by Lohr in the vanguard, and another at the rear. They were the best local guides in the darkness—and if something went wrong.

Somewhere between the van and the rear, he would find himself walking beside Obilot. She said, "Fighting Grelzers isn't the same as fighting Algarvians. It's like drinking spirits cut with too much water."

"We hurt the Algarvians when we hit the Grelzers, too," Garivald said.

"I know," she answered. "It's still not the same. I don't want to hurt Algarvians by hurting Grelzer traitors. I want to hurt Algarvians by hurting Algarvians." She kicked at the ground as if it were one of Mezentio's soldiers.

Not for the first time, Garivald wanted to ask what the redheads had done to her. Not for the first time, he found he lacked the nerve. He kept marching.

When they started to near Lohr, Tantris came over to him and said, "We ought to get off the road now, and go by way of the fields. If the traitors have sentries, they'll be less likely to spot us so."

He still wasn't giving orders. He'd lost some of his arrogance, sure enough. And his advice made sense. Garivald nodded and said, "Aye, we'll do it." He gave the orders.

No sentries challenged them. Garivald's confidence began to rise. No one had betrayed the attack to the men who followed King Raniero. He and his irregulars often knew what the Grelzers would do as soon as Raniero's men did, but that coin had two sides. *Who in my band is a traitor?* was a question that always ate at him.

Dawn had just begun to turn the eastern sky gray when they came up to Lohr. A man from the vanguard pointed out three or four houses. "Those are the ones the Grelzers use," he whispered to Garivald. He spoke with great confidence. Garivald assumed someone in the village had told him. Sure enough, this business of civil war was as much a matter of listening and hearing as it was of fighting.

"Forward!" Garivald called softly, and the irregulars loped into the sleeping village. Dogs began to bark. A little white one ran yapping at Garivald and made as if to bite his ankle. He blazed it. It let out a low wail of pain, then fell silent. He kicked its body aside and ran on.

A couple of villagers and a couple of Grelzer soldiers came out to see what the fuss was about. In the dim light, none of the irregulars tried to figure out who was who. They just started blazing. It wasn't a battle. It wasn't anything like a battle. In a very few minutes, Lohr was theirs.

The survivors they captured from the squad of Grelzers made Garivald sad. They could as easily have fought on his side as for the Algarvian puppet king of Grelz. But they'd made the other choice—the wrong choice, as it turned out—and they would have to pay for it. Tantris was looking at him, as if wondering whether he had the stomach to give the order.

He did, saying, "Blaze the traitors." A moment later, he added, "Blaze the firstman, too. He's been in bed with the Algarvians ever since they got here." None of that took long, either. Before the sun had risen, the irregulars were on their way back to their forest fastness.

Tantris came up to him, saying, "Very neat. You see what you can do."

Garivald nodded. "I also see you weren't joggling my elbow, the way you did when you tried to use Sadoc for more than he could give."

"Do I have to tell you again that everything you say will be remembered?" Tantris asked.

"Do you care to remember that I told you the truth?" Garivald answered. He stepped up his pace. Tantris didn't try to stay with him.

He caught up with Obilot just as the sun came red over the horizon. Her eyes, he thought, shone brighter than it did. "We did well there, even if they were only Grelzers," she said.

"Aye." Garivald nodded. Her words weren't much different from what Tantris had given him, but warmed him far more. He could have done without the regular's approval; at times, he would gladly have done without the regular altogether. But what Obilot thought mattered to him. All at once, hardly thinking what he was doing, he reached out and took her hand.

She blinked. Garivald waited to see what would happen next. If she decided she didn't like that, she was liable to do something much more emphatic than just telling him so. But she let his hand stay in hers. All she said was, "Took you long enough."

"I wanted to be sure," he answered, though he'd been anything but. Then he took his hand away, not wanting to push too hard.

The band got back under the trees without having lost a man—or a woman, either. Garivald left sentries behind to warn of a Grelzer counterattack if one came. The rest of the irregulars returned to the clearing for as much of a celebration as they could manage, though a lot of them wanted nothing but sleep.

Garivald caught Obilot's eye again. He wandered into the woods. If she followed, she did. If she didn't . . . He shrugged. Pushing Obilot when she didn't care to be pushed was a good way to end up dead.

But she did follow. When they found a tiny clearing far

enough from the main one, they paused and looked at each other. "Are you sure?" Garivald asked. He'd been away from his wife and family for more than a year. Obilot nodded. He thought she had no family left alive, though he wasn't sure. He took her in his arms. None of what they said to each other after that had anything to do with words.

Flying over the plains of southern Unkerlant, Count Sabrino felt a strong sense of having done all this before. By the way things looked, the war against Unkerlant, the war the Algarvians had thought they would win in the first campaigning season, would go on forever.

His mouth twisted. Appearances were liable to be deceiving, but not in the way for which his countrymen would have hoped. If they'd broken through to Cottbus, if they'd broken past Sulingen, maybe even if they'd torn the heart from the Unkerlanter defenses in the Durrwangen bulge . . .

But they hadn't. They hadn't done any of those things. And how many Algarvian behemoths lay rotting on the battlefields of the Durrwangen salient? Sabrino couldn't have said, not to the closest hundred, not even to the closest five hundred, not to save his own life. But he knew the answer just the same. *Too many.*

These days, the Algarvians had to hold on tightly to the behemoths they had left. If they incautiously threw them away, they'd have none at all. Oh, that wasn't quite true—but it came all too close. And it would be at least another year, more likely two or three, before new beasts came off the breeding farms in anything like adequate numbers.

Meanwhile . . . Meanwhile, the Unkerlanters still had behemoths and to spare. And they handled them better than they had when the war was new. *Why not?* Sabrino thought bitterly. *They've spent the past two years learning from us.*

They had behemoths. More came from their breeding farms in a steady stream. How many breeding farms did they have, there in the far west beyond the reach of any Algarvian dragon? Those same two words formed again in Sabrino's mind. *Too many.* They had footsoldiers in endless profusion, too. And they had mages willing to be as ruthless as—maybe more ruthless than—any who served King Mezentio.

No wonder, then, that Sabrino was flying a good deal north and east of Durrwangen these days. The Unkerlanters were the ones moving forward now, his own countrymen the ones who tried to slow them, tried to stop them, tried to turn them back. He wished they would have had more luck at it.

The Algarvians did have a counterattack going in now, a blow at the flank of an advancing Unkerlanter column. Sabrino knew a certain somber pride as he watched the footsoldiers down there far below crumple up the Unkerlanters. They were still better versed in the art of war than King Swemmel's men. Where they gained anything close to local equality, they could still drive the foe before them.

He spoke into his crystal: "Forward! If we take out their egg-tossers, our boys may be able to pin the Unkerlanters against the river and do a proper job of chewing them up."

Captain Orosio said, "Can't hurt to try. Sooner or later, we've got to stop these bastards. Might as well be now."

"That's right. We've got the edge here. We'd better take advantage of it." Sabrino said nothing of conquest. He said nothing of driving the enemy back to Durrwangen, let alone to Sulingen or Cottbus. His horizons had contracted. A local victory, an advance here instead of a retreat, would do well enough for now.

He spotted the egg-tossers in what had been a field of rye but was now overgrown and full of weeds. The dragonfliers of his wing behind him, he dove on them. For a few splendid minutes, everything went the way it had back in the first days of the war. One after another, the Algarvians released their eggs and then rose into the sky once more. Looking over his shoulder, Sabrino saw the bursts of sorcerous energy send the enemy egg-tossers and their crews flying in ruin.

"That's the way to do it," he said. The enemy would have a harder time hurting the Algarvian soldiers on the ground. He and his wing flew on toward the west, gaining height. There was the river, sure enough. He spoke into the crystal again: "We'll turn around and flame the crews we might have missed with our eggs. Then back to the dragon farm and we'll get ourselves some rest."

Rest. He laughed. He had trouble remembering what the word meant. He patted the scaly side of his dragon's neck. The vicious, stupid beast had trouble remembering, too. Of course, it had trouble remembering everything.

No sooner had that thought struck him than he spied the Unkerlanter dragons winging their way up out of the south, straight for his wing. They were very fast and flew in good formation—some of Swemmel's top dragonfliers, mounted on prime beasts. It was an honor of sorts, though one Sabrino could have done without. He shouted into the crystal, warning his men.

The Unkerlanters had the advantage of numbers and the advantage of height, as well as the advantage of fresh dragons. All Sabrino and his men had left to them was the advantage of skill. Up till now, it had always sufficed to let them hurt the foe worse than he hurt them, to bring most of them back safe to whichever dragon farm they were using that day.

"One more time, by the powers above," Sabrino said, and swung his dragon toward the closest Unkerlanter. However weary it was, it still hated its own kind; its scream of rage proved as much.

Sabrino blazed one of King Swemmel's dragonfliers off the back of his mount. The dragon, without control, went wild and struck out at the beast closest to it, which was also painted Unkerlanter rock-gray. Sabrino whooped. He'd just made life harder for the foe.

And then his own dragon twisted and convulsed beneath him, bellowing in the agony he'd inflicted on so many of his enemies. While he'd been dealing with the foe in front of him, he'd let an Unkerlanter dragon get close enough to his rear to flame. In any sort of even fight, it would have been a rookie mistake. Outnumbered as his countrymen were, it had to happen every so often. So he told himself, at any rate. Excuses aside, though, it was liable to kill him.

His dragon, he saw at once, wouldn't be able to stay in the air. He looked back. Sure enough, its right wing was badly burned. The only consolation he could draw was that it didn't plummet to earth at once, which would have put an immediate end to his career, too.

He tried to urge it back toward the east, toward the Algarvian lines. But, lost in its private wilderness of pain, the dragon paid no attention to the increasingly frantic signals he gave it with the goad. It flew straight for the river. *The water is cold,* it must have thought. *It will feel good on my hurt wing.*

"No, you miserable, stupid, stinking thing!" Sabrino howled. "You'll drown, and you'll drown me, too." He pounded at it with the goad.

Maybe he did a little good. Instead of coming down in the water, the dragon landed on the riverbank. Sabrino unfastened his harness and leaped off its back as it waded into the stream. Only then did he realize it had come down on the western side of the river, putting that stream and several miles of enemy-held country between himself and his countrymen.

Fast as he could, he got out of the furs and leather he wore to ward himself against the chill of the upper air. Drawn by the dragon, Unkerlanter soldiers were trotting toward him. They would finish him off if they got the chance. He didn't want to give it to them. Clad only in his drawers and clutching his stick, he plunged into the river.

He struck out for the eastern bank, swimming as strongly as he could. Even in late summer, the water was bitterly cold. The Unkerlanters shouted and started blazing. Puffs of steam rose from the river not far from Sabrino; their beams were plenty to boil it here and there. But they didn't get close enough to the water's edge to blaze with any great accuracy. For a while, Sabrino simply accepted that. He wasn't about to look back to see what was going on.

But then he didn't have to. His wounded dragon's bellows of pain and rage told him everything he wanted to know. Swemmel's soldiers would have to stalk it and kill it before they could worry too much about him. And, although it couldn't fly, it remained deadly dangerous on the ground.

Sabrino thought he could safely concentrate on his swimming.

He was worn when he splashed up onto the eastern bank. He lay there for a couple of minutes, gathering his strength. *I'm getting too old for these games,* he thought. But he wasn't so old that he felt like dying. Once he got his wind back, he climbed to his feet and started east. Somehow or other, he would have to get through the Unkerlanter line and back to his own.

First things first. He dove behind some bushes. A squad's worth of Unkerlanters were trotting toward the river. They were pointing at the dragon, and didn't see him. He supposed they were going to have some fun blazing at it. They couldn't do it much harm, not from this side of the stream. Of course, it couldn't flame them over here, either. Once they'd gone past him, Sabrino scurried east again.

He found the Unkerlanter in the bushes by almost stumbling over him. The fellow was squatting, his tunic hiked up, his stick beside him on the ground. He stared at Sabrino in the same horror and astonishment as Sabrino felt on coming across him. Then he grabbed for his stick. Sabrino blazed first. The Unkerlanter let out a moan and toppled.

Sabrino put on his rock-gray tunic and his boots, which were too big. He didn't look anything like an Unkerlanter, but he wouldn't stand out so much at long range wearing the tunic. The man he'd killed had some flat barley cakes in his belt pouch. Sabrino wolfed them down.

Should I lie low till nightfall? he wondered. In the end, he didn't dare. His dragon would draw more Unkerlanters, the same way amber drew feathers and bits of paper. The farther away from it he got, the better. And every step put him one step closer to his countrymen. *One step closer to the Unkerlanters' main line,* too, he thought. But he kept moving.

It almost cost him his life. A couple of Unkerlanters spotted him and started running after him. He blazed one of them, then ran like blazes himself. But the other soldier seemed to take two strides for every one of his. *I'm* much *too old for this,* Sabrino thought, heart thudding fit to burst.

The Unkerlanter kept blazing as he ran. He couldn't aim very well doing that; he charred lines in the grass and shrubs all around Sabrino. But then his beam caught the Algarvian dragonflier high in the back of the left shoulder. With a howl of pain, Sabrino fell forward on his face. With a howl of triumph, Swemmel's soldier dashed up to finish him off—and took a beam right in the chest. Wearing a look of absurd, indignant surprise, he crumpled.

"Never try to trick an old fox," Sabrino panted. Right at the moment, he felt like the oldest fox in the world. He robbed this Unkerlanter, too, and then cut the dead man's tunic into strips to bandage his wound. It hurt, but he didn't think it too serious. He also stuffed cloth into the toes of the boots he'd stolen to make them fit better.

Now he did hide till midnight. The Unkerlanter had an entrenching tool on his belt. Sabrino dug himself a scrape—awkwardly and painfully, with only one arm working well—and waited for darkness.

It came sooner than it would have at the height of the fighting for the Durrwangen bulge. Fall was on the way, and then another savage Unkerlanter winter. When night arrived, he scurried forward. He favored his left side, which had stiffened up. Every time he heard an Unkerlanter voice, he froze.

The front, fortunately, was fluid hereabouts. The Unkerlanters and his own men had foxholes and outposts, not solid trench lines. A determined—no, a desperate—man could sneak between them.

Dawn was painting the east red when someone called out a nervous challenge: "Halt! Who comes?"

Sabrino almost wept. The challenge was in Algarvian. "A friend," he said. "A dragonflier blazed down behind the enemy's line."

Silence. Then: "Advance and be recognized. Hands high." Because of the wound, Sabrino's left hand didn't want to go high. He raised it despite the pain. Moving forward as if surrendering, he let his own side capture him.

*   *   *

"Here you go, Constable." A baker offered Bembo a slice of cheese pie. "Try this and tell me what you think."

"Don't mind if I do." Bembo never minded taking free food and drink from the shops and taverns on his beat. He'd done it in Tricarico, and he did it here in Gromheort, too. He took a big bite and chewed thoughtfully. "Not bad," he said, and took another bite to prove it. "What all's in it?"

"Two kinds of cheese," the baker began. He spoke good Algarvian.

"Aye, I know that," Bembo said impatiently. "What livens it up?"

"Well, there's garlic and onions and leeks," the baker said, and Bembo nodded each time. Then the Forthwegian looked sly and set a finger by the side of his nose. "And there's a mystery ingredient. I don't know whether I ought to tell you or not."

By then, Bembo was finishing the slice of pie. "You'd better," he said, his mouth full. "You'll be sorry if you don't." Had the whoreson given him mouse turds, or something like that? Surely not—if he had, he wouldn't have told Bembo at all.

"All right, I'll talk," the baker said, as if he were a captive Bembo was belaboring. "It's dried chanterelle mushrooms."

"You're kidding." Bembo's stomach did a slow lurch. Like all Algarvians, he thought mushrooms disgusting. Forthwegians, on the other hand, were wild for them, and put them in everything but tea. Bembo's hand fell to the leather grip of his bludgeon. "I ought to loosen your teeth for you, feeding me those miserable things."

"Why?" the Forthwegian asked in what sounded like honest bewilderment. "You just said you liked the pie."

Bembo could hardly deny that. He did his best: "I liked it in spite of the mushrooms, not because of them."

"How do you know? Be honest, Constable. How *do* you know?" The baker speared a mushroom out of the pie with the point of the knife he'd used to slice it. He offered it to Bembo. "How can you really know till you try?"

"I'd sooner eat a snail," Bembo said, which was true—he liked snails fine, especially in butter and garlic. The Forthwegian baker made a horrible face. Bembo laughed at that, and wagged a finger at the fellow. "You see? I'm not the only one." But the mushroom remained on the end of the knife, a mute challenge to his manhood. He scowled, but then he ate it.

The little boy's way of handling such an unfortunate situation would have been to gulp the mushroom down without tasting it. Bembo was tempted to do just that, but made himself chew slowly and deliberately before swallowing. "Well?" the baker demanded. "What do you think?"

"I think you Forthwegians get too worked up over the cursed things, that's what," Bembo answered. "Not a whole lot of taste any which way."

"These are just the dried ones," the baker said. "When the fall rains come and the fresh mushrooms start growing, then . . ." He sighed, as Bembo might have sighed over the charms of a beautiful woman. Bembo was convinced he could have a lot more fun with a beautiful woman than any Forthwegian could with a mushroom.

"Well, I'm off," he said, wiping greasy fingers on his kilt. "No surprises next time, mind you, or you'll get a surprise you won't like so bloody well." He went on his way, hoping he'd put a little fear into the baker's heart. The strangled guffaw he heard as he closed the door behind him made him doubt it. He wasn't usually the sort who roused fear in people. Oraste, now . . . Oraste even roused fear in Bembo, his partner.

Bembo swaggered along, every now and then flourishing his club. Oraste, at the moment, roused fear in nobody; he was down with a nasty case of the grippe. Bembo hoped he wouldn't catch it. He feared he would, though. People who worked with people who got sick often got sick themselves. Nobody'd ever quite figured out why. It probably had something to do with the law of similarity.

Or maybe it's the law of contagion, Bembo thought. *Contagion. Get it?* He laughed. Without Oraste at his side, he had to tell jokes to himself. He found them funnier than Oraste would have. He was sure of that.

Seeing a company of Algarvian footsoldiers tramping toward the ley-line caravan depot, he stuck up his arm to halt traffic on the cross street. His countrymen cursed him as they passed. By now, he was used to that. They were on their way to Unkerlant, and he got to stay here in Gromheort. The way things were in Unkerlant these days, he wouldn't have wanted to go there himself.

Behind the Algarvians came another company in uniform: bearded Forthwegians who'd joined Plegmund's Brigade. Their countrymen, forced to wait at the cross street while they passed, cursed them more foully than the Algarvian sol-diers had cursed Bembo. Disciplined and stolid, the new recruits for the Brigade kept on marching. They puzzled Bembo. If some foreign king occupied Algarve, he couldn't see himself volunteering to fight for the fellow.

Of course, I'm a lover, not a fighter, he thought. He wouldn't have said that aloud had Oraste been tramping along beside him. His partner seldom found his jokes funny, but Oraste would have howled laughter at that.

A little storefront had a big sign in unintelligible Forthwegian. Below it, in smaller letters, were a couple of words of perfectly understandable Algarvian: *Healing Charms.* The paint that served as their background was a little newer, a little cleaner, than the rest of the sign. Bembo wondered if the sign had said the same thing in classical Kaunian before Gromheort changed hands.

He might have walked on by had he not chosen that moment to sneeze. He didn't want to spend several days on his cot aching and feverish and generally feeling as if he'd stepped in front of a ley-line caravan car. If a charm would stop his sickness before it really got started, he was all for it. He went inside.

Two men and a woman sat in a gloomy, nasty waiting room. They all looked up at him in varying degrees of alarm. He'd expected nothing less. "Relax," he told them, hoping they understood Algarvian—after the baker, he was feeling spoiled. "I'm here for the same reason you are."

One of the men murmured in Forthwegian. The other two people eased back into their seats. The woman chuckled nervously. The man who knew some Algarvian asked, "And why is that?"

"To keep myself from coming down with the grippe, of course," Bembo answered. He sneezed again. "Powers above, I hope I'm not too late."

"Oh," the man said. He translated once more. The other man said something. They all smiled. The man patted the chair next to him. "Here. You can go next."

"Thanks." Bembo took such privileges for granted. He sat down.

A few minutes later, the door to the back room opened. A man and a woman came out. The man took one look at Bembo and scooted past him, out the front door, and onto the street. That didn't surprise Bembo, either—the fellow was the type who would have dealt with constables before. The woman looked Bembo up and down, too. After a brittle silence, she asked, "What you want?" in halting Algarvian.

Before Bembo could speak, the man sitting by him said, "He's after your famous cure for the grippe."

"Ah." The woman nodded. She pointed to Bembo. "You come with me."

"Aye, Mistress," he answered, and followed her into the back room. It had the impressive disorder he'd seen before among mages of a certain type, although he would have been mightily surprised if she held any formal ranking. When she gestured, he sat down in one of the chairs. She sat in the other, which faced his.

"Grippe, eh?" she said.

"That's right," Bembo agreed. "My partner's down with it now, and I don't want to catch it myself."

Nodding again, she set her hand on his forehead. Her palm was cool and smooth. She clicked her tongue between her teeth. "You just in time—I hope," she said.

"Have I got a fever?" Bembo asked anxiously.

She held up her thumb and forefinger. "Little one," she answered. "*Now* little one. You not worry. I fix." She reached for a book. It was, Bembo saw, in Kaunian. He gave a mental shrug. Algarvian mages used the classical tongue, too.

After reading, she rummaged through her sorcerous supplies (had she not been a mage of sorts, Bembo would have thought of the stuff as junk). She bound a small, reddish rock and a bit of something fibrous into a silk bag, then hung it round his neck by a cord. Then she put a couple of teeth, one needlelike, the other thicker but still sharp, into another little sack and set that in his breast pocket.

"Bloodstone and sea sponge good against fever," she said. "Likewise fangs of serpent and crocodile." She stood and set both hands on top of his head. Some of her chant was in Forthwegian, some in Kaunian. When she was done, she gave Bembo a brisk nod and held out her right hand, palm up. "One broad silver bit."

He started to growl. But angering a mage, even a lesser one, was foolish. He paid. Not only did he pay, he said, "Thank you."

It wasn't what he was thinking. The healer had to know that. But nobody could blaze you for thinking. She said, "You're welcome."

When he came out into the front room, conversation stopped most abruptly. A couple of new people had come in while the healing mage was helping him. He thought they were talking back and forth in Kaunian, but he hadn't heard enough to be sure. He strode past them and out onto the street again.

The more he walked his beat, though, the more worried he got. If that was a place where disguised Kaunians gathered, had the healer tried to cure him or curse him? When he got back to the barracks, he put the question to a mage attached to the constabulary.

"Let's see the amulets she gave you," the fellow said. Bembo showed them to him. He nodded. "The substances are what they should be. I can check whether the spell was perverted some sort of way." The mage chanted, cocked his head to one side as if listening, and chanted some more. He glanced over at Bembo. "Far as I can tell, friend, you're not likely to get the grippe for a while. Everything's as it should be."

"Good," Bembo said. "The way things are nowadays, you can't be too careful."

"Well, I'm not going to tell you you're wrong there," the mage said. "But everything's fine this time."

Bembo intended to stop in and thank the healer—and probably frighten the life out of her customers—when he walked his beat the next day. But when he came to the little storefront, the door was ajar. He stuck his head inside. The door to the back room stood half open, too. He went back and peered into the gloom—no lamps shining now. And no litter of sorcerous apparatus there, either. The mage was gone, and she'd cleaned out all her stuff.

Bembo sighed. He wasn't even very surprised. He patted the amulets she'd given him. She'd been honest, and then she'd decided she had to run away. "Shows what honesty's worth," Bembo muttered. And if that wasn't a demon of a thought for a constable to have, he didn't know what was.

Spinello not only walked through the streets of Trapani with a limp, he walked through them with a cane. From what the healers said, he might get rid of the cane one day before too long. The limp, though, the limp looked to be here to stay.

There were compensations. He got pitying glances from women, and pity, for a man of enterprise, might easily be turned to some warmer emotion. The wound badge he wore on his tunic now supported a gold bar. He'd been awarded the Algarvian Sunburst, Second Grade, for gallantry in the face of the enemy, to go with his frozen-meat medal, and he had a colonel's three stars on his collar patches. When he went back to the front, he'd probably end up commanding a brigade.

He tried to straighten up and walk as if he hadn't been wounded. He could do it—for a couple of steps at a time. After that, it hurt too much. He would have traded rank and decorations for the smooth stride he'd once enjoyed in a heartbeat—*in half a heartbeat, by the powers above,* he thought. But the powers above didn't strike bargains like that, worse luck.

Going up the stairs to the Royal Cultural Museum made sweat spring out on his forehead. By the time he climbed them all and strode into the great rococo pile of a building, he was biting his lip against the pain. The ticket-seller, a nice-looking young woman, gave him a smile that could have been promising. But when Spinello said hello to her, he tasted blood in his mouth. He went on by, his own face grim.

As always, he made for the large gallery housing artifacts from the days of the Kaunian Empire. The spare, even severe, sensibility informing those busts and pots and coins and sorcerous tools and other articles of everyday life was as far removed from that inspiring the building in which they were housed as it possibly could have been. And yet, all things considered, Spinello preferred elegant simplicity to equally elegant extravagance.

As he always did in this gallery, Spinello paused in front of a two-handled drinking cup whose lines had always struck him as being as close to perfection as made no difference. Neither illustration nor memory ever did it justice. Every so often, he had to see it in the fired clay to remind himself what human hand and human will could shape.

"Spinello, isn't it?"

He was so lost in contemplation, he needed a moment to hear and recognize his own name. Then he turned and stared at the aged savant who'd been leaning on a cane longer than he had been alive. His own bow was awkward, but heartfelt. "Master Malindo!" he exclaimed. "What an honor! What a pleasant surprise!" *What a pleasant surprise to see you still breathing,* was what he meant. Malindo had been too old to serve in the Six Years' War, which surely put him up past ninety now.

"I go on," Malindo said in a creaky voice. "Are those a colonel's stars I see?"

"Aye." Spinello drew himself up with what he hoped was pardonable pride.

"A man of valor. A man of spirit," Malindo murmured. He paused, perhaps trying to find what he'd meant to say. *He is old,* Spinello thought. But then, quite visibly, the savant *did* find it. "And have you fought in the west?"

"Aye," Spinello repeated, this time in a different tone of voice.

Malindo reached out with his free hand, all wrinkled and veiny, and set it on the one Spinello used to hold his cane. "Then tell me—I beseech you, by the powers above—that what we hear of Algarve's dealings with Kaunians, dealings with the descendants of those who created *this*"—he wagged a finger at the cup—"is nothing but a lie, a filthy lie invented by our enemies."

Spinello couldn't nerve himself to lie to the old man. But he couldn't nerve himself to tell Malindo the truth, either. He stood mute.

Malindo sighed. He took his hand away from Spinello's. "What shall become of us?" he asked. Spinello didn't think the old man was talking to him. Malindo heaved another sigh, then slowly shuffled down the exhibit hall.

Try as he would, Spinello couldn't contemplate the cup the same way after that. The other Kaunian artifacts seemed somehow different, too. Cursing under his breath, he left the Royal Cultural Museum much sooner than he'd intended to. He wondered if he would ever be able to go back.

Two nights later, though, he hired a cab to take him through the darkened streets of Trapani to the royal palace. The last time he was wounded, he'd been too badly hurt to attend any of King Mezentio's receptions. This time, while not yet fit for field duty, he could—and did—display himself before his sovereign.

A somber servitor checked his name off a list. An even more somber mage muttered charms to test his cane before allowing him to go forward. "I haven't got a knife in there, nor a stick, either," Spinello said. "I could have told you as much, had you asked."

The mage bowed. "No doubt, your Excellency. An assassin could have told me as much, too, but he would have been lying. Best to take no chances, eh?"

"I suppose not," Spinello agreed with rather poor grace. But he added, "You didn't fret about such things when the war was new."

The mage shrugged. "Times are different now, sir." He waved Spinello past him.

Spinello went. What the fellow meant, of course, was, *The war news sounded a lot better then.* Who would have wanted to harm King Mezentio when Algarve's armies drove everything before them? No one, save perhaps some foreign hireling. Nowadays . . . Nowadays, there might well be Algarvians who'd lost enough to seek to avenge themselves on their sovereign. Spinello hoped not, but had to admit Mezentio was right to use the mage to help keep himself safe.

"Viscount Spinello!" a flunky bawled after Spinello murmured his name and rank to the man. A few heads turned his way. Most of the people already in the reception hall went on with what they were doing. A viscount limping along with the help of a cane was neither exotic nor prominent enough to be very interesting.

Officers and civilian functionaries drank and gossiped and eyed one another's women. The women drank and gossiped and eyed one another's men. And everyone, of course, eyed King Mezentio, who drifted through the room talking now with one man, now with another, or yet again with one of the better-looking women there.

After asking for a glass of wine and sipping it, Spinello looked at it in some surprise. "Something wrong, sir?" asked the servitor behind the bar.

"Wrong? No." Spinello shook his head. "But I've poured down too much in the way of Unkerlanter spirits, I think. Any drink that doesn't try to tear off the top of my skull hardly seems worth bothering with."

"Ha! That's the truth, by the powers above!" a soldier behind him boomed. The fellow also leaned on a cane, but would have been monstrous tall if straight. He wore a brigadier's rank badges, and had three gold bars under his wound badge. He went on, "After that stuff they brew from turnips and barley, wine isn't good for much but making you piss a lot."

"It does taste good," Spinello said, sipping again. For all the jolt it carried, it could have been water.

With a snort, the brigadier said, "My mistress tastes good, too, but that's not why I eat her." Had Spinello been drinking then, he would have sprayed wine over everything in front of him. As it was, he laughed loud enough to turn several heads his way.

One of those heads belonged to King Mezentio. He came over and asked, "And what is so funny here?"

"Your Majesty, you'll have to ask my superior here," Spinello answered. "He made the joke, and I would never dream of stealing it from him while he's close enough to listen to me do it."

Amusement flashed in Mezentio's hazel eyes. He turned to the brigadier, giving Spinello the long-nosed profile already familiar to him from the coins in his belt pouch. "Well, your Excellency?" Repeating himself didn't embarrass the brigadier one bit. And he made the king laugh. "Aye, that's good. That's very good," Mezentio said.

"I thought so," Spinello said: since he hadn't made the joke, he had to take credit for laughing at it. But maybe the wine he'd drunk had made him bolder than he'd believed, for he heard himself asking, "And when do we start making the Unkerlanters laugh out of the other side of their mouths again your Majesty?"

"If you have a way to do that, Colonel, leave a memorial with my officers," Mezentio replied. "I assure you, they will give it their closest attention."

He means it, Spinello realized, a wintry notion if ever there was one. The brigadier must have had the same thought, too, for he exclaimed, "We should have been readier when we struck them, then."

Now Mezentio looked right through him. "Thank you for your confidence in us, Carietto," the king said, for all the world as if he were Swemmel of Unkerlant, or perhaps twins. Spinello hadn't known the brigadier's name, but Mezentio did. Carietto, plainly, would never, ever, advance in rank again.

Spinello said, "Your Majesty, what can we do?"

"Keep fighting," King Mezentio said at once. "Make our foes bleed themselves white—and they will. Hold on till our mages strengthen their sorceries—and they will. Never admit we can be defeated. Fight with every fiber of our being so that victory comes to us—and it will."

He sounded very sure, very strong. Spinello saluted. So did Brigadier Carietto, not that it would do him any good. With a grin, Spinello said, "There may not be any Kaunians left by the time we're through."

"And so what?" Mezentio said. "How better to serve our ancient oppressors than to use them as weapons against the western barbarians? Algarve must save Derlavaian civilization, Colonel—and it will." He had a brandy in his hand. He knocked it back and strode away.

So much for old Malindo, Spinello thought. The savant, briefly, had made him feel guilty. Mezentio made him feel proud. Pride was better. He glanced over at Carietto. The brigadier looked like a man refusing to acknowledge he was wounded. He had pride, too. When he went back to the fighting, Spinello didn't think he would let himself live long.

"What were you talking about with the king?" That wasn't Carietto, but a woman about Spinello's own age. She had a wide, generous mouth, a nose with a tiny bend that made it more interesting than it would have been otherwise, and a figure her tight tunic and short kilt displayed to advantage.

Spinello bowed. "The war. Nothing important." He bowed again. "I would sooner talk about you, milady. I am Spinello. And your name is—?"

"Fronesia." She held out her hand.

After bowing over it once more, Spinello kissed it. "And whose friend are you, milady Fronesia?" he asked. "As lovely as you are, you must be someone's."

She smiled. "A colonel of dragonfliers' friend," she answered. "But Sabrino has been in the west forever and a day, and I grow lonely, to say nothing of bored. When I got myself invited here tonight, I hoped I would find a new friend. Was I right?"

Algarvian women had a way of coming straight to the point. So did Algarvian men. "Milady, with your looks"—Spinello's eyes traveled her curves—"you could have an array of friends, did you so choose. If you want one in particular, I am at your service."

Fronesia nodded. "If you're as generous as you are well-spoken, we should get on very well indeed, Colonel Spinello."

"There is generosity, and then there is generosity." Spinello looked her up and down again.

"My flat isn't far from here, Colonel," Fronesia said. "Shall we go back there and talk about it?"

"As long as we're there, we might as well talk, too," Spinello agreed. Laughing, they left together.

Ealstan had come up in the world. From bookkeeper, he'd advanced all the way to conspirator. If that wasn't progress, he didn't know what was. "I wish I'd found you a long time ago," he told Pybba.

"No, no, no." His boss shook his head. "Wish we'd been strong enough to give the stinking Algarvians a good boot in the balls when the war first started. Then we wouldn't have to play all these stupid games."

The pottery magnate was playing enough of them. Ealstan had thought as much when he first found the discrepancies in Pybba's books. He'd hoped as much. But even he hadn't had any notion of how deeply Pybba was involved in resisting King Mezentio's men in Forthweg. Nothing but admiration in his voice, he said, "I don't think anybody can write anything nasty about the Algarvians on a wall anywhere in Eoforwic unless you know about it before it happens."

"That's the idea." Pybba sounded smug: his usual growl with a purr mixed into it. The purr disappeared as he went on,

"Now shut up about what you're not supposed to be talking about and get back to work. If I don't make any money, I can't very well put any money into giving the redheads a hard time, now can I?"

Back to work Ealstan went, and utterly mundane work it was, too. But he didn't care. He'd scratched his itch to know. He'd done more than that. He'd started working to help drive Mezentio's men out of his kingdom. What more could he want? Nothing, or so he thought. If fighting the Algarvians also meant keeping track of invoices on fifty-seven different styles of teacup—and it did—he would cheerfully do that. If it wasn't his patriotic duty, he didn't know what it was.

And the news sheets had got very vague about how the fighting in Unkerlant was going. He took that as a good sign.

He'd been working in his new capacity for a few weeks when something odd struck him. That was almost literally true: he was walking home in the first rain of fall when the thought came to him. "The mushrooms will be springing up," he told Vanai when he got back to their flat.

"That's true." She clapped her hands together. "And I'll be able to go hunting them this year. Staying cooped up in the middle of mushroom season is something that shouldn't happen to anyone."

"Thanks to your sorcery, it won't happen to nearly so many people." Ealstan said went over and gave her a kiss. Then he paused, scratching his head.

"What is it?" Vanai asked.

"Nothing," Ealstan answered. "Or I don't think it's anything, anyway."

Vanai raised an eyebrow. But, rather to his relief, she did no more than raise an eyebrow. She didn't constantly push at him, for which he was duly grateful. Maybe that was because she'd never been able to push at her grandfather, by all the signs one of the least pushable men ever born. If so, it was one of the few things for which Ealstan would have thanked Brivibas had he been able. And, by all the signs, Brivibas wouldn't have appreciated his thanks.

A couple of days later, in casual tones, Ealstan said to Pybba, "Occurs to me you're missing something."

"Oh?" The pottery magnate raised a shaggy eyebrow. "What's that? Whatever it is, you'll tell me. You're the one who knows everything, after all."

Ealstan's cheeks heated. He hoped his beard kept Pybba from seeing him flush. But flushed or not, he stubbornly plowed ahead: "You want to do the redheads the most harm you can, right?"

"Not much point to kicking 'em halfway in the balls, is there?" his boss returned, and laughed at his own joke.

Ealstan chuckled, too, but went on, "Well, then, you *are* missing something. Who hates Mezentio's men more than anybody?"

Pybba jabbed a thumb at his own thick chest. "I do, by the powers above."

But Ealstan shook his head. "You don't hate them worse than the Kaunians do," he said. "And I haven't seen you doing anything to get the blonds to work alongside us Forthwegians. What they owe the Algarvians . . ."

"Kaunians? Blonds?" The pottery magnate might never have heard the names before. He scowled. "Weren't for the miserable Kaunians, we wouldn't have got into the war in the first place."

"Oh, by the powers above!" Ealstan clapped a hand to his forehead. "The Algarvians have been saying the same thing in their broadsheets ever since they beat us. Do you want to sound like them?"

"They're whoresons, aye—the Algarvians, I mean—but that doesn't make 'em wrong all the time," Pybba said. "I'd sooner trust my own kind, thank you very much."

"Kaunians are people, too," Ealstan said. His father had been saying that for as long as he could remember: long enough to make him take it for granted, anyway. But even if he took it for granted, he'd already seen that few of his fellow Forthwegians did.

Pybba proved not to be one of those few. He patted Ealstan

on the back and said, "I know you used to cast accounts for that half-breed musician. I suppose that's why you think the way you do. But most Kaunians are nothing but trouble, and you can take that to the bank. We'll kick the Algarvians out on their arses, we'll bring King Penda back, and everything will be fine."

Most Kaunians are nothing but trouble, and you can take that to the bank. What would Pybba say if he knew Ealstan's wife, whom he'd met as Thelberge, was really named Vanai? *He can't find out,* Ealstan thought—an obvious truth if ever there was one.

"Now get yourself back to work," Pybba said. "I'll do the thinking around here. You just cast the accounts."

"Right," Ealstan said tightly. He almost threw his job in the pottery magnate's face then and there. But if he left now, Pybba would realize his reasons had to do with Kaunians. He couldn't afford that. As he went back to the ledgers, tears of rage and frustration made the columns of numbers blur for a moment. He blinked till they went away. He'd found the underground, and now he found he didn't fit into it. That hurt almost too much to bear.

When he got home that evening, he poured out his troubles to Vanai. "No, you can't quit," his wife said, "even if Pybba has no use for Kaunians. If he has his way, people will despise us—the Forthwegians will, anyway. If the Algarvians win, we won't be around to despise. That makes things pretty simple, doesn't it?"

"It's not right," Ealstan insisted.

Vanai kissed him. "Of course it's not. But life hasn't been fair to us since the Kaunian Empire fell. Why should it start now? If Pybba and King Penda win, at least we get the chance to go on."

What Ealstan wanted to do was get drunk and stay drunk. *And if that doesn't prove I'm a Forthwegian, what would?* he thought. He didn't do it. He drank less wine with his supper than usual, in fact. But the temptation remained.

He felt Pybba's eye on him all the next morning. He went

about his work as stolidly as he could, and made no waves whatever. In the face of Vanai's relentless pragmatism, he didn't see what else he could do. When he didn't come out with anything radical, Pybba relaxed a little.

And then, a couple of days later, Ealstan jerked as if stung by a wasp. He looked around for Pybba. When he caught the pottery magnate's eye, Pybba was the one who flinched. "You've got that crazy look on your face again," he rumbled. "Mad Ealstan the Bookkeeper, that's you. Or that's what they'd've called you if you lived in King Plegmund's time, anyway."

Thinking of King Plegmund's time only made Ealstan scowl, no matter how glorious it had been for Forthweg. To him, Plegmund's time meant Plegmund's Brigade, and Plegmund's Brigade meant his cousin Sidroc, who'd killed his brother. Thinking of Plegmund's Brigade only convinced him his idea would work. He said, "Can we go into your office?"

"This had better be good," Pybba warned. Ealstan nodded. With obvious reluctance, his boss headed for the office. Ealstan followed him. Pybba slammed the door behind them. "Go ahead. You'd best knock me right out of my boots."

"I don't know whether I can or not," Ealstan said. "But I don't think we're doing everything with magecraft that we ought to be."

"You're right," the pottery magnate agreed. "I should have turned you into a paperweight or something else that can't talk a long time ago."

Ignoring that, Ealstan plowed ahead: "A mage could write something rude on one recruiting broadsheet for Plegmund's Brigade and then use the laws of similarity and contagion to make the same thing show up on every broadsheet all over Eoforwic."

"We are doing some of that kind of thing," Pybba said.

"Not enough," Ealstan returned. "Not nearly enough."

Pybba plucked at his beard. "It'd be hard on the mage if the redheads caught him," he said at last.

"It'd be hard on any of us if the redheads caught him," Ealstan answered. "Are we lawn-bowling with the Algarvians or fighting a war against them?"

The pottery magnate grunted. "Lawn-bowling, eh? All right, Mad Ealstan, get your arse back to your stool and start going over my books again."

That was all he would say. Ealstan wanted to push him harder, but decided he'd already done enough, or perhaps too much. He went back to the books. Pybba kept on calling him Mad Ealstan, which earned him some odd looks from the other men who worked for the magnate. Ealstan didn't let that worry him. If you weren't a little bit crazy, you couldn't work for Pybba very long.

When the next payday came, Pybba said, "Here. Make sure this goes on the books," and gave him another bonus. It was less than he'd got after being asked to look the other way about the discrepancies he'd found in Pybba's accounts, but it was a good deal better than a poke in the eye with a sharp stick.

A few days later, the Algarvians plastered a new recruiting broadsheet for Plegmund's Brigade all over Eoforwic. A FIGHT TO THE FINISH! it said. Two days after that, all those broadsheets suddenly sported a crude modification: A FIGHT FOR THE FINISHED! The Algarvians had paid Forthwegian laborers to put them up. Now they paid Forthwegians to take them down again.

"Aye, Mad Ealstan the Bookkeeper, by the powers above," Pybba said. Ealstan didn't say anything at all. He didn't say anything when Pybba gave him one more bonus the following payday, either. Nobody but him noticed the bonus, and nobody noticed his silence, either. Most people were silent around Pybba most of the time, and only exceptions got noticed. Ealstan knew what he'd done, and so did the magnate. Nothing else mattered.

Skarnu settled into a furnished room in the little town of Jurbarkas with the air of a man who'd known worse. When the silver in his pockets began to run low, he took odd jobs for the farmers around the town. He quickly proved he knew what he was doing, so he got more work than a lot of the drifters who looked for it in the market square.

Getting out into the countryside let him visit the farm near Jurbarkas run by a man who worked with the underground. After visiting, Skarnu wished he hadn't. Those fields grew rank and untended; the farmhouse stood empty. Three words had been daubed on the door in whitewash now rain streaked and fading: NIGHT AND FOG. Wherever the farmer had gone, he wouldn't be coming back. Skarnu hurried back to town as fast as he could.

Jurbarkas wasn't far from Pavilosta. That thought kept echoing and reechoing in Skarnu's mind. If Merkela hadn't had her baby—his baby—yet, she would any day now. But if he showed himself around those parts, he would be recognized. Even if the redheads didn't catch him, he might give them the excuse they needed to write NIGHT AND FOG on Merkela's door. He didn't want to do that, no matter what.

He wondered if Amatu would come after him. But as day followed day and nothing happened along those lines, he began to feel easier there. The returned exile was somebody else's worry now.

He did wonder a little that no one from the underground tried to get hold of him. But even that didn't worry him so much. He'd spent three years sticking pins in the Algarvians. He was willing—even eager—to let somebody else have a turn.

He stood in the market square at sunrise one morning. Despite the mug of hot tea he'd bought from a small eatery there, he shivered a little. Fall was in the air, even if the leaves hadn't started turning yet. Farmers came into town early, though, to get a full day's work from whomever they hired there and to keep from losing too much time themselves.

A fellow who wasn't a farmer walked up to Skarnu and said, "Hello, Pavilosta."

Only a man from the underground would have called him by the name of the hamlet near which he'd lived. "Well, well," he answered. "Hello yourself, Zarasai." That was also the name of a town, not a person. He didn't know the other man's real name, and hoped the fellow didn't know his. "What brings you here?"

"Somebody got wind that you were in these parts, even if you have been lying low," answered the other fellow from the underground. "I just came around to tell you lying low's a real good idea these days."

"Oh?" Skarnu said.

"That's right." The man from Zarasai nodded. "We've got trouble on the loose. Some madman is leaking to the redheads, leaking like a cursed sieve."

Skarnu rolled his eyes. "Just what we need. As if life weren't hard enough already." That got him another nod from the fellow who called himself Zarasai. Skarnu asked, "Who is the whoreson? Are we trying to kill him?"

"Of course we're trying to kill him. You think we're bloody daft?" "Zarasai" answered. "But the Algarvians are taking good care of him. If I were in their boots, curse them, I'd take good care of him, too. As for who he is, I haven't got a name to give him, but they say he's one of the fancy-trousers nobles who came back across the Strait of Valmiera from Lagoas to fight Mezentio's men. Then he changed his mind. He should have stayed down there in Setubal, powers below eat him."

"Powers below eat *me*," Skarnu exclaimed. The man from Zarasai raised a questioning eyebrow. Skarnu said, "That's got to be Amatu. The blundering idiot kept trying to get himself and everybody with him—including me—killed. He couldn't help acting like one of those nobles who want commoners to bow and scrape before 'em—that's what he was. Is. We finally fought about it. I gave him a good thumping, and we went our separate ways. I came here . . . and I guess he went to the redheads."

"I can see how you wouldn't have had any use for him," "Zarasai" said, "but he's singing like a nightingale now. We've lost at least half a dozen good men on account of him. And even a good man'll sing sometimes, if the Algarvians work on him long enough and hard enough. So we'll lose more, too, no doubt about it."

"Curse him," Skarnu repeated. "He wasn't important enough in the underground to suit him. He's important to the Algarvians, all right, the way a hook's important to a fisherman."

"Zarasai" said, "Sooner or later, he'll run out of names and places. After that, Mezentio's men will probably give him what he deserves."

"They couldn't possibly." Skarnu didn't try to hide his bitterness.

"Mm, maybe not," the other underground leader said. "But you're safe here, I think. If you parted from him, he won't know about this place, right? Sit tight, and we'll do our best to ride things out."

"I wish the redheads had caught him and not Lauzdonu over in Ventspils," Skarnu said. "He's not a coward. I don't think he would have had much to say if they'd just captured him. But he's a spoiled brat. He couldn't have everything he wanted from us, and so he went to get it from the Algarvians. Aye, he'd sing for them, sure enough."

"You've given us a name," "Zarasai" said. "That'll help. When we listen to the emanations from the Algarvians' crystals, maybe we'll hear it, so we'll know what they're doing with him. Maybe he'll have an accident. Aye, maybe he will. Here's hoping he does, anyhow." He slipped away. Skarnu didn't watch him go. The less Skarnu knew about anyone else's comings and goings, the less the Algarvians could tear out of him if they caught him and squeezed.

Lie low. Sit tight. Ride it out. At first, that all seemed good advice to Skarnu. But then he started to wonder, and to worry. He'd spent a lot of time with Amatu before they had their break. How much had he said about Merkela? Had he named her? Had he mentioned Pavilosta? If he had, would Amatu remember?

That seemed only too likely. And if he remembered, what would make him happier than betraying Skarnu's lover to the Algarvians? Nothing Skarnu could think of.

If he sat tight, if he lay low, he might save himself—and

abandon Merkela, abandon the child he'd never seen, and, not quite incidentally, abandon his old senior sergeant, Raunu, to the tender mercies of Mezentio's men, to say nothing of the Kaunian couple from Forthweg who'd escaped the sabotaged ley-line caravan that was carrying them to their death. Ever since he'd fled Merkela's farm, he'd told himself he would endanger her if he went back. Now he decided she would face worse danger if he stayed away. He left Jurbarkas without a backwards glance and went off down the road toward Pavilosta with a smile on his face.

He slept in a haystack that night, and had a chilly time of it: fall was on the way, sure enough. Because the night was cold, he woke in predawn grayness and got moving before the farmer knew he'd been there. After an hour or so, he came on a roadside tavern, and paid the proprietor an outrageous price for a sweet roll and a mug of hot herb tea thick with honey. Thus fortified, he set out again.

Before long, the road grew familiar. If he stayed on it, he would go straight into Pavilosta. He didn't want to do that; too many of the villagers knew who he was. The fewer folk who saw him, the fewer who might betray him to the Algarvians.

And so he left the road, heading down one narrow dirt track that looked no different from any of the others. The path, and others into which it led, took him around Pavilosta and toward Merkela's farm. He nodded to himself whenever he chose a new track; he knew these winding lanes as well as he knew the streets of Priekule. *Soon,* he thought. *Very soon.*

But the closer to the farm he got, the more fear fought with hope. What would he do if he found only an empty, abandoned farmhouse with NIGHT AND FOG scrawled on the door or the wall beside it? *Go mad,* was the answer that sprang to mind. Setting one foot in front of the other took endless distinct efforts of will.

"Powers above," he said softly, rounding the last bend. "There it is."

Tears sprang into his eyes: tears of relief, for smoke rose from the chimney. The fields were golden with ripening grain, the meadows emerald green. And that solid, stolid figure with the crook, keeping an eye on the sheep as they fed, could only belong to Raunu.

Skarnu hurried forward and climbed over the sun-faded wooden rails of the fence. Raunu trotted toward him, plainly ready to use that crook as a weapon. "Here now, stranger!" he shouted in a voice trained to carry through battlefield din. "What in blazes do you want?"

"I may be shabby, Sergeant, but I'm no stranger," Skarnu answered.

Raunu stopped in his tracks. Skarnu thought he might come to attention and salute, but he didn't. "No, Captain, you're no stranger," he agreed, "but you're an idiot to show your face in these parts. There's a hefty price on your head, there is. Nobody ever gave a fart about a sausage-seller's son"—he jerked a thumb at himself—"but a rebel marquis? The redheads want you bad."

"They're liable to care about you if you're here," Skarnu said, "you and Merkela and the Kaunians from Forthweg." He took a deep breath. "How is she?"

"Well enough, though she'll have that baby any day now," Raunu replied.

Skarnu nodded, but cursed softly under his breath. "That'll make moving fast harder, but we have to do it. I think—I'm pretty sure—this place has been betrayed to the Algarvians." In three or four sentences, he told of Amatu and what the other noble had done.

Raunu cursed, too, with a sergeant's fluency. "You're right—we can't stay. Come on back to the house with me, and tell your lady."

Merkela and Pernavai were kneading bread dough when Raunu and Skarnu walked in. Merkela looked up in surprise. "Why aren't you out in the—?" She broke off abruptly when she saw Skarnu behind the veteran sergeant. "What are you doing here?" she whispered, and then hurried to him.

She moved awkwardly; she was, as Raunu had said, very

great with child. When Skarnu took her in his arms, he had to lean forward over her swollen belly to kiss her. She was almost as tall as he. "You have to get away," he said. "The Algarvians know about this place—or they may, anyhow." And he told the story of Amatu again.

Merkela cursed as vividly as Skarnu had. "Nobles like that . . . If the redheads had smashed them, plenty of people would be glad to follow Mezentio." Her fury made Skarnu ashamed of his own high blood. Before he could say anything, she went on, "Aye, we have to leave. Pernavai, fetch Vatsyunas."

The woman from Forthweg nodded. She'd come to understand Valmieran well enough, even if she still spoke much more classical Kaunian. She hurried off to get her husband.

"We'll need to take the wagon," Skarnu said to Merkela. "You can't get far on foot." He too cursed Amatu with all the venom he had in him. That did no good.

"It'll make us easy to spot, easy to catch," Merkela protested.

"So would having you die by the roadside," Skarnu growled, and she subsided. They didn't run into a squad of Algarvians rushing to seize them as they rattled away from the farm. As far as Skarnu was concerned, that put them ahead of the game right there.

Sixteen

Count Lurcanio bowed to Krasta. "By your leave, milady, I should like to invite a guest to supper with us tonight," he said. "A nobleman—a Valmieran nobleman, to be perfectly plain."

He was scrupulous about remembering that the mansion and the serving staff were in fact Krasta's. He was more scrupulous about such things than a good many of his countrymen; had he chosen to commandeer rather than ask, what could she have done about it? Nothing, as she knew all too well. That was the essence of being occupied. And so she said, "Well, of course. Who is it?" She did hope she wouldn't have to endure one of the savage backwoods boors who seemed so fond of Algarve's cause. The idea of Valmierans fighting under Mezentio's banner still left her queasy.

But Lurcanio answered, "A count by the name of Amatu— affable fellow, I find, if a bit full of himself."

"Oh. Amatu. I know him, aye." Krasta didn't sigh in relief, but she felt like it. "He's from right here in Priekule. But . . ." Her voice trailed away. She frowned a little. "I haven't seen him—or I don't recall seeing him—in a very long time."

That held an unspoken question, something on the order of, *If he hasn't come to any of the functions that have gone on since Algarve occupied Valmiera, what's he doing here now?* Some nobles in the capital still stubbornly kept themselves aloof from Mezentio's men. Krasta wondered how Lurcanio would have gone about inviting one of them for supper.

"He's been away from the capital for some time," Lurcanio replied. "He's very glad to be home again, though, I will say."

"I should certainly hope so," Krasta exclaimed. "Why would anyone who could live in Priekule care to go anywhere else?"

Lurcanio didn't answer, from which she concluded he agreed with her. Though nothing else in Valmiera seemed to, her sense of superiority remained invincible. She went off to browbeat the cook into outdoing himself for a noble guest.

"Aye, milady, nothing but the best," the cook promised, his head bobbing up and down with a show of eagerness to please. "I've got a couple of fine beef tongues in the rest crate, if those would suit you for the main dish."

"The very thing!" Krasta's smile was not without a certain small malice. Algarvians had a way of looking down their noses at robust Valmieran cooking. Lurcanio could eat tongue tonight and like it—or at least pretend. She made sure the rest of the menu was along the same lines: fried parsnips with butter, sour cabbage, and a rhubarb pie for dessert. "Nothing spare and Algarvian tonight," she told the cook. "Tonight the guest is a countryman."

"Just as you say, milady, so it'll be," he replied.

"Well, of course," Krasta said. As long as she wasn't dealing with Lurcanio, her word remained law on her estate.

Having made sure of the cook, she went up to her bedchamber, shouting for Bauska as she went. The maidservant never got there fast enough to suit her. "I'm sorry, milady," she said when Krasta shouted at her rather than for her. "My little girl had soiled herself, and I was cleaning her off."

Krasta wrinkled her nose. "Is *that* what I smell?" she said, which was unfair: Bauska took good care of her bastard by an Algarvian officer, and the baby was not only cheerful and happy but gave promise of good looks. Krasta, however, worried very little about fairness. She went on, "Count Amatu is coming to supper tonight, and I want to impress him. What shall I wear?"

"How do you want to impress him?" Bauska asked. Krasta rolled her eyes. As far as she was concerned, only one way mattered. Bauska set out a gold silk tunic that looked transparent but wasn't quite and a pair of dark blue trousers in slashed velvet with side laces to get them to fit as tightly as possible. She added, "You might wear the black shoes with the heels, milady. They give your walk a certain something it wouldn't have otherwise."

"My walk already has everything it needs," Krasta said. But she did wear the shoes. They were even more uncomfortable than the trousers, which Bauska took savage pleasure in lacing till Krasta could hardly breathe. The serving woman looked disappointed when Krasta condescended to thank her for her help.

The way Colonel Lurcanio's eyes lit up when Krasta came downstairs was its own reward. He set a hand on the curve of her hip. "Perhaps I should send Amatu away and keep you all to myself tonight."

"Perhaps you should," she purred, looking up at him from under half-lowered eyelids.

But he laughed and patted her and shook his head. "No, he'll be here any moment, and I truly do want the two of you to meet . . . so long as I am chaperoning. You may have more in common than you think."

"What does that mean?" Krasta asked. "I don't like it when you make your little jokes and I don't know what's going on."

"You'll know soon enough, my sweet; I promise you that," Lurcanio said: more in the way of reassurance than he usually gave her.

Count Amatu knocked on the door a few minutes later. He bowed over Krasta's hand, then clasped wrists, Algarvian style, with Lurcanio. He was thinner than Krasta remembered, thinner and somehow harsher. He knocked back a brandy and nodded. "That opens your eyes," he said, and then, "I've had *my* eyes opened lately, by the powers above. That I have."

"How do you mean?" Krasta asked.

Amatu glanced over to Colonel Lurcanio, then asked her, "Have you seen your brother lately?"

"Skarnu?" Krasta exclaimed, as if she had some other brother, too. Count Amatu nodded. "No," she said. "I haven't seen him since he went off to fight in the war." That was true. "I've never been sure since whether he was alive or dead." That was anything but true, though she didn't think Lurcanio knew it. She knew her brother was alive and still doing something to resist the Algarvians. But what did Amatu know? She did her best to sound intrigued and pleased as she asked, "Why? Have you seen him? Where is he?"

"Oh, I've seen him, all right." Amatu didn't sound pleased about it, either. After muttering something under his breath that Krasta, perhaps fortunately, didn't catch, he went on, "He's down in the south somewhere, mucking about with those miserable bandits who don't know a lost cause when they see one."

"Is he? I had no idea." Krasta was very conscious of Lurcanio's eye on her. He'd invited Amatu here to see what she would do when she got this news. She had to let it seem a surprise. "I wish he'd chosen differently." And part of her did. Had he chosen differently, she wouldn't have had to think about how she'd chosen. One way and another, she'd learned too much about what the Algarvians were doing. That left her unhappy with herself: not a feeling she was used to having.

"They're hopeless, useless, worthless—the bandits, I mean," Amatu said with fine aristocratic scorn. "But your brother's having a fine time slumming, I will say. He's knocked up some peasant wench, and he couldn't be prouder if he'd taken one of King Gainibu's daughters to bed."

Now Krasta drew herself up very straight. "Skarnu and some woman off a farm? I don't believe you." She didn't think her brother immune to lust. Bad taste, however, was an altogether different question.

But Amatu said, "Only shows what you know. I heard him with my own ears—heard more than I ever want to, believe you me. He's as head over heels as if he'd invented this tart, and I'll take oath on that by the powers above."

He meant it. Krasta could see, could hear, as much. She asked, "How do you know all this? If he's with these bandits—were you with them, too?"

"For a little while," Amatu answered. "I spent some time down in Lagoas. When I came back across the Strait to Valmiera, I fell in with those people for a bit. But they haven't got the faintest idea what they're doing to the kingdom. They didn't want to listen to anybody who tried to tell them otherwise, either."

They didn't want to listen to you, and that's why you went over to the Algarvians, Krasta thought. She knew cattiness when she heard it; it came around too often in her own circle to let her mistake it. She was saved from having to say anything when a servant announced, "Milady, lords, supper is ready."

Amatu ate with good appetite, and did a good deal of drinking, too. When Lurcanio saw what the bill of fare was, he sent Krasta a reproachful look. She gave back her own most innocent stare, and said, "Don't you fancy our hearty Valmieran recipes?"

"*I* certainly do," Amatu said, and helped himself to another slice of tongue. He took a big spoonful of the onions the cook had boiled in the pot with the beef tongues. Lurcanio sighed, as if to say that even his own tool had turned in his hand and cut him. Krasta hid her smile.

After demolishing half the rhubarb pie himself, Amatu took his leave. Lurcanio sat in the dining hall, still sipping a cup of tea. He remarked, "You did not seem very excited about the news he had of your brother."

Krasta shrugged. "He seemed more interested in throwing it in my face than in really telling me anything about Skarnu, so I wouldn't give him the satisfaction. He doesn't like Skarnu much, does he?"

"One need hardly be a first-rank mage to see that," Lurcanio remarked. "Your brother, I gather, gave Amatu a good set of lumps before the count decided he might be better served on the Algarvian side."

"Did he?" Krasta said. "Well, good for him."

"I never claimed Amatu was the most lovable man ever born, though he does love himself rather well, would you not agreed?" Lurcanio said.

"Someone has to, I suppose," Krasta said. "He makes one."

"Sweet as ever," Lurcanio said, and Krasta smiled, as if at a compliment. Her Algarvian lover went on, "What do you think of what he did have to tell you?"

"I can't believe my brother would take up with a peasant girl," Krasta said. "It's . . . beneath his dignity."

"It also happens to be true," Lurcanio said. "Her name is Merkela. We were going to seize her, to use her as a lure to draw your brother, but she seems to have got wind of that, for she fled her farm."

"What would you have done with Skarnu if you'd caught him?" Krasta didn't want to ask the question, but didn't see how she could avoid it.

"Squeezed him for what he knew about the other bandits,

of course," Lurcanio answered. "We are fighting a war, after all. Still, we wouldn't have done anything, ah, drastic if he had come out and told us what we needed to learn. Does Amatu look much the worse for wear?"

"Well, no," Krasta admitted.

"There you are, then," Lurcanio said. But Krasta wondered if it were so simple. Amatu, unless she misread things, had had a bellyful of Algarve's foes and had gone to the redheads of his own accord. No wonder they'd taken it easy on him, then. Skarnu wouldn't have had that on his side of the ledger.

I went to the redheads of my own accord, too, Krasta thought. *No wonder they've taken it easy on me, then.* To her amazement—indeed, to something not far from her horror— she burst into tears.

Had Sidroc sat any closer to the fire, his tunic would have started smoldering. Fall here in southern Unkerlant was as bad as winter back in Gromheort. He'd seen what winter was like here. He never wanted to see it again, but he would, and soon . . . if he lived long enough.

He didn't want to think about that. He didn't want to think about anything. All he wanted was the simple animal pleasure of warmth. A pot atop the fire was starting to bubble. Pretty soon, he'd have the animal pleasure of food, too. For the moment—and what else mattered in a soldier's life?— things weren't so bad.

Sergeant Werferth got to his feet and stirred the pot with a big iron spoon that had come from an Unkerlanter peasant hut. "Pretty soon," he said, settling back down on his haunches again.

"Good," Sidroc said. A couple of other men from Pleg-mund's Brigade nodded.

Werferth let out a long sigh. "We were that close to smashing them," he said, holding up his thumb and forefinger almost touching. "*That* close, curse it."

Ceorl held up his thumb and forefinger the same way. "I'm about that close to starving," the ruffian said. "*That* close, curse it."

Everybody laughed: even Werferth, whose dignity as an underofficer was menaced; even Sidroc, who still despised Ceorl whenever the two of them weren't fighting the Unkerlanters. Werferth said, "I told you it'd be done soon. Did you think I was lying?"

Somewhere off in the distance—not too far—eggs burst. Everyone's head came up as the soldiers gauged the distance and direction of the noise. "Ours," Sidroc judged. He waited to see if anybody would argue with him. When no one did, he relaxed—a little.

Werferth said, "Powers below eat me if I know how we figure out who's tossing those eggs and what it means. The way things have been going, we're not even sure where in blazes we're at."

"Somewhere this side of the Gifhorn River," Sidroc said. "Somewhere this side of the western border of Grelz, too, or we'd have those fellows in the dark green tunics fighting on our side." They were somewhere a long way north and west of Durrwangen, but he didn't mention that. Everybody around the fire already knew it too well.

"We hope we would, anyhow," Werferth said. "From what I hear, the Grelzers are getting shaky."

"Fair-weather friends." Ceorl spat into the campfire. "Blaze a few of 'em to remind the rest who they work for and they won't give you much trouble."

Sidroc found himself nodding. Even though Ceorl was the one who'd said it, it made good sense to him. Werferth stirred the pot again, lifted out the spoon to taste a mouthful, and nodded. "It's done."

The stew was cabbage and buckwheat groats and turnips and meat from a dead unicorn, all boiled together with some salt. Back in Gromheort, Sidroc wouldn't have touched it. Here, he wolfed it down and held out his mess tin for more. His comrades were doing the same, so he didn't get much of a second helping.

A sentry called out a challenge. The Forthwegians by the fire grabbed for their sticks. Nobody from Plegmund's Brigade ever left his weapon out of reach, not even for a moment. Anybody who did that in this country was asking to get his throat cut. But the answer came back in Algarvian: "You are Plegmund's Brigade, is it not so? I've got letters for you: soldiers' post."

They greeted him almost as enthusiastically as if he were a woman of easy virtue. He got whatever stew was left in the pot, and a swig of spirits from somebody's water bottle. Once he figured out which squad from which company they were, he started passing out letters. Some of them got passed back to him, with remarks like, "He's dead," or, "He got wounded and taken off a couple weeks ago," that took the edge off the excitement of seeing mail.

Sidroc leaped in the air when the Algarvian called his name. He hadn't heard from Gromheort in a long time. The only person there who cared to write him was his father. The rest of his family were either dead or hated him, and that ran both ways.

Sure enough, the envelope the redhead handed him bore his father's familiar handwriting. It also bore a prewar Forthwegian value imprinted in one corner, and a green handstamp that said MILITARY POST over it. People who collected envelopes might have paid a fair bit of silver for this one. Sidroc wasn't any of those people, and so he tore it open to get at the letter inside.

My dear son, his father wrote. *It was good to hear from you, and good to hear that you came through the hard fighting around Durrwangen safe. I hope this finds you well. Powers above grant it be so. I am well enough, though a toothache will send me to the dentist when it gets bad enough.*

After I got your last letter, I paid a call on your dear Uncle Hestan. Sidroc grunted at that; Ealstan and Leofsig's father wasn't dear to him these days, nor he to Hestan. His own father went on, *I told him what you had to say to me about the Kaunian wench named Vanai, and about the way his precious son Ealstan had been panting after her for years. I also told him she was an Algarvian officer's plaything in Oyngestun.*

He only shrugged and said he didn't know anything about

it. He said he hadn't heard a word from Ealstan since the day you got hit in the head (however that happened) and the self-righteous little brat disappeared (however that happened).

I don't believe him. But you know Hestan too well, the same as I do. He never tells his face what he is thinking. A lot of people think he is clever just because they don't know what's going on inside his head. And he may even be clever, but he is not as smart as he thinks he is.

"Ha! That's the truth, by the powers above," Sidroc said, as if his father were standing there beside him.

I am afraid I will never be able to get to the bottom of this by myself, the letter went on. *Maybe I will see if the Algarvians are interested in getting to the bottom of it for me. Hestan is my own flesh and blood, but that gets hard to remember after all the names he's called me since things went sour between you and his sons.*

You are everything I have left. Stay safe. Stay warm. Be brave—I know you will. Love, your father.

"Powers below eat Uncle Hestan," Sidroc muttered. "Powers below eat Ealstan, too. He'd always suck up to the schoolmasters, and I'd get the stripes."

"Who's it from, Sidroc?" Sergeant Werferth asked. "Anything juicy in it?" The soldiers who got letters from sweethearts often read out the livelier bits to amuse their comrades.

But Sidroc shook his head. "Not a thing. It's just from my old man."

"Well, is he getting any?" Ceorl demanded. Sidroc shook his head again and put the letter in his belt pouch. Ceorl looked to be about to say something else. Sergeant Werferth set him to gathering more wood to throw on the fire. Werferth knew Sidroc and Ceorl had no love lost between them. He did his best not to give them any chance to quarrel.

"Halt! Who goes there?" the sentry called again.

"I have the honor to be Captain Baiardo," another Algarvian answered. "Do you have the honor to be the men of Plegmundo's—no, Plegmund's—Brigade?"

"Aye," the sentry answered. "Advance and be recognized, sir."

Sidroc turned to Sergeant Werferth. "Too bad they wouldn't let you keep the company, Sergeant. You've done as well with it as any of the redhead officers they put over us."

"Thanks." Werferth shrugged. "What can you do? They give the orders."

But Baiardo, when he came up to the fire, proved *not* to be the new company commander. Along with his rank badges, he wore that of a mage—he was an officer by courtesy, not by blood. And it took a lot of courtesy to reckon him an officer: he looked like an unmade bed. "Who's in charge here?" he asked, peering from one Forthwegian to another.

The men of Plegmund's Brigade wore their own king-dom's markings of rank; Sergeant Werferth's single chevrons couldn't have meant anything to Baiardo. "I am, sir," Werferth said resignedly. "What do you want?"

"I need a volunteer," Baiardo said.

Silence fell on the Forthwegians. They had seen plenty to teach them that the war was bad enough when they did what they had to do. Doing more than they had to do only made it worse. Baiardo looked expectantly from one soldier to the next. Maybe he hadn't seen all that much himself. Nobody could tell him no, not straight out. He was an Algarvian, and an officer—well, an officer of sorts—to boot. At last, Sergeant Werferth pointed to Sidroc and said, "He'll do whatever you need, sir."

"Splendid." Baiardo clapped his hands in what looked like real delight.

Sidroc thought it anything but splendid. He glared at Ba-iardo and Werferth in turn. Glaring, of course, was all he could do. Whatever happened to him would be better than what he'd get for disobeying an order. With a sigh, he asked the Algarvian mage, "What do you need from me, sir?"

If Baiardo noticed his reluctance, he didn't let it show. "Here." He unslung his pack and handed it to Sidroc. "Carry this. Come with me."

He's arrogant enough to make a proper Algarvian, Sidroc thought. The pack might have been stuffed with lead. He car-ried it and his own pack and his stick and followed Baiardo away from the fire. The mage blithely strode southwest. After a little while, Sidroc said, "Sir, if you keep going, you'll see the Unkerlanters closer than you ever wanted to."

"Their lines are close?" Baiardo sounded as if that hadn't occurred to him.

"You might say so, aye," Sidroc answered dryly. Baiardo clapped his hands again. "Powers above, keep quiet!" Sidroc hissed. "Are you trying to get both of us killed?" As far as he was concerned, Baiardo was welcome to do himself in, but Sidroc resented being included in his suicide.

But the mage shook his head and said, "No. Set down the pack"—an order Sidroc was glad to obey. Baiardo took from the heavy pack a laurel leaf of the sort often used in Forthwegian cookery and a small, dazzlingly bright opal. He wrapped the stone in the leaf and chanted first in Algarvian, then in classical Kaunian. Sidroc stared, for the mage's outline grew hazy, indistinct; at last, Baiardo almost disappeared. "Stay here," he told Sidroc. "Wait for me." Still in that wraithlike state, he started for the Unkerlanters' line.

How long do I wait? Sidroc wondered. Baiardo wasn't fully invisible. If Swemmel's soldiers were alert, they would spot him. If they did, Sidroc was liable to have a very long wait indeed. Muttering a curse under his breath, he started digging a hole. He felt naked on the Unkerlanter plain without one. The dirt he dug up made a breastwork in front of his scrape. It wouldn't protect him if a regiment of Unkerlanters came roaring after Baiardo, but it might keep a sniper from parting his hair with a beam.

He'd just scrambled down into the hole when a voice spoke out of thin air behind him: "We can go back now." He whirled, and there stood Baiardo, as haggard and unkempt as ever, putting the laurel leaf and the opal back into his pack. The mage added, "I got what I came for."

"And you almost got blazed before you could deliver it, whatever it was, you cursed fool," Sidroc said angrily. "Don't you have any sense at all?"

Baiardo gave that serious consideration. "I doubt it," he said at last. "It doesn't always help in my business."

They trudged back toward the fire, Baiardo pleased with himself, Sidroc still a little—maybe more than a little—twitchy. The mage, he noticed, had sense enough not to carry his own pack when he didn't have to. He left that to Sidroc.

"Welcome back," people kept telling Fernao, in Kuusaman and in classical Kaunian. Some of them added, "How well you are moving!"

"Thank you," Fernao said, over and over. The mages and the cooks and maids in the hostel in the Naantali district were just being polite, and he knew it. He would never move well again, not as long as he lived. Maybe he was moving a little better than he had when he went off to Setubal. Maybe. He remained imperfectly convinced.

Ilmarinen helped him put things in perspective. The master mage patted him on the back and said, "Well, after so much time off in that miserable little no-account excuse for a city, you must be glad to come back here, to a place where interesting things are happening."

His classical Kaunian was so fast and colloquial—so much like a living language in his mouth—that at first Fernao thought he meant the Naantali district was the sleepy place and Setubal the one where things happened. When he realized Ilmarinen had said the opposite, he laughed out loud. "You always have that knack for turning things upside down," he told the Kuusaman mage. His own Kaunian remained formal: a language he could use, but not one in which he felt at home.

"I don't know what you're talking about," Ilmarinen answered. "I always speak plain sense. Is it my fault the rest of the world isn't ready to see it most of the time?"

Pekka came into the dining room in time to hear that. "A madman's ravings always seem sensible to him," she remarked, not without affection.

Ilmarinen snorted and waved to a serving woman. "A mug of ale, Linna," he called before turning back to Pekka. "You sound as if sense were sensible in magecraft. A thing has to work. It doesn't have to be sensible."

"Oh, nonsense," Fernao said. "Otherwise, theoretical sorcery would be a dry well."

"A lot of the time, it is," Ilmarinen retorted, reveling in his heresy. "A lot of the time, what we do is figure out after the fact why an experiment that had no business working did work in spite of what we—wrongly—thought we knew." He waved. "If that weren't so, what would we all be doing here?"

Fernao hesitated. Ilmarinen enjoyed tossing eggs into a conversation. But being outrageous wasn't necessarily the same as being wrong.

Pekka, now, wagged a finger under Ilmarinen's nose, as if he were a naughty little boy. "We can also go from pure theory to practical sorcery. If that isn't sense, what is it?"

"Luck," Ilmarinen answered. "And speaking of luck . . ." Linna came up with the mug of ale. "Here it is now. Thank you, sweetheart." He bowed to the serving girl. He hadn't given up chasing her—or maybe he had while Fernao was away, and then started up again. You never could tell with Ilmarinen.

Linna went off without a backwards glance. Plainly, the next time Ilmarinen caught her would be the first. Whatever else Fernao couldn't tell about the master mage, that was glaringly obvious.

Ilmarinen took a long pull at the ale. "Curse King Mezentio," he ground out. "Curse him and all his clever mages. Now the rest of the world has to deal with the question of how in blazes to beat him without being as vile as he is."

"King Swemmel worries about that not at all," Fernao pointed out, which only prompted Ilmarinen to make a horrible face at him.

"We are still fighting King Mezentio, too, and we have resorted to none of his barbarism," Pekka said primly.

Ilmarinen got down to the bottom of his mug and smacked it down on the table almost hard enough to shatter it. He said, "We've also got the luxury of the Strait of Valmiera between us and the worst Mezentio can do. The Unkerlanters, poor buggers, don't. What'll we do when we've got big armies in the field against Algarve?"

"A good deal of the answer to that depends on whether we succeed here, would you not agree?" Fernao said. Pekka nodded; she agreed, at any rate.

But Ilmarinen, contrary as usual, said, "Suppose we fail here. Sooner or later, we'll still have big armies in the field against the Algarvians. Sure as Mezentio's got a pointy nose, they'll start killing Kaunians to try to stop us. What do we do then?"

That was a large, important question. The only time the Lagoans and Kuusamans had had a large army in the field against Algarve after Mezentio's men unveiled their murderous magic was down in the land of the Ice People. Sure as sure, the Algarvians had tried to turn back their foes by butchering blonds. But the magic had gone wrong, there on the austral continent. It had come down on the Algarvians' heads, not those of their foes. That wouldn't happen on the mainland of Derlavai. Too many massacres had proved as much.

Pekka said, "We cannot match them in murder. That is the best argument I know for mastering them with magecraft."

"Suppose we fail," Ilmarinen repeated. "We'll be fighting Mezentio's men even so. What do we do when they start killing? We had better think about that, you know—I don't mean us here alone, but also the Seven here and King Vitor and his counselors in that small town of yours, Fernao. The day *is* coming. We've all heard the name Habakkuk—no use pretending we haven't."

"I have heard the name, but I do not know what it means," Fernao said.

"My husband works with Habakkuk, and I do not know what he does," Pekka added. "I do not ask, any more than he asks me what I do."

"You are the soul of virtue." Ilmarinen's voice was sour. "Well, *I* know, because I have no virtue save perhaps that of thinking backwards and upside down. I will spare your tender virgin ears the details, but I trust I do not shock you when I say Habakkuk isn't intended to make Mezentio sleep easier of nights."

"If Mezentio can sleep at all, after the things he has done, his conscience is made of cast iron," Fernao said, "and doubtless he can, so doubtless it is."

"All right, then." Ilmarinen took his usual pleasure in making himself as difficult as possible. "Thanks to Habakkuk, among other things, we come to grips with Algarve on land. Mezentio's mages kill Kaunians to throw us back. What comes next?"

"There are blocking spells," Fernao said. "If you and Siuntio had not used them then, we probably would not be here to have this discussion."

"Aye, they helped—some," Ilmarinen answered. "How would you like to be a foolish young man, more balls than brains, trying to kill other foolish young men in a different uniform, with your mages helping you with a spell that leaks as much as it shields? Before very long, wouldn't you sooner take after them than after the enemy soldiers? I would, and I wouldn't take long to get there, either."

"Master Ilmarinen, you have just shown why we so badly have to succeed," Pekka said.

"No." The master mage shook his head. "I've shown why we so badly *need* to succeed. But have to?" He shook his head again. "Life does not come with a guarantee, except that it will end. What I tried to show you was that we'd better find some answers somewhere else in case we don't find them here. But you don't want to listen to that. And so . . ." He got to his feet, gave Fernao and Pekka nicely matched mocking bows, and departed.

"I am always so grateful for such encouragement," Pekka said.

"As am I," Fernao agreed. He made as if to rise and follow Ilmarinen. "And now, if you will excuse me, I think I shall go back to my room and slit my wrists."

Pekka stared at him, then laughed when she realized he was joking. "Be careful with what you say," she warned. "I took you seriously for a moment."

"He asks interesting questions, does he not?" Fernao said.

"If he were as interested in answering them as he is in asking them . . ." He shrugged. "If that were so, he would not be Ilmarinen."

"No—he would come closer to being Siuntio," Pekka said. "And Siuntio is the mage we need most right now. Every day without him proves that." Her hands folded into fists. "Powers below eat the Algarvians. Curse their magic."

Fernao nodded. But the question Ilmarinen had posed kept rattling around in his mind, whether he wanted it to or not. "If we fail here, how *do* our kingdoms beat the Algarvians without sinking into the swamp that has already taken them?"

"I do not know," Pekka said. "If we do sink down into the swamp with the Algarvians, does it matter in the end whether we win or lose?"

"To us, aye, it matters." Fernao held up a hand to show he hadn't finished and to keep Pekka from arguing. "To the world, it probably does not."

Pekka pondered that, then slowly nodded. "If Algarve beats Unkerlant, we have Mezentio's minions eyeing us from across the Strait of Valmiera. And if Unkerlant beats Algarve, we have Swemmel's minions eyeing us instead. But the one set would not be much different from the other, would it?"

"The Algarvians would tell you more about the differences than you would ever want to hear," Fernao answered. "So would the Unkerlanters. My opinion is that they would not matter much."

"I think you are right," Pekka said. "You see through the show to the essential. That is what makes you a good mage."

"Thank you," Fernao said. "Praise from the praiseworthy is praise indeed." That was a proverb in classical Kaunian. He brought it out as if he'd thought of it on the spur of the moment.

Kuusamans were swarthy; he couldn't be sure whether Pekka blushed. But, by the way she murmured, "You do me too much honor," he judged he'd succeeded in embarrassing her. He didn't mind. He wanted her to know he thought well of her. Even more, he wanted her to think well of him. He wished he could come right out and say that. He knew he would ruin everything if he did.

He sighed, both because of that and for other reasons. "One way or another," he said, "the world will not be the same after this war ends."

Pekka thought about that, then shook her head. "No. One way *and* another, the world will not be the same after this war ends. We are changing too many things ever to be the same again."

"True enough," Fernao said. "Too true, if anything." He waved in the direction of the blockhouse. "If all goes well, we help set the tone of the changes. That is no small privilege."

"That is no small responsibility." Pekka sighed. "I wish it were not on my shoulders. But what we wish for and what we get are not always the same. I know that I can deal with the world the way it is, no matter how much I wish it were otherwise."

Fernao inclined his head to her. "We are lucky to have such a leader." Part of that was flattery. A larger part was anything but.

"If we were lucky, we would still have Siuntio," Pekka answered. "Whenever we run into trouble, I ask myself how he might fix it. I hope I am right more often than I am wrong."

"You could do worse," Fernao said.

"I know," Pekka said bleakly. "And, one of these days, I probably will." Try as he would, Fernao found no flattering answer for that.

When Istvan looked up at the night sky from the island of Becsehely, he had no trouble seeing the stars. The didn't glitter so brilliantly as they did in the clear, cold air of his own mountain valley, but they were there, from horizon to horizon. "It almost seems strange," he remarked to Szonyi. "After so long in the accursed woods of western Unkerlant, I'd got used to seeing a star here, a star there, but most of them blotted out by branches overhead."

"Aye." Szonyi's fingers writhed in a sign to avert evil. "Me, too. No wonder I felt forsaken by the stars while I was there."

"No wonder at all." Some of Istvan's shiver had to do with the night air, which was moist and chilly. More sprang from dread and loathing of the forest he and his companions had finally escaped. "There are places in those woods that no star saw for years at a time."

"Can't say that here." Szonyi's waved encompassed all of Becsehely—not that there was a whole lot to encompass. "It's not much like Obuda, is it? Before we got to this place, I always thought, well, an island is an island, you know what I mean? But it doesn't look like it works that way."

The gold frame to Captain Kun's spectacles glittered in the firelight as he turned his head toward Szonyi. "After you had one woman," he asked, "did you think all women were the same, too?"

He probably wanted to anger Szonyi. But the big trooper just laughed and said, "After my first one? Aye, of course I did. I found out different pretty fast. Now I'm finding out different about islands, too."

"He's got you there, Kun," Istvan said with a laugh.

"I suppose so—if you're daft enough to assume one island is like another to begin with," Kun answered.

"Enough." Istvan put a sergeant's snap in his voice. "Let's hope this island won't be anything like Obuda. Let's hope—and let's make sure—we don't lose it to the stinking Kuusamans, the way we lost Obuda."

He peered west through the darkness, as if expecting to spot a fleet of Kuusaman ley-line cruisers and patrol boats and transports and dragon haulers bearing down on Becsehely. Gyongyos had lost a good many islands besides Obuda to Kuusamo this past year; Ekrekek Arpad had vowed to the stars that the warrior race would lose no more.

I am the instrument of Arpad's vow, Istvan thought. *An instrument of his vow, anyway.* In the forests of Unkerlant, he'd often feared that the Ekrekek had joined the stars in forsaking him. Here, by contrast, he felt as if he were serving under his sovereign's eye.

After a while, he wrapped himself in a blanket and slept. When he woke, he wondered if Ekrekek Arpad had blinked: a thick fog covered Becsehely. All the Kuusaman ships in the world could have sailed past half a mile offshore, and he never would have known it. More fog streamed from his nose and mouth every time he exhaled. When he inhaled, he could taste the sea almost as readily as if he were a fish swimming in it.

Not far away, a bell began ringing. Istvan's stomach rumbled. "Follow your ears, boys," he told the troopers in his squad. "Try not to break your necks before you get there."

His boots scrunched on gravel and squelched through mud as he made his own way toward the bell. The fog muffled his footsteps. It muffled the bell, too, and the endless slap of the sea on the beach perhaps a quarter of a mile away. Becsehely was low and flat. Had it not lain along a ley line, it wouldn't have been worth visiting at all—but then, as far as Istvan was concerned, the same held true for every island in the Bothnian Ocean.

There was the cookfire—and there was a queue of men with mess kits. Istvan took his place in it. The man in front of him turned and said, "Good morning, Sergeant."

"Oh!" Istvan said. "Good morning, Captain Frigyes. I'm sorry, sir—a man wouldn't know his own mother in this fog."

"Can't argue with you there," his company commander replied. "You'd almost think the Kuusamans magicked it up on purpose."

"Sir?" Istvan said in some alarm. "You don't suppose—?"

Frigyes shook his head. "No, I don't suppose that. Our mages would be screaming their heads off were it so. They aren't. That means it isn't."

Istvan considered. "Aye. That makes sense." He peered out into the fog with new suspicion just the same.

A bored-looking cook filled his mess tin with a stew of millet and lentils and bits of fish. He ate methodically, then went down to the beach and washed the tin in the ocean. Becsehely boasted only a handful of springs; fresh water was too precious to waste on washing.

Toward mid-morning, the fog lifted. The sky remained gray. So did the sea. Becsehely seemed gray, too. Most of the gravel was that color, and the grass and bushes, fading in the fall, were more yellowish gray than green.

An observation tower stood on the high ground—such as it was—at the center of the island. Sentries with spyglasses swept the horizon, not that they would have done much good in the swaddling fog. But dowsers and other mages stood by to warn against trouble then. Istvan hoped whatever warning they might give would be enough.

A dragon flapped into the air from the farm beyond the tower. Istvan expected it to vanish into the clouds, but it didn't. It flew in a wide spiral below them: one more sentry, to spy out the Kuusamans before they drew too close to Becsehely. Sentries were all very well, but . . .

Istvan turned to Captain Frigyes and said, "I wish we had more dragons on this stars-forsaken island, sir."

"Well, Sergeant, so do I, when you get right down to it," Frigyes answered. "But Becsehely doesn't have enough growing on it to support much in the way of cattle or pigs or even"—he made a revolted face—"goats. That means we have to ship in meat for the dragons, same as we have to bring in food for us. We can only afford so many of the miserable beasts."

"Miserable is right." Istvan remembered unpleasant days on Obuda, mucking out dragon farms. With a frown, he went on, "The stinking Kuusamans bring whole shiploads of dragons with 'em wherever they go."

"I know that. We all know that—much too well, in fact," Frigyes said. "It's one of the reasons they've given us so much trouble in the islands. We'll be able to do it ourselves before too long."

"That'd be about time, sir," Istvan said. *We'll be able to do it before too long* was a phrase that had got a lot of Gyongyosian soldiers killed before their time.

"We are a warrior race," Frigyes said, disapproval strong in his voice. "We shall prevail."

"Aye, sir," Istvan answered. He couldn't very well say anything else, not without denying Gyongyos' heritage. But he'd seen over and over again, on Obuda and in the woods of western Unkerlant, that warrior virtues, however admirable, could be overcome by sound strategy or strong sorcery.

Despite the tower, despite the dragons, despite the dowsers, no one on Becsehely spied the approaching Kuusaman flotilla till it launched its dragons at the island. Mist and rain clung to Becsehely, thwarting the men with the spyglass, thwarting the dragonfliers, and even thwarting the dowsers, who had to try to detect the motion of ships through the motions of millions of falling raindrops. Dowsers had techniques for noting one kind of motion while screening out others; maybe the Kuusamans had techniques for making ships seem more like rain.

Whatever the explanation, the first thing the garrison knew of the flotilla was eggs falling out of the sky and bursting all over the island. The observation tower went down in ruin when a lucky hit smashed its supports. More eggs burst near the dragon farm, but the dragonfliers got at least some of their beasts into the air to challenge the Kuusamans.

Frigyes' whistle wailed through the din. "To the beach!" he yelled. "Stand by to repel invaders!"

"Come on, you lugs!" Istvan shouted to his squad. "If they don't make it ashore, they can't hurt us, right?"

More eggs burst close by, making all the Gyongyosians dive for holes in the ground. As dirt pattered down on them, Szonyi said, "Who says they can't?"

"Come on!" Istvan repeated, and they were up and running again. He and Kun—and Szonyi, too—had spent a lot of time harping on how important it was to keep the Kuusamans from landing. He knew a certain amount of pride that the rest of the squad took them seriously. Everybody loved the stars, but no one wanted them to take and cherish his spirit right then.

The Kuusaman dragons had already given the trenches by the beach a pretty good pounding. Istvan wasn't fussy—any hole in the ground, whether a proper trench or the crater left by a bursting egg, would do fine. He jumped down into one, then peered out again, wondering how close the invasion fleet was, and what sort of defending vessels Gyongyos had in these waters. He remembered only too well how the Kuusamans had fought their way onto the beaches of Obuda.

He spied no enemy ships gliding along the ley line toward Becsehely, no landing boats leaving larger ships and approaching the island on a broad front propelled by sails or oars. Corporal Kun saw—or rather, didn't see—the same thing, and spoke with some relief: "Just a raid from their dragon haulers."

"Aye." Istvan sounded relieved, too. The dragons might kill him, but without landing boats in the water there wasn't the certainty of a life-and-death struggle for the island. Sooner or later, the accursed beasts would fly back to the ships that had brought them, and the raid would end.

"Demon of a lot of dragons overhead for just a raid," Kun said.

That was also true. Istvan shrugged. "They must have brought more of those ships along than usual. Aren't we lucky?"

And then they *were* lucky, for one of the heavy sticks mounted on Becsehely blazed a Kuusaman dragon out of the sky. It fell into the sea just offshore and thrashed out its death agony there. Painted pale blue and light green, it might almost have been a sea creature itself. If its dragonflier hadn't been dead when it smashed down, its writhings would surely have crushed him.

Eventually, a soldier managed to blaze the dragon through one of its great, glaring eyes. It shuddered and lay still. A moment later, another dragon plunged into the sea, and then one onto the stony soil of the island behind Istvan. He shook his fist in triumph. "By the stars, nothing's going to come cheap for the stinking Kuusamans here."

The foe must have decided the same thing, for the dragons flew off toward the west. Only later did Istvan pause to wonder whether Becsehely was worth having for anybody at all.

Talsu walked through the streets of Skrunda thinking about spells of undoing. There had to be a way to get more out of them than he'd yet seen. He was convinced of that. But he wasn't yet sure what it might be.

A news-sheet vendor waved a leaf of paper at him. "Gyongyos crushes Kuusaman air pirates!" the fellow called. "Read the whole exciting story!"

Instead of answering, Talsu just kept walking. If he'd said no, the vendor would have done his best to turn it into an argument, hoping to entice him to buy the news sheet that way. But silence gave the fellow nothing to grip. He glared at Talsu. Talsu ignored that, too.

As soon as he turned a corner, though, he cursed under his breath. The vendor had made him fall away from the ley line his thought had been following. Whatever the answer he'd sought, he wouldn't find it right away.

FINE SILVERSMITHING BY KUGU, a shopfront sign said, and then below, in smaller letters, JEWELRY MADE AND REPAIRED. CUSTOM FLATWARE. POTS & BOWLS OUR SPECIALTY. The shop was closed.

"Pest-holes and betrayals, our specialty," Talsu muttered under his breath. He wanted to let his face show exactly what he thought of the silversmith. But he couldn't even do that, because he was meeting Kugu for supper at an eatery that should be . . . He brightened. "There it is." He'd walked past the Dragon Inn any number of times. He'd never gone inside, not till now. It came as close to being a fine eatery as any place Skrunda boasted.

His nostrils twitched at the smell of roasting meat as he opened the door. He didn't suppose the inn cooked with a real dragon: stoves and grills surely gave better—to say nothing of safer—results. But food and flame did come together here. His belly rumbled. He didn't eat much meat back home.

As if by sorcery, a waiter appeared at his elbow. "May I help you, sir?" The tone was polite but wary. He got the feeling he'd be out on the street in a hurry if the fellow didn't like his answer.

But the waiter relaxed when he said, "I'm dining with Master Kugu."

"Ah. Of course. Come with me, then, if you'd be so kind. The gentleman is waiting for you." The waiter led him to a booth in the back where Kugu did indeed sit waiting. With a bow, the fellow said, "Enjoy your meal, sir," and vanished as suddenly as he'd appeared.

Kugu rose and clasped Talsu's hand. "Good of you to join me," he murmured. "Let me pour you some wine." He did, then raised his goblet in salute. "Your very good health."

"Thanks. And yours." With straight-faced hypocrisy, Talsu drank. His eyebrows rose. He didn't get to enjoy wine like this at home: a full-bodied vintage, with just a touch of lime to give it the tartness Jelgavans craved. He thought he could get tiddly on the bouquet alone.

"Order whatever suits your fancy: it's my pleasure," Kugu said. "The leg of mutton is very fine, if you care for it. They don't stint the garlic."

"That sounds good," Talsu agreed, and he did choose it when the waiter came back with an inquiring look on his face. So did Kugu. Talsu had all he could do not to gape like a fool when his supper arrived. Aye, that much meat could have fed his father and mother and sister and wife—and him to boot—for a couple of days, or so he thought. It was tender as lamb but far more flavorful; it seemed to melt off the bone. In an amazingly short time, nothing but that bone remained on the plate.

"I trust that met with your approval?" Kugu asked as the waiter carried the plate away. The silversmith had also demolished his supper. Talsu nodded; he was too full to speak. But he discovered he still had room for the brandied cherries the man brought back. They were potent. After only three or four, his eyes started to cross. Kugu ate them, too, but they didn't look to bother him. He said, "Shall we get down to business?"

"Aye. We might as well," Talsu agreed. He would have agreed to anything about then, regardless of how he felt about the silversmith.

Kugu's smile reached his mouth but not his eyes. "You alarmed the occupying authorities, you know."

"How could I have done that?" Talsu asked. "Powers above, I was in a dungeon. I was about as alarming as a mouse in a trap."

"Mice don't write denunciations," Kugu said patiently, as if he'd had nothing to do with Talsu's ending up in a dungeon. "You named people the Algarvians thought were safe. They did some checking and found out that some of those people weren't so safe after all. Do you wonder that they started worrying?"

Talsu shrugged. "If I'd told them a pack of lies, I'd still be in that miserable place." *And I remember who put me there. Aye, I remember.*

"I understand that," the silversmith said, more patiently still. "But when they found out they'd trusted some of the wrong people, they started checking everybody they'd trusted. They even checked me, if you can imagine."

Talsu didn't trust himself to say anything to that. Any reply he gave would have sounded sardonic, and he didn't dare make Kugu any more suspicious than he was already. He sat there and waited.

Kugu nodded, as if acknowledging a clever ploy. He went on, "And so, you see, we have to show we can work together. Then the Algarvians will know they can trust both of us. That's something they need to know. There's a lot of treason in this kingdom."

He spoke very earnestly, as if he meant treason against Jelgava rather than treason against her occupiers. Maybe he confused the two. Maybe Talsu had come closer to getting him in serious trouble than he'd thought possible, too. He hoped so. He wanted Kugu in serious trouble, however it happened. He wasn't the least bit fussy about that. "What have you got in mind?" he asked.

Kugu returned a question for a question: "Do you know Zverinu the banker?"

"I know of him. Who doesn't?" Talsu answered. He didn't point out how unlikely it was for a tailor's son to have made the acquaintance of probably the richest man in Skrunda.

"That will do," Kugu said. Maybe he really did know

Zverinu. Talsu had seen that he knew some surprising people. For now, he went on, "If we both denounce him, a few days apart, the Algarvians are bound to haul him in. That will make us look good in their eyes. It'll make us look busy, if you know what I mean?"

"Has he done anything that needs denouncing?" Talsu asked. If Kugu said aye, he would find some excuse not to do anything of the sort.

But the silversmith only shrugged, as Talsu had a while before. "Who knows? By the time the Algarvians are done digging, though, they'll find something. You can bet on that."

Talsu abruptly wondered if he'd be sick all over the table in front of him. This was fouler than anything he'd imagined. It felt like wading in sewage. Worse still was being unable to show what he thought. He spoke carefully: "The Algarvians are liable to know I don't know anything about Zverinu."

"Not if you phrase the denunciation the right way." Kugu taught treason with the same methodical thoroughness he gave classical Kaunian. "You can say you heard him on the street, or in the market square, or any place where you could both plausibly be. You can even say you had to ask somebody who he was. That's a nice touch, in fact. It makes things feel real."

"I'll see what I can come up with." Talsu gulped the fine wine Kugu was buying. That first denunciation had got him out of the dungeon, but it hadn't got him out of trouble. If anything, it had got him in deeper.

"All right." Kugu emptied his own goblet. "Don't take too long, though. They're keeping an eye on both of us. It's a hard, cold world, and a man has to get along as best he can."

A man has to get along as best he can. Talsu had lived by that rule in the army. The idea of living by it to the extent of turning against his own kingdom filled him with loathing. But all he said was, "Aye." Here he was, getting along with Kugu as best he could till he found some way to pay back the silversmith.

Kugu set coins on the table, some with King Donalitu's image, more with that of King Mainardo, the younger brother of King Mezentio. If nothing else, Talsu had made him spend a good deal of his, or perhaps Algarve's, money. That wasn't so bad, but it wasn't enough, not nearly.

In the cool evening twilight outside the eatery, Kugu asked, "Do you want to lead off with your denunciation, or shall I go first?"

"You go ahead," Talsu answered. "Yours will be better than mine; it's bound to be. So mine can add on to what you've already said." The longer he delayed, the more time he had to come up with something to undo Kugu.

But the silversmith took Talsu's flattery, if that was what it was, as no more than his due. Nodding, he said, "I give my language lessons tomorrow. I'll work on mine over the next couple of days after that and turn it in. That gives you plenty of time to get something ready."

"All right," Talsu said, though it wasn't. "I'd better get back before curfew catches me."

"Before long, you won't need to worry about that," Kugu said. "People will know who you are." Confident as if he were a redhead, he strode away.

So did Talsu, less confidently. He was thinking furiously as he went back to his father's tailor's shop and his room above it. He kept right on thinking furiously all the next day. He was thinking so hard, he wasn't worth much at work. Traku scolded him: "How many times are you going to use the undo spell, son? The idea is to get it right the first time, not to see how many different kinds of mistake you can fix."

"I'm sorry." Talsu didn't like lying to his father, but he didn't know what else to do. He wanted to see just how many things he could undo, and in how many ways.

His father and his mother and his sister and Gailisa all squawked at him when he went out that night, but he did a good job of pretending to be deaf. He also did a good job of evading patrols as he made his way to Kugu's house. Skrunda was his town. In the mandatory darkness of night, he knew how to disappear.

He didn't knock on Kugu's door. He waited across the street, hidden in a deeper shadow. Several language students went in. They didn't see him, any more than the Algarvian constables had. He lurked there till he was sure Kugu would be immersed in his classical Kaunian lesson and then, very quietly, he began to chant.

Odds are, I'm wasting my time, he thought. Undoing spells were funny business. Could he make what worked with cloth work on a man, too? He'd twiddled up a spell as best he knew how, but he knew he didn't know much. Could he really undo Kugu's mask of virtue and patriotism and make him reveal himself to the men he taught for what he really was? Even if he could, would he ever know he'd done it? Might he have to write his denunciation even if he succeeded?

He hadn't known if he would get answers to any of those questions, but he got answers to all of them, and in short order, too. Without warning, furious shouts and screams from inside Kugu's house shattered the stillness of the night. Crashes and thuds followed immediately thereafter. The front door flew open. The silversmith's students fled into the night.

Talsu slipped away, too, still unseen. He wondered how by word or deed he'd made Kugu betray himself. He would never know, and it didn't matter, but he still wondered. When he got back home, he found his whole family waiting anxiously for him. He grinned, greeted them with two words— "He's undone"—and laughed loud and long.

The crystallomancer nodded to Rathar. "Go ahead, lord Marshal. His Majesty awaits you."

"So I see," Rathar said: King Swemmel's pale, long-faced image peered out of the crystal at him. He took a deep breath and went on, "Your Majesty, as I greet you I stand on the soil of the Duchy of Grelz."

"Ah." The king's eyes glittered. "We are pleased to hear that, Marshal. Aye, we are very pleased indeed."

Rathar bowed. "So I hoped. And the Algarvians continue to fall back before us."

He might as well not have spoken, for the king talked right through him: "We would have been better pleased still, though, had Grelz never fallen to the invader in the first place."

"So would I, your Majesty." That was true, even if Rathar knew how lucky Unkerlant was to have survived the first dreadful year of fighting against the redheads. "Your armies are doing their best to make amends."

"Aye." The king sounded as if that best were not nearly good enough. But then he brightened. "Inside Grelz," he murmured, at least half to himself. "The time comes for a great burning and boiling and flaying of traitors."

"As you say, your Majesty." Rathar knew there were traitors aplenty in Grelz. His men had already run up against Grelzer soldiers: men of good Unkerlanter blood wearing dark green tunics and fighting for Raniero, the Algarvian puppet king. Some of those companies and battalions broke and fled when the first eggs burst near them. Some fought his men harder and with more grim determination than any Algarvians. That was what Swemmel's reign had sown, and what it now reaped.

If Swemmel himself realized as much, he gave no sign of it. "Carry on, then, Marshal," he said. "Purify the land. Purify it with fire and water and sweet-edged steel." Before Rathar could answer, the king's image disappeared. The crystal flared and then became nothing but an inert globe of glass.

"Do you require any other connections, lord Marshal?" the crystallomancer asked.

"What?" Rathar said absently. Then he shook his head. "No. Not right now."

He took his umbrella and left the ruined house where the crystallomancer had set up shop. Rain thrummed on the umbrella's canvas when he stepped outside. His boots squelched in mud. Two years before, the fall rains and mud had slowed Mezentio's men on their drive toward Cottbus. Now they slowed the Unkerlanters in their assault on the invaders. Rain and mud were impartial. *Curse them,* Rathar thought, squelching again.

Every house in this village was wrecked, to a greater or

lesser degree. The Algarvians had fought hard to hold the place before sullenly, stubbornly withdrawing. *Curse them, too,* Rathar thought. Nothing in this summer's drive toward the east had been easy. The redheads never had enough men or behemoths or dragons to halt his men for long, but they always knew what to do with the ones they had. Despite the rain, the stench of death was strong here.

Eggs burst, somewhere not far away. No, the redheads hadn't given up, nor the Grelzers they led, either. If they could stop the Unkerlanters, they would. And if they couldn't, they would make King Swemmel's soldiers pay the highest possible price for going forward. He'd seen that, too.

"Urra!" a peasant shouted as Rathar walked down the street toward what had probably been the firstman's house. Rathar nodded at him and went on. The peasant was gray-haired and limped. Maybe he'd been wounded in the Six Years' War. That might keep Swemmel's impressers from hauling him into the army once the front moved a little farther east. The younger, haler men in the village, though, those of them that were left, would probably be wearing rock-gray and carrying sticks before long.

Those of them that were left. A sour expression on his face, Rathar surveyed the village. Aye, it had been fought over. But he'd been through plenty of other villages that had been fought over. Once the fighting was over, the peasants came back from wherever they'd been hiding and got on with their lives. Here in Grelz, a lot of them didn't. A lot of them fled east with the retreating Algarvians. He'd seen some of that before, in lands to the south and west. He'd never seen it to the degree he was seeing it here, however.

How bad would it be if the Algarvians had set up a local noble as king, and not King Mezentio's first cousin? he wondered. No way to know, of course, but he suspected it would have been a good deal worse. As things were, a lot of Grelzers still remained loyal to the throne of Unkerlant. Had they had one of their own set above them, not some foreign overlord . . .

Algarvians were arrogant. It was their worst failing. They

hadn't thought they would need to worry about how the Grelzers felt. And so Raniero got to wear a fancy crown and call himself king—and plenty of men who might have put up with a Grelzer puppet went into the woods and fought for Swemmel.

Rathar stomped on over to the firstman's house, scraping mud from his boots off against the doorsill. General Vatran looked up from a mug of tea—fortified tea, for Rathar's nose caught the tang of spirits. "Well?" Vatran asked. "I trust his Majesty was pleased to learn where we are?"

"Aye, so he was," Rathar agreed. "Much easier to explain advances than retreats, by the powers above."

"I believe it." Vatran lifted his mug in salute. "May we have many more advances to explain, then."

"That would be very fine." Rathar raised his voice a little: "Ysolt, can I get a mug of tea, too? And a good slug of whatever Vatran poured into it?"

"Coming up, lord Marshal." The headquarters cook had been plucking a chicken. Now she went over to the brass kettle hanging above the fire and poured tea for Rathar. As she brought it to him, she went on, "You'll have to pry the brandy out of the general. That's his, not ours." She went back to the bird, rolling her formidable haunches as she walked.

Rathar held out the mug to Vatran. "How about it, General?"

Vatran undid the flask he wore on his belt. "Here you go, lord Marshal. If this doesn't make your eyes open wide, you're dead."

Rathar undid the stopper, sniffed, and then coughed. "That's strong, all right." He poured some into the tea and handed the flask back to General Vatran. With caution exaggerated enough to make Vatran laugh, he raised the mug to his lips. "Ahh!" he said. "Well, you're right. That's the straight goods."

"You bet it is. It'll put hair on your chest." Vatran pulled open the neck of his tunic and peered down at himself. "Works for me, anyway." Rathar knew Vatran had a thick thatch of white hair there. Most Unkerlanter men were pretty hairy. Of course, most Unkerlanter men drank a good deal, too. Maybe the one had something to do with the other.

Vatran said, "All right, now that we're inside Grelz, what does the king want us to do next?"

"Purify the land," he said," Rathar answered, and took another sip of tea. He coughed again. "Pouring these spirits over it ought to do the trick there." While Vatran laughed once more, the marshal went on, "Past that, he didn't give any detailed orders."

"Good," Vatran murmured—but only after glancing around to make sure Ysolt was out of earshot. Rathar nodded. He hated nothing worse than Swemmel's trying to direct the campaign from Cottbus. The king often couldn't resist sticking his oar in, but he usually made things worse, not better. In more normal tones, Vatran asked, "What have you got in mind, then?"

"I want to strike for Herborn," Rathar said.

That made Vatran's bushy white eyebrows fly up toward his hairline. Rathar had been sure it would, which was one of the reasons he hadn't mentioned it till now. "During the fall mud-time, lord Marshal?" Vatran said. "Do you really think we've got a chance of bringing it off?"

"I do, by the powers above," Rathar answered, "and one of the reasons I do is that the Algarvians won't think we'd dare try. We're better in the mud, the same as we're better in the snow. We have to be. We deal with them every year. If we can crack the crust and get a couple of columns moving fast, we can cut off a lot of redheads."

"That's the game they like to play against us," Vatran said.

"It's a good game," Rathar said. "And I'll tell you something else, too: it's a lot more fun when you're on the giving end than when you've got to take it."

"That's the truth!" Vatran boomed. "Getting our own back feels pretty cursed good; bugger me if it doesn't. But speaking of buggers, what about the Grelzers? They're flesh of our flesh, bone of our bone. They know what to do in mud and snow, even if Mezentio's men don't."

Rathar cursed. "You're right," he said reluctantly. "But I still think we can do it. From everything we've seen, the Grelzers are just footsoldiers. They're light on horses and unicorns, they haven't got any behemoths the scouts have seen, and they haven't got much in the way of egg-tossers. The redheads have been using 'em to hold down the country-side, not to do any real fighting. Send General Gurmun through 'em with a column of behemoths and they'll shatter like glass."

"Here's hoping." Vatran rubbed his chin, considering. "It could be, I suppose. You're really going to try it?"

"Aye, I'm really going to try it. Even if it doesn't go the way we hope it will, the Algarvians can't knock us back very far." Rathar cocked his head to one side in some astonishment, listening to what he'd just said.

Vatran's face bore a bemused look, too. "You know, I think you may be right," he said. "That's what the cursed redheads were saying about us a couple of years ago."

"I know," Rathar said. "They turned out to be wrong. We have to keep hammering them. That's the best hope we've got of turning out to be right." He nodded to himself. "Sure enough: I'm going for Herborn."

"Command me, then, lord Marshal," Vatran said. "If you've got the stomach for pushing forward even through mud, I'll help you ram the knife home."

"Good," Rathar told him. "I'll need all the help I can—" He broke off and turned toward the front door, through which a panting young lieutenant of crystallomancers had just come. "Hello! What's this about?"

"Lord Marshal." The young officer saluted. "We're getting reports from the front that the Algarvians have started pulling some of their units out of the line and taking them back to the east."

"What?" Rathar exclaimed. "Why in blazes are they doing that? Have they forgotten they're still fighting us?"

"I don't know why, sir," the crystallomancer said. "I just know what's reported to me."

"Well, whatever the reason—" Rathar smacked his fist into the palm of his other hand. "Whatever the reason, we'll make 'em pay for it."

Seventeen

꩜

"Come on, my beauty." Cornelu urged his leviathan forward as if he were urging a lover into his bedchamber. "Come on, my sweet." He stroked, he caressed, he cajoled, trying to get every bit of speed he could out of the beast.

And the leviathan gave him everything he asked, which was more than he could say about Janira back in Setubal. On it swam, toward Sibiu, toward—if the powers above proved kind—a return from exile after close to three and a half bitter years.

"This time," he murmured, "*this* time I won't swim up onto Tirgoviste because I had my mount killed out from under me. This time, *this* time"—he caressed the words, too— "if the powers above be kind, I'm coming home to a free kingdom. A freed kingdom, anyhow."

He ordered the leviathan up into a tailstand so he could see farther. There straight ahead lay Sigisoara, the easternmost of Sibiu's five main islands. He wished he'd been ordered to Tirgoviste, but his wishes counted for nothing in the eyes of the Lagoan Admiralty. And there, coming along every ley line that bore on the islands of Sibiu from east, southeast, and south, glided perhaps the largest fleet the world had ever seen: Sibian and Kuusaman warships of every size shepherding transports full of soldiers. Cornelu's was but one of a pod of leviathans helping to protect both the transports and the warships.

And there overhead, also warding the grand fleet from Algarvian attack, flew the greatest swarm of dragons Cornelu had ever seen. He didn't know how it measured in the historical scheme of things. He did know he'd never seen so many dragons accompanying a naval expedition. He couldn't imagine how the Lagoans and Kuusamans had got so many of the huge, fractious beasts aboard ship.

All at once, as if drawn by a lodestone, his head swung to the left, toward the south. He stroked the leviathan, commanding it to stay up on its tail longer so he could get a better look. At first, his hand went to the rubber pouch he wore on his belt—he intended to get out his crystal and scream a warning to the fleet. Of all things the ships didn't need, a great, drifting iceberg in their midst was among the worst.

After a moment, though, he realized the iceberg wasn't drifting. Instead, it glided east along the ley line under at least as much control as a cruiser. Its upper surface wasn't sharp and jagged, as it would have been in nature, but low and smooth and flat. Even as Cornelu watched, a dragon landed on the ice and two more, both painted in Lagoan scarlet and gold, took off. A chunk of ice that size could carry a lot of dragons—aye, and their handlers, too.

For a couple of heartbeats, Cornelu simply gaped at that. Then he remembered a name he'd heard on his journey down to the mages' base at the eastern edge of the land of the Ice People. "Habakkuk!" he exclaimed. He didn't *know* that that name went with the iceberg-turned-dragon-hauler, but it struck him as a good bet. What else but ice would those mages have been working on, down there on the austral continent?

He still had no idea why they'd had him bring egg casings full of sawdust to their base. *If I ever see one of them again, I'll have to ask,* he thought.

Right now, he had more urgent things to worry about. He let his leviathan slide back down into the sea, which it did with an indignant wriggle that told him it thought he'd made it stand on its tail far too long. "I am sorry," he told it. "You don't understand how strange that iceberg is."

The leviathan wriggled again, as if to say, *An iceberg is an iceberg. What else can it be?* Up till he'd seen this one, Cornelu would have thought the same thing. Now he saw that the question had a different answer, but it wasn't one he could explain to his mount.

With a snap of its toothy jaws, the leviathan gulped down a

squid as long as his arm. Then it swam on. Did it think Cornelu had arranged the treat? He didn't know—it couldn't tell him—but it didn't complain when, a few minutes later, he ordered it to lift its head, and him, high out of the water again.

Sigisoara island was closer now, close enough to let him see flashes of light and puffs of smoke as eggs burst near its south- and east-facing beaches. Boatloads of Kuusaman and Lagoan soldiers were leaving the transports and making for those beaches. Cornelu yelled himself hoarse as the leviathan sank back into the sea.

Tears stung his eyes, tears that felt more astringent than the endless miles of salt water all around. "At last," he murmured. "By the powers above, at last." He wished the Sibians could have freed themselves. That failing, having others— even having Lagoans—restore their freedom struck him as good enough. He shook a fist to the northwest, in the direction of Trapani. *Take that, Mezentio,* he thought. *Aye, take that and more besides.*

Here and there, eggs burst among the oncoming boats. Some of the Algarvians still on Sibiu were trying to give rather than take. An Algarvian dragon swooped down on a landing boat, flamed all the Lagoans in it, and left it burning on the water. A couple of Kuusaman dragons drove the enemy beast away, but too late, too late.

Still, Mezentio's men weren't putting up much of a fight. More than a year and a half before, Cornelu had been part of the force that raided Sibiu to distract the Algarvians while another fleet carried a Lagoan army to the land of the Ice People. Then the enemy had hit back hard. Had that raid been an invasion, it would have failed miserably.

Now . . . Now the Algarvians didn't seem to have so much with which to strike the invaders. Cornelu had seen as much on his last trip to Sibiu on leviathanback. His laugh was hard and cold. "That's what you get for taking on Unkerlant," he said, and laughed again.

Algarve had been recruiting Sibians to help fight its battles when he was there. He supposed they would mostly have gone to Unkerlant, too, the fools. How many of them crouched low in holes in the ground along with their Algarvian overlords, looking at vengeance here out on the ocean? However many traitors there were, Cornelu wished he could kill them all himself. Since he couldn't, he hoped the dragons overhead, the eggs tossed from the warships ashore, and the soldiers landing on the beaches would do the job for him.

He'd had his hopes dashed too many times in this war: his hopes for how the war would go, his hopes for his kingdom, his hopes for his marriage and his happiness. He was afraid to have hopes any more, for fear something would go wrong and ruin them anew.

Did King Burebistu have hopes? Like Gainibu of Valmiera, he'd been an Algarvian captive the past three years and more. Like Gainibu, he probably counted himself lucky that Mezentio hadn't booted him off the throne and replaced him with some Algarvian royal relative he wanted to get out of his hair. What was the King of Sibiu doing now? Something useful? Rallying the people in the palace against the Algarvian occupiers? Maybe. If Sibiu was lucky, just maybe.

But then Cornelu stopped worrying about Burebistu or anything farther away than the Algarvian ley-line frigate sliding down from the north toward the landing boats. Its egg-tossers and heavy sticks tore at the invaders; no Lagoan or Kuusaman warships were close enough to deal with it right away.

"I am," Cornelu said, and then, to his leviathan, "We are." He urged his mount forward. The frigate was faster than the leviathan, but if he could get to the ley line ahead of the ship's path and wait . . . If he could do that, he might give a good many of Mezentio's men a very thin time of it indeed.

He slid under the leviathan's belly, ready to loosen the egg slung there and fasten it to the frigate's hull. But he reached the ley line just too late; the frigate had already glided past. He couldn't even curse, not underwater, but red rage filled his thoughts.

As much from rage as for any other reason, he ordered the leviathan after the ley-line frigate. As long as the frigate kept going, it would leave the leviathan behind; it was, after all, steel and sorcery, not mere flesh and blood. But the frigate slowed when it got in among the landing boats. With so many targets all around, its captain wanted to make sure he missed none. Eggs started bursting near the frigate from ships that had seen the danger to the soldiers, but none struck home.

If one of those eggs burst too close to the leviathan, it could do as much harm as if the Algarvians tossed it. That was Cornelu's first thought. His second was, *If one of those eggs bursts too close to me* . . . But he had his duty, and a fine warm hatred of Mezentio's men to boot. He urged the leviathan forward.

"Now," he muttered, and tapped out the intricate signal that ordered the animal to dive deep and come up under the frigate's hull. When it did, he was waiting. He freed the egg from its sling and attached it to the Algarvian warship. Sorcery and lodestones held it to the ship. He sent the leviathan away as fast as it would go.

More eggs burst close by, which frightened it into swimming faster. He was glad it did. That meant it had got plenty far away when the egg he'd affixed to the frigate burst. It was a larger egg than the ones being tossed; Cornelu had no doubt which one it was. He urged the leviathan to the surface and looked back. When he saw the ley-line frigate sinking with a broken back, he pumped a fist in the air and shouted, "Take that, you son of a whore!"

A moment later, a puff of steam roiled the seawater by him, and then another and another. Soldiers in the surviving landing boats were blazing at him, not sure whose side he was on and not inclined to take chances finding out. He ordered the leviathan to submerge once more. He didn't suppose he could blame the Kuusamans and Lagoans bobbing on the sea. Blame them or not, though, he didn't want them killing him.

They blazed at him again when the leviathan surfaced once more, but by then he was too far away for their beams to be dangerous. And by then, he was cheering again, for boats were beaching themselves on Sigisoara and soldiers scrambling out of them. He approved of the soldiers, as long as they were going after the Algarvians and not him.

More Algarvian patrol boats came forth, these from the harbor at Lehliu, the port on the southeast coast of Sigisoara. None got close enough to do the landing boats any harm, though their crews pressed the attack with typical Algarvian dash and courage. Kuusaman dragons sank a couple, while well-positioned warships wrecked the rest.

As the day drew to a close, Cornelu used his crystal to call the Lagoan officer in charge of leviathan patrols: the very man, as it happened, who'd introduced the plan for the attack on Sibiu to him and his fellow exiles in the Admiralty offices in Setubal. "How do we fare, sir?" Cornelu asked. "I am not going to approach a ley-line cruiser to try to find out. The sailors would slay me before they bothered asking questions."

"You think so, eh?" the Lagoan said—in Algarvian, which probably gave his security mages nightmares. "Well, you're probably right. We fare very well, as a matter of face. Mezentio's men weren't expecting us—weren't expecting us at all, by every sign we can gather. Sigisoara and Tirgoviste are ours already, or near enough as makes no difference. We'll hold all five islands by this time tomorrow, and we'll be able to hold them against anything Algarve is likely to throw at us. As far as I can see, Commander, your kingdom's on the way to being free."

Would Sibiu truly be free, with Lagoan and Kuusaman soldiers holding the Algarvians at bay? It was bound to be freer. For now, that would do. "Powers above be praised," Cornelu said. "I can go home again." He could, aye. He needed a moment to remember that he might not want to.

An early fall rain—early for Bishah, at any rate—had turned the road between Hajjaj's estate in the hills and the capital of Zuwayza to mud. The foreign minister was almost perfectly content to stay where he was. His contentment would have been complete had the roof not developed a couple of what seemed like inevitable leaks.

"There ought to be an ordinance against roofers, as against any other frauds and cheats," he fumed. "And, of course, they can't come out to fix the damage till the rain stops, at which point no one needs them anymore." He was content to be isolated from Bishah, aye. He didn't care so much to have Bishah isolated from him.

His majordomo didn't point that out. Instead, Tewfik said, "Well, young fellow, it's not so bad as it could be. When you get as old as I am, you'll realize that." Hajjaj was no youngster himself—was anything but a youngster, in fact. But he was likely to be dead by the time he got as old as Tewfik. The family servitor looked ready to go on forever.

A younger, sprier servant came up to them and told Hajjaj, "Your Excellency, your secretary would speak to you by crystal."

"I'm coming," Hajjaj said. "Run on ahead and tell him I'll be right there." The servant, perhaps a third of Hajjaj's age, hurried away. The Zuwayzi foreign minister followed at a more stately pace. *Stately,* he thought. *That's a pretty-sounding word old men use when they mean slow.*

Hajjaj's back twinged when he sat down on the carpet in front of the crystal. "Hello, your Excellency," Qutuz said from out of the globe of glass. "How are you today?"

"Fine, thanks, except that my roof leaks and the roofers are thieves," Hajjaj replied. "What's come up?" Something had to have, or Qutuz wouldn't have called him. On the crystal, unlike in person, he didn't have to go through long courtesies before getting to the point.

Qutuz said, "Your Excellency, I have waiting on another crystal Minister Hadadezer of Ortah. He wishes to speak with you, and was disappointed to learn you hadn't come down to the palace today. I have a mage waiting to transfer his emanations to your crystal there, if you give me leave."

"By all means," Hajjaj said at once. "Talking with the Ortaho is always a treat." Because of the swamps and mountains that warded Ortah, it had always been all but immune to pressure from the outside, even though it lay between Algarve and Unkerlant. Ortaho foreign relations were a luxury, not a necessity as they were in the rest of the world. Hajjaj couldn't help wishing Zuwayza might say the same. He asked, "Do you know what he has in mind?"

"No, your Excellency." Qutuz shook his head. "But just let me give the word to the mage here, and you can find out for yourself." He turned away and said, "Go ahead," to someone Hajjaj couldn't see.

A moment later, Qutuz's image faded from the crystal. But light didn't flare from it, as it would have were the etheric connection broken. After a pause of a few heartbeats, a new image formed in the crystal: that of a man whose long white beard began to grow just below his eyes, and whose hairline was hardly separable from his eyebrows. Most savants reckoned the Ortahoin cousins to the Ice People of the austral continent.

Hajjaj gave Hadadezer a seated bow. "Good day, your Excellency," he said in Algarvian, a language the Ortaho minister also used. "As always, it is a privilege to speak to you. I should be delighted to enjoy the privilege more often."

"You are too kind," Hadadezer replied. "You will, I hope, remember our conversation this past winter."

"Aye, I do indeed," Hajjaj said. Sulingen had been on the point of falling then. "It was a worrisome time."

"Worrisome." The minister from Ortah nodded. "The very word. It surely was. You may perhaps also remember the concerns of my sovereign, King Ahinadab."

"I do recall them," Hajjaj agreed soberly. "You are perhaps wise not to speak of them too openly. It is probably that no one but ourselves is picking up these emanations, but it is not certain." Ahinadab had worried that, for the first time in generations, war might bear down on his kingdom in the aftermath of the Algarvian defeat. To Hajjaj, that proved the King of Ortah was no fool.

Now, speaking like a man in mortal torment, Hadadezer said, "What King Ahinadab feared has now come to pass. Algarvian soldiers have begun retreating into Ortah to escape the Unkerlanters, and King Swemmel's men are hard on their heels."

"Oh, my dear fellow!" Hajjaj said, as he had the winter before when Hadadezer spoke of his sovereign's concern. "Do I understand, then, that Ortah lacks the strength to keep them out?"

Ever so mournfully, the Ortaho minister nodded. "King Ahinadab has sent protests in the strongest terms to both Trapani and Cottbus." His eyebrows—they were separate from his hair after all—bristled in humiliated fury. "Ortah is a kingdom, not a road." More bristling. "But neither Mezentio nor Swemmel pays the least attention. Each, in fact, demanded that we declare war on the other."

"Oh, my dear fellow!" Hajjaj said again. Zuwayza lacked Ortah's natural defenses, and had had to suffer some generations of Unkerlanter overlordship. But King Shazli didn't have to worry about getting attacked by both sides at once. With real curiosity, Hajjaj asked, "What will your sovereign do?"

"I do not know," Hadadezer answered. "King Ahinadab does not yet know, either. If we say aye to either kingdom, we put ourselves in that king's hands and make an enemy of the other."

"And if you say no to both kings, you make enemies of them both," Hajjaj said.

"My sovereign is only too painfully aware of that as well," Hadadezer said. "As I told you last winter, I am no skilled diplomat. Ortah has no skilled diplomats. We have never needed skilled diplomats: the land is our shield. But with so many behemoths and dragons about, with so much more strong magecraft loosed in this war, we cannot be sure the land will ward us anymore."

"I think you are wise to worry," Hajjaj agreed. "In this war, men have taken nature by the neck and not the other way round, or not nearly so much as when men knew less than they do today."

Oh, nature could still work its will, and he knew as much. Every Algarvian who'd fought through an Unkerlanter winter would have agreed with him, too. So would the Unkerlanters who'd invaded desert Zuwayza. Still, what he'd said was more nearly true than not.

Hadadezer said, "Because we of Ortah are no diplomats, my king bade me ask you, the finest of the age, what you would do in his place."

"You do me too much honor," Hajjaj murmured. As he had

when Hadadezer's image first appeared before him, he bowed where he sat. The Ortaho minister inclined his head in turn. Carefully, Hajjaj said, "I am not in your king's place, nor can I be."

"I understand that. He also understands it," Hadadezer replied. "He makes no promises to follow what you propose. Still, he would know."

"Very well." Now Hajjaj spoke with some relief. He wouldn't have wanted the responsibility for the Ortahoin blindly obeying whatever he said. After he thought for a bit, he started ticking off points on his fingers: "You could fight as best you can. Or you could flee into the most rugged parts of the land and *let* the rest be a road."

"No," Hadadezer said firmly. "If we did that, we would never recover the land we gave up once the fighting ended."

What makes you think you will keep it all anyhow? Hajjaj wondered. But he said, "That could be. You could stay neutral and hope for the best. Or you could pick one side or the other. If you choose the winner, you may not be devoured afterwards. If you pick the loser . . . well, with your landscape, you still may not be devoured afterwards. That is better luck than most kingdoms have."

Hadadezer said, "We have been at peace a long time. All we ask is to be let alone. But who will hear us when we ask it? No one. Not a soul. The world has become a cruel, hard place."

"I wish I could say you were wrong, your Excellency," Hajjaj answered sadly. "But I fear—worse, I know—you are right. I also fear things will get worse before they get better, if they ever get better."

"I fear the same," the Ortaho minister said. "You will give my king no advice?"

"I have set forth the courses he might take," Hajjaj said. "In propriety, I can do no more than that."

With obvious reluctance, Hadadezer nodded. "Very well. I understand how you might feel that way, though I would be lying if I said I did not wish you to go further. Thank you for your time and for your patience, your Excellency. I bid you good day."

His image faded out of the crystal. Once more, though, it did not flare: the etheric connection remained intact. After a moment, Hajjaj saw Qutuz's face again. "Were you able to listen to any of that?" the Zuwayzi foreign minister asked.

"Aye, your Excellency." Qutuz suddenly looked anxious. "Why? Would you rather I hadn't?"

"No, no. It doesn't matter. I doubt Marquis Balastro would kidnap you and torture you or offer you lickerish Algarvian lasses to find out what Hadadezer had to say. It's only that . . ." Hajjaj's voice trailed away. He was more than a little horrified to find himself on the edge of tears. "Wasn't it the saddest thing you ever heard?"

"That it was," his secretary said. "Poor fellow hasn't a clue. By the way he made it sound, his king hasn't a clue, either. Not a clue in the whole kingdom, or his Excellency wouldn't have come crying to you."

"No, none," Hajjaj agreed. "Ortah's been able to stay apart from the rest of Derlavai too long. Nobody there knows how to do anything else." With seeming irrelevance, he added, "I read an account once of an island the Valmierans—I think it was the Valmierans—found in the Great Northern Sea."

Qutuz's eyebrows rose. "Your Excellency?" he asked, obviously hoping Hajjaj would make himself clear.

The Zuwayzi foreign minister did his best: "It was an uninhabited island—uninhabited by people, anyhow. It was full of birds that looked like big doves, doves the size of dogs, so big they couldn't fly. If I remember rightly, the Valmierans called them solitaires, or maybe it was Solitary Island. I haven't thought of it in years."

"Why couldn't they fly?" Qutuz still sounded confused.

"They'd lost the need, you might say. They had no enemies there," Hajjaj replied. "The Ortahoin, who've lost the need to deal with their neighbors, put me in mind of them."

"Ah." Qutuz still didn't seem altogether clear about where his superior was going, but he found the right question to ask: "What happened to these big birds, then?"

Hajjaj grimaced. "They were good to eat. The Valmierans hunted them till none was left—they couldn't get away, after all. The island wasn't very big, and they couldn't fly to another one. All we know of them now, we know from a few skins and feathers in a museum in Priekule." He paused. "If I were you, I wouldn't tell this tale to Hadadezer."

"I promise," Qutuz said solemnly.

When Pekka walked into the refectory in the hostel in the Naantali district, she found Fernao fighting his way through a Kuusaman news sheet. What with the news sheet, a Kuusaman-Lagoan lexicon, and, almost incidentally, the grilled herring and scrambled eggs and hot tea in front of him, he was as busy a man with breakfast as Pekka had ever seen.

Somehow, he wasn't too busy to notice her come in. He smiled at her and waved the news sheet in the air, almost upsetting his teacup. "Habakkuk!" he exclaimed.

"Aye, Habakkuk." Pekka turned the word into a happy, three-syllable squeak.

"That is brilliant sorcery. Brilliant, I say." Fernao spoke in classical Kaunian so he wouldn't have to pause and search for a word or two every sentence. "Sawdust and ice for strengthening the landing surface the dragons use. More magecraft, drawing energy from the ley lines to keep the icebergs frozen in warm seas. Aye, brilliant. Sea fights will never be the same, now that so many dragons can be carried across the water so quickly."

"You talk like an admiral," Pekka said. The term literally meant *general on the ocean*; the ancient Kaunian Empire had been far stronger on land than at sea.

Fernao waved the news sheet again. "I do not need to be an admiral to see what splendid magecraft went into this." He read from the sheet: " 'Not least because of their dominance in the air, Kuusaman and Lagoan forces had little trouble overwhelming the relatively weak Algarvian garrisons on the five main islands of Sibiu.' "

"You read that very well," Pekka said. "Your accent is much better than it used to be. How much did you understand?"

"Almost all—now." Fernao tapped the lexicon. "Not so much before I worked my way through it."

"All right." Pekka nodded. "If you stay here too much longer, though, we will make a Kuusaman of you in spite of yourself."

"Though I would have to clip my ponytail, there are probably worse fates. And I already have some of the seeming." Fernao rested his index finger by one narrow, slanted eye to show what he meant. Those eyes argued powerfully that he did have some Kuusaman blood. Then he waved to the seat across from his at the table. "Will you join me? You must have come here to eat, not to talk shop."

"Nothing wrong with talking shop," Pekka said as she did sit down. "But you will have to move that news sheet if I am to have enough room for my breakfast." When a serving girl came up to her, she ordered smoked salmon scrambled with eggs and her own mug of tea.

The tea arrived very quickly. She had to wait a little longer for the rest of her breakfast. As she sat chatting with Fernao, she noticed that neither of them said a word about Leino, though they both knew her husband had had a lot to do with the icebergs-turned-dragon-carriers that went by the name of Habakkuk. Fernao had praised the magecraft without praising the mages who worked it. As for her, she was proud as could be of Leino. But she didn't have much to say about him to Fernao, any more than she'd had much to say about Fernao when she went home to Leino.

But those shouldn't be inverses of each other, she thought. Before she had much chance to wonder why she'd acted as if they were, Ilmarinen came in and started raising a fuss. "Why are we here?" he said loudly. "What are we doing wasting our time in the middle of nowhere?"

"I do not know about you," Fernao said, buttering a slice of dark brown bread. "As for me, I am eating breakfast, and enjoying it, too."

"So am I." Pekka looked up over the rim of her mug of tea at Ilmarinen. "Do you have anything in particular in mind that we should be doing but are not, Master? Or are you just angry at the world this morning?"

He glared at her. "You're not my mother. You're not going

to pat me on the head and tell me everything's all right and get me to go back to work like a good little boy."

"No?" In fact, Pekka was in the habit of treating him rather as if he were Uto, but she'd never told him that. She was tempted now, just to see the look on his face. "What would you have me do, then?"

"Leave me alone!" Ilmarinen shouted, loud enough to make everyone in the refectory, mages and servants alike, stare at him.

Fernao surged to his feet. Pekka noted that he put only a little weight on his cane. Not so long before, he couldn't have done anything without it. "Now see here," he began, looming over Ilmarinen.

"Sit down," Pekka told him, her voice not sharp but flat. He looked astonished. *Of course he's astonished,* Pekka thought. *He thinks he's helping me.* She didn't look at him. She didn't repeat herself. She just waited. The Lagoan mage sank back into his seat. Pekka's gaze swung back to Ilmarinen. "I suggest you also sit down. Have breakfast. Whatever you are upset about will still be here when you have finished. Standing around and screaming at one another is a game for mountain apes or Algarvians, not for civilized men." She spoke in classical Kaunian, partly for Fernao's benefit, partly because it helped her sound dispassionate.

Like Fernao before him, Ilmarinen sat down before he quite seemed to realize he'd done it. Pekka waved for a serving girl. She wasn't sorry the one she got was Linna, for whom Ilmarinen still yearned. She hoped the master mage wouldn't want to make a bigger fool of himself in front of the girl. And he didn't; he ordered breakfast, much more like a civilized man than a shrieking mountain ape.

Pekka nodded. "And have some tea, Master, have some bergamot tea. It will help soothe you." She nodded to Linna to make sure the serving girl added the tea to Ilmarinen's order. Linna hurried off and brought the tea before anything else. The look she gave Pekka wasn't quite conspiratorial, but it came close.

As the fragrant leaves steeped, Ilmarinen muttered something under his breath. "What was that?" Fernao asked, though Pekka wished he would have let it ride.

Ilmarinen repeated himself, a little louder: "Seven Princes and a Princess—Pekka of Naantali."

"Nonsense," Pekka said, "nonsense or maybe treason, depending on whether Prince Renavall, whose district this is, finds himself in a merciful mood."

Ilmarinen took a couple of somber sips of tea and shook his head. "I have no trouble disobeying princes. I *enjoy* disobeying princes, by the powers above. But I obeyed you. Why do you suppose that is?" He sounded puzzled, almost bewildered.

"Because you know you were making an idiot of yourself?" Pekka suggested.

"That seldom stops me," Ilmarinen answered.

"Aye, we have seen as much," Fernao said.

Ilmarinen turned a baleful eye his way. "I'm not the only one at this table who's doing it," he snapped. "I'm just the only one who's not ashamed to admit it." Fernao turned very red. With his fair skin, the flush was easy to see.

Something close to desperation in her voice, Pekka said, "Enough!" She hoped she wasn't flushing, too. If she was, she hoped it didn't show. She went on, "Master Ilmarinen, you came in and said we were wasting our time. You said it at the top of your lungs. Suppose you either explain yourself or apologize."

"Suppose I do neither one." Ilmarinen sounded as if he was enjoying himself again.

Pekka shrugged. She kept on speaking classical Kaunian: "If you would sooner disrupt the work than join it, you may leave, sir. We have snow on the ground again. Sending you by sleigh to the nearest ley-line caravan depot would be easy—nothing easier, in fact. You could be in Yliharma day after tomorrow. You would not be wasting your time, or ours, there."

"I am Ilmarinen," he said. "Have you forgotten?" What he meant was, *Do you think you can accomplish anything without my brilliance?*

"I remember all too well. You make me remember all too well with your disruptions," Pekka answered. "I am the mage who leads this project. Have you forgotten? If your disruptions cost more than you give, we are better off without you, no matter who you are."

"Aye," Fernao growled.

But Pekka waved him to silence. "This is between Master Ilmarinen and me. How now, Master Ilmarinen? Do you follow where I lead here, or do you go your own carefree way somewhere else?"

She wondered if she'd pushed it too hard, if Ilmarinen *would* leave in a huff. If he did, could they go forward? He was, unquestionably, the most brilliant living mage in Kuusamo. He was also, as unquestionably, the most difficult. She waited. Ilmarinen said, "I would like a third choice."

"I know. But those are the two you have," Pekka said.

"Then I obey," Ilmarinen said. "I even apologize, which is not something you will hear from me every day." In token of obedience, he slipped out of his seat and went to one knee before Pekka, as if she were truly one of the Seven Princes . . . and he were a woman.

She snorted. "You overact," she said, now in quick Kuusaman, rather hoping Fernao couldn't follow. "And you know what that posture means."

"Of course I do," he answered in the same tongue as he sat in the chair again. "But so what? It's fun no matter who's doing it to whom."

Now Pekka knew she was blushing. Very much to her relief, she saw Fernao hadn't caught all of the byplay. She returned to classical Kaunian: "Enough of that, too. More than enough, Master Ilmarinen. I ask you again: why do you say we are wasting our time here? I expect an answer."

"You know why. Both of you know why." Ilmarinen pointed to her and to Fernao in turn. "Our experiment brought fresh green grass here in dead of winter. If we can do that, we can go the other way as well."

"We are not grass," Pekka said. "And we have no notion from which summer the grass came hither."

Ilmarinen waved his hand. "That is a detail. One reason we don't know is because we haven't tried to find out. That's why I say we're wasting time."

Fernao spoke up: "You were the one who showed similarity and contagion have an inverse relationship, not a direct one. If the relationship is not direct, what works in one direction will fail in the other. Calculations to that effect are very plain, would you not agree?"

"Without experiment, I agree to nothing," Ilmarinen said. "Calculation springs from experiment, not the other way round. Without the experiment of Mistress Pekka here, the landscape would have a good many fewer holes in it, Master Siuntio would still be alive, and you would be back in Lagoas where you belong."

"That will be quite enough of that," Pekka snapped. To her surprise, Ilmarinen inclined his head in—another apology? She had trouble believing that, but she didn't know what else it could be. Then Fernao started to say something. He and Pekka got on very well—sometimes, she feared, almost too well—most of the time, but now she pointed her index finger at him as if it were a stick, since she was sure he was about to aim a barb at Ilmarinen. "Do not even start," she said sternly. "We have had too much quarreling among ourselves as is. Do you understand me?"

"Aye." After a moment's hesitation, Fernao added, "Mistress Pekka." He looked as apologetic as Ilmarinen had.

For a heartbeat or two, Pekka simply accepted that and was glad of it. Then she stared down at her own hands in something very much like wonder. *By the powers above,* she thought, a little—more than a little—dazed. *I'm leading them. I really am.*

Grelz boiled and bubbled like a pot of cabbage soup too long on the fire. Grelzer soldiers trudged west, to try to help Algarve and keep the land a kingdom. Unkerlanter soldiers battled their way east, to try to make it into a duchy once more. And the peasants who made up the bulk of the population were caught in the middle, as peasants all too often were during wartime.

Some of them, those who would soon have lived under puppet King Raniero than fierce King Swemmel, fled east ahead of the oncoming Unkerlanter army and the retreating Algarvians and Grelzers. In the mud time, the roads would have been bad without them. With them clogging those roads, the redheads and their Grelzer hounds had an even harder time getting men and beasts and supplies to the front.

With so many strangers on the move, Garivald's band of irregulars could operate far more freely than they had before. Most of the time, a stranger's appearance in a peasant village brought gossip and speculation. Having lived his whole life up till the war in Zossen, a village much like any other, Garivald understood that in his bones. But things were different now. With strangers everywhere, what difference did one more make?

"Our army's still moving," Garivald told Tantris as reports from the outside world trickled into the woods where the irregulars denned. "Not easy to press forward in the mud time. I ought to know."

"Marshal Rathar's no ordinary soldier," the Unkerlanter regular replied. "He can make men do things they couldn't manage most of the time."

"The ground's starting to freeze every now and then," Garivald said. "That'll make things easier—at least till the first big blizzard."

"Easier for both sides," Tantris said. "When it's mud, we've got the edge on the redheads."

"Oh, aye, no doubt," Garivald agreed. "We can move a little, and the stinking Algarvians can hardly move at all."

He'd intended that for sarcasm, but Tantris took him literally and nodded. "If you can get any kind of advantage, no matter how small, you grab it with both hands," he said. "That's how you win."

For once, Obilot agreed with him. "We have the best chance to hurt the Algarvians now," she told Garivald inside the tent the two of them had started sharing. "The real army is getting close. Mezentio's whoresons will be careless of us. They'll have bigger things, worse things, on their minds."

"Aye." Garivald knew he sounded abstracted. He couldn't help it. If the army wasn't so far away from here, it was even closer to Zossen . . . Zossen, where his wife and son and daughter lived. One of these days, he would have to go back, which meant that one of these days there would be no place for Obilot in his life.

He reached for her. She came to him, a smile on her face. They made love under a couple of blankets; it was cold in the tent, and getting colder. At the moment when she stiffened and shuddered and her arms tightened around him, she whispered his name with a kind of wonder in her voice he'd never heard from anyone else. He missed his wife and children, but he would miss her, too, if this ever had to end.

Afterwards, he asked her, "Do you think about what life will be like once the army takes back all of Grelz?"

"When there's no more need for irregulars, you mean?" she asked, and he nodded. She shrugged. "No, not very much. What's the point? I haven't got anything to go back to. Everything I had once upon a time, the redheads smashed."

Garivald still didn't know what she'd had. He supposed she'd been a wife, as Annore was his wife back in Zossen. Maybe she'd been a mother, too. And maybe it wasn't just her family that didn't exist anymore. Maybe it was her whole village. The Algarvians had never been shy about giving out lessons like that.

"Curse them," he muttered.

"We'll do worse than curse them," Obilot answered, "or maybe better. We'll hurt them instead." She spoke of that with a savage relish at least as passionate as anything she'd said while she lay in his arms.

And she left the woods the next morning to go spy out the roads and the nearby villages. Both the Algarvians and the Grelzers paid less attention to women than they did to men. In a way, that made sense, for more women were less dangerous than most men. But Obilot was different from most women.

When she came back the next day, excitement glowed on her face. "We *can* hurt them," she said. "We can hurt them badly. They're mustering at Pirmasens for a strike against the head of the column of regulars moving east."

That made Tantris' eyes glow. "Aye, that's what we'll do," he said. "That's what we're for."

"How many of them are mustering at Pirmasens?" Garivald asked.

"I don't know exactly," Obilot replied. "A couple of regiments, anyhow. Algarvians and Grelzers both."

He stared. "Powers above!" he exclaimed. "What can we do against a couple of regiments of real soldiers? They'd squash us like bugs."

But Obilot shook her head. "We can't fight them, no. But there are only two bridges over the streams south of Pirmasens. If we can knock those into the water, the redheads and the traitors can't get where they're going."

"That's right." Sadoc nodded. The peasant who made such a disastrous mage went on, "I'm from those parts. They'd have to spend a while building bridges if we take out the ones that are standing."

Tantris nodded, too. Tantris, in fact, all but licked his chops. "If this isn't the sort of thing a band of irregulars can do, what is?" he asked Garivald. He still didn't try giving orders, though. Maybe he'd really learned.

"We can try it, aye," Garivald said. "A good thing you managed to get us a few eggs—they'll help." Tantris actually had been worth something there. Back in the days when Munderic led the band, he'd had connections among disaffected Grelzer soldiers that got eggs for the irregulars. Garivald hadn't been able to match that. But Tantris, being a regular, had sources of supply farther west, and they'd come through.

Sadoc said, "I want to get out there and fight. I want to make the Algarvians and the traitors pay. That's all I've ever wanted."

It wasn't any such thing. Once upon a time—not very long before—he'd wanted to slay Garivald with sorcery. All he'd managed to do was kill Tantris' comrade instead. He was far more dangerous to the foe with a stick in his hand than with a spell. Maybe he'd really learned, too.

Garivald scratched his chin. "If we're going to wreck the bridges, we'll have to move by night. We can't let anybody catch us hauling eggs by daylight. Anyone sees us doing that, we're dead men."

Tantris stirred but didn't speak. Garivald could guess what he was thinking: that wrecking the bridges counted for more than losing a few irregulars. That was probably how real soldiers had to think. If not thinking that way meant Garivald wasn't a real soldier, he wouldn't lose any sleep over it. And he saw the rest of the band nodding their heads in agreement with him. They wanted to make the Algarvians and their puppets suffer. They didn't want to do any dying themselves.

Some of them would, no matter what they wanted. Garivald was pretty sure of that, even as he got the irregulars moving a little past midnight. He hoped they weren't dwelling on it. But if they wrecked those bridges south of Pirmasens, the enemy would have a good idea of where they were—and would stand between them and the shelter of the woods. Getting back wouldn't be so easy.

Getting to the bridges was another matter. Nights were long now, long and cold and dark: plenty of time for marching, plenty of darkness for concealment. Clouds overhead threatened snow. Garivald hoped they would hold off. *That'd be just what we need,* he thought: *a bunch of tracks saying, Here we are—come blaze us!*

They carried four eggs, two for each bridge, with each egg yoked between two men with carrying poles and rope. Every so often, new pairs would take them; they weren't light, and Garivald didn't want anyone exhausted. He also sent out scouts well ahead of the main body of irregulars: here of all times, he couldn't afford to be surprised.

Tantris came up to him and remarked, "I've seen real officers who didn't arrange their men half so well."

"Have you?" Garivald said, and the regular nodded. Garivald let out a thoughtful grunt. "No wonder the Algarvians drove us so hard during the first days of the war, then."

"You may make fine songs, but your mouth will be the death of you one day," Tantris said. Garivald didn't answer. He just kept trudging along. When the time came to take one egg's carrying poles on his shoulders for a while, he did it without hesitation. A real officer probably wouldn't have, but he wasn't one, so he didn't care.

He sent a runner up to the scouts with orders to swing wide around Pirmasens. The glow from the campfires there was plenty to warn him away from the place. The runner came back with word that the scouts had already swung wide on their own. Garivald wondered if regular soldiers would have. He didn't ask Tantris.

When they got to the first bridge, they planted an egg at each end. The second bridge lay a few hundred yards upstream. When they got there, Sadoc murmured, "I feel a power point. All I have to do is say the word, and—"

"No!" Garivald hissed frantically. To his vast relief, Tantris said the same thing in the same tone of voice. Sadoc muttered something else, but the louder mutter of the rain-swollen river swept it away.

Tantris went off by himself into the darkness. The eggs were *his;* he knew the spell that would make them burst, and he jealously guarded the knowledge. Garivald made out only one word from him—"Now!"— and then four nearly simultaneous roars shattered the night and shattered the bridges. Chunks of wood rained down on the irregulars. Someone let out a yowl of pain. Nobody would cross the river by either of those ways for a good long while.

But then, even before Garivald could order the irregulars back toward the woods, challenges rang out and beams began to flicker in the night. The Grelzers *had* had patrols on the move—he'd just been lucky enough to miss them. Now . . . Now there were a lot of shouts of "Raniero!" and a lot of men rushing down from Pirmasens to join the hunt for the bridge-wreckers. Garivald's mouth went dry. Some Grelzer soldiers would sooner surrender than fight. Some were very good men indeed. *My luck to run into that kind again,* he thought. *And they can pin us against the river. We can't use those stinking bridges, either.*

The Grelzers plainly intended to do just that. Garivald had no idea how to stop them. If Tantris did, he kept it as secret as the bursting spell. Another thought ran through Garivald's mind. *We're going to die here. We're all going to die here.* A beam zipped past him. For a moment, the air smelled of thunderstorms.

No sooner had that crossed his mind than lightning smote the Grelzers, not once but again and again. Each crash of cloven air dwarfed the roars that had come from the bursting eggs. No snow. No rain. Only bolt after bolt of lightning, peal after peal of thunder.

Through those peals, Garivald heard someone laughing like a man possessed. *Sadoc,* he realized. Awe—or perhaps the aftereffects of lightning—made the hair prickle up on his arms and at the nape of his neck. *He's found himself at last.* And then, as the Grelzer soldiers fled howling in fear, *Well, for sure he picked the right time.*

As the ley-line caravan glided to a stop on the eastern outskirts of Eoforwic, Vanai squeezed Ealstan's hand in excitement. "Oh, I can hardly wait!" she exclaimed.

He was grinning, too. They both got to their feet and descended from the caravan car. They both popped open umbrellas; it was drizzling. The misty rain hid all but the nearest houses. There weren't so many, anyhow; the city faded away into meadows and orchards and farmland—exactly the sort of landscape Vanai wanted now.

Along with her umbrella, she clutched a wickerwork basket. Ealstan had one just like it. Vanai jumped in the air from sheer high spirits. "Mushrooms!" she squealed, as if it were a magic word. And so, for her, it was.

"Aye." Ealstan nodded. They walked away from the caravan stop. Their shoes got muddy. Neither of them cared. They both had on old pairs. They weren't the only ones who'd got off at this stop, either. Half a carload of eager Forthwegians scattered to pursue their kingdom's favorite fall sport.

"You don't know what this means to me," Vanai said once the other mushroom hunters were out of earshot.

"Maybe a little," Ealstan said. "I remember how excited you were after you found the sorcery last year, just to be able to go to a park and look for mushrooms there. This has to be even better."

"It is." Vanai gave him a quick kiss. He did try to understand in his head. Maybe he even succeeded there. But how could he understand in his belly what being cooped up inside that flat for most of a year had been like? How could he understand the fear she'd felt every time somebody walked along the hall past the door? A pause, a knock, could have meant the end for her. It hadn't happened, but it could have. She'd know that in *her* belly.

Her husband's thoughts were traveling a different ley line. "There in the park, that was where you got your Forthwegian name," Ealstan said. "It was the first one that popped into my head when we ran into Ethelhelm and his friends."

"Thelberge." Vanai tasted it, then shrugged. "It took me by surprise then. I'm used to it by now, or pretty much so, anyway. Everybody who calls me anything calls me Thelberge these days—except you, every once in a while."

"I like you as Vanai," he said seriously. "I always have, you know." Despite the chilly drizzle, that warmed her. Ealstan shifted his basket to the hand that also held the umbrella so he could put his free arm around her. He went on, "You've had a better year than Ethelhelm did, and that's the truth."

"I know." Her shiver had nothing to do with the weather, either. "I wonder what's become of him since he ran away from everything. He had nerve, there in the street in Eoforwic when his spell wore off. He started singing and playing and bluffed his way through."

"If he'd had more nerve earlier, it might not have come to that." Ealstan had never had much bend to him. As far as he was concerned, things were right or they were wrong, and that was that. "But he wanted to stay rich even though the Algarvians were running the kingdom, and he ended up paying the price."

"You can't blame him too much," Vanai said. "Most people just want to get along as best they can. He did better than almost anybody else with Kaunian blood in Forthweg . . . for a while, anyhow."

"Aye. For a while." Ealstan sounded grim.

Part of that, Vanai knew, was what he reckoned friendship betrayed. She said, "Maybe we haven't heard the last of him yet."

"Maybe," Ealstan said. "If he has any sense, though, he'll go on lying low. The Algarvians would be on him like a blaze if he started making waves. And Pybba would know about him, too, if he were trying to give the redheads a hard time. Pybba hasn't heard a thing."

"Would he tell you if he had?" Vanai asked.

Before Ealstan answered, he stooped to pick some meadow mushrooms and toss them into his basket. Then he said, "Would he tell me? I don't know. But there would likely be some sign of it in his books, and there isn't. You poke through a fellow's books, you can find all sorts of things if you know how to look."

"You could, maybe," Vanai said. He spoke with great assurance. His father had trained him well. At nineteen, he was a match for any bookkeeper in Eoforwic.

And how did your grandfather train you? Vanai asked herself. *If there were need for a junior historian of the Kaunian Empire, you might fill the bill. Since the Algarvians have made it illegal to write Kaunian—and a capital offense to be Kaunian—you're not good for much right now.*

She walked on for another couple of paces, then stopped so abruptly that Ealstan kept going on for a bit before realizing she wasn't following. He turned back in surprise. "What's wrong?"

"Nothing." She'd been feeling flutters in her belly the past few days, maybe even the past week. She'd put them down to gas and a sour stomach; her digestion wasn't all it might have been. But this wasn't gas. She knew what it was, knew what it had to be. "Nothing's wrong. The baby just kicked me."

Ealstan looked as astonished as he had when she'd first told him she was pregnant. Then he hurried back to her and set his own hand on her belly. Vanai looked around, ready to be embarrassed, but she couldn't see anyone else, which meant no one else could see him do such an intimate thing. He said, "Do you suppose he'll do it again?"

"How should I know?" Vanai said, startled into laughter. "It's not anything I can make him do."

"No, I guess not." Ealstan sounded as if that hadn't occurred to him till she pointed it out.

But then, with his palm still pressed against her tunic, the baby did stir again within her. "There!" she said. "Did you feel that?"

"Aye." Now wonder filled his face. "What does it feel like to you?"

Vanai thought about that. "It doesn't feel *like* anything else," she said at last. "It feels *as if* somebody tiny is moving around inside me, and he's not very careful where he puts his feet." She laughed and set her hand on top of his. "That really is what's going on."

Ealstan nodded. "Now it does seem you're going to have a baby. It didn't feel quite real before, somehow."

"It did to me!" Vanai exclaimed. For a moment, she was angry at him for being so dense. She'd gone through four months of sleepiness, of nausea, of tender breasts. She'd gone through four months without the usual monthly reminder that she wasn't pregnant. But all of that, she reminded herself, had been *her* concern, not Ealstan's. All he could note from firsthand experience was, this past week or so, a very slight bulge in her lower abdomen and, now, a flutter under his hand.

He must have been thinking along with her there, for he said, "I can't have the baby, you know. All I can do is watch."

She cocked her head to one side and smiled at him. "Oh, you had a little more to do with it than that." Ealstan coughed and spluttered, as she'd hoped he would. She went on, "The baby isn't going anywhere for months, even if he thinks he is. We'll only be out here hunting mushrooms for a few hours. Can we do that now?"

"All right." Ealstan looked astonished again. The baby was uppermost—overwhelmingly uppermost—in his thoughts. He had to be amazed it wasn't so overwhelmingly uppermost in hers. But she'd had those months to get used to the idea, while he'd admitted a minute before that it hadn't seemed real to him till now.

"Come on." She pointed ahead. "Are those oaks there? I think they are. Maybe we'll find some oyster mushrooms growing on their trunks."

"Maybe we will." Ealstan slipped his arm around her waist—she still had a waist. "We did back there in that grove between Gromheort and Oyngestun." He grinned at her. "We found all sorts of interesting things in that oak grove."

"I don't know what you're talking about," Vanai said. They both laughed. They'd first met in that grove of oaks. They'd first traded mushrooms there, too. And, a couple of years later, they'd first made love in the shade of those trees. Vanai smiled at Ealstan. "A good thing it wasn't drizzling that one day, or everything that's happened since would have been different."

"That's so." Ealstan wasn't smiling anymore; he frowned as he worked through the implications of what she'd said. "Strange to think how something you can't control, like the weather, can change your whole life."

"Tell it to the Algarvians," Vanai said savagely. "In summer, they go forward in Unkerlant. In winter, they go back." Before Ealstan could answer, she made her own commentary to that: "Except this year, powers below eat them, they couldn't go forward in summer. They tried, but they couldn't."

"No." Ealstan's voice held the same fierce, gloating joy as hers. "Nothing came easy for them this year. And now there's fighting down in Sibiu, too. I don't think that's going so well for the redheads, either, or they'd say more about it in the news sheets."

"Here's hoping you're right," Vanai said. "The thinner they spread themselves, the better." She stooped and plucked up a couple of horse mushrooms, slightly more flavorful cousins to ordinary meadow mushrooms. As she put them in her basket, she sighed. "I don't think there are as many interesting kinds around Eoforwic as there were back where we came from."

"I think you're right." Ealstan started to add something else, but broke off and looked at her with an expression she'd come to recognize. Sure enough, he said, "Your sorcery's slipped again."

Vanai's mouth twisted. "It shouldn't have. I renewed it not long before we walked to the caravan stop."

"Well, it has," her husband said. "Is it my imagination, or has the spell been fading faster since you got pregnant?"

"I don't know," Vanai said. "Maybe. It's a good thing nobody's close by, that's all." Now she hurried for the shelter of the oaks—not that they gave much shelter, with most of the leaves off the branches. She took out her two precious lengths of yarn, twirled them together, and made the spell anew. "Is it all right?" she asked.

"Aye." Ealstan nodded. Now he looked thoughtful. "I wonder why it isn't holding so long these days. Maybe because you've got more life energy in you now, and so the spell has more to cover."

"It could be. It sounds logical," Vanai said. "But I hope you're wrong. I hope I just didn't cast the spell quite right. I could have lost the disguise on the caravan car, not out here where no one but you saw me." Her shiver, again, had nothing to do with the chilly, nasty weather. "That would have been very bad."

"Forward!" Sergeant Leudast shouted. "Aye, forward, by the powers above!" Since the great battles in the Durrwangen bulge, he'd shouted the order to advance again and again. It still tasted sweet as honey, still felt strong as spirits, in his mouth. He might almost have been telling a pretty woman he loved her.

But the men holed up in the village ahead didn't love him or his comrades. The ragged banners flapping in the chilly breeze there were green and gold—the colors of what the Algarvians called the Kingdom of Grelz. As far as Leudast was concerned, that kingdom didn't exist. The Grelzers blazing at his company from those battered huts had a different opinion.

"Death to the traitors!" Captain Recared yelled. Somewhere in the long fight between Durrwangen and westcentral Grelz, a promotion had finally caught up with him. Leudast couldn't remember where. It didn't matter to him. Promotion or no, Recared kept doing the same job. Leudast kept doing the same job, too, and nobody would ever promote him to lieutenant's rank. He was sure of that. He had neither the bloodlines nor the pull to become an officer. "Death to the traitors!" Recared cried again, from behind a pale-barked birch tree.

Leudast crawled over toward Recared. Somebody in the village saw the motion and blazed at him. The ground was wet: steam puffed up where the beam bit, a few feet in front of his head. He froze. In southern Unkerlant, with winter coming on fast, that could easily be a literal as well as a metaphorical statement. After shivering for half a minute, he dashed forward again, and found shelter behind another tree trunk. The Grelzer blazed at him again, and missed again.

"Death to those who follow the false king!" Captain Recared roared.

"Sir," Leudast said, and then, when Recared didn't notice him right away, "Sir!"

"Eh?" That second time, he'd spoken loud enough to make Recared jump. The young regimental commander turned his head. "Oh, it's you, Sergeant. What do you want?"

"Sir, if you don't mind, don't shout about death so much," Leudast answered. "It just makes the cursed Grelzers fight harder, if you know what I mean. Sometimes they'll surrender, if you give 'em the chance."

Recared chewed on that: visibly, for Leudast watched his jaw muscles work. At last, he said, "But they deserve death."

"Aye, most of 'em do." Leudast didn't want to argue with his superior; he just wanted him to shut up. "But if you tell 'em ahead of time that they'll get it, then they've got no reason not to fight as hard as they can to keep from falling into our hands. Do you see what I'm saying?"

The winter before, Recared wouldn't have. Now, reluctantly, he nodded, though he said, "I still have to make our men want to fight."

"Haven't you noticed how it is, sir?" Leudast asked. "Advancing makes a big difference there." Unkerlanter egg-tossers began pelting the enemy-held village. Leudast grinned wider at each burst. "And so does efficiency. They see we really can lick the whoresons on the other side."

"Of course we can," Recared exclaimed, as if the first two desperate summers of the war against Algarve had never happened. He knew how to take advantage of the egg-tossers, though. He raised his voice to a shout again: "They've got to keep their heads down, boys, so we can take 'em. Forward! King Swemmel and victory!"

"Swemmel and victory!" Leudast echoed, also at the top of his lungs. Nothing wrong with that war cry, nothing at all. A lot of Unkerlant—and a good big stretch of the Duchy of Grelz here—had been recaptured behind it.

Recared ran forward—he was brave enough and to spare. Leudast followed him. So did everybody within earshot, and then the rest of the Unkerlanter soldiers who saw their comrades moving. "Urra!" they shouted, and, "Swemmel and victory!"

Shouts rose from inside the village: "Raniero!" and "Swemmel the murderer!" Advancing Unkerlanters went down. Some howled out cries that held no words, only pain. Others lay very still. These Grelzers weren't about to surrender regardless of what the Unkerlanters yelled.

They'd buried eggs in the mud in front of their village, too. An Unkerlanter soldier trod on one. He shrieked briefly as the released energies consumed him. Leudast cursed. His own countrymen had stalled Algarvian attacks in the Durrwangen salient with belt after belt of hidden eggs. Having the stratagem turned against them seemed anything but fair.

Then Recared pointed south of the village and said the happiest words any Unkerlanter footsoldier could use: "Behemoths! Our behemoths, by the powers above!"

Even with snowshoes spreading their weight, even with the way made easier with brush and logs spread in front of them, the great beasts made slower, rougher going in the mud than they had on the hard ground of summer. But they moved forward faster than men could, and they and their armored crewmen were much harder to kill than ordinary footsoldiers.

Leudast said, "Let's go with them and bypass this place. Once we get behind it, it won't be worth anything to the Grelzers anymore."

Recared frowned. "We ought to go straight at the enemy. He's right there in front of us."

"And we're right here in front of him, where he's got the best blaze at us," Leudast answered. "When the Algarvians were driving us, they'd go around the places that fought hard and let them wither on the vine. They'd advance where we were weak, and we couldn't be strong everywhere."

"That's so," Recared said thoughtfully. He hadn't been there to go through most of that, but he knew about it. A great many of the soldiers who had gone through it were dead; Leudast knew how lucky he was to be among the exceptions. To his relief, Recared nodded again, blew his whistle, and shouted for his men to swing south of the village and go with the behemoths. "The men who come after us, the ones who aren't good enough to fight in the first rank, can mop up these traitors," he declared.

As Leudast hurried toward the behemoths, he wondered if the Grelzers would sally to try to stop them. But the men who followed King Mezentio's cousin stayed under cover; they knew they'd get slaughtered out in the open. Leudast expected them to get slaughtered anyway, but now it would take longer and cost more.

The Unkerlanters pressed on for another couple of miles before a well-aimed beam from a heavy stick left one of their behemoths kicking its way toward death in the mud. Another beam, not so well aimed, threw up a great gout of nasty-smelling steam between a couple of other behemoths. All the crews frantically pointed ahead. When Leudast saw Algarvian behemoths at the edge of some woods, he threw himself flat in the muck. The redheads didn't seem to have so many behemoths left these days, but they used the ones they did have with as much deadly panache as ever.

Still, two and a half years of war had taught King Swemmel's soldiers several painful but important lessons. Their behemoths didn't charge straight at the Algarvian beasts. Some of them traded beams and sticks with the Algarvians from a distance. That let the others sidle around to the flank. Leudast had watched this dance of death before. He knew what the right counter would be: having more behemoths waiting to engage the Unkerlanters trying the flanking move. The Algarvians didn't have them. That meant they could either withdraw or die where they stood.

They chose to withdraw. Someplace else, someplace where they found odds that looked better, they would challenge the Unkerlanters again. In the meanwhile . . . "Forward!" Leudast shouted, scrambling up out of the mud. He wasn't that much filthier than the men around him, and his voice lent him authority.

Not long before nightfall, his squad and a couple of others fought their way into a village neither the Grelzers nor the Algarvians defended very hard. Captain Recared strode for the firstman's house, to make his headquarters there. He found the place empty, the door standing open. "Where's the firstman?" he asked a dumpy woman looking out the window of the hut next door.

She jerked a thumb toward the east. "He done run off," she answered, her Grelzer accent thick as syrup in Leudast's ears. "He were in bed with the Algarvians, he were." She sniffed. "His daughter were in bed with anything that walked on two legs and weren't quite dead. Little slut."

Recared nodded and went inside. Leudast nodded, too—wearily. He heard that story, or one just like it, in every village the Unkerlanters recaptured. All those villages had the same look: a lot of houses abandoned because the peasants had fled east to stay under Algarvian protection, hardly any men fit for soldiers showing themselves on the street.

The first few times he'd heard peasants tell tales of woe, he'd been sympathetic. Now . . . Now sympathy came harder. A lot of these people had run away rather than returning to King Swemmel's rule. From what Leudast had seen, a lot of the ones who'd stayed behind had done so only because they hadn't found the chance to flee.

No sooner had that thought crossed his mind than a scuffle broke out in a house not far away: curses and thumps and a shout of pain. "Think we ought to do anything about that, Sergeant?" one of his men asked.

Leudast shrugged and then shook his head. "I think it'll sort itself out without us. When it does . . ."

He proved a good prophet. A couple of minutes later, three middle-aged men half led, half dragged one of their contemporaries up before him. "Ascovind here, he done sucked up to the Algarvians and to the miserable little tinpot king they made," one of the captors said. "He ought to get what's coming to him."

"That's a filthy lie!" Ascovind shouted, twisting and trying to break free. "I never done nothing like that."

"Liar!" all three of the men shouted at the same time. One added, "He done told the Grelzers where irregulars hid out. Hurt 'em powerful bad, I bet."

"What do you want me to do about it?" Leudast asked the men. "You can save him for King Swemmel's inspectors when they get here, or else you can knock him over the head yourselves. Makes no difference to me one way or the other."

They dragged Ascovind away. Presently, they came back and he didn't. Leudast had seen the like there a good many times, too. Ascovind should have run off, but he'd probably thought his neighbors wouldn't turn on him when they got the chance. As far as Leudast was concerned, that made him a fool as well as a traitor; he'd probably deserved whatever the other villagers had given him.

And he wouldn't be the only one. Men who'd cursed King Swemmel or who'd just tried to get along; women who'd opened their legs to an Algarvian or to a Grelzer soldier; men and women nobody much liked—aye, the inspectors would be busy here. They'd be busy lots of places. Leudast was glad of his uniform. Nobody could suspect him of treason, not for anything.

The soldiers took as much food as they could find. They had to, to feed themselves. None of the villagers dared say a word. These men in filthy rock-gray who represented King Swemmel could start calling them traitors, too. Leudast shared some of the black bread he got with the prettiest girl he saw. Later, she shared herself with him. They hadn't made the bargain in words, but it was nonetheless real.

Recared's whistle shrilled before sunrise the next morning. "Forward!" he shouted. Forward Leudast went, on toward Herborn.

Eighteen

Bembo was sleeping the deep, restful sleep of a man with a clean conscience—or perhaps of a man with no conscience—when someone shattered that rest by rudely shaking him awake. His eyes flew open. So did his mouth, to curse whoever would perpetrate such an enormity. But the curses died before they saw the light of day: Sergeant Pesaro loomed over him, fat face filled with fury.

"Get your arse out of the sack, you son of a whore," Pesaro

snarled. "Come with me this instant—this instant, do you hear?"

"Aye, Sergeant," Bembo answered meekly, and came, even though he wore only his light tunic and kilt and the barracks was chilly. He followed Pesaro into the sergeant's office, where, shivering, he plucked up his always indifferent courage enough to ask, "What—what is it?"

The worst he could think of was that Pesaro had found out how he'd spirited away the parents of Doldasai the Kaunian courtesan. By the fearsome expression on Pesaro's face, this was liable to be even worse than that. Pesaro snatched a leaf of paper off his desk and waved it in Bembo's face. "Do you see this?" he shouted. "*Do* you?"

"Uh, no, Sergeant," Bembo said. "Not unless you hold it still." Thus reminded, Pesaro did. Bembo read the first few lines. His eyes widened. "By the powers above," he whispered. "My leave's come through."

Pesaro's glare grew more baleful yet. "Aye, it has, you stinking sack of moldy mushrooms," he ground out. "*Your* leave has come through. Nobody else's has, not in this whole barracks, not in this whole stinking town. Not even *mine*. Powers below eat you, *you* get to go back to Tricarico for ten mortal days and enjoy yourself in civilization while the rest of us stay stuck with the fornicating Forthwegians."

He looked about to tear the precious paper to shreds. To forestall   such a disaster, Bembo snatched it out of his hands. "Thank you, Sergeant!" he exclaimed. "I feel like a man who just won the lottery." That was no exaggeration; he knew how unlikely leaves were. All but babbling, he went on, "I'm sure yours will come through very soon. Not just sure—positive." Aye, he was babbling. He didn't care.

"Ha!" Pesaro tossed his head in magnificent, jowl-wobbling contempt. "Go on, get out of my sight. I'll be jealous of you every minute you're gone—and if you're even one minute late coming back to duty, you'll pay. Oh, how you'll pay."

Nodding, doing his best not to gloat, Bembo fled. He

dressed. He packed. He collected all his back pay. He hurried to the ley-line caravan depot and waited for an eastbound caravan. He'd just scrambled aboard it when he realized he hadn't bothered waiting for breakfast. If that didn't speak to his desperation for escape, he didn't know what did.

Almost all the Algarvians in his caravan car were soldiers who'd got leave from the endless grinding war against Unkerlant. Some of them, seeing his constable's uniform, cursed him for a coward and a slacker. He'd heard that before, whenever soldiers passed through Gromheort. Here, he had to grin and bear it—either that or pick a fight and get beaten to a pulp.

But some of the soldiers, instead of reviling him, just called him a lucky dog. They shared food with him, and fiery Unkerlanters spirits, too. By the time the ley-line caravan had got well into Algarve, Bembo leaned back in his seat with a glazed look on his face.

He found he had little trouble figuring out just when the caravan entered his native kingdom. It wasn't so much that redheads replaced swarthy, bearded Forthwegians in the fields. That did happen, but it wasn't what he noticed. What he noticed was something starker: women replaced men.

"Where are all the men?" he exclaimed. "Gone to fight King Swemmel?"

One of the fellows who'd been feeding him spirits shook his head. "Oh, no, buddy, not all of them. By now, a good many are dead." Bembo started to laugh, then choked on it. The soldier wasn't joking.

Changing caravans in Dorgali, a good-sized town in south-central Algarve, came as more than a little relief. Most of the men under fifty in the depot wore uniforms, but some didn't. And hearing women and children use his own language as their birthspeech was music to Bembo's ears after a couple of years of listening to sonorous Forthwegian and occasional classical Kaunian.

Best of all, the civilians among whom Bembo sat on the trip to Tricarico didn't blame him for not being a soldier. Some of them, in fact, started to take his constable's uniform for that of the army. He wouldn't have denied it if a woman hadn't pointed him out for what he really was. But even she didn't do it in a mean way; she said, "You're serving King Mezentio beyond the frontier, too, just as if you were a soldier."

"Why, so I am, dear," Bembo said. "I couldn't have put it better, or even so well, myself." He flirted with her till she got off the caravan car a couple of hours later. That made him snap his fingers in disappointment; if she'd stayed on till Tricarico, something interesting might have developed.

He let out a long sigh of pleasure, like that of a lover returning to his beloved, when the conductor called, "Tricarico, folks! All out for Tricarico!" He grabbed his bag and hurried down onto the platform of the depot. It was, he saw, the platform from which he'd left for Forthweg a couple of years before. He kicked at the paving stones as he left the depot and hurried out into the city—his city.

There were the Bradano Mountains, indenting the eastern skyline. He didn't have to worry about blond Jelgavans swarming out of them, as he had in the early days of the war. He didn't have to worry about Jelgavan dragons anymore, either.

And *there* was a cab. He waved to it. The driver stopped. Bembo hopped in. "The Duke's Delight," he told the hackman, naming a hostel he'd have no trouble affording. He'd had to give up his flat when he went off to the west.

"You'll be from around these parts," the driver said, flicking the horse's reins.

"How do you know?" Bembo asked.

"Way you talk," the fellow answered. "And nobody who wasn't would know of a dive like that." Bembo laughed. He also got the last laugh, by shorting the driver's tip to pay him back for his crack.

Once he'd got himself a room at the hostel, Bembo walked down the hall to take a bath, then changed into wrinkled civilian clothes and went back out to promenade through the streets of Tricarico. *How shabby everything looks,* he thought. *How worn.* That took him by surprise; after so long in battered Gromheort, he'd expected his home town to sparkle by comparison.

As he'd seen on his caravan journey across Algarve, few men between seventeen and fifty were on the streets. Of those who were, many limped or were short a hand or wore an eye patch or sometimes a black mask. Bembo grimaced whenever he saw men who'd come back from the war something less than a full man. They made him feel guilty for his free if not especially graceful stride.

After so long looking at dumpy Forthwegian women and the occasional blond Kaunian, Bembo had thought he would enjoy himself back in his home town. But his own countrywomen seemed tired and drab, too. Too many of them wore the dark gray of someone who'd lost a husband or brother or father or son.

Powers above, he thought. *The Forthwegians are having a better time of it than my own folk.* For a moment, that seemed impossible. Then, all at once, it made sense. *Of course they are. They're out of the war. They aren't losing loved ones anymore— well, except for the Kaunians in Forthweg, anyhow. We have to go right on taking it in the teeth till we finally win.* Lurid broadsheets shouted, THE KAUNIANS STARTED THIS WAR, BUT WE WILL FINISH IT! Others cried, THE STRUGGLE AGAINST KAUNI- ANITY NEVER ENDS! They were pasted on every vertical surface, and gave Tricarico most of what little color it had. People hurried past them head down, not bothering to read.

Another thought occurred to Bembo: *or we have to go on taking it till we lose.* He resolutely shoved that one to the back of his mind.

He wasn't walking a beat here. He had to keep reminding himself of that. Whether he was or he wasn't, though, he soon found himself back at the constabulary station where he'd spent so much time before going to Gromheort. He hadn't seemed to belong anywhere else.

He went up the stairs and into the beat-up old building with hope thudding in his heart. He got his first jolt when he opened the door: that wasn't Sergeant Pesaro sitting behind the desk in the front hall. *Of course not, you idiot,* Bembo jeered at himself. *You left Pesaro back in Forthweg.* He didn't recognize the fellow in the sergeant's familiar seat.

The constable didn't recognize him, either. "What do you want, pal?" he asked in tones suggesting that Bembo had no business wanting anything and would be wise to take himself elsewhere in a hurry.

I'm not in uniform, Bembo realized. He fished in his belt pouch and found the card that identified him as a constable from Tricarico. Displaying it, he said, "I've been on duty in Forthweg the past couple of years. Lightning finally struck— they gave me leave."

"And you came back to a constabulary station?" the man in Pesaro's seat said incredulously. "Haven't you got better things to do with yourself?"

"Curse me if I know for sure," Bembo answered. "Tricarico looks dead and about halfway buried. What's wrong with everybody, anyway?"

"War news isn't so good," the other constable said.

"I know, but that's not it, or not all of it," Bembo insisted. With a shrug, he went on, "Here, at least, I know some people."

"Go on, then," said the constable behind the desk. "Just don't bother anybody who's working, that's all."

Bembo didn't dignify that with a reply. He hurried down the hall to the big room where clerks and sketch artists worked. A lot of the clerks he'd known were gone, with women taking their places. Most of the time, that would have cheered Bembo, but now he was looking for familiar faces. The jeers and insults he got from the handful of people who recognized him felt better than blank stares from even pretty strangers.

"Where's Saffa?" he asked one of the clerks who hadn't gone off to war when he didn't see the artist. "The army can't have taken *her.*"

"She had a baby a couple weeks ago," the fellow answered. "She'll be back before too long, I expect."

"A baby!" Bembo exclaimed. "I didn't even know she'd got married."

"Who said anything about married?" the clerk replied. That made Bembo laugh. It also made him wonder why, if Saffa was going to fall into bed with somebody, she hadn't fallen into bed with him. *Life isn't fair,* he thought, and pushed on farther into the station.

Frontino the warder hastily stuck a trashy historical romance into his desk drawer when Bembo came in. Then he pulled it out again, saying, "Oh, it's you. I thought it might be somebody important," as if the constable had never gone away. He got up and clasped Bembo's wrist.

"Nice to see some things haven't changed," Bembo said. "You're still a lazy good-for-nothing."

"And you're still an old windbag," Frontino retorted fondly.

Again, trading insults made Bembo feel at home. His wave encompassed the whole constabulary station, the whole town, the whole kingdom. "It's not the same as it was, is it?"

Frontino pondered that. Bembo wondered how the warder was supposed to judge, when he spent most of his time shut away in the gaol he ran. But he didn't take long to nod and say, "It's been better, sure enough." Bembo nodded, too. All at once, he looked forward to getting back to Gromheort.

A baby's thin, angry wail woke Skarnu in the middle of the night. Merkela stirred beside him in the narrow, crowded bed. "Hush," she told the baby in the cradle. "Just hush."

The baby wasn't inclined to listen. Skarnu hadn't thought he would be. He didn't suppose Merkela had thought so, either. With a weary sigh, she got out of bed and lifted their son from that cradle. "What does he want?" Skarnu asked. "Is he wet, or is he just hungry?"

"I'll find out," she answered, and then, a moment later, "He's wet. I hope I don't wake him up too much changing him." She laid the baby on the bed and found a fresh rag with which to wrap his middle. "Hush, Gedominu," she murmured again, but the baby didn't want to hush.

"He's hungry," Skarnu said.

Merkela sighed. "I know." She sat down beside the baby, picked him up, and gave him her breast. He nursed avidly—

and noisily. Skarnu tried to go back to sleep, but couldn't. He listened to his son eat. The baby was named for Merkela's dead husband, whom the Algarvians had blazed. It wasn't the name Skarnu would have chosen, but Merkela hadn't given him much choice. He could live with it. Gedominu had been a brave man.

Little Gedominu's sucking slowed, then stopped. Merkela raised him to her shoulder and patted him till he gave forth with a surprisingly deep belch. She set him back in the cradle and lay down beside Skarnu again.

"Not too bad," she said, yawning.

"No, not too," Skarnu agreed. Little Gedominu was only a couple of weeks old. Already, Skarnu and Merkela had learned the difference between good nights and bad, fussy feedings and others. Skarnu went on, "One of him and two of us. He only outnumbers us by a little."

No matter how sleepy she was, Merkela noticed that. "Ha!" she said: not laughter but an exclamation. "That isn't funny."

"I didn't think it was," Skarnu replied. A new thought crossed his mind. "Powers above! How do you suppose people with twins or triplets manage?"

Merkela noticed that, too. "I don't know," she said. "They probably just go mad, wouldn't you think?" She yawned again. Skarnu started to answer, but checked himself when her breathing grew slow and regular. She had the knack for falling asleep at once—or maybe, taking care of Gedominu, she was too weary to do anything else.

Gedominu woke once more in the night, and then again at first light. That left Skarnu shambling and red-eyed from lack of sleep, and Merkela a good deal worse. As she put a pot on the wood-burning stove to make tea, she said, "It might have been simpler just to let the Algarvians catch us."

She'd never said anything like that while they were on the farm. But then, she hadn't had to contend with a new baby while they were on the farm, either. Skarnu went over and set a hand on her shoulder. "Things will straighten out," he said. "Sooner or later, they have to."

"I suppose so." Even though Gedominu lay in the cradle, awake but quiet, Merkela sounded anything but convinced. When she waved her arm, she almost hit Skarnu and she almost hit a couple of walls; the flat wasn't very big. That, to her, was part of the problem. She burst out, "How do towns-folk stand living cooped up like this all their lives? Why don't they run screaming through the streets?"

Her farmhouse hadn't been very large, either, but when she looked out the windows there she saw her fields and meadows and the trees across the road. When she looked out the one small, grimy window here, all she saw were the cobbles of the street below and, across that street, another block of flats of grimy yellowish brown bricks much like the ones here.

"Erzvilkas isn't much of a town," Skarnu said with what he reckoned commendable understatement, "and this isn't much of a flat, either. We'll do better as soon as we get the chance. For now, though, we're safe from the redheads, and that's what matters most."

Merkela only grunted and poured two mugs of tea. She took a jar of honey and spooned some into her mug, then passed it to Skarnu, who did the same. He sipped the hot, sweet, strong brew. It drove back the worst of his weariness.

But it couldn't drive away his worries. They'd escaped the Algarvians, aye. That wasn't the same as saying they were safe from them. Skarnu knew as much, whether Merkela did or not. When Merkela fled the farm, she'd left everything behind. Algarvian mages could use her clothes or her cooking gear and the law of contagion to help find her. You didn't have to be a mage to know that objects once in contact remained in contact. Fortunately, you did have to be a mage to do anything about it.

Algarvian mages were spread thin these days. The war wasn't going so well for the redheads. Maybe they wouldn't worry so much about one renegade Valmieran noble. In the larger scheme of things, Skarnu wasn't that important. So he hoped they would reckon the odds, anyway.

It all boiled down to, how badly did they want him? He

sighed. The other side of the coin was, they were liable to want him quite a bit with both his sister and Amatu howling for his blood. He didn't dare get too sure he was safe.

Merkela's thought followed a different ley line. After another sip of tea, she said, "How long can they keep holding down our kingdom? Sibiu is free again, or just about."

"Aye, I think so." Skarnu nodded. "The news sheets would talk more about the fighting there if it were going better for Algarve. But the Sibs didn't free themselves: Lagoas and Kuusamo beat King Mezentio and took the kingdom away from him. And it's a lot easier to invade some islands in the middle of the sea than to put soldiers ashore on the Derlavaian mainland."

For a moment, Merkela looked as if she hated him. "I want to be free again," she said. "I want that so much, I'd—" Before she could say what she might do, Gedominu started to whimper. Merkela laughed ruefully. "Nobody who wants to be free should ever have a baby." She picked him up and held him in the crook of her elbow. Maybe that was what he wanted, for he quieted down.

"Where'd that honey jar go?" Skarnu got up and opened it. He tore a piece off a loaf of black bread, dipped it in the honey, and ate it. Back before the war, he would have turned up his nose at the idea of such a breakfast. Now he knew that any breakfast at all was a long way toward being a good one.

"Fix some of that for me, too, would you?" Merkela said. Skarnu nodded and did. Gedominu stared up at his mother, as if trying to understand what she'd just said.

His intent expression made Skarnu start to laugh. "The world must be a demon of a confusing place for babies," he remarked as he handed Merkela the bread and honey.

"Of course it is," Merkela said. "It's a demon of a confusing place for everybody." She took a bite. Gedominu was still watching, wide-eyed. She shook her head at him. "You can't have any of this. Not till you get bigger."

The baby's face screwed up. He started to cry. Skarnu started to laugh. "That'll teach you to tell him what he can't do," he said. Merkela jiggled Gedominu up and down and from side to side. He subsided. She let out a sigh of relief.

Someone knocked on the door, a quick, hard, urgent knock.

Skarnu had been about to pour himself another cup of tea. He froze. So did Merkela, with a bite of bread halfway to her mouth. Nobody in Erzvilkas had any business here at this hour.

The knock came again. Skarnu grabbed a knife and went to the door. "Who is it?" he growled, his voice clotted with suspicion.

"*Not* the redheads, and cursed lucky for you."

Hearing that rough reply, Skarnu unbarred the door and worked the latch. Sure enough, Raunu stood in the hallway. Skarnu looked him up and down. "No, you're not the redheads," he agreed. "But if you're here now, you don't think they're very far behind you."

"They're sniffing around, all right," the veteran sergeant agreed. "Time for you and yours to pack up and go."

"What about you?" Skarnu demanded. "What about the Kaunians from Forthweg?"

Patiently, Raunu said, "I'm not a captain. I'm not a marquis. As far as the Algarvians are concerned, people like me are two for a copper. And Vatsyunas and Pernavai are just a loose end. You, though, you're a prize. And your lady's bait."

"He's right," Merkela said from behind Skarnu. "We have to go." She held little Gedominu in her arms, and also carried a sack full of diapers. "When there's no other choice, we run, and then we strike again another time."

Raunu smiled at her and gave her half a bow, as if her veins, not Skarnu's, held noble blood. "That's good sense. You've always shown good sense, as long as I've known you." He turned back to Skarnu. "Come *on*, Captain. We've a mage of sorts downstairs, ready to block the redheads' searching as best she can."

"A mage of sorts?" In spite of everything, Skarnu smiled. "That sounds—interesting." But the smile slipped. He was worried about Merkela. "*Can* you flee again, so soon out of childbed?" he asked her.

"Of course I can," she said at once. "I have to. Do you think I want to fall into the Algarvians' hands?"

He had no answer to that. "Let's go, then," he said roughly. Raunu's shoulders rose and straightened, as if he'd just had a burden lifted from them. He hurried for the stairs. Skarnu and Merkela followed. When they got to the stairway, Skarnu took the baby and the sack of cloths. Merkela didn't protest, a telling measure of how worn she was.

Out on the street, a carriage waited. Skarnu let out his own sigh of relief when he saw it. No matter how fiercely insistent she was, Merkela couldn't have got far on foot.

Also waiting was Raunu's "mage of sorts." She couldn't have been above fifteen, her figure half formed, her hair stringy, pimples splashing her cheeks and chin. In a low voice, Skarnu said, "*She's* going to hold the Algarvian wizards off our trail?"

It wasn't low enough; the girl heard him. She flushed, but spoke steadily: "I think I can do that, aye. The techniques for breaking affinities have improved remarkably since the days of the Six Years' War."

Skarnu stared. She certainly spoke as if she knew what she was doing. Raunu let out a soft grunt of laughter. He said, "I've been pretty impressed with Palasta, I have."

"Maybe I see why," Skarnu answered, and bowed to her.

"Get you gone," Palasta told him. "That's the point of this business, after all. From now on, powers above willing, the Algarvians will have a harder time coming after you."

Raunu had already helped Merkela up into the carriage. Now he slapped Skarnu on the back and gave him a little push. Skarnu handed Merkela Gedominu and the bag of cloths, then scrambled up beside her. The driver—another man from the underground—flicked the reins. The carriage started to roll.

Fleeing again, Skarnu thought bitterly. He reached out and set his hand on Merkela's. This time, at least, he had what mattered most to him.

* * *

The silversmith's shop that had been Kugu's remained closed. Every so often, Talsu would walk by, just for the satisfaction of seeing it locked and dark and quiet. He knew better than to do that very often. Someone might note it and report him to the Algarvians. He was grimly certain Kugu hadn't been the only collaborator in Skrunda.

He'd wondered if the redheads would come around asking questions of him after Kugu's untimely demise. So far, they hadn't. A forensic mage could have assured them he hadn't been in the room when the silversmith perished. That was true. But truth, here, had many layers.

He also knew Algarve still had foes in his home town. He wondered if Kugu's former students were among the men responsible for the new graffiti he saw on so many walls these days. HABAKKUK! they read, and HABAKKUK IS COMING! And he wondered what in blazes Habakkuk was.

"Whatever it is, Mezentio's men don't like it," Gailisa said when Talsu wondered out loud at supper one evening. "Have you seen them putting together gangs of people they drag off the street to paint it out wherever they find it?"

Talsu nodded. "Aye, I have. That's got to mean it's something good for Jelgava." He laughed. "Feels funny, hoping for something without knowing what I'm hoping for."

"I know what I'm hoping for," Traku said, dipping a piece of barley bread in garlic-flavored olive oil. "I'm hoping for more orders of winter gear from Algarvians heading off to Unkerlant. That wouldn't make me unhappy at all, Habakkuk or no Habakkuk."

"I won't say you're wrong there, because you're right." Talsu nodded again. "But it's such a funny name or word or whatever it is. It doesn't sound Jelgavan at all."

"Is it classical Kaunian?" his father asked.

"It's nothing Kugu ever taught me, anyhow," Traku answered, "and Kugu taught me all sorts of things." He paused, recalling some of the painful lessons he'd learned from the silversmith. Then he said, "Pass me the bread and oil, would you please?"

His mother beamed. "That's good. That's very good," Ausra said. "High time you got some meat back on your bones."

Talsu knew better than to argue with his mother about such things. Later, in the small room that now seemed even smaller because he shared it with Gailisa, he asked his wife, "Am I still as skinny as all that?"

"There's certainly more to you than there was when you first came home," Gailisa said after a brief pause for thought. "Back then, I think your shadow took up more room in bed than you did. But you're still skinnier than you were before the Algarvians grabbed you."

He lay down on the bed and grinned up at her. "If I take up more room now than I used to, maybe you can get on top tonight."

Gailisa stuck out her tongue at him. "I did that anyhow when you came back—or have you forgotten? I didn't want you working too hard. Now . . ." Her eye's sparkled as she started to undo the toggles on her tunic. "Well, why not?"

She'd just gone off to her father's grocery store the next morning when an Algarvian captain strode into the tailor's shop. "Good morning, sir," Traku said to him. "And what can we do for you today?" He didn't ask the redhead if he was looking for something warm. The Algarvian might have taken that as gloating over a trip to Unkerlant, which would have cost Traku business.

But this particular Algarvian turned out not to be going to Unkerlant. Pointing to Talsu, he spoke in good Jelgavan: "You are Talsu son of Traku, is it not so?"

"Aye," Talsu answered. As his father had, he asked, "What can I do for you today, sir?"—but he feared he knew the answer.

Sure enough, the Algarvian said, "We haven't heard much from you. We'd hoped for more—quite a lot more."

"I'm sorry, sir," replied Talsu, who was anything but. "I've just stayed close to home and minded my own business. I haven't heard anything much."

With a frown, the Algarvian said, "That's not why we ordered you turned loose, you know. We expected to get some use out of you."

"And so you have, by the powers above," Traku put in. "I couldn't have done half as much for you people without my son here stitching right beside me."

"That's not what I meant," the redhead said pointedly.

"I don't care," Traku growled.

"Father—" Talsu said in some alarm. He didn't want to go back to the dungeon himself, no, but he didn't want to send his father there on his account, either.

But Traku wasn't inclined to listen to him, either. Glaring at the Algarvian, he went on, "I don't care what you meant, I tell you. Go ask the soldiers who've left this sunny land of ours for Unkerlant. Ask them about their tunics and kilts and capes and cloaks. Ask them if Talsu's done something worth doing for them. Then come back here and complain, if you've got the nerve."

Now the Algarvian captain frankly stared at him. Odds were; nobody in Jelgava had ever dared talk back to him before. He didn't seem to know what to make of it. At last, he said, "You play a dangerous game."

Still furious, Traku shook his head. "I'm not playing games at all. For you, maybe, it's a game. For me and my son, it's our lives and our livelihood. Why don't you cursed well leave us alone and let us mind our own business, like Talsu here said?"

He was shouting, shouting loud enough to make Ausra come halfway down the stairs to find out what was going on. When Talsu's mother saw the redhead in the shop, she let out a horrified gasp and retreated in a hurry. Talsu sighed in relief. He'd feared she would lay into the Algarvian the same way his father had.

The captain said, "There is service, and then there is service. You are trying to tell me that one kind is worth as much as another. In this, you . . ." Then, to Talsu's astonishment, he grinned. "In this, you may be right. I do not say you are; I say you may be. Someone of higher rank than I will make the final decision." He bowed and strolled out of the shop.

Talsu gaped at his father. "That was one of the bravest things I ever saw," he said.

"Was it?" Traku shrugged. "I don't know anything about that. All I know is, I was too little to go off and fight the redheads in the last war, and I get bloody sick of bending my neck and going, 'Aye, sir,' whenever they come through the door. So I told this son of a whore a couple of plain truths, that's all."

"That's not all," Talsu said. "You know the risk you were running."

"What risk?" Traku didn't want to take him seriously. "You went after the Algarvians with a stick in your hands. That, now, that was running a risk. This isn't so much, not even close." He coughed once or twice. "There've been times when I've sounded like it was your fault Jelgava didn't lick those Algarvian buggers. I know there have. I'm sorry for it."

Talsu tried to remember if he'd ever heard his father apologize for anything before. He didn't think so. He didn't quite know how to respond, either. He finally said, "Don't worry about it. I never have."

That was true, though perhaps not in a way Traku would have cared to know. Talsu discounted everything his father had to say about the war precisely because Traku hadn't seen it for himself. What soldier ever born took seriously a civilian's opinions about fighting?

They went back to work in companionable silence. After a while, Ausra appeared on the stairs again, Laitsina behind her. When the two women didn't see the Algarvian, they came all the way down. "Is everything all right?" they asked together.

"Everything is fine," Traku said gruffly. "Sometimes it's a little harder to make people see sense than it is other times, that's all."

"You made . . . an Algarvian see sense?" Laitsina sounded as if she couldn't believe her ears.

"He sure did." Talsu thumped his father on the shoulder.

Traku, to his astonishment, blushed like a girl. Ausra came over and kissed her husband on the cheek. That made Traku blush more than ever.

Ausra and Laitsina went upstairs again. Talsu and Traku looked at each other before they started work again. Maybe the Algarvian captain had seen sense, aye. But maybe he'd just gone for reinforcements—more redheads, or perhaps some Jelgavan constables. Or maybe his superiors would overrule him. Having been in the army, Talsu knew how easily that could happen.

But the Algarvian didn't come back, with or without reinforcements. As the day wore on toward evening, Talsu began to believe he wouldn't. When Gailisa came back from the grocer's shop, Talsu told her how brave Traku had been. She clapped her hands together and kissed Traku on the cheek, too. That made Talsu's father turn even redder than the kiss from his own wife had.

Supper was barley porridge enlivened with garlic, olives, cheese, raisins, and wine: food for hard times. Talsu remembered that huge piece of mutton he'd eaten with Kugu. Then he shrugged. The company was better here. When he went off to his cramped little bedchamber with Gailisa, that thought occurred to him again, rather more forcefully. He kissed her.

"What was that for?" she asked, smiling.

"Just because," Talsu answered. *Because you're not Kugu* struck him as the wrong thing to say. He did add, "I like kissing you."

"Do you?" Gailisa gave him a sidelong look. "What else would you like?"

They found something they both liked. As a result, they were sleeping soundly when eggs started falling on Skrunda. The first bursts made Talsu sit bolt upright, instantly wide awake. After his time in the army, he would never mistake that sound, and never fail to respond to it, either.

"Downstairs!" he exclaimed, springing out of bed. "We've got to get downstairs! Powers above, I wish we had a cellar to hide in." He heard his parents and sister calling out in their bedrooms. "Downstairs!" he cried again, this time at the top of his lungs. "We'll hide behind the counter. It's good and thick—better than nothing."

Only later did he stop to think that going downstairs in pitch blackness was liable to be more dangerous than having an egg burst close by. But the whole family got down safe. They huddled behind the counter, chilly and frightened and crowded and uncomfortable. "The news sheets will be screaming about air pirates tomorrow," Traku predicted.

"Not if one of these eggs bursts on their office, they won't," Laitsina said.

"I hope some of them burst on the Algarvians here in town," Talsu said. "Otherwise, the Lagoans or Kuusamans up there on those dragons are just wasting their eggs."

"Why are they bothering us?" his mother wailed as an egg came down close by and made the building shake. "We haven't done anything to them."

Talsu did his best to think like a general, and a foreign general at that. "If they strike at Jelgava," he said, "that makes it harder for the Algarvians to pull men out of our kingdom and send them to Unkerlant." He paused. "That means Father and I won't sell the redheads so many cloaks."

"Curse the foreigners, in that case!" Traku exclaimed. Maybe he meant it. Maybe he was joking. Maybe he was doing both at once. Any which way, Talsu laughed in spite of the death raining down on his home town. *May it strike the Algarvians indeed, just as my sister said,* he thought, and hoped the powers above were listening.

Colonel Spinello's ley-line caravan glided to a stop in a battered city in eastern Forthweg—not that there were any cities in Forthweg, eastern or western, that weren't battered. The corporal doing conductor duty bawled, "This here is Gromheort. Two-hour layover—we're picking up some men and some horses here. Two-hour layover."

"Gromheort," Spinello murmured. He'd been through this place before, when he was posted in Oyngestun back in the days when the war was easy. When he thought of Oyngestun, he thought of the Kaunian girl he'd enjoyed there. He'd whiled away a lot of bitter hours in Unkerlant telling stories about Vanai.

Gromheort was the biggest Forthwegian town near the Algarvian border. Almost without a doubt, the Kaunians from Oyngestun would have been brought here, to make it easier for the Algarvians to ship them west for sacrifice. If Vanai was here, if he could find her and bring her back . . . *She won't be sacrificed, and I won't have to sleep with some dumpy Unkerlanter peasant wench,* Spinello thought. *It'll work out fine for both of us.*

He got up and limped to the door of the caravan car. His leg still wasn't everything it might have been. But he could use it. And Algarve, these days, needed every man even remotely able to fight to throw into the battle against King Swemmel.

Outside the depot, a news-sheet vendor was waving a copy of his wares and shouting in Forthwegian. Spinello had only a smattering of Forthwegian, but he got the gist: Algarvian dragons striking hard at Sibiu. His mouth twisted. Some of the more ignorant or more forgetful Forthwegians might take that as an Algarvian victory. But if Lagoas and Kuusamo hadn't swooped down on the island kingdom, Algarvian dragons would have had no need to set upon it.

He saw no obvious Kaunians on the street. But what did that prove? He'd heard about the sorcery that let them look like Forthwegians, and about the trouble it had caused the occupying authorities. When he spotted a plump, redheaded constable in tunic and kilt, he waved to the man. "You, there!"

For a moment, he thought the fat constable would pretend he hadn't heard, but the fellow didn't quite dare. "Aye, Colonel?" he said, coming up. "What do you want?"

"Do you by any chance know for a fact whether the Kaunians from a no-account village called Oyngestun were brought here for safekeeping?" Spinello asked.

"I do know that." The constable's chest swelled with self-importance, till it stuck out almost as far as his belly. "Helped bring those blonds in myself."

"Did you?" That was better than Spinello had hoped for. "Good! Do you chance to recall a girl named Vanai, then? She'd be worth recalling."

And sure enough, the constable nodded. "She live with an old foof named Brivibas, didn't she? Cute little piece."

"That's right," Spinello agreed. "His granddaughter. I'm bound for Unkerlant, and I want to get her out of the Kaunian quarter here and take her along to keep my bed warm."

"Don't blame you a bit," the constable said, "but I don't think you can do it."

"Don't tell me she's been shipped west!" Spinello exclaimed. "That would be a horrible waste."

"I can't prove it one way or the other," the constable replied. "I'll tell you this, though: that Brivibas whoreson is dead as shoe leather. I caught him myself—me, Bembo. Bastard put on his sorcerous disguise—you know the blonds do?" He waited for Spinello to nod, then, looking smug, went on, "That disguise doesn't do anything for a voice, and I recognized his. He hanged himself in his gaol cell, and nobody misses him a bit, not so far as I can see."

Spinello missed Brivibas—he missed him a good deal. Brivibas was a key to getting Vanai to do what he wanted. Sooner than watch her dusty old granddad kill himself as a roadbuilder, she'd peeled off her clothes and opened her legs. Spinello sighed. "So you don't think anybody could find Vanai in a hurry?"

"Not a chance." The constable—Bembo—paused again, frowning. "In fact, come to think of it, she never got hauled into Gromheort at all. If I remember right, she ran off before we cleaned all the Kaunians out of Oyngestun."

"Powers above!" Spinello glared at him. "Why didn't you say that sooner? Who'd she run off with? Some boy?" Maybe that fellow from Plegmund's Brigade had known what he was talking about after all.

"I don't know all the ins and outs of it." Bembo laughed loudly at his own wit. "If it weren't for her mouthy old grandfather, I might not remember her at all. It's not like I ever laid her or anything."

"All right. All right." Spinello, who had, knew when to give up. He turned, cursing under his breath at a good idea wasted, and went back to the depot.

Before long, the ley-line caravan was gliding west across Forthweg again. It stopped in Eoforwic to pick up more reinforcements, then slid on toward the fighting front. Towns and villages in western Forthweg and in Unkerlant had taken even more damage, and more recent damage, than those farther east. Swemmel's men might not have fought skillfully, but they'd fought hard from the very beginning.

And they—or their brethren who practiced the nasty art of the guerrilla—kept right on making themselves difficult. The caravan had to halt twice before it got to the front, for Unkerlanter irregulars had burst eggs on the ley line and overloaded its energy-carrying capacity. Algarvian mages had to put the damage right, and there weren't enough of them to go around.

At last, a day and a half later than he should have, Spinello got down from the caravan car in the wreckage of a town named Pewsum. A sergeant was standing on the platform at the depot, holding up a leaf of paper with his name printed on it in big letters. "I'm Spinello," he said, cane in one hand, carpetbag in the other.

The sergeant saluted. "Pleased to meet you, sir. Welcome to the brigade. Here, let me get that for you." He relieved Spinello of the carpetbag. "Now if you'll just come with me, I've got a wagon waiting."

"Efficiency," Spinello remarked, and the sergeant grinned at him. Algarvians did their best to practice what King Swemmel preached. But the locally built wagon testified to genuine Unkerlanter efficiency—it was high-wheeled and curve-bottomed, and could go through mud that bogged down any Algarvian vehicle. As the sergeant flicked the reins and the horses got moving, Spinello said, "We can't have too many of these wagons, no matter how we get 'em. Nothing like 'em in the fall or the spring."

"That's the truth, sir. Powers above be praised that you see it," the driver said. "Sometimes we can get them from units that think something has to come from Trapani to be any good. If our neighbors want to be fools, it's no skin off our noses."

"No, indeed," Spinello said, but then he checked himself. "The way things are nowadays, nobody Algarvian can afford to be a fool. We have to leave that for the Unkerlanters." After a few seconds of very visible thought, the sergeant nodded.

Brigade headquarters lay in a little village called Ubach, a couple of miles northwest of Pewsum. Getting there took more than an hour; though Unkerlanter wagons could get through the mud, nothing could get through it very fast. The sergeant pointed to the firstman's house. "That'll be yours, sir. I'll let the regimental commanders know you're here, so you can meet them."

"Thanks." Spinello looked around Ubach with something less than overwhelming curiosity. He'd already seen more Unkerlanter villages than he'd ever wanted. A few peasants tramped along the streets, doing their best to keep their long tunics out of the mud. Some nodded to him as the wagon sloshed by. Rather more pretended he didn't exist. He'd seen all that before, too. And then he did a double take. Seeing a pretty young Kaunian girl in Ubach was the last thing he'd expected. She reminded him achingly of Vanai, though she was even younger and, he thought, even prettier. Pointing her way, he asked, "What's she doing here?"

"Oh, Yadwigai?" The sergeant blew her a kiss. He raised his voice: "Hello, sweetheart!"

The blond girl—Yadwigai—waved back. "Hello, Sergeant," she called in good Algarvian. "Is that the new colonel there?"

"Aye, it is," the sergeant answered, and blew her another kiss.

"Is she yours?" Spinello poked the sergeant in the ribs. "You lucky dog."

"Oh, no, sir!" The soldier driving him sounded shocked.

"Ah." Spinello nodded wisely. "A pet for one of the officers, then." He sighed, wishing again that he'd been lucky enough to get his hands on Vanai during the layover at Gromheort.

But the sergeant shook his head once more. "No, sir," he repeated. "Yadwigai isn't anybody's—not any one man's, I mean. She belongs to the brigade."

"Really?" Spinello knew he sounded astonished. He'd seen more camp followers than he'd ever wanted to, too. Yadwigai had none of their hard, bitter look. If anything, she put him in mind of a prosperous merchant's daughter: happy and right on the edge of being spoiled.

"Aye, sir," the sergeant replied, and then, realizing what Spinello had to mean, "No, sir—not like that! She's not our whore. We'd kill anybody who tried doing anything like that with her. She's our . . . our luck, I guess you might say."

Spinello scratched his head. "You'd better tell me more," he said at last. The sergeant had to know what happened to most of the Kaunians the Algarvians brought into Unkerlant. Spinello wondered if Yadwigai did.

"Well, it's like this, sir," the sergeant said, halting the wagon in front of the firstman's house. "We picked her up in a village in western Forthweg when we first started fighting Swemmel's buggers, and we've brought her along ever since. We've had good fortune ever since, too, and I don't think there's a man among us who wouldn't die to help keep her safe. She's . . . sweet, sir. You know what I'm saying?"

"All right, Sergeant. I won't mess with your good-luck charm." Spinello could see that any other answer would land him in trouble with his new brigade before he met anyone in it but this fellow driving him.

He got down from the wagon and went into the firstman's hut. Along with the benches against the walls that marked Unkerlanter peasant houses, the main room held an Algarvian-issue cot, folding table, and chairs. A map was tacked down on the table. Spinello studied it while the sergeant brought in his carpetbag, set it down beside the cot, and went out again.

Officers started coming in to greet their new commander a

few minutes later. The brigade was made up of five regiments. Majors led four of them, a captain the fifth. Spinello nodded to himself. He'd led a regiment as a major, too.

"Very pleased to make your acquaintance, gentlemen," he said, bowing. "By what I saw on the map, we have a good deal of work ahead of us to make sure King Swemmel's whoresons stay where they belong, but I think we can bring it off. I tell you frankly, I'd be a lot more worried if we didn't have Yadwigai here to make sure everything turned out all right."

The officers stared. Then they broke into broad smiles. A couple of them even clapped their hands. Spinello smiled, too, at least as much at himself as at his subordinates. Sure as sure, he'd got his new command off on the right foot.

"With your kind permission, milady," Colonel Lurcanio said, bowing, "I should like to invite Count Amatu to supper again tomorrow night."

Krasta drummed her fingers on the frame of the doorway in which she was standing. "Must you?" she said. "I don't like hearing my brother cursed in the house that is—was—his home."

"I understand that." Lurcanio bowed again. "I shall do my best to persuade Amatu to be moderate. But I should be grateful if you would say aye. He needs to feel . . . welcome in Priekule."

"He needs to feel not quite everybody hates him, you mean." Krasta tossed her head. "If he curses Skarnu, I *will* hate him, and I *will* let him know about it. Even you don't do that."

"For which praise, such as it is, I thank you." Lurcanio bowed once more. "Professionally speaking, I quite admire your brother. He is as slippery as olive oil. We thought we had him again not long ago, but he slipped through our fingers again."

"Did he?" Krasta kept her voice as neutral as she could. She was glad the Algarvians hadn't caught Skarnu, but knew

Lurcanio could and would make her unhappy for showing it. Changing the subject and yielding on the side issue struck her as a good idea; with a theatrical sigh, she said, "I suppose Amatu is welcome—tomorrow night, you said?—if he behaves himself."

"You are gracious and generous," Colonel Lurcanio said— qualities few people had accused Krasta of having. He went on, "Might I also beg one more favor? Would it be possible for your cook to serve something other than beef tongue?"

Krasta's eyes sparkled. "Why, of course," she said, and her prompt agreement made Lurcanio bow yet again. Krasta kissed him on the cheek and hurried into the kitchen. "Count Amatu will be coming for supper again tomorrow night," she told the cook. "Do you by any chance have some tripe in the rest crate there?"

He nodded. "Aye, milady. I do indeed." He hesitated, then said, "From what I know of Algarvians, the colonel will be less happy at eating tripe than Count Amatu will."

"But Amatu is our honored guest, and so his wishes must come first." Krasta batted her eyes in artful artlessness. She doubted she convinced the cook. If Lurcanio asked him why he'd prepared a supper unlikely to be to an Algarvian's taste, though, he had only to repeat what she said and she would stay out of trouble. She hoped she would stay out of trouble, anyhow.

The cook dipped his head. "Aye, milady. And I suppose you will want the side dishes to come from the countryside, too." He didn't quite smile, but something in his face told Krasta he knew what she was up to, sure enough.

All she said was, "I'm certain Count Amatu would enjoy that. Pickled beets, perhaps." Lurcanio wouldn't be happy with tripe and pickled beets or whatever else the cook came up with, but she didn't think he would be so unhappy as to do something drastic.

Still, having given the cook his instructions, Krasta thought she might be wise to get out of the house for a while. She ordered her driver to take her into Priekule. "Aye, milady," he said. "Let me harness the horses for you, and we'll be on our way."

He took the opportunity to don a broad-brimmed hat and throw on a heavy cloak, too. The slight sloshing noise Krasta heard between hoofbeats came from somewhere by his left hip: a flask under the cloak, she realized. That would also help keep him warm. Thinking of Lurcanio discomfited put Krasta in such a good mood, she didn't even snap at the driver for drinking on the job.

He stopped the carriage on a side street just off the Avenue of Equestrians. Krasta looked back over her shoulder as she hurried toward Priekule's toniest boulevard of shops. He'd already tilted the flask to his lips. It wouldn't slosh nearly so much on the way back to the mansion. It might not slosh at all. She shrugged. What could you expect from commoners but drunkenness?

She shrugged again, much less happily, when she started up the Avenue of Equestrians toward the park where the Kaunian Column of Victory had stood from the days of the Kaunian Empire till a couple of winters before, when the Algarvians demolished it on the grounds that it reflected poorly on their barbarous ancestors. She'd got used to the column's no longer being there, though its destruction had infuriated her. The shrug came from the sorry state of the shops. She'd been unhappy about that ever since Algarve occupied the capital of Valmiera.

More shopfronts were vacant now than ever before. More of the ones that still had goods had nothing Krasta wanted. No matter how many Valmieran women—aye, and men, too—wore Algarvian-style kilts these days, she couldn't bring herself to do it. She'd had kilts in her closet before the war, but that had been fashion, not compulsion. She hated compulsion, or at least being on the receiving end of it.

A couple of Algarvian soldiers ogled her. They did no more than that, for which she was duly grateful. She sneered at a Valmieran girl in a very short kilt, though she suspected the redheads would like the girl fine. And she started to sneer at a Valmieran man in an almost equally short kilt till he waved at her and she saw it was Viscount Valnu.

"Hello, sweetheart!" he cried, hurrying up to kiss her on the cheek. "How much of your money have you wasted this afternoon?"

"None, yet," Krasta answered. "I haven't found anything worth spending it on."

"What a tragedy!" Valnu exclaimed. "In that case, why don't you buy me a mug of ale, and maybe even a bite to eat to go with it?" He waved. They stood in front of an eatery called Classical Cuisine. "Maybe it'll have dormice in honey," he said.

"If they do, I'll get you a big plate of them," Krasta promised. But, since Valnu had made it plain she'd be doing the buying, she held the door open for him instead of the other way round. He took the point, and kissed her on the cheek again as he walked past her into the eatery.

She ordered ale for both of them, and—no dormice appearing on the bill of fare—strips of smoked and salted beef to go with it. "I thank you," Valnu said, and raised his mug in salute.

"It's all right," Krasta said. "It's rather better than all right, in fact."

"Really?" The tip of Valnu's rather sharp pink tongue appeared between his lips for a moment. "What *have* you got in mind, darling?"

He meant, *Do you want to go to bed with me, darling?* Krasta did want to, but didn't dare. She had to get in her digs at her Algarvian lover less directly. "I'm going to feed Lurcanio tripe tomorrow night," she answered, "and he'll have to eat it and make as if he likes it."

"You are?" Valnu said. "He will? How did you manage that?"

"I didn't, or not mostly. Lurcanio did it himself, and to himself," Krasta replied. "He's invited Count Amatu to supper again, and Amatu, say what you will about him, eats like a Valmieran. Do you know him?"

"I used to, back before the war. Haven't seen much of him since," Valnu said.

Krasta sighed and gulped down her ale. "I wish I could say the same. He's a bit of a bore these days. More than a bit, if you want to know the truth."

Valnu finished his ale, too. Instead of ordering another round for both of them, as Krasta expected him to, he got up and fluttered his fingers at her. "I'm terribly sorry, my love, but I must dash," he said. "One of my dear friends will beat me to a pulp if he thinks I've stood him up." He shrugged a comic shrug. "What can one do?"

"Pick different friends?" Krasta suggested. Instead of getting angry, Valnu only laughed and slid out of the eatery. Krasta bit down on a strip of smoked meat with quite unnecessary violence.

A waiter came up to her. "Will there be anything else, milady?"

"No," she snarled, and strode out of Classical Cuisine herself.

Not even buying a new hat made her feel better. The hat sported a jaunty peacock feather leaping up from the band— an Algarvian style, although that, perhaps fortunately, didn't occur to her. Her driver hadn't got too drunk to take her back to her mansion. The horse knew the way, whether the driver was sure of it or not.

Lurcanio praised the hat. That made Krasta feel a little guilty about the supper she'd planned for the next evening, but only a little: not enough to change the menu. If Lurcanio would inflict Amatu on her, she would inflict tripe on him.

Amatu, for a wonder, did have the sense not to talk much about Skarnu when he came. Maybe Lurcanio really had warned him to keep his mouth shut. Whatever the reason, it made him much better company. And he praised the tripe to the skies, and made a pig of himself over it. That made him better company still. Colonel Lurcanio, by contrast, picked at his supper and drank more than he was in the habit of doing.

"So sorry to see you go," Krasta told Amatu when he took his leave. To her surprise, she meant it.

"I'd be delighted to come again," he answered. "You set a fine table—eh, Colonel?" He turned to Lurcanio. The Algarvian's nod was halfhearted at best. Krasta hid a smile by swigging from her mug of ale.

Amatu's driver had had his supper with Krasta's servants. She never even thought to wonder what they had eaten. The count's carriage rattled off toward the heart of Priekule. Standing in the doorway, Krasta watched till it was out of sight—which, in the all-encompassing darkness that pervaded nights to foil Lagoan dragons, did not take long.

When she closed the door and turned around, she almost bumped into Lurcanio, who stood closer behind her than she'd thought. She let out a startled squeak. Lurcanio said, "I trust you were amused, serving up another supper not to my taste."

"I served it for Count Amatu. *He* certainly seemed to enjoy it." But Krasta, eyeing Lurcanio, judged it the wrong moment for defiance, and so changed her course. Putting a throaty purr in her voice, she asked, "And what would *you* enjoy, Colonel?" and set a hand on his arm.

Up in her bedchamber, he showed her what he would enjoy. She enjoyed it, too; he did know what he was doing, even if he couldn't do it quite so often as a younger man might have. Tonight, unusually, he fell asleep beside her instead of going back to his own bed. Maybe he'd put down even more ale with the supper he'd disliked than Krasta had thought. She fell asleep, too, pleased in more ways than one.

Some time in the middle of the night, someone pounded on the bedchamber door, someone who shouted Lurcanio's name and a spate of unintelligible Algarvian. Lurcanio sprang out of bed still naked and hurried to the door, also exclaiming in his own language. Then he remembered Valmieran, and called to Krasta as if she were a servant: "Light the lamp. I need to find my clothes."

"*I* need to go back to sleep," she complained, but she didn't dare disobey. Blinking in the sudden light, she asked, "What on earth is worth making a fuss about at this hour?"

"Amatu is dead," Lurcanio answered, pulling up his kilt. "Rebel bandits ambushed him on his way home from here. Powers below eat the bandits, we needed that man. His driver's dead, too." He threw on his tunic and rapidly buttoned it. "Tell me, milady, did you mention to anyone—to anyone at all, mind you—that the count would visit here tonight?"

"Only to the cook, so he would know to make something special," Krasta replied around a yawn.

Lurcanio shook his head. "He is safe enough. He can't fart without our knowing it, let alone betray us. You are certain of that?"

"Of course I am—as certain as I am that I'm sleepy," Krasta said. Lurcanio cursed in Valmieran, and then, as if that didn't satisfy him, said several things in Algarvian that certainly sounded incandescent. And Krasta, yawning again, realized she'd just told a lie, though she hadn't intended to. She'd mentioned Amatu to Viscount Valnu when they went into that place called Classical Cuisine. Which meant . . .

Which means I hold Valnu's life in the hollow of my hand, Krasta thought. *I wonder what I ought to do with it.*

Cornelu would rather have entered Tirgoviste harbor aboard his own leviathan. But the Lagoan and Kuusaman naval patrols around the harbor were attacking all leviathans without warning; the Algarvians had already sneaked in a couple and sunk several warships. And so Cornelu stood on the foredeck of a Lagoan ley-line frigate and watched the wharves and piers come nearer.

Speaking Algarvian, a Lagoan lieutenant said, "Coming home must feel good for you, eh, Commander?"

"My kingdom no longer has King Mezentio's hobnailed boot on its neck," Cornelu replied, also in the language of the enemy. "That feels very good indeed." Thinking he'd got agreement, the Lagoan nodded and went away.

The frigate glided up to its assigned berth, a pretty piece of work by its captain and the mages who kept it afloat. Sailors on the pier caught bow lines and stern lines and made the ship fast. When the gangplank thudded down, Cornelu was the first man off the ship. He'd had a new sea-green uniform tunic and kilt made up in Sigisoara town, so that he looked every inch a proper Sibian officer—well, almost every inch, for the truly observant would have noticed he still wore Lagoan-issue shoes.

He cursed when he got a close look at the harbor buildings. They'd taken a beating when the Algarvians first seized the city, and had been allowed to decay. It would be a while before Tirgoviste became a first-class port again. "Whoresons," he muttered under his breath.

But he had more reasons, and more urgent and intimate reasons, for cursing Mezentio's men than what they'd done to the harbor district. Three Algarvian officers had been billeted in the house his wife and daughter shared, and he feared—no, he was all too certain—Costache had been more than friendly with them.

Away from the harbor, Tirgoviste town looked better. The town had yielded to Algarve once the harbor installations fell, and the Algarvians hadn't made much of a stand here after Lagoan and Kuusaman soldiers gained a foothold elsewhere on Tirgoviste island. Cornelu didn't know whether to be grateful to them for that or to sneer at them for their faintheartedness.

Tirgoviste town rose rapidly from the sea. Cornelu was panting by the time he began to near his own house. Then he got a chance to rest, for a squad of Kuusamans herded a couple of companies' worth of Algarvian captives past him, and he had to stop till they went by. The Algarvians towered over their slight, swarthy captors, but that didn't matter. The Kuusamans were the ones with the sticks.

A small crowd formed to watch the Algarvians tramp past. A few people shouted curses at Mezentio's defeated troopers, but only a few. Most just stood silently. And then, behind Cornelu, somebody said, "Look at our fancy officer, back from overseas. He's all decked out now, but he couldn't run away fast enough when the Algarvians came."

Cornelu whirled, fists clenched, fury on his face. But he couldn't tell which Sibian had spoken, and no one pointed at the wretch who'd impugned his courage. The last of the captives went by, opening the intersection again. Cornelu let his hands drop. He couldn't fight everybody, however much he wanted to. And he knew he'd have a fight a few blocks ahead. He turned back around and walked on.

Algarvian recruiting broadsheets still clung to walls and fences. Cornelu spat at one of them. Then he wondered why he bothered. They belonged to a different world—and not just a different world now, but a dead one.

He turned onto his own street. He'd envisioned knocking on the door, having Costache open it and watching astonishment spread over her face. But there she was in front of the house, carrying something out to the gutter in a dustpan—a dead rat, he saw as he got closer.

What the dustpan held wasn't the first thing he noticed, however much he wished it would have been. The way her belly bulged was.

She dumped the rat into the gutter, then looked up and saw him. She froze, bent out over the street, as if a sorcerer had turned her to stone. Then, slowly and jerkily, she straightened. She did her best to put a welcoming smile on her face, but it cracked and slid away and she gave up trying to hold it. When she said, "You came back," it sounded more like accusation than welcome.

"Aye." Cornelu had never imagined he could despise anyone so much. And he'd loved her once. He knew he had. But that made things worse, not better. So much worse. "Did you think I wouldn't?"

"Of course I did," Costache answered. "Nobody thought the Algarvians would lose the war, and you were never coming home if they won." She dropped the dustpan: a clatter of tin. Her hands folded over her swollen stomach. "Curse you, do you think I'm the only one who's going to have a baby on account of Mezentio's men?"

"No, but you're mine." Cornelu corrected himself: "You *were* mine. And it wasn't as if you thought I was dead. You knew I was still around. You saw me. You ate with me. And you still did—*that.*" He pointed to her belly as if it were a crime somehow separate from the woman he'd wooed and married . . . and lost.

"Oh, aye, I saw you." Scorn roughened Costache's voice

till it cut into Cornelu like the teeth of a saw. "I saw you filthy and unshaven and stinking like the hillman you were pretending to be. Is it any wonder I never wanted anything to do with you after that?"

He clapped a hand to his forehead. "You stupid slut!" he shouted. "I couldn't very well go around in uniform then. Do you think I wanted to end up in a captives' camp, or more likely blazed?"

Instead of answering right away, Costache looked all around, as if to see which neighbors were likely drinking in the scandal. That also seemed to remind her of the dustpan, which she picked up. "Oh, come inside, will you?" she said impatiently. "You don't have to do this in front of everyone, do you?"

"Why not?" Cornelu slapped her in the face. "Don't you think you deserve to be shamed?"

Her hand flew to her cheek. "I think . . ." She grimaced—not with pain, he thought, but with disgust, and not self-disgust—disgust at him. "What I think doesn't matter anymore, does it? It never will anymore, will it?" She walked up the path to the house, not caring, or at least pretending not to care, whether Cornelu followed.

He did, still almost too furious to speak. In the front room, Brindza was playing with a doll—the gift of an Algarvian officer? Of the father of her half brother or sister to come? Cornelu's own daughter shied away from him and said, "Mama, who is the strange man in the funny clothes?"

"Brindza, I am your father," Cornelu said, but he could see that didn't mean anything to her.

"Go on back to your bedroom now, sweetheart," Cornelu told her. "We'll talk about it later." Brindza did as she was told. Cornelu wished Costache would have done the same. He looked down at himself. Sibian naval uniform—funny clothes? Maybe so. Brindza might never have seen it before. That spoke unhappy volumes about the state of Cornelu's kingdom.

Costache went into the kitchen. He heard her getting down goblets, and knew exactly the cupboard from which she was getting them. He knew which cupboard held the wine and ale and spirits, too. Costache came back carrying two goblets full of wine. She thrust one of them at him. "Here. This will be bad enough any which way. We may as well blur it a little."

"I don't want to drink with you." But Cornelu took the goblet. Whether with her or not, he did want to drink. He took a big swig, then made a face. "Powers above, that's foul. The Algarvians sent all their best vintages here, didn't they?"

"I gave you what I have," Costache answered.

"You gave everybody what you have, didn't you?" Cornelu pointed at her belly as he finished the wine. Costache's mouth tightened. He went on, "And you're going to pay for it, too, by the powers above. Sibiu's free again. Anyone who sucked up to the Algarvians"—he started to say something else along those lines, but the thought so infuriated him, he choked on the words—"is going to pay."

She just stood there, watching him. *She has nerve, curse her,* he thought angrily. "I don't suppose I could say anything that would make you change your mind," she observed.

"Ha!" He clapped a hand to his forehead. "Not likely! What'll you tell me, how handsome the Algarvian was? How good he was?"

That got home. Costache flushed till the handprint on her cheek seemed to fade. She said, "I could talk about how lonely I was, and how afraid, too."

"Aye, you could," Cornelu said. "You might even get some softheaded, softhearted fool to believe it, too. But so what? You won't even get me to listen."

"I didn't think so," Costache said tonelessly. "You never had any forgiveness in you. And I'm sure you never got into bed with anyone all the time you were away."

"We're not talking about me. We're talking about you," Cornelu snapped. "I'm not carrying an Algarvian's bastard. You miserable little whore, you were sleeping with Mezentio's men when you knew I was on Tirgoviste island. Do you even know which one put the baby in you?"

"How do you know what I was doing or what I wasn't?" she asked.

"How do I know? They were chasing me, that's how!" Cornelu howled. "I came down here out of the hills hoping I'd find some way to shake free of them and bring you and Brindza along with me. And what did I find? What did I find? You telling the Algarvians how much they'd enjoy it, that's what!"

He took a couple of quick steps across the room and slapped her again. She staggered. The goblet flew out of her hand and shattered on the floor. She straightened, the whole side of her face red now. "Did you enjoy that?" she asked.

"Aye," he growled, breathing hard. He might have been in battle. His heart pounded. His stomach churned. He raised his hand to hit her once more. Then, quite suddenly, his stomach did more than churn. It knotted. Horrible pain filled him. He bent double, clutching at his belly. The next thing he knew, he'd crumpled to the floor.

Costache stood over him, looking down. Calmly, she said, "The warning on the packet was true. It *does* work on people the same way it works on rats."

"You poisoned me," he choked, tasting blood in his mouth. He tried to reach for her, to grab her, to pull her down, but his hands obeyed him only slowly, oh so slowly.

She stepped back, not very far. She didn't need to step back very far. "So I did," she told him, calm still. "I knew what you'd be like, and I was right." Her voice seemed to come from farther and father away.

Cornelu stared up at her. "You won't—get away—with it." His own words seemed to come from farther and farther away, too.

"I have a chance," she said. He tried to answer. This time, no words came. He still stared up, but he saw nothing at all.

Nineteen

ᗉᗰᗊᗯ

"Cee that that gets translated into Algarvian," Hajjaj told his
secretary, "but let me review the translation before we
send it on to Marquis Balastro, and then . . . Are you listening to me?"

"I'm sorry, your Excellency." Qutuz had cocked his head
to one side and seemed to be listening not to the Zuwayzi foreign minister but to something outside King Shazli's palace.
"Is that thunder?"

"Nonsense," Hajjaj said. Aye, fall and winter were the
rainy season in Zuwayza, but the day—the whole week—had
been fine and dry and sunny. But then his ears also caught the
low rumble the younger man had heard before him. He
frowned. "That *is* thunder. But it can't be."

He and Qutuz both found the answer more slowly than they
should have. They both found it at the same time, too. "Eggs!"
Qutuz blurted, while Hajjaj exclaimed, "The Unkerlanters!"

Ever since the war began, King Swemmel's dragonfliers
had occasionally visited Bishah. They hadn't come in large
numbers; they could hardly afford to, not with Unkerlant
locked in a life-or-death struggle against Algarve. As far as
Hajjaj could tell, they'd mounted the attacks more to remind
the Zuwayzin that Swemmel hadn't forgotten about them
than for any other reason. The Unkerlanter dragons had also
done their best to hit the Algarvian ministry in Bishah, but
they'd never quite succeeded.

Hajjaj didn't need long to realize this morning would be
different. "They're dropping a good many eggs today, aren't
they?" he remarked, doing his best to stay calm—or at least
not to show he was anything else but.

"Aye, your Excellency, so they are." Qutuz took his cue from Hajjaj, but he had less practice at seeming dispassionate while actually frightened or furious.

More roars of bursting eggs beat against Hajjaj's ears. They were coming closer to the palace now, too, so he no longer had any doubt what they were. The ground started shaking under his fundament, as if at an earthquake. Pen cases and leaves of paper on his desk trembled and quivered.

"Perhaps," Qutuz said, "we ought to look for shelter."

"Where?" Hajjaj asked, not at all rhetorically. He'd read that people in Setubal and Sulingen and other places that often came under attack from the air took refuge in cellars. Cellars, however, had never been a part of Zuwayzi architecture, and no one had ever dreamt the Unkerlanters would really pummel Bishah.

"I'm getting under my desk," Qutuz declared, and hurried off to do just that. Hajjaj nodded approval. It wasn't a bad notion at all. He crawled under his own. For once, he wished he were in the habit of working at it in a chair rather than sitting on the floor; he would have had more room under there. His joints creaked as he tried to fold himself into as small a space as he could.

Then the first eggs fell on the royal palace. For the next little while, Hajjaj had nothing whatever to do with whether he lived or died. The ground shook. Windows blew out. Walls fell in. Chunks of the roof came crashing down. One of them landed where he'd been sitting while talking with his secretary. Another came down on the desk, but wasn't heavy enough to crush it—and, incidentally, Hajjaj.

Someone was screaming. After a moment, Hajjaj realized that was his own voice. He bit down hard on his lower lip to make himself stop. Then he wondered why he bothered. Plenty of people, surely, were screaming right now. But he kept on biting his lip instead. *Pride is a strange thing,* he thought, *a strange thing, but a very strong one.*

An eternity later—an eternity probably measurable as a couple of minutes—the eggs stopped landing on and around the palace and started falling farther north in Bishah. Hajjaj had to fight his way out from under the desk; some of the rubble all but caged him there.

"Qutuz!" he called. "Are you all right?"

"Aye, your Excellency." The secretary came running into Hajjaj's office. "Powers above be praised that *you're* safe."

"I'm well enough," Hajjaj said, "but you're bleeding." He pointed to a gash on Qutuz's left calf.

His secretary looked down at it. When he looked up again, astonishment filled his face. "I didn't even know it was there," he said.

"Well, it needs bandaging—that's plain." Hajjaj used a letter-opener to cut up cushions to get cloth to wrap around Qutuz's leg. He would have had a simpler time of it had either of them worn clothes.

"I thank you, your Excellency," Qutuz said. "There are bound to be plenty of people hurt a lot worse than I am. We'd better see what we can do for them."

"You're right." Hajjaj went over to the little closet that opened onto his office. His ceremonial wardrobe lay in chaos on the floor. He didn't care. He tossed his secretary a couple of tunics and kilts and grabbed some for himself. Seeing Qutuz's bewilderment, he spoke aloud his thought of a moment before: "Bandages."

"Ah." Qutuz's face cleared. "That's clever. That's very clever."

"It's cleverness I wish we didn't need," Hajjaj said grimly. "Come on. Let's make for the audience chamber and the throne room." That was as close as he would come to admitting he was worried about King Shazli. His secretary's eyes widened, but Qutuz didn't worry out loud, either.

And they both had plenty to do before they got anywhere near the throne room. People were down and groaning in the hallways. Some of them, the ones with broken bones, needed more than bandaging. Some were beyond all help. Hajjaj and Qutuz found not only bodies but buried bodies and pieces of bodies. Before long, their sandals left bloody footprints at every stride.

Someone around the corner of a corridor barked peremptory orders: "Get that rubble off him! Grab that roof beam and lift! Maybe we can still save his leg!"

Hajjaj's heart leaped within him. He knew that voice. "Your Majesty!" he called. Behind him, Qutuz whooped.

"Is that you, Hajjaj?" the king asked. "Powers above be praised you're whole and hale. Powers below eat the Unkerlanters for doing this to us." He went back to the rescue he was leading: "Heave there, all of you." A shriek—not King Shazli's—followed. "Easy there, my friend," Shazli said. "It'll be better now."

Dust and dirt and blood covered Shazli when Hajjaj finally reached his side. But the king needed no fancy trappings to gain obedience. When he gave a command, everyone who heard hurried to carry it out. People respected him for the man he was as well as for the rank he held.

"Very good indeed to see you in one piece, your Excellency," he told Hajjaj when the foreign minister reached his side. "Swemmel's whoresons have struck us a heavy blow here."

"Aye, your Majesty." Hajjaj knew more than a little gratitude that the king didn't blame him for the Unkerlanter attack—or, if he did, didn't say so in public.

"We are going to have to strengthen our defenses against dragons around the city," Shazli said. "If the Unkerlanters did this once, they'll come back to do it again."

"That's . . . true, your Majesty." Hajjaj bowed with no small respect. "I hadn't thought so far ahead." That such a thing could happen once to Bishah was appalling enough. That it might happen again and again . . . He shivered.

"Do you know whether General Ikhshid lives?" King Shazli asked.

"I'm sorry, but no," Hajjaj answered. "I have no idea. The eggs stopped falling, and the first thing I wanted to do was make sure you were safe."

"Here I stand." Shazli had lived the softest of soft lives. He was inclined to be pudgy, and had never looked particularly impressive. But there was iron in him. "King Swemmel will think he can put fear in us, so that we will do whatever he wants. He will find he is wrong. He will find he cannot make us bend our necks by dropping eggs from the sky."

Several of the people in the damaged hallway clapped their hands. Hajjaj almost clapped himself. He did bow again. "This is the spirit that led your father to reclaim our freedom after the Unkerlanters ruled us for so long."

King Shazli nodded. "And we shall stay free, come what may. Are we not still the men of the desert our forefathers were in days gone by?"

"Even so, your Majesty," Hajjaj replied, though he and the king both knew the Zuwayzin were no such thing. This generation was more urban, and more like townsfolk in the rest of Derlavai, than any before it. But Shazli had to know saying such things was the best way to rally his people.

Neither of them mentioned that the king's father had needed to free Zuwayza because the Unkerlanters had been strong enough to hold it down for generations, and neither of them mentioned that enough blows like the one the Unkerlanters had just delivered might break any people's will—to say nothing of ability—to keep on fighting. Hajjaj understood both those things painfully well. This did not seem the best time to ask Shazli whether he did, too.

"I shall find out what we need to learn about Ikhshid," the king said. He pointed at Hajjaj. "I want you to find a crystallomancer and speak to Marquis Balastro. Assure him we are still in the fight, and see what help we can hope to get from Algarve."

"As you say." Hajjaj's cough had nothing to do with the dust and smoke in the air. It was pure diplomacy. "Seeing how things are going for them in their own fight against Unkerlant, I don't know what they'll be able to spare us."

Shazli, fortunately, recognized a diplomatic cough when he heard one. "You may tell the marquis that we need tools to stay in the fight. They have more dragons than we do. They also have more highly trained mages than we do; they're bound to be better off when it comes to things like heavy sticks that can knock a dragon out of the sky."

"Every word you say there is true," Hajjaj agreed. "I'll do what I can." He nodded to Qutuz. "To the crystallomancers." His secretary nodded and followed.

One of the thick mud-brick walls of the crystallomancers' office had a new, yard-wide hole in it. Some of their tables were overturned; some of their crystals were bright, jagged shards on the floor; some of them were bleeding. But one of the men who hadn't been hurt quickly established an etheric connection with the Algarvian ministry. Balastro's image stared out of a surviving crystal at Hajjaj. "Good to see you in one piece, your Excellency," the redhead said.

"And you," Hajjaj answered. "King Shazli expects the Unkerlanters to pay us more such calls."

"I shouldn't be surprised," Balastro said. "They missed me this time, so they'll have to come back and try again."

Hajjaj smiled at his self-importance, which was partly an act and partly typical of a lot of Algarvians. The Zuwayzi foreign minister said, "Any help you can give us, we'll be grateful for and put to good use. We have the men to serve heavy sticks and the men to fly dragons, if only we could get them. Then the Unkerlanters wouldn't have such an easy time of it."

"I'll pass that along," Balastro said. "When we haven't got enough of anything ourselves, I don't know what they'll say about it back in Trapani. But I'll pass it on with my recommendation that they give you all they can." His eyes narrowed. He was shrewd, was Balastro. "After all, we have to keep you fighting Swemmel, too."

"You and King Shazli see things much alike here," Hajjaj said. "I am glad of it." *And I hope it does some good. But will it? Will anything?*

Captain Orosio stuck his head into Colonel Sabrino's tent. "Sir, the field post is here," the squadron commander said.

"Is it?" Sabrino rose from his folding chair. He winced. The blazed shoulder he'd taken escaping the Unkerlanters after his dragon was flamed out of the sky still pained him. He wore a wound badge along with his other decorations now.

He knew how lucky he was to be alive, and savored survival with Algarvian gusto. "Let's see what we've got, then."

He wore the furs and leather in which he would have flown into the frigid upper air. It was frigid enough down here on the ground in the Kingdom of Grelz. *The third winter of the war against Unkerlant,* he thought with a sort of dull wonder. He'd never imagined, not that first heady summer when the Algarvians plunged ahead on their western adventure, that the war against King Swemmel could last into its third winter. He'd found a lot of things here that he'd never imagined then.

The postman, who wasn't a dragonflier, looked cold, but Algarvian soldiers who stayed on the ground weren't always freezing, as they had that first dreadful winter, for which they'd been so woefully unprepared. The fellow saluted as Sabrino came up to him. "Here you go, Colonel," he said, and handed the wing commander an envelope.

"Thanks." Sabrino recognized the handwriting at once. To Orosio, he said, "From my wife."

"Ah." Orosio stepped back a couple of paces to give him privacy to read it.

Opening the envelope with gloved hands was a clumsy business, but Sabrino managed. Inside were two pages closely written in Gismonda's clear, precise script. As was her way, she came straight to the point. *I have good reason to believe that your mistress has taken up with another man,* she told him. *Fronesia has been seen too much with an infantry officer—some say a major, others a colonel—to leave any doubt that he has seen too much of her. That being so, I suggest you let him pay for her flat and her extravagances.*

"And so I shall," Sabrino muttered.

"What's that, sir?" Oraste asked.

"Cut off my mistress' support," Sabrino answered. "My wife tells me some colonel of footsoldiers, or whatever he may be, is getting the benefits from her these days. If he's getting the benefits, by the powers above, he can bloody well pay the freight, too."

"I should say so." But Orosio's rather heavy features

clouded. "As long as you're sure your wife's telling the truth, that is."

Sabrino nodded. "Oh, aye, without a doubt. Gismonda has never given me any trouble about Fronesia. I should hope she wouldn't. My dear fellow, do you know a proper Algarvian noble who *hasn't* got a mistress or two?—aside from the handful who have boys on the side instead, I mean."

"Well . . ." Captain Orosio hesitated, then said, "There's me."

Sabrino slapped him on the back. "And we know what your problem is: you've been here fighting a war and serving your kingdom. You get back to civilization, you'll need to carry a constable's club to beat the women back."

"Maybe." Orosio kicked at the frozen dirt like a youth just beginning to think about girls. "It'd be nice."

Sabrino slapped him on the back again. "It'll happen," he said, wondering if it would. Orosio was a nobleman, all right, or he'd have had an even harder time making officer's rank than he had, but you needed to squint hard at his pedigree to be sure of it. He'd have risen further and faster otherwise, for he was a first-rate soldier. There were times when Sabrino was glad Orosio hadn't been in position to hope for a wing of his own to command; he was too useful and able a subordinate to want to lose.

"Well, maybe," Orosio said again. He knew what held him back. He could hardly help knowing. After another kick at the dirt, he went on, "The way our losses are these days, we're getting more out-and-out commoners as officers than we probably ever did in all our history till now."

"It could be," Sabrino agreed. "The Six Years' War was hard on our noble families, too. Put it together with this one, and . . ." He sighed. "When the war is over, the king will have to grant a lot of patents of nobility, just to keep the ranks from getting too thin."

"I suppose so." Orosio's laugh sent fog spurting from his mouth. "And then the families who were noble before the war will spend the next five hundred years looking down their noses at the new ones."

"That's the truth." Sabrino laughed, too. But, as happened so often these days, the laughter didn't want to stick. "Better that than having some other king tell us who our nobles will be and who they won't be."

In centuries gone by, Valmiera and Jelgava and Forthweg and even Yanina had meddled in Algarvian affairs, backing now this local prince, now that one, as puppet or cat's-paw. Once upon a time, Sibiu had ruled a broad stretch of the coastline of southern Algarve. Those bad days, those days when a man was embarrassed to admit he was an Algarvian, were gone. Algarve had taken its right place in the sun, a kingdom among kingdoms, a great kingdom among great kingdoms.

But Algarve didn't hold Sibiu anymore. And, not far away, eggs burst, a quick, hard drumbeat of noise. Sabrino's head swung in that direction as he gauged the sound and what it might mean. So did Orosio's. "Unkerlanters," Orosio said.

"Aye." Sabrino hated to nod. "They didn't even let the mud slow them down this autumn. Now that the ground's hard again, I don't know how we're going to hold them out of Herborn."

"Neither do I," Orosio said. "But we'd cursed well better, because we'll have a demon of a time hanging on to the rest of Grelz if we lose it."

"Oh, it's not quite so bad as that, I wouldn't say—not good, mind you, but not so bad as that," Sabrino said. Orosio looked glum and cold and disbelieving and said not a word. Sabrino had been hoping for an argument. Silence, skeptical silence, gave him nothing to push against.

A crystallomancer hurried over to his tent and stuck his head inside. Not seeing him, the fellow drew back in confusion. "Here I am," Sabrino called, and waved. "What's gone wrong now?" He assumed something had, or the fellow wouldn't have been looking for him.

With a salute, the crystallomancer said, "Sir, the wing is ordered to attack the Unkerlanter ground forces now pushing their way into map square Green-Three."

"Green-Three? Powers below eat me if I remember where

that is," Sabrino said. "Tell the dragon handlers to load eggs onto the beasts. Orosio, call out the dragonfliers, and I'll go find out what in blazes we're supposed to be doing."

While the crystallomancer and Orosio shouted, Sabrino went back to his tent and unfolded the situation map. For a moment, he didn't see any square labeled Green-Three, and he wondered whether the crystallomancer had got the order straight. Then he noticed that the vertical column of squares labeled *Green* lay east of Herborn, not west where he'd been looking. He cursed under his breath. No, the capital of the Kingdom of Grelz wasn't going to hold. If the Unkerlanters were already beyond Herborn, the fight had to be to keep a corridor open so the troops in the city could pull out.

No help for it, he thought. *If we lose Herborn* and *those men, we'll be worse off than if we just lose Herborn.*

He hurried out of the tent again, shouting orders of his own. "Come on, you whoresons!" he yelled to the men of his wing. "Time to make some Unkerlanters sorry they were ever born."

Even now, after so many bitter battles, his dragonfliers gave him a cheer. Somehow, that rocked him. He had trouble believing they had anything to cheer about, or that he'd done anything to deserve those shouts. Waving a mittened hand, he scrambled up onto his dragon and took his place at the base of its neck. The dragon's screech rang high and shrill in his ears. It was younger and smaller than the beast he'd taken into all the fights before it got blazed out of the sky—younger and smaller and, if such a thing was possible, stupider, too.

He whacked it with the goad. It screeched again, this time in fury, and sprang into the air as if hoping to shake him off. He grinned. An angry dragon was a dragon that would fly hard. He activated his crystal and spoke to his squadron leaders: "Green-Three, boys, just like the crystallomancer said. North and east of Herborn."

Would the words slide by without the officers' fully noticing what he'd just said? He hoped so. But no such luck. "North and *east?*" Captain Orosio exclaimed. "Colonel, that doesn't sound good at all, not even a little bit."

"I wish I could tell you you were wrong, but I'm afraid you're right," Sabrino said. "Nothing we can do about it, though, except hit Swemmel's bastards as hard as we can and help our own boys down on the ground."

Orosio didn't answer that. As far as Sabrino could see, it had no answer. They flew on over the ruined landscape of the Kingdom—*not* the Duchy (*not yet*, thought Sabrino)—of Grelz. Two and a half years before, the Unkerlanters had fought hard to hold back the Algarvians. Little of what those battles wrecked was rebuilt, and now Sabrino's countrymen were doing everything they could to keep the Unkerlanters from retaking this stretch of land. If anything hereabouts was left standing by the time these battles were through, Sabrino would have been amazed.

Then he stopped worrying about the local landscape. There down below, just emerging from forest onto open ground, was the head of an Unkerlanter column—surely the force against which his wing had been sent. A few Algarvian behemoths out on the frozen fields started tossing eggs at Swemmel's soldiers, but they wouldn't be able to stall the Unkerlanters for long, not without help they wouldn't.

"Come on!" Sabrino shouted into his crystal. He pointed for good measure. "There they are. Now we make 'em sorry they aren't somewhere else."

Like most of its kind, his new dragon was happy enough to stoop on the enemy, as if it imagined itself a madly outsized kestrel. Getting it to pull up, he knew, would be another problem. It wanted to sink its claws into a behemoth and fly off with the great beast, armor and crew and all: it had not the wit to see such was far beyond even its great strength.

Sabrino loosed the eggs slung beneath the dragon and hit it with the goad. It screeched angrily, but did finally decide to rise rather than flying into the ground. More eggs burst behind Sabrino as the rest of his dragonfliers also loosed their loads of death on the Unkerlanters. He looked back over his shoulder and nodded in solid professional satisfaction. Battered and undermanned though it was, his wing still did a solid professional job. They'd well and truly smashed in the head of this column. Swemmel's men wouldn't be coming forward here, not for a while.

But then more Unkerlanters emerged from the woods north and east of the column the dragonfliers had just attacked. And, as his dragon gained height, Sabrino saw still more men and beasts, some in rock-gray, some in white winter smocks over rock-gray, moving up from the south toward those soldiers coming out of the forest.

Sabrino didn't know whether to groan or to curse. He did both at once, with great feeling. "Powers below eat them!" he shouted to the uncaring sky. "They've got Herborn trapped in one of their stinking kettles!"

"Herborn surrounded." Fernao sounded out the Kuusaman words with care as he fought his way through the news sheet from Yliharma. "Large force of Algarvians trapped inside Unkerlanter lines. Demand for surrender refused."

"I've heard Lagoans who sounded worse," Ilmarinen said. Coming from him, any praise was high praise.

Fernao dipped his head. "Thank you," he said in Kuusaman. He went on in classical Kaunian, in which he remained more fluent: "Reading the news sheets, I learn many military terms. But they are not much use to me in speaking of ordinary things."

"Oh, I don't know." Ilmarinen looked around the refectory till he spotted the serving girl for whom he'd conceived an as yet unrequited passion. Waving to get her attention, he called, "Hey, Linna! If I surround you, will you surrender?"

"You are not asleep, Master Ilmarinen. You are awake," Linna answered. "You are not talking in your dreams, however much you wish you were."

"I see," Fernao said. "Aye, I followed that well enough."

"I was afraid you would," Ilmarinen said glumly. "That wench must spend an hour every morning stropping her tongue to make it sharper." He took a sip of tea, then asked, "Let me see that news sheet, will you?" Fernao passed it to him; Ilmarinen was bound to make smoother, faster going of it than he could. And, sure enough, the Kuusaman master mage soon grunted. "Here's a sweet little story: a Sibian woman who was pregnant by an Algarvian fed her husband rat poison when he came home and found out what she'd been up to."

"Sweet, aye." Fernao had a pretty good idea why Ilmarinen had picked that particular story. He had no intention of admitting as much, since that would also have meant admitting Ilmarinen had a point.

When Fernao said no more, Ilmarinen grunted again and went on, "Aye, poor Commander, ah, Cornelu won't be riding leviathans for King Burebistu any more, and his not-so-loving wife will end up a head shorter. Bad business all the way around."

"Cornelu?" Fernao exclaimed—the name got his notice. "Oh, that poor bugger!"

"You knew him?" Now Ilmarinen sounded surprised.

"Not well, but aye, I knew him," Fernao answered. "He was the leviathan-rider who pulled King Penda of Forthweg and me out of Mizpah, down in the land of the Ice People, when it was on the point of falling to the Yaninans."

"Ah." Ilmarinen nodded. "I suspect that, if we knew more of these webs of casual acquaintance, we could do more with the law of contagion than we've managed up till now. If I had to guess, I'd say that would be for the generation of mages after you."

"It could be." Fernao eyed Ilmarinen with admiration no less genuine for being reluctant. No one could ever say Ilmarinen thought small. In a couple of sentences, he'd proposed a program of research that might well keep a whole generation of mages busy.

Before Fernao could say anything else, Pekka strode into the refectory and spoke in ringing tones: "My fellow mages, we are leaving for the blockhouse in a quarter of an hour. You will be ready." The Kuusaman verb had a form that expressed absolute certainty; Pekka used it then.

And Fernao *was* ready in a quarter of an hour—done with his breakfast and decked in furs a man of the Ice People wouldn't have disdained. As he dressed, he wondered whether Ilmarinen, who'd lingered in the dining hall, could possibly get to the front door of the hostel within the appointed time. But he found Ilmarinen there before him. The master mage gave a superior smirk, as if to say he knew he'd put one over on Fernao.

Everyone was there: all the theoretical sorcerers who would conduct the next experiment that sprang from the unity at the heart of the Two Laws, the secondary sorcerers who would project their spell to the animals, the sorcerers who would keep the animals from freezing till the spell went forth, and the contingent of mages who would do their best to protect the theoretical sorcerers against any onslaught from Algarve.

Pekka didn't look pleased to find everyone ready on time. She looked as if that were nothing less than her due. Maybe that was what leading meant. "And off we go," she said. "The weather is very fine today."

She came from Kajaani, of course, on the southern coast of Kuusamo. That meant her standards differed from Fernao's. As far as he was concerned, it was bloody cold outside. But several of the other Kuusamans nodded, so he supposed he was the odd man out here.

Odd man out or not, he was glad to snuggle under more furs in a sleigh. He was also glad to snuggle under them beside Pekka. Snuggle down beside her was all he did. Without a word, without a gesture, she'd made it plain that anything else would cost them the friendship they'd built up since he came to Kuusamo. He didn't think that was because she wasn't interested in him. On the contrary—he thought she was, and sternly wouldn't let herself be.

In an abstract way, he admired that . . . which made it no less frustrating. Still, he didn't suppose he wanted to put her husband Leino in a situation like the one from which poor, luckless Cornelu hadn't escaped. No, he didn't want that at all. *All I want is to go to bed with her.* If only things were so simple. But he knew too well they weren't.

Pekka said, "In spite of everything, we do make progress. We shall be sending the energies farther from the site of the sorcery than we have ever tried before." She paused before adding, "Almost far enough to be useful in the field."

"Almost," Fernao said. But his comment was rather gloomier than hers: "Almost is one of the saddest words in the language—in any language. It speaks of hopes with nothing to show for them."

"We are already releasing nearly as much energy with our sorcery as the Algarvians are with their murderous magecraft," Pekka said. "And our magic is far cleaner than theirs."

"I know," Fernao replied—the last thing he wanted to do was affront her. "But they still have more control over theirs than we do with ours. We do not yet know how to project the energies from our spell across the Strait of Valmiera, for instance, and we know too well that Mezentio's mages can."

As usual, speaking classical Kaunian gave the conversation a certain air of detachment—some, but not enough here. Pekka's shiver had nothing to do with the icy air through which the sleigh glided. "Aye, we do know that too well," she agreed with a grimace. "Were it not so, we would still have Siuntio on our side, and not a day goes by in which I do not miss him."

"I know," Fernao said again. He might have dragged Siuntio out of the blockhouse when it started to collapse and burn during the Algarvian sorcerous attack. He'd dragged Pekka out instead. She still didn't realize he'd been closer to Siuntio than to her. No matter how much he wanted to bed her, he would never tell her that.

Ptarmigan fluttered away from the sleigh, wings whistling as they took flight. "They are in their full winter plumage now," Pekka said. "The rabbits and the ferrets will be white, too."

"So they will, here," Fernao said. "Up by Setubal—and on the Derlavaian mainland farther north, too—many of them will stay brown the whole winter long. I wonder how they know to go white here, where it snows more, but not to where the winters are milder."

"Savants have puzzled over that for a long time," Pekka said. "They have never yet found an answer that satisfies me."

"Nor me," Fernao agreed. "It almost tempts me to think some inborn sorcerous power is hidden inside animals. But if it is there, no mage has ever been able to detect it, and that makes me not believe in any such thing."

"You are a modern rational man, and I feel the same way you do," Pekka said. "No wonder, though, that our superstitious ancestors thought beasts had the same potential for using magic as people did."

"No wonder at all," Fernao said.

Before he or Pekka could say anything more, the driver reined in and spoke two words of Kuusaman: "We're here."

Fernao got down from the sleigh and extended a mittened hand to Pekka. She set her own mittened hand in his as she alighted. That was the contact of ordinary politeness, and she did not shy away from it. Even through two thick layers of felted wool, her touch warmed him.

Braziers warmed the blockhouse—not nearly so well, as far as Fernao was concerned. Filling it with mages did a better job: did, in fact, too good a job. People shed cloaks and jackets. Fernao started sweating after taking off his coat. He joined the grumbling about how warm it was. But then Pekka's voice crisply cut through that grumbling: "Let us begin, shall we? Crystallomancer, please be so kind as to check with the mages handling the animals. Is everything ready?"

She spoke to the woman in Kuusaman, but Fernao found he had no trouble following her. After a moment, the crystallomancer replied, "They are ready at your convenience, Mistress."

"Good," Pekka said, and recited the ancient phrases with which Kuusamans preceded every sorcery. The other mages in the blockhouse repeated the phrases with her—everyone but Fernao. Nobody bothered him for not joining in the ritual, though one mage or another would sometimes tease him about it back at the hostel.

Before Pekka could begin the spell itself, Ilmarinen let out a sharp bark of warning: "Look out!" Fernao's head came up. He peered north, as if he could see to the Strait of Valmiera, let alone across it. He sensed no sorcerous disturbance, not yet. A moment later, though, one of the mages charged with defending against Algarvian wizardry also exclaimed.

And then Fernao felt it, too—that cantrip that tasted of iron and brimstone and blood, so much blood; that smelled of powers above only knew how many open graves. He couldn't join the Kuusaman mages in their defense against it—their ways were not his. His ways, to his shame, were closer to the school of sorcery that had spawned such monstrousness.

"No!" he shouted in Lagoan, a cry of rejection hardly different from its Algarvian equivalent. He launched his own angry counterspell at Mezentio's mages. He didn't think it would do much good, but he didn't see how it could hurt, either. Then, to his astonishment, he felt his spell lifted, reinforced. He was almost startled enough to break off the chant. Ilmarinen waved for him to continue. So did Pekka. She was incanting furiously.

But she's not aiming at the Algarvians, a tiny part of his mind thought. *She's going on with the magic she would have tried anyhow.* He didn't dwell on that. He dwelt on nothing but his own magecraft, and on the astonishing boost Ilmarinen was giving it. He couldn't see to the Strait of Valmiera, no, but he felt as if he might reach it and cross it.

He wanted to loose his bolt of sorcerous power, but felt someone—Ilmarinen again?—delaying him, making him hold back. Then he could delay no more—but when he launched it, he also launched all the tremendous energy from the spell Pekka had shaped. Unlike the Kuusamans, the Algarvian mages had been ready only for attack; they hadn't dreamt they would need to defend. Fernao felt the sorcerous counterstroke shatter them. He cried out in triumph and pitched forward on his face in a faint.

"We did it!" Pekka exclaimed for about the dozenth time since the mages returned to their hostel. "We truly did it! I didn't think we could, but we did it!"

"So we did." Fernao spoke in classical Kaunian rather than Kuusaman. He still looked pale and drawn, though a couple of mugs of ale had gone some way toward restoring his color. "Not quite the experiment we had in mind when we went to the blockhouse, but success is never an orphan: only failure has to look for a father."

"It was your success," Pekka said. "Everyone else thought only of holding off the Algarvians. You were the one who struck back."

He shrugged. "Ilmarinen here helped. And I have Algarvic blood in me, and I am trained in Algarvic-style magecraft. I hoped they would prove all sword and no shield, and I was lucky enough to be right. It turned out better than I thought it would, in fact."

"It turned out better than I dreamt it could," Pekka exclaimed. She sipped from a small goblet of brandy flavored with almond paste. "The Algarvians will not try to strike us again any time soon, not that way."

Ilmarinen gave her a sour stare. "If you gush any more, my dear, you'll turn into a hot spring."

She reminded herself that Fernao had needed the master mage's help to launch his counterspell at Mezentio's mages. That helped her keep her temper now. "The Algarvians are the ones gushing hot tears now," she said. "We put a lot of their sorcerers out of business today."

"Well, so we did." But even that didn't much impress Ilmarinen. He went on, "It won't bring the Kaunians they killed back to life, though."

"Did I say it would?" Pekka returned. "But it may give them less reason to kill more of them. That also counts for something."

Perhaps because of the brandy, she felt her temper slipping out from under her control whether she wanted it to or not. Had Ilmarinen argued further, she would have scorched him. To her relief, he didn't, or not very much, anyhow. He said, "Aye, I suppose that's true, not that it does the poor blond buggers they sacrificed this time any good." Then he gulped the last of the ale in his mug, slammed it down on the table, and stalked away.

Fernao stared after him. "I almost think he would be happier if we were losing than he is to have struck the Algarvians a solid sorcerous blow," the Lagoan mage observed.

With a sigh, Pekka answered, "I fear you are exactly right. He would feel more needed were that so, and we would be more inclined to make the kind of experiments he wants." She shrugged. "As things are, I am the one who judges what is important and what is not, and I say that what we did here today was one of the most important things we have ever done."

"I think you are right," Fernao said. "We proved we could project that power a long way—a lot farther than we would have tried had the Algarvians not pushed us."

"Everything we have done up till now, we have done because the Algarvians are pushing us," Pekka said. "This time, though, we pushed back."

"Aye." Fernao turned in his chair till he was facing north and ever so slightly west. He pointed in that same direction. "Along this bearing—this is the direction from which their attack came, and the direction along which we aimed our answer. If we sent a dragon flying along this line, I wonder what its flier would see after it got to the coast of Valmiera."

"We ought to do that," Pekka said, and scribbled a note to herself. "We ought to find out what our magic does in the field rather than on the testing range, as we have been using it here."

"When do you suppose we really shall start using it in the field?" Fernao asked. He passed the back of his hand across his forehead, as if wiping away sweat. "I do not know how often any one mage would want to serve as the channel through which that energy runs. Once was plenty for me, I think."

"This strike was a makeshift," Pekka said. "It might be easier if we planned it more beforehand."

"It might." But Fernao did not sound convinced.

Pekka went on, "I cannot answer your question yet, not altogether. I can say this, though: before we start work in the field, we shall have to train more mages to use these spells—ordinary practical mages, I mean, not theoretical sorcerers like the ones we have gathered here. That will take some time." She scribbled another note. "It is something we ought to think about beginning, though, is it not?"

Fernao nodded. "It may well be."

She only half heard the answer. *Ordinary practical mages,* she thought. *Mages like Leino, to whom I just happen to be married. Could he have done what Fernao did there today? He might have—he likely would have—had the presence of mind. Would he have had the strength, the will?*

Angry at herself for raising the question in those terms, she knocked back the rest of her brandy. Fernao raised an eyebrow. *And what does that mean?* she asked herself. *Is he surprised to see me guzzle so, or is he hoping I'm doing it to give myself an excuse to do something with him?*

Is *that why I'm doing it?*

Pekka got to her feet—indeed, almost sprang to her feet. The refectory swayed a little when she did: sure enough, she'd had more brandy than she thought. "I," she declared, "am going upstairs to bed. To sleep," she added, so as not to leave Fernao in any possible doubt about what she meant.

If he offered to escort her . . . *I'll have to pretend to be angrier than I am,* Pekka thought. But Fernao nodded. "I intend to do the same thing in a little while," he said. "I have not drunk quite enough yet, though."

"Try not to have too thick a head come morning," Pekka warned. "You will need to draft a report on what we did today."

"I remember," Fernao answered, and Pekka had to fight against a giggle. The Lagoan mage might have been Uto dutifully saying, *Aye, Mother.* Pekka got to her feet and hurried away. She'd had that thought about Ilmarinen a good many times. What did it mean when she also started having it about the other mages with whom she worked? *That you think being in charge of them means mothering them?* She wasn't sure she liked that. She was sure they wouldn't if they found out about it.

She almost ran to the stairway, as if running from her own thoughts. Had she had long legs like Fernao's, she would have gone up the stairs two at a time. As things were, she just climbed them as fast as she could. That proved plenty fast to startle two people embracing halfway up to the second floor.

Ilmarinen and . . . Linna? Pekka wondered if she'd drunk enough to start seeing things. Then Ilmarinen demanded, "Did you *have* to come by at the most inconvenient possible moment?" and his annoyance convinced her her imagination hadn't run wild after all.

"I didn't intend to," Pekka answered. "I am allowed to go up to my own room, you know."

"I suppose so." Ilmarinen sounded as if he supposed nothing of the sort. He turned back to the serving girl. "And how would you like to go up to my own room?"

"Better that than blocking the stairway," Pekka said.

Linna didn't say anything right away. Pekka hoped she wouldn't have to listen to Ilmarinen begging. That didn't suit her image of the way a master mage should act. Of course, a lot of the things Ilmarinen did failed to suit her image, and he cared not a fig. But humiliation seemed somehow worse than outrageousness.

Then Linna answered, "Well, why not? I've already come this far." Ilmarinen beamed and kicked up his heels like a frisky young reindeer. Pekka thought he would have carried Linna up the stairs if she'd shown any sign of wanting him to. The next question was, would he measure up once he lay down beside her? For his sake, Pekka hoped so. If he didn't, he was liable to be devastated.

She let the two of them go up the stairs ahead of her. Now that she'd escaped Fernao, any more rushing seemed pointless. She walked past Ilmarinen's chamber on the way to her own, but made a point of not listening to whatever was going on in there. Officially, it was none of her business. And Ilmarinen's attitude the next time she saw him would tell her everything she needed to know, anyhow.

The inside of her own room, bare and spare, was not the most welcoming place in which she'd ever found herself. Hoping to lose herself in the intricate business of trying to record events exactly as they'd happened, she inked a pen and began to write. But, after she'd set down a couple of sentences, she shook her head and pushed the leaf of paper away.

"He's saved your life twice, maybe three times now," she said aloud, as if someone had denied it. "This last time, he may have saved everything. Why are you running away from him, then?"

Part of her knew the answer to that. The rest, the larger part, proved not to want to think about it. Looking out the window, she saw it was snowing again. She ran a finger under the collar of her tunic. It felt unpleasantly warm inside the hostel—certainly inside her room. She set down the pen. With a sigh that was the next thing to a sob, she got up and headed for the refectory.

When she walked past Ilmarinen's room, Linna's giggle gave her pause. Indeed, it almost sent her running back to her own chamber. But she shook her head and kept going. She wondered if she would bump into Fernao on the stairway, and what would happen if she did.

She didn't. And when she went back into the refectory and looked around, she didn't see him there, either.

She stood in the entranceway looking around till one of the serving women came up to her and asked, "May I help you with anything, Mistress Pekka?"

Pekka jumped as if the woman had asked her something shameful. "No," she said, louder and more sharply than she'd intended. "I was just . . . looking for someone, that's all."

"Ah." The serving woman nodded. "Master Fernao went up to his chamber a couple of minutes ago."

"Did he?" Pekka said, and the woman nodded again. *She knows whom I'd be looking for, does she? She probably knows why I'd be looking for him, too. And she probably knows why better than I do myself.*

"Aye, he did." The woman nodded again. She sounded very certain—more certain than Pekka was herself. Oh, she understood why she might be—no, why she was—looking for Fernao. What she didn't know was whether she wanted to do anything about her understanding.

The serving woman eyed her curiously, as if to say, *I told you where he was. Why are you wasting your time here?*

When Pekka turned to go, out of the corner of her eye she spied the other woman nodding. She shook her own head. *You may think you know everything that's going on, but you're wrong this time.*

She did go back upstairs, but not to Fernao's room. Whatever she was thinking, she wasn't ready to be so brazen as that. *Not quite,* she told herself, whether with relief or disappointment even she couldn't tell. When she attacked the report again, in earnest this time, she got a lot of work done.

Captain Recared had a new cry now: "Hold them!" It was one Sergeant Leudast was delighted to echo. The Unkerlanters had drawn their ring all the way around Herborn. If they could keep it shut tight, the Algarvian forces trapped inside would beat themselves to death trying to break out.

"Hold them!" Leudast shouted. Along with the rest of the men in the regiment, he'd done a prodigious lot of marching to move east as far and as fast as he had. Now he faced west again, to keep the redheads and their Grelzer puppets from pulling the stopper out of the bottle that contained them.

Eggs kicked up clouds of snow when they burst in and around the Grelzer village his company was holding. Fragments of metal from the eggshells whined through the air. But instead of cratering the ground, as they would have in summertime, the eggs only knocked holes about the size and depth of a small washtub in it; it was frozen too hard for anything more.

"Here they come!" somebody shouted.

Leudast peered out from the hut in which he sheltered. Sure enough, the Algarvians and Grelzers were trying to press home their attack against the village. They had better gear now than they'd used the first winter of the war in Unkerlant: they all wore white snow smocks, and almost all of them snowshoes. Some of them shouted, "Mezentio!" Others, presumably the Grelzers, yelled, "Raniero!"

"Plenty of time," Leudast called to his men as the enemy slogged across the snow-covered fields outside the village. "Make sure you've got a good target before you start blazing."

Before the Algarvians and Grelzers even got into stick range of the village, Unkerlanter egg-tossers started pounding them. Leudast knew a moment's abstract pity for the foe. With the ground hard as iron, the soldiers out there couldn't very well dig holes in which to shelter from the eggs. They had to take whatever the Unkerlanters could dish out.

Rock-gray dragons dropped out of the sky on the redheads and the traitors who fought on their side. More eggs burst, these delivered with pinpoint precision and released only a few feet above the enemy's heads. Flame yellow as the sun—and far hotter than the winter sun down here in Grelz—burst from the dragons' jaws. Leudast watched a kilted Algarvian blacken and writhe and shrink in on himself like a moth that had just flown into a campfire.

Recared's whistle screamed. "Forward—now!" the regimental commander shouted. "If we hit them hard, we can break them."

A bit more than a year earlier, battling down in the wreckage of Sulingen, Leudast would have laughed at the thought of breaking Algarvians. Overwhelming them, certainly. But breaking them? Making them run? It would have seemed impossible. A lot had happened since then. "Aye!" he shouted. "We *can* do it, by the powers above! Urra! King Swemmel! Urra!"

The Unkerlanters burst from the village and rushed at the redheads. Eggs kept falling on the enemy, helping to pin him in place. Some of the Algarvians tried to flee anyway, and were flung aside when eggs bust near then. Others threw their sticks down in the snow, raised their hands, and went willingly enough into captivity. And some of the redheads, good, stubborn, resourceful soldiers that they were, held on as long as they could to let their comrades escape.

Fighting alongside Mezentio's soldiers were men who looked like Leudast and his comrades, but who wore dark green tunics rather than rock-gray under their snow smocks. Few Grelzers tried to surrender. Few of those who did try succeeded. The men who'd chosen Raniero over Swemmel had discovered the Unkerlanters weren't much interested in taking them alive.

"Keep your eyes and ears open," Leudast warned the soldiers in his company. "You see somebody you don't know, watch him, especially if he talks with a Grelzer accent. The traitors will strip our dead for their tunics so they get the chance to sneak out of the fight."

He knew he wasn't the only Unkerlanter passing along that warning. He also knew a few perfectly loyal Unkerlanter soldiers who chanced to spring from Grelz would get blazed because their countrymen went for sticks without bothering to ask questions first. His broad shoulders moved up and down in a shrug. As long as the Grelzers got rooted out, he didn't much care what else happened.

Captain Recared hadn't been the sole commander to order a counterattack. Shouting "Urra!" and King Swemmel's name, Unkerlanter soldiers stormed forward all along the line. Instead of trying to break out of the cauldron around Herborn in which they were trapped, the Algarvians and Grelzers had to try to hold back a foe who outnumbered them in men, in egg-tossers, in horses and unicorns, in behemoths, and in dragons.

They tried. They tried bravely. But they could not hold. Here and there, they would form a line and battle the Unkerlanters in front of them to a standstill—for a while. But then Swemmel's soldiers would find a way around one flank or the other, and the Algarvians and Grelzers would have to give ground again: either that or be slaughtered where they stood.

The progress Leudast's countrymen made left him slightly dazed. That evening, he sat down to barley cakes and garlicky sausage filched from an Algarvian sergeant he'd captured. Toasting a length of sausage over a fire on a stick, he said, "Curse me if they're not starting to fall apart."

Captain Recared had some sausage, too. He pulled it away from the flames, examined it, and then thrust it back to cook some more. "Aye, they are," he agreed while the sausage sizzled and dripped grease into the fire. "By this time tomorrow, they'll have figured out that they can't pound their way through our ring. They'll start trying to sneak through in small bands. We have to smash as many of them as we can. Every soldier we kill or capture now is one more we won't have to worry about later on."

"I understand, sir," Leudast said. "And when they're hungry and scared and their sticks are low on charges, they're a lot easier to deal with than when they've got their peckers up."

"That's right. That's just right." Recared nodded. He took his sausage off the fire and looked at it again. With another nod, he began to eat.

He proved a good prophet, for over the next couple of days the spirit did leak out of the Algarvians, like water leaking from a cracked jar. They stopped standing up to the Unkerlanters and started trying to escape whenever and however they could. When they couldn't run and couldn't hide, they surrendered in a hurry, glad to do it before something worse happened to them

After a couple of days of that, Leudast was as rich as he'd ever been in all his born days. He didn't suppose it would last; when he came to a place where he could spend the money he was taking from captured Algarvian officers, he probably would. But a heavy belt pouch wasn't the worst thing in the world, either.

One of his men asked, "Sergeant, what do we do with the coins we take that have false King Raniero on 'em?"

"Well, Kiun, if I were you, I'd lose the Grelzer copper," Leudast answered. "It'll never be worth anything on its own, if you know what I mean. But silver's silver, even if it is stamped with Raniero's pointy-nosed face. Somebody'll melt it down for you and give you what it's worth in metal, even if not in coin."

"Ah." The soldier nodded. "Thanks. That makes good sense."

The next morning, Leudast's company came on the tracks of a squad of men trying to make their way east. With snow on the ground, following the trail was child's play. Before long, his troopers caught up with the fleeing Algarvians. A couple of men started blazing at the redheads. As soon as steam puffed up from the smoke around them, the Algarvians raised their hands in surrender.

"Aye, you have us," one of them said in pretty good Unkerlanter as Leudast and his men came up: a bald fellow in his late middle years who wore a colonel's uniform. "We can run no more."

"You'd best believe it, pal." Leudast cocked his head to one side. "You talk funny." The officer's accent wasn't a typical Algarvian trill, but something else, something familiar.

"I was, in the last war, colonel of a regiment of Forthwegians in Algarvian service," the redhead answered.

"That's it, sure enough." Leudast nodded. His own home village, up in the north, wasn't so far from the Forthwegian border. No wonder he thought he'd heard that accent before—he had.

"Sergeant—" Kiun, the fellow who'd asked him about Grelzer money, plucked at his sleeve. "Sergeant, powers below eat me if that's not Raniero his own self."

"What?" Leudast shook himself free. "You're out of your fornicating . . ." But his voice trailed away. He shuffled a couple of paces sideways so he could look at the Algarvian in profile. His lips pursed in a soundless whistle. The captive in the colonel's uniform certainly had the right beaky nose. "*Are* you Raniero?"

A couple of the captive's comrades exclaimed in Algarvian. But he shook his head and drew himself up very straight. "I have that honor, aye." He bowed. "And to whom do I present myself?"

Numbly, Leudast gave his own name. He gestured with his stick. "You come along with me." What would they give the man who'd just captured the King of Grelz? He didn't know—he had no idea—but he looked forward to finding out. He also waved to a couple of his own men, who were all staring wide-eyed at Raniero. "You boys come along, too." He didn't want his prisoner stolen out from under him. He made sure he included Kiun—the trooper also deserved a reward.

A lieutenant well back of the line glared at him. "Why

didn't you just send your captive to the rear, Sergeant?" he growled, meaning, *Why do you think you deserve to get out of the fight for a while?*

"Sir, this isn't just any captive," Leudast answered. "This is Raniero, who calls himself King of Grelz." The lieutenant's glare turned to a gape. He didn't have the presence of mind to ask to accompany Leudast.

Raniero's name was the password that got Leudast taken from division headquarters to army headquarters to a battered firstman's house in a village that looked to have changed hands a good many times. The soldier who came out of the house had iron-gray hair and big stars on the collar tabs of his tunic. Marshal Rathar eyed the captive, nodded, and told Leudast, "That's Raniero, all right."

Leudast saluted. "Aye, sir," he said.

Rathar seemed to forget about him then. He spoke to Raniero in Algarvian, and King Mezentio's cousin answered in the same language. But Rathar wasn't one to forget his own men for long. After giving Raniero what looked like a sympathetic pat on the back, he turned to Leudast and asked, "And what do you expect for bringing this fellow in, eh, Sergeant?"

"Sir, whatever seems right to you," Leudast answered. "I've figured you were fair-minded ever since we fought side by side for a little while up in the Zuwayzi desert." He didn't expect the marshal to remember him, but he wanted Rathar to know they'd met before. And he added, "Kiun here was the one who first recognized him."

"A pound of gold and sergeant's rank for him. And, Lieutenant Leudast, how does five pounds of gold on top of a promotion sound for you?" Rathar asked.

Leudast had expected gold, though he'd thought one pound likelier than five for himself. The promotion was a delightful surprise. "Me?" he squeaked. "An officer?" Officer's rank wasn't quite so much the preserve of bluebloods in Unkerlant's army as in Algarve's—King Swemmel had killed too many nobles to make that practical—but it wasn't something to which a peasant could normally aspire, either. "An officer," Leudast repeated. *If I live through the war, I've got it made,* he thought dizzily. *If.*

Vanai had heard that there came a time when a woman actually enjoyed carrying a child. During the first third of her pregnancy, she wouldn't have believed it, not for anything. When she hadn't been nauseated, she'd been exhausted; sometimes she'd been both at once. Her breasts had pained her all the time. There had been days when she'd not cared to do anything but lie on her back with her tunic off and with a bucket beside her.

This middle stretch seemed better, though. She could eat anything. She could clean her teeth without wondering if she would lose what she'd eaten last. She didn't feel as if she needed to prop her eyelids open with little sticks.

And the baby moving inside her was something she never took for granted. Maybe, in a way, Ealstan had been right: no matter how emphatically she'd known before that she was with child, its kicks and pokes did make that undeniably real, the more so as they got stronger and more vigorous with each passing week.

And ... "Just as well I'm Thelberge in a Forthwegian-style tunic these days," she told Ealstan over supper one evening. "If I still wore trousers, I'd have to buy new ones, because I wouldn't be able to fit into the ones I had been wearing anymore."

He nodded. "I've noticed. With the tunic, though, it hardly shows, even yet."

"With the tunic, no," Vanai said. "Without it . . ." She shrugged. Her body had stayed much the same ever since she became a woman. To watch it change, to feel it change, almost from day to day was disconcerting, to say the very least.

Ealstan shrugged, too. "I like the way you look without your tunic just fine, believe me."

Vanai did believe him. She'd heard of men who lost interest in their wives when the women were expecting a baby. That hadn't happened with Ealstan, who remained as eager as ever. In fact, from the look in his eye now ... The supper dishes got cleaned rather later than they might have.

When they woke up the next morning, Ealstan spoke in classical Kaunian, as if to emphasize his words: "You look like Vanai again, not like Thelberge."

"Do I?" Vanai spoke Forthwegian, annoyed Forthwegian: "But I renewed the spell just before we went to sleep, and you told me I'd got it right. It really isn't holding as long as it used to."

"I don't know what to tell you." Ealstan returned to Forthwegian, too. "You need to be careful, that's all." He got out of bed and put on fresh drawers and a clean tunic. "And I need to get going, or Pybba will have me for breakfast when I get to his office. He just about lives there, and he thinks everybody else should, too."

"I *am* careful," Vanai insisted. "I have to be." She got out of bed, too. "Here, I'll fix your breakfast."

It didn't take much fixing: barley bread with olive oil, some raisins on the side, and a cup of wine to wash things down. Vanai ate with Ealstan, and then, while he shifted from foot to foot with impatience to be gone, went through the spell that let her look like a Forthwegian. When she was through, he said, "There you are, sure enough—you look like my sister again."

She didn't even let that annoy her, not this morning. "As long as I don't look like a Kaunian, everything's fine," she said. "I spent too much time cooped up in this flat. I don't care to do it again."

"If you have to, you have to," Ealstan answered. "Better that than getting caught, wouldn't you say?" He brushed his lips across hers. "I really do have to go. By the powers above, don't do anything foolish."

That *did* make her angry. "I don't intend to," she said, biting the words off between her teeth. "Going out and making sure we don't starve doesn't count as foolish to me. I hope it doesn't to you, either."

"No," Ealstan admitted. "But getting caught does. I've bought food for us before. I can do it again."

"Everything will be fine," Vanai repeated. "Go on. You're the one worrying about being late." She shoved him out the door.

Once he was gone, she washed the handful of breakfast dishes. Then, more than a little defiantly, she put money in her handbag and went out the door herself. *I won't be caged up anymore. I won't, curse it,* she thought.

No one paid any attention to her when she left the lobby of her block of flats and went down the stairs to the sidewalk. Why should anyone have paid attention to her? She looked as much like a Forthwegian as anyone else on the street.

How many of the other people on the street also were sorcerously disguised Kaunians? Vanai had no way to tell. In Forthweg as a whole, about one in ten had shared her blood before the Derlavaian War began. More Kaunians had lived in and around Eoforwic than anywhere else. On the other hand, the redheads had already shipped a lot of Kaunians off to Unkerlant, to fuel the Algarvian there with their life energy. How many? Vanai had no way to know that, either, and wished the question had never crossed her mind.

A pair of Algarvian constables came up the street toward her. One of them reached out, as if to pat her on the bottom. She squeaked indignantly and sidestepped before he could. He laughed. So did his pal. Vanai glared at them, which only made them laugh harder. The fellow who'd tried to feel her up blew her a farewell kiss over his shoulder as he kept on walking his beat.

So long as he keeps walking, Vanai, thought. It wasn't just that she didn't want him groping her. He might have noticed she felt different to his hand from the way she looked to his eye. Her spell affected only her visual appearance; Ealstan had remarked on that more than once. She couldn't afford to let an Algarvian discover it, no matter how much like a Forthwegian she looked.

And I have to hurry, she reminded herself. *I can't know how long I'm going to keep on looking like a Forthwegian, not anymore.* Her hand went to her belly in an involuntary gesture of annoyance. She was convinced her being with child was what weakened the magecraft. It hadn't changed a bit from the day she perfected it till she found herself pregnant. Now . . . For all she knew, the baby inside her looked as if it were fully Forthwegian, too.

Smiling at that, she walked on toward the market square. Before she got there, she went past more Algarvian constables. These fellows weren't grinning and doing their best to be friendly. They were grabbing men off the street for a work gang, pointing toward walls and fences, and shouting, "Getting those down!" in their rudimentary Forthwegian.

Those were broadsheets. Vanai hurried forward to get a look at them before they all came down. DEATH TO THOSE WHO MURDER KAUNIANS! screamed one in lurid red characters. Another cried, VENGEANCE ON ALGARVE!

She couldn't even stare. She had to keep walking. *It's got to be Kaunians who put those up,* she thought. *Of course it's got to be Kaunians—how many Forthwegians care about us?*

But no Kaunian underground had shown itself since Algarve overran Forthweg, or none to speak of. How could such a thing start now, with so many Kaunians already gone? However it had happened, Vanai was savagely delighted to learn of it, a delight that only grew stronger because it had to stay hidden.

In the market square, she bought olive oil and almonds and green onions and a good-sized bream. She was just starting off toward her block of flats when an egg burst back where the Algarvians were making the Forthwegian work gang strip the broadsheets off the walls.

It was a big egg. The roar of its bursting was more a blow against the ears than an ordinary noise. The next thing Vanai knew, she was on her knees. She'd dropped the jar, and it had shattered, oil spilling and sliding across the cobbles of the market square. She cursed as she got to her feet. She wasn't the only one who'd fallen, or the only one who'd had something break, either.

When she staggered upright, she first started back toward the stall where she'd bought the olive oil. Then she started thinking straight, and realized she had more important things to worry about. Chief among them was that she couldn't afford to be recognized as a Kaunian at this of all moments. Forthwegians and Algarvians alike would assume she'd helped plant the egg, and she probably wouldn't last long enough to get shipped west.

That meant she had to return to the flat as fast as she could. Only when she headed back across the square did she realize how lucky she'd been not to have stood closer to the egg when it burst. Some people were down and shrieking. Other people, and parts of people, lay motionless. Blood was everywhere, puddling between cobblestones and splashed up onto walls and stalls the sorcerous energies hadn't knocked down.

The street by which she'd entered the square, the street on which the Forthwegians had been pulling down broadsheets, suddenly had an opening twice as wide as it had been. Fewer people—fewer whole people, anyway—and more body parts lay closer to where the egg must have been hidden. Gulping, trying to avert her eyes, Vanai picked her way past them, and past the crater the egg had blown in the ground.

By some miracle, one of the Algarvian constables who'd been on the street had survived. His tunic and kilt were half torn off him. Blood streamed down his face, and from cuts on his arms and legs. But he was up and walking, and in that state of eerie calm where he hardly seemed aware of his own injuries.

"Stinking Kaunians sneaking back from Zuwayza must've done this," he said to Vanai in Algarvian, as if to a superior. "Zuwayzin are supposed to be allies, curse 'em." He spat—spat red—and then noticed to whom he was talking. "Powers above, you probably don't understand a word I'm saying." Off he staggered, looking for an officer to brief.

But Vanai followed Algarvian well enough. She thought the constable was very likely right. The difference was, he hated the Kaunian raiders, while she hoped they would do more and worse.

People were rushing toward the burst. Some paused to help wounded men and women. Nobody took any special notice of unhurt or slightly hurt folk coming away. Vanai wasn't the only one—far from it. For all she knew, she wasn't the only Kaunian hurrying to get out of the public eye before concealing sorcery concealed no more.

Her street. Her block. The entrance to her block of flats. The stairway up to the dingy lobby. The stairway up to her flat. The hallway. Her front door. Her front door, opening. Her front door, closed behind her.

She took the almonds and the onions and the bream into the kitchen. Then she poured herself a full mug of wine and gulped it down. It would probably make her go to sleep in the middle of the day. She didn't care. She would probably look like a Kaunian when she woke up, too. She didn't care about that, either—not now. What difference did it make, here inside the flat where she was safe?

Twenty

Unkerlanter dragons swarmed above Herborn. Unkerlanter mages swarmed inside the reclaimed capital of Grelz and to the east of it. They had plenty of Unkerlanter victims ready to sacrifice if the Algarvians chose a sorcerous strike at Herborn during King Swemmel's moment of triumph. Common sense said nothing could go wrong.

Marshal Rathar had learned not to trust common sense. "I'm worried," he told General Vatran.

Vatran, to his relief, didn't pat him on the shoulder and go, *Everything will be fine.* Instead, the veteran officer screwed up his face and said, "I'm worried, too, lord Marshal. If the Algarvians get wind of what's going on here this afternoon, they'll turn this place upside down to stop it." Looking around, he added, "Of course, between the two sides, they and we've pretty much turned Herborn upside down already—and inside out, too, come to that."

"True enough." Rathar looked around, too. Herborn was one of the oldest towns in Unkerlant. An Algarvian merchant prince—or, some said, an Algarvian bandit chief—had set himself up here as king in the land more than eight hundred years before. Ever since, the city had had an Algarvian look to it, though a native dynasty soon supplanted the foreigners. Extravagantly ornamented, skyward-leaping towers always put visitors in mind of places farther east.

In the battles for Herborn, though—when the Algarvians took it from Unkerlant in the first months of the war, and now when King Swemmel's soldiers took it back—a lot of those skyward-leaping towers had been groundward-falling. Others yet stood but looked as if they'd had chunks bitten out of them. Still others were only fire-ravaged skeletons of what they had been.

The stink of stale smoke lingered in the air. So did the stink of death. That would have been worse had the weather been warmer.

It was still too warm to suit Rathar. "I wish we'd have a blizzard," he grumbled. "That'd make his Majesty put things off." He cast a hopeful eye westward, the direction from which bad weather was likeliest to come. But none looked like coming today.

Vatran shook his head. "For one thing, his Majesty doesn't give a fart if all the Algarvian captives he's got—well, all but one—freeze to death while he's parading 'em."

"I know *that*," Rathar said impatiently. "But he wouldn't care to go up on a reviewing stand and watch 'em in the middle of a snowstorm."

"Mm, maybe not," Vatran allowed. "Still and all, though, if he put things off, it'd give the redheads longer to find out what we're about."

That made Rathar nod, however little he wanted to. "Aye, you're right," he said. "If we have to do it, we'd best get it over with as soon as may be. If the king will—"

Vatran gave him a shot in the ribs with an elbow. The general had known him a long time, but that didn't excuse such uncouth familiarity. Rathar started to say so, in no certain terms. Then he too saw King Swemmel coming up, surrounded by a squad of hard-faced bodyguards. He bowed very low. "Your Majesty," he murmured. Beside him, Vatran did the same.

"Marshal. General," Swemmel said. He wore a tunic and cloak of military cut but royal splendor: even in the wan winter sunlight, their threadwork of cloth-of-gold, their encrusting pearls and rubies and polished, faceted chunks of jet glittered dazzlingly. So did the heavy crown on his head. He waved. "We are pleased with the aspect of this, our city of Herborn."

"Your Majesty?" This time, Rathar exclaimed in astonishment. Swemmel's guards caught the tone. Their faces went harder yet. Several of them growled, down deep in their throats, like any wolves. They knew lese majesty when they heard it.

But the king, for once, felt expansive enough to overlook it. He waved again. "Aye, we are pleased," he repeated. "Most of all are we pleased with that." He pointed to the tallest surviving tower of the duke's palace, the palace that had been Raniero's till not long before. Unkerlant's banner—white, black, and crimson—fluttered above it.

"Ah." Rathar nodded, as he had to Vatran. Now he understood what Swemmel meant. Hoping to take advantage of his sovereign's good humor, he asked, "Your Majesty, may I say a word?"

Swemmel's bodyguards growled again. Whatever Rathar was about to say, they could tell it would be something their master didn't care to hear. King Swemmel could tell as much, too. "Say on," he replied, icy warning in his voice.

Most of the king's courtiers would have found something harmless to ask him after that response. Doing anything else took more nerve than facing the Algarvians in battle. But Rathar would speak his mind every now and then, and did so now: "Your Majesty, what you have planned for the end of the parade—"

"Shall go forward," King Swemmel broke in. "It is our will. Our will shall assuredly be done."

"It will make the war harder to fight from now on," Rathar said. "We'll see no quarter, not anymore." He glanced over to Vatran. Vatran plainly wished he hadn't. But the white-haired general nodded agreement.

Swemmel snapped his fingers. "There is no quarter between us and Algarve now," he said. "There has been none since Mezentio treacherously hurled his armies across our border."

That held some truth. But Rathar wondered if Swemmel remembered he'd also been planning to attack the redheads, back three summers before. Much of Mezentio's treachery lay in striking first. With peasant stubbornness, Rathar tried once more: "Your Majesty . . ."

Slowly and deliberately, his contempt as vast as it was regal, King Swemmel turned his back. His guards didn't just growl. They snarled. Without looking at Rathar again, the king said what he'd said before: "Our will shall assuredly be done." He strode off, not giving his marshal any chance to reply. Some of the guards looked as if they wanted to blaze Rathar for his presumption.

Once they were out of earshot, General Vatran said, "Well, you tried."

"I know." Rathar kicked at the ground. It was icy; he almost fell when his booted foot slid more than he'd expected. "I wish he would have listened. Sometimes he does."

"But not today," Vatran said.

"No, not today." Rathar kicked again, more carefully this time. "But we're the ones who'll have to pay the price because he didn't."

"Hard to imagine how we could pay a price much bigger than we're paying now," Vatran said, which also held its share of truth and more.

Broadsheets summoned the people of Herborn to the parade route. Unkerlanter soldiers with megaphones also ordered them out of their homes—those who still had homes standing, at any rate. Watching the men and women coming up to line the street, Rathar wondered how many, not so long before, had waved gold-and-green flags and cheered then-King Raniero. More than a few: of that he was certain. The smart ones would already have burnt those, and whatever else gold and green they owned. If Swemmel's inspectors found such things, it would go hard on whoever had them.

Rathar's own place was on the reviewing stand, at his sovereign's side. It stood not far from the ducal palace, on the edge of Herborn's central square. That square was smaller than Cottbus', but large enough and to spare. Grelzers lined the square, too, though guards kept them well away from the reviewing stand.

King Swemmel imperiously raised his arm. "Let us begin!" he cried.

A band began the triumphal parade. Horns and drums blared out the Unkerlanter national hymn. Rathar wondered if the musicians would follow that with the hymn of the Duchy of Grelz, but they didn't. Maybe Swemmel didn't want the folk of Herborn thinking about being Grelzers at all, whether inhabitants of a separate duchy or of a separate kingdom. Maybe he just wanted them to think of themselves as belonging to the kingdom of Unkerlant—and maybe he was shrewd to want them to think of themselves so.

Instead of the hymn for the Duchy of Grelz, the band played a medley of patriotic songs that had grown popular in these parts since the Algarvians overran the region. Somebody, Rathar remembered, had said they were written by a local peasant or irregular or something of the sort. He wondered if that was true. It struck him as being too pat for plausibility, and so likelier a tale that came from Cottbus. Swemmel was shrewd enough to come up with something like that, and paid plenty of writers to come up with such things for him.

After the musicians came a regiment of behemoths, their armor clattering upon them, their heavy strides shaking the ground—the timbers of the reviewing stand vibrated beneath

Rathar's feet. Nothing could have been better calculated to overawe folk who still had doubts about whom they wanted to rule over them. What the locals wanted didn't count for much, of course. King Swemmel had returned, and did not intend to be dislodged again.

And after the behemoths came a great shambling mob of Algarvian captives, herded along by spruced-up Unkerlanter soldiers. A herald bellowed scornfully: "Behold the conquering heroes!" Scrawny, unshaven, filthy, some of them bandaged, all of them in shabby, tattered tunics and kilts, they looked like what they were: men who'd fought a war as hard and as long as they could, fought it and lost it.

In high good humor, Swemmel turned to Rathar and said, "Our mines and quarries shall have labor to spare for years to come."

"Aye, your Majesty," the marshal said abstractedly. He was watching the dragons overhead more than the luckless captives. Several of them broke off their spirals and flew east. No Algarvian dragons appeared above Herborn. If any tried to come over the town, the dragons painted rock-gray drove them back.

No Grelzer captives appeared on the streets of Herborn. If Grelzers hadn't been able to sneak out of the fight and find civilian clothes, they'd seldom left it alive.

An elegant troop of unicorn cavalry followed the mass of Algarvian captives. They were beautiful to look upon, even if not much use in the field. And after them strode the high-ranking Algarvian officers Swemmel's soldiers had captured in the Herborn pocket: colonels and brigadiers and generals. They were better dressed and better fed than their countrymen of lower estate, but if anything seemed even glummer.

Last of all, separated from them by more tough-looking Unkerlanter footsoldiers, Raniero—briefly King of Grelz—marched all alone. The band, the behemoths, the ordinary captives, the unicorn cavalry, the high Algarvian officers . . . all left the square in front of the ducal palace. Raniero and his guards remained. Silence fell.

In the midst of that silence, certain servitors of Swemmel's wheeled a large brass kettle, nearly full of water, into the center of the square. Other servitors piled coal, a great deal of coal, beneath the kettle and lit it. Still others set up a sort of a stand by the kettle; one broad plank projected out over the polished brass vessel. The guards took Raniero up onto the platform, but not yet onto the final plank. Like everyone else, they waited for the water in the kettle to boil.

Raniero had courage. Across the square, he waved to King Swemmel. Rathar murmured, "Your Majesty, I beg you—do not do this thing."

"Be silent," Swemmel said furiously. "Be silent, or join him there." Biting his lip, Rathar was silent.

At length, one of the Unkerlanter soldiers on the platform with Raniero held up his hand. King Swemmel nodded. "Let the usurper perish!" he shouted in a great voice. "Let all who rise against us perish!" He had spoken the identical words when putting his brother Kyot to death at the end of the Twinkings War.

Raniero had courage indeed. Instead of making the guards hurl him into the kettle—as even Kyot had done—he marched out over it, waved to Swemmel again, and with a cry of "Farewell!" leaped into the seething, steaming water.

Courage failed him then, of course. His shrieks ripped through the square, but not for long. Swemmel let out a breathy grunt, as he might have after a woman. "That was fine," he murmured, his eyes shining. "Aye, very fine indeed."

Rathar was glad the breeze blew from him toward the kettle, not the other way round. Even so, he did not think he would eat boiled beef or pork again any time soon.

Sidroc stumbled as he came up to the campfire, so that he kicked a little snow onto Sergeant Werferth. Werferth shook a fist at him. "All right, you son of a whore, now you've done it!" he shouted. "Just for that, I order you boiled alive!"

"Oh, come off it, Sergeant," Sidroc said. "I have to be an Algarvian, and a prince to boot, to rate anything so fancy. Why don't you just blaze me and get it over with?"

"Nah, that's what the Unkerlanters do to Grelzers they catch," Werferth said. "You ought to get something juicier."

Ceorl was cooking some horsemeat and buckwheat groats in his mess tin, using a branch as a handle. He said. "The Unkerlanters are liable to do that to us if they catch us, too. We look too much like them."

Sidroc plucked at his beard. Unkerlanters shaved. Forthwegians didn't. When he'd lived in Gromheort, that had seemed plenty to distinguish between his own people and the bumpkins and semisavages of Unkerlant. But when he was in the midst of fighting a war against those bumpkins and semisavages, and when they seldom got a chance to shave because they spent so much time in the field, having a beard didn't seem enough differentiation.

Not that the Unkerlanters wouldn't kill him for being a Forthwegian, too. But they sometimes showed mercy to men from Plegmund's Brigade. To Grelzers who'd fought for King Raniero—dead Raniero now—hardly ever.

Squatting down by the fire, Sidroc said, "Word going around is that we're getting a counterattack ready."

"Aye, well, we'd bloody well better do something," Ceorl said. "If we don't, they'll throw us out of Grelz altogether. Maybe we weren't so cursed smart, joining the Brigade. Looks like Algarve's losing the war."

"Shut your trap," Werferth said flatly. "You're only lucky it was a couple of your squadmates heard that, not somebody who'd report you." He eyed Sidroc. Reluctantly, Sidroc nodded to show he wouldn't. He didn't like Ceorl, not even a little, but the ruffian was a good man to have along in a brawl.

"Ahh, bugger it." Ceorl spat into the fire. "What difference does it make? Not a one of us is ever going to get home to Forthweg anyway. Who cares if our side kills us, or the other bastards do?"

Sidroc waited for Werferth to pitch a fit. But the veteran

sergeant only sighed. "Odds are you're right. Powers below eat you for saying so out loud, though."

"Why?" Ceorl sounded genuinely curious.

"Why? I'll tell you why," Werferth answered. "Because we've got to go on fighting like we're on the edge of winning this war, that's why. Because we'll get ourselves killed quicker if we don't, that's why. Because we still might beat the odds, too, that's why."

Ceorl dug into the meat and groats he'd cooked up. His mouth full, he said, "Fat chance."

"No, I think the sergeant's right," Sidroc said.

Ceorl sneered. "Of course you do. He's arguing with me. If he said the sky was green, you'd figure he was right."

"Oh, futter yourself," Sidroc said. "I think he's right on account of I think he's right, and on account of the Algarvians. They're sneakier than the Unkerlanters, and they're smarter, too. The war's not over yet, not by a long blaze. If they kill enough stinking Kaunians . . ."

"It won't make a counterfeit copper's worth of difference," Ceorl said. "Swemmel's boys will just kill as many of their own people as they need to, to even things out. Haven't we already seen that?"

"Maybe they'll come up with some other kind of magecraft, then. *I* don't know," Sidroc said. "What I do know is, one Algarvian is worth two or three Unkerlanters. We've seen that plenty of times. Powers above, one of us is worth two or three of Swemmel's men, too."

"Of course we are," Ceorl said—had he said anything else, he would have had Werferth arguing with him again, too. "Trouble is, one of us is worth two or three Unkerlanters, and then that fourth or fifth Unkerlanter ups and kicks us in the balls. We've seen that plenty of times, too—tell me we haven't."

Sidroc grunted. He couldn't tell Ceorl any such thing, and he knew it. He gave the best comeback he could: "They've got to run out of soldiers sooner or later."

"Sooner would be better," Sergeant Werferth said.

Neither Ceorl nor Sidroc wanted to quarrel with that. Not

far away, a sentry called out a challenge in Algarvian. All three men by the fire grabbed for their sticks, not that those had been very far away. The answer came back in Algarvian, too. Neither Sidroc, Werferth, nor Ceorl relaxed. For one thing, the Unkerlanters sometimes found soldiers who could speak the language of their enemies. For another, Algarvians who didn't know the men of Plegmund's Brigade went right on taking them for Unkerlanters.

Not this time, though, not even when the sentry let out a happy yelp in Forthwegian—"Behemoths!"—that the red-heads could easily have taken for Unkerlanter. Sidroc and his comrades exclaimed in delight. Behemoths with Algarvians aboard them had been too rare since so many died trying to smash their way through the Durrwangen bulge.

"I wonder who's going short so the beasts can come here," Werferth said.

"I don't, Sergeant," Sidroc answered. "I don't even care. All I know is, for once *we're* not going to go short."

"That's right, by the powers above," Ceorl said. Not for the first time, having Ceorl agree with him made Sidroc wonder if he was wrong.

On snowshoes, the behemoths' strides were surprisingly quiet. The white surcoats the beasts wore—the equivalent of the soldiers' snow smocks—helped muffle the clank and clat-ter of their chainmail. But they drew the men of Plegmund's Brigade and their Algarvian officers just the same.

And the Algarvians who crewed the behemoths retained the cheerful arrogance of earlier days. They waved to the Forthwegians as if to younger brothers. "You boys come along with us," one of them called, "and we'll do a proper job of smashing up the Unkerlanters."

"That's right," said a redhead on a different behemoth. "They haven't got a chance of standing up against us once we get rolling. You know that."

Sidroc knew nothing of the sort. What he knew was that, had the war been going just the way the Algarvians wanted, Plegmund's Brigade would never have come to the front line at all. It would have stayed in Grelz hunting irregulars, as it had started out doing. Well, now it was back in Grelz after a year and more of some of the most desperate fighting in the war, and it was facing the full weight of King Swemmel's army.

But, and especially after Ceorl's gloom, that Algarvian good cheer hit Sidroc like a strong slug of spirits. Mezentio's men *had* gone forward against the Unkerlanters. Why shouldn't they go forward against them again?

Algarvian footsoldiers came up with the behemoths. Some of them—new men, by their trim uniforms and unhaggard faces—gave the troopers of Plegmund's Brigade suspicious stares. "Are these fellows really on our side?" one of them asked, as if the bearded men in long tunics couldn't possibly be expected to understand his language.

"Aye, we are," Sidroc said. "And we'll stay that way as long as you don't ask idiot questions like that." The redhead glared at him. Sidroc was no older, but he'd seen things the Algarvian hadn't yet imagined. He looked through the newcomer as if he didn't exist. A couple of Mezentio's veterans talked to their countryman and calmed him down.

Somewhere not far away, the Algarvians had gathered together a good many egg-tossers, too. They all started flinging death at the Unkerlanters at once. "They'd never lay on so much just for us," Ceorl grumbled. "Put their own people into the fight, though, and they care a lot more."

That was probably true. Sidroc shook his head. No, that was certainly true. "Nothing we can do about it but make the most of it now," he said.

Whistles shrilled. The Algarvian behemoths lumbered forward, straight through the hole the egg-tossers had torn in the Unkerlanter line. Footsoldiers—Algarvians and the men of Plegmund's Brigade together—accompanied the behemoths.

Maybe the men who rode those behemoths knew what they were talking about. King Swemmel's soldiers seemed astonished to find Algarvians attacking. Whenever the Unkerlanters were astonished, they had trouble. Some of them fought, stubborn as always. But a good many fled, and a good many surrendered.

"Forward!" Algarvian officers shouted, again and again. "Keep up with the behemoths!"

Sidroc did his best. Despite the snow on the ground, sweat streamed down his face. His legs ached. But he was advancing again. He blazed at an Unkerlanter before the fellow could blaze at an Algarvian behemoth. The Unkerlanter went down. Sidroc whooped with glee.

A couple of days later, Swemmel's soldiers tried to rally at the outskirts of what was either a large village or a small town. They had egg-tossers in the place. Eggs flew through the air, kicking up fans of snow—and a few Algarvian soldiers—when they burst. The counterattack slowed and threatened to stall. Sidroc cursed. "Just when things looked like they were starting to go our way—"

"Aye," Werferth agreed mournfully. "Maybe that whoreson of a Ceorl was right. This is how it works for the redheads these days. They don't—*we* don't—have enough to smash the Unkerlanters flat when we're supposed to."

But he was wrong. The Algarvians had always been good at making their egg-tossers keep up with advancing soldiers. Now more eggs burst in and around the Unkerlanter-held town than came out of it. One by one, the Unkerlanter egg-tossers fell silent, suppressed by the eggs flung at them. Lately, Algarvian dragons had seemed almost as scarce in the air as Algarvian behemoths were on the ground. But a wing of them stooped on the town like kestrels. With eggs and flame, they left it a smoking ruin. Only then did officers blow their whistles and shout, "Forward!"

Behemoths advanced with the footsoldiers, tossing still more eggs on the enemy. Even before the Algarvians and the men of Plegmund's Brigade got into the village, white flags started flying. Unkerlanter soldiers stumbled toward them, hands high.

"I'll be a son of a whore," Sidroc said in something approaching awe. "Haven't seen anything like this in I don't know when."

"Forward!" an Algarvian officer not far away shouted. "Keep moving! Don't waste a heartbeat! Push 'em hard! We'll take Herborn back yet!"

Three or four days before; Sidroc would have thought him a madman. Then, like everyone else, he'd been wondering how far the Algarvians would have to retreat before finally finding a line they could hold. Now . . . Now, for the time being at least, they had the bit between their teeth again. He trudged on past burning peasant huts and Unkerlanter corpses. He didn't know how far he and his comrades could go, but he was interested again in finding out.

An enormous wolf with fangs dripping blood had a long, sly face that looked a lot like King Swemmel's. So no Forthwegian could miss the point, the artist who'd painted the wolf on the broadsheet had thoughtfully labeled it UNKERLANT. A stalwart Algarvian shepherd with a stout spear stood between that fearsome wolf and a flock of sheep altogether too precious and sweet to be believable. They too had a label: DERLAVAIAN CIVILIZATION.

Ealstan studied the broadsheet with a connoisseur's appraising eye. In four and a half years of war, he'd seen a lot of them. At last, with the grudged respect one gave a clever foe, he nodded. This was one of Algarve's better efforts. Few Forthwegians loved their cousins to the west. The broadsheet might prompt his countrymen to think of the redheads as their protectors.

But so what? Ealstan thought, and his face twisted into a grin almost as fearsome as the Swemmel-wolf's. *So what, by the powers above? If the Unkerlanters keep pounding Mezentio's men, what Forthweg thinks about them won't matter. The Algarvians are losing.* That was sweet as honey to him. Ever since the Algarvians overwhelmed the Forthwegian army—and so many others afterwards—he'd wondered if they *could* lose, and feared they couldn't.

Still wearing that grin, he turned away from the broadsheet and walked down the street. A news-sheet vendor on a corner shouted, "Read about the Algarvian counterattack in the

Kingdom of Grelz! Herborn threatened! Swemmel flees to Cottbus with his tail between his legs! Heroes of Plegmund's Brigade!"

Ealstan strode past him as if he didn't exist. He wondered how many times he'd done that, in Gromheort and now in Eoforwic. Too many—he knew that. He pretended newssheet vendors didn't exist whenever the Algarvians moved forward. And whenever he thought of Plegmund's Brigade, he hoped his cousin was dead: horribly dead and a long time dying, with any luck at all.

PYBBA'S POTTERTY! screeched a sign ever so much larger and gaudier than any broadsheet the Algarvians had ever put up. This wasn't the enormous warehouse down by the Twegen River, but the home of Pybba's kilns and his offices. The only pots and plates the magnate sold here were the ones that came out of the kilns too badly botched to go to the warehouse or to any shop, no matter how shoddy. OUR MISTAKES—CHEAP! another sign proclaimed. Pybba did a brisk business with them. Pybba, as far as Ealstan could tell, did a brisk business with everything.

He was prowling through the offices when Ealstan came in. "You're late," he growled, though Ealstan was no such thing. "What took you so long?"

"I was looking at a new broadsheet," Ealstan answered.

"Wasting time," Pybba said. "Sit your arse down in front of the books. That's what you're supposed to be doing, not leering at Algarvian tripe. I bet it had naked women on it. The redheads are shameless buggers."

A couple of men who'd beaten Ealstan into the pottery works laughed. Pybba was reliably loud and reliably vulgar. Ealstan perched on a tall stool and got to work. His boss' legitimate books were quite complex enough. The others . . .

Before long, Pybba let out a roar from inside his sanctum: "Ealstan! Get your arse in here this minute, curse you, and see if you can't bring your brains with it."

More snickers came from Ealstan's coworkers as he got

down from the stool. They weren't without sympathy; before long, Pybba would be bellowing at somebody else, and everyone knew it. "What is it?" Ealstan asked, standing in the doorway.

"Shut the cursed door," the pottery magnate rumbled. Ealstan did. Pybba's voice suddenly dropped: "Which broadsheet were you talking about? The one with the wolf?"

"Aye." Ealstan nodded. "Is there another one?"

"After the Kaunians burst that egg? You'd best believe there is, boy. It shows a monster peeking out from behind a mask that looks a little like you."

"A Kaunian monster," Ealstan said. This time, Pybba nodded. Ealstan's lip curled. "That's disgusting."

"It's a pretty fair broadsheet," Pybba answered. "Maybe not quite as strong as the one with the wolf, but close. Who's got any use for Kaunians, anyhow?"

He certainly didn't; Ealstan knew as much. Picking his words with care, Ealstan observed, "If the Algarvians hate the blonds, they've probably got something going for them."

"Fat chance," Pybba said. "All right. I just wanted to find out if you knew something I didn't. You don't." He raised his voice to an angry yell: "So get your miserable carcass back to work!"

Part of the reason for that yell was to make sure nobody outside wondered what Pybba and Ealstan were talking about in their quiet conversation. The rest was because Pybba was fed up with Ealstan. Ealstan knew that too well. He'd tried again and again to get his boss to pay some attention to the Kaunians in Eoforwic and in Forthweg generally. Who in all the kingdom had better reason to hate the occupiers and work against them? Nobody Ealstan could see. But Pybba didn't care. Despising Kaunians himself, he refused to see them as allies.

He wants a Forthwegian kingdom when the Algarvians get thrown out, Ealstan realized as he went back to the ledgers. *Not a Kingdom of Forthweg, the way it was before the war, but a* Forthwegian *kingdom, without Kaunians. The Algar-*

vians, as far as he's concerned, are solving the Kaunian problem for him.

That thought was chillier than Forthwegian winters commonly got. For a moment, Ealstan was tempted to throw his job in Pybba's face and find other work. But he'd already seen that Pybba could make it hard for him to find bookkeeping work.

And Vanai wouldn't want him to quit. He'd already seen that, too. She would want him to keep doing everything he could to drive Mezentio's men out of Forthweg. Whatever happened after that, it would be better than having the Algarvians running the kingdom. He didn't like that line of reasoning—loving his wife as he did, he wanted nothing less than full equality for all Kaunians—but he couldn't find any holes in it.

From somewhere in the vast pottery works came a large, almost musical crash, as of a good many crocks and chamber pots and dishes meeting an untimely demise. One of the fellows who worked near Ealstan—his job was writing catchy slogans for the wares Pybba produced—grinned and said, "Get out the red ink, my friend. There go some of the profits."

Pybba heard the crash, too. Pybba, by all the signs, heard everything. He flew out of his inner sanctum like an egg flying out of a tosser. "Powers above, that's coming out of somebody's pay!" he roared. "Just let me get my mitts on the butterfingered bunghole who buggered that up. Probably greased his hand so he could play with himself, the son of a whore!" And he rushed off to find out exactly what had gone wrong and who was to blame for it.

"So calm." Ealstan rolled his eyes. "So restrained."

The slogan writer—his name was Baldred—chuckled. "Never a dull moment around this place. Of course, sometimes you wish there were."

"Why would you want that?" Ealstan wondered. "I've got so I *like* having my hair set on fire about three times a day. Hardly seems like I'm doing anything unless somebody's screaming at me to do more."

"Oh, it's not so bad as that," Baldred said. He was about halfway between Ealstan's age and Pybba's—in his mid-thirties—with white hairs in his beard still so few that he ostentatiously plucked them out whenever he found them. "As long as you do the work of four men, he'll pay you for two. What more could you want?"

"That's about the size of it," Ealstan agreed. He thought Baldred worked on Pybba's unofficial business as well as that pertaining to pottery, but he wasn't sure. Because he wasn't sure, he never mentioned it to the slogan-writer. Every now and again, he wondered whether Baldred wondered about him.

Pybba stomped back into the offices, a stormcloud on his face. But no cringing employee followed him to pick up whatever pay he was owed and then leave forever. Irked at Pybba, Ealstan kept at his work and didn't ask the obvious question. Baldred did: "What happened?"

"Fornicating stray dog came round a corner going one way at the same time as one of our boys came round it going the other," Pybba said. "Aye, he tripped over the stinking thing. Powers below eat him, what else could he do? Three or four people saw it, and the poor bastard's got a scraped knee on one leg and a dog bite on the other one."

"Ah," Baldred said wisely. "No wonder you didn't fire him, then."

The pottery magnate's scowl grew more fearsome yet; he'd doubtless roared out of the office intending to do exactly that. "You tend to your knitting," he rumbled, "or I'll bloody well fire you. Not a thing to say I can't do that."

Baldred got very busy very fast. Pybba eyed him long enough to make sure he *was* busy, then went into his own office and slammed the door behind him, hard enough to make little waves in Ealstan's inkwell. "Charming as always," Ealstan murmured.

"But of course." Baldred shrugged. "I'm not going to worry about it. Before too long, he'll pitch a fit at somebody else instead. Tell me I'm wrong."

"Can't do it." Ealstan got back to work, too.

A few minutes later, the outer door opened. Ealstan looked up, still expecting the potter who'd had the unfortunate encounter with the stray dog. What he expected was not what he got. What he got was an Algarvian colonel with spiky waxed mustaches. Ealstan wondered if he ought to run or if he ought to scream for Pybba to run. Before he could do either, the redhead swept off his hat, bowed, and spoke in pretty good Forthwegian: "I require to see the gentleman Pybba, if you would be so kind."

"Aye, I'll get him for you," Ealstan answered. "May I ask why?"

"I seek to purchase pots." The Algarvian raised an eyebrow. "If I wanted flowers, you may be sure I would go elsewhere."

Ears burning, Ealstan descended from his stool and went to fetch Pybba. "Pots?" the pottery magnate said. "I'll give him—" He shook his head and followed Ealstan out again. Eyeing the Algarvian with no great warmth, he asked, "What sort of pots have you got in mind?"

"Small ones." The officer gestured. "Ones to fit the palm of the hand and the fingers, so. Round, or nearly round, with snug-fitting lids."

"Haven't got anything just like that in stock," Pybba answered. "It'd have to be a special order—unless some sugar bowls would do?"

"Let me see them," the Algarvian said.

"Come with me," Pybba told him. "I've got some samples in the next room."

"Good. Very good. Take me to them, if you please."

When Pybba and the redhead came back from the samples room, the pottery magnate wore a sandbagged expression. "Fifty thousand sugar bowls, style seventeen," he said hoarsely, and turned to stare at the colonel. "Why would anybody want fifty thousand sugar bowls?"

"For a very large tea party, of course," the Algarvian said blandly.

That wasn't the truth, of course. Ealstan wondered what the truth was, and who would get hurt finding out.

* * *

"Rain pouring down on us,"Sergeant Istvan complained, squelching along a muddy trench on the little island of Becsehely. "Water all around us." His wave encompassed the Bothnian Ocean not far away. "We might as well grow fins and turn into fish."

Szonyi shook his head, which made water fly off his waxed cloth cap. "I'd sooner turn into a dragon and fly away from this miserable place."

"Probably safer to turn into a fish," Corporal Kun observed. "The Kuusamans have too many dragons between us and the stars." He pointed upward.

"No stars to see now, not with this rain," Szonyi said. "No dragons to see, either, and I don't miss 'em one fornicating bit." Kun had disagreed with him about which impossible choice was better to make, but not even Kun could argue about that.

With a sigh, Istvan said, "If we were only fighting the Kuusamans, we'd do fine. And if we were only fighting the Unkerlanters, we'd do fine, too. But we're fighting both of 'em, and we're not doing so fine."

"We'll send you back to the capital," Kun said. "You can teach the foreign ministry how to run its business."

"It'd mean I didn't have you in my hair anymore." Istvan scratched. Something gave under his fingernail. He grunted in considerable satisfaction. "There's one louse that's not in my hair from now on." The satisfaction evaporated. "Stars only know how many I've still got, though."

"We all have 'em." Szonyi scratched, too. "You'd think the wizards would come up with a charm that could keep the lice off a fellow for more than a day or two at a time." He scowled at Kun, as if to say he blamed the mage's apprentice for the problem.

Kun shrugged. "I can't do anything about it—except scratch, just like everybody else." He did.

Lajos came up the trench. "Assembly!" the youngster called. "Captain Frigyes wants to talk to the whole company."

"Where?" Istvan asked. "When?"

"Right now," Lajos answered. "Back there, not far from the messfires." He pointed in the direction from which he'd come. At the moment, the rain had put out the fires.

Istvan nodded to the other two veterans who'd been through so much with him. "You heard the man," he said as Lajos went on to pass the word to more men in the company. "Let's find out what the captain's got to say." He slogged down the trench once more. Kun and Szonyi followed.

Captain Frigyes stood waiting while the soldiers gathered. He wore a rain cape. Instead of using the hood or a cap like Szonyi's, he had on a broad-brimmed felt hat in the Algarvian style. Even though the feather in the hatband was sadly draggled, the headgear, cocked at a jaunty angle, gave him a dashing air he couldn't have got without it.

He returned Istvan's salute, and then those of his companions. "What's up, sir?" Istvan asked.

"I'll tell it all once," Captain Frigyes answered. "That way, I won't have to go over pieces of it three or four different times. You'll hear soon enough, Sergeant—I promise you that." Istvan nodded. What the company commander said made good sense. Even if it hadn't, of course, he couldn't have done anything about it.

A lieutenant, another sergeant, two corporals, and even a cheeky common soldier asked Frigyes more or less the same question as they came up. He gave them the same answer, or lack of answer. Istvan felt better to find out he wasn't the only nosy one in the company.

When just about everyone had gathered in front of Frigyes, he nodded to his soldiers and said, "Men, it's time to stop beating around the bush. Nobody talks about it much, but we all know the war isn't going as well for Gyongyos as it ought to be. We've got two foes, and we can't hit either one so hard as we'd like." Istvan preened in front of Szonyi and Kun. He'd said the same thing. Maybe he really did deserve a job in the foreign ministry.

Frigyes went on, "Most of you fought in the forests of Un-kerlant. Some of you remember how, summer before last, we were on the edge of breaking out of the forest and into the open country beyond, and the magic the Unkerlanters made to help halt us."

Not likely I'd ever forget that, Istvan thought. The other longtimers in the company were nodding. Kun had a look of something close to horror on his face. Having at least a small fragment of a mage's talent, he'd not only felt the spell, he'd understood how the Unkerlanters had done what they'd done.

For those who didn't, Frigyes spelled it out: "King Swemmel's mages slay their own folk—the ones they reckon useless—to fuel that magecraft. The Algarvians use the same spell, but power it with the life energy of those they've conquered. Neither of those is, or could ever be, the proper Gyongyosian path."

"Stars be praised!" Kun murmured beside Istvan.

But Frigyes went on, "Still, we need to use that spell if we are to hold back the grinning dwarfs of Kuusamo."

Kun gasped. "No!"

"Aye," Frigyes said, though Istvan didn't think he could possibly have heard Kun. "We need it, for it has proved itself far stronger than any sorcery we have. But the essence of the spell is its use of life energy, not the murder of those who have done nothing to deserve it to gain that life energy."

"What's he talking about?" Kun whispered to Istvan.

Istvan looked at him in surprise. "Don't you know?" Kun was a city man. If this was what being a city man meant, Istvan was just as well pleased to come from a mountain valley. He understood how a proper Gyongyosian was supposed to think.

For Kun and any others who didn't, Captain Frigyes spelled it out again: "We are seeking volunteers among the warriors of Gyongyos. If you say aye, your name will go on a list to be held against time of need. Should the need arise, you will serve Gyongyos one last time, and the glorious stars above will remember your name and your heroism forevermore. Who now will step forward to show you are willing—

no, to show you are eager—to serve Gyongyos in her time of need?"

"Madness," Kun said, though still quietly.

"No," Istvan said. "Our duty." His hand shot into the air. He wasn't the first, but he wasn't far behind, either. More and more hands went up after his, Szonyi's among them, till about two thirds of the company had volunteered.

"Stout fellows. I expected nothing less," Frigyes said. "Hold those hands high while I write down your names. I knew I could rely on you. I knew Gyongyos could rely on you. All through our army, officers are asking this question today. All through our army, I'm sure they're finding heroes."

Muttering under his breath, Kun raised his hand, too. "There you are!" Istvan said. "I knew you had a warrior's spirit in you."

"Warrior's spirit, my arse," Kun said. "If all you fools say aye, you'll hate me for saying no. That's the long and short of it."

He probably wasn't the only one to think like that; either, and he probably wasn't wrong. More and more hands went up, till only a few stubborn or fearful soldiers refused to volunteer. Frigyes had been no fool to ask all the men at the same time. They shamed one another forward.

When at last no more hands rose, the company commander nodded approval. "I knew you were warriors," he said. "If the stars be kind, as I hope they will, your names on this list will be only names and nothing more. But should the need arise to give of ourselves for Ekrekek Arpad, I know we will go bravely, and of our own free will. And I want you men to know one thing." He held up the list of names he'd taken. "My own name is here among yours. I am willing to give my life for Gyongyos, too. Dismissed!"

"That's a brave man, by the stars," Szonyi said as he and Kun and Istvan walked off together. "He put his name right down with ours."

Kun gave him a pitying look. Then the city man glanced over to Istvan. "You see it, don't you, Sergeant?"

"See what?" Istvan asked. "Szonyi's right—Captain Frigyes *is* brave."

"He's brave in battle. Nobody could say anything about that," Kun admitted. "But volunteering to be sacrificed doesn't prove anything about him one way or the other."

"No?" Szonyi asked. "You want your throat cut if Gyongyos gets in trouble? *I* don't, and I don't suppose the captain does, either."

Kun sighed, as if wondering why he met all the stupidity in the world. Szonyi started to get angry. Istvan sympathized with Szonyi. "What *are* you going on about?" he asked Kun. "Do you think the captain didn't put his name down on the list when he said he did? You'd better not think that." He started to get angry, too: angry at Kun, because he didn't want to be angry at the man who led them into battle.

"I don't think that, not for a minute," Kun said. "Don't you see, though? It doesn't matter."

"You keep saying it doesn't matter. I see that," Istvan answered. "The more you say it, the more I want to give you a clout in the eye. I see that, too. So either start talking sense or else shut up."

"All right, by the stars, I'll make sense." Now Kun sounded angry, too, and spoke with savage irony: "There's one captain for every hundred common soldiers, more or less. It's harder to be a captain than a common soldier. You have to do and know everything a common soldier does and knows, and a lot more besides. So when the time comes for the mages to start cutting throats, if it ever does, are they going to start cutting common soldiers' throats, or captains'? Which can they replace easier if they have to use them up?"

"Oh." Istvan walked on for a few paces. He felt foolish. He felt worse than foolish—he felt stupid. He glanced over at Szonyi. Szonyi wasn't saying anything, just tramping along with his head down and a half glum, half furious expression on his face. With a sigh, Istvan nodded to Kun. "Well, you're right."

That made Szonyi speak up: "I still want to give you a set

of lumps. Maybe now more than ever."

"Why? For being right?" Kun asked. "Where's the justice there?"

"For being right in the wrong tone of voice," Istvan said. "You do that a lot."

"No, that's not it, not this time." Szonyi shook his big head. Water flew from the brim of his cap. "For making me see Captain Frigyes was talking sly himself. I don't want anybody saying one thing when he means something else, or when he doesn't mean anything at all."

"Clouds hide the truth," Kun said. "The stars shine down on it. They send out their light for us to see by."

Like everything Kun said, that sounded wise. Szonyi grunted and finally, reluctantly, nodded. Istvan wasn't so sure. Even as a sergeant, he'd seen that the tricks by which men led other men weren't so simple. Casting light on those tricks made leading harder. Considering the way the war was going, maybe Kun should have kept his mouth shut.

Garivald had never seen so many Unkerlanter soldiers in all his born days. They swarmed through the forest west of Herborn and clogged the roads north and south of the woods. With every passing day, the band of irregulars he led looked less and less important. In fact, it hardly seemed his band at all any more. Tantris gave more orders than he did, and seemed happier doing it.

No matter how happy Tantris seemed, people started slipping away from the band under cover of night. A couple of years before, they'd slipped into the woods the same way to join the irregulars. The first couple of inspectors—or were they impressers?—joined Tantris not long after Herborn fell to King Swemmel's soldiers. Garivald didn't like the way they huddled with the regular. He didn't like the way they looked at him, either.

After darkness fell that night, he spoke to Obilot in a low whisper: "I'm going to get away while I still have the chance."

She nodded. "You think they mean to shove a uniform tunic on you." It wasn't a question.

"I think they mean to shove a uniform tunic on me and send me wherever it's hottest and get me killed," Garivald answered. "After all, I've led fighters who weren't taking orders straight from King Swemmel's men."

"You're going to slide off?" Obilot said.

"I already said so," he answered. "I'm not going to waste a minute, either—I don't intend to be here when the sun comes up tomorrow." He took her hand. "This isn't the way I wanted to say goodbye, but . . ."

"I'll come with you, if you want," she said.

Garivald stared. "But—" he said again.

"But I'm a woman?" Obilot asked. "But they won't shove a uniform tunic on me? So what? I wish they would. It'd let me go on killing Algarvians. But you're right; they won't. And so I'll come with you. If you want."

"You know where I'll be going," Garivald said slowly.

"Back to Zossen," Obilot answered. "Back to your wife and your children. Aye, I know. That's why I said what I said the way I said it."

"What will you do once I get there?" he asked.

Obilot shrugged. "I don't know. That'll be partly up to you, anyhow. But maybe you could use somebody to watch your back on the way—and we'll have another few days together, anyhow. Past that . . ." She shrugged again. "I never have worried much about what happens next. When it happens, I'll worry about it."

"All right." Garivald kissed her. Part of him was ashamed of himself: he might lie with her a couple of more times on the way back to Annore, his wife. But another part of him eagerly looked forward to that. And yet another part warned he might well need a companion, and maybe a fellow fighter, before he got to Zossen. "Let's wait till midnight or so, and then we'll see if we can sneak off."

Getting out of camp, going from leader of the band of irregulars to fugitive, proved easier than he'd expected. No one challenged him as he slipped away. Tantris and the inspectors snored drunkenly by a fire. *So much for efficiency,* Garivald thought. Obilot joined him a few minutes after he left his hut. "If they really want to, they'll be able to follow our tracks in the snow," she said.

"I know." Garivald grimaced. "The Algarvians and the Grelzers could do the same thing in wintertime." Now he was worried about pursuit from his own side, from the side he still preferred to the expelled enemy and their puppets. He started away from the encampment. "Let's get to a road. Then our tracks won't be the only ones."

"How far is Zossen?" Obilot asked as they slipped through the trees.

"I don't know. Forty, fifty, sixty miles—something like that," Garivald answered with a shrug. "I was never more than a day's walk away from it till the redheads grabbed and and took me off to Herborn. They were going to boil me the way King Swemmel boiled Raniero, but Munderic waylaid 'em when they cut through the woods instead of going around. So I've seen Zossen and I've seen the forest and what's around it, but I haven't hardly seen whatever's in between, if you know what I mean."

Obilot nodded. "I hadn't been far from my village before the Algarvians came, either. Just to the market town. I don't think anything's left of either one of them. Our army fought there, but we didn't win."

"They were going to make a stand in Zossen, too," Garivald said. "But before they could, they heard the redheads had outflanked them, and so they fell back."

An icy breeze blew out of the west. Garivald steered by it. It was all he had, with clouds covering the stars. Somewhere not far away, an owl hooted. "I'd rather hear that than wolves," Obilot remarked.

"Aye." Garivald was carrying his stick, but his head went up and down anyway. A few paces later, he added, "Some of the wolves in these woods go on two legs, not four." Obilot laughed, not that he'd been joking. She had her stick, too.

They were both yawning when they emerged from the forest a couple of hours later. But they kept going till they struck the road. Even in the middle of the night, it had plenty of traffic: wagons and unicorns and behemoths and columns of marching men, all heading east. Garivald had to spring off to the side of the road again and again to keep from being trampled.

At sunrise, they came to a tent city that hadn't been there a few days before and probably wouldn't be there in another few days. "Can you spare us any bread?" Obilot called to the soldiers.

Had Garivald asked, the troopers likely would have cursed him or worse. But a woman's voice worked wonders. They got black bread and ham and butter and pickled onions. "Go on back to your farm, if there's anything left of it," one of the soldiers said in a northern accent. "Here's hoping you find some pieces worth picking up."

"Thanks," Garivald said. "Powers above keep you safe."

"Same to you," the soldier answered. "I may see you again one of these days. Wherever your farm's at, the inspectors and impressers'll be paying you a call sooner or later. They want everybody to join the fun—that's how things work."

"That's how things work," Garivald repeated bitterly as he and Obilot walked west against the flow of military traffic. "The worst of it is, he's right. Some locusts have two legs, too. Don't they know they have to leave *some* people on the land to keep everybody from starving?"

"Nobody from Cottbus knows anything." Now that Obilot was back under King Swemmel's rule, she mocked his officials, too.

They slept for a few hours in a wrecked peasant hut, lying in each other's arms under both their cloaks. When they woke and went back to the road, they couldn't go down it for quite a while: a great column of Algarvian captives filled it. Some of the redheads looked glum. Some seemed relieved just to be alive. And a few, with the lighthearted Algarvian arrogance Garivald had seen before, were doing their best to make a lark of it, singing and grinning and acting the fool.

"What'll happen to these bastards?" he called to one of the Unkerlanters herding the captives along.

"Oh, they're for the mines, every stinking one of 'em," the soldier answered. "Let 'em grub out brimstone and quicksilver and coal, so we get some use out of 'em. A short life and a not so merry one."

"Even that's too good for them," Obilot said. "I wish they had just one neck, so we could take off all their heads at once." The guard laughed and nodded. Any of the redheads who understood were probably less amused.

Garivald and Obilot fell in behind the column. They walked at whatever pace they chose. The Algarvians walked at the faster pace the guards set. Every so often, one wouldn't be able to keep up anymore. Garivald and Obilot walked past redheaded corpses in the roadway. Obilot kicked the first couple they passed. After that, she didn't bother.

A strange cracking noise made Garivald turn around to see what it was. Another, smaller, column of captives was gaining on him. These weren't Algarvians. They were men who looked a lot like him. They looked a lot like their captors, too. But their uniform tunics weren't rock-gray. They were dark green. Some of the Grelzers who'd been fighting for Raniero still lived, then.

Their guards hustled them forward, driving them even faster than the Unkerlanters in charge of the Algarvian captives. Garivald and Obilot scrambled out of the roadway to let them pass. And Garivald discovered what that cracking noise was: one of the guards carried not a stick but a whip, which he brought down again and again on the back of a Grelzer captive.

"Mercy!" the captive cried, in accents much like Garivald's.

"Mercy? For you?" His tormentor laughed. "By the time we're finished with you and your pals, filth, you'll end up envying Raniero, you will." The whip came down.

The Grelzer dashed forward, not in a run for freedom but straight toward an oncoming behemoth. As the beast raised a great foot, he dove under it. Red smeared the road when the behemoth took another step. The Unkerlanter guardsman cursed. Someone had escaped him.

Toward evening, Obilot again begged food from soldiers. "Here," one of the men said. "We can spare you and your man a tent for the night, too." To their own, they could be kindly. To their own who'd turned against them . . . Garivald fought to forget the sound the behemoth's foot had made as it crushed the life from the Grelzer captive.

Only a few peasants were left in the villages by the side of the road. Garivald asked an old man, "How far to Zossen?"

"Never heard of it," the fellow answered.

A couple of hours later, another old man said, "Zossen? A day, I think—maybe not even."

"No, a day and a half, easy," a woman insisted. They started to argue.

She turned out to be closer to right. Early the following morning, Garivald began recognizing the countryside. He might have done it sooner, but the fighting looked to have been heavy in these parts. He and Obilot walked on. Some time in the middle of the afternoon, he said, "Around that next bend, there'll be Zossen."

Obilot stopped. She looked at him. "You'll want to go on by yourself," she said. Rather miserably, Garivald nodded. He'd fought for his life with Obilot as well as lain beside her, but all his life before the Algarvians snatched him lay ahead. He wouldn't have come back if he hadn't wanted that. "Go on, then," Obilot told him. "I'll come along in a little while. We'll see how things are when I get there." When he still hesitated, she pushed him. "Go on, I told you. I knew how things were when we left the woods."

"All right." Garivald trudged on along the path. When he looked back over his shoulder, Obilot stood in the middle of the road, cradling her stick in a way that said she'd used it many times before and was ready to use it again if anyone bothered her.

But Garivald was looking ahead, eagerly looking ahead, when he rounded that last bend. Obilot was behind him now, in the path and in the past. Ahead of him lay the field he and his fellow peasants worked and . . .

Nothing.

When he looked to where the village had stood, nothing was what he saw. The Algarvians must have made a stand here. Not a house still stood: not his hut, not Waddo the firstman's two-story home, not his friend Dagulf's. None. The buildings of Zossen—the houses, the smithy, the tavern—were erased as if they had never been.

The people? His wife? His son and daughter? Maybe they'd fled. He shook his head. He knew what the odds were. Far more likely—likely almost to the point of certainty—they'd died with their village.

He was still standing, still staring, when he heard footsteps behind him. He turned. Obilot came up and put a hand on his arm. "I'm sorry," she said. "Now you have nothing, too, just like me."

"Aye." Garivald's voice was still dull with shock. He and Obilot stood side by side surveying the devastation, both their lives in ruin.

Vanai was cooking rabbit stew with prunes and dried mushrooms when Ealstan gave the coded knock at their door. She hurried over to unbar it and let him in. When she did, his face glowed with excitement. That made her smile, too. She kissed him and then asked, "What's happened? Something has. I can see it."

"You'll never guess," he said.

She looked at him in amused annoyance. "I was hoping I wouldn't have to."

"You know how Herborn's fallen to the Unkerlanters," he said.

"Oh, aye." Vanai nodded. "The news sheets finally admitted that a couple of days ago, when they couldn't not admit it anymore, if you know what I mean."

"That's right—and the Algarvians and Plegmund's stinking Brigade were going to chase the Unkerlanters out again any minute now. I lose track of the lies sometimes," Ealstan said. "Well, Pybba knows more than the news sheets do. For instance, had you heard the Unkerlanters caught King Mezentio's cousin Raniero, the fellow he'd named King of Grelz?"

"No!" Vanai kissed Ealstan again, this time for bringing home such wonderful news. "What are they going to do to him?" To her way of thinking—Brivibas' way of thinking, too, but her grandfather never entered her mind—the Unkerlanters were barbarous enough to be capable of anything.

"They've already done it," Ealstan told her. "That's the real news. They held a ceremony in Herborn and boiled him alive."

"Oh." For once, the lurch Vanai's stomach gave had nothing to do with her pregnancy. "That's . . ." She didn't know quite what it was. "I wouldn't wish it on . . ." *Why wouldn't you wish it on an Algarvian?* she wondered. *You've wished plenty of worse things on them, and what they've done to your own folk makes them deserve every one.* "Good riddance," she said at last.

"Aye, just so," Ealstan said. "That's how they serve up rebels. And they slaughter their own folk when . . . to strike back at the Algarvians."

When the Algarvians slaughter Kaunians, he hadn't said, even if he'd started to. He tried to spare her feelings. And Forthwegians looked down on their cousins to the west hardly less than the Kaunians of Forthweg did. The only difference was, the Kaunians of Forthweg looked down on the Forthwegians, too.

Ealstan went into the kitchen and came back with two mugs of wine. He handed Vanai one and raised the other in a toast: "Down with Algarve!" He drank.

"Down with Algarve!" Vanai would always drink to that. The mere idea made any wine sweeter.

Over supper, Ealstan said, "One of these days before too long, Swemmel's men are bound to strike blows in the north to match the ones they're making down in Grelz."

"Is that something else Pybba knows but the news sheets don't?" Vanai asked.

He shook his head. "No. I wish it were. But it stands to reason, doesn't it? They'll want to run the redheads out of all of their kingdom, not just part of it."

"If they do run them out of Unkerlant, they'll run them back into Forthweg—and then they'll come after them," Vanai said. "That stands to reason, too."

"Aye." To her surprise, Ealstan didn't look so happy about it. He explained why: "We don't get rid of our occupiers. We only trade one set for another."

"It's a good trade," Vanai said. Ealstan nodded, but with something less than full enthusiasm. It would certainly be a good trade for Forthweg's surviving Kaunians; the Unkerlanters didn't much care about Kaunianity one way or the other. But an Unkerlanter occupation might not be such a good trade for the Forthwegians themselves. The men of Swemmel's kingdom liked them no better than they liked Unkerlanters.

Wistfully, Ealstan said, "It would be nice if King Penda could just come back."

Vanai reached across the table and set her hand on his. "Aye, it would," she said, giving him—and Penda—the benefit of the doubt as he'd given it to the idea of an Unkerlanter occupation.

As she was washing the supper dishes, Ealstan came up behind her and began to caress her. "Be careful," she warned him.

"I am," he said, and he was. Vanai had trouble concentrating on the dishes. Her breasts had grown more tender since she'd started expecting a baby, but they'd also grown more sensitive. After a little while, she decided the dishes could wait. She turned and put her arms around Ealstan.

Forthwegian-style tunics were easier to get out of than the short tunics and trousers she'd worn back in Oyngestun. Certain post-imperial Kaunian writers had used that truth to sneer at the morals of Forthwegian women. Back in the bedchamber, Vanai simply found it convenient.

Afterwards, she rubbed her upper lip; Ealstan's mustache had tickled her when their lips clung while they made love. "I'm happy with you," he said.

"Good," she answered. "I'm happy with you, too." She kissed him again, careless of that vicious mustache. She meant it. The accursed Algarvian officer who'd introduced her to what passed between man and woman might have been—probably had been—more skilled in this and that than Ealstan was. But so what? It wasn't even that Spinello hadn't wanted her to have pleasure. He had—so her pleasure could give him more. But his own delight came first, always. Ealstan wanted to give her pleasure for her sake, not his. He might have given a little less, but she took ever so much more.

Spinello went off to Unkerlant, she reminded herself. *With any luck at all, he's dead, horribly dead, or else crippled or in torment from his wounds. A lot of Algarvian officers go to Unkerlant. Not so many come back in one piece.*

"What are you thinking?" Ealstan asked. He would do that every once in a while, after lovemaking or just out of the blue.

Usually, Vanai felt obligated to answer with the truth. Tonight, she gave him only part of it: "I love you."

As she'd known it would be, that was the part he wanted to hear. He squeezed her to him. "I'm glad," he said. "I don't know where I'd be without you."

You'd be back in Gromheort with your family, she thought. *If you weren't already married to some Forthwegian girl, you'd be pledged to one. You're too good a catch not to be. I ought to know.*

But where would I be without you? Maybe I would have lasted long enough in the Kaunian district in Gromheort to come up with the spell that lets Kaunians look like Forthwegians. Maybe. Or maybe somebody else would have come up with it by now. Maybe. She tried to make herself believe either of those things. It wasn't easy. *Odds are, Mezentio's men would have shipped me west. I wouldn't be here worrying about it. I wouldn't be anywhere at all.*

She clung to Ealstan. "I'm very lucky," she said.

He squeezed her again, this time till she could hardly breathe. "You make me lucky," he said. Vanai didn't know whether to laugh or to cry at that. It was absurd, but magnificently absurd. The baby kicked. "I felt that!" Ealstan exclaimed, which was hardly surprising, considering how tight he held her. "He's getting stronger."

"That's what he's supposed to do," Vanai answered. "He's getting bigger, too." She rolled away from Ealstan and onto her back, then lifted her head so she could look at herself. Her belly definitely bulged now. Pretty soon, even her baggy Forthwegian tunics wouldn't be able to hide her pregnancy any more. "And so am I."

He set his hand on the swelling below her navel. "That's what you're supposed to do, too." Before very long, his hand wandered lower. He was still young enough to be able to make love about as often as the thought crossed his mind.

As he began to stroke her, Vanai said, "This is how my belly started getting big in the first place."

Laughing, Ealstan shook his head. "My hand had nothing to do with that." But, what with what followed, Vanai wasn't wrong, either. Both of them slept soundly that night.

When they woke, it was later in the morning than usual. Vanai wasn't surprised when Ealstan told her her sorcerous disguise had slipped. She repaired it while he gobbled bread and almonds and wine for breakfast. "Is everything all right?" she asked when she finished the spell.

He nodded. "Fine," he said with his mouth full. "Pybba's going to burst like an egg if I don't get to work on time."

"No, he won't," Vanai said. "He knows you do good work, and he knows you do plenty of work, too. You just take him too seriously when he starts roaring and bellowing."

"If you'd listened to him roaring and bellowing as much as I have, you'd take him seriously, too." Ealstan dug a finger into one ear, as if to say listening to Pybba had left him half deaf. From her own brief meeting with the pottery magnate, Vanai could readily believe that. Ealstan gave her a quick kiss tasting of wine and hurried out the door. She rolled her eyes. He talked about listening to Pybba, but he hadn't listened to her.

She ate her own breakfast at a more leisurely clip. Then she put some silver in her handbag and went downstairs. Her thoughts of the evening before convinced her she needed a couple of new tunics, cut even more loosely than the ones she already owned. Forthwegian women just didn't display the contours of their bodies. If she was to seem a proper Forthwegian woman, she couldn't, either.

Down on the streets, news-sheet vendors shouted out their headlines. They still said nothing about King Raniero boiled alive. Their cry was, "Algarvian drive toward Herborn storms on! Plegmund's brave Brigade spearheads assault!" Vanai did not buy a news sheet.

She did buy a couple of tunics in a linen-wool blend. They would do for any but very cold days, and she could wear a cloak over them then. Picking colors was harder than it had been before she donned a Forthwegian appearance, and took a while. Forthwegians could and did wear stronger colors than she would have chosen while she still looked like her fair-haired Kaunian self. The shopgirl seemed to mean it when she particularly praised the green of one tunic, which left Vanai pleased with herself as she headed back to the flat with her purchases.

She didn't have far to go, but she'd got less than halfway when she noticed people staring at her. She wondered why, but not for more than a couple of strides. Then panic seized her. The spell must have worn off, leaving her looking like what she really was. In Eoforwic these days, what she really was could easily prove fatal.

Vanai began to run. Only a couple of blocks to the flat. If she could just get inside . . . She hurried past the apothecary's where she dared not stop anymore, rounded a corner—and almost ran over two Algarvian constables.

They were startled, but not too startled to grab her. "Well, well, what having we here?" one of them said. But he knew. They both knew too well. "You coming with us, Kaunian. Magic not working, eh? You arresting." Vanai screamed and kicked and clawed, but she couldn't get away. And no one on the street tried to help her. No one at all. Somehow, that was the worst of it.

Harry Turtledove, the master of
alternate history, turns his talents to
one of fantasy's most beloved sagas:

Robert E. Howard's Conan!

CONAN OF
VENARIUM

———————— ⟊⟊⟊ ————————

The *origin* of the might barbarian—
available soon in hardcover
from Tor Books

Read on for a thrilling preview!

Chapter 1

The Coming of the Aquilonians

Iron belled on iron. Sparks flew. Mordec struck again, harder than ever. The blacksmith grunted in satisfaction and, hammer still clenched in his great right hand, lifted the red-hot sword blade from the anvil with the tongs in his left. Nodding, he watched the color slowly fade from the iron. "I'll not need to thrust it back into the fire, Conan," he said. "You can rest easy at the bellows."

"All right, Father." Conan was not sorry to step back from the forge. Sweat ran down his bare chest. Though the day was not warm—few days in Cimmeria were warm—hard work by the forge made a man or a boy forget the weather outside. At twelve, the blacksmith's son stood on the border of manhood. He was already as tall as some of the men in the village of Duthil, and his own labor at Mordec's side had given him thews some of those men might envy.

Yet next to his father, Conan's beardless cheeks were not all that marked him as a stripling. For Mordec was a giant of a man, well over six feet, but so thick through the shoulders and chest that he did not seem so tall. A square-cut mane of thick black hair, now streaked with gray, almost covered the blacksmith's volcanic blue eyes. Mordec's close-trimmed beard was also beginning to go gray, and had one long white streak marking the continuation of a scar that showed on his cheek. His voice was a deep bass rumble, which made Conan's unbroken treble all the shriller by comparison.

From the back of the smithy, from the rooms where the blacksmith and his family lived, a woman called, "Mordec! Come here. I need you."

Mordec's face twisted with a pain he never would have

shown if wounded by sword or spear or arrow. "Go tend to your mother, son," he said roughly. "It's really you Verina wants to see, anyhow."

"But she called you," said Conan.

"Go, I said." Mordec set down the blacksmith's hammer and folded his hand into a fist. "Go, or you'll be sorry."

Conan hurried away. A buffet from his father might stretch him senseless on the rammed-earth floor of the smithy, for Mordec did not always know his own strength. And Conan dimly understood that his father did not want to see his mother in her present state; Verina was slowly and lingeringly dying of some ailment of the lungs that neither healers nor wizards had been able to reverse. But Mordec, lost in his own torment, did not grasp how watching Conan's mother fail by inches flayed the boy.

As usual, Verina lay in bed, covered and warmed by the cured hides of panthers and wolves Mordec had slain on hunting trips. "Oh," she said. "Conan." She smiled, though her lips had a faint bluish cast that had been absent even a few weeks before.

"What do you need, Mother?" he asked.

"Some water, please," said Verina. "I didn't want to trouble you." Her voice held the last word an instant longer than it might have.

Conan did not notice, though Mordec surely would have. "I'll get it for you," he said, and hurried to the pitcher on the rough-hewn cedar table near the hearth. He poured an earthenware cup full and brought it back to the bedchamber.

"Thank you. You're a good—" Verina broke off to cough. The racking spasm went on and on. Her thin shoulders shook with it. A little pink-tinged froth appeared at the corner of her mouth. At last, she managed to whisper, "The water."

"Here." Conan wiped her mouth and helped her sit up. He held the cup to her lips.

She took a few swallows—fewer than he would have wanted to see. But when she spoke again, her voice was stronger: "That is better. I wish I could—" She broke off again, this time in surprise. "What's that?"

Running feet pounded along the dirt track that served Duthil for a main street. "The Aquilonians!" a hoarse voice bawled. "The Aquilonians have crossed into Cimmeria!"

"The Aquilonians!" Conan's voice, though still unbroken, crackled with ferocity and raw blood lust. "By Crom, they'll pay for this! We'll make them pay for this!" He eased Verina down to the pillow once more. "I'm sorry, Mother. I have to go." He dashed away to hear the news.

"Conan—" she called after him, her voice fading. He did not hear her. Even if she had screamed, he would not have heard her. The electrifying news drew him as a lodestone draws iron.

Mordec had already hurried out of the smithy. Conan joined his father in the street. Other Cimmerians came spilling from their homes and shops: big men, most of them, dark-haired, with eyes of gray or blue that crackled like blazing ice at the news. As one, they rounded on the newcomer, crying, "Tell us more."

"I will," he said, "and gladly." He was older than Mordec, for his hair and beard were white. He must have run a long way, but was not breathing unduly hard. He carried a staff with a crook on the end, and wore a herder's sheepskin coat that reached halfway down his thighs. "I'm Fidach, of Aedan's clan. With my brother, I tend sheep on one of the valleys below the tree line."

Nods came from the men of Duthil. Aedan's clan dwelt hard by the border with Aquilonia—and, now and again, sneaked across it for sheep or cattle or the red joy of slaughtering men of foreign blood. "Go on," said Mordec. "You were tending your sheep, you say, and then—"

"And then the snout end of the greatest army I've ever seen thrust itself into the valley," said Fidach. "Aquilonian knights, and archers from the Bossonian Marches, and those damned stubborn spearmen out of Gunderland who like retreat hardly better than we do. A whole great swarm of them, I tell you. This is no raid. They're come to stay, unless we drive them forth."

A low growl rose from the men of Duthil: the growl that

might have come from a panther's throat when it sighted prey. "We'll drive them forth, all right," said someone, and in a heartbeat every man in the village had taken up the cry.

"Hold," said Mordec, and Conan saw with pride how his father needed only the one word to make every head turn his way. The blacksmith went on, "We will not drive out the invaders by ourselves, not if they have come with an army. We will need to gather men from several clans, from several villages." He looked around at his comrades. "Eogannan! Glemmis! Can you leave your work here for a few days?"

"With Aquilonians loose in Cimmeria, we can," declared Glemmis. Eogannan, a man nearly of Mordec's size, was sparing of speech, but he nodded.

"Stout fellows," said Mordec. "Glemmis, go to Uist. Eogannan, you head for Nairn. Neither one of those places is more than a couple of days from here. Let the folk there know we've been invaded, if they've not already heard. Tell them to spread the word to other villages beyond them. When we strike the foe, we must strike him with all our strength."

Eogannan simply nodded again and strode off down the road toward Nairn, trusting to luck and to his own intimate knowledge of the countryside for food along the way. Glemmis briefly ducked back into his home before setting out. He left Duthil with a leather sack slung over one shoulder: Conan supposed it would hold oatcakes or a loaf of rye bread and smoked meat to sustain him on the journey.

"This is well done," said Fidach. "And if you have sent men to Uist and Nairn, I will go on to Lochnagar, off to the northwest. My wife's father's family springs from those parts. I will have no trouble finding kinsfolk to guest with when I get there. We shall meet again, and blood our swords in the Aquilonians' throats." With that for a farewell, he trotted away, his feet pounding in a steady pace that would eat up the miles.

The men of Duthil stayed in the street. Some looked after Fidach, others toward the south, toward the border with Aquilonia, the border their southern neighbors had crossed. A sudden grim purpose informed the Cimmerians. Until the invaders were expelled from their land, none of them would rest easy.

"Bring your swords and spears and axes to the smithy," said Mordec. "I'll sharpen them for you, and I'll ask nothing for it. What we can do to drive out the Aquilonians, let each man do, and count not the cost. For whatever it may be, it is less than the cost of slavery."

"Mordec speaks like a clan chief." That was Balarg the weaver, whose home stood only a few doors down from Mordec's. The words were respectful; the tone was biting. Mordec and Balarg were the two leading men of Duthil, with neither willing to admit the other might be *the* leading man in the village.

"I speak like a man with a notion of what needs doing," rumbled Mordec. "And how I might speak otherwise—" He broke off and shook his big head. "However that might be, I will not speak so now, not with the word the shepherd brought."

"Speak as you please," said Balarg. He was younger than Mordec, and handsomer, and surely smoother. "I will answer—you may rely on it."

"No." Mordec shook his head again. "The war needs both of us. Our own feuds can wait."

"Let it be so, then." Again, Balarg sounded agreeable. But even as he spoke, he turned away from the blacksmith.

Conan burned to avenge the insult to his father. He burned to, but made himself hold back. For one thing, Mordec only shrugged—and, if the fight against the invaders meant his feud with Balarg could wait, it surely meant Conan's newly discovered feud with the weaver could wait as well. And, for another, Balarg's daughter, Tarla, was just about Conan's age—and, the past few months, the blacksmith's son had begun to look at her in a way different from the way he had looked at any girl when he was smaller.

Men began going back into their houses. Women began exclaiming when their husbands and brothers gave them the news Fidach had brought. The exclamations were of rage, not of dismay; Cimmerian women, no strangers to war, loved freedom no less than their menfolk.

Mordec set a large hand on Conan's shoulder, saying, "Come back to the smithy, son. Until the warriors march against the Aquilonians, we will be busier than we ever have."

"Yes, Father." Conan nodded. "Swords and spears and axes, the way you said, and helms, and mailshirts—"

"Helms, aye," said Mordec. "A helm can be forged of two pieces of iron and riveted up the center. But a byrnie is a different business. Making any mail is slow, and making good mail is slower. Each ring must be shaped, and joined to its neighbors, and riveted so it cannot slip its place. In the time I would need to finish one coat of mail, I cold do so many other things, making the armor would not be worth my while. Would it were otherwise, but—" The blacksmith shrugged.

When they walked into the smithy, they found Conan's mother standing by the forge. Conan exclaimed in surprise; she seldom left her bed these days. Mordec might have been rooted in the doorway. Conan started toward Verina to help her back to the bedchamber. She held up a bony hand. "Wait," she said. "Tell me more of the Aquilonians. I heard the shouting in the street, but I could not make out the words."

"They have come into our country," said Mordec.

Verina's mouth narrowed. So did her eyes. "You will fight them." It was no question; she might have been stating a law of nature.

"We will all fight them: everyone from Duthil, everyone from the surrounding villages, everyone who hears the news and can come against them with a weapon to hand," said Mordec. Conan nodded, but his father paid him no heed.

His mother's long illness might have stolen her bodily vigor, but not that of her spirit. Her eyes flamed hotter than the fire inside the forge. "Good," she said. "Slay them all, save for one you let live to flee back over the border to bring his folk word of their kinsmen's ruin."

Conan smacked a fist into the callused palm of his other hand. "By Crom, we will!"

Mordec chuckled grimly. "The rooks and ravens will feast soon enough, Verina. You would have watched them glut themselves on another field twelve years gone by, were you not busy birthing this one here." He pointed to Conan.

"Women fight their battles, too, though men know it not," said Verina. Then she began to cough again; she had been fighting that battle for years, and would not win it. But she mastered the fit, even though, while it went on, she swayed on her feet.

"Here, Mother, go back and rest," said Conan. "The battle ahead is one for men."

He helped Verina to the bedchamber and helped her ease herself down into the bed. "Thank you, my son," she whispered. "You are a good boy."

Conan, just then, was not thinking of being a good boy. Visions of blood and slaughter filled his head, of clashing swords and cloven flesh and spouting blood, of foes in flight before him, of black birds fluttering down to feast on bloated bodies, of battles and of heroes, and of men uncounted crying out his name.

Granth son of Biemur swung an axe—not at some foeman's neck but at the trunk of a spruce. The blade bit. A chunk of pale wood came free when he pulled out the axehead. He paused in the work for a moment, leaning on the long-handled axe and scowling down at his blistered palms. "If I'd wanted to be a carpenter, I could have gone to work for my uncle," he grumbled.

His cousin Vulth was attacking a pine not far away. "You go in for the soldier's trade, you learn a bit of all the others with it," he said. He gave the pine a couple of more strokes. It groaned and tottered and fell—in the open space between Vulth and Granth, just where he had planned it. He walked along the length of the trunk, trimming off the big branches with the axe.

And Granth got to work again, too, for he had spied Sergeant Nopel coming their way. Looking busy when the sergeant was around was something all soldiers learned in a hurry—or, if they did not, they soon learned to be sorry. As Vulth's pine had a moment before, the spruce dropped neatly to the ground. Granth started trimming branches. The spicy scent of spruce sap filled his nostrils.

"Aye, keep at it, you dogs," said Nopel. "We'll be glad of a palisade one of these nights, and of wood for watchfires. Mitra, but I hate this gloomy forest."

"Where are the barbarians?" asked Vulth. "Since those herders by the stream a few days ago, we've hardly seen a stinking Cimmerian."

"Maybe they've run away." Granth always liked to look on the bright side of things.

Nopel laughed in his face; sergeants got to be sergeants not least by forgetting there was or ever had been any such thing as a bright side. "They're around. They're barbarians, but they're not cowards—oh, no, they're not. I wish they were. They're waiting and watching and gathering. They'll strike when they're ready—and when they think we're not."

Granth grunted. "I still say building a little fort every time we camp for the night is more trouble than it's worth." He went back to the base of the trimmed trunk and began to shape it into a point.

"It's a craven's way of fighting," agreed Vulth, who was doing the same thing to the pine. The woods rang with the sound of axes. Vulth went on, "Count Stercus brought us up here to fight the Cimmerians. So why don't we fight them, instead of chopping lumber for them to use once we've moved on?"

"Count Stercus is no craven," said Nopel. "There are some who'd name him this or that or the other thing, sure enough, but no one's ever called him a coward. And when we're in the middle of enemy country, with wild men skulking all about, a fortified camp is a handy thing to have, whether you gents care for the notion or not." He gave Granth and Vulth a mincing, mock-aristocratic bow, then growled, "So get on with it!" and stalked off to harry some other soldiers.

After the cousins had shaped the felled trunks into several stakes sharpened at both ends and a little taller than they were, they hauled them back to the encampment. Archers and pikemen guarded the warriors who had set aside their weapons for spades and were digging a ditch around the camp. Inside the ditch, a palisade of stakes was already going up. The ones Granth and Vulth brought were tipped upright and placed in waiting postholes with the rest.

"I wouldn't want to attack a camp like this. I admit it," said Vulth. "You'd have to be crazy to try."

"Maybe you're right." Granth did not want to admit any more than that—or, indeed, even so much. But he could hardly deny that the campsite looked more formidable every minute. He could not deny that it was well placed, either: on a rise, with a spring bubbling out of the ground inside the palisade. The axemen had cleared the dark Cimmerian forest back far enough from the ditch and the wall of stakes that the wild men lurking in the woods could not hope to take the army by surprise.

But then a lanky Bossonian straightening the stakes of the palisade said, "I wouldn't want to attack a camp like this, either, but that doesn't mean the damned Cimmerians will leave us alone. The difference between them and us is, they really are crazy, and they'll do crazy things."

"They're barbarians, and we're coming into their land," said Granth. "They're liable to try to kill without counting the cost."

"That's what I just said, isn't it?" The Bossonian paused in his work long enough to set hands on hips. "If trying to kill without worrying about whether you fall yourself isn't crazy, Mitra smite me if I know what would be."

Another sergeant, also a Bossonian, set hands on hips, too. "If standing around talking without worrying about whether you work isn't lazy, Mitra smite me if I know what would be. So work, you good-for-nothing dog!" The lanky man hastily got back to it. The sergeant rounded on Granth and Vulth. "You lugs were just rattling your teeth, too. If you've got more stakes, bring 'em. If you don't, go cut 'em. Don't let me catch you standing around, though, or I'll make you sorry you were ever born. You hear me?" His voice rose to an irascible roar.

"Yes, Sergeant," chorused the two Gundermen. They hurried off to collect more of the stakes they had already prepared, only to discover that their comrades had already hauled those back to the encampment. Granth swore; cutting trees down was harder work than carrying stakes already cut. "Can't trust anyone," he complained, forgetting that only the day before he and Vulth had cheerfully absconded with three stakes someone else had trimmed.

As darkness began to fall—impossible to say precisely when the sun set, for the clouds and mists of Cimmeria obscured both sunrise and sunset—a long, mournful note blown on the trumpet recalled the Aquilonian soldiers to the camp. Savory steam rose from big iron pots bubbling over cookfires. Rubbing their bellies to show how hungry they were, men lined up to get their suppers.

"Mutton stew?" asked Granth, sniffing.

"Mutton stew," answered a Bossonian who had just had his tin panikin filled. He spoke with resignation. Mutton was what most of the army had eaten ever since crossing into Cimmeria. The forage here was not good enough to support many cattle. Even the sheep were small and scrawny.

A cook spooned stew into Granth's panikin. He stepped aside to let the cook feed the next soldier, then dug in with his horn spoon. The meat was tough and stringy and gamy. The barley that went with it had come up from the Aquilonian side of the border in supply wagons. Cimmeria's scanty fields held mostly rye and oats; the short growing season did not always allow barley, let alone wheat, to ripen.

Had Granth got a supper like this at an inn down in Gunderland, he would have snarled at the innkeeper. On campaign, he was glad he had enough to fill his belly. Anything more than that was better than a bonus; it came near enough to being a miracle.

Someone asked, "What are we calling this camp?" Count Stercus had named each successive encampment after an estate that belonged to him or to one of his friends. Granth supposed it made as good a way as any other to remember which was which.

"Venarium," answered another soldier. "This one's Camp Venarium."

Mordec methodically set his iron cap on his head. He wore a long knife—almost a shortsword—on his belt. A long-handled war axe and a round wooden shield faced with leather and bossed with iron leaned against the brickwork of the forge. A leather wallet carried enough oatcakes and smoked meat to feed him for several days.

Conan was anything but methodical. He sprang into the air in frustration and fury. "Take me with you!" he shouted, not for the first time. "Take me with you, Father!"

"No," growled Mordec.

But the one word, which would usually have silenced his son, had no effect here. "Take me with you!" cried Conan once more. "I can fight. By Crom, I can! I'm bigger than a lot of the men in Duthil, and stronger, too!"

"No," said Mordec once again, deeper and more menacingly than before. Again, though, Conan shook his head, desperate to accompany his father against the invading Aquilonians. Mordec shook his head, too, as if bedeviled by gnats rather than by a boy who truly was bigger and stronger than many of the grown men in the village. Reluctantly, Mordec spoke further: "You were born on a battlefield, son. I don't care to see you die on one."

"I wouldn't die!" The idea did not seem real to Conan. "I'd make the southrons go down like grain before the scythe."

And so he might—for a while. Mordec knew it. But no un-tried boy would last long against a veteran who had practiced his bloody trade twice as long as his foe had lived. And no one, boy or veteran, was surely safe against flying arrows and javelins. "When I say no, I mean no. You're too young. You'll stay here in Duthil where you belong, and you'll take care of your mother."

That struck home; the blacksmith saw as much. But Conan was too wild to go to war to heed even such a potent command. "I won't!" he said shrilly. "I won't, and you can't make me. After you leave, I'll run off and join the army, too."

The next thing he knew, he was lying on the ground by the forge. His head spun. His ears rang. His father stood over him, breathing hard, ready to hit him again if he had to. "You will do no such thing," declared Mordec. "You will do what I tell you, and nothing else. Do you hear me?"

Instead of answering in words, Conan sprang up and grabbed for his father's axe. For the moment, he was ready to do murder for the sake of going to war. But even as his hand closed on the axe handle, Mordec's larger, stronger hand closed on his wrist. Conan tried to twist free, tried and failed. Then he hit his father. He had told the truth—he did have the strength of an ordinary man. The blacksmith, however, was no ordinary man. He took his son's buffet without changing expression.

"So you want to see what it's really like, do you?" asked Mordec. "All right, by Crom. I'll let you have a taste."

He had hit Conan before; as often as not, nothing but his hand would gain and hold the boy's attention. But he had never given him such a cold-blooded, thorough, methodical beating as he did now. Conan tried to fight back for as long as he could. Mordec kept hitting him until he had no more fight left in him. The blacksmith aimed to make the boy cry out for mercy, but Conan set his jaw and suffered in silence, plainly as intent on dying before he showed weakness as Mordec was on breaking him.

And Conan might have died then, for his father, afraid he would fall to an enemy's weapons, was not at all afraid to kill him for pride's sake. After the beating had gone on for some long and painful time, though, Verina came out of the bedchamber. "Hold!" she croaked. "Would you slay what's most like you?"

Mordec stared at her. Rage suddenly rivered out of him, pouring away like ale from a cracked cup. He knelt by his bruised and bloodied son. "You will stay here," he said, half commanding, half pleading.

Conan did not say no. Conan, then, could not have said anything, for his father had beaten him all but senseless. He saw the smithy through a red haze of anguish.

Taking his silence for acquiescence, Mordec filled a dipper with cold water and held it to his battered lips. Conan took a mouthful. He wanted to spit it in his father's face, but animal instinct made him swallow instead. Mordec did not take the dipper away. Conan drained it dry.

"You are as hard on your son as you are on everything else," said Verina with a bubbling sigh.

"Life is hard," answered Mordec. "Anyone who will not see that is a fool: no, worse than a fool—a blind man."

"Life is hard, aye," agreed his wife. "I am not blind; I can see that, too. But I can also see that you are blind, blind to the way you make it harder than it need be."

With a grunt, the blacksmith got to his feet. He towered over Verina. Scowling, he replied, "I am not the only one in this home of whom that might be said."

"And if I fight you, will you beat me as you beat the boy?" asked Verina. "What point to that? All you have to do is wait; before long the sickness in my lungs will slay me and set you free."

"You twist everything I say, everything I do," muttered Mordec, at least as much to himself as to her. Fighting the Aquilonians would seem simple when set against the long, quiet (but no less deadly for being quiet) war he had waged with his wife.

"All you want to do is spill blood," said Verina. "You would be as happy slaying Cimmerians as you are going off to battle Aquilonians."

"Not so," said Mordec. "These are thieves who come into our land. You know that yourself. They would take what little we have and send it south to add to their own riches. They would, but they will not. I go to join the muster of the clans." He strode forward, snatched up his axe and shield and wallet, and stormed forth from the smithy, a thunderstorm of fury on his face.

"No good will come of this!" called Verina, but the black-smith paid no heed.

Conan heard his father and mother quarrel as if from very far away. The pain of the beating made everything else seem small and unimportant. He tried to get to his feet, but found he lacked the strength. He lay in the dirt, even his ardor to go forth to battle quelled for the moment.

Verina stooped beside him. His mother held a bowl full of water and a scrap of cloth. She wet the cloth and gently scrubbed at his face. The rag, which had been the brownish gray of undyed wool, came away crimson. She soaked it in the bowl, wrung it nearly dry, and went back to what she was doing. "There," she said at last. "You're young—you'll heal."

With an effort, Conan managed to sit up. "I still want to go and fight, no matter what Father says," he mumbled through cut and swollen lips.

But his mother shook her head. "Mordec was right." She made a sour face. "Not words I often say, but true. However great you've grown, you are yet too young to go to war." And Conan, who would have and nearly had fought to the death against his father, accepted Verina's words without a murmur.

Also coming soon
in hardcover from Tor:

JAWS OF
DARKNESS

The next volume of
Harry Turtledove's masterful epic
of a world at war